THE CANTERBURY TALES

Geoffrey Chaucer

COLLINS
CLASSICS

Harper Press
An imprint of HarperCollins*Publishers*
1 London Bridge Street,
London SE1 9GF

This Harper Press paperback edition published 2011

A catalogue record for this book is available from the British Library

ISBN: 978-0-00-744944-6

Printed and bound by CPI Group (UK) Ltd, Croydon, CR0 4YY

MIX
Paper from
responsible sources
FSC™ C007454

Life & Times section © HarperCollins*Publishers* Ltd.
Gerard Cheshire asserts his moral rights as author of the Life & Times section
Classic Literature: Words and Phrases adapted from
Collins English Dictionary
Typesetting in Kalix by Palimpsest Book Production Limited,
Falkirk, Stirlingshire

History of Collins

In 1819, millworker William Collins from Glasgow, Scotland, set up a company for printing and publishing pamphlets, sermons, hymn books and prayer books. That company was Collins and was to mark the birth of HarperCollins Publishers as we know it today. The long tradition of Collins dictionary publishing can be traced back to the first dictionary William published in 1824, *Greek and English Lexicon*. Indeed, from 1840 onwards, he began to produce illustrated dictionaries and even obtained a licence to print and publish the Bible.

Soon after, William published the first Collins novel, *Ready Reckoner*, however it was the time of the Long Depression, where harvests were poor, prices were high, potato crops had failed and violence was erupting in Europe. As a result, many factories across the country were forced to close down and William chose to retire in 1846, partly due to the hardships he was facing.

Aged 30, William's son, William II took over the business. A keen humanitarian with a warm heart and a generous spirit, William II was truly 'Victorian' in his outlook. He introduced new, up-to-date steam presses and published affordable editions of Shakespeare's works and *Pilgrim's Progress*, making them available to the masses for the first time. A new demand for educational books meant that success came with the publication of travel books, scientific books, encyclopaedias and dictionaries. This demand to be educated led to the later publication of atlases and Collins also held the monopoly on scripture writing at the time.

In the 1860s Collins began to expand and diversify

and the idea of 'books for the millions' was developed. Affordable editions of classical literature were published and in 1903 Collins introduced 10 titles in their Collins Handy Illustrated Pocket Novels. These proved so popular that a few years later this had increased to an output of 50 volumes, selling nearly half a million in their year of publication. In the same year, The Everyman's Library was also instituted, with the idea of publishing an affordable library of the most important classical works, biographies, religious and philosophical treatments, plays, poems, travel and adventure. This series eclipsed all competition at the time and the introduction of paperback books in the 1950s helped to open that market and marked a high point in the industry.

HarperCollins is and has always been a champion of the classics and the current Collins Classics series follows in this tradition – publishing classical literature that is affordable and available to all. Beautifully packaged, highly collectible and intended to be reread and enjoyed at every opportunity.

Life & Times

Middle English

Middle English is the term used to describe the English language that developed following the Norman Conquest (1066). After invading Britain and making it their own, the Normans spoke French, which had become the language of nobility and authority, and scholars spoke Latin, which was the universal language of Europe. The Anglo-Saxons spoke Middle English, which was the language of the lay population. This linguistic period lasted until 1485 when the Plantagenet era came to a close with the death of King Richard III. Fifteen years prior to Richard's death a new form of English called Chancery Standard had been established, which was based on the London dialect. When the Tudor era began with King Henry VII it marked the official transition from Middle English to Chancery Standard. The Age of Discovery had begun as maritime explorers expanded the known world. London had become an important centre for trade, so it made commercial sense to have London English as the official language.

Geoffrey Chaucer (circa 1343–1400) is widely acknowledged as the person who standardized vernacular Middle English by writing many works that used the native tongue of the 14th century, as opposed to the official languages of French and Latin. Chaucer's life spanned the second half of the 14th century, some 300 years after the Normans had invaded Britain and made it their own. During Chaucer's time, Middle English was rising through the ranks of society because commoners were becoming educated and achieving higher social status. Chaucer was himself a civil servant, polymath and philosopher who had been born into a family of vintners. He would have been considered middle class in modern England. Chaucer's name was derived from the

French *chausseur* which means 'shoe maker', so he evidently had Norman ancestry.

The Black Death (bubonic plague) swept through Europe between 1348 and 1350, which had a profound effect on English society during Chaucer's childhood. Roughly half of the adult population had been killed by the disease, and this meant that the lower classes had greater opportunity to succeed, because the nobility found themselves with fewer commoners to work for them and fewer of their own to administrate. The way was therefore paved for the likes of Chaucer to use their intelligence and education to secure more important roles.

The Canterbury Tales

Chaucer's works of literature are considered useful documents of a language that was destined to be consigned to history less than a century later. Of his works, *The Canterbury Tales* is probably the best known and was written towards the end of his life. Written in poetic verse, with the remainder in prose, the book is a collection of stories. At the time it was common practice for people to make Christian pilgrimages to Canterbury Cathedral to visit the site where Thomas Beckett was slain in 1170. This involved following the Pilgrims' Way, of which there were several, depending on where the pilgrim was travelling from. In Chaucer's case, he would have followed the route from Southwark Cathedral, London, to Canterbury in Kent.

Walking the London Pilgrims' Way is the theme that ties *The Canterbury Tales* together. Chaucer is both a pilgrim in the story and the narrator of the book. He describes his encounters with other pilgrims and some of them tell their own stories. There is thus a main tale of the journey and various other tales within. The tales within the tale include *The Knight's Tale, The Miller's Tale, The Wife of Bath's Tale*,

The Pardoner's Tale and *The Nun's Priest's Tale*. As the pilgrimage attracted a broad cross-section of society Chaucer chose the perfect scenario for incorporating characters from diverse backgrounds. This, in turn, enabled him to assemble a series of tales that impart ethical and moral advice and guidance to the reader, though also imbued with a good deal of wit and humour.

In *The Nun's Priest's Tale* the characters are anthropomorphic animals – chickens and a fox. A cockerel named Chanticleer has a dream that he will be taken by a fox, but his hen wife, Pertelote, dismisses the dream as nonsense. The fox duly catches Chanticleer with flattery, by telling him he has a beautiful voice and grabbing him while he is distracted by his own crowing. However, the cockerel manages to escape from the fox's mouth by flattering the fox into boasting about his cunning to those who have set out to rescue Chanticleer. The tale is one of *touché* as both male characters are outwitted by their own vanity. The chickens have French names. *Chanticleer* means to 'sing clearly' in French, while *Pertelote* means to 'confuse someone's fate'.

The Wife of Bath's Tale is about dilemma or a choice between two undesirable options – Morton's fork, as it is sometimes termed. On pain of death, a knight, who is accused of rape, is sent on a quest. His queen sends him to discover what women really want. After a year he finally meets an old hag who tells him that women desire sovereignty over their husbands. However, the forfeit he has to pay for her wisdom is to marry her. She then gives him a choice – he can have an unattractive but faithful wife, or he can have an attractive but unfaithful wife. He concedes that it is an impossible choice and that she therefore has sovereignty over him. The hag then transforms into an attractive and faithful wife, knowing she has the power in their relationship.

It seems that there may also have been an element of allegory in this tale, as there is evidence that Chaucer was himself accused of rape. Perhaps writing the tale was a kind of catharsis for the author. Whether he was innocent or guilty, he seems to have used the tale as a philosophical expression of his view about the relationship between men and women. In fact, many of the tales address marriage, sex, infidelity and so on. It seems that the fundamental themes of human society have changed little over the centuries and they are, and will continue to be the staples of literature.

The Miller's Tale was particularly racy in this regard. John the carpenter has a wife who is far younger than he and very attractive, too. The lodger Nicholas manages to sleep with her, abusing John's trust in him. However, the town clerk Absalon is also interested in the wife. When he visits her home at night and asks for a kiss she presents her posterior through the window, which he kisses before realizing her joke. He returns with a red hot iron to burn her buttocks, but this time Nicholas presents his bottom and duly has it burnt. John is labelled a cuckold by the townsfolk when they wake to Nicholas' screams of pain – a cuckold being a man with an unfaithful wife. Nicholas is seen to have been divinely punished for taking advantage of another man's wife.

Chaucer's work often seems lewd and ribald, especially when one considers that the overall theme is one of Christian homage. An example is the use of *queynte* which was the common vernacular for female genitalia at the time and survives today, in its modern form, as a profanity of the first order. However, Medieval England was a relatively coarse culture in comparison with today, so Chaucer was merely reporting what he witnessed every day. Society was learning to become more refined and sophisticated. Etiquette, courtesy, politeness and civility were matters that concerned only those who had the luxury of leisure time to consider their behaviour in the eyes of others, which inevitably meant that such affectations also served to separate the ruling classes from the rest.

The Church attempted to instil in the masses a sense

that common good behaviour was expected of them by their Christian god. The Ten Commandments and phrases such as 'cleanliness is next to godliness' were used to instruct the lay population in this regard. At the top of the list was the warning that those who committed sin would go to Hell in the afterlife, so the consequences of vice were also addressed by Chaucer. In *The Pardoner's Tale* characters feature who indulge in gambling, drunkenness, gluttony and swearing. They are visited by a mysterious old man who represents death. Chaucer's message is clear – that their god will punish them for their sins if they fail to mend their ways.

In a world that was rife with illness and death, and where people were still a long way from having a scientific understanding, it is hardly surprising that so much emphasis was placed on the observance of supernatural doctrine. People genuinely believed that their Christian god was the overseer of their fate, yet they struggled with their mortal wants and desires because life was so hard. In *The Canterbury Tales* Chaucer was documenting the human condition of his historical age – evidently behaviour that is still reflected in the human condition to this day.

THE
CANTERBURY
TALES

CONTENTS

THE CANTERBURY TALES

THE GENERAL PROLOGUE

When that Aprilis, with his showers swoot*,   *sweet
The drought of March hath pierced to the root,
And bathed every vein in such licour,
Of which virtue engender'd is the flower;
When Zephyrus eke with his swoote breath
Inspired hath in every holt* and heath   *grove, forest
The tender croppes* and the younge sun   *twigs, boughs
Hath in the Ram his halfe course y-run,
And smalle fowles make melody,
That sleepen all the night with open eye,
(So pricketh them nature in their corages*);   *hearts,
    inclinations
Then longe folk to go on pilgrimages,
And palmers for to seeke strange strands,
To *ferne hallows couth* in sundry lands; *distant saints
    known*
And specially, from every shire's end
Of Engleland, to Canterbury they wend,
The holy blissful Martyr for to seek,
That them hath holpen*, when that they were sick. *helped

Befell that, in that season on a day,
In Southwark at the Tabard as I lay,
Ready to wenden on my pilgrimage
To Canterbury with devout corage,
At night was come into that hostelry
Well nine and twenty in a company
Of sundry folk, *by aventure y-fall* *who had by chance fallen*
In fellowship, and pilgrims were they all, *into company.*
That toward Canterbury woulde ride.
The chamber, and the stables were wide,
And *well we weren eased at the best.* *we were well provided
with the best*
And shortly, when the sunne was to rest,
So had I spoken with them every one,
That I was of their fellowship anon,
And made forword* early for to rise, *promise
To take our way there as I you devise*. *describe, relate

But natheless, while I have time and space,
Ere that I farther in this tale pace,
Me thinketh it accordant to reason,
To tell you alle the condition
Of each of them, so as it seemed me,
And which they weren, and of what degree;
And eke in what array that they were in:
And at a Knight then will I first begin.

A Knight there was, and that a worthy man,
That from the time that he first began
To riden out, he loved chivalry,
Truth and honour, freedom and courtesy.
Full worthy was he in his Lorde's war,
And thereto had he ridden, no man farre*, *farther
As well in Christendom as in Heatheness,
And ever honour'd for his worthiness

At Alisandre he was when it was won.
Full often time he had the board begun
Above alle nations in Prusse.
In Lettowe had he reysed,* and in Russe, *journeyed
No Christian man so oft of his degree.
In Grenade at the siege eke had he be
Of Algesir, and ridden in Belmarie.
At Leyes was he, and at Satalie,
When they were won; and in the Greate Sea
At many a noble army had he be.
At mortal battles had he been fifteen,
And foughten for our faith at Tramissene.
In listes thries, and aye slain his foe.
This ilke* worthy knight had been also *same
Some time with the lord of Palatie,
Against another heathen in Turkie:
And evermore *he had a sovereign price*. *He was held in
        very high esteem.*
And though that he was worthy he was wise,
And of his port as meek as is a maid.
He never yet no villainy ne said
In all his life, unto no manner wight.
He was a very perfect gentle knight.
But for to telle you of his array,
His horse was good, but yet he was not gay.
Of fustian he weared a gipon*, *short doublet
Alle *besmotter'd with his habergeon,* *soiled by his coat of
        mail.*
For he was late y-come from his voyage,
And wente for to do his pilgrimage.

With him there was his son, a younge Squire,
A lover, and a lusty bacheler,
With lockes crulle* as they were laid in press. *curled
Of twenty year of age he was I guess.

3

Of his stature he was of even length,
And *wonderly deliver*, and great of strength. *wonderfully
     nimble*
And he had been some time in chevachie*, *cavalry raids
In Flanders, in Artois, and Picardie,
And borne him well, *as of so little space*, *in such a short time*
In hope to standen in his lady's grace.
Embroider'd was he, as it were a mead
All full of freshe flowers, white and red.
Singing he was, or fluting all the day;
He was as fresh as is the month of May.
Short was his gown, with sleeves long and wide.
Well could he sit on horse, and faire ride.
He coulde songes make, and well indite,
Joust, and eke dance, and well pourtray and write.
So hot he loved, that by nightertale* *night-time
He slept no more than doth the nightingale.
Courteous he was, lowly, and serviceable,
And carv'd before his father at the table.

A Yeoman had he, and servants no mo'
At that time, for *him list ride so* *it pleased him so to ride*
And he was clad in coat and hood of green.
A sheaf of peacock arrows bright and keen
Under his belt he bare full thriftily.
Well could he dress his tackle yeomanly:
His arrows drooped not with feathers low;
And in his hand he bare a mighty bow.
A nut-head had he, with a brown visiage:
Of wood-craft coud* he well all the usage: *knew
Upon his arm he bare a gay bracer*, *small shield
And by his side a sword and a buckler,
And on that other side a gay daggere,
Harnessed well, and sharp as point of spear:
A Christopher on his breast of silver sheen.

An horn he bare, the baldric was of green:
A forester was he soothly* as I guess. *certainly

There was also a Nun, a Prioress,
That of her smiling was full simple and coy;
Her greatest oathe was but by Saint Loy;
And she was cleped* Madame Eglentine. *called
Full well she sang the service divine,
Entuned in her nose full seemly;
And French she spake full fair and fetisly* *properly
After the school of Stratford atte Bow,
For French of Paris was to her unknow.
At meate was she well y-taught withal;
She let no morsel from her lippes fall,
Nor wet her fingers in her sauce deep.
Well could she carry a morsel, and well keep,
That no droppe ne fell upon her breast.
In courtesy was set full much her lest*. *pleasure
Her over-lippe wiped she so clean,
That in her cup there was no farthing* seen *speck
Of grease, when she drunken had her draught;
Full seemely after her meat she raught*: *reached out her hand
And *sickerly she was of great disport*, *surely she was of a
       lively disposition*
And full pleasant, and amiable of port,
And *pained her to counterfeite cheer *took pains to assume
Of court,* and be estately of mannere, a courtly disposition*
And to be holden digne* of reverence. *worthy
But for to speaken of her conscience,
She was so charitable and so pitous,* *full of pity
She woulde weep if that she saw a mouse
Caught in a trap, if it were dead or bled.
Of smalle houndes had she, that she fed
With roasted flesh, and milk, and *wastel bread.* *finest white
       bread*

5

But sore she wept if one of them were dead,
Or if men smote it with a yarde* smart: *staff
And all was conscience and tender heart.
Full seemly her wimple y-pinched was;
Her nose tretis;* her eyen gray as glass; *well-formed
Her mouth full small, and thereto soft and red;
But sickerly she had a fair forehead.
It was almost a spanne broad I trow;
For *hardily she was not undergrow*. *certainly she was not
    small*
Full fetis* was her cloak, as I was ware. *neat
Of small coral about her arm she bare
A pair of beades, gauded all with green;
And thereon hung a brooch of gold full sheen,
On which was first y-written a crown'd A,
And after, *Amor vincit omnia.* *love conquers all*
Another Nun also with her had she,
That was her chapelleine, and priestes three.

A Monk there was, a fair *for the mast'ry*, *above all others*
An out-rider, that loved venery*; *hunting
A manly man, to be an abbot able.
Full many a dainty horse had he in stable:
And when he rode, men might his bridle hear
Jingeling in a whistling wind as clear,
And eke as loud, as doth the chapel bell,
There as this lord was keeper of the cell.
The rule of Saint Maur and of Saint Benet,
Because that it was old and somedeal strait
This ilke* monk let olde thinges pace, *same
And held after the newe world the trace.
He *gave not of the text a pulled hen,* *he cared nothing
for the text*
That saith, that hunters be not holy men:
Ne that a monk, when he is cloisterless;

Is like to a fish that is waterless;
This is to say, a monk out of his cloister.
This ilke text held he not worth an oyster;
And I say his opinion was good.
Why should he study, and make himselfe wood* *mad
Upon a book in cloister always pore,
Or swinken* with his handes, and labour, *toil
As Austin bid? how shall the world be served?
Let Austin have his swink to him reserved.
Therefore he was a prickasour* aright: *hard rider
Greyhounds he had as swift as fowl of flight;
Of pricking* and of hunting for the hare *riding
Was all his lust,* for no cost would he spare. *pleasure
I saw his sleeves *purfil'd at the hand* *worked at the end
    with a fur*
With gris, and that the finest of the land. *called "gris"*
And for to fasten his hood under his chin,
He had of gold y-wrought a curious pin;
A love-knot in the greater end there was.
His head was bald, and shone as any glass,
And eke his face, as it had been anoint;
He was a lord full fat and in good point;
His eyen steep,* and rolling in his head, *deep-set
That steamed as a furnace of a lead.
His bootes supple, his horse in great estate,
Now certainly he was a fair prelate;
He was not pale as a forpined* ghost; *wasted
A fat swan lov'd he best of any roast.
His palfrey was as brown as is a berry.

A Friar there was, a wanton and a merry,
A limitour, a full solemne man.
In all the orders four is none that can* *knows
So much of dalliance and fair language.
He had y-made full many a marriage

Of younge women, at his owen cost.
Unto his order he was a noble post;
Full well belov'd, and familiar was he
With franklins *over all* in his country, *everywhere*
And eke with worthy women of the town:
For he had power of confession,
As said himselfe, more than a curate,
For of his order he was licentiate.
Full sweetely heard he confession,
And pleasant was his absolution.
He was an easy man to give penance,
There as he wist to have a good pittance: *where he knew
     he would get good payment*
For unto a poor order for to give
Is signe that a man is well y-shrive.
For if he gave, he *durste make avant*, *dared to boast*
He wiste* that the man was repentant. *knew
For many a man so hard is of his heart,
He may not weep although him sore smart.
Therefore instead of weeping and prayeres,
Men must give silver to the poore freres.
His tippet was aye farsed* full of knives *stuffed
And pinnes, for to give to faire wives;
And certainly he had a merry note:
Well could he sing and playen *on a rote*; *from memory*
Of yeddings* he bare utterly the prize. *songs
His neck was white as is the fleur-de-lis.
Thereto he strong was as a champion,
And knew well the taverns in every town.
And every hosteler and gay tapstere,
Better than a lazar* or a beggere, *leper
For unto such a worthy man as he
Accordeth not, as by his faculty,
To have with such lazars acquaintance.
It is not honest, it may not advance,

As for to deale with no such pouraille*, *offal, refuse
But all with rich, and sellers of vitaille*. *victuals
And *ov'r all there as* profit should arise, *in every place where*
Courteous he was, and lowly of service;
There n'as no man nowhere so virtuous.
He was the beste beggar in all his house:
And gave a certain farme for the grant,
None of his bretheren came in his haunt.
For though a widow hadde but one shoe,
So pleasant was his *In Principio*,
Yet would he have a farthing ere he went;
His purchase was well better than his rent.
And rage he could and play as any whelp,
In lovedays; there could he muchel* help. *greatly
For there was he not like a cloisterer,
With threadbare cope as is a poor scholer;
But he was like a master or a pope.
Of double worsted was his semicope*, *short cloak
That rounded was as a bell out of press.
Somewhat he lisped for his wantonness,
To make his English sweet upon his tongue;
And in his harping, when that he had sung,
His eyen* twinkled in his head aright, *eyes
As do the starres in a frosty night.
This worthy limitour was call'd Huberd.

A Merchant was there with a forked beard,
In motley, and high on his horse he sat,
Upon his head a Flandrish beaver hat.
His bootes clasped fair and fetisly*. *neatly
His reasons aye spake he full solemnly,
Sounding alway th' increase of his winning.
He would the sea were kept for any thing
Betwixte Middleburg and Orewell
Well could he in exchange shieldes* sell *crown coins

9

This worthy man full well his wit beset*; *employed
There wiste* no wight** that he was in debt, *knew **man
So *estately was he of governance* *so well he managed*
With his bargains, and with his chevisance*. *business contract
For sooth he was a worthy man withal,
But sooth to say, I n'ot* how men him call. *know not

A Clerk there was of Oxenford* also, *Oxford
That unto logic hadde long y-go*. *devoted himself
As leane was his horse as is a rake,
And he was not right fat, I undertake;
But looked hollow*, and thereto soberly**. *thin; **poorly
Full threadbare was his *overest courtepy*, *uppermost short
    cloak*
For he had gotten him yet no benefice,
Ne was not worldly, to have an office.
For him was lever* have at his bed's head *rather
Twenty bookes, clothed in black or red,
Of Aristotle, and his philosophy,
Than robes rich, or fiddle, or psalt'ry.
But all be that he was a philosopher,
Yet hadde he but little gold in coffer,
But all that he might of his friendes hent*, *obtain
On bookes and on learning he it spent,
And busily gan for the soules pray
Of them that gave him wherewith to scholay* *study
Of study took he moste care and heed.
Not one word spake he more than was need;
And that was said in form and reverence,
And short and quick, and full of high sentence.
Sounding in moral virtue was his speech,
And gladly would he learn, and gladly teach.

A Sergeant of the Law, wary and wise,
That often had y-been at the Parvis,

There was also, full rich of excellence.
Discreet he was, and of great reverence:
He seemed such, his wordes were so wise,
Justice he was full often in assize,
By patent, and by plein* commission; *full
For his science, and for his high renown,
Of fees and robes had he many one.
So great a purchaser was nowhere none.
All was fee simple to him, in effect
His purchasing might not be in suspect* *suspicion
Nowhere so busy a man as he there was
And yet he seemed busier than he was
In termes had he case' and doomes* all *judgements
That from the time of King Will were fall.
Thereto he could indite, and make a thing
There coulde no wight *pinch at* his writing. *find fault with*
And every statute coud* he plain by rote *knew
He rode but homely in a medley* coat, *multicoloured
Girt with a seint* of silk, with barres small; *sash
Of his array tell I no longer tale.

A Frankelin* was in this company; *rich landowner
White was his beard, as is the daisy.
Of his complexion he was sanguine.
Well lov'd he in the morn a sop in wine.
To liven in delight was ever his won*, *wont
For he was Epicurus' owen son,
That held opinion, that plein* delight *full
Was verily felicity perfite.
An householder, and that a great, was he;
Saint Julian he was in his country.
His bread, his ale, was alway *after one*; *pressed on one*
A better envined* man was nowhere none; *stored with wine
Withoute bake-meat never was his house,
Of fish and flesh, and that so plenteous,

It snowed in his house of meat and drink,
Of alle dainties that men coulde think.
After the sundry seasons of the year,
So changed he his meat and his soupere.
Full many a fat partridge had he in mew*, *cage
And many a bream, and many a luce* in stew** *pike
    **fish-pond
Woe was his cook, *but if* his sauce were *unless*
Poignant and sharp, and ready all his gear.
His table dormant* in his hall alway *fixed
Stood ready cover'd all the longe day.
At sessions there was he lord and sire.
Full often time he was *knight of the shire* *Member of
    Parliament*
An anlace*, and a gipciere** all of silk, *dagger **purse
Hung at his girdle, white as morning milk.
A sheriff had he been, and a countour
Was nowhere such a worthy vavasour.

An Haberdasher, and a Carpenter,
A Webbe*, a Dyer, and a Tapiser**, *weaver **tapestry-maker
Were with us eke, cloth'd in one livery,
Of a solemn and great fraternity.
Full fresh and new their gear y-picked* was. *spruce
Their knives were y-chaped* not with brass, *mounted
But all with silver wrought full clean and well,
Their girdles and their pouches *every deal*. *in every part*
Well seemed each of them a fair burgess,
To sitten in a guild-hall, on the dais.
Evereach, for the wisdom that he can*, *knew
Was shapely* for to be an alderman. *fitted
For chattels hadde they enough and rent,
And eke their wives would it well assent:
And elles certain they had been to blame.
It is full fair to be y-clep'd madame,

And for to go to vigils all before,
And have a mantle royally y-bore.

A Cook they hadde with them for the nones*, *occasion
To boil the chickens and the marrow bones,
And powder merchant tart and galingale.
Well could he know a draught of London ale.
He could roast, and stew, and broil, and fry,
Make mortrewes, and well bake a pie.
But great harm was it, as it thoughte me,
That, on his shin a mormal* hadde he. *ulcer
For blanc manger, that made he with the best

A Shipman was there, *wonned far by West*: *who dwelt far
        to the West*
For ought I wot, be was of Dartemouth.
He rode upon a rouncy*, as he couth, *hack
All in a gown of falding* to the knee. *coarse cloth
A dagger hanging by a lace had he
About his neck under his arm adown;
The hot summer had made his hue all brown;
And certainly he was a good fellow.
Full many a draught of wine he had y-draw
From Bourdeaux-ward, while that the chapmen sleep;
Of nice conscience took he no keep.
If that he fought, and had the higher hand,
By water he sent them home to every land. *he drowned his
        prisoners*
But of his craft to reckon well his tides,
His streames and his strandes him besides,
His herberow*, his moon, and lodemanage**, *harbourage
        **pilotage
There was none such, from Hull unto Carthage
Hardy he was, and wise, I undertake:
With many a tempest had his beard been shake.

13

He knew well all the havens, as they were,
From Scotland to the Cape of Finisterre,
And every creek in Bretagne and in Spain:
His barge y-cleped was the Magdelain.

With us there was a Doctor of Physic;
In all this worlde was there none him like
To speak of physic, and of surgery:
For he was grounded in astronomy.
He kept his patient a full great deal
In houres by his magic natural.
Well could he fortune* the ascendent   *make fortunate
Of his images for his patient,.
He knew the cause of every malady,
Were it of cold, or hot, or moist, or dry,
And where engender'd, and of what humour.
He was a very perfect practisour
The cause y-know,* and of his harm the root,   *known
Anon he gave to the sick man his boot*   *remedy
Full ready had he his apothecaries,
To send his drugges and his lectuaries
For each of them made other for to win
Their friendship was not newe to begin
Well knew he the old Esculapius,
And Dioscorides, and eke Rufus;
Old Hippocras, Hali, and Gallien;
Serapion, Rasis, and Avicen;
Averrois, Damascene, and Constantin;
Bernard, and Gatisden, and Gilbertin.
Of his diet measurable was he,
For it was of no superfluity,
But of great nourishing, and digestible.
His study was but little on the Bible.
In sanguine* and in perse** he clad was all   *red **blue
Lined with taffeta, and with sendall*.   *fine silk

And yet *he was but easy of dispense*: *he spent very little*
He kept *that he won in the pestilence*. *the money he made
    during the plague*
For gold in physic is a cordial;
Therefore he loved gold in special.

A good Wife was there of beside Bath,
But she was somedeal deaf, and that was scath*. *damage; pity
Of cloth-making she hadde such an haunt*, *skill
She passed them of Ypres, and of Gaunt.
In all the parish wife was there none,
That to the off'ring* before her should gon, *the offering at mass
And if there did, certain so wroth was she,
That she was out of alle charity
Her coverchiefs* were full fine of ground *head-dresses
I durste swear, they weighede ten pound
That on the Sunday were upon her head.
Her hosen weren of fine scarlet red,
Full strait y-tied, and shoes full moist* and new *fresh
Bold was her face, and fair and red of hue.
She was a worthy woman all her live,
Husbands at the church door had she had five,
Withouten other company in youth;
But thereof needeth not to speak as nouth*. *now
And thrice had she been at Jerusalem;
She hadde passed many a strange stream
At Rome she had been, and at Bologne,
In Galice at Saint James, and at Cologne;
She coude* much of wand'rng by the Way. *knew
Gat-toothed* was she, soothly for to say. *buck-toothed
Upon an ambler easily she sat,
Y-wimpled well, and on her head an hat
As broad as is a buckler or a targe.
A foot-mantle about her hippes large,
And on her feet a pair of spurres sharp.

In fellowship well could she laugh and carp* *jest, talk
Of remedies of love she knew perchance
For of that art she coud* the olde dance. *knew

A good man there was of religion,
That was a poore Parson of a town:
But rich he was of holy thought and werk*. *work
He was also a learned man, a clerk,
That Christe's gospel truly woulde preach.
His parishens* devoutly would he teach. *parishioners
Benign he was, and wonder diligent,
And in adversity full patient:
And such he was y-proved *often sithes*. *oftentimes*
Full loth were him to curse for his tithes,
But rather would he given out of doubt,
Unto his poore parishens about,
Of his off'ring, and eke of his substance.
He could in little thing have suffisance. *he was satisfied
with very little*
Wide was his parish, and houses far asunder,
But he ne left not, for no rain nor thunder,
In sickness and in mischief to visit
The farthest in his parish, *much and lit*, *great and small*
Upon his feet, and in his hand a staff.
This noble ensample to his sheep he gaf*, *gave
That first he wrought, and afterward he taught.
Out of the gospel he the wordes caught,
And this figure he added yet thereto,
That if gold ruste, what should iron do?
For if a priest be foul, on whom we trust,
No wonder is a lewed* man to rust: *unlearned
And shame it is, if that a priest take keep,
To see a shitten shepherd and clean sheep:
Well ought a priest ensample for to give,
By his own cleanness, how his sheep should live.

He sette not his benefice to hire,
And left his sheep eucumber'd in the mire,
And ran unto London, unto Saint Paul's,
To seeke him a chantery for souls,
Or with a brotherhood to be withold:* *detained
But dwelt at home, and kepte well his fold,
So that the wolf ne made it not miscarry.
He was a shepherd, and no mercenary.
And though he holy were, and virtuous,
He was to sinful men not dispitous* *severe
Nor of his speeche dangerous nor dign* *disdainful
But in his teaching discreet and benign.
To drawen folk to heaven, with fairness,
By good ensample, was his business:
But it were any person obstinate, *but if it were*
What so he were of high or low estate,
Him would he snibbe* sharply for the nones**. *reprove
    **nonce, occasion
A better priest I trow that nowhere none is.
He waited after no pomp nor reverence,
Nor maked him a *spiced conscience*, *artificial conscience*
But Christe's lore, and his apostles' twelve,
He taught, and first he follow'd it himselve.

With him there was a Ploughman, was his brother,
That had y-laid of dung full many a fother*. *ton
A true swinker* and a good was he, *hard worker
Living in peace and perfect charity.
God loved he beste with all his heart
At alle times, were it gain or smart*, *pain, loss
And then his neighebour right as himselve.
He woulde thresh, and thereto dike*, and delve, *dig ditches
For Christe's sake, for every poore wight,
Withouten hire, if it lay in his might.
His tithes payed he full fair and well,

17

Both of his *proper swink*, and his chattel** *his own labour*
    **goods
In a tabard* he rode upon a mare. *sleeveless jerkin

There was also a Reeve, and a Millere,
A Sompnour, and a Pardoner also,
A Manciple, and myself, there were no mo'.

The Miller was a stout carle for the nones,
Full big he was of brawn, and eke of bones;
That proved well, for *ov'r all where* he came, *wheresoever*
At wrestling he would bear away the ram.
He was short-shouldered, broad, a thicke gnarr*, *stump of
    wood
There was no door, that he n'old* heave off bar, *could not
Or break it at a running with his head.
His beard as any sow or fox was red,
And thereto broad, as though it were a spade.
Upon the cop* right of his nose he had *head
A wart, and thereon stood a tuft of hairs
Red as the bristles of a sowe's ears.
His nose-thirles* blacke were and wide. *nostrils
A sword and buckler bare he by his side.
His mouth as wide was as a furnace.
He was a jangler, and a goliardais*, *buffoon
And that was most of sin and harlotries.
Well could he steale corn, and tolle thrice
And yet he had a thumb of gold, pardie.
A white coat and a blue hood weared he
A baggepipe well could he blow and soun',
And therewithal he brought us out of town.

A gentle Manciple was there of a temple,
Of which achatours* mighte take ensample *buyers
For to be wise in buying of vitaille*. *victuals

For whether that he paid, or took *by taile*, *on credit*
Algate* he waited so in his achate**, *always **purchase
That he was aye before in good estate.
Now is not that of God a full fair grace
That such a lewed* mannes wit shall pace** *unlearned **surpass
The wisdom of an heap of learned men?
Of masters had he more than thries ten,
That were of law expert and curious:
Of which there was a dozen in that house,
Worthy to be stewards of rent and land
Of any lord that is in Engleland,
To make him live by his proper good,
In honour debtless, *but if he were wood*, *unless he were
    mad*
Or live as scarcely as him list desire;
And able for to helpen all a shire
In any case that mighte fall or hap;
And yet this Manciple *set their aller cap* *outwitted them
    all*

The Reeve was a slender choleric man
His beard was shav'd as nigh as ever he can.
His hair was by his eares round y-shorn;
His top was docked like a priest beforn
Full longe were his legges, and full lean
Y-like a staff, there was no calf y-seen
Well could he keep a garner* and a bin* *storeplaces for grain
There was no auditor could on him win
Well wist he by the drought, and by the rain,
The yielding of his seed and of his grain
His lorde's sheep, his neat*, and his dairy *cattle
His swine, his horse, his store, and his poultry,
Were wholly in this Reeve's governing,
And by his cov'nant gave he reckoning,
Since that his lord was twenty year of age;

There could no man bring him in arrearage
There was no bailiff, herd, nor other hine* *servant
That he ne knew his *sleight and his covine* *tricks and
    cheating*
They were adrad* of him, as of the death *in dread
His wonning* was full fair upon an heath *abode
With greene trees y-shadow'd was his place.
He coulde better than his lord purchase
Full rich he was y-stored privily
His lord well could he please subtilly,
To give and lend him of his owen good,
And have a thank, and yet* a coat and hood. *also
In youth he learned had a good mistere* *trade
He was a well good wright, a carpentere
This Reeve sate upon a right good stot*, *steed
That was all pomely* gray, and highte** Scot. *dappled
    **called
A long surcoat of perse* upon he had, *sky-blue
And by his side he bare a rusty blade.
Of Norfolk was this Reeve, of which I tell,
Beside a town men clepen* Baldeswell, *call
Tucked he was, as is a friar, about,
And ever rode the *hinderest of the rout*. *hindmost of the
    group*

A Sompnour* was there with us in that place, *summoner
That had a fire-red cherubinnes face,
For sausefleme* he was, with eyen narrow. *red or pimply
As hot he was and lecherous as a sparrow,
With scalled browes black, and pilled* beard: *scanty
Of his visage children were sore afeard.
There n'as quicksilver, litharge, nor brimstone,
Boras, ceruse, nor oil of tartar none,
Nor ointement that woulde cleanse or bite,
That him might helpen of his whelkes* white, *pustules

Nor of the knobbes* sitting on his cheeks. *buttons
Well lov'd he garlic, onions, and leeks,
And for to drink strong wine as red as blood.
Then would he speak, and cry as he were wood;
And when that he well drunken had the wine,
Then would he speake no word but Latin.
A fewe termes knew he, two or three,
That he had learned out of some decree;
No wonder is, he heard it all the day.
And eke ye knowen well, how that a jay
Can clepen* "Wat," as well as can the Pope. *call
But whoso would in other thing him grope*, *search
Then had he spent all his philosophy,
Aye, *Questio quid juris*, would he cry.

He was a gentle harlot* and a kind; *a low fellow
A better fellow should a man not find.
He woulde suffer, for a quart of wine,
A good fellow to have his concubine
A twelvemonth, and excuse him at the full.
Full privily a *finch eke could he pull*. *"fleece" a man*
And if he found owhere* a good fellaw, *anywhere
He woulde teache him to have none awe
In such a case of the archdeacon's curse;
But if a manne's soul were in his purse; *unless*
For in his purse he should y-punished be.
"Purse is the archedeacon's hell," said he.
But well I wot, he lied right indeed:
Of cursing ought each guilty man to dread,
For curse will slay right as assoiling* saveth; *absolving
And also 'ware him of a *significavit*.
In danger had he at his owen guise
The younge girles of the diocese,
And knew their counsel, and was of their rede*. *counsel
A garland had he set upon his head,

21

As great as it were for an alestake*: *The post of an alehouse sign
A buckler had he made him of a cake.

With him there rode a gentle Pardonere
Of Ronceval, his friend and his compere,
That straight was comen from the court of Rome.
Full loud he sang, "Come hither, love, to me"
This Sompnour *bare to him a stiff burdoun*, *sang the bass*
Was never trump of half so great a soun'.
This Pardoner had hair as yellow as wax,
But smooth it hung, as doth a strike* of flax: *strip
By ounces hung his lockes that he had,
And therewith he his shoulders oversprad.
Full thin it lay, by culpons* one and one, *locks, shreds
But hood for jollity, he weared none,
For it was trussed up in his wallet.
Him thought he rode all of the *newe get*, *latest fashion*
Dishevel, save his cap, he rode all bare.
Such glaring eyen had he, as an hare.
A vernicle* had he sew'd upon his cap. *image of Christ
His wallet lay before him in his lap,
Bretful* of pardon come from Rome all hot. *brimful
A voice he had as small as hath a goat.
No beard had he, nor ever one should have.
As smooth it was as it were new y-shave;
I trow he were a gelding or a mare.
But of his craft, from Berwick unto Ware,
Ne was there such another pardonere.
For in his mail* he had a pillowbere**, *bag **pillowcase
Which, as he saide, was our Lady's veil:
He said, he had a gobbet* of the sail *piece
That Sainte Peter had, when that he went
Upon the sea, till Jesus Christ him hent*. *took hold of
He had a cross of latoun* full of stones, *copper
And in a glass he hadde pigge's bones.

But with these relics, whenne that he fond
A poore parson dwelling upon lond,
Upon a day he got him more money
Than that the parson got in moneths tway;
And thus with feigned flattering and japes*, *jests
He made the parson and the people his apes.
But truely to tellen at the last,
He was in church a noble ecclesiast.
Well could he read a lesson or a story,
But alderbest* he sang an offertory: *best of all
For well he wiste, when that song was sung,
He muste preach, and well afile* his tongue, *polish
To winne silver, as he right well could:
Therefore he sang full merrily and loud.

Now have I told you shortly in a clause
Th' estate, th' array, the number, and eke the cause
Why that assembled was this company
In Southwark at this gentle hostelry,
That highte the Tabard, fast by the Bell.
But now is time to you for to tell
How that we baren us that ilke night, *what we did that
      same night*
When we were in that hostelry alight.
And after will I tell of our voyage,
And all the remnant of our pilgrimage.
But first I pray you of your courtesy,
That ye *arette it not my villainy*, *count it not rudeness
      in me*
Though that I plainly speak in this mattere.
To tellen you their wordes and their cheer;
Not though I speak their wordes properly.
For this ye knowen all so well as I,
Whoso shall tell a tale after a man,
He must rehearse, as nigh as ever he can,

Every word, if it be in his charge,
All speak he ne'er so rudely and so large; *let him speak*
Or elles he must tell his tale untrue,
Or feigne things, or finde wordes new.
He may not spare, although he were his brother;
He must as well say one word as another.
Christ spake Himself full broad in Holy Writ,
And well ye wot no villainy is it.
Eke Plato saith, whoso that can him read,
The wordes must be cousin to the deed.
Also I pray you to forgive it me,
All have I not set folk in their degree, *although I have*
Here in this tale, as that they shoulden stand:
My wit is short, ye may well understand.

Great cheere made our Host us every one,
And to the supper set he us anon:
And served us with victual of the best.
Strong was the wine, and well to drink us lest*. *pleased
A seemly man Our Hoste was withal
For to have been a marshal in an hall.
A large man he was with eyen steep*, *deep-set.
A fairer burgess is there none in Cheap:
Bold of his speech, and wise and well y-taught,
And of manhoode lacked him right naught.
Eke thereto was he right a merry man,
And after supper playen he began,
And spake of mirth amonges other things,
When that we hadde made our reckonings;
And saide thus; "Now, lordinges, truly
Ye be to me welcome right heartily:
For by my troth, if that I shall not lie,
I saw not this year such a company
At once in this herberow*, am is now. *inn
Fain would I do you mirth, *an I wist* how. *if I knew*

And of a mirth I am right now bethought.
To do you ease*, and it shall coste nought. *pleasure
Ye go to Canterbury; God you speed,
The blissful Martyr *quite you your meed*; *grant you what
    you deserve*
And well I wot, as ye go by the way,
Ye *shapen you* to talken and to play: *intend to*
For truely comfort nor mirth is none
To ride by the way as dumb as stone:
And therefore would I make you disport,
As I said erst, and do you some comfort.
And if you liketh all by one assent
Now for to standen at my judgement,
And for to worken as I shall you say
To-morrow, when ye riden on the way,
Now by my father's soule that is dead,
But ye be merry, smiteth off mine head. *unless you are merry,
    smite off my head*
Hold up your hands withoute more speech.

Our counsel was not longe for to seech*: *seek
Us thought it was not worth to *make it wise*, *discuss it at
    length*
And granted him withoute more avise*, *consideration
And bade him say his verdict, as him lest.
Lordings (quoth he), now hearken for the best;
But take it not, I pray you, in disdain;
This is the point, to speak it plat* and plain. *flat
That each of you, to shorten with your way
In this voyage, shall tellen tales tway,
To Canterbury-ward, I mean it so,
And homeward he shall tellen other two,
Of aventures that whilom have befall.
And which of you that bear'th him best of all,
That is to say, that telleth in this case

Tales of best sentence and most solace,
Shall have a supper *at your aller cost* *at the cost of you all*
Here in this place, sitting by this post,
When that ye come again from Canterbury.
And for to make you the more merry,
I will myselfe gladly with you ride,
Right at mine owen cost, and be your guide.
And whoso will my judgement withsay,
Shall pay for all we spenden by the way.
And if ye vouchesafe that it be so,
Tell me anon withoute wordes mo"*, *more
And I will early shape me therefore."

This thing was granted, and our oath we swore
With full glad heart, and prayed him also,
That he would vouchesafe for to do so,
And that he woulde be our governour,
And of our tales judge and reportour,
And set a supper at a certain price;
And we will ruled be at his device,
In high and low: and thus by one assent,
We be accorded to his judgement.
And thereupon the wine was fet* anon. *fetched
We drunken, and to reste went each one,
Withouten any longer tarrying
A-morrow, when the day began to spring,
Up rose our host, and was *our aller cock*, *the cock to wake
        us all*
And gather'd us together in a flock,
And forth we ridden all a little space,
Unto the watering of Saint Thomas:
And there our host began his horse arrest,
And saide; "Lordes, hearken if you lest.
Ye *weet your forword,* and I it record. *know your promise*
If even-song and morning-song accord,

Let see now who shall telle the first tale.
As ever may I drinke wine or ale,
Whoso is rebel to my judgement,
Shall pay for all that by the way is spent.
Now draw ye cuts*, ere that ye farther twin**.   *lots **go
He which that hath the shortest shall begin."

"Sir Knight (quoth he), my master and my lord,
Now draw the cut, for that is mine accord.
Come near (quoth he), my Lady Prioress,
And ye, Sir Clerk, let be your shamefastness,
Nor study not: lay hand to, every man."
Anon to drawen every wight began,
And shortly for to tellen as it was,
Were it by a venture, or sort*, or cas**,   *lot **chance
The sooth is this, the cut fell to the Knight,
Of which full blithe and glad was every wight;
And tell he must his tale as was reason,
By forword, and by composition,
As ye have heard; what needeth wordes mo'?
And when this good man saw that it was so,
As he that wise was and obedient
To keep his forword by his free assent,
He said; "Sithen* I shall begin this game,   *since
Why, welcome be the cut in Godde's name.
Now let us ride, and hearken what I say."
And with that word we ridden forth our way;
And he began with right a merry cheer
His tale anon, and said as ye shall hear.

THE KNIGHT'S TALE

Whilom*, as olde stories tellen us,   *formerly
There was a duke that highte* Theseus.   *was called
Of Athens he was lord and governor,

And in his time such a conqueror
That greater was there none under the sun.
Full many a riche country had he won.
What with his wisdom and his chivalry,
He conquer'd all the regne of Feminie,
That whilom was y-cleped Scythia;
And weddede the Queen Hippolyta
And brought her home with him to his country
With muchel* glory and great solemnity, *great
And eke her younge sister Emily,
And thus with vict'ry and with melody
Let I this worthy Duke to Athens ride,
And all his host, in armes him beside.

And certes, if it n'ere* too long to hear, *were not
I would have told you fully the mannere,
How wonnen* was the regne of Feminie, *won
By Theseus, and by his chivalry;
And of the greate battle for the nonce
Betwixt Athenes and the Amazons;
And how assieged was Hippolyta,
The faire hardy queen of Scythia;
And of the feast that was at her wedding
And of the tempest at her homecoming.
But all these things I must as now forbear.
I have, God wot, a large field to ear* *plough;
And weake be the oxen in my plough;
The remnant of my tale is long enow.
I will not *letten eke none of this rout*. *hinder any of this company*
Let every fellow tell his tale about,
And let see now who shall the supper win.
There *as I left*, I will again begin. *where I left off*

This Duke, of whom I make mentioun,
When he was come almost unto the town,

In all his weal, and in his moste pride,
He was ware, as he cast his eye aside,
Where that there kneeled in the highe way
A company of ladies, tway and tway,
Each after other, clad in clothes black:
But such a cry and such a woe they make,
That in this world n'is creature living,
That hearde such another waimenting* *lamenting
And of this crying would they never stenten*, *desist
Till they the reines of his bridle henten*. *seize
"What folk be ye that at mine homecoming
Perturben so my feaste with crying?"
Quoth Theseus; "Have ye so great envy
Of mine honour, that thus complain and cry?
Or who hath you misboden*, or offended? *wronged
Do telle me, if it may be amended;
And why that ye be clad thus all in black?"

The oldest lady of them all then spake,
When she had swooned, with a deadly cheer*, *countenance
That it was ruthe* for to see or hear. *pity
She saide; "Lord, to whom fortune hath given
Vict'ry, and as a conqueror to liven,
Nought grieveth us your glory and your honour;
But we beseechen mercy and succour.
Have mercy on our woe and our distress;
Some drop of pity, through thy gentleness,
Upon us wretched women let now fall.
For certes, lord, there is none of us all
That hath not been a duchess or a queen;
Now be we caitives*, as it is well seen: *captives
Thanked be Fortune, and her false wheel,
That *none estate ensureth to be wele*. *assures no
    continuance of prosperous estate*
And certes, lord, t'abiden your presence

Here in this temple of the goddess Clemence
We have been waiting all this fortenight:
Now help us, lord, since it lies in thy might.

"I, wretched wight, that weep and waile thus,
Was whilom wife to king Capaneus,
That starf* at Thebes, cursed be that day: *died
And alle we that be in this array,
And maken all this lamentatioun,
We losten all our husbands at that town,
While that the siege thereabouten lay.
And yet the olde Creon, wellaway!
That lord is now of Thebes the city,
Fulfilled of ire and of iniquity,
He for despite, and for his tyranny,
To do the deade bodies villainy*, *insult
Of all our lorde's, which that been y-slaw, *slain
Hath all the bodies on an heap y-draw,
And will not suffer them by none assent
Neither to be y-buried, nor y-brent*, *burnt
But maketh houndes eat them in despite."
And with that word, withoute more respite
They fallen groff,* and cryden piteously; *grovelling
"Have on us wretched women some mercy,
And let our sorrow sinken in thine heart."

This gentle Duke down from his courser start
With hearte piteous, when he heard them speak.
Him thoughte that his heart would all to-break,
When he saw them so piteous and so mate* *abased
That whilom weren of so great estate.
And in his armes he them all up hent*, *raised, took
And them comforted in full good intent,
And swore his oath, as he was true knight,
He woulde do *so farforthly his might* *as far as his power went*

Upon the tyrant Creon them to wreak*, *avenge
That all the people of Greece shoulde speak,
How Creon was of Theseus y-served,
As he that had his death full well deserved.
And right anon withoute more abode* *delay
His banner he display'd, and forth he rode
To Thebes-ward, and all his host beside:
No ner* Athenes would he go nor ride, *nearer
Nor take his ease fully half a day,
But onward on his way that night he lay:
And sent anon Hippolyta the queen,
And Emily her younge sister sheen* *bright, lovely
Unto the town of Athens for to dwell:
And forth he rit*; there is no more to tell. *rode

The red statue of Mars with spear and targe* *shield
So shineth in his white banner large
That all the fieldes glitter up and down:
And by his banner borne is his pennon
Of gold full rich, in which there was y-beat* *stamped
The Minotaur which that he slew in Crete
Thus rit this Duke, thus rit this conqueror
And in his host of chivalry the flower,
Till that he came to Thebes, and alight
Fair in a field, there as he thought to fight.
But shortly for to speaken of this thing,
With Creon, which that was of Thebes king,
He fought, and slew him manly as a knight
In plain bataille, and put his folk to flight:
And by assault he won the city after,
And rent adown both wall, and spar, and rafter;
And to the ladies he restored again
The bodies of their husbands that were slain,
To do obsequies, as was then the guise*. *custom

But it were all too long for to devise*   *describe
The greate clamour, and the waimenting*,   *lamenting
Which that the ladies made at the brenning*   *burning
Of the bodies, and the great honour
That Theseus the noble conqueror
Did to the ladies, when they from him went:
But shortly for to tell is mine intent.
When that this worthy Duke, this Theseus,
Had Creon slain, and wonnen Thebes thus,
Still in the field he took all night his rest,
And did with all the country as him lest*.   *pleased
To ransack in the tas* of bodies dead,   *heap
Them for to strip of *harness and of **weed,   *armour **clothes
The pillers* did their business and cure,   *pillagers
After the battle and discomfiture.
And so befell, that in the tas they found,
Through girt with many a grievous bloody wound,
Two younge knightes *ligging by and by*   *lying side by side*
Both in *one armes*, wrought full richely: *the same armour*
Of whiche two, Arcite hight that one,
And he that other highte Palamon.
Not fully quick*, nor fully dead they were,   *alive
But by their coat-armour, and by their gear,
The heralds knew them well in special,
As those that weren of the blood royal
Of Thebes, and *of sistren two y-born*.   *born of two sisters*
Out of the tas the pillers have them torn,
And have them carried soft unto the tent
Of Theseus, and he full soon them sent
To Athens, for to dwellen in prison
Perpetually, he *n'olde no ranson*.   *would take no ransom*
And when this worthy Duke had thus y-done,
He took his host, and home he rit anon
With laurel crowned as a conquerour;

And there he lived in joy and in honour
Term of his life; what needeth wordes mo'?
And in a tower, in anguish and in woe,
Dwellen this Palamon, and eke Arcite,
For evermore, there may no gold them quite* *set free

Thus passed year by year, and day by day,
Till it fell ones in a morn of May
That Emily, that fairer was to seen
Than is the lily upon his stalke green,
And fresher than the May with flowers new
(For with the rose colour strove her hue;
I n'ot* which was the finer of them two), *know not
Ere it was day, as she was wont to do,
She was arisen, and all ready dight*, *dressed
For May will have no sluggardy a-night;
The season pricketh every gentle heart,
And maketh him out of his sleep to start,
And saith, "Arise, and do thine observance."

This maketh Emily have remembrance
To do honour to May, and for to rise.
Y-clothed was she fresh for to devise;
Her yellow hair was braided in a tress,
Behind her back, a yarde long I guess.
And in the garden at *the sun uprist* *sunrise
She walketh up and down where as her list.
She gathereth flowers, party* white and red, *mingled
To make a sotel* garland for her head, *subtle, well-arranged
And as an angel heavenly she sung.
The greate tower, that was so thick and strong,
Which of the castle was the chief dungeon
(Where as these knightes weren in prison,
Of which I tolde you, and telle shall),

Was even joinant* to the garden wall, *adjoining
There as this Emily had her playing.

Bright was the sun, and clear that morrowning,
And Palamon, this woful prisoner,
As was his wont, by leave of his gaoler,
Was ris'n, and roamed in a chamber on high,
In which he all the noble city sigh*, *saw
And eke the garden, full of branches green,
There as this fresh Emelia the sheen
Was in her walk, and roamed up and down.
This sorrowful prisoner, this Palamon
Went in his chamber roaming to and fro,
And to himself complaining of his woe:
That he was born, full oft he said, Alas!
And so befell, by aventure or cas*, *chance
That through a window thick of many a bar
Of iron great, and square as any spar,
He cast his eyes upon Emelia,
And therewithal he blent* and cried, Ah! *started aside
As though he stungen were unto the heart.
And with that cry Arcite anon up start,
And saide, "Cousin mine, what aileth thee,
That art so pale and deadly for to see?
Why cried'st thou? who hath thee done offence?
For Godde's love, take all in patience
Our prison*, for it may none other be. *imprisonment
Fortune hath giv'n us this adversity'.
Some wick'* aspect or disposition *wicked
Of Saturn, by some constellation,
Hath giv'n us this, although we had it sworn,
So stood the heaven when that we were born,
We must endure; this is the short and plain."

This Palamon answer'd, and said again:
"Cousin, forsooth of this opinion
Thou hast a vain imagination.
This prison caused me not for to cry;
But I was hurt right now thorough mine eye
Into mine heart; that will my bane* be.   *destruction
The fairness of the lady that I see
Yond in the garden roaming to and fro,
Is cause of all my crying and my woe.
I *n'ot wher* she be woman or goddess,   *know not whether*
But Venus is it, soothly* as I guess",   *truly
And therewithal on knees adown he fill,
And saide: "Venus, if it be your will
You in this garden thus to transfigure
Before me sorrowful wretched creature,
Out of this prison help that we may scape.
And if so be our destiny be shape
By etern word to dien in prison,
Of our lineage have some compassion,
That is so low y-brought by tyranny."

And with that word Arcite *gan espy*   *began to look forth*
Where as this lady roamed to and fro
And with that sight her beauty hurt him so,
That if that Palamon was wounded sore,
Arcite is hurt as much as he, or more.
And with a sigh he saide piteously:
"The freshe beauty slay'th me suddenly
Of her that roameth yonder in the place.
And but* I have her mercy and her grace,   *unless
That I may see her at the leaste way,
I am but dead; there is no more to say."
This Palamon, when he these wordes heard,
Dispiteously* he looked, and answer'd: *angrily
"Whether say'st thou this in earnest or in play?"

35

"Nay," quoth Arcite, "in earnest, by my fay*. *faith
God help me so, *me lust full ill to play*." *I am in no humour
    for jesting*
This Palamon gan knit his browes tway.
"It were," quoth he, "to thee no great honour
For to be false, nor for to be traitour
To me, that am thy cousin and thy brother
Y-sworn full deep, and each of us to other,
That never for to dien in the pain,
Till that the death departen shall us twain,
Neither of us in love to hinder other,
Nor in none other case, my leve* brother; *dear
But that thou shouldest truly farther me
In every case, as I should farther thee.
This was thine oath, and mine also certain;
I wot it well, thou dar'st it not withsayn*, *deny
Thus art thou of my counsel out of doubt,
And now thou wouldest falsely be about
To love my lady, whom I love and serve,
And ever shall, until mine hearte sterve* *die
Now certes, false Arcite, thou shalt not so
I lov'd her first, and tolde thee my woe
As to my counsel, and my brother sworn
To farther me, as I have told beforn.
For which thou art y-bounden as a knight
To helpe me, if it lie in thy might,
Or elles art thou false, I dare well sayn,"

This Arcite full proudly spake again:
"Thou shalt," quoth he, "be rather* false than I, *sooner
And thou art false, I tell thee utterly;
For par amour I lov'd her first ere thou.
What wilt thou say? *thou wist it not right now* *even now
    thou knowest not*
Whether she be a woman or goddess.

Thine is affection of holiness,
And mine is love, as to a creature:
For which I tolde thee mine aventure
As to my cousin, and my brother sworn
I pose*, that thou loved'st her beforn: *suppose
Wost* thou not well the olde clerke's saw, *know'st
That who shall give a lover any law?
Love is a greater lawe, by my pan,
Than may be giv'n to any earthly man:
Therefore positive law, and such decree,
Is broke alway for love in each degree
A man must needes love, maugre his head.
He may not flee it, though he should be dead,
All be she maid, or widow, or else wife. *whether she be*
And eke it is not likely all thy life
To standen in her grace, no more than I
For well thou wost thyselfe verily,
That thou and I be damned to prison
Perpetual, us gaineth no ranson.
We strive, as did the houndes for the bone;
They fought all day, and yet their part was none.
There came a kite, while that they were so wroth,
And bare away the bone betwixt them both.
And therefore at the kinge's court, my brother,
Each man for himselfe, there is no other.
Love if thee list; for I love and aye shall
And soothly, leve brother, this is all.
Here in this prison musten we endure,
And each of us take his Aventure."

Great was the strife and long between these tway,
If that I hadde leisure for to say;
But to the effect: it happen'd on a day
(To tell it you as shortly as I may),
A worthy duke that hight Perithous

That fellow was to the Duke Theseus
Since thilke* day that they were children lite** *that **little
Was come to Athens, his fellow to visite,
And for to play, as he was wont to do;
For in this world he loved no man so;
And he lov'd him as tenderly again.
So well they lov'd, as olde bookes sayn,
That when that one was dead, soothly to sayn,
His fellow went and sought him down in hell:
But of that story list me not to write.
Duke Perithous loved well Arcite,
And had him known at Thebes year by year:
And finally at request and prayere
Of Perithous, withoute ranson
Duke Theseus him let out of prison,
Freely to go, where him list over all,
In such a guise, as I you tellen shall
This was the forword*, plainly to indite, *promise
Betwixte Theseus and him Arcite:
That if so were, that Arcite were y-found
Ever in his life, by day or night, one stound* *moment
In any country of this Theseus,
And he were caught, it was accorded thus,
That with a sword he shoulde lose his head;
There was none other remedy nor rede*. *counsel
But took his leave, and homeward he him sped;
Let him beware, his necke lieth *to wed*. *in pledge*

How great a sorrow suff'reth now Arcite!
The death he feeleth through his hearte smite;
He weepeth, waileth, crieth piteously;
To slay himself he waiteth privily.
He said; "Alas the day that I was born!
Now is my prison worse than beforn:
Now is me shape eternally to dwell *it is fixed for me*

Not in purgatory, but right in hell.
Alas! that ever I knew Perithous.
For elles had I dwelt with Theseus
Y-fettered in his prison evermo'.
Then had I been in bliss, and not in woe.
Only the sight of her, whom that I serve,
Though that I never may her grace deserve,
Would have sufficed right enough for me.
"O deare cousin Palamon," quoth he,
"Thine is the vict'ry of this aventure,
Full blissfully in prison to endure:
In prison? nay certes, in paradise.
Well hath fortune y-turned thee the dice,
That hast the sight of her, and I th' absence.
For possible is, since thou hast her presence,
And art a knight, a worthy and an able,
That by some cas*, since fortune is changeable, *chance
Thou may'st to thy desire sometime attain.
But I that am exiled, and barren
Of alle grace, and in so great despair,
That there n'is earthe, water, fire, nor air,
Nor creature, that of them maked is,
That may me helpe nor comfort in this,
Well ought I *sterve in wanhope* and distress. *die in despair*
Farewell my life, my lust*, and my gladness. *pleasure
Alas, *why plainen men so in commune *why do men so often
      complain*
Of purveyance of God, or of Fortune, *of God's providence?*
That giveth them full oft in many a guise
Well better than they can themselves devise?
Some man desireth for to have richess,
That cause is of his murder or great sickness.
And some man would out of his prison fain,
That in his house is of his meinie* slain. *servants
Infinite harmes be in this mattere.

We wot never what thing we pray for here.
We fare as he that drunk is as a mouse.
A drunken man wot well he hath an house,
But he wot not which is the right way thither,
And to a drunken man the way is slither*.   *slippery
And certes in this world so fare we.
We seeke fast after felicity,
But we go wrong full often truely.
Thus we may sayen all, and namely* I,   *especially
That ween'd*, and had a great opinion,   *thought
That if I might escape from prison
Then had I been in joy and perfect heal,
Where now I am exiled from my weal.
Since that I may not see you, Emily,
I am but dead; there is no remedy."

Upon that other side, Palamon,
When that he wist Arcite was agone,
Much sorrow maketh, that the greate tower
Resounded of his yelling and clamour
The pure* fetters on his shinnes great *very
Were of his bitter salte teares wet.

"Alas!" quoth he, "Arcite, cousin mine,
Of all our strife, God wot, the fruit is thine.
Thou walkest now in Thebes at thy large,
And of my woe thou *givest little charge*.   *takest little heed*
Thou mayst, since thou hast wisdom and manhead*,   *manhood,
    courage
Assemble all the folk of our kindred,
And make a war so sharp on this country
That by some aventure, or some treaty,
Thou mayst have her to lady and to wife,
For whom that I must needes lose my life.
For as by way of possibility,

Since thou art at thy large, of prison free,
And art a lord, great is thine avantage,
More than is mine, that sterve here in a cage.
For I must weep and wail, while that I live,
With all the woe that prison may me give,
And eke with pain that love me gives also,
That doubles all my torment and my woe."

Therewith the fire of jealousy upstart
Within his breast, and hent* him by the heart   *seized
So woodly*, that he like was to behold   *madly
The box-tree, or the ashes dead and cold.
Then said; "O cruel goddess, that govern
This world with binding of your word etern*   *eternal
And writen in the table of adamant
Your parlement* and your eternal grant,   *consultation
What is mankind more *unto you y-hold*   *by you esteemed
Than is the sheep, that rouketh* in the fold!   *lie huddled
        together
For slain is man, right as another beast;
And dwelleth eke in prison and arrest,
And hath sickness, and great adversity,
And oftentimes guiltless, pardie*   *by God
What governance is in your prescience,
That guiltless tormenteth innocence?
And yet increaseth this all my penance,
That man is bounden to his observance
For Godde's sake to *letten of his will*,   *restrain his desire*
Whereas a beast may all his lust fulfil.
And when a beast is dead, he hath no pain;
But man after his death must weep and plain,
Though in this worlde he have care and woe:
Withoute doubt it maye standen so.
"The answer of this leave I to divines,
But well I wot, that in this world great pine* is;   *pain, trouble

GEOFFREY CHAUCER

Alas! I see a serpent or a thief
That many a true man hath done mischief,
Go at his large, and where him list may turn.
But I must be in prison through Saturn,
And eke through Juno, jealous and eke wood*, *mad
That hath well nigh destroyed all the blood
Of Thebes, with his waste walles wide.
And Venus slay'th me on that other side
For jealousy, and fear of him, Arcite."

Now will I stent* of Palamon a lite**, *pause **little
And let him in his prison stille dwell,
And of Arcite forth I will you tell.
The summer passeth, and the nightes long
Increase double-wise the paines strong
Both of the lover and the prisonere.
I n'ot* which hath the wofuller mistere**. *know not
    **condition
For, shortly for to say, this Palamon
Perpetually is damned to prison,
In chaines and in fetters to be dead;
And Arcite is exiled *on his head* *on peril of his head*
For evermore as out of that country,
Nor never more he shall his lady see.
You lovers ask I now this question,
Who lieth the worse, Arcite or Palamon?
The one may see his lady day by day,
But in prison he dwelle must alway.
The other where him list may ride or go,
But see his lady shall he never mo'.
Now deem all as you liste, ye that can,
For I will tell you forth as I began.

When that Arcite to Thebes comen was,
Full oft a day he swelt*, and said, "Alas!" *fainted

For see this lady he shall never mo'.
And shortly to concluden all his woe,
So much sorrow had never creature
That is or shall be while the world may dure.
His sleep, his meat, his drink is *him byraft*, *taken away
from him*
That lean he wex*, and dry as any shaft. *became
His eyen hollow, grisly to behold,
His hue sallow, and pale as ashes cold,
And solitary he was, ever alone,
And wailing all the night, making his moan.
And if he hearde song or instrument,
Then would he weepen, he might not be stent*. *stopped
So feeble were his spirits, and so low,
And changed so, that no man coulde know
His speech, neither his voice, though men it heard.
And in his gear* for all the world he far'd *behaviour
Not only like the lovers' malady
Of Eros, but rather y-like manie* *madness
Engender'd of humours melancholic,
Before his head in his cell fantastic.
And shortly turned was all upside down,
Both habit and eke dispositioun,
Of him, this woful lover Dan* Arcite. *Lord
Why should I all day of his woe indite?
When he endured had a year or two
This cruel torment, and this pain and woe,
At Thebes, in his country, as I said,
Upon a night in sleep as he him laid,
Him thought how that the winged god Mercury
Before him stood, and bade him to be merry.
His sleepy yard* in hand he bare upright; *rod
A hat he wore upon his haires bright.
Arrayed was this god (as he took keep*) *notice
As he was when that Argus took his sleep;

And said him thus: "To Athens shalt thou wend*; *go
There is thee shapen* of thy woe an end." *fixed, prepared
And with that word Arcite woke and start.
"Now truely how sore that e'er me smart,"
Quoth he, "to Athens right now will I fare.
Nor for no dread of death shall I not spare
To see my lady that I love and serve;
In her presence *I recke not to sterve.*" *do not care if I die*
And with that word he caught a great mirror,
And saw that changed was all his colour,
And saw his visage all in other kind.
And right anon it ran him ill his mind,
That since his face was so disfigur'd
Of malady the which he had endur'd,
He mighte well, if that he *bare him low,* *lived in lowly fashion*
Live in Athenes evermore unknow,
And see his lady wellnigh day by day.
And right anon he changed his array,
And clad him as a poore labourer.
And all alone, save only a squier,
That knew his privity* and all his cas**, *secrets **fortune
Which was disguised poorly as he was,
To Athens is he gone the nexte* way. *nearest
And to the court he went upon a day,
And at the gate he proffer'd his service,
To drudge and draw, what so men would devise*. *order
And, shortly of this matter for to sayn,
He fell in office with a chamberlain,
The which that dwelling was with Emily.
For he was wise, and coulde soon espy
Of every servant which that served her.
Well could he hewe wood, and water bear,
For he was young and mighty for the nones*, *occasion
And thereto he was strong and big of bones
To do that any wight can him devise.

A year or two he was in this service,
Page of the chamber of Emily the bright;
And Philostrate he saide that he hight.
But half so well belov'd a man as he
Ne was there never in court of his degree.
He was so gentle of conditioun,
That throughout all the court was his renown.
They saide that it were a charity
That Theseus would *enhance his degree*, *elevate him in rank*
And put him in some worshipful service,
There as he might his virtue exercise.
And thus within a while his name sprung
Both of his deedes, and of his good tongue,
That Theseus hath taken him so near,
That of his chamber he hath made him squire,
And gave him gold to maintain his degree;
And eke men brought him out of his country
From year to year full privily his rent.
But honestly and slyly* he it spent, *discreetly, prudently
That no man wonder'd how that he it had.
And three year in this wise his life be lad*, *led
And bare him so in peace and eke in werre*, *war
There was no man that Theseus had so derre*. *dear
And in this blisse leave I now Arcite,
And speak I will of Palamon a lite*. *little

In darkness horrible, and strong prison,
This seven year hath sitten Palamon,
Forpined*, what for love, and for distress. *pined, wasted away
Who feeleth double sorrow and heaviness
But Palamon? that love distraineth* so, *afflicts
That wood* out of his wits he went for woe, *mad
And eke thereto he is a prisonere
Perpetual, not only for a year.

Who coulde rhyme in English properly
His martyrdom? forsooth*, it is not I; *truly
Therefore I pass as lightly as I may.
It fell that in the seventh year, in May
The thirde night (as olde bookes sayn,
That all this story tellen more plain),
Were it by a venture or destiny
(As when a thing is shapen* it shall be), *settled, decreed
That soon after the midnight, Palamon
By helping of a friend brake his prison,
And fled the city fast as he might go,
For he had given drink his gaoler so
Of a clary, made of a certain wine,
With *narcotise and opie* of Thebes fine, *narcotics and opium*
That all the night, though that men would him shake,
The gaoler slept, he mighte not awake:
And thus he fled as fast as ever he may.
The night was short, and *faste by the day* *close at hand was
        the day*
That needes cast he must himself to hide*. *during which he
        must cast about, or contrive, to conceal himself.*
And to a grove faste there beside
With dreadful foot then stalked Palamon.
For shortly this was his opinion,
That in the grove he would him hide all day,
And in the night then would he take his way
To Thebes-ward, his friendes for to pray
On Theseus to help him to warray*. *make war
And shortly either he would lose his life,
Or winnen Emily unto his wife.
This is th' effect, and his intention plain.

Now will I turn to Arcite again,
That little wist how nighe was his care,
Till that Fortune had brought him in the snare.

The busy lark, the messenger of day,
Saluteth in her song the morning gray;
And fiery Phoebus riseth up so bright,
That all the orient laugheth at the sight,
And with his streames* drieth in the greves** *rays **groves
The silver droppes, hanging on the leaves;
And Arcite, that is in the court royal
With Theseus, his squier principal,
Is ris'n, and looketh on the merry day.
And for to do his observance to May,
Remembering the point* of his desire, *object
He on his courser, starting as the fire,
Is ridden to the fieldes him to play,
Out of the court, were it a mile or tway.
And to the grove, of which I have you told,
By a venture his way began to hold,
To make him a garland of the greves*, *groves
Were it of woodbine, or of hawthorn leaves,
And loud he sang against the sun so sheen*. *shining bright
"O May, with all thy flowers and thy green,
Right welcome be thou, faire freshe May,
I hope that I some green here getten may."
And from his courser*, with a lusty heart, *horse
Into the grove full hastily he start,
And in a path he roamed up and down,
There as by aventure this Palamon
Was in a bush, that no man might him see,
For sore afeard of his death was he.
Nothing ne knew he that it was Arcite;
God wot he would have *trowed it full lite*. *full little
     believed it*
But sooth is said, gone since full many years,
The field hath eyen*, and the wood hath ears, *eyes
It is full fair a man *to bear him even*, *to be on his guard*
For all day meeten men at *unset steven*. *unexpected time*

47

Full little wot Arcite of his fellaw,
That was so nigh to hearken of his saw*, *saying, speech
For in the bush he sitteth now full still.
When that Arcite had roamed all his fill,
And *sungen all the roundel* lustily, *sang the roundelay*
Into a study he fell suddenly,
As do those lovers in their *quainte gears*, *odd fashions*
Now in the crop*, and now down in the breres**, *tree-top **briars
Now up, now down, as bucket in a well.
Right as the Friday, soothly for to tell,
Now shineth it, and now it raineth fast,
Right so can geary* Venus overcast *changeful
The heartes of her folk, right as her day
Is gearful*, right so changeth she array. *changeful
Seldom is Friday all the weeke like.
When Arcite had y-sung, he gan to sike*, *sigh
And sat him down withouten any more:
"Alas!" quoth he, "the day that I was bore!
How longe, Juno, through thy cruelty
Wilt thou warrayen* Thebes the city? *torment
Alas! y-brought is to confusion
The blood royal of Cadm' and Amphion:
Of Cadmus, which that was the firste man,
That Thebes built, or first the town began,
And of the city first was crowned king.
Of his lineage am I, and his offspring
By very line, as of the stock royal;
And now I am *so caitiff and so thrall*, *wretched and enslaved*
That he that is my mortal enemy,
I serve him as his squier poorely.
And yet doth Juno me well more shame,
For I dare not beknow* mine owen name, *acknowledge
But there as I was wont to hight Arcite,
Now hight I Philostrate, not worth a mite.
Alas! thou fell Mars, and alas! Juno,

Thus hath your ire our lineage all fordo*   *undone, ruined
Save only me, and wretched Palamon,
That Theseus martyreth in prison.
And over all this, to slay me utterly,
Love hath his fiery dart so brenningly*   *burningly
Y-sticked through my true careful heart,
That shapen was my death erst than my shert.
Ye slay me with your eyen, Emily;
Ye be the cause wherefore that I die.
Of all the remnant of mine other care
Ne set I not the *mountance of a tare*,   *value of a straw*
So that I could do aught to your pleasance."

And with that word he fell down in a trance
A longe time; and afterward upstart
This Palamon, that thought thorough his heart
He felt a cold sword suddenly to glide:
For ire he quoke*, no longer would he hide.   *quaked
And when that he had heard Arcite's tale,
As he were wood*, with face dead and pale,   *mad
He start him up out of the bushes thick,
And said: "False Arcite, false traitor wick*,   *wicked
Now art thou hent*, that lov'st my lady so,   *caught
For whom that I have all this pain and woe,
And art my blood, and to my counsel sworn,
As I full oft have told thee herebeforn,
And hast bejaped* here Duke Theseus,   *deceived, imposed upon
And falsely changed hast thy name thus;
I will be dead, or elles thou shalt die.
Thou shalt not love my lady Emily,
But I will love her only and no mo';
For I am Palamon thy mortal foe.
And though I have no weapon in this place,
But out of prison am astart* by grace,   *escaped
I dreade* not that either thou shalt die,   *doubt

Or else thou shalt not loven Emily.
Choose which thou wilt, for thou shalt not astart."

This Arcite then, with full dispiteous* heart,   *wrathful
When he him knew, and had his tale heard,
As fierce as lion pulled out a swerd,
And saide thus; "By God that sitt'th above,
N'ere it that thou art sick, and wood for love,   *were it not*
And eke that thou no weap'n hast in this place,
Thou should'st never out of this grove pace,
That thou ne shouldest dien of mine hand.
For I defy the surety and the band,
Which that thou sayest I have made to thee.
What? very fool, think well that love is free;
And I will love her maugre* all thy might.   *despite
But, for thou art a worthy gentle knight,
And *wilnest to darraine her by bataille*,   *will reclaim her by
    combat*
Have here my troth, to-morrow I will not fail,
Without weeting* of any other wight,   *knowledge
That here I will be founden as a knight,
And bringe harness* right enough for thee;   *armour and arms
And choose the best, and leave the worst for me.
And meat and drinke this night will I bring
Enough for thee, and clothes for thy bedding.
And if so be that thou my lady win,
And slay me in this wood that I am in,
Thou may'st well have thy lady as for me."
This Palamon answer'd, "I grant it thee."
And thus they be departed till the morrow,
When each of them hath *laid his faith to borrow*.   *pledged
    his faith*

O Cupid, out of alle charity!
O Regne* that wilt no fellow have with thee!   *queen

Full sooth is said, that love nor lordeship
Will not, *his thanks*, have any fellowship. *thanks to him*
Well finden that Arcite and Palamon.
Arcite is ridd anon unto the town,
And on the morrow, ere it were daylight,
Full privily two harness hath he dight*, *prepared
Both suffisant and meete to darraine* *contest
The battle in the field betwixt them twain.
And on his horse, alone as he was born,
He carrieth all this harness him beforn;
And in the grove, at time and place y-set,
This Arcite and this Palamon be met.
Then change gan the colour of their face;
Right as the hunter in the regne* of Thrace *kingdom
That standeth at a gappe with a spear
When hunted is the lion or the bear,
And heareth him come rushing in the greves*, *groves
And breaking both the boughes and the leaves,
Thinketh, "Here comes my mortal enemy,
Withoute fail, he must be dead or I;
For either I must slay him at the gap;
Or he must slay me, if that me mishap:"
So fared they, in changing of their hue
As far as either of them other knew. *When they recognised
        each other afar off*
There was no good day, and no saluting,
But straight, withoute wordes rehearsing,
Evereach of them holp to arm the other,
As friendly, as he were his owen brother.
And after that, with sharpe speares strong
They foined* each at other wonder long. *thrust
Thou mightest weene*, that this Palamon *think
In fighting were as a wood* lion, *mad
And as a cruel tiger was Arcite:
As wilde boars gan they together smite,

51

That froth as white as foam, *for ire wood*. *mad with anger*
Up to the ancle fought they in their blood.
And in this wise I let them fighting dwell,
And forth I will of Theseus you tell.

The Destiny, minister general,
That executeth in the world o'er all
The purveyance*, that God hath seen beforn; *foreordination
So strong it is, that though the world had sworn
The contrary of a thing by yea or nay,
Yet some time it shall fallen on a day
That falleth not eft* in a thousand year. *again
For certainly our appetites here,
Be it of war, or peace, or hate, or love,
All is this ruled by the sight* above. *eye, intelligence, power
This mean I now by mighty Theseus,
That for to hunten is so desirous —
And namely* the greate hart in May — *especially
That in his bed there dawneth him no day
That he n'is clad, and ready for to ride
With hunt and horn, and houndes him beside.
For in his hunting hath he such delight,
That it is all his joy and appetite
To be himself the greate harte's bane* *destruction
For after Mars he serveth now Diane.
Clear was the day, as I have told ere this,
And Theseus, with alle joy and bliss,
With his Hippolyta, the faire queen,
And Emily, y-clothed all in green,
On hunting be they ridden royally.
And to the grove, that stood there faste by,
In which there was an hart, as men him told,
Duke Theseus the straighte way doth hold,
And to the laund* he rideth him full right, *plain
There was the hart y-wont to have his flight,

And over a brook, and so forth on his way.
This Duke will have a course at him or tway
With houndes, such as him lust* to command. *pleased
And when this Duke was come to the laund,
Under the sun he looked, and anon
He was ware of Arcite and Palamon,
That foughte breme*, as it were bulles two. *fiercely
The brighte swordes wente to and fro
So hideously, that with the leaste stroke
It seemed that it woulde fell an oak,
But what they were, nothing yet he wote*. *knew
This Duke his courser with his spurres smote,
And at a start he was betwixt them two, *suddenly*
And pulled out a sword and cried, "Ho!
No more, on pain of losing of your head.
By mighty Mars, he shall anon be dead
That smiteth any stroke, that I may see!
But tell to me what mister* men ye be, *manner, kind
That be so hardy for to fighte here
Withoute judge or other officer,
As though it were in listes royally.
This Palamon answered hastily,
And saide: "Sir, what needeth wordes mo'?
We have the death deserved bothe two,
Two woful wretches be we, and caitives,
That be accumbered* of our own lives, *burdened
And as thou art a rightful lord and judge,
So give us neither mercy nor refuge.
And slay me first, for sainte charity,
But slay my fellow eke as well as me.
Or slay him first; for, though thou know it lite*, *little
This is thy mortal foe, this is Arcite
That from thy land is banisht on his head,
For which he hath deserved to be dead.
For this is he that came unto thy gate

And saide, that he highte Philostrate.
Thus hath he japed* thee full many year,   *deceived
And thou hast made of him thy chief esquier;
And this is he, that loveth Emily.
For since the day is come that I shall die
I make pleinly* my confession,   *fully, unreservedly
That I am thilke* woful Palamon,   *that same
That hath thy prison broken wickedly.
I am thy mortal foe, and it am I
That so hot loveth Emily the bright,
That I would die here present in her sight.
Therefore I aske death and my jewise*.   *judgement
But slay my fellow eke in the same wise,
For both we have deserved to be slain."

This worthy Duke answer'd anon again,
And said, "This is a short conclusion.
Your own mouth, by your own confession
Hath damned you, and I will it record;
It needeth not to pain you with the cord;
Ye shall be dead, by mighty Mars the Red.

The queen anon for very womanhead
Began to weep, and so did Emily,
And all the ladies in the company.
Great pity was it as it thought them all,
That ever such a chance should befall,
For gentle men they were, of great estate,
And nothing but for love was this debate
They saw their bloody woundes wide and sore,
And cried all at once, both less and more,
"Have mercy, Lord, upon us women all."
And on their bare knees adown they fall
And would have kissed his feet there as he stood,
Till at the last *aslaked was his mood*   *his anger was appeased*

(For pity runneth soon in gentle heart);
And though at first for ire he quoke and start
He hath consider'd shortly in a clause
The trespass of them both, and eke the cause:
And although that his ire their guilt accused
Yet in his reason he them both excused;
As thus; he thoughte well that every man
Will help himself in love if that he can,
And eke deliver himself out of prison.
Of women, for they wepten ever-in-one:* *continually
And eke his hearte had compassion
And in his gentle heart he thought anon,
And soft unto himself he saide: "Fie
Upon a lord that will have no mercy,
But be a lion both in word and deed,
To them that be in repentance and dread,
As well as-to a proud dispiteous* man *unpitying
That will maintaine what he first began.
That lord hath little of discretion,
That in such case *can no division*: *can make no distinction*
But weigheth pride and humbless *after one*." *alike*
And shortly, when his ire is thus agone,
He gan to look on them with eyen light*, *gentle, lenient*
And spake these same wordes *all on height.* *aloud*

"The god of love, ah! benedicite*, *bless ye him
How mighty and how great a lord is he!
Against his might there gaine* none obstacles, *avail, conquer
He may be called a god for his miracles
For he can maken at his owen guise
Of every heart, as that him list devise.
Lo here this Arcite, and this Palamon,
That quietly were out of my prison,
And might have lived in Thebes royally,
And weet* I am their mortal enemy, *knew

And that their death li'th in my might also,
And yet hath love, *maugre their eyen two*, *in spite of their eyes*
Y-brought them hither bothe for to die.
Now look ye, is not this an high folly?
Who may not be a fool, if but he love?
Behold, for Godde's sake that sits above,
See how they bleed! be they not well array'd?
Thus hath their lord, the god of love, them paid
Their wages and their fees for their service;
And yet they weene for to be full wise,
That serve love, for aught that may befall.
But this is yet the beste game* of all, *joke
That she, for whom they have this jealousy,
Can them therefor as muchel thank as me.
She wot no more of all this *hote fare*, *hot behaviour*
By God, than wot a cuckoo or an hare.
But all must be assayed hot or cold;
A man must be a fool, or young or old;
I wot it by myself *full yore agone*: *long years ago*
For in my time a servant was I one.
And therefore since I know of love's pain,
And wot how sore it can a man distrain*, *distress
As he that oft hath been caught in his last*, *snare
I you forgive wholly this trespass,
At request of the queen that kneeleth here,
And eke of Emily, my sister dear.
And ye shall both anon unto me swear,
That never more ye shall my country dere* *injure
Nor make war upon me night nor day,
But be my friends in alle that ye may.
I you forgive this trespass *every deal*. *completely*
And they him sware *his asking* fair and well, *what he asked*
And him of lordship and of mercy pray'd,
And he them granted grace, and thus he said:

"To speak of royal lineage and richess,
Though that she were a queen or a princess,
Each of you both is worthy doubteless
To wedde when time is; but natheless
I speak as for my sister Emily,
For whom ye have this strife and jealousy,
Ye wot* yourselves, she may not wed the two *know
At once, although ye fight for evermo:
But one of you, *all be him loth or lief,* *whether or not he
    wishes*
He must *go pipe into an ivy leaf*: *"go whistle"*
This is to say, she may not have you both,
All be ye never so jealous, nor so wroth.
And therefore I you put in this degree,
That each of you shall have his destiny
As *him is shape*; and hearken in what wise *as is decreed
    for him*
Lo hear your end of that I shall devise.
My will is this, for plain conclusion
Withouten any replication*, *reply
If that you liketh, take it for the best,
That evereach of you shall go where *him lest*, *he pleases*
Freely without ransom or danger;
And this day fifty weekes, *farre ne nerre*, *neither more nor
    less*
Evereach of you shall bring an hundred knights,
Armed for listes up at alle rights
All ready to darraine* her by bataille, *contend for
And this behete* I you withoute fail *promise
Upon my troth, and as I am a knight,
That whether of you bothe that hath might,
That is to say, that whether he or thou
May with his hundred, as I spake of now,
Slay his contrary, or out of listes drive,
Him shall I given Emily to wive,

To whom that fortune gives so fair a grace.
The listes shall I make here in this place.
And God so wisly on my soule rue, *may God as surely have
        mercy on my soul*
As I shall even judge be and true.
Ye shall none other ende with me maken
Than one of you shalle be dead or taken.
And if you thinketh this is well y-said,
Say your advice*, and hold yourselves apaid**. *opinion
        **satisfied
This is your end, and your conclusion."
Who looketh lightly now but Palamon?
Who springeth up for joye but Arcite?
Who could it tell, or who could it indite,
The joye that is maked in the place
When Theseus hath done so fair a grace?
But down on knees went every *manner wight*, *kind of person*
And thanked him with all their heartes' might,
And namely* these Thebans *ofte sithe*. *especially *oftentimes*
And thus with good hope and with hearte blithe
They take their leave, and homeward gan they ride
To Thebes-ward, with his old walles wide.

I trow men woulde deem it negligence,
If I forgot to telle the dispence* *expenditure
Of Theseus, that went so busily
To maken up the listes royally,
That such a noble theatre as it was,
I dare well say, in all this world there n'as*. *was not
The circuit a mile was about,
Walled of stone, and ditched all without.
*Round was the shape, in manner of compass,
Full of degrees, the height of sixty pas
That when a man was set on one degree
He letted* not his fellow for to see. *hindered

Eastward there stood a gate of marble white,
Westward right such another opposite.
And, shortly to conclude, such a place
Was never on earth made in so little space,
For in the land there was no craftes-man,
That geometry or arsmetrike* can**, *arithmetic **knew
Nor pourtrayor*, nor carver of images, *portrait painter
That Theseus ne gave him meat and wages
The theatre to make and to devise.
And for to do his rite and sacrifice
He eastward hath upon the gate above,
In worship of Venus, goddess of love,
Done make an altar and an oratory; *caused to be made*
And westward, in the mind and in memory
Of Mars, he maked hath right such another,
That coste largely of gold a fother*. *a great amount
And northward, in a turret on the wall,
Of alabaster white and red coral
An oratory riche for to see,
In worship of Diane of chastity,
Hath Theseus done work in noble wise.
But yet had I forgotten to devise* *describe
The noble carving, and the portraitures,
The shape, the countenance of the figures
That weren in there oratories three.

First in the temple of Venus may'st thou see
Wrought on the wall, full piteous to behold,
The broken sleepes, and the sikes* cold, *sighes
The sacred teares, and the waimentings*, *lamentings
The fiery strokes of the desirings,
That Love's servants in this life endure;
The oathes, that their covenants assure.
Pleasance and Hope, Desire, Foolhardiness,
Beauty and Youth, and Bawdry and Richess,

Charms and Sorc'ry, Leasings* and Flattery, *falsehoods
Dispence, Business, and Jealousy,
That wore of yellow goldes* a garland, *sunflowers
And had a cuckoo sitting on her hand,
Feasts, instruments, and caroles and dances,
Lust and array, and all the circumstances
Of Love, which I reckon'd and reckon shall
In order, were painted on the wall,
And more than I can make of mention.
For soothly all the mount of Citheron,
Where Venus hath her principal dwelling,
Was showed on the wall in pourtraying,
With all the garden, and the lustiness*. *pleasantness
Nor was forgot the porter Idleness,
Nor Narcissus the fair of *yore agone*, *olden times*
Nor yet the folly of King Solomon,
Nor yet the great strength of Hercules,
Th' enchantments of Medea and Circes,
Nor of Turnus the hardy fierce courage,
The rich Croesus *caitif in servage.* *abased into slavery*
Thus may ye see, that wisdom nor richess,
Beauty, nor sleight, nor strength, nor hardiness
Ne may with Venus holde champartie*, *divided possession
For as her liste the world may she gie*. *guide
Lo, all these folk so caught were in her las* *snare
Till they for woe full often said, Alas!
Suffice these ensamples one or two,
Although I could reckon a thousand mo'.

The statue of Venus, glorious to see
Was naked floating in the large sea,
And from the navel down all cover'd was
With waves green, and bright as any glass.
A citole in her right hand hadde she,
And on her head, full seemly for to see,

A rose garland fresh, and well smelling,
Above her head her doves flickering
Before her stood her sone Cupido,
Upon his shoulders winges had he two;
And blind he was, as it is often seen;
A bow he bare, and arrows bright and keen.

Why should I not as well eke tell you all
The portraiture, that was upon the wall
Within the temple of mighty Mars the Red?
All painted was the wall in length and brede* *breadth
Like to the estres* of the grisly place *interior chambers
That hight the great temple of Mars in Thrace,
In thilke* cold and frosty region, *that
There as Mars hath his sovereign mansion.
In which there dwelled neither man nor beast,
With knotty gnarry* barren trees old *gnarled
Of stubbes sharp and hideous to behold;
In which there ran a rumble and a sough*, *groaning noise
As though a storm should bursten every bough:
And downward from an hill under a bent* *slope
There stood the temple of Mars Armipotent,
Wrought all of burnish'd steel, of which th' entry
Was long and strait, and ghastly for to see.
And thereout came *a rage and such a vise*, *such a furious
    voice*
That it made all the gates for to rise.
The northern light in at the doore shone,
For window on the walle was there none
Through which men mighten any light discern.
The doors were all of adamant etern,
Y-clenched *overthwart and ende-long* *crossways and
    lengthways*
With iron tough, and, for to make it strong,
Every pillar the temple to sustain

61

Was tunne-great*, of iron bright and sheen. *thick as a tun (barrel)
There saw I first the dark imagining
Of felony, and all the compassing;
The cruel ire, as red as any glede*, *live coal
The picke-purse, and eke the pale dread;
The smiler with the knife under the cloak,
The shepen* burning with the blacke smoke *stable
The treason of the murd'ring in the bed,
The open war, with woundes all be-bled;
Conteke* with bloody knife, and sharp menace. *contention, discord
All full of chirking* was that sorry place. *creaking, jarring noise
The slayer of himself eke saw I there,
His hearte-blood had bathed all his hair:
The nail y-driven in the shode* at night, *hair of the head
The colde death, with mouth gaping upright.
Amiddes of the temple sat Mischance,
With discomfort and sorry countenance;
Eke saw I Woodness* laughing in his rage, *Madness
Armed Complaint, Outhees*, and fierce Outrage; *Outcry
The carrain* in the bush, with throat y-corve**, *corpse **slashed
A thousand slain, and not *of qualm y-storve*; *dead of sickness*
The tyrant, with the prey by force y-reft;
The town destroy'd, that there was nothing left.
Yet saw I brent* the shippes hoppesteres, *burnt
The hunter strangled with the wilde bears:
The sow freting* the child right in the cradle; *devouring
The cook scalded, for all his longe ladle.
Nor was forgot, *by th'infortune of Mart* *through the misfortune of war*
The carter overridden with his cart;
Under the wheel full low he lay adown.
There were also of Mars' division,
The armourer, the bowyer*, and the smith, *maker of bows

That forgeth sharp swordes on his stith*.   *anvil
And all above depainted in a tower
Saw I Conquest, sitting in great honour,
With thilke* sharpe sword over his head   *that
Hanging by a subtle y-twined thread.
Painted the slaughter was of Julius,
Of cruel Nero, and Antonius:
Although at that time they were yet unborn,
Yet was their death depainted there beforn,
By menacing of Mars, right by figure,
So was it showed in that portraiture,
As is depainted in the stars above,
Who shall be slain, or elles dead for love.
Sufficeth one ensample in stories old,
I may not reckon them all, though I wo'ld.

The statue of Mars upon a carte* stood   *chariot
Armed, and looked grim as he were wood*,   *mad
And over his head there shone two figures
Of starres, that be cleped in scriptures,
That one Puella, that other Rubeus.
This god of armes was arrayed thus:
A wolf there stood before him at his feet
With eyen red, and of a man he eat:
With subtle pencil painted was this story,
In redouting* of Mars and of his glory.   *reverance, fear

Now to the temple of Dian the chaste
As shortly as I can I will me haste,
To telle you all the descriptioun.
Depainted be the walles up and down
Of hunting and of shamefast chastity.
There saw I how woful Calistope,
When that Dian aggrieved was with her,
Was turned from a woman to a bear,

And after was she made the lodestar*: *pole star
Thus was it painted, I can say no far*; *farther
Her son is eke a star as men may see.
There saw I Dane turn'd into a tree,
I meane not the goddess Diane,
But Peneus' daughter, which that hight Dane.
There saw I Actaeon an hart y-maked*, *made
For vengeance that he saw Dian all naked:
I saw how that his houndes have him caught,
And freten* him, for that they knew him not. *devour
Yet painted was, a little farthermore
How Atalanta hunted the wild boar;
And Meleager, and many other mo',
For which Diana wrought them care and woe.
There saw I many another wondrous story,
The which me list not drawen to memory.
This goddess on an hart full high was set*, *seated
With smalle houndes all about her feet,
And underneath her feet she had a moon,
Waxing it was, and shoulde wane soon.
In gaudy green her statue clothed was,
With bow in hand, and arrows in a case*. *quiver
Her eyen caste she full low adown,
Where Pluto hath his darke regioun.
A woman travailing was her beforn,
But, for her child so longe was unborn,
Full piteously Lucina gan she call,
And saide; "Help, for thou may'st best of all."
Well could he painte lifelike that it wrought;
With many a florin he the hues had bought.
Now be these listes made, and Theseus,
That at his greate cost arrayed thus
The temples, and the theatre every deal*, *part
When it was done, him liked wonder well.

But stint* I will of Theseus a lite**, *cease speaking **little
And speak of Palamon and of Arcite.
The day approacheth of their returning,
That evereach an hundred knights should bring,
The battle to darraine* as I you told; *contest
And to Athens, their covenant to hold,
Hath ev'reach of them brought an hundred knights,
Well-armed for the war at alle rights.
And sickerly* there trowed** many a man, *surely **believed
That never, sithen* that the world began, *since
For to speaken of knighthood of their hand,
As far as God hath maked sea and land,
Was, of so few, so noble a company.
For every wight that loved chivalry,
And would, *his thankes, have a passant name*, *thanks to his
     own efforts, have a surpassing name*
Had prayed, that he might be of that game,
And well was him, that thereto chosen was.
For if there fell to-morrow such a case,
Ye knowe well, that every lusty knight,
That loveth par amour, and hath his might
Were it in Engleland, or elleswhere,
They would, their thankes, willen to be there,
T' fight for a lady; Benedicite,
It were a lusty* sighte for to see. *pleasing
And right so fared they with Palamon;
With him there wente knightes many one.
Some will be armed in an habergeon,
And in a breast-plate, and in a gipon*; *short doublet.
And some will have *a pair of plates* large; *back and front
     armour*
And some will have a Prusse* shield, or targe; *Prussian
Some will be armed on their legges weel;
Some have an axe, and some a mace of steel.
There is no newe guise*, but it was old. *fashion

Armed they weren, as I have you told,
Evereach after his opinion.
There may'st thou see coming with Palamon
Licurgus himself, the great king of Thrace:
Black was his beard, and manly was his face.
The circles of his eyen in his head
They glowed betwixte yellow and red,
And like a griffin looked he about,
With kemped* haires on his browes stout;   *combed
His limbs were great, his brawns were hard and strong,
His shoulders broad, his armes round and long.
And as the guise* was in his country,   *fashion
Full high upon a car of gold stood he,
With foure white bulles in the trace.
Instead of coat-armour on his harness,
With yellow nails, and bright as any gold,
He had a beare's skin, coal-black for old*.   *age
His long hair was y-kempt behind his back,
As any raven's feather it shone for black.
A wreath of gold *arm-great*, of huge weight,   *thick as a man's
     arm*
Upon his head sate, full of stones bright,
Of fine rubies and clear diamants.
About his car there wente white alauns*,   *greyhounds
Twenty and more, as great as any steer,
To hunt the lion or the wilde bear,
And follow'd him, with muzzle fast y-bound,
Collars of gold, and torettes* filed round.   *rings
An hundred lordes had he in his rout*   *retinue
Armed full well, with heartes stern and stout.

With Arcite, in stories as men find,
The great Emetrius the king of Ind,
Upon a *steede bay* trapped in steel,   *bay horse*
Cover'd with cloth of gold diapred* well,   *decorated

66

Came riding like the god of armes, Mars.
His coat-armour was of *a cloth of Tars*, *a kind of silk*
Couched* with pearls white and round and great *trimmed
His saddle was of burnish'd gold new beat;
A mantelet on his shoulders hanging,
Bretful* of rubies red, as fire sparkling. *brimful
His crispe hair like ringes was y-run,
And that was yellow, glittering as the sun.
His nose was high, his eyen bright citrine*, *pale yellow
His lips were round, his colour was sanguine,
A fewe fracknes* in his face y-sprent**, *freckles **sprinkled
Betwixte yellow and black somedeal y-ment* *mixed
And as a lion he *his looking cast* *cast about his eyes*
Of five and twenty year his age I cast* *reckon
His beard was well begunnen for to spring;
His voice was as a trumpet thundering.
Upon his head he wore of laurel green
A garland fresh and lusty to be seen;
Upon his hand he bare, for his delight,
An eagle tame, as any lily white.
An hundred lordes had he with him there,
All armed, save their heads, in all their gear,
Full richely in alle manner things.
For trust ye well, that earles, dukes, and kings
Were gather'd in this noble company,
For love, and for increase of chivalry.
About this king there ran on every part
Full many a tame lion and leopart.
And in this wise these lordes *all and some* *all and sundry*
Be on the Sunday to the city come
Aboute prime, and in the town alight.

This Theseus, this Duke, this worthy knight
When he had brought them into his city,
And inned* them, ev'reach at his degree, *lodged

He feasteth them, and doth so great labour
To *easen them*, and do them all honour, *make them
    comfortable*
That yet men weene* that no mannes wit *think
Of none estate could amenden* it. *improve
The minstrelsy, the service at the feast,
The greate giftes to the most and least,
The rich array of Theseus' palace,
Nor who sate first or last upon the dais.
What ladies fairest be, or best dancing
Or which of them can carol best or sing,
Or who most feelingly speaketh of love;
What hawkes sitten on the perch above,
What houndes liggen* on the floor adown, *lie
Of all this now make I no mentioun
But of th'effect; that thinketh me the best
Now comes the point, and hearken if you lest.* *please

The Sunday night, ere day began to spring,
When Palamon the larke hearde sing,
Although it were not day by houres two,
Yet sang the lark, and Palamon right tho* *then
With holy heart, and with an high courage,
Arose, to wenden* on his pilgrimage *go
Unto the blissful Cithera benign,
I meane Venus, honourable and digne*. *worthy
And in her hour he walketh forth a pace
Unto the listes, where her temple was,
And down he kneeleth, and with humble cheer* *demeanour
And hearte sore, he said as ye shall hear.

"Fairest of fair, O lady mine Venus,
Daughter to Jove, and spouse of Vulcanus,
Thou gladder of the mount of Citheron!
For thilke love thou haddest to Adon

Have pity on my bitter teares smart,
And take mine humble prayer to thine heart.
Alas! I have no language to tell
Th'effecte, nor the torment of mine hell;
Mine hearte may mine harmes not betray;
I am so confused, that I cannot say.
But mercy, lady bright, that knowest well
My thought, and seest what harm that I feel.
Consider all this, and *rue upon* my sore,   *take pity on*
As wisly* as I shall for evermore   *truly
Enforce my might, thy true servant to be,
And holde war alway with chastity:
That make I mine avow*, so ye me help.   *vow, promise
I keepe not of armes for to yelp,*   *boast
Nor ask I not to-morrow to have victory,
Nor renown in this case, nor vaine glory
Of *prize of armes*, blowing up and down,   *praise for valour*
But I would have fully possessioun
Of Emily, and die in her service;
Find thou the manner how, and in what wise.
I *recke not but* it may better be   *do not know whether*
To have vict'ry of them, or they of me,
So that I have my lady in mine arms.
For though so be that Mars is god of arms,
Your virtue is so great in heaven above,
That, if you list, I shall well have my love.
Thy temple will I worship evermo',
And on thine altar, where I ride or go,
I will do sacrifice, and fires bete*.   *make, kindle
And if ye will not so, my lady sweet,
Then pray I you, to-morrow with a spear
That Arcite me through the hearte bear
Then reck I not, when I have lost my life,
Though that Arcite win her to his wife.
This is th' effect and end of my prayere, —

Give me my love, thou blissful lady dear."
When th' orison was done of Palamon,
His sacrifice he did, and that anon,
Full piteously, with alle circumstances,
All tell I not as now his observances. *although I tell not
    now*
But at the last the statue of Venus shook,
And made a signe, whereby that he took
That his prayer accepted was that day.
For though the signe shewed a delay,
Yet wist he well that granted was his boon;
And with glad heart he went him home full soon.

The third hour unequal that Palamon
Began to Venus' temple for to gon,
Up rose the sun, and up rose Emily,
And to the temple of Dian gan hie.
Her maidens, that she thither with her lad*, *led
Th' incense, the clothes, and the remnant all
That to the sacrifice belonge shall,
The hornes full of mead, as was the guise;
There lacked nought to do her sacrifice.
Smoking* the temple full of clothes fair, *draping
This Emily with hearte debonnair* *gentle
Her body wash'd with water of a well.
But how she did her rite I dare not tell;
But* it be any thing in general; *unless
And yet it were a game* to hearen all *pleasure
To him that meaneth well it were no charge:
But it is good a man to *be at large*. *do as he will*
Her bright hair combed was, untressed all.
A coronet of green oak cerriall
Upon her head was set full fair and meet.
Two fires on the altar gan she bete,
And did her thinges, as men may behold

In Stace of Thebes, and these bookes old.
When kindled was the fire, with piteous cheer
Unto Dian she spake as ye may hear.

"O chaste goddess of the woodes green,
To whom both heav'n and earth and sea is seen,
Queen of the realm of Pluto dark and low,
Goddess of maidens, that mine heart hast know
Full many a year, and wost* what I desire, *knowest
To keep me from the vengeance of thine ire,
That Actaeon aboughte* cruelly: *earned; suffered from
Chaste goddess, well wottest thou that I
Desire to be a maiden all my life,
Nor never will I be no love nor wife.
I am, thou wost*, yet of thy company, *knowest
A maid, and love hunting and venery*, *field sports
And for to walken in the woodes wild,
And not to be a wife, and be with child.
Nought will I know the company of man.
Now help me, lady, since ye may and can,
For those three formes that thou hast in thee.
And Palamon, that hath such love to me,
And eke Arcite, that loveth me so sore,
This grace I pray thee withoute more,
As sende love and peace betwixt them two:
And from me turn away their heartes so,
That all their hote love, and their desire,
And all their busy torment, and their fire,
Be queint*, or turn'd into another place. *quenched
And if so be thou wilt do me no grace,
Or if my destiny be shapen so
That I shall needes have one of them two,
So send me him that most desireth me.
Behold, goddess of cleane chastity,
The bitter tears that on my cheekes fall.

Since thou art maid, and keeper of us all,
My maidenhead thou keep and well conserve,
And, while I live, a maid I will thee serve."

The fires burn upon the altar clear,
While Emily was thus in her prayere:
But suddenly she saw a sighte quaint*.   *strange
For right anon one of the fire's queint*   *went out
And quick'd* again, and after that anon   *and revived
That other fire was queint, and all agone:
And as it queint, it made a whisteling,
As doth a brande wet in its burning.
And at the brandes end outran anon
As it were bloody droppes many one:
For which so sore aghast was Emily,
That she was well-nigh mad, and gan to cry,
For she ne wiste what it signified;
But onely for feare thus she cried,
And wept, that it was pity for to hear.
And therewithal Diana gan appear
With bow in hand, right as an hunteress,
And saide; "Daughter, stint* thine heaviness.   *cease
Among the goddes high it is affirm'd,
And by eternal word writ and confirm'd,
Thou shalt be wedded unto one of tho*   *those
That have for thee so muche care and woe:
But unto which of them I may not tell.
Farewell, for here I may no longer dwell.
The fires which that on mine altar brenn*,   *burn
Shall thee declaren, ere that thou go henne*,   *hence
Thine aventure of love, as in this case."
And with that word, the arrows in the case*   *quiver
Of the goddess did clatter fast and ring,
And forth she went, and made a vanishing,
For which this Emily astonied was,

And saide; "What amounteth this, alas!
I put me under thy protection,
Diane, and in thy disposition."
And home she went anon the nexte* way. *nearest
This is th' effect, there is no more to say.

The nexte hour of Mars following this
Arcite to the temple walked is
Of fierce Mars, to do his sacrifice
With all the rites of his pagan guise.
With piteous* heart and high devotion *pious
Right thus to Mars he said his orison
"O stronge god, that in the regnes* old *realms
Of Thrace honoured art, and lord y-hold* *held
And hast in every regne, and every land
Of armes all the bridle in thine hand,
And *them fortunest as thee list devise*, *send them fortune
    as you please*
Accept of me my piteous sacrifice.
If so be that my youthe may deserve,
And that my might be worthy for to serve
Thy godhead, that I may be one of thine,
Then pray I thee to *rue upon my pine*, *pity my anguish*
For thilke* pain, and thilke hote fire, *that
In which thou whilom burned'st for desire
Whenne that thou usedest* the beauty *enjoyed
Of faire young Venus, fresh and free,
And haddest her in armes at thy will:
And though thee ones on a time misfill*, *were unlucky
When Vulcanus had caught thee in his las*, *net
And found thee ligging* by his wife, alas! *lying
For thilke sorrow that was in thine heart,
Have ruth* as well upon my paine's smart. *pity
I am young and unconning*, as thou know'st, *ignorant, simple
And, as I trow*, with love offended most *believe

That e'er was any living creature:
For she, that doth* me all this woe endure, *causes
Ne recketh ne'er whether I sink or fleet* *swim
And well I wot, ere she me mercy hete*, *promise, vouchsafe
I must with strengthe win her in the place:
And well I wot, withoute help or grace
Of thee, ne may my strengthe not avail:
Then help me, lord, to-morr'w in my bataille,
For thilke fire that whilom burned thee,
As well as this fire that now burneth me;
And do* that I to-morr'w may have victory. *cause
Mine be the travail, all thine be the glory.
Thy sovereign temple will I most honour
Of any place, and alway most labour
In thy pleasance and in thy craftes strong.
And in thy temple I will my banner hong*, *hang
And all the armes of my company,
And evermore, until that day I die,
Eternal fire I will before thee find
And eke to this my vow I will me bind:
My beard, my hair that hangeth long adown,
That never yet hath felt offension* *indignity
Of razor nor of shears, I will thee give,
And be thy true servant while I live.
Now, lord, have ruth upon my sorrows sore,
Give me the victory, I ask no more."

The prayer stint* of Arcite the strong, *ended
The ringes on the temple door that hong,
And eke the doores, clattered full fast,
Of which Arcite somewhat was aghast.
The fires burn'd upon the altar bright,
That it gan all the temple for to light;
A sweete smell anon the ground up gaf*, *gave
And Arcite anon his hand up haf*, *lifted

And more incense into the fire he cast,
With other rites more and at the last
The statue of Mars began his hauberk ring;
And with that sound he heard a murmuring
Full low and dim, that saide thus, "Victory."
For which he gave to Mars honour and glory.
And thus with joy, and hope well to fare,
Arcite anon unto his inn doth fare.
As fain* as fowl is of the brighte sun. *glad

And right anon such strife there is begun
For thilke* granting, in the heav'n above, *that
Betwixte Venus the goddess of love,
And Mars the sterne god armipotent,
That Jupiter was busy it to stent*: *stop
Till that the pale Saturnus the cold,
That knew so many of adventures old,
Found in his old experience such an art,
That he full soon hath pleased every part.
As sooth is said, eld* hath great advantage, *age
In eld is bothe wisdom and usage*: *experience
Men may the old out-run, but not out-rede*. *outwit
Saturn anon, to stint the strife and drede,
Albeit that it is against his kind,* *nature
Of all this strife gan a remedy find.
"My deare daughter Venus," quoth Saturn,
"My course*, that hath so wide for to turn, *orbit
Hath more power than wot any man.
Mine is the drowning in the sea so wan;
Mine is the prison in the darke cote*, *cell
Mine the strangling and hanging by the throat,
The murmur, and the churlish rebelling,
The groyning*, and the privy poisoning. *discontent
I do vengeance and plein* correction, *full
I dwell in the sign of the lion.

Mine is the ruin of the highe halls,
The falling of the towers and the walls
Upon the miner or the carpenter:
I slew Samson in shaking the pillar:
Mine also be the maladies cold,
The darke treasons, and the castes* old: *plots
My looking is the father of pestilence.
Now weep no more, I shall do diligence
That Palamon, that is thine owen knight,
Shall have his lady, as thou hast him hight*. *promised
Though Mars shall help his knight, yet natheless
Betwixte you there must sometime be peace:
All be ye not of one complexion,
That each day causeth such division,
I am thine ayel*, ready at thy will; *grandfather
Weep now no more, I shall thy lust* fulfil." *pleasure
Now will I stenten* of the gods above, *cease speaking
Of Mars, and of Venus, goddess of love,
And telle you as plainly as I can
The great effect, for which that I began.

Great was the feast in Athens thilke* day; *that
And eke the lusty season of that May
Made every wight to be in such pleasance,
That all that Monday jousten they and dance,
And spenden it in Venus' high service.
But by the cause that they shoulde rise
Early a-morrow for to see that fight,
Unto their reste wente they at night.
And on the morrow, when the day gan spring,
Of horse and harness* noise and clattering *armour
There was in the hostelries all about:
And to the palace rode there many a rout* *train, retinue
Of lordes, upon steedes and palfreys.
There mayst thou see devising* of harness *decoration

So uncouth* and so rich, and wrought so weel *unkown, rare
Of goldsmithry, of brouding*, and of steel; *embroidery
The shieldes bright, the testers*, and trappures** *helmets
    **trappings
Gold-hewen helmets, hauberks, coat-armures;
Lordes in parements* on their coursers, *ornamental garb;
Knightes of retinue, and eke squiers,
Nailing the spears, and helmes buckling,
Gniding* of shieldes, with lainers** lacing; *polishing **lanyards
There as need is, they were nothing idle:
The foamy steeds upon the golden bridle
Gnawing, and fast the armourers also
With file and hammer pricking to and fro;
Yeomen on foot, and knaves* many one *servants
With shorte staves, thick* as they may gon**; *close **walk
Pipes, trumpets, nakeres*, and clariouns, *drums
That in the battle blowe bloody souns;
The palace full of people up and down,
There three, there ten, holding their questioun*, *conversation
Divining* of these Theban knightes two. *conjecturing
Some saiden thus, some said it shall he so;
Some helden with him with the blacke beard,
Some with the bald, some with the thick-hair'd;
Some said he looked grim, and woulde fight:
He had a sparth* of twenty pound of weight. *double-headed axe
Thus was the halle full of divining* *conjecturing
Long after that the sunne gan up spring.
The great Theseus that of his sleep is waked
With minstrelsy, and noise that was maked,
Held yet the chamber of his palace rich,
Till that the Theban knightes both y-lich* *alike
Honoured were, and to the palace fet*. *fetched
Duke Theseus is at a window set,
Array'd right as he were a god in throne:
The people presseth thitherward full soon

Him for to see, and do him reverence,
And eke to hearken his hest* and his sentence**. *command
    **speech
An herald on a scaffold made an O,
Till the noise of the people was y-do*: *done
And when he saw the people of noise all still,
Thus shewed he the mighty Duke's will.
"The lord hath of his high discretion
Considered that it were destruction
To gentle blood, to fighten in the guise
Of mortal battle now in this emprise:
Wherefore to shape* that they shall not die, *arrange,
    contrive
He will his firste purpose modify.
No man therefore, on pain of loss of life,
No manner* shot, nor poleaxe, nor short knife *kind of
Into the lists shall send, or thither bring.
Nor short sword for to stick with point biting
No man shall draw, nor bear it by his side.
And no man shall unto his fellow ride
But one course, with a sharp y-grounden spear:
Foin if him list on foot, himself to wear. *He who wishes can
    fence on foot to defend himself*
And he that is at mischief shall be take, and he that is in
    peril shall be taken*
And not slain, but be brought unto the stake,
That shall be ordained on either side;
Thither he shall by force, and there abide.
And if *so fall* the chiefetain be take *should happen*
On either side, or elles slay his make*, *equal, match
No longer then the tourneying shall last.
God speede you; go forth and lay on fast.
With long sword and with mace fight your fill.
Go now your way; this is the lordes will.
The voice of the people touched the heaven,

So loude cried they with merry steven*: *sound
God save such a lord that is so good,
He willeth no destruction of blood.

Up go the trumpets and the melody,
And to the listes rode the company
By ordinance, throughout the city large, *in orderly array*
Hanged with cloth of gold, and not with sarge*. *serge
Full like a lord this noble Duke gan ride,
And these two Thebans upon either side:

And after rode the queen and Emily,
And after them another company
Of one and other, after their degree.
And thus they passed thorough that city
And to the listes came they by time:
It was not of the day yet fully prime*. *between 6 and
    9 a.m.
When set was Theseus full rich and high,
Hippolyta the queen and Emily,
And other ladies in their degrees about,
Unto the seates presseth all the rout.
And westward, through the gates under Mart,
Arcite, and eke the hundred of his part,
With banner red, is enter'd right anon;
And in the selve* moment Palamon *self-same
Is, under Venus, eastward in the place,
With banner white, and hardy cheer* and face *expression
In all the world, to seeken up and down
So even* without variatioun *equal
There were such companies never tway.
For there was none so wise that coulde say
That any had of other avantage
Of worthiness, nor of estate, nor age,
So even were they chosen for to guess.

And *in two ranges faire they them dress*. *they arranged
    themselves in two rows*
When that their names read were every one,
That in their number guile* were there none, *fraud
Then were the gates shut, and cried was loud;
"Do now your devoir, younge knights proud"
The heralds left their pricking* up and down *spurring their
    horses
Now ring the trumpet loud and clarioun.
There is no more to say, but east and west
In go the speares sadly* in the rest; *steadily
In go the sharpe spurs into the side.
There see me who can joust, and who can ride.
There shiver shaftes upon shieldes thick;
He feeleth through the hearte-spoon the prick.
Up spring the speares twenty foot on height;
Out go the swordes as the silver bright.
The helmes they to-hewen, and to-shred*; *strike in pieces
Out burst the blood, with sterne streames red.
With mighty maces the bones they to-brest*. *burst
He through the thickest of the throng gan threst*. *thrust
There stumble steedes strong, and down go all.
He rolleth under foot as doth a ball.
He foineth* on his foe with a trunchoun, *forces himself
And he him hurtleth with his horse adown.
He through the body hurt is, and *sith take*, *afterwards
    captured*
Maugre his head, and brought unto the stake,
As forword* was, right there he must abide. *covenant
Another led is on that other side.
And sometime doth* them Theseus to rest, *caused
Them to refresh, and drinken if them lest*. *pleased
Full oft a day have thilke Thebans two *these
Together met and wrought each other woe:
Unhorsed hath each other of them tway* *twice

There is no tiger in the vale of Galaphay,
When that her whelp is stole, when it is lite* *little
So cruel on the hunter, as Arcite
For jealous heart upon this Palamon:
Nor in Belmarie there is no fell lion,
That hunted is, or for his hunger wood* *mad
Or for his prey desireth so the blood,
As Palamon to slay his foe Arcite.
The jealous strokes upon their helmets bite;
Out runneth blood on both their sides red,
Sometime an end there is of every deed
For ere the sun unto the reste went,
The strong king Emetrius gan hent* *sieze, assail
This Palamon, as he fought with Arcite,
And made his sword deep in his flesh to bite,
And by the force of twenty is he take,
Unyielding, and is drawn unto the stake.
And in the rescue of this Palamon
The strong king Licurgus is borne down:
And king Emetrius, for all his strength
Is borne out of his saddle a sword's length,
So hit him Palamon ere he were take:
But all for nought; he was brought to the stake:
His hardy hearte might him helpe naught,
He must abide when that he was caught,
By force, and eke by composition*. *the bargain
Who sorroweth now but woful Palamon
That must no more go again to fight?
And when that Theseus had seen that sight
Unto the folk that foughte thus each one,
He cried, "Ho! no more, for it is done!
I will be true judge, and not party.
Arcite of Thebes shall have Emily,
That by his fortune hath her fairly won."
Anon there is a noise of people gone,

For joy of this, so loud and high withal,
It seemed that the listes shoulde fall.

What can now faire Venus do above?
What saith she now? what doth this queen of love?
But weepeth so, for wanting of her will,
Till that her teares in the listes fill* *fall
She said: "I am ashamed doubteless."
Saturnus saide: "Daughter, hold thy peace.
Mars hath his will, his knight hath all his boon,
And by mine head thou shalt be eased soon."
The trumpeters with the loud minstrelsy,
The heralds, that full loude yell and cry,
Be in their joy for weal of Dan* Arcite. *Lord
But hearken me, and stinte noise a lite,
What a miracle there befell anon
This fierce Arcite hath off his helm y-done,
And on a courser for to shew his face
He *pricketh endelong* the large place, *rides from end to
    end*
Looking upward upon this Emily;
And she again him cast a friendly eye
(For women, as to speaken *in commune*, *generally*
They follow all the favour of fortune),
And was all his in cheer*, as his in heart. *countenance
Out of the ground a fire infernal start,
From Pluto sent, at request of Saturn
For which his horse for fear began to turn,
And leap aside, and founder* as he leap *stumble
And ere that Arcite may take any keep*, *care
He pight* him on the pummel** of his head. *pitched **top
That in the place he lay as he were dead.
His breast to-bursten with his saddle-bow.
As black he lay as any coal or crow,
So was the blood y-run into his face.

Anon he was y-borne out of the place
With hearte sore, to Theseus' palace.
Then was he carven* out of his harness. *cut
And in a bed y-brought full fair and blive* *quickly
For he was yet in mem'ry and alive,
And always crying after Emily.

Duke Theseus, with all his company,
Is come home to Athens his city,
With alle bliss and great solemnity.
Albeit that this aventure was fall*, *befallen
He woulde not discomforte* them all *discourage
Then said eke, that Arcite should not die,
He should be healed of his malady.
And of another thing they were as fain*. *glad
That of them alle was there no one slain,
All* were they sorely hurt, and namely** one, *although
    **especially
That with a spear was thirled* his breast-bone. *pierced
To other woundes, and to broken arms,
Some hadden salves, and some hadden charms:
And pharmacies of herbs, and eke save* *sage, Salvia
    officinalis
They dranken, for they would their lives have.
For which this noble Duke, as he well can,
Comforteth and honoureth every man,
And made revel all the longe night,
Unto the strange lordes, as was right.
Nor there was holden no discomforting,
But as at jousts or at a tourneying;
For soothly there was no discomfiture,
For falling is not but an aventure*. *chance, accident
Nor to be led by force unto a stake
Unyielding, and with twenty knights y-take
One person all alone, withouten mo',

And harried* forth by armes, foot, and toe, *dragged, hurried
And eke his steede driven forth with staves,
With footmen, bothe yeomen and eke knaves*, *servants
It was *aretted him no villainy:* *counted no disgrace to him*
There may no man *clepen it cowardy*. *call it cowardice*
For which anon Duke Theseus *let cry*, – *caused to be proclaimed*
To stenten* alle rancour and envy, – *stop
The gree* as well on one side as the other, *prize, merit
And either side alike as other's brother:
And gave them giftes after their degree,
And held a feaste fully dayes three:
And conveyed the kinges worthily
Out of his town a journee* largely *day's journey
And home went every man the righte way,
There was no more but "Farewell, Have good day."
Of this bataille I will no more indite
But speak of Palamon and of Arcite.

Swelleth the breast of Arcite and the sore
Increaseth at his hearte more and more.
The clotted blood, for any leache-craft* *surgical skill
Corrupteth and is *in his bouk y-laft* *left in his body*
That neither *veine blood nor ventousing*, *blood-letting or cupping*
Nor drink of herbes may be his helping.
The virtue expulsive or animal,
From thilke virtue called natural,
Nor may the venom voide, nor expel
The pipes of his lungs began to swell
And every lacert* in his breast adown *sinew, muscle
Is shent* with venom and corruption. *destroyed
Him gaineth* neither, for to get his life, *availeth
Vomit upward, nor downward laxative;
All is to-bursten thilke region;

Nature hath now no domination.
And certainly where nature will not wirch,* *work
Farewell physic: go bear the man to chirch.* *church
This all and some is, Arcite must die.
For which he sendeth after Emily,
And Palamon, that was his cousin dear,
Then said he thus, as ye shall after hear.

"Nought may the woful spirit in mine heart
Declare one point of all my sorrows' smart
To you, my lady, that I love the most:
But I bequeath the service of my ghost
To you aboven every creature,
Since that my life ne may no longer dure.
Alas the woe! alas, the paines strong
That I for you have suffered and so long!
Alas the death, alas, mine Emily!
Alas departing* of our company! *the severance
Alas, mine hearte's queen! alas, my wife!
Mine hearte's lady, ender of my life!
What is this world? what aske men to have?
Now with his love, now in his colde grave
Al one, withouten any company.
Farewell, my sweet, farewell, mine Emily,
And softly take me in your armes tway,
For love of God, and hearken what I say.
I have here with my cousin Palamon
Had strife and rancour many a day agone,
For love of you, and for my jealousy.
And Jupiter so *wis my soule gie*, *surely guides my soul*
To speaken of a servant properly,
With alle circumstances truely,
That is to say, truth, honour, and knighthead,
Wisdom, humbless*, estate, and high kindred, *humility
Freedom, and all that longeth to that art,

85

So Jupiter have of my soul part,
As in this world right now I know not one,
So worthy to be lov'd as Palamon,
That serveth you, and will do all his life.
And if that you shall ever be a wife,
Forget not Palamon, the gentle man."

And with that word his speech to fail began.
For from his feet up to his breast was come
The cold of death, that had him overnome*.   *overcome
And yet moreover in his armes two
The vital strength is lost, and all ago*.   *gone
Only the intellect, withoute more,
That dwelled in his hearte sick and sore,
Gan faile, when the hearte felte death;
Dusked* his eyen two, and fail'd his breath.   *grew dim
But on his lady yet he cast his eye;
His laste word was; "Mercy, Emily!"
His spirit changed house, and wente there,
As I came never I cannot telle where.
Therefore I stent*, I am no divinister**;   *refrain **diviner
Of soules find I nought in this register.
Ne me list not th' opinions to tell
Of them, though that they writen where they dwell;
Arcite is cold, there Mars his soule gie.*   *guide
Now will I speake forth of Emily.

Shriek'd Emily, and howled Palamon,
And Theseus his sister took anon
Swooning, and bare her from the corpse away.
What helpeth it to tarry forth the day,
To telle how she wept both eve and morrow?
For in such cases women have such sorrow,
When that their husbands be from them y-go*,   *gone
That for the more part they sorrow so,

Or elles fall into such malady,
That at the laste certainly they die.
Infinite be the sorrows and the tears
Of olde folk, and folk of tender years,
In all the town, for death of this Theban:
For him there weepeth bothe child and man.
So great a weeping was there none certain,
When Hector was y-brought, all fresh y-slain,
To Troy: alas! the pity that was there,
Scratching of cheeks, and rending eke of hair.
"Why wouldest thou be dead?" these women cry,
"And haddest gold enough, and Emily."
No manner man might gladden Theseus,
Saving his olde father Egeus,
That knew this worlde's transmutatioun,
As he had seen it changen up and down,
Joy after woe, and woe after gladness;
And shewed him example and likeness.
"Right as there died never man," quoth he,
"That he ne liv'd in earth in some degree*,   *rank, condition
Right so there lived never man," he said,
"In all this world, that sometime be not died.
This world is but a throughfare full of woe,
And we be pilgrims, passing to and fro:
Death is an end of every worldly sore."
And over all this said he yet much more
To this effect, full wisely to exhort
The people, that they should them recomfort.
Duke Theseus, with all his busy cure*,   *care
Casteth about, where that the sepulture *deliberates*
Of good Arcite may best y-maked be,
And eke most honourable in his degree.
And at the last he took conclusion,
That there as first Arcite and Palamon
Hadde for love the battle them between,

That in that selve* grove, sweet and green, *self-same
There as he had his amorous desires,
His complaint, and for love his hote fires,
He woulde make a fire*, in which th' office *funeral pyre
Of funeral he might all accomplice;
And *let anon command* to hack and hew *immediately gave
    orders*
The oakes old, and lay them *on a rew* *in a row*
In culpons*, well arrayed for to brenne**. *logs **burn
His officers with swifte feet they renne* *run
And ride anon at his commandement.
And after this, Duke Theseus hath sent
After a bier, and it all oversprad
With cloth of gold, the richest that he had;
And of the same suit he clad Arcite.
Upon his handes were his gloves white,
Eke on his head a crown of laurel green,
And in his hand a sword full bright and keen.
He laid him *bare the visage* on the bier, *with face uncovered*
Therewith he wept, that pity was to hear.
And, for the people shoulde see him all,
When it was day he brought them to the hall,
That roareth of the crying and the soun'.
Then came this woful Theban, Palamon,
With sluttery beard, and ruggy ashy hairs,
In clothes black, y-dropped all with tears,
And (passing over weeping Emily)
The ruefullest of all the company.
And *inasmuch as* the service should be *in order that*
The more noble and rich in its degree,
Duke Theseus let forth three steedes bring,
That trapped were in steel all glittering.
And covered with the arms of Dan Arcite.
Upon these steedes, that were great and white,
There satte folk, of whom one bare his shield,

Another his spear in his handes held;
The thirde bare with him his bow Turkeis*, *Turkish.
Of brent* gold was the case** and the harness: *burnished
    **quiver
And ride forth *a pace* with sorrowful cheer** *at a foot pace*
    **expression
Toward the grove, as ye shall after hear.

The noblest of the Greekes that there were
Upon their shoulders carried the bier,
With slacke pace, and eyen red and wet,
Throughout the city, by the master* street, *main
That spread was all with black, and wondrous high
Right of the same is all the street y-wrie.* *covered
Upon the right hand went old Egeus,
And on the other side Duke Theseus,
With vessels in their hand of gold full fine,
All full of honey, milk, and blood, and wine;
Eke Palamon, with a great company;
And after that came woful Emily,
With fire in hand, as was that time the guise*, *custom
To do th' office of funeral service.

High labour, and full great appareling* *preparation
Was at the service, and the pyre-making,
That with its greene top the heaven raught*, *reached
And twenty fathom broad its armes straught*: *stretched
This is to say, the boughes were so broad.
Of straw first there was laid many a load.
But how the pyre was maked up on height,
And eke the names how the trees hight*, *were called
As oak, fir, birch, asp*, alder, holm, poplere, *aspen
Willow, elm, plane, ash, box, chestnut, lind*, laurere, *linden,
    lime
Maple, thorn, beech, hazel, yew, whipul tree,

How they were fell'd, shall not be told for me;
Nor how the goddes* rannen up and down *the forest deities
Disinherited of their habitatioun,
In which they wonned* had in rest and peace, *dwelt
Nymphes, Faunes, and Hamadryades;
Nor how the beastes and the birdes all
Fledden for feare, when the wood gan fall;
Nor how the ground aghast* was of the light, *terrified
That was not wont to see the sunne bright;
Nor how the fire was couched* first with stre**, *laid **straw
And then with dry stickes cloven in three,
And then with greene wood and spicery*, *spices
And then with cloth of gold and with pierrie*, *precious stones
And garlands hanging with full many a flower,
The myrrh, the incense with so sweet odour;
Nor how Arcite lay among all this,
Nor what richess about his body is;
Nor how that Emily, as was the guise*, *custom
Put in the fire of funeral service; *appplied the torch*
Nor how she swooned when she made the fire,
Nor what she spake, nor what was her desire;
Nor what jewels men in the fire then cast
When that the fire was great and burned fast;

Nor how some cast their shield, and some their spear,
And of their vestiments, which that they wear,
And cuppes full of wine, and milk, and blood,
Into the fire, that burnt as it were wood*; *mad
Nor how the Greekes with a huge rout* *procession
Three times riden all the fire about
Upon the left hand, with a loud shouting,
And thries with their speares clattering;
And thries how the ladies gan to cry;
Nor how that led was homeward Emily;
Nor how Arcite is burnt to ashes cold;

Nor how the lyke-wake* was y-hold   *wake
All thilke* night, nor how the Greekes play   *that
The wake-plays*, ne keep** I not to say: *funeral games **care
Who wrestled best naked, with oil anoint,
Nor who that bare him best *in no disjoint*.   *in any contest*
I will not tell eke how they all are gone
Home to Athenes when the play is done;
But shortly to the point now will I wend*,   *come
And maken of my longe tale an end.

By process and by length of certain years
All stinted* is the mourning and the tears   *ended
Of Greekes, by one general assent.
Then seemed me there was a parlement
At Athens, upon certain points and cas*:   *cases
Amonge the which points y-spoken was
To have with certain countries alliance,
And have of Thebans full obeisance.
For which this noble Theseus anon
Let* send after the gentle Palamon,   *caused
Unwist* of him what was the cause and why: *unknown
But in his blacke clothes sorrowfully
He came at his commandment *on hie*;   *in haste*
Then sente Theseus for Emily.
When they were set*, and hush'd was all the place   *seated
And Theseus abided* had a space   *waited
Ere any word came from his wise breast
His eyen set he there as was his lest,   *he cast his eyes
    wherever he pleased*
And with a sad visage he sighed still,
And after that right thus he said his will.
"The firste mover of the cause above
When he first made the faire chain of love,
Great was th' effect, and high was his intent;
Well wist he why, and what thereof he meant:

For with that faire chain of love he bond* *bound
The fire, the air, the water, and the lond
In certain bondes, that they may not flee:
That same prince and mover eke," quoth he,
"Hath stablish'd, in this wretched world adown,
Certain of dayes and duration
To all that are engender'd in this place,
Over the whiche day they may not pace*, *pass
All may they yet their dayes well abridge.
There needeth no authority to allege
For it is proved by experience;
But that me list declare my sentence*. *opinion
Then may men by this order well discern,
That thilke* mover stable is and etern. *the same
Well may men know, but that it be a fool,
That every part deriveth from its whole.
For nature hath not ta'en its beginning
Of no *partie nor cantle* of a thing, *part or piece*
But of a thing that perfect is and stable,
Descending so, till it be corruptable.
And therefore of His wise purveyance* *providence
He hath so well beset* his ordinance,
That species of things and progressions
Shallen endure by successions,
And not etern, withouten any lie:
This mayst thou understand and see at eye.
Lo th' oak, that hath so long a nourishing
From the time that it 'ginneth first to spring,
And hath so long a life, as ye may see,
Yet at the last y-wasted is the tree.
Consider eke, how that the harde stone
Under our feet, on which we tread and gon*, *walk
Yet wasteth, as it lieth by the way.
The broade river some time waxeth drey*. *dry
The great townes see we wane and wend*. *go, disappear

Then may ye see that all things have an end.
Of man and woman see we well also, —
That needes in one of the termes two, —
That is to say, in youth or else in age, —
He must be dead, the king as shall a page;
Some in his bed, some in the deepe sea,
Some in the large field, as ye may see:
There helpeth nought, all go that ilke* way: *same
Then may I say that alle thing must die.
What maketh this but Jupiter the king?
The which is prince, and cause of alle thing,
Converting all unto his proper will,
From which it is derived, sooth to tell
And hereagainst no creature alive,
Of no degree, availeth for to strive.
Then is it wisdom, as it thinketh me,
To make a virtue of necessity,
And take it well, that we may not eschew*,   *escape
And namely what to us all is due.
And whoso grudgeth* ought, he doth folly,   *murmurs at
And rebel is to him that all may gie*.   *direct, guide
And certainly a man hath most honour
To dien in his excellence and flower,
When he is sicker* of his goode name.   *certain
Then hath he done his friend, nor him*, no shame   *himself
And gladder ought his friend be of his death,
When with honour is yielded up his breath,
Than when his name *appalled is for age*;   *decayed by old age*
For all forgotten is his vassalage*.   *valour, service
Then is it best, as for a worthy fame,
To dien when a man is best of name.
The contrary of all this is wilfulness.
Why grudge we, why have we heaviness,
That good Arcite, of chivalry the flower,
Departed is, with duty and honour,

Out of this foule prison of this life?
Why grudge here his cousin and his wife
Of his welfare, that loved him so well?
Can he them thank? nay, God wot, neverdeal*, — *not a jot
That both his soul and eke themselves offend*, *hurt
And yet they may their lustes* not amend**. *desires **control
What may I conclude of this longe serie*, *string of remarks
But after sorrow I rede* us to be merry, *counsel
And thanke Jupiter for all his grace?
And ere that we departe from this place,
I rede that we make of sorrows two
One perfect joye lasting evermo':
And look now where most sorrow is herein,
There will I first amenden and begin.
"Sister," quoth he, "this is my full assent,
With all th' advice here of my parlement,
That gentle Palamon, your owen knight,
That serveth you with will, and heart, and might,
And ever hath, since first time ye him knew,
That ye shall of your grace upon him rue*, *take pity
And take him for your husband and your lord:
Lend me your hand, for this is our accord.
Let see now of your womanly pity. *make display*
He is a kinge's brother's son, pardie*. *by God
And though he were a poore bachelere,
Since he hath served you so many a year,
And had for you so great adversity,
It muste be considered, *'lieveth me*. *believe me*
For gentle mercy *oweth to passen right*." *ought to be rightly
    directed*
Then said he thus to Palamon the knight;
"I trow there needeth little sermoning
To make you assente to this thing.
Come near, and take your lady by the hand."
Betwixte them was made anon the band,

That hight matrimony or marriage,
By all the counsel of the baronage.
And thus with alle bliss and melody
Hath Palamon y-wedded Emily.
And God, that all this wide world hath wrought,
Send him his love, that hath it dearly bought.
For now is Palamon in all his weal,
Living in bliss, in riches, and in heal*.   *health
And Emily him loves so tenderly,
And he her serveth all so gentilly,
That never was there worde them between
Of jealousy, nor of none other teen*.   *cause of anger
Thus endeth Palamon and Emily
And God save all this faire company.

THE MILLER'S TALE

When that the Knight had thus his tale told
In all the rout was neither young nor old,
That he not said it was a noble story,
And worthy to be *drawen to memory*;   *recorded*
And *namely the gentles* every one.   *especially the gentlefolk*
Our Host then laugh'd and swore, "So may I gon,*   *prosper
This goes aright; *unbuckled is the mail;*   *the budget is opened*
Let see now who shall tell another tale:
For truely this game is well begun.
Now telleth ye, Sir Monk, if that ye conne*,   *know
Somewhat, to quiten* with the Knighte's tale."   *match
The Miller that fordrunken was all pale,
So that unnethes* upon his horse he sat,   *with difficulty
He would avalen* neither hood nor hat,   *uncover
Nor abide* no man for his courtesy,   *give way to
But in Pilate's voice he gan to cry,
And swore by armes, and by blood, and bones,
"I can a noble tale for the nones*   *occasion,

With which I will now quite* the Knighte's tale." *match
Our Host saw well how drunk he was of ale,
And said; "Robin, abide, my leve* brother, *dear
Some better man shall tell us first another:
Abide, and let us worke thriftily."
"By Godde's soul," quoth he, "that will not I,
For I will speak, or elles go my way!"
Our Host answer'd; "*Tell on a devil way*; *devil take you!*
Thou art a fool; thy wit is overcome."
"Now hearken," quoth the Miller, "all and some:
But first I make a protestatioun.
That I am drunk, I know it by my soun':
And therefore if that I misspeak or say,
Wite it the ale of Southwark, I you pray: *blame it on*
For I will tell a legend and a life
Both of a carpenter and of his wife,
How that a clerk hath *set the wrighte's cap*." *fooled the
    carpenter*
The Reeve answer'd and saide, "*Stint thy clap*, *hold your
    tongue*
Let be thy lewed drunken harlotry.
It is a sin, and eke a great folly
To apeiren* any man, or him defame, *injure
And eke to bringe wives in evil name.
Thou may'st enough of other thinges sayn."
This drunken Miller spake full soon again,
And saide, "Leve brother Osewold,
Who hath no wife, he is no cuckold.
But I say not therefore that thou art one;
There be full goode wives many one.
Why art thou angry with my tale now?
I have a wife, pardie, as well as thou,
Yet *n'old I*, for the oxen in my plough, *I would not*
Taken upon me more than enough,
To deemen* of myself that I am one; *judge

I will believe well that I am none.
An husband should not be inquisitive
Of Godde's privity, nor of his wife.
So he may finde Godde's foison* there,   *treasure
Of the remnant needeth not to enquere."

What should I more say, but that this Millere
He would his wordes for no man forbear,
But told his churlish* tale in his mannere;   *boorish, rude
Me thinketh, that I shall rehearse it here.
And therefore every gentle wight I pray,
For Godde's love to deem not that I say
Of evil intent, but that I must rehearse
Their tales all, be they better or worse,
Or elles falsen* some of my mattere.   *falsify
And therefore whoso list it not to hear,
Turn o'er the leaf, and choose another tale;
For he shall find enough, both great and smale,
Of storial* thing that toucheth gentiless,   *historical, true
And eke morality and holiness.
Blame not me, if that ye choose amiss.
The Miller is a churl, ye know well this,
So was the Reeve, with many other mo',
And harlotry* they tolde bothe two.   *ribald tales
Avise you now, and put me out of blame;   *be warned*
And eke men should not make earnest of game*.   *jest, fun

THE TALE

Whilom there was dwelling in Oxenford
A riche gnof*, that *guestes held to board*,   *miser *took in
    boarders*
And of his craft he was a carpenter.
With him there was dwelling a poor scholer,
Had learned art, but all his fantasy

Was turned for to learn astrology.
He coude* a certain of conclusions   *knew
To deeme* by interrogations,   *determine
If that men asked him in certain hours,
When that men should have drought or elles show'rs:
Or if men asked him what shoulde fall
Of everything, I may not reckon all.

This clerk was called Hendy* Nicholas; *gentle, handsome
Of derne* love he knew and of solace;   *secret, earnest
And therewith he was sly and full privy,
And like a maiden meek for to see.
A chamber had he in that hostelry
Alone, withouten any company,
Full *fetisly y-dight* with herbes swoot*,   *neatly decorated*
   *sweet
And he himself was sweet as is the root
Of liquorice, or any setewall*.   *valerian
His *Almagest*, and bookes great and small,
His astrolabe, belonging to his art,
His augrim stones, layed fair apart
On shelves couched* at his bedde's head,   *laid, set
His press y-cover'd with a falding* red.   *coarse cloth
And all above there lay a gay psalt'ry
On which he made at nightes melody,
So sweetely, that all the chamber rang:
And *Angelus ad Virginem* he sang.
And after that he sung the *Kinge's Note*;
Full often blessed was his merry throat.
And thus this sweete clerk his time spent
After *his friendes finding and his rent.*   *Attending to his
      friends, and providing for the cost of his lodging*
This carpenter had wedded new a wife,
Which that he loved more than his life:
Of eighteen year, I guess, she was of age.

Jealous he was, and held her narr'w in cage,
For she was wild and young, and he was old,
And deemed himself belike* a cuckold. *perhaps
He knew not Cato, for his wit was rude,
That bade a man wed his similitude.
Men shoulde wedden after their estate,
For youth and eld* are often at debate. *age
But since that he was fallen in the snare,
He must endure (as other folk) his care.
Fair was this younge wife, and therewithal
As any weasel her body gent* and small. *slim, neat
A seint* she weared, barred all of silk, *girdle
A barm-cloth* eke as white as morning milk *apron
Upon her lendes*, full of many a gore**. *loins **plait
White was her smock*, and broider'd all before, *robe or
        gown
And eke behind, on her collar about
Of coal-black silk, within and eke without.
The tapes of her white volupere* *head-kerchief
Were of the same suit of her collere;
Her fillet broad of silk, and set full high:
And sickerly* she had a likerous** eye. *certainly **lascivious
Full small y-pulled were her browes two,
And they were bent*, and black as any sloe. *arched
She was well more *blissful on to see* *pleasant to look upon*
Than is the newe perjenete* tree; *young pear-tree
And softer than the wool is of a wether.
And by her girdle hung a purse of leather,
Tassel'd with silk, and *pearled with latoun*. *set with brass
        pearls*
In all this world to seeken up and down
There is no man so wise, that coude thenche* *fancy, think of
So gay a popelot*, or such a wench. *puppet
Full brighter was the shining of her hue,
Than in the Tower the noble* forged new. *a gold coin

But of her song, it was as loud and yern*, *lively
As any swallow chittering on a bern*. *barn
Thereto* she coulde skip, and *make a game* *also *romp*
As any kid or calf following his dame.
Her mouth was sweet as braket, or as methe* *mead
Or hoard of apples, laid in hay or heath.
Wincing* she was as is a jolly colt, *skittish
Long as a mast, and upright as a bolt.
A brooch she bare upon her low collere,
As broad as is the boss of a bucklere.
Her shoon were laced on her legges high;
She was a primerole,* a piggesnie, *primrose
For any lord t' have ligging* in his bed, *lying
Or yet for any good yeoman to wed.

Now, sir, and eft* sir, so befell the case, *again
That on a day this Hendy Nicholas
Fell with this younge wife to rage* and play, *toy, play the
    rogue
While that her husband was at Oseney,
As clerkes be full subtle and full quaint.
And privily he caught her by the queint,* *cunt
And said; "Y-wis,* but if I have my will, *assuredly
For *derne love of thee, leman, I spill."* *for earnest love of
    thee my mistress, I perish*
And helde her fast by the haunche bones,
And saide "Leman, love me well at once,
Or I will dien, all so God me save."
And she sprang as a colt doth in the trave:
And with her head she writhed fast away,
And said; "I will not kiss thee, by my fay*. *faith
Why let be," quoth she, "let be, Nicholas,
Or I will cry out harow and alas!
Do away your handes, for your courtesy."
This Nicholas gan mercy for to cry,

And spake so fair, and proffer'd him so fast,
That she her love him granted at the last,
And swore her oath by Saint Thomas of Kent,
That she would be at his commandement,
When that she may her leisure well espy.
"My husband is so full of jealousy,
That but* ye waite well, and be privy, *unless
I wot right well I am but dead," quoth she.
"Ye muste be full derne* as in this case." *secret
"Nay, thereof care thee nought," quoth Nicholas:
"A clerk had *litherly beset his while*, *ill spent his time*
But if he could a carpenter beguile." *unless
And thus they were accorded and y-sworn
To wait a time, as I have said beforn.
When Nicholas had done thus every deal*, *whit
And thwacked her about the lendes* well, *loins
He kiss'd her sweet, and taketh his psalt'ry
And playeth fast, and maketh melody.
Then fell it thus, that to the parish church,
Of Christe's owen workes for to wirch*, *work
This good wife went upon a holy day;
Her forehead shone as bright as any day,
So was it washen, when she left her werk.

Now was there of that church a parish clerk,
The which that was y-cleped Absolon.
Curl'd was his hair, and as the gold it shone,
And strutted* as a fanne large and broad; *stretched
Full straight and even lay his jolly shode*. *head of hair
His rode* was red, his eyen grey as goose, *complexion
With Paule's windows carven on his shoes
In hosen red he went full fetisly*. *daintily, neatly
Y-clad he was full small and properly,
All in a kirtle* of a light waget*; *girdle **sky blue
Full fair and thicke be the pointes set,

And thereupon he had a gay surplice,
As white as is the blossom on the rise*. *twig
A merry child he was, so God me save;
Well could he letten blood, and clip, and shave,
And make a charter of land, and a quittance.
In twenty manners could he trip and dance,
After the school of Oxenforde tho*, *then
And with his legges caste to and fro;
And playen songes on a small ribible*; *fiddle
Thereto he sung sometimes a loud quinible* *treble
And as well could he play on a gitern.* *guitar
In all the town was brewhouse nor tavern,
That he not visited with his solas*, *mirth, sport
There as that any *garnard tapstere* was. *licentious barmaid*
But sooth to say he was somedeal squaimous* *squeamish
Of farting, and of speeche dangerous.
This Absolon, that jolly was and gay,
Went with a censer on the holy day,
Censing* the wives of the parish fast; *burning incense for
And many a lovely look he on them cast,
And namely* on this carpenter's wife: *especially
To look on her him thought a merry life.
She was so proper, and sweet, and likerous.
I dare well say, if she had been a mouse,
And he a cat, he would *her hent anon*. *have soon caught
    her*
This parish clerk, this jolly Absolon,
Hath in his hearte such a love-longing!
That of no wife took he none offering;
For courtesy he said he woulde none.
The moon at night full clear and brighte shone,
And Absolon his gitern hath y-taken,
For paramours he thoughte for to waken,
And forth he went, jolif* and amorous, *joyous
Till he came to the carpentere's house,

A little after the cock had y-crow,
And *dressed him* under a shot window, *stationed himself.*
That was upon the carpentere's wall.
He singeth in his voice gentle and small;
"Now, dear lady, if thy will be,
I pray that ye will rue* on me;" *take pity
Full well accordant to his giterning.
This carpenter awoke, and heard him sing,
And spake unto his wife, and said anon,
What Alison, hear'st thou not Absolon,
That chanteth thus under our bower* wall?" *chamber
And she answer'd her husband therewithal;
"Yes, God wot, John, I hear him every deal."
This passeth forth; what will ye bet* than well? *better

From day to day this jolly Absolon
So wooeth her, that him is woebegone.
He waketh all the night, and all the day,
To comb his lockes broad, and make him gay.
He wooeth her *by means and by brocage*, *by presents and
    by agents*
And swore he woulde be her owen page.
He singeth brokking* as a nightingale. *quavering
He sent her piment, mead, and spiced ale,
And wafers* piping hot out of the glede**: *cakes **coals
And, for she was of town, he proffer'd meed.
For some folk will be wonnen for richess,
And some for strokes, and some with gentiless.
Sometimes, to show his lightness and mast'ry,
He playeth Herod on a scaffold high.
But what availeth him as in this case?
So loveth she the Hendy Nicholas,
That Absolon may *blow the bucke's horn*: *"go whistle"*
He had for all his labour but a scorn.
And thus she maketh Absolon her ape,

And all his earnest turneth to a jape*.   *jest
Full sooth is this proverb, it is no lie;
Men say right thus alway; the nighe sly
Maketh oft time the far lief to be loth.
For though that Absolon be wood* or wroth   *mad
Because that he far was from her sight,
This nigh Nicholas stood still in his light.
Now bear thee well, thou Hendy Nicholas,
For Absolon may wail and sing "Alas!"

And so befell, that on a Saturday
This carpenter was gone to Oseney,
And Hendy Nicholas and Alison
Accorded were to this conclusion,
That Nicholas shall *shape him a wile*   *devise a stratagem*
The silly jealous husband to beguile;
And if so were the game went aright,
She shoulde sleepen in his arms all night;
For this was her desire and his also.
And right anon, withoute wordes mo',
This Nicholas no longer would he tarry,
But doth full soft unto his chamber carry
Both meat and drinke for a day or tway.
And to her husband bade her for to say,
If that he asked after Nicholas,
She shoulde say, "She wist* not where he was;   *knew
Of all the day she saw him not with eye;
She trowed* he was in some malady,   *believed
For no cry that her maiden could him call
He would answer, for nought that might befall."
Thus passed forth all thilke* Saturday,   *that
That Nicholas still in his chamber lay,
And ate, and slept, and didde what him list
Till Sunday, that* the sunne went to rest.   *when
This silly carpenter *had great marvaill*   *wondered greatly*

Of Nicholas, or what thing might him ail,
And said; "I am adrad*, by Saint Thomas! *afraid, in dread
It standeth not aright with Nicholas:
God shielde that he died suddenly. *heaven forbid!*
This world is now full fickle sickerly*. *certainly
I saw to-day a corpse y-borne to chirch,
That now on Monday last I saw him wirch*. *work
Go up," quod he unto his knave*, "anon; *servant.
Clepe* at his door, or knocke with a stone: *call
Look how it is, and tell me boldely."
This knave went him up full sturdily,
And, at the chamber door while that he stood,
He cried and knocked as that he were wood:* *mad
"What how? what do ye, Master Nicholay?
How may ye sleepen all the longe day?"
But all for nought, he hearde not a word.
An hole he found full low upon the board,
Where as the cat was wont in for to creep,
And at that hole he looked in full deep,
And at the last he had of him a sight.
This Nicholas sat ever gaping upright,
As he had kyked* on the newe moon. *looked
Adown he went, and told his master soon,
In what array he saw this ilke* man. *same

This carpenter to *blissen him* began, *bless, cross himself*
And said: "Now help us, Sainte Frideswide.
A man wot* little what shall him betide. *knows
This man is fall'n with his astronomy
Into some woodness* or some agony. *madness
I thought aye well how that it shoulde be.
Men should know nought of Godde's privity*. *secrets
Yea, blessed be alway a lewed* man, *unlearned
That *nought but only his believe can*. *knows no more than
    his "credo."*

105

So far'd another clerk with astronomy:
He walked in the fieldes for to *pry
Upon* the starres, what there should befall, *keep watch on*
Till he was in a marle pit y-fall.
He saw not that. But yet, by Saint Thomas!
Me rueth sore of Hendy Nicholas: *I am very sorry for*
He shall be *rated of* his studying, *chidden for*
If that I may, by Jesus, heaven's king!
Get me a staff, that I may underspore* *lever up
While that thou, Robin, heavest off the door:
He shall out of his studying, as I guess."
And to the chamber door he gan him dress* *apply himself.
His knave was a strong carl for the nonce,
And by the hasp he heav'd it off at once;
Into the floor the door fell down anon.
This Nicholas sat aye as still as stone,
And ever he gap'd upward into the air.
The carpenter ween'd* he were in despair, *thought
And hent* him by the shoulders mightily, *caught
And shook him hard, and cried spitously;* *angrily
"What, Nicholas? what how, man? look adown:
Awake, and think on Christe's passioun.
I crouche thee from elves, and from wights"*. *witches
Therewith the night-spell said he anon rights*, *properly
On the four halves* of the house about, *corners
And on the threshold of the door without.
"Lord Jesus Christ, and Sainte Benedight,
Blesse this house from every wicked wight,
From the night mare, the white Pater-noster;
Where wonnest* thou now, Sainte Peter's sister?" *dwellest
And at the last this Hendy Nicholas
Gan for to sigh full sore, and said; "Alas!
Shall all time world be lost eftsoones* now?" *forthwith
This carpenter answer'd; "What sayest thou?
What? think on God, as we do, men that swink.*" *labour

This Nicholas answer'd; "Fetch me a drink;
And after will I speak in privity
Of certain thing that toucheth thee and me:
I will tell it no other man certain."

This carpenter went down, and came again,
And brought of mighty ale a large quart;
And when that each of them had drunk his part,
This Nicholas his chamber door fast shet*, *shut
And down the carpenter by him he set,
And saide; "John, mine host full lief* and dear, *loved
Thou shalt upon thy truthe swear me here,
That to no wight thou shalt my counsel wray*: *betray
For it is Christes counsel that I say,
And if thou tell it man, thou art forlore:* *lost
For this vengeance thou shalt have therefor,
That if thou wraye* me, thou shalt be wood**." *betray **mad
"Nay, Christ forbid it for his holy blood!"
Quoth then this silly man; "I am no blab,* *talker
Nor, though I say it, am I *lief to gab*. *fond of speech*
Say what thou wilt, I shall it never tell
To child or wife, by him that harried Hell."

"Now, John," quoth Nicholas, "I will not lie,
I have y-found in my astrology,
As I have looked in the moone bright,
That now on Monday next, at quarter night,
Shall fall a rain, and that so wild and wood*, *mad
That never half so great was Noe's flood.
This world," he said, "in less than half an hour
Shall all be dreint*, so hideous is the shower: *drowned
Thus shall mankinde drench*, and lose their life." *drown
This carpenter answer'd; "Alas, my wife!
And shall she drench? alas, mine Alisoun!"
For sorrow of this he fell almost adown,

And said; "Is there no remedy in this case?"

"Why, yes, for God," quoth Hendy Nicholas;

"If thou wilt worken after *lore and rede*; *learning and
    advice*

Thou may'st not worken after thine own head.

For thus saith Solomon, that was full true:

Work all by counsel, and thou shalt not rue*. *repent

And if thou worke wilt by good counseil,

I undertake, withoute mast or sail,

Yet shall I save her, and thee, and me.

Hast thou not heard how saved was Noe,

When that our Lord had warned him beforn,

That all the world with water *should be lorn*?" *should
    perish*

"Yes," quoth this carpenter, "*full yore ago*." *long since*

"Hast thou not heard," quoth Nicholas, "also

The sorrow of Noe, with his fellowship,

That he had ere he got his wife to ship?

*Him had been lever, I dare well undertake,

At thilke time, than all his wethers black,

That she had had a ship herself alone.

And therefore know'st thou what is best to be done?

This asketh haste, and of an hasty thing

Men may not preach or make tarrying.

Anon go get us fast into this inn* *house

A kneading trough, or else a kemelin*, *brewing-tub

For each of us; but look that they be large,

In whiche we may swim* as in a barge: *float

And have therein vitaille suffisant

But for one day; fie on the remenant;

The water shall aslake* and go away *slacken, abate

Aboute prime* upon the nexte day. *early morning

But Robin may not know of this, thy knave*, *servant

Nor eke thy maiden Gill I may not save:

Ask me not why: for though thou aske me

I will not telle Godde's privity.
Sufficeth thee, *but if thy wit be mad*, *unless thou be out
      of thy wits*
To have as great a grace as Noe had;
Thy wife shall I well saven out of doubt.
Go now thy way, and speed thee hereabout.
But when thou hast for her, and thee, and me,
Y-gotten us these kneading tubbes three,
Then shalt thou hang them in the roof full high,
So that no man our purveyance* espy: *foresight, providence
And when thou hast done thus as I have said,
And hast our vitaille fair in them y-laid,
And eke an axe to smite the cord in two
When that the water comes, that we may go,
And break an hole on high upon the gable
Into the garden-ward, over the stable,
That we may freely passe forth our way,
When that the greate shower is gone away.
Then shalt thou swim as merry, I undertake,
As doth the white duck after her drake:
Then will I clepe,* 'How, Alison? How, John? *call
Be merry: for the flood will pass anon.'
And thou wilt say, 'Hail, Master Nicholay,
Good-morrow, I see thee well, for it is day.'
And then shall we be lordes all our life
Of all the world, as Noe and his wife.
But of one thing I warne thee full right,
Be well advised, on that ilke* night, *same
When we be enter'd into shippe's board,
That none of us not speak a single word,
Nor clepe nor cry, but be in his prayere,
For that is Godde's owen heste* dear. *command
Thy wife and thou must hangen far atween*, *asunder
For that betwixte you shall be no sin,
No more in looking than there shall in deed.

This ordinance is said: go, God thee speed
To-morrow night, when men be all asleep,
Into our kneading tubbes will we creep,
And sitte there, abiding Godde's grace.
Go now thy way, I have no longer space
To make of this no longer sermoning:
Men say thus: Send the wise, and say nothing:
Thou art so wise, it needeth thee nought teach.
Go, save our lives, and that I thee beseech."

This silly carpenter went forth his way,
Full oft he said, "Alas!" and "Well-a-day!",
And to his wife he told his privity,
And she was ware, and better knew than he
What all this *quainte cast was for to say*.   *strange contrivance
      meant*
But natheless she fear'd as she would dey,
And said: "Alas! go forth thy way anon.
Help us to scape, or we be dead each one.
I am thy true and very wedded wife;
Go, deare spouse, and help to save our life."
Lo, what a great thing is affection!
Men may die of imagination,
So deeply may impression be take.
This silly carpenter begins to quake:
He thinketh verily that he may see
This newe flood come weltering as the sea
To drenchen* Alison, his honey dear.   *drown
He weepeth, waileth, maketh *sorry cheer*;   *dismal
      countenance*
He sigheth, with full many a sorry sough.*   *groan
He go'th, and getteth him a kneading trough,
And after that a tub, and a kemelin,
And privily he sent them to his inn:
And hung them in the roof full privily.

With his own hand then made he ladders three,
To climbe by *the ranges and the stalks* *the rungs and the
      uprights*
Unto the tubbes hanging in the balks*; *beams
And victualed them, kemelin, trough, and tub,
With bread and cheese, and good ale in a jub*, *jug
Sufficing right enough as for a day.
But ere that he had made all this array,
He sent his knave*, and eke his wench** also, *servant **maid
Upon his need* to London for to go. *business
And on the Monday, when it drew to night,
He shut his door withoute candle light,
And dressed* every thing as it should be. *prepared
And shortly up they climbed all the three.
They satte stille well *a furlong way*. *the time it would take
      to walk a furlong*
"Now, Pater noster, clum," said Nicholay,
And "clum," quoth John; and "clum," said Alison:
This carpenter said his devotion,
And still he sat and bidded his prayere,
Awaking on the rain, if he it hear.
The deade sleep, for weary business,
Fell on this carpenter, right as I guess,
About the curfew-time, or little more,
For *travail of his ghost* he groaned sore, *anguish of
      spirit*
And eft he routed, for his head mislay. *and then he snored,
      for his head lay awry*
Adown the ladder stalked Nicholay;
And Alison full soft adown she sped.
Withoute wordes more they went to bed,
There as the carpenter was wont to lie: *where*
There was the revel, and the melody.
And thus lay Alison and Nicholas,
In business of mirth and in solace,

Until the bell of laudes* gan to ring, *morning service, at 3 a.m.
And friars in the chancel went to sing.

This parish clerk, this amorous Absolon,
That is for love alway so woebegone,
Upon the Monday was at Oseney
With company, him to disport and play;
And asked upon cas* a cloisterer** *occasion **monk
Full privily after John the carpenter;
And he drew him apart out of the church,
And said, "I n'ot;* I saw him not here wirch** *know not **work
Since Saturday; I trow that he be went
For timber, where our abbot hath him sent.
And dwellen at the Grange a day or two:
For he is wont for timber for to go,
Or else he is at his own house certain.
Where that he be, I cannot *soothly sayn.*" *say certainly*
This Absolon full jolly was and light,
And thought, "Now is the time to wake all night,
For sickerly* I saw him not stirring *certainly
About his door, since day began to spring.
So may I thrive, but I shall at cock crow
Full privily go knock at his window,
That stands full low upon his bower* wall: *chamber
To Alison then will I tellen all
My love-longing; for I shall not miss
That at the leaste way I shall her kiss.
Some manner comfort shall I have, parfay*, *by my faith
My mouth hath itched all this livelong day:
That is a sign of kissing at the least.
All night I mette* eke I was at a feast. *dreamt
Therefore I will go sleep an hour or tway,
And all the night then will I wake and play."
When that the first cock crowed had, anon
Up rose this jolly lover Absolon,

And him arrayed gay, *at point devise.* *with exact care*
But first he chewed grains and liquorice,
To smelle sweet, ere he had combed his hair.
Under his tongue a true love he bare,
For thereby thought he to be gracious.

Then came he to the carpentere's house,
And still he stood under the shot window;
Unto his breast it raught*, it was so low; *reached
And soft he coughed with a semisoun'.* *low tone
"What do ye, honeycomb, sweet Alisoun?
My faire bird, my sweet cinamome*, *cinnamon, sweet spice
Awaken, leman* mine, and speak to me. *mistress
Full little thinke ye upon my woe,
That for your love I sweat *there as* I go. *wherever
No wonder is that I do swelt* and sweat. *faint
I mourn as doth a lamb after the teat
Y-wis*, leman, I have such love-longing, *certainly
That like a turtle* true is my mourning. *turtle-dove
I may not eat, no more than a maid."
"Go from the window, thou jack fool," she said:
"As help me God, it will not be, 'come ba* me.' *kiss
I love another, else I were to blame,
Well better than thee, by Jesus, Absolon.
Go forth thy way, or I will cast a stone;
And let me sleep; *a twenty devil way'"*. *twenty devils take ye!*
"Alas!" quoth Absolon, "and well away!
That true love ever was so ill beset:
Then kiss me, since that it may be no bet*, *better
For Jesus' love, and for the love of me."
"Wilt thou then go thy way therewith?", quoth she.
"Yea, certes, leman," quoth this Absolon.
"Then make thee ready," quoth she, "I come anon."
And unto Nicholas she said *full still*: *in a low voice*
"Now peace, and thou shalt laugh anon thy fill."

This Absolon down set him on his knees,
And said; "I am a lord at all degrees:
For after this I hope there cometh more;
Leman, thy grace, and, sweete bird, thine ore.*" *favour
The window she undid, and that in haste.
"Have done," quoth she, "come off, and speed thee fast,
Lest that our neighebours should thee espy."
Then Absolon gan wipe his mouth full dry.
Dark was the night as pitch or as the coal,
And at the window she put out her hole,
And Absolon him fell ne bet ne werse,
But with his mouth he kiss'd her naked erse
Full savourly. When he was ware of this,
Aback he start, and thought it was amiss;
For well he wist a woman hath no beard.
He felt a thing all rough, and long y-hair'd,
And saide; "Fy, alas! what have I do?"
"Te he!" quoth she, and clapt the window to;
And Absolon went forth at sorry pace.
"A beard, a beard," said Hendy Nicholas;
"By God's corpus, this game went fair and well."
This silly Absolon heard every deal*, *word
And on his lip he gan for anger bite;
And to himself he said, "I shall thee quite"*. *requite, be even
    with
Who rubbeth now, who frotteth* now his lips *rubs
With dust, with sand, with straw, with cloth, with chips,
But Absolon? that saith full oft, "Alas!
My soul betake I unto Sathanas,
But me were lever* than all this town," quoth he *rather
"I this despite awroken* for to be. *revenged
Alas! alas! that I have been y-blent*." *deceived
His hote love is cold, and all y-quent.* *quenched
For from that time that he had kiss'd her erse,
Of paramours he *sette not a kers,* *cared not a rush*

For he was healed of his malady;
Full often paramours he gan defy,
And weep as doth a child that hath been beat.
A softe pace he went over the street
Unto a smith, men callen Dan* Gerveis, *master
That in his forge smithed plough-harness;
He sharped share and culter busily.
This Absolon knocked all easily,
And said; "Undo, Gerveis, and that anon."
"What, who art thou?" "It is I, Absolon."
"What? Absolon, what? Christe's sweete tree*, *cross
Why rise so rath*? hey! Benedicite, *early
What aileth you? some gay girl, God it wote,
Hath brought you thus upon the viretote:
By Saint Neot, ye wot well what I mean."
This Absolon he raughte* not a bean *recked, cared
Of all his play; no word again he gaf*, *spoke
For he had more tow on his distaff
Than Gerveis knew, and saide; "Friend so dear,
That hote culter in the chimney here
Lend it to me, I have therewith to don*: *do
I will it bring again to thee full soon."
Gerveis answered; "Certes, were it gold,
Or in a poke* nobles all untold, *purse
Thou shouldst it have, as I am a true smith.
Hey! Christe's foot, what will ye do therewith?"
"Thereof," quoth Absolon, "be as be may;
I shall well tell it thee another day:"
And caught the culter by the colde stele*. *handle
Full soft out at the door he gan to steal,
And went unto the carpentere's wall
He coughed first, and knocked therewithal
Upon the window, light as he did ere*. *before
This Alison answered; "Who is there
That knocketh so? I warrant him a thief."

"Nay, nay," quoth he, "God wot, my sweete lefe*, *love
I am thine Absolon, my own darling.
Of gold," quoth he, "I have thee brought a ring,
My mother gave it me, so God me save!
Full fine it is, and thereto well y-grave*: *engraved
This will I give to thee, if thou me kiss."
Now Nicholas was risen up to piss,
And thought he would *amenden all the jape*; *improve the joke*
He shoulde kiss his erse ere that he scape:
And up the window did he hastily,
And out his erse he put full privily
Over the buttock, to the haunche bone.
And therewith spake this clerk, this Absolon,
"Speak, sweete bird, I know not where thou art."
This Nicholas anon let fly a fart,
As great as it had been a thunder dent*; *peal, clap
That with the stroke he was well nigh y-blent*; *blinded
But he was ready with his iron hot,
And Nicholas amid the erse he smote.
Off went the skin an handbreadth all about.
The hote culter burned so his tout*, *breech
That for the smart he weened* he would die; *thought
As he were wood*, for woe he gan to cry, *mad
"Help! water, water, help for Godde's heart!"

This carpenter out of his slumber start,
And heard one cry "Water," as he were wood*, *mad
And thought, "Alas! now cometh Noe's flood."
He sat him up withoute wordes mo'
And with his axe he smote the cord in two;
And down went all; he found neither to sell
Nor bread nor ale, till he came to the sell*, *threshold
Upon the floor, and there in swoon he lay.
Up started Alison and Nicholay,·
And cried out an "harow!" in the street.

The neighbours alle, bothe small and great
In ranne, for to gauren* on this man,   *stare
That yet in swoone lay, both pale and wan:
For with the fall he broken had his arm.
But stand he must unto his owen harm,
For when he spake, he was anon borne down
With Hendy Nicholas and Alisoun.
They told to every man that he was wood*;   *mad
He was aghaste* so of Noe's flood,   *afraid
Through phantasy, that of his vanity
He had y-bought him kneading-tubbes three,
And had them hanged in the roof above;
And that he prayed them for Godde's love
To sitten in the roof for company.
The folk gan laughen at his phantasy.
Into the roof they kyken* and they gape,   *peep, look.
And turned all his harm into a jape*.   *jest
For whatsoe'er this carpenter answer'd,
It was for nought, no man his reason heard.
With oathes great he was so sworn adown,
That he was holden wood in all the town.
For every clerk anon right held with other;
They said, "The man was wood, my leve* brother;"   *dear
And every wight gan laughen at his strife.
Thus swived* was the carpentere's wife,   *enjoyed
For all his keeping* and his jealousy;   *care
And Absolon hath kiss'd her nether eye;
And Nicholas is scalded in the tout.
This tale is done, and God save all the rout*.   *company

THE REEVE'S TALE

WHEN folk had laughed all at this nice case
Of Absolon and Hendy Nicholas,
Diverse folk diversely they said,

But for the more part they laugh'd and play'd;* *were diverted
And at this tale I saw no man him grieve,
But it were only Osewold the Reeve.
Because he was of carpenteres craft,
A little ire is in his hearte laft*; *left
He gan to grudge* and blamed it a lite.** *murmur **little.
"So the* I," quoth he, "full well could I him quite** *thrive **match
With blearing* of a proude miller's eye, *dimming
If that me list to speak of ribaldry.
But I am old; me list not play for age;
Grass time is done, my fodder is now forage.
This white top* writeth mine olde years; *head
Mine heart is also moulded* as mine hairs; *grown mouldy
And I do fare as doth an open-erse*; *medlar
That ilke* fruit is ever longer werse, *same
Till it be rotten *in mullok or in stre*. *on the ground or in straw*
We olde men, I dread, so fare we;
Till we be rotten, can we not be ripe;
We hop* away, while that the world will pipe; *dance
For in our will there sticketh aye a nail,
To have an hoary head and a green tail,
As hath a leek; for though our might be gone,
Our will desireth folly ever-in-one*: *continually
For when we may not do, then will we speak,
Yet in our ashes cold does fire reek.* *smoke
Four gledes* have we, which I shall devise**, *coals ** describe
Vaunting, and lying, anger, covetise*. *covetousness
These foure sparks belongen unto eld.
Our olde limbes well may be unweld*, *unwieldy
But will shall never fail us, that is sooth.
And yet have I alway a coltes tooth,
As many a year as it is passed and gone
Since that my tap of life began to run;
For sickerly*, when I was born, anon *certainly
Death drew the tap of life, and let it gon:

And ever since hath so the tap y-run,
Till that almost all empty is the tun.
The stream of life now droppeth on the chimb.
The silly tongue well may ring and chime
Of wretchedness, that passed is full yore*: *long
With olde folk, save dotage, is no more."

When that our Host had heard this sermoning,
He gan to speak as lordly as a king,
And said; "To what amounteth all this wit?
What? shall we speak all day of holy writ?
The devil made a Reeve for to preach,
As of a souter* a shipman, or a leach**. *cobbler **surgeon
Say forth thy tale, and tarry not the time:
Lo here is Deptford, and 'tis half past prime:
Lo Greenwich, where many a shrew is in.
It were high time thy tale to begin."

"Now, sirs," quoth then this Osewold the Reeve,
I pray you all that none of you do grieve,
Though I answer, and somewhat set his hove*, *hood
For lawful is *force off with force to shove.* *to repel force by force*
This drunken miller hath y-told us here
How that beguiled was a carpentere,
Paraventure* in scorn, for I am one: *perhaps
And, by your leave, I shall him quite anon.
Right in his churlish termes will I speak,
I pray to God his necke might to-break.
He can well in mine eye see a stalk,
But in his own he cannot see a balk."

THE TALE

At Trompington, not far from Cantebrig,* *Cambridge
There goes a brook, and over that a brig,

Upon the whiche brook there stands a mill:
And this is *very sooth* that I you tell. *complete truth*
A miller was there dwelling many a day,
As any peacock he was proud and gay:
Pipen he could, and fish, and nettes bete*, *prepare
And turne cups, and wrestle well, and shete*. *shoot
Aye by his belt he bare a long pavade*, *poniard
And of his sword full trenchant was the blade.
A jolly popper* bare he in his pouch; *dagger
There was no man for peril durst him touch.
A Sheffield whittle* bare he in his hose. *small knife
Round was his face, and camuse* was his nose. *flat
As pilled* as an ape's was his skull. *peeled, bald.
He was a market-beter* at the full. *brawler
There durste no wight hand upon him legge*, *lay
That he ne swore anon he should abegge*. *suffer the
    penalty

A thief he was, for sooth, of corn and meal,
And that a sly, and used well to steal.
His name was *hoten deinous Simekin* *called "Disdainful
    Simkin"*
A wife he hadde, come of noble kin:
The parson of the town her father was.
With her he gave full many a pan of brass,
For that Simkin should in his blood ally.
She was y-foster'd in a nunnery:
For Simkin woulde no wife, as he said,
But she were well y-nourish'd, and a maid,
To saven his estate and yeomanry:
And she was proud, and pert as is a pie*. *magpie
A full fair sight it was to see them two;
On holy days before her would he go
With his tippet* y-bound about his head; *hood
And she came after in a gite* of red, *gown

And Simkin hadde hosen of the same.
There durste no wight call her aught but Dame:
None was so hardy, walking by that way,
That with her either durste *rage or play*, *use freedom*
But if he would be slain by Simekin *unless
With pavade, or with knife, or bodekin.
For jealous folk be per'lous evermo':
Algate* they would their wives *wende so*. *unless *so behave*
And eke for she was somewhat smutterlich*, *dirty
She was as dign* as water in a ditch, *nasty
And all so full of hoker*, and bismare**. *ill-nature **abusive
    speech
Her thoughte that a lady should her spare*, *not judge her
    hardly
What for her kindred, and her nortelrie* *nurturing,
    education
That she had learned in the nunnery.

One daughter hadde they betwixt them two
Of twenty year, withouten any mo,
Saving a child that was of half year age,
In cradle it lay, and was a proper page.* *boy
This wenche thick and well y-growen was,
With camuse* nose, and eyen gray as glass; *flat
With buttocks broad, and breastes round and high;
But right fair was her hair, I will not lie.
The parson of the town, for she was fair,
In purpose was to make of her his heir
Both of his chattels and his messuage,
And *strange he made it* of her marriage. *he made it a
    matter of difficulty*
His purpose was for to bestow her high
Into some worthy blood of ancestry.
For holy Church's good may be dispended* *spent
On holy Church's blood that is descended.

121

Therefore he would his holy blood honour
Though that he holy Churche should devour.

Great soken* hath this miller, out of doubt, *toll taken for
    grinding
With wheat and malt, of all the land about;
And namely* there was a great college *especially
Men call the Soler Hall at Cantebrege,
There was their wheat and eke their malt y-ground.
And on a day it happed in a stound*, *suddenly
Sick lay the manciple* of a malady, *steward
Men *weened wisly* that he shoulde die. *thought certainly*
For which this miller stole both meal and corn
An hundred times more than beforn.
For theretofore he stole but courteously,
But now he was a thief outrageously.
For which the warden chid and made fare*, *fuss
But thereof *set the miller not a tare*; *he cared not a rush*
He *crack'd his boast,* and swore it was not so. *talked big*

Then were there younge poore scholars two,
That dwelled in the hall of which I say;
Testif* they were, and lusty for to play; *headstrong
And only for their mirth and revelry
Upon the warden busily they cry,
To give them leave for but a *little stound*, *short time*
To go to mill, and see their corn y-ground:
And hardily* they durste lay their neck, *boldly
The miller should not steal them half a peck
Of corn by sleight, nor them by force bereave* *take away
And at the last the warden give them leave:
John hight the one, and Alein hight the other,
Of one town were they born, that highte Strother,
Far in the North, I cannot tell you where.
This Alein he made ready all his gear,

And on a horse the sack he cast anon:
Forth went Alein the clerk, and also John,
With good sword and with buckler by their side.
John knew the way, him needed not no guide,
And at the mill the sack adown he lay'th.

Alein spake first; "All hail, Simon, in faith,
How fares thy faire daughter, and thy wife."
"Alein, welcome," quoth Simkin, "by my life,
And John also: how now, what do ye here?"
"By God, Simon," quoth John, "need has no peer*. *equal
Him serve himself behoves that has no swain*, *servant
Or else he is a fool, as clerkes sayn.
Our manciple I hope* he will be dead, *expect
So workes aye the wanges* in his head: *cheek-teeth
And therefore is I come, and eke Alein,
To grind our corn and carry it home again:
I pray you speed us hence as well ye may."
"It shall be done," quoth Simkin, "by my fay.
What will ye do while that it is in hand?"
"By God, right by the hopper will I stand,"
Quoth John, "and see how that the corn goes in.
Yet saw I never, by my father's kin,
How that the hopper wagges to and fro."
Alein answered, "John, and wilt thou so?
Then will I be beneathe, by my crown,
And see how that the meale falls adown
Into the trough, that shall be my disport*: *amusement
For, John, in faith I may be of your sort;
I is as ill a miller as is ye."

This miller smiled at their nicety*, *simplicity
And thought, "All this is done but for a wile.
They weenen* that no man may them beguile, *think
But by my thrift yet shall I blear their eye,

For all the sleight in their philosophy.
The more *quainte knackes* that they make, *odd little tricks*
The more will I steal when that I take.
Instead of flour yet will I give them bren*. *bran
The greatest clerks are not the wisest men,
As whilom to the wolf thus spake the mare:
Of all their art ne count I not a tare."
Out at the door he went full privily,
When that he saw his time, softly.
He looked up and down, until he found
The clerkes' horse, there as he stood y-bound
Behind the mill, under a levesell:* *arbour
And to the horse he went him fair and well,
And stripped off the bridle right anon.
And when the horse was loose, he gan to gon
Toward the fen, where wilde mares run,
Forth, with "Wehee!" through thick and eke through thin.
This miller went again, no word he said,
But did his note*, and with these clerkes play'd, *business
Till that their corn was fair and well y-ground.
And when the meal was sacked and y-bound,
Then John went out, and found his horse away,
And gan to cry, "Harow, and well-away!
Our horse is lost: Alein, for Godde's bones,
Step on thy feet; come off, man, all at once:
Alas! our warden has his palfrey lorn.*" *lost
This Alein all forgot, both meal and corn;
All was out of his mind his husbandry*. *careful watch over
    the corn*
"What, which way is he gone?" he gan to cry.
The wife came leaping inward at a renne*, *run
She said; "Alas! your horse went to the fen
With wilde mares, as fast as he could go.
Unthank* come on his hand that bound him so *ill luck, a
    curse

And his that better should have knit the rein."
"Alas!" quoth John, "Alein, for Christes pain
Lay down thy sword, and I shall mine also.
I is full wight*, God wate**, as is a roe. *swift **knows
By Godde's soul he shall not scape us bathe*. *both
Why n' had thou put the capel* in the lathe**? *horse **barn
Ill hail, Alein, by God thou is a fonne.*" *fool
These silly clerkes have full fast y-run
Toward the fen, both Alein and eke John;
And when the miller saw that they were gone,
He half a bushel of their flour did take,
And bade his wife go knead it in a cake.
He said; "I trow, the clerkes were afeard,
Yet can a miller *make a clerkes beard,* *cheat a scholar*
For all his art: yea, let them go their way!
Lo where they go! yea, let the children play:
They get him not so lightly, by my crown."
These silly clerkes runnen up and down
With "Keep, keep; stand, stand; jossa*, warderere. *turn
Go whistle thou, and I shall keep* him here." *catch
But shortly, till that it was very night
They coulde not, though they did all their might,
Their capel catch, he ran alway so fast:
Till in a ditch they caught him at the last.

Weary and wet, as beastes in the rain,
Comes silly John, and with him comes Alein.
"Alas," quoth John, "the day that I was born!
Now are we driv'n till hething* and till scorn. *mockery
Our corn is stol'n, men will us fonnes* call, *fools
Both the warden, and eke our fellows all,
And namely* the miller, well-away!" *especially
Thus plained John, as he went by the way
Toward the mill, and Bayard* in his hand. *the bay horse
The miller sitting by the fire he fand*. *found

For it was night, and forther* might they not, *go their way
But for the love of God they him besought
Of herberow* and ease, for their penny. *lodging
The miller said again, "If there be any,
Such as it is, yet shall ye have your part.
Mine house is strait, but ye have learned art;
Ye can by arguments maken a place
A mile broad, of twenty foot of space.
Let see now if this place may suffice,
Or make it room with speech, as is your guise.*" *fashion
"Now, Simon," said this John, "by Saint Cuthberd
Aye is thou merry, and that is fair answer'd.
I have heard say, man shall take of two things,
Such as he findes, or such as he brings.
But specially I pray thee, hoste dear,
Gar us have meat and drink, and make us cheer,
And we shall pay thee truly at the full:
With empty hand men may not hawkes tull*. *allure
Lo here our silver ready for to spend."

This miller to the town his daughter send
For ale and bread, and roasted them a goose,
And bound their horse, he should no more go loose:
And them in his own chamber made a bed.
With sheetes and with chalons* fair y-spread, *blankets
Not from his owen bed ten foot or twelve:
His daughter had a bed all by herselve,
Right in the same chamber *by and by*: *side by side*
It might no better be, and cause why,
There was no *roomer herberow* in the place. *roomier
    lodging*
They suppen, and they speaken of solace,
And drinken ever strong ale at the best.
Aboute midnight went they all to rest.
Well had this miller varnished his head;

Full pale he was, fordrunken, and *nought red*. *without his
  wits*
He yoxed*, and he spake thorough the nose, *hiccuped
As he were in the quakke*, or in the pose**. *grunting **catarrh
To bed he went, and with him went his wife,
As any jay she light was and jolife,* *jolly
So was her jolly whistle well y-wet.
The cradle at her beddes feet was set,
To rock, and eke to give the child to suck.
And when that drunken was all in the crock* *pitcher
To bedde went the daughter right anon,
To bedde went Alein, and also John.
There was no more; needed them no dwale.
This miller had, so wisly* bibbed ale, *certainly
That as a horse he snorted in his sleep,
Nor of his tail behind he took no keep*. *heed
His wife bare him a burdoun*, a full strong; *bass
Men might their routing* hearen a furlong. *snoring

The wenche routed eke for company.
Alein the clerk, that heard this melody,
He poked John, and saide: "Sleepest thou?
Heardest thou ever such a song ere now?
Lo what a compline is y-mell* them all. *among
A wilde fire upon their bodies fall,
Who hearken'd ever such a ferly* thing? *strange
Yea, they shall have the flow'r of ill ending!
This longe night there *tides me* no rest. *comes to me*
But yet no force*, all shall be for the best. *matter
For, John," said he, "as ever may I thrive,
If that I may, yon wenche will I swive*. *enjoy carnally
Some easement* has law y-shapen** us *satisfaction **provided
For, John, there is a law that sayeth thus,
That if a man in one point be aggriev'd,
That in another he shall be relievd.

Our corn is stol'n, soothly it is no nay,
And we have had an evil fit to-day.
And since I shall have none amendement
Against my loss, I will have easement:
By Godde's soul, it shall none, other be."
This John answer'd; "Alein, *avise thee*:   *have a care*
The miller is a perilous man," he said,
"And if that he out of his sleep abraid*,   *awaked
He mighte do us both a villainy*."   *mischief
Alein answer'd; "I count him not a fly.
And up he rose, and by the wench he crept.
This wenche lay upright, and fast she slept,
Till he so nigh was, ere she might espy,
That it had been too late for to cry:
And, shortly for to say, they were at one.
Now play, Alein, for I will speak of John.

This John lay still a furlong way or two,
And to himself he made ruth* and woe.   *wail
"Alas!" quoth he, "this is a wicked jape*;   *trick
Now may I say, that I is but an ape.
Yet has my fellow somewhat for his harm;
He has the miller's daughter in his arm:
He auntred* him, and hath his needes sped,   *adventured
And I lie as a draff-sack in my bed;
And when this jape is told another day,
I shall be held a daffe* or a cockenay   *coward
I will arise, and auntre* it, by my fay: *attempt
Unhardy is unsely, as men say."
And up he rose, and softely he went
Unto the cradle, and in his hand it hent*,   *took
And bare it soft unto his beddes feet.
Soon after this the wife *her routing lete*,   *stopped snoring*
And gan awake, and went her out to piss
And came again and gan the cradle miss

And groped here and there, but she found none.
"Alas!" quoth she, "I had almost misgone
I had almost gone to the clerkes' bed.
Ey! Benedicite, then had I foul y-sped."
And forth she went, till she the cradle fand.
She groped alway farther with her hand
And found the bed, and *thoughte not but good* *had no
    suspicion*
Because that the cradle by it stood,
And wist not where she was, for it was derk;
But fair and well she crept in by the clerk,
And lay full still, and would have caught a sleep.
Within a while this John the Clerk up leap
And on this goode wife laid on full sore;
So merry a fit had she not had *full yore*. *for a long time*
He pricked hard and deep, as he were mad.

This jolly life have these two clerkes had,
Till that the thirde cock began to sing.
Alein wax'd weary in the morrowing,
For he had swonken* all the longe night, *laboured
And saide; "Farewell, Malkin, my sweet wight.
The day is come, I may no longer bide,
But evermore, where so I go or ride,
I is thine owen clerk, so have I hele.*" *health
"Now, deare leman*," quoth she, "go, fare wele: *sweetheart
But ere thou go, one thing I will thee tell.
When that thou wendest homeward by the mill,
Right at the entry of the door behind
Thou shalt a cake of half a bushel find,
That was y-maked of thine owen meal,
Which that I help'd my father for to steal.
And goode leman, God thee save and keep."
And with that word she gan almost to weep.
Alein uprose and thought, "Ere the day daw

I will go creepen in by my fellaw:"
And found the cradle with his hand anon.
"By God!" thought he, "all wrong I have misgone:
My head is *totty of my swink* to-night, *giddy from my
    labour*
That maketh me that I go not aright.
I wot well by the cradle I have misgo';
Here lie the miller and his wife also."
And forth he went a twenty devil way
Unto the bed, there as the miller lay.
He ween'd* t' have creeped by his fellow John, *thought
And by the miller in he crept anon,
And caught him by the neck, and gan him shake,
And said; "Thou John, thou swines-head, awake
For Christes soul, and hear a noble game!
For by that lord that called is Saint Jame,
As I have thries in this shorte night
Swived the miller's daughter bolt-upright,
While thou hast as a coward lain aghast*." *afraid
"Thou false harlot," quoth the miller, "hast?
Ah, false traitor, false clerk," quoth he,
"Thou shalt be dead, by Godde's dignity,
Who durste be so bold to disparage* *disgrace
My daughter, that is come of such lineage?"
And by the throate-ball* he caught Alein, *Adam's apple
And he him hent* dispiteously** again, *seized **angrily
And on the nose he smote him with his fist;
Down ran the bloody stream upon his breast:
And in the floor with nose and mouth all broke
They wallow, as do two pigs in a poke.
And up they go, and down again anon,
Till that the miller spurned* on a stone, *stumbled
And down he backward fell upon his wife,
That wiste nothing of this nice strife:
For she was fall'n asleep a little wight* *while

With John the clerk, that waked had all night:
And with the fall out of her sleep she braid*.   *woke
"Help, holy cross of Bromeholm," she said;
"In manus tuas! Lord, to thee I call.
Awake, Simon, the fiend is on me fall;
Mine heart is broken; help; I am but dead:
There li'th one on my womb and on mine head.
Help, Simkin, for these false clerks do fight"
This John start up as fast as e'er he might,
And groped by the walles to and fro
To find a staff; and she start up also,
And knew the estres* better than this John,   *apartment
And by the wall she took a staff anon:
And saw a little shimmering of a light,
For at an hole in shone the moone bright,
And by that light she saw them both the two,
But sickerly* she wist not who was who,   *certainly
But as she saw a white thing in her eye.
And when she gan this white thing espy,
She ween'd* the clerk had wear'd a volupere**;   *supposed
     **night-cap
And with the staff she drew aye nere* and nere*,   *nearer
And ween'd to have hit this Alein at the full,
And smote the miller on the pilled* skull;   *bald
That down he went, and cried, "Harow! I die."
These clerkes beat him well, and let him lie,
And greithen* them, and take their horse anon,   *make ready,
     dress
And eke their meal, and on their way they gon:
And at the mill door eke they took their cake
Of half a bushel flour, full well y-bake.

Thus is the proude miller well y-beat,
And hath y-lost the grinding of the wheat;
And payed for the supper *every deal*   *every bit*

Of Alein and of John, that beat him well;
His wife is swived, and his daughter als*; *also
Lo, such it is a miller to be false.
And therefore this proverb is said full sooth,
"*Him thar not winnen well* that evil do'th, *he deserves not
    to gain*
A guiler shall himself beguiled be:"
And God that sitteth high in majesty
Save all this Company, both great and smale.
Thus have I quit* the Miller in my tale. *made myself quits
    with

THE COOK'S TALE

THE Cook of London, while the Reeve thus spake,
For joy he laugh'd and clapp'd him on the back:
"Aha!" quoth he, "for Christes passion,
This Miller had a sharp conclusion,
Upon this argument of herbergage.* *lodging
Well saide Solomon in his language,
Bring thou not every man into thine house,
For harbouring by night is perilous.
Well ought a man avised for to be *a man should take good
    heed*
Whom that he brought into his privity.
I pray to God to give me sorrow and care
If ever, since I highte* Hodge of Ware, *was called
Heard I a miller better *set a-work*; *handled
He had a jape* of malice in the derk. *trick
But God forbid that we should stinte* here, *stop
And therefore if ye will vouchsafe to hear
A tale of me, that am a poore man,
I will you tell as well as e'er I can
A little jape that fell in our city."

Our Host answer'd and said; "I grant it thee.
Roger, tell on; and look that it be good,
For many a pasty hast thou letten blood,
And many a Jack of Dover hast thou sold,
That had been twice hot and twice cold.
Of many a pilgrim hast thou Christe's curse,
For of thy parsley yet fare they the worse.
That they have eaten in thy stubble goose:
For in thy shop doth many a fly go loose.
Now tell on, gentle Roger, by thy name,
But yet I pray thee be not *wroth for game*; *angry with my
    jesting*
A man may say full sooth in game and play."
"Thou sayst full sooth," quoth Roger, "by my fay;
But sooth play quad play, as the Fleming saith,
And therefore, Harry Bailly, by thy faith,
Be thou not wroth, else we departe* here, *part company
Though that my tale be of an hostelere.* *innkeeper
But natheless, I will not tell it yet,
But ere we part, y-wis* thou shalt be quit." *assuredly
And therewithal he laugh'd and made cheer,
And told his tale, as ye shall after hear.

THE TALE

A prentice whilom dwelt in our city,
And of a craft of victuallers was he:
Galliard* he was, as goldfinch in the shaw**, *lively **grove
Brown as a berry, a proper short fellow:
With lockes black, combed full fetisly.* *daintily
And dance he could so well and jollily,
That he was called Perkin Revellour.
He was as full of love and paramour,
As is the honeycomb of honey sweet;
Well was the wenche that with him might meet.

At every bridal would he sing and hop;
He better lov'd the tavern than the shop.
For when there any riding was in Cheap,
Out of the shoppe thither would he leap,
And, till that he had all the sight y-seen,
And danced well, he would not come again;
And gather'd him a meinie* of his sort, *company of fellows
To hop and sing, and make such disport:
And there they *sette steven* for to meet *made
    appointment*
To playen at the dice in such a street.
For in the towne was there no prentice
That fairer coulde cast a pair of dice
Than Perkin could; and thereto *he was free* *he spent money
    liberally*
Of his dispence, in place of privity. *where he would not be
    seen*
That found his master well in his chaffare,* *merchandise
For oftentime he found his box full bare.
For, soothely, a prentice revellour,
That haunteth dice, riot, and paramour,
His master shall it in his shop abie*, *suffer for
All* have he no part of the minstrelsy. *although
For theft and riot they be convertible,
All can they play on *gitern or ribible.* *guitar or rebeck*
Revel and truth, as in a low degree,
They be full wroth* all day, as men may see. *at variance

This jolly prentice with his master bode,
Till he was nigh out of his prenticehood,
All were he snubbed* both early and late, *rebuked
And sometimes led with revel to Newgate.
But at the last his master him bethought,
Upon a day when he his paper sought,
Of a proverb, that saith this same word;

Better is rotten apple out of hoard,
Than that it should rot all the remenant:
So fares it by a riotous servant;
It is well lesse harm to let him pace*, *pass, go
Than he shend* all the servants in the place. *corrupt
Therefore his master gave him a quittance,
And bade him go, with sorrow and mischance.
And thus this jolly prentice had his leve*: *desire
Now let him riot all the night, or leave*. *refrain
And, for there is no thief without a louke,
That helpeth him to wasten and to souk* *spend
Of that he bribe* can, or borrow may, *steal
Anon he sent his bed and his array
Unto a compere* of his owen sort, *comrade
That loved dice, and riot, and disport;
And had a wife, that held *for countenance* *for
    appearances*
A shop, and swived* for her sustenance. *prostituted herself
  . . . .

THE MAN OF LAW'S TALE

Our Hoste saw well that the brighte sun
Th' arc of his artificial day had run
The fourthe part, and half an houre more;
And, though he were not deep expert in lore,
He wist it was the eight-and-twenty day
Of April, that is messenger to May;
And saw well that the shadow of every tree
Was in its length of the same quantity
That was the body erect that caused it;
And therefore by the shadow he took his wit*, *knowledge
That Phoebus, which that shone so clear and bright,
Degrees was five-and-forty clomb on height;
And for that day, as in that latitude,

It was ten of the clock, he gan conclude;
And suddenly he plight* his horse about. *pulled

"Lordings," quoth he, "I warn you all this rout*, *company
The fourthe partie of this day is gone.
Now for the love of God and of Saint John
Lose no time, as farforth as ye may.
Lordings, the time wasteth night and day,
And steals from us, what privily sleeping,
And what through negligence in our waking,
As doth the stream, that turneth never again,
Descending from the mountain to the plain.
Well might Senec, and many a philosopher,
Bewaile time more than gold in coffer.
For loss of chattels may recover'd be,
But loss of time shendeth* us", quoth he. *destroys

"It will not come again, withoute dread,
No more than will Malkin's maidenhead,
When she hath lost it in her wantonness.
Let us not moulde thus in idleness.
Sir Man of Law," quoth he, "so have ye bliss,
Tell us a tale anon, as forword* is. *the bargain
Ye be submitted through your free assent
To stand in this case at my judgement.
Acquit you now, and *holde your behest*; *keep your
    promise*
Then have ye done your devoir* at the least." *duty
"Hoste," quoth he, "*de par dieux jeo asente*;
To breake forword is not mine intent.
Behest is debt, and I would hold it fain,
All my behest; I can no better sayn.
For such law as a man gives another wight,
He should himselfe usen it by right.
Thus will our text: but natheless certain

I can right now no thrifty* tale sayn, *worthy
But Chaucer (though he *can but lewedly* *knows but imperfectly*
    imperfectly*
On metres and on rhyming craftily)
Hath said them, in such English as he can,
Of olde time, as knoweth many a man.
And if he have not said them, leve* brother, *dear
In one book, he hath said them in another
For he hath told of lovers up and down,
More than Ovide made of mentioun
In his Epistolae, that be full old.
Why should I telle them, since they he told?
In youth he made of Ceyx and Alcyon,
And since then he hath spoke of every one
These noble wives, and these lovers eke.
Whoso that will his large volume seek
Called the Saintes' Legend of Cupid:
There may he see the large woundes wide
Of Lucrece, and of Babylon Thisbe;
The sword of Dido for the false Enee;
The tree of Phillis for her Demophon;
The plaint of Diane, and of Hermion,
Of Ariadne, and Hypsipile;
The barren isle standing in the sea;
The drown'd Leander for his fair Hero;
The teares of Helene, and eke the woe
Of Briseis, and Laodamia;
The cruelty of thee, Queen Medea,
Thy little children hanging by the halse*, *neck
For thy Jason, that was of love so false.
Hypermnestra, Penelop', Alcest',
Your wifehood he commendeth with the best.
But certainly no worde writeth he
Of *thilke wick* example of Canace, *that wicked*
That loved her own brother sinfully;

(Of all such cursed stories I say, Fy),
Or else of Tyrius Apollonius,
How that the cursed king Antiochus
Bereft his daughter of her maidenhead;
That is so horrible a tale to read,
When he her threw upon the pavement.
And therefore he, *of full avisement*, *deliberately,
    advisedly*
Would never write in none of his sermons
Of such unkind* abominations; *unnatural
Nor I will none rehearse, if that I may.
But of my tale how shall I do this day?
Me were loth to be liken'd doubteless
To Muses, that men call Pierides
(Metamorphoseos wot what I mean),
But natheless I recke not a bean,
Though I come after him with hawebake*; *lout
I speak in prose, and let him rhymes make."
And with that word, he with a sober cheer
Began his tale, and said as ye shall hear.

THE TALE

O scatheful harm, condition of poverty,
With thirst, with cold, with hunger so confounded;
To aske help thee shameth in thine hearte;
If thou none ask, so sore art thou y-wounded,
That very need unwrappeth all thy wound hid.
Maugre thine head thou must for indigence
Or steal, or beg, or borrow thy dispence*. *expense

Thou blamest Christ, and sayst full bitterly,
He misdeparteth* riches temporal; *allots amiss
Thy neighebour thou witest* sinfully, *blamest
And sayst, thou hast too little, and he hath all:

"Parfay (sayst thou) sometime he reckon shall,
When that his tail shall *brennen in the glede*, *burn in the
    fire*
For he not help'd the needful in their need."

Hearken what is the sentence of the wise:
Better to die than to have indigence.
Thy selve neighebour will thee despise, *that same*
If thou be poor, farewell thy reverence.
Yet of the wise man take this sentence,
Alle the days of poore men be wick"*, *wicked, evil
Beware therefore ere thou come to that prick*. *point

If thou be poor, thy brother hateth thee,
And all thy friendes flee from thee, alas!
O riche merchants, full of wealth be ye,
O noble, prudent folk, as in this case,
Your bagges be not fill'd with *ambes ace,* *two aces*
But with *six-cinque*, that runneth for your chance; *six-five*
At Christenmass well merry may ye dance.

Ye seeke land and sea for your winnings,
As wise folk ye knowen all th' estate
Of regnes*; ye be fathers of tidings, *kingdoms
And tales, both of peace and of debate*: *contention, war
I were right now of tales desolate*, *barren, empty.
But that a merchant, gone in many a year,
Me taught a tale, which ye shall after hear.

In Syria whilom dwelt a company
Of chapmen rich, and thereto sad* and true, *grave, steadfast
Clothes of gold, and satins rich of hue.
That widewhere* sent their spicery, *to distant parts
Their chaffare* was so thriftly** and so new, *wares
    **advantageous

139

That every wight had dainty* to chaffare**   *pleasure **deal
With them, and eke to selle them their ware.

Now fell it, that the masters of that sort
Have *shapen them* to Rome for to wend,   *determined,
    prepared*
Were it for chapmanhood* or for disport,   *trading
None other message would they thither send,
But come themselves to Rome, this is the end:
And in such place as thought them a vantage
For their intent, they took their herbergage.*   *lodging

Sojourned have these merchants in that town
A certain time as fell to their pleasance:
And so befell, that th' excellent renown
Of th' emperore's daughter, Dame Constance,
Reported was, with every circumstance,
Unto these Syrian merchants in such wise,
From day to day, as I shall you devise*   *relate

This was the common voice of every man
"Our emperor of Rome, God him see*,   *look on with favour
A daughter hath, that since the world began,
To reckon as well her goodness and beauty,
Was never such another as is she:
I pray to God in honour her sustene*,   *sustain
And would she were of all Europe the queen.

"In her is highe beauty without pride,
And youth withoute greenhood* or folly: *childishness,
    immaturity
To all her workes virtue is her guide;
Humbless hath slain in her all tyranny:
She is the mirror of all courtesy,

Her heart a very chamber of holiness,
Her hand minister of freedom for almess*." *almsgiving

And all this voice was sooth, as God is true;
But now to purpose* let us turn again. *our tale
These merchants have done freight their shippes new,
And when they have this blissful maiden seen,
Home to Syria then they went full fain,
And did their needes*, as they have done yore,* *business
        **formerly
And liv'd in weal*; I can you say no more. *prosperity

Now fell it, that these merchants stood in grace* *favour
Of him that was the Soudan* of Syrie: *Sultan
For when they came from any strange place
He would of his benigne courtesy
Make them good cheer, and busily espy* *inquire
Tidings of sundry regnes*, for to lear** *realms **learn
The wonders that they mighte see or hear.

Amonges other thinges, specially
These merchants have him told of Dame Constance
So great nobless, in earnest so royally,
That this Soudan hath caught so great pleasance*
        *pleasure
To have her figure in his remembrance,
That all his lust*, and all his busy cure**, *pleasure **care
Was for to love her while his life may dure.

Paraventure in thilke* large book, *that
Which that men call the heaven, y-written was
With starres, when that he his birthe took,
That he for love should have his death, alas!
For in the starres, clearer than is glass,

Is written, God wot, whoso could it read,
The death of every man withoute dread.* *doubt

In starres many a winter therebeforn
Was writ the death of Hector, Achilles,
Of Pompey, Julius, ere they were born;
The strife of Thebes; and of Hercules,
Of Samson, Turnus, and of Socrates
The death; but mennes wittes be so dull,
That no wight can well read it at the full.

This Soudan for his privy council sent,
And, *shortly of this matter for to pace*, *to pass briefly by*
He hath to them declared his intent,
And told them certain, but* he might have grace *unless
To have Constance, within a little space,
He was but dead; and charged them in hie* *haste
To shape* for his life some remedy. *contrive

Diverse men diverse thinges said;
And arguments they casten up and down;
Many a subtle reason forth they laid;
They speak of magic, and abusion*; *deception
But finally, as in conclusion,
They cannot see in that none avantage,
Nor in no other way, save marriage.

Then saw they therein such difficulty
By way of reason, for to speak all plain,
Because that there was such diversity
Between their bothe lawes, that they sayn,
They trowe* that no Christian prince would fain** *believe
    **willingly
Wedden his child under our lawe sweet,
That us was given by Mahound* our prophete. *Mahomet

And he answered: "Rather than I lose
Constance, I will be christen'd doubteless
I must be hers, I may none other choose,
I pray you hold your arguments in peace,
Save my life, and be not reckeless
To gette her that hath my life in cure,* *keeping
For in this woe I may not long endure."

What needeth greater dilatation?
I say, by treaty and ambassadry,
And by the Pope's mediation,
And all the Church, and all the chivalry,
That in destruction of Mah'metry,* *Mahometanism
And in increase of Christe's lawe dear,
They be accorded* so as ye may hear; *agreed

How that the Soudan, and his baronage,
And all his lieges, shall y-christen'd be,
And he shall have Constance in marriage,
And certain gold, I n'ot* what quantity, *know not
And hereto find they suffisant surety.
The same accord is sworn on either side;
Now, fair Constance, Almighty God thee guide!

Now woulde some men waiten, as I guess,
That I should tellen all the purveyance*, *provision
The which the emperor of his noblesse
Hath shapen* for his daughter, Dame Constance. *prepared
Well may men know that so great ordinance
May no man tellen in a little clause,
As was arrayed for so high a cause.

Bishops be shapen with her for to wend,
Lordes, ladies, and knightes of renown,
And other folk enough, this is the end.

And notified is throughout all the town,
That every wight with great devotioun
Should pray to Christ, that he this marriage
Receive *in gree*, and speede this voyage. *with good will,
    favour*

The day is comen of her departing, —
I say the woful fatal day is come,
That there may be no longer tarrying,
But forward they them dressen* all and some. *prepare to set
    out*
Constance, that was with sorrow all o'ercome,
Full pale arose, and dressed her to wend,
For well she saw there was no other end.

Alas! what wonder is it though she wept,
That shall be sent to a strange nation
From friendes, that so tenderly her kept,
And to be bound under subjection
of one, she knew not his condition?
Husbands be all good, and have been *of yore*, *of old*
That knowe wives; I dare say no more.

"Father," she said, "thy wretched child Constance,
Thy younge daughter, foster'd up so soft,
And you, my mother, my sov'reign pleasance
Over all thing, out-taken* Christ *on loft*, *except *on high*
Constance your child her recommendeth oft
Unto your grace; for I shall to Syrie,
Nor shall I ever see you more with eye.

"Alas! unto the barbarous nation
I must anon, since that it is your will:
But Christ, that starf* for our redemption, *died
So give me grace his hestes* to fulfil. *commands

I, wretched woman, *no force though I spill!* *no matter
    though I perish*
Women are born to thraldom and penance,
And to be under mannes governance."

I trow at Troy when Pyrrhus brake the wall,
Or Ilion burnt, or Thebes the city,
Nor at Rome for the harm through Hannibal,
That Romans hath y-vanquish'd times three,
Was heard such tender weeping for pity,
As in the chamber was for her parting;
But forth she must, whether she weep or sing.

O firste moving cruel Firmament,
With thy diurnal sway that crowdest* aye, *pushest together,
    drivest
And hurtlest all from East till Occident
That naturally would hold another way;
Thy crowding set the heav'n in such array
At the beginning of this fierce voyage,
That cruel Mars hath slain this marriage.

Unfortunate ascendant tortuous,
Of which the lord is helpless fall'n, alas!
Out of his angle into the darkest house;
O Mars, O Atyzar, as in this case;
O feeble Moon, unhappy is thy pace.* *progress
Thou knittest thee where thou art not receiv'd,
Where thou wert well, from thennes art thou weiv'd.

Imprudent emperor of Rome, alas!
Was there no philosopher in all thy town?
Is no time bet* than other in such case? *better
Of voyage is there none election,
Namely* to folk of high condition, *especially

Not *when a root is of a birth y-know?* *when the nativity is
    known*
Alas! we be too lewed*, or too slow. *ignorant

To ship was brought this woeful faire maid
Solemnely, with every circumstance:
"Now Jesus Christ be with you all," she said.
There is no more, but "Farewell, fair Constance."
She *pained her* to make good countenance. *made an
    effort*
And forth I let her sail in this manner,
And turn I will again to my matter.

The mother of the Soudan, well of vices,
Espied hath her sone's plain intent,
How he will leave his olde sacrifices:
And right anon she for her council sent,
And they be come, to knowe what she meant,
And when assembled was this folk *in fere*, *together*
She sat her down, and said as ye shall hear.

"Lordes," she said, "ye knowen every one,
How that my son in point is for to lete* *forsake
The holy lawes of our Alkaron*, *Koran
Given by God's messenger Mahomete:
But one avow to greate God I hete*, *promise
Life shall rather out of my body start,
Than Mahomet's law go out of mine heart.

"What should us tiden* of this newe law, *betide, befall
But thraldom to our bodies, and penance,
And afterward in hell to be y-draw,
For we *renied Mahound our creance?* *denied Mahomet our
    belief*
But, lordes, will ye maken assurance,

As I shall say, assenting to my lore*? *advice
And I shall make us safe for evermore."

They sworen and assented every man
To live with her and die, and by her stand:
And every one, in the best wise he can,
To strengthen her shall all his friendes fand.* *endeavour
And she hath this emprise taken in hand,
Which ye shall heare that I shall devise*; *relate
And to them all she spake right in this wise.

"We shall first feign us *Christendom to take*; *embrace
    Christianity*
Cold water shall not grieve us but a lite*: *little
And I shall such a feast and revel make,
That, as I trow, I shall the Soudan quite.* *requite, match
For though his wife be christen'd ne'er so white,
She shall have need to wash away the red,
Though she a fount of water with her led."

O Soudaness*, root of iniquity, *Sultaness
Virago thou, Semiramis the second!
O serpent under femininity,
Like to the serpent deep in hell y-bound!
O feigned woman, all that may confound
Virtue and innocence, through thy malice,
Is bred in thee, as nest of every vice!

O Satan envious! since thilke day
That thou wert chased from our heritage,
Well knowest thou to woman th' olde way.
Thou madest Eve to bring us in servage*: *bondage
Thou wilt fordo* this Christian marriage: *ruin
Thine instrument so (well-away the while!)
Mak'st thou of women when thou wilt beguile.

This Soudaness, whom I thus blame and warray*, *oppose,
    censure
Let privily her council go their way:
Why should I in this tale longer tarry?
She rode unto the Soudan on a day,
And said him, that she would *reny her lay,* *renounce her creed*
And Christendom of priestes' handes fong*, *take
Repenting her she heathen was so long;

Beseeching him to do her that honour,
That she might have the Christian folk to feast:
"To please them I will do my labour."
The Soudan said, "I will do at your hest,*" *desire
And kneeling, thanked her for that request;
So glad he was, he wist* not what to say. *knew
She kiss'd her son, and home she went her way.

Arrived be these Christian folk to land
In Syria, with a great solemne rout,
And hastily this Soudan sent his sond,* *message
First to his mother, and all the realm about,
And said, his wife was comen out of doubt,
And pray'd them for to ride again* the queen, *to meet
The honour of his regne* to sustene. *realm

Great was the press, and rich was the array
Of Syrians and Romans met *in fere*. *in company*
The mother of the Soudan rich and gay
Received her with all so glad a cheer* *face
As any mother might her daughter dear
And to the nexte city there beside
A softe pace solemnely they ride.

Nought, trow I, the triumph of Julius
Of which that Lucan maketh such a boast,

Was royaller, or more curious,
Than was th' assembly of this blissful host
But O this scorpion, this wicked ghost,* *spirit
The Soudaness, for all her flattering
Cast* under this full mortally to sting. *contrived

The Soudan came himself soon after this,
So royally, that wonder is to tell,
And welcomed her with all joy and bliss.
And thus in mirth and joy I let them dwell.
The fruit of his matter is that I tell;
When the time came, men thought it for the best
That revel stint,* and men go to their rest. *cease

The time is come that this old Soudaness
Ordained hath the feast of which I told,
And to the feast the Christian folk them dress
In general, yea, bothe young and old.
There may men feast and royalty behold,
And dainties more than I can you devise;
But all too dear they bought it ere they rise.

O sudden woe, that ev'r art successour
To worldly bliss! sprent* is with bitterness *sprinkled
Th' end of our joy, of our worldly labour;
Woe *occupies the fine* of our gladness. *seizes the end*
Hearken this counsel, for thy sickerness*: *security
Upon thy glade days have in thy mind
The unware* woe of harm, that comes behind. *unforeseen

For, shortly for to tell it at a word,
The Soudan and the Christians every one
Were all *to-hewn and sticked* at the board, *cut to pieces*
But it were only Dame Constance alone.
This olde Soudaness, this cursed crone,

Had with her friendes done this cursed deed,
For she herself would all the country lead.

Nor there was Syrian that was converted,
That of the counsel of the Soudan wot*, *knew
That was not all to-hewn, ere he asterted*: *escaped
And Constance have they ta'en anon foot-hot*, *immediately
And in a ship all steereless,* God wot, *without rudder
They have her set, and bid her learn to sail
Out of Syria *again-ward to Itale.* *back to Italy*

A certain treasure that she thither lad,* *took
And, sooth to say, of victual great plenty,
They have her giv'n, and clothes eke she had
And forth she sailed in the salte sea:
O my Constance, full of benignity,
O emperores younge daughter dear,
He that is lord of fortune be thy steer*! *rudder, guide

She bless'd herself, and with full piteous voice
Unto the cross of Christ thus saide she;
"O dear, O wealful* altar, holy cross, *blessed, beneficent
Red of the Lambes blood, full of pity,
That wash'd the world from old iniquity,
Me from the fiend and from his clawes keep,
That day that I shall drenchen* in the deepe. *drown

"Victorious tree, protection of the true,
That only worthy were for to bear
The King of Heaven, with his woundes new,
The white Lamb, that hurt was with a spear;
Flemer* of fiendes out of him and her *banisher, driver out
On which thy limbes faithfully extend,
Me keep, and give me might my life to mend."

Yeares and days floated this creature
Throughout the sea of Greece, unto the strait
Of Maroc*, as it was her a venture: *Morocco; Gibraltar
On many a sorry meal now may she bait,
After her death full often may she wait*, *expect
Ere that the wilde waves will her drive
Unto the place *there as* she shall arrive. *where

Men mighten aske, why she was not slain?
Eke at the feast who might her body save?
And I answer to that demand again,
Who saved Daniel in the horrible cave,
Where every wight, save he, master or knave*, *servant
Was with the lion frett*, ere he astart?** *devoured ** escaped
No wight but God, that he bare in his heart.

God list* to shew his wonderful miracle *it pleased
In her, that we should see his mighty workes:
Christ, which that is to every harm triacle*, *remedy, salve
By certain meanes oft, as knowe clerkes*, *scholars
Doth thing for certain ende, that full derk is
To manne's wit, that for our, ignorance
Ne cannot know his prudent purveyance*. *foresight

Now since she was not at the feast y-slaw,* *slain
Who kepte her from drowning in the sea?
Who kepte Jonas in the fish's maw,
Till he was spouted up at Nineveh?
Well may men know, it was no wight but he
That kept the Hebrew people from drowning,
With drye feet throughout the sea passing.

Who bade the foure spirits of tempest,
That power have t' annoye land and sea,
Both north and south, and also west and east,

Annoye neither sea, nor land, nor tree?
Soothly the commander of that was he
That from the tempest aye this woman kept,
As well when she awoke as when she slept.

Where might this woman meat and drinke have?
Three year and more how lasted her vitaille*? *victuals
Who fed the Egyptian Mary in the cave
Or in desert? no wight but Christ *sans faille.* *without fail*
Five thousand folk it was as great marvaille
With loaves five and fishes two to feed
God sent his foison* at her greate need. *abundance

She drived forth into our ocean
Throughout our wilde sea, till at the last
Under an hold*, that nempnen** I not can, *castle **name
Far in Northumberland, the wave her cast
And in the sand her ship sticked so fast
That thennes would it not in all a tide:
The will of Christ was that she should abide.

The Constable of the castle down did fare* *go
To see this wreck, and all the ship he sought*, *searched
And found this weary woman full of care;
He found also the treasure that she brought:
In her language mercy she besought,
The life out of her body for to twin*, *divide
Her to deliver of woe that she was in.

A manner Latin corrupt was her speech,
But algate* thereby was she understond. *nevertheless
The Constable, when him list no longer seech*, *search
This woeful woman brought he to the lond.
She kneeled down, and thanked *Godde's sond*; *what God
    had sent*

But what she was she would to no man say
For foul nor fair, although that she should dey.* *die

She said, she was so mazed in the sea,
That she forgot her minde, by her truth.
The Constable had of her so great pity
And eke his wife, that they wept for ruth:* *pity
She was so diligent withoute slouth
To serve and please every one in that place,
That all her lov'd, that looked in her face.

The Constable and Dame Hermegild his wife
Were Pagans, and that country every where;
But Hermegild lov'd Constance as her life;
And Constance had so long sojourned there
In orisons, with many a bitter tear,
Till Jesus had converted through His grace
Dame Hermegild, Constabless of that place.

In all that land no Christians durste rout;* *assemble
All Christian folk had fled from that country
Through Pagans, that conquered all about
The plages* of the North by land and sea. *regions, coasts
To Wales had fled the *Christianity
Of olde Britons,* dwelling in this isle; *the Old Britons who
    were Christians*
There was their refuge for the meanewhile.

But yet n'ere* Christian Britons so exiled, *there were
That there n'ere* some which in their privity not
Honoured Christ, and heathen folk beguiled;
And nigh the castle such there dwelled three:
And one of them was blind, and might not see,
But* it were with thilk** eyen of his mind, *except **those
With which men maye see when they be blind.

Bright was the sun, as in a summer's day,
For which the Constable, and his wife also,
And Constance, have y-take the righte way
Toward the sea a furlong way or two,
To playen, and to roame to and fro;
And in their walk this blinde man they met,
Crooked and old, with eyen fast y-shet.* *shut

"In the name of Christ," cried this blind Briton,
"Dame Hermegild, give me my sight again!"
This lady *wax'd afrayed of that soun',* *was alarmed by that cry*
Lest that her husband, shortly for to sayn,
Would her for Jesus Christe's love have slain,
Till Constance made her hold, and bade her wirch* *work
The will of Christ, as daughter of holy Church

The Constable wax'd abashed* of that sight, *astonished
And saide; *"What amounteth all this fare?"* *what means all
    this ado?*
Constance answered; "Sir, it is Christ's might,
That helpeth folk out of the fiendes snare:"
And *so farforth* she gan our law declare, *with such effect*
That she the Constable, ere that it were eve,
Converted, and on Christ made him believe.

This Constable was not lord of the place
Of which I speak, there as he Constance fand,* *found
But kept it strongly many a winter space,
Under Alla, king of Northumberland,
That was full wise, and worthy of his hand
Against the Scotes, as men may well hear;
But turn I will again to my mattere.

Satan, that ever us waiteth to beguile,
Saw of Constance all her perfectioun,

And *cast anon how he might quite her while;* *considered
    how to have revenge on her*
And made a young knight, that dwelt in that town,
Love her so hot of foul affectioun,
That verily him thought that he should spill* *perish
But* he of her might ones have his will. *unless

He wooed her, but it availed nought;
She woulde do no sinne by no way:
And for despite, he compassed his thought
To make her a shameful death to dey;* *die
He waiteth when the Constable is away,
And privily upon a night he crept
In Hermegild's chamber while she slept.

Weary, forwaked* in her orisons, *having been long
    awake
Sleepeth Constance, and Hermegild also.
This knight, through Satanas' temptation;
All softely is to the bed y-go,* *gone
And cut the throat of Hermegild in two,
And laid the bloody knife by Dame Constance,
And went his way, there God give him mischance.

Soon after came the Constable home again,
And eke Alla that king was of that land,
And saw his wife dispiteously* slain, *cruelly
For which full oft he wept and wrung his hand;
And ill the bed the bloody knife he fand
By Dame Constance: Alas! what might she say?
For very woe her wit was all away.

To King Alla was told all this mischance
And eke the time, and where, and in what wise
That in a ship was founden this Constance,

As here before ye have me heard devise:* *describe
The kinges heart for pity *gan agrise,* *to be grieved, to
    tremble*
When he saw so benign a creature
Fall in disease* and in misaventure. *distress

For as the lamb toward his death is brought,
So stood this innocent before the king:
This false knight, that had this treason wrought,
Bore her in hand that she had done this thing: *accused her
    falsely*
But natheless there was great murmuring
Among the people, that say they cannot guess
That she had done so great a wickedness.

For they had seen her ever virtuous,
And loving Hermegild right as her life:
Of this bare witness each one in that house,
Save he that Hermegild slew with his knife:
This gentle king had *caught a great motife* *been greatly
    moved by the evidence*
Of this witness, and thought he would inquere
Deeper into this case, the truth to lear.* *learn

Alas! Constance, thou has no champion,
Nor fighte canst thou not, so well-away!
But he that starf* for our redemption, *died
And bound Satan, and yet li'th where he lay,
So be thy stronge champion this day:
For, but Christ upon thee miracle kithe,* *show
Withoute guilt thou shalt be slain *as swithe.* *immediately*

She set her down on knees, and thus she said;
"Immortal God, that savedest Susanne
From false blame; and thou merciful maid,

Mary I mean, the daughter to Saint Anne,
Before whose child the angels sing Osanne,* *Hosanna
If I be guiltless of this felony,
My succour be, or elles shall I die."

Have ye not seen sometime a pale face
(Among a press) of him that hath been lad* *led
Toward his death, where he getteth no grace,
And such a colour in his face hath had,
Men mighte know him that was so bestad* *bested,
    situated
Amonges all the faces in that rout?
So stood Constance, and looked her about.

O queenes living in prosperity,
Duchesses, and ye ladies every one,
Have some ruth* on her adversity! *pity
An emperor's daughter, she stood alone;
She had no wight to whom to make her moan.
O blood royal, that standest in this drede,* *danger
Far be thy friendes in thy greate need!

This king Alla had such compassioun,
As gentle heart is full filled of pity,
That from his eyen ran the water down
"Now hastily do fetch a book," quoth he;
"And if this knight will sweare, how that she
This woman slew, yet will we us advise* *consider
Whom that we will that shall be our justice."

A Briton book, written with Evangiles,* *the Gospels
Was fetched, and on this book he swore anon
She guilty was; and, in the meanewhiles,
An hand him smote upon the necke bone,
That down he fell at once right as a stone:

And both his eyen burst out of his face
In sight of ev'rybody in that place.

A voice was heard, in general audience,
That said; "Thou hast deslander'd guilteless
The daughter of holy Church in high presence;
Thus hast thou done, and yet *hold I my peace?"* *shall I be
    silent?*
Of this marvel aghast was all the press,
As mazed folk they stood every one
For dread of wreake,* save Constance alone. *vengeance

Great was the dread and eke the repentance
Of them that hadde wrong suspicion
Upon this sely* innocent Constance; *simple, harmless
And for this miracle, in conclusion,
And by Constance's mediation,
The king, and many another in that place,
Converted was, thanked be Christe's grace!

This false knight was slain for his untruth
By judgement of Alla hastily;
And yet Constance had of his death great ruth;* *compassion
And after this Jesus of his mercy
Made Alla wedde full solemnely
This holy woman, that is so bright and sheen,
And thus hath Christ y-made Constance a queen.

But who was woeful, if I shall not lie,
Of this wedding but Donegild, and no mo',
The kinge's mother, full of tyranny?
Her thought her cursed heart would burst in two;
She would not that her son had done so;

Her thought it a despite that he should take
So strange a creature unto his make.* *mate, consort

Me list not of the chaff nor of the stre* *straw
Make so long a tale, as of the corn.
What should I tellen of the royalty
Of this marriage, or which course goes beforn,
Who bloweth in a trump or in an horn?
The fruit of every tale is for to say;
They eat and drink, and dance, and sing, and play.

They go to bed, as it was skill* and right; *reasonable
For though that wives be full holy things,
They muste take in patience at night
Such manner* necessaries as be pleasings *kind of
To folk that have y-wedded them with rings,
And lay *a lite* their holiness aside *a little of*
As for the time, it may no better betide.

On her he got a knave* child anon, *male
And to a Bishop and to his Constable eke
He took his wife to keep, when he is gone
To Scotland-ward, his foemen for to seek.
Now fair Constance, that is so humble and meek,
So long is gone with childe till that still
She held her chamb'r, abiding Christe's will

The time is come, a knave child she bare;
Mauricius at the font-stone they him call.
This Constable *doth forth come* a messenger, *caused to
        come forth*
And wrote unto his king that clep'd was All',
How that this blissful tiding is befall,
And other tidings speedful for to say

He* hath the letter, and forth he go'th his way. *i.e. the
    messenger

This messenger, to *do his avantage,* *promote his own interest*
Unto the kinge's mother rideth swithe,* *swiftly
And saluteth her full fair in his language.
"Madame," quoth he, "ye may be glad and blithe,
And thanke God an hundred thousand sithe;* *times
My lady queen hath child, withoute doubt,
To joy and bliss of all this realm about.

"Lo, here the letter sealed of this thing,
That I must bear with all the haste I may:
If ye will aught unto your son the king,
I am your servant both by night and day."
Donegild answer'd, "As now at this time, nay;
But here I will all night thou take thy rest,
To-morrow will I say thee what me lest.*" *pleases

This messenger drank sadly* ale and wine, *steadily
And stolen were his letters privily
Out of his box, while he slept as a swine;
And counterfeited was full subtilly
Another letter, wrote full sinfully,
Unto the king, direct of this mattere
From his Constable, as ye shall after hear.

This letter said, the queen deliver'd was
Of so horrible a fiendlike creature,
That in the castle none so hardy* was *brave
That any while he durst therein endure:
The mother was an elf by aventure
Become, by charmes or by sorcery,
And every man hated her company.

Woe was this king when he this letter had seen,
But to no wight he told his sorrows sore,
But with his owen hand he wrote again,
"Welcome the sond* of Christ for evermore *will, sending
To me, that am now learned in this lore:
Lord, welcome be thy lust* and thy pleasance, *will,
    pleasure
My lust I put all in thine ordinance.

"Keepe* this child, albeit foul or fair, *preserve
And eke my wife, unto mine homecoming:
Christ when him list may send to me an heir
More agreeable than this to my liking."
This letter he sealed, privily weeping.
Which to the messenger was taken soon,
And forth he went, there is no more to do'n.* *do

O messenger full fill'd of drunkenness,
Strong is thy breath, thy limbes falter aye,
And thou betrayest alle secretness;
Thy mind is lorn,* thou janglest as a jay; *lost
Thy face is turned in a new array;* *aspect
Where drunkenness reigneth in any rout,* *company
There is no counsel hid, withoute doubt.

O Donegild, I have no English dign* *worthy
Unto thy malice, and thy tyranny:
And therefore to the fiend I thee resign,
Let him indite of all thy treachery
Fy, mannish,* fy! O nay, by God I lie; *unwomanly woman
Fy, fiendlike spirit! for I dare well tell,
Though thou here walk, thy spirit is in hell.

This messenger came from the king again,
And at the kinge's mother's court he light,* *alighted

And she was of this messenger full fain,* *glad
And pleased him in all that e'er she might.
He drank, and *well his girdle underpight*; *stowed away
    (liquor)
He slept, and eke he snored in his guise under his girdle*
All night, until the sun began to rise.

Eft* were his letters stolen every one, *again
And counterfeited letters in this wise:
The king commanded his Constable anon,
On pain of hanging and of high jewise,* *judgement
That he should suffer in no manner wise
Constance within his regne* for to abide *kingdom
Three dayes, and a quarter of a tide;

But in the same ship as he her fand,
Her and her younge son, and all her gear,
He shoulde put, and crowd* her from the land, *push
And charge her, that she never eft come there.
O my Constance, well may thy ghost* have fear, *spirit
And sleeping in thy dream be in penance,* *pain, trouble
When Donegild cast* all this ordinance.** *contrived **plan,
    plot

This messenger, on morrow when he woke,
Unto the castle held the nexte* way, *nearest
And to the constable the letter took;
And when he this dispiteous* letter sey,** *cruel **saw
Full oft he said, "Alas, and well-away!
Lord Christ," quoth he, "how may this world endure?
So full of sin is many a creature.

"O mighty God, if that it be thy will,
Since thou art rightful judge, how may it be
That thou wilt suffer innocence to spill,* *be destroyed

And wicked folk reign in prosperity?
Ah! good Constance, alas! so woe is me,
That I must be thy tormentor, or dey* *die
A shameful death, there is no other way.

Wept bothe young and old in all that place,
When that the king this cursed letter sent;
And Constance, with a deadly pale face,
The fourthe day toward her ship she went.
But natheless she took in good intent
The will of Christ, and kneeling on the strond* *strand, shore
She saide, "Lord, aye welcome be thy sond* *whatever thou
  sendest

"He that me kepte from the false blame,
While I was in the land amonges you,
He can me keep from harm and eke from shame
In the salt sea, although I see not how
As strong as ever he was, he is yet now,
In him trust I, and in his mother dere,
That is to me my sail and eke my stere."* *rudder, guide

Her little child lay weeping in her arm
And, kneeling, piteously to him she said
"Peace, little son, I will do thee no harm:"
With that her kerchief off her head she braid,* *took, drew
And over his little eyen she it laid,
And in her arm she lulled it full fast,
And unto heav'n her eyen up she cast.

"Mother," quoth she, "and maiden bright, Mary,
Sooth is, that through a woman's eggement* *incitement,
  egging on
Mankind was lorn,* and damned aye to die; *lost
For which thy child was on a cross y-rent:* *torn, pierced

163

Thy blissful eyen saw all his torment,
Then is there no comparison between
Thy woe, and any woe man may sustene.

"Thou saw'st thy child y-slain before thine eyen,
And yet now lives my little child, parfay:* *by my faith
Now, lady bright, to whom the woeful cryen,
Thou glory of womanhood, thou faire may,* *maid
Thou haven of refuge, bright star of day,
Rue* on my child, that of thy gentleness *take pity
Ruest on every rueful* in distress. *sorrowful person

"O little child, alas! what is thy guilt,
That never wroughtest sin as yet, pardie?* *par Dieu; by
        God
Why will thine harde* father have thee spilt?** *cruel
        **destroyed
O mercy, deare Constable," quoth she,
"And let my little child here dwell with thee:
And if thou dar'st not save him from blame,
So kiss him ones in his father's name."

Therewith she looked backward to the land,
And saide, "Farewell, husband rutheless!"
And up she rose, and walked down the strand
Toward the ship, her following all the press:* *multitude
And ever she pray'd her child to hold his peace,
And took her leave, and with an holy intent
She blessed her, and to the ship she went.

Victualed was the ship, it is no drede,* *doubt
Abundantly for her a full long space:
And other necessaries that should need* *be needed
She had enough, heried* be Godde's grace: *praised
For wind and weather, Almighty God purchase,* *provide

And bring her home; I can no better say;
But in the sea she drived forth her way.

Alla the king came home soon after this
Unto the castle, of the which I told,
And asked where his wife and his child is;
The Constable gan about his heart feel cold,
And plainly all the matter he him told
As ye have heard; I can tell it no better;
And shew'd the king his seal, and eke his letter

And saide; "Lord, as ye commanded me
On pain of death, so have I done certain."
The messenger tormented* was, till he   *tortured
Muste beknow,* and tell it flat and plain,   *confess
From night to night in what place he had lain;
And thus, by wit and subtle inquiring,
Imagin'd was by whom this harm gan spring.

The hand was known that had the letter wrote,
And all the venom of the cursed deed;
But in what wise, certainly I know not.
Th' effect is this, that Alla, *out of drede,*   *without doubt*
His mother slew, that may men plainly read,
For that she traitor was to her liegeance:*   *allegiance
Thus ended olde Donegild with mischance.

The sorrow that this Alla night and day
Made for his wife, and for his child also,
There is no tongue that it telle may.
But now will I again to Constance go,
That floated in the sea in pain and woe
Five year and more, as liked Christe's sond,* *decree, command
Ere that her ship approached to the lond.*   *land

Under an heathen castle, at the last,
Of which the name in my text I not find,
Constance and eke her child the sea upcast.
Almighty God, that saved all mankind,
Have on Constance and on her child some mind,
That fallen is in heathen hand eftsoon* *again
In point to spill, as I shall tell you soon! *in danger of
    perishing*
Down from the castle came there many a wight
To gauren* on this ship, and on Constance: *gaze, stare
But shortly from the castle, on a night,
The lorde's steward, — God give him mischance, —
A thief that had *renied our creance,* *denied our faith*
Came to the ship alone, and said he would
Her leman* be, whether she would or n'ould. *illicit lover

Woe was this wretched woman then begone;
Her child cri'd, and she cried piteously:
But blissful Mary help'd her right anon,
For, with her struggling well and mightily,
The thief fell overboard all suddenly,
And in the sea he drenched* for vengeance, *drowned
And thus hath Christ unwemmed* kept Constance.
    *unblemished

O foul lust of luxury! lo thine end!
Not only that thou faintest* manne's mind, *weakenest
But verily thou wilt his body shend.* *destroy
Th' end of thy work, or of thy lustes blind,
Is complaining: how many may men find,
That not for work, sometimes, but for th' intent
To do this sin, be either slain or shent?

How may this weake woman have the strength
Her to defend against this renegate?

O Goliath, unmeasurable of length,
How mighte David make thee so mate?* *overthrown
So young, and of armour so desolate,* *devoid
How durst he look upon thy dreadful face?
Well may men see it was but Godde's grace.

Who gave Judith courage or hardiness
To slay him, Holofernes, in his tent,
And to deliver out of wretchedness
The people of God? I say for this intent
That right as God spirit of vigour sent
To them, and saved them out of mischance,
So sent he might and vigour to Constance.

Forth went her ship throughout the narrow mouth
Of *Jubaltare and Septe,* driving alway, *Gibraltar and
    Ceuta*
Sometime west, and sometime north and south,
And sometime east, full many a weary day:
Till Christe's mother (blessed be she aye)
Had shaped* through her endless goodness *resolved,
    arranged
To make an end of all her heaviness.

Now let us stint* of Constance but a throw,** *cease
    speaking **short time
And speak we of the Roman emperor,
That out of Syria had by letters know
The slaughter of Christian folk, and dishonor
Done to his daughter by a false traitor,
I mean the cursed wicked Soudaness,
That at the feast *let slay both more and less.* *caused both
    high and low to be killed*
For which this emperor had sent anon
His senator, with royal ordinance,

And other lordes, God wot, many a one,
On Syrians to take high vengeance:
They burn and slay, and bring them to mischance
Full many a day: but shortly this is th' end,
Homeward to Rome they shaped them to wend.

This senator repaired with victory
To Rome-ward, sailing full royally,
And met the ship driving, as saith the story,
In which Constance sat full piteously:
And nothing knew he what she was, nor why
She was in such array; nor she will say
Of her estate, although that she should dey.* *die

He brought her unto Rome, and to his wife
He gave her, and her younge son also:
And with the senator she led her life.
Thus can our Lady bringen out of woe
Woeful Constance, and many another mo':
And longe time she dwelled in that place,
In holy works ever, as was her grace.

The senatores wife her aunte was,
But for all that she knew her ne'er the more:
I will no longer tarry in this case,
But to King Alla, whom I spake of yore,
That for his wife wept and sighed sore,
I will return, and leave I will Constance
Under the senatores governance.

King Alla, which that had his mother slain,
Upon a day fell in such repentance;
That, if I shortly tell it shall and plain,
To Rome he came to receive his penitance,
And put him in the Pope's ordinance

In high and low, and Jesus Christ besought
Forgive his wicked works that he had wrought.

The fame anon throughout the town is borne,
How Alla king shall come on pilgrimage,
By harbingers that wente him beforn,
For which the senator, as was usage,
Rode *him again,* and many of his lineage, *to meet him*
As well to show his high magnificence,
As to do any king a reverence.

Great cheere* did this noble senator *courtesy
To King Alla and he to him also;
Each of them did the other great honor;
And so befell, that in a day or two
This senator did to King Alla go
To feast, and shortly, if I shall not lie,
Constance's son went in his company.

Some men would say, at request of Constance
This senator had led this child to feast:
I may not tellen every circumstance,
Be as be may, there was he at the least:
But sooth is this, that at his mother's hest* *behest
Before Alla during *the meates space,* *meal time*
The child stood, looking in the kinges face.

This Alla king had of this child great wonder,
And to the senator he said anon,
"Whose is that faire child that standeth yonder?"
"I n'ot,"* quoth he, "by God and by Saint John; *know not
A mother he hath, but father hath he none,
That I of wot:" and shortly in a stound* *short time
He told to Alla how this child was found.

"But God wot," quoth this senator also,
"So virtuous a liver in all my life
I never saw, as she, nor heard of mo'
Of worldly woman, maiden, widow or wife:
I dare well say she hadde lever* a knife *rather
Throughout her breast, than be a woman wick',* *wicked
There is no man could bring her to that prick.* *point

Now was this child as like unto Constance
As possible is a creature to be:
This Alla had the face in remembrance
Of Dame Constance, and thereon mused he,
If that the childe's mother *were aught she* *could be she*
That was his wife; and privily he sight,* *sighed
And sped him from the table *that he might.* *as fast as he could*

"Parfay,"* thought he, "phantom** is in mine head. *by my faith
     **a fantasy
I ought to deem, of skilful judgement,
That in the salte sea my wife is dead."
And afterward he made his argument,
"What wot I, if that Christ have hither sent
My wife by sea, as well as he her sent
To my country, from thennes that she went?"

And, after noon, home with the senator.
Went Alla, for to see this wondrous chance.
This senator did Alla great honor,
And hastily he sent after Constance:
But truste well, her liste not to dance.
When that she wiste wherefore was that sond,* *summons
Unneth* upon her feet she mighte stand. *with difficulty

When Alla saw his wife, fair he her gret,* *greeted
And wept, that it was ruthe for to see,

For at the firste look he on her set
He knew well verily that it was she:
And she, for sorrow, as dumb stood as a tree:
So was her hearte shut in her distress,
When she remember'd his unkindeness.

Twice she swooned in his owen sight,
He wept and him excused piteously:
"Now God," quoth he, "and all his hallows bright* *saints
So wisly* on my soule have mercy, *surely
That of your harm as guilteless am I,
As is Maurice my son, so like your face,
Else may the fiend me fetch out of this place."

Long was the sobbing and the bitter pain,
Ere that their woeful heartes mighte cease;
Great was the pity for to hear them plain,* *lament
Through whiche plaintes gan their woe increase.
I pray you all my labour to release,
I may not tell all their woe till to-morrow,
I am so weary for to speak of sorrow.

But finally, when that the *sooth is wist,* *truth is known*
That Alla guiltless was of all her woe,
I trow an hundred times have they kiss'd,
And such a bliss is there betwixt them two,
That, save the joy that lasteth evermo',
There is none like, that any creature
Hath seen, or shall see, while the world may dure.

Then prayed she her husband meekely
In the relief of her long piteous pine,* *sorrow
That he would pray her father specially,
That of his majesty he would incline
To vouchesafe some day with him to dine:

She pray'd him eke, that he should by no way
Unto her father no word of her say.

Some men would say, how that the child Maurice
Did this message unto the emperor:
But, as I guess, Alla was not so nice,* *foolish
To him that is so sovereign of honor
As he that is of Christian folk the flow'r,
Send any child, but better 'tis to deem
He went himself; and so it may well seem.

This emperor hath granted gentilly
To come to dinner, as he him besought:
And well rede* I, he looked busily *guess, know
Upon this child, and on his daughter thought.
Alla went to his inn, and as him ought
Arrayed* for this feast in every wise, *prepared
As farforth as his cunning may suffice. *as far as his skill*

The morrow came, and Alla gan him dress,* *make ready
And eke his wife, the emperor to meet:
And forth they rode in joy and in gladness,
And when she saw her father in the street,
She lighted down and fell before his feet.
"Father," quoth she, "your younge child Constance
Is now full clean out of your remembrance.

"I am your daughter, your Constance," quoth she,
"That whilom ye have sent into Syrie;
It am I, father, that in the salt sea
Was put alone, and damned* for to die. *condemned
Now, goode father, I you mercy cry,
Send me no more into none heatheness,
But thank my lord here of his kindeness."

Who can the piteous joye tellen all,
Betwixt them three, since they be thus y-met?
But of my tale make an end I shall,
The day goes fast, I will no longer let.* *hinder
These gladde folk to dinner be y-set;
In joy and bliss at meat I let them dwell,
A thousand fold well more than I can tell.

This child Maurice was since then emperor
Made by the Pope, and lived Christianly,
To Christe's Churche did he great honor:
But I let all his story passe by,
Of Constance is my tale especially,
In the olde Roman gestes* men may find *histories
Maurice's life, I bear it not in mind.

This King Alla, when he his time sey,* *saw
With his Constance, his holy wife so sweet,
To England are they come the righte way,
Where they did live in joy and in quiet.
But little while it lasted, I you hete,* *promise
Joy of this world for time will not abide,
From day to night it changeth as the tide.

Who liv'd ever in such delight one day,
That him not moved either conscience,
Or ire, or talent, or *some kind affray,* *some kind of
    disturbance*
Envy, or pride, or passion, or offence?
I say but for this ende this sentence,* *judgment, opinion*
That little while in joy or in pleasance
Lasted the bliss of Alla with Constance.

For death, that takes of high and low his rent,
When passed was a year, even as I guess,

173

Out of this world this King Alla he hent,* *snatched
For whom Constance had full great heaviness.
Now let us pray that God his soule bless:
And Dame Constance, finally to say,
Toward the town of Rome went her way.

To Rome is come this holy creature,
And findeth there her friendes whole and sound:
Now is she scaped all her aventure:
And when that she her father hath y-found,
Down on her knees falleth she to ground,
Weeping for tenderness in hearte blithe
She herieth* God an hundred thousand sithe.** *praises
    **times

In virtue and in holy almes-deed
They liven all, and ne'er asunder wend;
Till death departeth them, this life they lead:
And fare now well, my tale is at an end
Now Jesus Christ, that of his might may send
Joy after woe, govern us in his grace
And keep us alle that be in this place.

THE WIFE OF BATH'S TALE

Experience, though none authority* *authoritative texts
Were in this world, is right enough for me
To speak of woe that is in marriage:
For, lordings, since I twelve year was of age,
(Thanked be God that *is etern on live),* *lives eternally*
Husbands at the church door have I had five,
For I so often have y-wedded be,
And all were worthy men in their degree.
But me was told, not longe time gone is
That sithen* Christe went never but ones *since

174

To wedding, in the Cane* of Galilee, *Cana
That by that ilk* example taught he me, *same
That I not wedded shoulde be but once.
Lo, hearken eke a sharp word for the nonce,* *occasion
Beside a welle Jesus, God and man,
Spake in reproof of the Samaritan:
"Thou hast y-had five husbandes," said he;
"And thilke* man, that now hath wedded thee, *that
Is not thine husband:" thus said he certain;
What that he meant thereby, I cannot sayn.
But that I aske, why the fifthe man
Was not husband to the Samaritan?
How many might she have in marriage?
Yet heard I never tellen *in mine age* *in my life*
Upon this number definitioun.
Men may divine, and glosen* up and down; *comment
But well I wot, express without a lie,
God bade us for to wax and multiply;
That gentle text can I well understand.
Eke well I wot, he said, that mine husband
Should leave father and mother, and take to me;
But of no number mention made he,
Of bigamy or of octogamy;
Why then should men speak of it villainy?* *as if it were a
    disgrace

Lo here, the wise king Dan* Solomon, *Lord
I trow that he had wives more than one;
As would to God it lawful were to me
To be refreshed half so oft as he!
What gift* of God had he for all his wives? *special favour,
    licence
No man hath such, that in this world alive is.
God wot, this noble king, *as to my wit,* *as I understand*
The first night had many a merry fit

With each of them, so *well was him on live.* *so well he
    lived*
Blessed be God that I have wedded five!
Welcome the sixth whenever that he shall.
For since I will not keep me chaste in all,
When mine husband is from the world y-gone,
Some Christian man shall wedde me anon.
For then th' apostle saith that I am free
To wed, *a' God's half,* where it liketh me. *on God's part*
He saith, that to be wedded is no sin;
Better is to be wedded than to brin.* *burn
What recketh* me though folk say villainy** *care **evil
Of shrewed* Lamech, and his bigamy? *impious, wicked
I wot well Abraham was a holy man,
And Jacob eke, as far as ev'r I can.* *know
And each of them had wives more than two;
And many another holy man also.
Where can ye see, *in any manner age,* *in any period*
That highe God defended* marriage *forbade
By word express? I pray you tell it me;
Or where commanded he virginity?
I wot as well as you, it is no dread,* *doubt
Th' apostle, when he spake of maidenhead,
He said, that precept thereof had he none:
Men may counsel a woman to be one,* *a maid
But counseling is no commandement;
He put it in our owen judgement.
For, hadde God commanded maidenhead,
Then had he damned* wedding out of dread;** *condemned
    **doubt
And certes, if there were no seed y-sow,* *sown
Virginity then whereof should it grow?
Paul durste not commanden, at the least,
A thing of which his Master gave no hest.* *command
The dart* is set up for virginity; *goal

Catch whoso may, who runneth best let see.
But this word is not ta'en of every wight,
But there as God will give it of his might. *except where*
I wot well that th' apostle was a maid,
But natheless, although he wrote and said,
He would that every wight were such as he,
All is but counsel to virginity.
And, since to be a wife he gave me leave
Of indulgence, so is it no repreve* *scandal, reproach
To wedde me, if that my make* should die, *mate, husband
Without exception* of bigamy; *charge, reproach
All were it good no woman for to touch *though it might be*
(He meant as in his bed or in his couch),
For peril is both fire and tow t'assemble
Ye know what this example may resemble.
This is all and some, he held virginity
More profit than wedding in frailty:
(*Frailty clepe I, but if* that he and she *frailty I call it, unless*
Would lead their lives all in chastity),
I grant it well, I have of none envy
Who maidenhead prefer to bigamy;
It liketh them t' be clean in body and ghost;* *soul
Of mine estate* I will not make a boast. *condition

For, well ye know, a lord in his household
Hath not every vessel all of gold;
Some are of tree, and do their lord service.
God calleth folk to him in sundry wise,
And each one hath of God a proper gift,
Some this, some that, as liketh him to shift.* *appoint,
    distribute
Virginity is great perfection,
And continence eke with devotion:
But Christ, that of perfection is the well,* *fountain
Bade not every wight he should go sell

All that he had, and give it to the poor,
And in such wise follow him and his lore:* *doctrine
He spake to them that would live perfectly, —
And, lordings, by your leave, that am not I;
I will bestow the flower of mine age
In th' acts and in the fruits of marriage.
Tell me also, to what conclusion* *end, purpose
Were members made of generation,
And of so perfect wise a wight* y-wrought? *being
Trust me right well, they were not made for nought.
Glose whoso will, and say both up and down,
That they were made for the purgatioun
Of urine, and of other thinges smale,
And eke to know a female from a male:
And for none other cause? say ye no?
Experience wot well it is not so.
So that the clerkes* be not with me wroth, *scholars
I say this, that they were made for both,
That is to say, *for office, and for ease* *for duty and for
    pleasure*
Of engendrure, there we God not displease.
Why should men elles in their bookes set,
That man shall yield unto his wife her debt?
Now wherewith should he make his payement,
If he us'd not his silly instrument?
Then were they made upon a creature
To purge urine, and eke for engendrure.
But I say not that every wight is hold,* *obliged
That hath such harness* as I to you told, *equipment
To go and use them in engendrure;
Then should men take of chastity no cure.* *care
Christ was a maid, and shapen* as a man, *fashioned
And many a saint, since that this world began,
Yet ever liv'd in perfect chastity.
I will not vie* with no virginity. *contend

Let them with bread of pured* wheat be fed, *purified
And let us wives eat our barley bread.
And yet with barley bread, Mark tell us can,
Our Lord Jesus refreshed many a man.
In such estate as God hath *cleped us,* *called us to
I'll persevere, I am not precious,* *over-dainty
In wifehood I will use mine instrument
As freely as my Maker hath it sent.
If I be dangerous* God give me sorrow; *sparing of my favours
Mine husband shall it have, both eve and morrow,
When that him list come forth and pay his debt.
A husband will I have, I *will no let,* *will bear no hindrance*
Which shall be both my debtor and my thrall,* *slave
And have his tribulation withal
Upon his flesh, while that I am his wife.
I have the power during all my life
Upon his proper body, and not he;
Right thus th' apostle told it unto me,
And bade our husbands for to love us well;
All this sentence me liketh every deal.* *whit

Up start the Pardoner, and that anon;
"Now, Dame," quoth he, "by God and by Saint John,
Ye are a noble preacher in this case.
I was about to wed a wife, alas!
What? should I bie* it on my flesh so dear? *suffer for
Yet had I lever* wed no wife this year." *rather
"Abide,"* quoth she; "my tale is not begun *wait in patience
Nay, thou shalt drinken of another tun
Ere that I go, shall savour worse than ale.
And when that I have told thee forth my tale
Of tribulation in marriage,
Of which I am expert in all mine age,
(This is to say, myself hath been the whip),
Then mayest thou choose whether thou wilt sip

Of *thilke tunne,* that I now shall broach. *that tun*
Beware of it, ere thou too nigh approach,
For I shall tell examples more than ten:
Whoso will not beware by other men,
By him shall other men corrected be:
These same wordes writeth Ptolemy;
Read in his *Almagest*, and take it there."
"Dame, I would pray you, if your will it were,"
Saide this Pardoner, "as ye began,
Tell forth your tale, and spare for no man,
And teach us younge men of your practique."
"Gladly," quoth she, "since that it may you like.
But that I pray to all this company,
If that I speak after my fantasy,
To take nought agrief* what I may say; *to heart
For mine intent is only for to play."

Now, Sirs, then will I tell you forth my tale.
As ever may I drinke wine or ale
I shall say sooth; the husbands that I had
Three of them were good, and two were bad
The three were goode men, and rich, and old
Unnethes mighte they the statute hold *they could with
      difficulty obey the law*
In which that they were bounden unto me.
Yet wot well what I mean of this, pardie.* *by God
As God me help, I laugh when that I think
How piteously at night I made them swink,* *labour
But, *by my fay, I told of it no store:* *by my faith, I held it
      of no account*
They had me giv'n their land and their treasor,
Me needed not do longer diligence
To win their love, or do them reverence.
They loved me so well, by God above,
That I *tolde no dainty* of their love. *cared nothing for*

A wise woman will busy her ever-in-one* *constantly
To get their love, where that she hath none.
But, since I had them wholly in my hand,
And that they had me given all their land,
Why should I take keep* them for to please, *care
But* it were for my profit, or mine ease? *unless
I set them so a-worke, by my fay,
That many a night they sange, well-away!
The bacon was not fetched for them, I trow,
That some men have in Essex at Dunmow.
I govern'd them so well after my law,
That each of them full blissful was and fawe* *fain
To bringe me gay thinges from the fair.
They were full glad when that I spake them fair,
For, God it wot, I *chid them spiteously.* *rebuked them angrily*
Now hearken how I bare me properly.

Ye wise wives, that can understand,
Thus should ye speak, and *bear them wrong on hand,* *make
                them believe falsely*
For half so boldely can there no man
Swearen and lien as a woman can.
(I say not this by wives that be wise,
But if it be when they them misadvise.)** *unless* **act
                unadvisedly
A wise wife, if that she can* her good, *knows
Shall *beare them on hand* the cow is wood, *make them believe*
And take witness of her owen maid
Of their assent: but hearken how I said.
"Sir olde kaynard, is this thine array?
Why is my neigheboure's wife so gay?
She is honour'd *over all where* she go'th, *wheresoever
I sit at home, I have no *thrifty cloth.* *good clothes*
What dost thou at my neigheboure's house?
Is she so fair? art thou so amorous?

What rown'st* thou with our maid? benedicite, *whisperest
Sir olde lechour, let thy japes* be. *tricks
And if I have a gossip, or a friend
(Withoute guilt), thou chidest as a fiend,
If that I walk or play unto his house.
Thou comest home as drunken as a mouse,
And preachest on thy bench, with evil prefe:* *proof
Thou say'st to me, it is a great mischief
To wed a poore woman, for costage:* *expense
And if that she be rich, of high parage;* * birth
Then say'st thou, that it is a tormentry
To suffer her pride and melancholy.
And if that she be fair, thou very knave,
Thou say'st that every holour* will her have; *whoremonger
She may no while in chastity abide,
That is assailed upon every side.
Thou say'st some folk desire us for richess,
Some for our shape, and some for our fairness,
And some, for she can either sing or dance,
And some for gentiless and dalliance,
Some for her handes and her armes smale;
Thus goes all to the devil, by thy tale;
Thou say'st, men may not keep a castle wall
That may be so assailed *over all.* *everywhere*
And if that she be foul, thou say'st that she
Coveteth every man that she may see;
For as a spaniel she will on him leap,
Till she may finde some man her to cheap;* *buy
And none so grey goose goes there in the lake,
(So say'st thou) that will be without a make.* *mate
And say'st, it is a hard thing for to weld *wield, govern
A thing that no man will, *his thankes, held.* *hold with his
    goodwill*
Thus say'st thou, lorel,* when thou go'st to bed,
      *good-for-nothing

And that no wise man needeth for to wed,
Nor no man that intendeth unto heaven.
With wilde thunder dint* and fiery leven** *stroke
    **lightning
Mote* thy wicked necke be to-broke. *may
Thou say'st, that dropping houses, and eke smoke,
And chiding wives, make men to flee
Out of their owne house; ah! ben'dicite,
What aileth such an old man for to chide?
Thou say'st, we wives will our vices hide,
Till we be fast,* and then we will them shew. *wedded
Well may that be a proverb of a shrew.* *ill-tempered wretch
Thou say'st, that oxen, asses, horses, hounds,
They be *assayed at diverse stounds,* *tested at various seasons*
Basons and lavers, ere that men them buy,
Spoones, stooles, and all such husbandry,
And so be pots, and clothes, and array,* *raiment
But folk of wives make none assay,
Till they be wedded, — olde dotard shrew! —
And then, say'st thou, we will our vices shew.
Thou say'st also, that it displeaseth me,
But if * that thou wilt praise my beauty, *unless
And but* thou pore alway upon my face, *unless
And call me faire dame in every place;
And but* thou make a feast on thilke** day *unless **that
That I was born, and make me fresh and gay;
And but thou do to my norice* honour, *nurse
And to my chamberere* within my bow'r, *chamber-maid
And to my father's folk, and mine allies;* *relations
Thus sayest thou, old barrel full of lies.
And yet also of our prentice Jenkin,
For his crisp hair, shining as gold so fine,
And for he squireth me both up and down,
Yet hast thou caught a false suspicioun:
I will him not, though thou wert dead to-morrow.

But tell me this, why hidest thou, *with sorrow,* *sorrow on
    thee!*
The keyes of thy chest away from me?
It is my good* as well as thine, pardie. *property
What, think'st to make an idiot of our dame?
Now, by that lord that called is Saint Jame,
Thou shalt not both, although that thou wert wood,*
    *furious
Be master of my body, and my good,* *property
The one thou shalt forego, maugre* thine eyen. *in spite of
What helpeth it of me t'inquire and spyen?
I trow thou wouldest lock me in thy chest.
Thou shouldest say, 'Fair wife, go where thee lest;
Take your disport; I will believe no tales;
I know you for a true wife, Dame Ales.'* *Alice
We love no man, that taketh keep* or charge *care
Where that we go; we will be at our large.
Of alle men most blessed may he be,
The wise astrologer Dan* Ptolemy, *Lord
That saith this proverb in his *Almagest*:
'Of alle men his wisdom is highest,
That recketh not who hath the world in hand.'
By this proverb thou shalt well understand,
Have thou enough, what thar* thee reck or care *needs,
    behoves
How merrily that other folkes fare?
For certes, olde dotard, by your leave,
Ye shall have [pleasure] right enough at eve.
He is too great a niggard that will werne* *forbid
A man to light a candle at his lantern;
He shall have never the less light, pardie.
Have thou enough, thee thar* not plaine** thee *need **complain
Thou say'st also, if that we make us gay
With clothing and with precious array,
That it is peril of our chastity.

And yet, — with sorrow! — thou enforcest thee,
And say'st these words in the apostle's name:
'In habit made with chastity and shame* *modesty
Ye women shall apparel you,' quoth he,
'And not in tressed hair and gay perrie,* *jewels
As pearles, nor with gold, nor clothes rich.'
After thy text nor after thy rubrich
I will not work as muchel as a gnat.
Thou say'st also, I walk out like a cat;
For whoso woulde singe the catte's skin
Then will the catte well dwell in her inn;* *house
And if the catte's skin be sleek and gay,
She will not dwell in house half a day,
But forth she will, ere any day be daw'd,
To shew her skin, and go a caterwaw'd.* *caterwauling
This is to say, if I be gay, sir shrew,
I will run out, my borel* for to shew. *apparel, fine clothes
Sir olde fool, what helpeth thee to spyen?
Though thou pray Argus with his hundred eyen
To be my wardecorps,* as he can best *bodyguard
In faith he shall not keep me, *but me lest:* *unless I please*
Yet could I *make his beard,* so may I the.* *make a jest of
    him* *thrive

"Thou sayest eke, that there be thinges three,
Which thinges greatly trouble all this earth,
And that no wighte may endure the ferth:* *fourth
O lefe* sir shrew, may Jesus short** thy life. *pleasant **shorten
Yet preachest thou, and say'st, a hateful wife
Y-reckon'd is for one of these mischances.
Be there *none other manner resemblances* *no other kind of
    comparison*
That ye may liken your parables unto,
But if a silly wife be one of tho?* *those
Thou likenest a woman's love to hell;

To barren land where water may not dwell.
Thou likenest it also to wild fire;
The more it burns, the more it hath desire
To consume every thing that burnt will be.
Thou sayest, right as wormes shend* a tree,   *destroy
Right so a wife destroyeth her husbond;
This know they well that be to wives bond."

Lordings, right thus, as ye have understand,
Bare I stiffly mine old husbands on hand,   *made them
    believe*
That thus they saiden in their drunkenness;
And all was false, but that I took witness
On Jenkin, and upon my niece also.
O Lord! the pain I did them, and the woe,
Full guilteless, by Godde's sweete pine;*   *pain
For as a horse I coulde bite and whine;
I coulde plain,* an'** I was in the guilt,   *complain **even
    though
Or elles oftentime I had been spilt*   *ruined
Whoso first cometh to the nilll, first grint;*   *is ground
I plained first, so was our war y-stint.*   *stopped
They were full glad to excuse them full blive*   *quickly
Of things that they never *aguilt their live.*   *were guilty in
    their lives*
Of wenches would I *beare them on hand,*   *falsely accuse
    them*
When that for sickness scarcely might they stand,
Yet tickled I his hearte for that he
Ween'd* that I had of him so great cherte:**   *thought
    **affection
I swore that all my walking out by night
Was for to espy wenches that he dight:*   *adorned
Under that colour had I many a mirth.
For all such wit is given us at birth;

Deceit, weeping, and spinning, God doth give
To women kindly,* while that they may live. *naturally
And thus of one thing I may vaunte me,
At th' end I had the better in each degree,
By sleight, or force, or by some manner thing,
As by continual murmur or grudging,* *complaining
Namely* a-bed, there hadde they mischance, *especially
There would I chide, and do them no pleasance:
I would no longer in the bed abide,
If that I felt his arm over my side,
Till he had made his ransom unto me,
Then would I suffer him do his nicety.* *folly
And therefore every man this tale I tell,
Win whoso may, for all is for to sell;
With empty hand men may no hawkes lure;
For winning would I all his will endure,
And make me a feigned appetite,
And yet in bacon* had I never delight: *i.e. of Dunmow
That made me that I ever would them chide.
For, though the Pope had sitten them beside,
I would not spare them at their owen board,
For, by my troth, I quit* them word for word *repaid
As help me very God omnipotent,
Though I right now should make my testament
I owe them not a word, that is not quit* *repaid
I brought it so aboute by my wit,
That they must give it up, as for the best
Or elles had we never been in rest.
For, though he looked as a wood* lion, *furious
Yet should he fail of his conclusion.
Then would I say, "Now, goode lefe* tak keep** *dear **heed
How meekly looketh Wilken oure sheep!
Come near, my spouse, and let me ba* thy cheek *kiss
Ye shoulde be all patient and meek,
And have a *sweet y-spiced* conscience, *tender, nice*

Since ye so preach of Jobe's patience.
Suffer alway, since ye so well can preach,
And but* ye do, certain we shall you teach* *unless
That it is fair to have a wife in peace.
One of us two must bowe* doubteless: *give way
And since a man is more reasonable
Than woman is, ye must be suff'rable.
What aileth you to grudge* thus and groan? *complain
Is it for ye would have my [love] alone?
Why, take it all: lo, have it every deal,* *whit
Peter! shrew* you but ye love it well *curse
For if I woulde sell my *belle chose*, *beautiful thing*
I coulde walk as fresh as is a rose,
But I will keep it for your owen tooth.
Ye be to blame, by God, I say you sooth."
Such manner wordes hadde we on hand.

Now will I speaken of my fourth husband.
My fourthe husband was a revellour;
This is to say, he had a paramour,
And I was young and full of ragerie,* *wantonness
Stubborn and strong, and jolly as a pie.* *magpie
Then could I dance to a harpe smale,
And sing, y-wis,* as any nightingale, *certainly
When I had drunk a draught of sweete wine.
Metellius, the foule churl, the swine,
That with a staff bereft his wife of life
For she drank wine, though I had been his wife,
Never should he have daunted me from drink:
And, after wine, of Venus most I think.
For all so sure as cold engenders hail,
A liquorish mouth must have a liquorish tail.
In woman vinolent* is no defence,** *full of wine *resistance
This knowe lechours by experience.
But, lord Christ, when that it rememb'reth me

Upon my youth, and on my jollity,
It tickleth me about mine hearte-root;
Unto this day it doth mine hearte boot,* *good
That I have had my world as in my time.
But age, alas! that all will envenime,* *poison, embitter
Hath me bereft my beauty and my pith:* *vigour
Let go; farewell; the devil go therewith.
The flour is gon, there is no more to tell,
The bran, as I best may, now must I sell.
But yet to be right merry will I fand.* *try
Now forth to tell you of my fourth husband,
I say, I in my heart had great despite,
That he of any other had delight;
But he was quit,* by God and by Saint Joce: *requited, paid
    back
I made for him of the same wood a cross;
Not of my body in no foul mannere,
But certainly I made folk such cheer,
That in his owen grease I made him fry
For anger, and for very jealousy.
By God, in earth I was his purgatory,
For which I hope his soul may be in glory.
For, God it wot, he sat full oft and sung,
When that his shoe full bitterly him wrung.* *pinched
There was no wight, save God and he, that wist
In many wise how sore I did him twist.
He died when I came from Jerusalem,
And lies in grave under the *roode beam:* *cross*
Although his tomb is not so curious
As was the sepulchre of Darius,
Which that Apelles wrought so subtlely.
It is but waste to bury them preciously.
Let him fare well, God give his soule rest,
He is now in his grave and in his chest.

Now of my fifthe husband will I tell:
God let his soul never come into hell.
And yet was he to me the moste shrew;* *cruel,
    ill-tempered
That feel I on my ribbes all *by rew,* *in a row
And ever shall, until mine ending day.
But in our bed he was so fresh and gay,
And therewithal so well he could me glose,* *flatter
When that he woulde have my belle chose,
Though he had beaten me on every bone,
Yet could he win again my love anon.
I trow, I lov'd him better, for that he
Was of his love so dangerous* to me. *sparing, difficult
We women have, if that I shall not lie,
In this matter a quainte fantasy.
Whatever thing we may not lightly have,
Thereafter will we cry all day and crave.
Forbid us thing, and that desire we;
Press on us fast, and thenne will we flee.
With danger* utter we all our chaffare;** *difficulty
    **merchandise
Great press at market maketh deare ware,
And too great cheap is held at little price;
This knoweth every woman that is wise.
My fifthe husband, God his soule bless,
Which that I took for love and no richess,
He some time was *a clerk of Oxenford,* *a scholar of Oxford*
And had left school, and went at home to board
With my gossip,* dwelling in oure town: *godmother
God have her soul, her name was Alisoun.
She knew my heart, and all my privity,
Bet than our parish priest, so may I the.* *thrive
To her betrayed I my counsel all;
For had my husband pissed on a wall,
Or done a thing that should have cost his life,

To her, and to another worthy wife,
And to my niece, which that I loved well,
I would have told his counsel every deal.* *jot
And so I did full often, God it wot,
That made his face full often red and hot
For very shame, and blam'd himself, for he
Had told to me so great a privity.* *secret
And so befell that ones in a Lent
(So oftentimes I to my gossip went,
For ever yet I loved to be gay,
And for to walk in March, April, and May
From house to house, to heare sundry tales),
That Jenkin clerk, and my gossip, Dame Ales,
And I myself, into the fieldes went.
Mine husband was at London all that Lent;
I had the better leisure for to play,
And for to see, and eke for to be sey* *seen
Of lusty folk; what wist I where my grace* *favour
Was shapen* for to be, or in what place? *appointed
Therefore made I my visitations
To vigilies,* and to processions, *festival-eves
To preachings eke, and to these pilgrimages,
To plays of miracles, and marriages,
And weared upon me gay scarlet gites.* *gowns
These wormes, nor these mothes, nor these mites
On my apparel frett* them never a deal** *fed **whit
And know'st thou why? for they were used* well. *worn
Now will I telle forth what happen'd me:
I say, that in the fieldes walked we,
Till truely we had such dalliance,
This clerk and I, that of my purveyance* *foresight
I spake to him, and told him how that he,
If I were widow, shoulde wedde me.
For certainly, I say for no bobance,* *boasting
Yet was I never without purveyance* *foresight

Of marriage, nor of other thinges eke:
I hold a mouse's wit not worth a leek,
That hath but one hole for to starte* to, *escape
And if that faile, then is all y-do.* *done
I bare him on hand he had enchanted me *falsely assured
    him*
(My dame taughte me that subtilty);
And eke I said, I mette* of him all night, *dreamed
He would have slain me, as I lay upright,
And all my bed was full of very blood;
But yet I hop'd that he should do me good;
For blood betoken'd gold, as me was taught.
And all was false, I dream'd of him right naught,
But as I follow'd aye my dame's lore,
As well of that as of other things more.
But now, sir, let me see, what shall I sayn?
Aha! by God, I have my tale again.
When that my fourthe husband was on bier,
I wept algate* and made a sorry cheer,** *always
    **countenance
As wives must, for it is the usage;
And with my kerchief covered my visage;
But, for I was provided with a make,* *mate
I wept but little, that I undertake* *promise
To churche was mine husband borne a-morrow
With neighebours that for him made sorrow,
And Jenkin, oure clerk, was one of tho:* *those
As help me God, when that I saw him go
After the bier, methought he had a pair
Of legges and of feet so clean and fair,
That all my heart I gave unto his hold.* *keeping
He was, I trow, a twenty winter old,
And I was forty, if I shall say sooth,
But yet I had always a colte's tooth.
Gat-toothed I was, and that became me well,

I had the print of Sainte Venus' seal.
As help me God, I was a lusty one,
And fair, and rich, and young, and *well begone:* *in a good way*
For certes I am all venerian* *under the influence of Venus
In feeling, and my heart is martian;* *under the influence of Mars
Venus me gave my lust and liquorishness,
And Mars gave me my sturdy hardiness.
Mine ascendant was Taure,* and Mars therein: *Taurus
Alas, alas, that ever love was sin!
I follow'd aye mine inclination
By virtue of my constellation:
That made me that I coulde not withdraw
My chamber of Venus from a good fellow.
Yet have I Marte's mark upon my face,
And also in another privy place.
For God so wisly* be my salvation, *certainly
I loved never by discretion,
But ever follow'd mine own appetite,
All* were he short, or long, or black, or white, *whether
I took no keep,* so that he liked me, *heed
How poor he was, neither of what degree.
What should I say? but that at the month's end
This jolly clerk Jenkin, that was so hend,* *courteous
Had wedded me with great solemnity,
And to him gave I all the land and fee
That ever was me given therebefore:
But afterward repented me full sore.
He woulde suffer nothing of my list.* *pleasure
By God, he smote me ones with his fist,
For that I rent out of his book a leaf,
That of the stroke mine eare wax'd all deaf.
Stubborn I was, as is a lioness,
And of my tongue a very jangleress,* *prater

And walk I would, as I had done beforn,
From house to house, although he had it sworn:* *had sworn to
For which he oftentimes woulde preach prevent it
And me of olde Roman gestes* teach *stories
How that Sulpitius Gallus left his wife
And her forsook for term of all his
For nought but open-headed* he her say** *bare-headed
        **saw
Looking out at his door upon a day.
Another Roman told he me by name,
That, for his wife was at a summer game
Without his knowing, he forsook her eke.
And then would he upon his Bible seek
That ilke* proverb of Ecclesiast, *same
Where he commandeth, and forbiddeth fast,
Man shall not suffer his wife go roll about.
Then would he say right thus withoute doubt:
"Whoso that buildeth his house all of sallows,* *willows
And pricketh his blind horse over the fallows,
And suff'reth his wife to *go seeke hallows,* *make
        pilgrimages*
Is worthy to be hanged on the gallows."
But all for nought; I *sette not a haw* *cared nothing for*
Of his proverbs, nor of his olde saw;
Nor would I not of him corrected be.
I hate them that my vices telle me,
And so do more of us (God wot) than I.
This made him wood* with me all utterly; *furious
I woulde not forbear* him in no case. *endure
Now will I say you sooth, by Saint Thomas,
Why that I rent out of his book a leaf,
For which he smote me, so that I was deaf.
He had a book, that gladly night and day
For his disport he would it read alway;
He call'd it *Valerie, and Theophrast,*

And with that book he laugh'd alway full fast.
And eke there was a clerk sometime at Rome,
A cardinal, that highte Saint Jerome,
That made a book against Jovinian,
Which book was there; and eke Tertullian,
Chrysippus, Trotula, and Heloise,
That was an abbess not far from Paris;
And eke the Parables* of Solomon, *Proverbs
Ovide's *Art*, and bourdes* many one; *jests
And alle these were bound in one volume.
And every night and day was his custume
(When he had leisure and vacation
From other worldly occupation)
To readen in this book of wicked wives.
He knew of them more legends and more lives
Than be of goodde wives in the Bible.
For, trust me well, it is an impossible
That any clerk will speake good of wives,
(*But if* it be of holy saintes' lives) *unless
Nor of none other woman never the mo'.
Who painted the lion, tell it me, who?
By God, if women haddde written stories,
As clerkes have within their oratories,
They would have writ of men more wickedness
Than all the mark of Adam may redress
The children of Mercury and of Venus,
Be in their working full contrarious.
Mercury loveth wisdom and science,
And Venus loveth riot and dispence.* *extravagance
And for their diverse disposition,
Each falls in other's exaltation.
As thus, God wot, Mercury is desolate
In Pisces, where Venus is exaltate,
And Venus falls where Mercury is raised.
Therefore no woman by no clerk is praised.

The clerk, when he is old, and may not do
Of Venus' works not worth his olde shoe,
Then sits he down, and writes in his dotage,
That women cannot keep their marriage.
But now to purpose, why I tolde thee
That I was beaten for a book, pardie.

Upon a night Jenkin, that was our sire,*   *goodman
Read on his book, as he sat by the fire,
Of Eva first, that for her wickedness
Was all mankind brought into wretchedness,
For which that Jesus Christ himself was slain,
That bought us with his hearte-blood again.
Lo here express of women may ye find
That woman was the loss of all mankind.
Then read he me how Samson lost his hairs
Sleeping, his leman cut them with her shears,
Through whiche treason lost he both his eyen.
Then read he me, if that I shall not lien,
Of Hercules, and of his Dejanire,
That caused him to set himself on fire.
Nothing forgot he of the care and woe
That Socrates had with his wives two;
How Xantippe cast piss upon his head.
This silly man sat still, as he were dead,
He wip'd his head, and no more durst he sayn,
But, "Ere the thunder stint* there cometh rain."   *ceases
Of Phasiphae, that was queen of Crete,
For shrewedness* he thought the tale sweet.   *wickedness
Fy, speak no more, it is a grisly thing,
Of her horrible lust and her liking.
Of Clytemnestra, for her lechery
That falsely made her husband for to die,
He read it with full good devotion.
He told me eke, for what occasion

Amphiorax at Thebes lost his life:
My husband had a legend of his wife
Eryphile, that for an ouche* of gold   *clasp, collar
Had privily unto the Greekes told,
Where that her husband hid him in a place,
For which he had at Thebes sorry grace.
Of Luna told he me, and of Lucie;
They bothe made their husbands for to die,
That one for love, that other was for hate.
Luna her husband on an ev'ning late
Empoison'd had, for that she was his foe:
Lucia liquorish lov'd her husband so,
That, for he should always upon her think,
She gave him such a manner* love-drink,   *sort of
That he was dead before it were the morrow:
And thus algates* husbands hadde sorrow.   *always
Then told he me how one Latumeus
Complained to his fellow Arius
That in his garden growed such a tree,
On which he said how that his wives three
Hanged themselves for heart dispiteous.
"O leve* brother," quoth this Arius,   *dear
"Give me a plant of thilke* blessed tree,   *that
And in my garden planted shall it be."
Of later date of wives hath he read,
That some have slain their husbands in their bed,
And let their *lechour dight them* all the night,   *lover ride
     them*
While that the corpse lay on the floor upright:
And some have driven nails into their brain,
While that they slept, and thus they have them slain:
Some have them given poison in their drink:
He spake more harm than hearte may bethink.
And therewithal he knew of more proverbs,
Than in this world there groweth grass or herbs.

"Better" (quoth he) "thine habitation
Be with a lion, or a foul dragon,
Than with a woman using for to chide."
"Better" (quoth he) "high in the roof abide,
Than with an angry woman in the house,
They be so wicked and contrarious:
They hate that their husbands loven aye."
He said, "A woman cast her shame away
When she cast off her smock;" and farthermo',
"A fair woman, but* she be chaste also,   *except
Is like a gold ring in a sowe's nose."
Who coulde ween,* or who coulde suppose   *think
The woe that in mine heart was, and the pine?*   *pain
And when I saw that he would never fine*   *finish
To readen on this cursed book all night,
All suddenly three leaves have I plight*   *plucked
Out of his book, right as he read, and eke
I with my fist so took him on the cheek,
That in our fire he backward fell adown.
And he up start, as doth a wood* lion,   *furious
And with his fist he smote me on the head,
That on the floor I lay as I were dead.
And when he saw how still that there I lay,
He was aghast, and would have fled away,
Till at the last out of my swoon I braid,*   *woke
"Oh, hast thou slain me, thou false thief?" I said
"And for my land thus hast thou murder'd me?
Ere I be dead, yet will I kisse thee."
And near he came, and kneeled fair adown,
And saide, "Deare sister Alisoun,
As help me God, I shall thee never smite:
That I have done it is thyself to wite,*   *blame
Forgive it me, and that I thee beseek."*   *beseech
And yet eftsoons* I hit him on the cheek,   *immediately;
    again

And saidde, "Thief, thus much am I awreak.* *avenged
Now will I die, I may no longer speak."

But at the last, with muche care and woe
We fell accorded* by ourselves two: *agreed
He gave me all the bridle in mine hand
To have the governance of house and land,
And of his tongue, and of his hand also.
I made him burn his book anon right tho.* *then
And when that I had gotten unto me
By mast'ry all the sovereignty,
And that he said, "Mine owen true wife,
Do *as thee list,* the term of all thy life, *as pleases thee*
Keep thine honour, and eke keep mine estate;"
After that day we never had debate.
God help me so, I was to him as kind
As any wife from Denmark unto Ind,
And also true, and so was he to me:
I pray to God that sits in majesty
So bless his soule, for his mercy dear.
Now will I say my tale, if ye will hear. —

The Friar laugh'd when he had heard all this:
"Now, Dame," quoth he, "so have I joy and bliss,
This is a long preamble of a tale."
And when the Sompnour heard the Friar gale,* *speak
"Lo," quoth this Sompnour, "Godde's armes two,
A friar will intermete* him evermo': *interpose
Lo, goode men, a fly and eke a frere
Will fall in ev'ry dish and eke mattere.
What speak'st thou of perambulation?* *preamble
What? amble or trot; or peace, or go sit down:
Thou lettest* our disport in this mattere." *hinderest
"Yea, wilt thou so, Sir Sompnour?" quoth the Frere;
"Now by my faith I shall, ere that I go,

Tell of a Sompnour such a tale or two,
That all the folk shall laughen in this place."
"Now do, else, Friar, I beshrew* thy face," *curse
Quoth this Sompnour; "and I beshrewe me,
But if* I telle tales two or three *unless
Of friars, ere I come to Sittingbourne,
That I shall make thine hearte for to mourn:
For well I wot thy patience is gone."
Our Hoste cried, "Peace, and that anon;"
And saide, "Let the woman tell her tale.
Ye fare* as folk that drunken be of ale. *behave
Do, Dame, tell forth your tale, and that is best."
"All ready, sir," quoth she, "right as you lest,* *please
If I have licence of this worthy Frere."
"Yes, Dame," quoth he, "tell forth, and I will hear."

THE TALE

In olde dayes of the king Arthour,
Of which that Britons speake great honour,
All was this land full fill'd of faerie;* *fairies
The Elf-queen, with her jolly company,
Danced full oft in many a green mead
This was the old opinion, as I read;
I speak of many hundred years ago;
But now can no man see none elves mo',
For now the great charity and prayeres
Of limitours,* and other holy freres, *begging friars
That search every land and ev'ry stream
As thick as motes in the sunne-beam,
Blessing halls, chambers, kitchenes, and bowers,
Cities and burghes, castles high and towers,
Thorpes* and barnes, shepens** and dairies, *villages **stables
This makes that there be now no faeries:
For *there as* wont to walke was an elf, *where*

There walketh now the limitour himself,
In undermeles* and in morrowings**, *evenings **mornings
And saith his matins and his holy things,
As he goes in his limitatioun.* *begging district
Women may now go safely up and down,
In every bush, and under every tree;
There is none other incubus but he;
And he will do to them no dishonour.

And so befell it, that this king Arthour
Had in his house a lusty bacheler,
That on a day came riding from river:
And happen'd, that, alone as she was born,
He saw a maiden walking him beforn,
Of which maiden anon, maugre* her head, *in spite of
By very force he reft her maidenhead:
For which oppression was such clamour,
And such pursuit unto the king Arthour,
That damned* was this knight for to be dead *condemned
By course of law, and should have lost his head;
(Paraventure such was the statute tho),* *then
But that the queen and other ladies mo'
So long they prayed the king of his grace,
Till he his life him granted in the place,
And gave him to the queen, all at her will
To choose whether she would him save or spill* *destroy
The queen thanked the king with all her might;
And, after this, thus spake she to the knight,
When that she saw her time upon a day.
"Thou standest yet," quoth she, "in such array,* *a position
That of thy life yet hast thou no surety;
I grant thee life, if thou canst tell to me
What thing is it that women most desiren:
Beware, and keep thy neck-bone from the iron* *executioner's
  axe

And if thou canst not tell it me anon,
Yet will I give thee leave for to gon
A twelvemonth and a day, to seek and lear* *learn
An answer suffisant* in this mattere. *satisfactory
And surety will I have, ere that thou pace,* *go
Thy body for to yielden in this place."
Woe was the knight, and sorrowfully siked;* *sighed
But what? he might not do all as him liked.
And at the last he chose him for to wend,* *depart
And come again, right at the yeare's end,
With such answer as God would him purvey:* *provide
And took his leave, and wended forth his way.

He sought in ev'ry house and ev'ry place,
Where as he hoped for to finde grace,
To learne what thing women love the most:
But he could not arrive in any coast,
Where as he mighte find in this mattere
Two creatures *according in fere.* *agreeing together*
Some said that women loved best richess,
Some said honour, and some said jolliness,
Some rich array, and some said lust* a-bed, *pleasure
And oft time to be widow and be wed.
Some said, that we are in our heart most eased
When that we are y-flatter'd and y-praised.
He *went full nigh the sooth,* I will not lie; *came very near
   the truth*
A man shall win us best with flattery;
And with attendance, and with business
Be we y-limed,* bothe more and less. *caught with bird-lime
And some men said that we do love the best
For to be free, and do *right as us lest,* *whatever we please*
And that no man reprove us of our vice,
But say that we are wise, and nothing nice,* *foolish
For truly there is none among us all,

If any wight will claw us on the gall,
That will not kick, for that he saith us sooth:
Assay,* and he shall find it, that so do'th. *try
For be we never so vicious within,
We will be held both wise and clean of sin.
And some men said, that great delight have we
For to be held stable and eke secre,* *discreet
And in one purpose steadfastly to dwell,
And not bewray* a thing that men us tell. *give away
But that tale is not worth a rake-stele.* *rake-handle
Pardie, we women canne nothing hele,* *hide
Witness on Midas; will ye hear the tale?
Ovid, amonges other thinges smale* *small
Saith, Midas had, under his longe hairs,
Growing upon his head two ass's ears;
The whiche vice he hid, as best he might,
Full subtlely from every man's sight,
That, save his wife, there knew of it no mo';
He lov'd her most, and trusted her also;
He prayed her, that to no creature
She woulde tellen of his disfigure.
She swore him, nay, for all the world to win,
She would not do that villainy or sin,
To make her husband have so foul a name:
She would not tell it for her owen shame.
But natheless her thoughte that she died,
That she so longe should a counsel hide;
Her thought it swell'd so sore about her heart
That needes must some word from her astart
And, since she durst not tell it unto man
Down to a marish fast thereby she ran,
Till she came there, her heart was all afire:
And, as a bittern bumbles* in the mire, *makes a humming
     noise
She laid her mouth unto the water down

"Bewray me not, thou water, with thy soun'"
Quoth she, "to thee I tell it, and no mo',
Mine husband hath long ass's eares two!
Now is mine heart all whole; now is it out;
I might no longer keep it, out of doubt."
Here may ye see, though we a time abide,
Yet out it must, we can no counsel hide.
The remnant of the tale, if ye will hear,
Read in Ovid, and there ye may it lear.* *learn

This knight, of whom my tale is specially,
When that he saw he might not come thereby,
That is to say, what women love the most,
Within his breast full sorrowful was his ghost.* *spirit
But home he went, for he might not sojourn,
The day was come, that homeward he must turn.
And in his way it happen'd him to ride,
In all his care,* under a forest side, *trouble, anxiety
Where as he saw upon a dance go
Of ladies four-and-twenty, and yet mo',
Toward this ilke* dance he drew full yern,** *same **eagerly
The hope that he some wisdom there should learn;
But certainly, ere he came fully there,
Y-vanish'd was this dance, he knew not where;
No creature saw he that bare life,
Save on the green he sitting saw a wife,
A fouler wight there may no man devise.* *imagine, tell
Against* this knight this old wife gan to rise, *to meet
And said, "Sir Knight, hereforth* lieth no way. *from here
Tell me what ye are seeking, by your fay.
Paraventure it may the better be:
These olde folk know muche thing." quoth she.
"My léve* mother," quoth this knight, "certain, *dear
I am but dead, but if* that I can sayn *unless
What thing it is that women most desire:

Could ye me wiss,* I would well *quite your hire."* *instruct
    reward you
"Plight me thy troth here in mine hand," quoth she,
"The nexte thing that I require of thee
Thou shalt it do, if it be in thy might,
And I will tell it thee ere it be night."
"Have here my trothe," quoth the knight; "I grant."
"Thenne," quoth she, "I dare me well avaunt,* *boast, affirm
Thy life is safe, for I will stand thereby,
Upon my life the queen will say as I:
Let see, which is the proudest of them all,
That wears either a kerchief or a caul,
That dare say nay to that I shall you teach.
Let us go forth withoute longer speech
Then *rowned she a pistel* in his ear, *she whispered a
    secret*
And bade him to be glad, and have no fear.

When they were come unto the court, this knight
Said, he had held his day, as he had hight,* *promised
And ready was his answer, as he said.
Full many a noble wife, and many a maid,
And many a widow, for that they be wise, —
The queen herself sitting as a justice, —
Assembled be, his answer for to hear,
And afterward this knight was bid appear.
To every wight commanded was silence,
And that the knight should tell in audience,
What thing that worldly women love the best.
This knight he stood not still, as doth a beast,
But to this question anon answer'd
With manly voice, that all the court it heard,
"My liege lady, generally," quoth he,
"Women desire to have the sovereignty
As well over their husband as their love

And for to be in mast'ry him above.
This is your most desire, though ye me kill,
Do as you list, I am here at your will."
In all the court there was no wife nor maid
Nor widow, that contraried what he said,
But said, he worthy was to have his life.
And with that word up start that olde wife
Which that the knight saw sitting on the green.

"Mercy," quoth she, "my sovereign lady queen,
Ere that your court departe, do me right.
I taughte this answer unto this knight,
For which he plighted me his trothe there,
The firste thing I would of him requere,
He would it do, if it lay in his might.
Before this court then pray I thee, Sir Knight,"
Quoth she, "that thou me take unto thy wife,
For well thou know'st that I have kept* thy life. *preserved
If I say false, say nay, upon thy fay."* *faith
This knight answer'd, "Alas, and well-away!
I know right well that such was my behest.* *promise
For Godde's love choose a new request
Take all my good, and let my body go."
"Nay, then," quoth she, "I shrew* us bothe two, *curse
For though that I be old, and foul, and poor,
I n'ould* for all the metal nor the ore, *would not
That under earth is grave,* or lies above *buried
But if thy wife I were and eke thy love."
"My love?" quoth he, "nay, my damnation,
Alas! that any of my nation
Should ever so foul disparaged be.
But all for nought; the end is this, that he
Constrained was, that needs he muste wed,
And take this olde wife, and go to bed.

Now woulde some men say paraventure
That for my negligence I do no cure*   *take no pains
To tell you all the joy and all th' array
That at the feast was made that ilke* day.   *same
To which thing shortly answeren I shall:
I say there was no joy nor feast at all,
There was but heaviness and muche sorrow:
For privily he wed her on the morrow;
And all day after hid him as an owl,
So woe was him, his wife look'd so foul
Great was the woe the knight had in his thought
When he was with his wife to bed y-brought;
He wallow'd, and he turned to and fro.
This olde wife lay smiling evermo',
And said, "Dear husband, benedicite,
Fares every knight thus with his wife as ye?
Is this the law of king Arthoures house?
Is every knight of his thus dangerous?*   *fastidious, niggardly
I am your owen love, and eke your wife
I am she, which that saved hath your life
And certes yet did I you ne'er unright.
Why fare ye thus with me this firste night?
Ye fare like a man had lost his wit.
What is my guilt? for God's love tell me it,
And it shall be amended, if I may."
"Amended!" quoth this knight; "alas, nay, nay,
It will not be amended, never mo';
Thou art so loathly, and so old also,
And thereto* comest of so low a kind,   *in addition
That little wonder though I wallow and wind;*   *writhe, turn
    about
So woulde God, mine hearte woulde brest!"*   *burst
"Is this," quoth she, "the cause of your unrest?"
"Yea, certainly," quoth he; "no wonder is."
"Now, Sir," quoth she, "I could amend all this,

If that me list, ere it were dayes three,
So well ye mighte bear you unto me. *if you could conduct
    yourself well towards me*
But, for ye speaken of such gentleness
As is descended out of old richess,
That therefore shalle ye be gentlemen;
Such arrogancy is *not worth a hen.* *worth nothing
Look who that is most virtuous alway,
Prive and apert, and most intendeth aye *in private and
    public*
To do the gentle deedes that he can;
And take him for the greatest gentleman.
Christ will,* we claim of him our gentleness, *wills, requires
Not of our elders* for their old richess. *ancestors
For though they gave us all their heritage,
For which we claim to be of high parage,* *birth, descent
Yet may they not bequeathe, for no thing,
To none of us, their virtuous living
That made them gentlemen called to be,
And bade us follow them in such degree.
Well can the wise poet of Florence,
That highte Dante, speak of this sentence:* *sentiment
Lo, in such manner* rhyme is Dante's tale. *kind of
'Full seld'* upriseth by his branches smale *seldom
Prowess of man, for God of his goodness
Wills that we claim of him our gentleness;'
For of our elders may we nothing claim
But temp'ral things that man may hurt and maim.
Eke every wight knows this as well as I,
If gentleness were planted naturally
Unto a certain lineage down the line,
Prive and apert, then would they never fine* *cease
To do of gentleness the fair office
Then might they do no villainy nor vice.
Take fire, and bear it to the darkest house

Betwixt this and the mount of Caucasus,
And let men shut the doores, and go thenne,* *thence
Yet will the fire as fair and lighte brenne* *burn
As twenty thousand men might it behold;
Its office natural aye will it hold, *it will perform its natural
       duty*
On peril of my life, till that it die.
Here may ye see well how that gentery* *gentility, nobility
Is not annexed to possession,
Since folk do not their operation
Alway, as doth the fire, lo, *in its kind* *from its very nature*
For, God it wot, men may full often find
A lorde's son do shame and villainy.
And he that will have price* of his gent'ry, *esteem, honour
For* he was boren of a gentle house, *because
And had his elders noble and virtuous,
And will himselfe do no gentle deedes,
Nor follow his gentle ancestry, that dead is,
He is not gentle, be he duke or earl;
For villain sinful deedes make a churl.
For gentleness is but the renomee* *renown
Of thine ancestors, for their high bounte,* *goodness, worth
Which is a strange thing to thy person:
Thy gentleness cometh from God alone.
Then comes our very* gentleness of grace; *true
It was no thing bequeath'd us with our place.
Think how noble, as saith Valerius,
Was thilke* Tullius Hostilius, *that
That out of povert' rose to high
Read in Senec, and read eke in Boece,
There shall ye see express, that it no drede* is, *doubt
That he is gentle that doth gentle deedes.
And therefore, leve* husband, I conclude, *dear
Albeit that mine ancestors were rude,
Yet may the highe God, — and so hope I, —

Grant me His grace to live virtuously:
Then am I gentle when that I begin
To live virtuously, and waive* sin.   *forsake

"And whereas ye of povert' me repreve,*   *reproach
The highe God, on whom that we believe,
In wilful povert' chose to lead his life:
And certes, every man, maiden, or wife
May understand that Jesus, heaven's king,
Ne would not choose a virtuous living.
Glad povert' is an honest thing, certain;   *poverty cheerfully
    endured*
This will Senec and other clerkes sayn
Whoso that *holds him paid of* his povert',   *is satisfied with*
I hold him rich though he hath not a shirt.
He that coveteth is a poore wight
For he would have what is not in his might
But he that nought hath, nor coveteth to have,
Is rich, although ye hold him but a knave.*   *slave, abject wretch
Very povert' is sinne, properly.   *the only true poverty is sin*
Juvenal saith of povert' merrily:
The poore man, when he goes by the way
Before the thieves he may sing and play
Povert' is hateful good, and, as I guess,
A full great *bringer out of business;*   *deliver from trouble*
A great amender eke of sapience
To him that taketh it in patience.
Povert' is this, although it seem elenge*   *strange
Possession that no wight will challenge
Povert' full often, when a man is low,
Makes him his God and eke himself to know
Povert' a spectacle* is, as thinketh me   *a pair of spectacles
Through which he may his very* friendes see.   *true
And, therefore, Sir, since that I you not grieve,
Of my povert' no more me repreve.*   *reproach

"Now, Sir, of elde* ye repreve me: *age
And certes, Sir, though none authority* *text, dictum
Were in no book, ye gentles of honour
Say, that men should an olde wight honour,
And call him father, for your gentleness;
And authors shall I finden, as I guess.
Now there ye say that I am foul and old,
Then dread ye not to be a cokewold.* *cuckold
For filth, and elde, all so may I the,* *thrive
Be great wardens upon chastity.
But natheless, since I know your delight,
I shall fulfil your wordly appetite.
Choose now," quoth she, "one of these thinges tway,
To have me foul and old till that I dey,* *die
And be to you a true humble wife,
And never you displease in all my life:
Or elles will ye have me young and fair,
And take your aventure of the repair* *resort
That shall be to your house because of me, —
Or in some other place, it may well be?
Now choose yourselfe whether that you liketh.

This knight adviseth* him and sore he siketh,** *considered
        **sighed
But at the last he said in this mannere;
"My lady and my love, and wife so dear,
I put me in your wise governance,
Choose for yourself which may be most pleasance
And most honour to you and me also;
I *do no force* the whether of the two: *care not
For as you liketh, it sufficeth me."
"Then have I got the mastery," quoth she,
"Since I may choose and govern as me lest."* *pleases
"Yea, certes wife," quoth he, "I hold it best."
"Kiss me," quoth she, "we are no longer wroth,* *at variance

For by my troth I will be to you both;
This is to say, yea, bothe fair and good.
I pray to God that I may *sterve wood,* *die mad*
But* I to you be all so good and true, *unless
As ever was wife since the world was new;
And but* I be to-morrow as fair to seen, *unless
As any lady, emperess or queen,
That is betwixt the East and eke the West
Do with my life and death right as you lest.* *please
Cast up the curtain, and look how it is."

And when the knight saw verily all this,
That she so fair was, and so young thereto,
For joy he hent* her in his armes two: *took
His hearte bathed in a bath of bliss,
A thousand times *on row* he gan her kiss: *in succession*
And she obeyed him in every thing
That mighte do him pleasance or liking.
And thus they live unto their lives' end
In perfect joy; and Jesus Christ us send
Husbandes meek and young, and fresh in bed,
And grace to overlive them that we wed.
And eke I pray Jesus to short their lives,
That will not be governed by their wives.
And old and angry niggards of dispence,* *expense
God send them soon a very pestilence!

THE FRIAR'S TALE

This worthy limitour, this noble Frere,
He made always a manner louring cheer* *countenance
Upon the Sompnour; but for honesty* *courtesy
No villain word as yet to him spake he:
But at the last he said unto the Wife:
"Dame," quoth he, "God give you right good life,

Ye have here touched, all so may I the,* *thrive
In school matter a greate difficulty.
Ye have said muche thing right well, I say;
But, Dame, here as we ride by the way,
Us needeth not but for to speak of game,
And leave authorities, in Godde's name,
To preaching, and to school eke of clergy.
But if it like unto this company,
I will you of a Sompnour tell a game;
Pardie, ye may well knowe by the name,
That of a Sompnour may no good be said;
I pray that none of you be *evil paid;* *dissatisfied*
A Sompnour is a runner up and down
With mandements* for fornicatioun, *mandates, summonses*
And is y-beat at every towne's end."
Then spake our Host; "Ah, sir, ye should be hend* *civil, gentle
And courteous, as a man of your estate;
In company we will have no debate:
Tell us your tale, and let the Sompnour be."
"Nay," quoth the Sompnour, "let him say by me
What so him list; when it comes to my lot,
By God, I shall him quiten* every groat! *pay him off
I shall him telle what a great honour
It is to be a flattering limitour
And his office I shall him tell y-wis".
Our Host answered, "Peace, no more of this."
And afterward he said unto the frere,
"Tell forth your tale, mine owen master dear."

THE TALE

Whilom* there was dwelling in my country *once on a time
An archdeacon, a man of high degree,
That boldely did execution,
In punishing of fornication,

Of witchecraft, and eke of bawdery,
Of defamation, and adultery,
Of churche-reeves,* and of testaments, *churchwardens
Of contracts, and of lack of sacraments,
And eke of many another manner* crime, *sort of
Which needeth not rehearsen at this time,
Of usury, and simony also;
But, certes, lechours did he greatest woe;
They shoulde singen, if that they were hent;* *caught
And smale tithers were foul y-shent,* *troubled, put to shame
If any person would on them complain;
There might astert them no pecunial pain.
For smalle tithes, and small offering,
He made the people piteously to sing;
For ere the bishop caught them with his crook,
They weren in the archedeacon's book;
Then had he, through his jurisdiction,
Power to do on them correction.

He had a Sompnour ready to his hand,
A slier boy was none in Engleland;
For subtlely he had his espiaille,* *espionage
That taught him well where it might aught avail.
He coulde spare of lechours one or two,
To teache him to four and twenty mo'.
For, — though this Sompnour wood* be as a hare, — *furious,
    mad
To tell his harlotry I will not spare,
For we be out of their correction,
They have of us no jurisdiction,
Ne never shall have, term of all their lives.

"Peter; so be the women of the stives,"* *stews
Quoth this Sompnour, "y-put out of our cure."* *care

214

"Peace, with mischance and with misaventure,"
Our Hoste said, "and let him tell his tale.
Now telle forth, and let the Sompnour gale,*   *whistle; bawl
Nor spare not, mine owen master dear."

This false thief, the Sompnour (quoth the Frere),
Had always bawdes ready to his hand,
As any hawk to lure in Engleland,
That told him all the secrets that they knew, —
For their acquaintance was not come of new;
They were his approvers* privily.   *informers
He took himself at great profit thereby:
His master knew not always what he wan.*   *won
Withoute mandement, a lewed* man   *ignorant
He could summon, on pain of Christe's curse,
And they were inly glad to fill his purse,
And make him greate feastes at the nale.*   *alehouse
And right as Judas hadde purses smale,*   *small
And was a thief, right such a thief was he,
His master had but half *his duety.*   *what was owing him*
He was (if I shall give him his laud)
A thief, and eke a Sompnour, and a bawd.
And he had wenches at his retinue,
That whether that Sir Robert or Sir Hugh,
Or Jack, or Ralph, or whoso that it were
That lay by them, they told it in his ear.
Thus were the wench and he of one assent;
And he would fetch a feigned mandement,
And to the chapter summon them both two,
And pill* the man, and let the wenche go.   *plunder, pluck
Then would he say, "Friend, I shall for thy sake
Do strike thee out of oure letters blake;*   *black
Thee thar* no more as in this case travail;   *need
I am thy friend where I may thee avail."
Certain he knew of bribers many mo'

215

Than possible is to tell in yeare's two:
For in this world is no dog for the bow,
That can a hurt deer from a whole know,
Bet* than this Sompnour knew a sly lechour, *better
Or an adult'rer, or a paramour:
And, for that was the fruit of all his rent,
Therefore on it he set all his intent.

And so befell, that once upon a day.
This Sompnour, waiting ever on his prey,
Rode forth to summon a widow, an old ribibe,
Feigning a cause, for he would have a bribe.
And happen'd that he saw before him ride
A gay yeoman under a forest side:
A bow he bare, and arrows bright and keen,
He had upon a courtepy* of green, *short doublet
A hat upon his head with fringes blake.* *black
"Sir," quoth this Sompnour, "hail, and well o'ertake."
"Welcome," quoth he, "and every good fellow;
Whither ridest thou under this green shaw?"* shade
Saide this yeoman; "wilt thou far to-day?"
This Sompnour answer'd him, and saide, "Nay.
Here faste by," quoth he, "is mine intent
To ride, for to raisen up a rent,
That longeth to my lorde's duety."
"Ah! art thou then a bailiff?" "Yea," quoth he.
He durste not for very filth and shame
Say that he was a Sompnour, for the name.
"*De par dieux*," quoth this yeoman, "leve* brother, *dear
Thou art a bailiff, and I am another.
I am unknowen, as in this country.
Of thine acquaintance I will praye thee,
And eke of brotherhood, if that thee list.* *please
I have gold and silver lying in my chest;
If that thee hap to come into our shire,

All shall be thine, right as thou wilt desire."
"Grand mercy,"* quoth this Sompnour, "by my faith." *great
    thanks
Each in the other's hand his trothe lay'th,
For to be sworne brethren till they dey.* *die
In dalliance they ride forth and play.

This Sompnour, which that was as full of jangles,*
    *chattering
As full of venom be those wariangles,* * butcher-birds
And ev'r inquiring upon every thing,
"Brother," quoth he, "where is now your dwelling,
Another day if that I should you seech?"* *seek, visit
This yeoman him answered in soft speech;
"Brother," quoth he, "far in the North country,
Where as I hope some time I shall thee see
Ere we depart I shall thee so well wiss,* *inform
That of mine house shalt thou never miss."
"Now, brother," quoth this Sompnour, "I you pray,
Teach me, while that we ride by the way,
(Since that ye be a bailiff as am I,)
Some subtilty, and tell me faithfully
For mine office how that I most may win.
And *spare not* for conscience or for sin, *conceal nothing*
But, as my brother, tell me how do ye."
"Now by my trothe, brother mine," said he,
As I shall tell to thee a faithful tale:
My wages be full strait and eke full smale;
My lord is hard to me and dangerous,* *niggardly
And mine office is full laborious;
And therefore by extortion I live,
Forsooth I take all that men will me give.
Algate* by sleighte, or by violence, *whether
From year to year I win all my dispence;
I can no better tell thee faithfully."

Now certes," quoth this Sompnour, "so fare* I; *do
I spare not to take, God it wot,
But if it be too heavy or too hot. *unless*
What I may get in counsel privily,
No manner conscience of that have I.
N'ere* mine extortion, I might not live, *were it not for
For of such japes* will I not be shrive.** *tricks **confessed
Stomach nor conscience know I none;
I shrew* these shrifte-fathers** every one. *curse **confessors
Well be we met, by God and by St Jame.
But, leve brother, tell me then thy name,"
Quoth this Sompnour. Right in this meane while
This yeoman gan a little for to smile.

"Brother," quoth he, "wilt thou that I thee tell?
I am a fiend, my dwelling is in hell,
And here I ride about my purchasing,
To know where men will give me any thing.
My purchase is th' effect of all my rent *what I can gain is
    my sole revenue*
Look how thou ridest for the same intent
To winne good, thou reckest never how,
Right so fare I, for ride will I now
Into the worlde's ende for a prey."

"Ah," quoth this Sompnour, "benedicite! what say y'?
I weened ye were a yeoman truly. *thought
Ye have a manne's shape as well as I
Have ye then a figure determinate
In helle, where ye be in your estate?"* *at home
"Nay, certainly," quoth he, there have we none,
But when us liketh we can take us one,
Or elles make you seem* that we be shape *believe
Sometime like a man, or like an ape;
Or like an angel can I ride or go;

218

It is no wondrous thing though it be so,
A lousy juggler can deceive thee.
And pardie, yet can I more craft* than he." *skill, cunning
"Why," quoth the Sompnour, "ride ye then or gon
In sundry shapes and not always in one?"
"For we," quoth he, "will us in such form make.
As most is able our prey for to take."
"What maketh you to have all this labour?"
"Full many a cause, leve Sir Sompnour,"
Saide this fiend. "But all thing hath a time;
The day is short and it is passed prime,
And yet have I won nothing in this day;
I will intend* to winning, if I may, *apply myself
And not intend our thinges to declare:
For, brother mine, thy wit is all too bare
To understand, although I told them thee.
But for thou askest why laboure we: *because*
For sometimes we be Godde's instruments
And meanes to do his commandements,
When that him list, upon his creatures,
In divers acts and in divers figures:
Withoute him we have no might certain,
If that him list to stande thereagain.* *against it
And sometimes, at our prayer have we leave
Only the body, not the soul, to grieve:
Witness on Job, whom that we did full woe,
And sometimes have we might on both the two, —
This is to say, on soul and body eke,
And sometimes be we suffer'd for to seek
Upon a man and do his soul unrest
And not his body, and all is for the best,
When he withstandeth our temptation,
It is a cause of his salvation,
Albeit that it was not our intent
He should be safe, but that we would him hent.* *catch

219

And sometimes be we servants unto man,
As to the archbishop Saint Dunstan,
And to th'apostle servant eke was I."
"Yet tell me," quoth this Sompnour, "faithfully,
Make ye you newe bodies thus alway
Of th' elements?" The fiend answered, "Nay:
Sometimes we feign, and sometimes we arise
With deade bodies, in full sundry wise,
And speak as reas'nably, and fair, and well,
As to the Pythoness did Samuel:
And yet will some men say it was not he.
I *do no force of* your divinity. *set no value upon*
But one thing warn I thee, I will not jape,* jest
Thou wilt *algates weet* how we be shape: *assuredly know*
Thou shalt hereafterward, my brother dear,
Come, where thee needeth not of me to lear.* *learn
For thou shalt by thine own experience
Conne in a chair to rede of this sentence, *learn to
        understand what I have said*
Better than Virgil, while he was alive,
Or Dante also. Now let us ride blive,* *briskly
For I will holde company with thee,
Till it be so that thou forsake me."
"Nay," quoth this Sompnour, "that shall ne'er betide.
I am a yeoman, that is known full wide;
My trothe will I hold, as in this case;
For though thou wert the devil Satanas,
My trothe will I hold to thee, my brother,
As I have sworn, and each of us to other,
For to be true brethren in this case,
And both we go *abouten our purchase.* *seeking what we
        may pick up*
Take thou thy part, what that men will thee give,
And I shall mine, thus may we bothe live.
And if that any of us have more than other,

Let him be true, and part it with his brother."
"I grante," quoth the devil, "by my fay."
And with that word they rode forth their way,
And right at th'ent'ring of the towne's end,
To which this Sompnour shope* him for to wend,**   *shaped **go
They saw a cart, that charged was with hay,
Which that a carter drove forth on his way.
Deep was the way, for which the carte stood:
The carter smote, and cried as he were wood,*   *mad
"Heit Scot! heit Brok! what, spare ye for the stones?
The fiend" (quoth he) "you fetch body and bones,
As farforthly* as ever ye were foal'd,   *sure
So muche woe as I have with you tholed.*   *endured
The devil have all, horses, and cart, and hay."
The Sompnour said, "Here shall we have a prey,"
And near the fiend he drew, *as nought ne were,*   *as if
    nothing were the matter*
Full privily, and rowned* in his ear: *whispered
"Hearken, my brother, hearken, by thy faith,
Hearest thou not, how that the carter saith?
Hent* it anon, for he hath giv'n it thee,   *seize
Both hay and cart, and eke his capels* three."   *horses
"Nay," quoth the devil, "God wot, never a deal,*   *whit
It is not his intent, trust thou me well;
Ask him thyself, if thou not trowest* me,   *believest
Or elles stint* a while and thou shalt see."   *stop
The carter thwack'd his horses on the croup,
And they began to drawen and to stoop.
"Heit now," quoth he; "there, Jesus Christ you bless,
And all his handiwork, both more and less!
That was well twight,* mine owen liart,** boy,   *pulled **grey
I pray God save thy body, and Saint Loy!
Now is my cart out of the slough, pardie."
"Lo, brother," quoth the fiend, "what told I thee?
Here may ye see, mine owen deare brother,

221

The churl spake one thing, but he thought another.
Let us go forth abouten our voyage;
Here win I nothing upon this carriage."

When that they came somewhat out of the town,
This Sompnour to his brother gan to rown;
"Brother," quoth he, "here wons* an old rebeck, *dwells
That had almost as lief to lose her neck.
As for to give a penny of her good.
I will have twelvepence, though that she be wood,* *mad
Or I will summon her to our office;
And yet, God wot, of her know I no vice.
But for thou canst not, as in this country,
Winne thy cost, take here example of me."
This Sompnour clapped at the widow's gate:
"Come out," he said, "thou olde very trate;* *trot
I trow thou hast some friar or priest with thee."
"Who clappeth?" said this wife; "benedicite,
God save you, Sir, what is your sweete will?"
"I have," quoth he, "of summons here a bill.
Up* pain of cursing, looke that thou be *upon
To-morrow before our archdeacon's knee,
To answer to the court of certain things."
"Now Lord," quoth she, "Christ Jesus, king of kings,
So wisly* helpe me, *as I not may.* *surely *as I cannot*
I have been sick, and that full many a day.
I may not go so far," quoth she, "nor ride,
But I be dead, so pricketh it my side.
May I not ask a libel, Sir Sompnour,
And answer there by my procuratour
To such thing as men would appose* me?" *accuse
"Yes," quoth this Sompnour, "pay anon, let see,
Twelvepence to me, and I will thee acquit.
I shall no profit have thereby but lit:* *little
My master hath the profit and not I.

Come off, and let me ride hastily;
Give me twelvepence, I may no longer tarry."

"Twelvepence!" quoth she; "now lady Sainte Mary
So wisly* help me out of care and sin,   *surely
This wide world though that I should it win,
No have I not twelvepence within my hold.
Ye know full well that I am poor and old;
Kithe your almes upon me poor wretch."   *show your charity*
"Nay then," quoth he, "the foule fiend me fetch,
If I excuse thee, though thou should'st be spilt."* *ruined
"Alas!" quoth she, "God wot, I have no guilt."
"Pay me," quoth he, "or, by the sweet Saint Anne,
As I will bear away thy newe pan
For debte, which thou owest me of old, —
When that thou madest thine husband cuckold, —
I paid at home for thy correction."
"Thou liest," quoth she, "by my salvation;
Never was I ere now, widow or wife,
Summon'd unto your court in all my life;
Nor never I was but of my body true.
Unto the devil rough and black of hue
Give I thy body and my pan also."
And when the devil heard her curse so
Upon her knees, he said in this mannere;
"Now, Mabily, mine owen mother dear,
Is this your will in earnest that ye say?"
"The devil," quoth she, "so fetch him ere he dey,* *die
And pan and all, but* he will him repent."   *unless
"Nay, olde stoat,* that is not mine intent,"   *polecat
Quoth this Sompnour, "for to repente me
For any thing that I have had of thee;
I would I had thy smock and every cloth."
"Now, brother," quoth the devil, "be not wroth;
Thy body and this pan be mine by right.

Thou shalt with me to helle yet tonight,
Where thou shalt knowen of our privity*   *secrets
More than a master of divinity."

And with that word the foule fiend him hent.*   *seized
Body and soul, he with the devil went,
Where as the Sompnours have their heritage;
And God, that maked after his image
Mankinde, save and guide us all and some,
And let this Sompnour a good man become.
Lordings, I could have told you (quoth this Frere),
Had I had leisure for this Sompnour here,
After the text of Christ, and Paul, and John,
And of our other doctors many a one,
Such paines, that your heartes might agrise,*   *be horrified
Albeit so, that no tongue may devise,* —   *relate
Though that I might a thousand winters tell, —
The pains of thilke* cursed house of hell   *that
But for to keep us from that cursed place
Wake we, and pray we Jesus, of his grace,
So keep us from the tempter, Satanas.
Hearken this word, beware as in this case.
The lion sits *in his await* alway *on the watch*
To slay the innocent, if that he may.
Disposen aye your heartes to withstond
The fiend that would you make thrall and bond;
He may not tempte you over your might,
For Christ will be your champion and your knight;
And pray, that this our Sompnour him repent
Of his misdeeds ere that the fiend him hent.*   *seize

THE SOMPNOUR'S TALE

The Sompnour in his stirrups high he stood,
Upon this Friar his hearte was so wood,*   *furious

That like an aspen leaf he quoke* for ire: *quaked,
   trembled
"Lordings," quoth he, "but one thing I desire;
I you beseech, that of your courtesy,
Since ye have heard this false Friar lie,
As suffer me I may my tale tell
This Friar boasteth that he knoweth hell,
And, God it wot, that is but little wonder,
Friars and fiends be but little asunder.
For, pardie, ye have often time heard tell,
How that a friar ravish'd was to hell
In spirit ones by a visioun,
And, as an angel led him up and down,
To shew him all the paines that there were,
In all the place saw he not a frere;
Of other folk he saw enough in woe.
Unto the angel spake the friar tho;* *then
'Now, Sir,' quoth he, 'have friars such a grace,
That none of them shall come into this place?'
'Yes' quoth the angel; 'many a millioun:'
And unto Satanas he led him down.
'And now hath Satanas,' said he, 'a tail
Broader than of a carrack is the sail.
Hold up thy tail, thou Satanas,' quoth he,
'Shew forth thine erse, and let the friar see
Where is the nest of friars in this place.'
And *less than half a furlong way of space* *immediately*
Right so as bees swarmen out of a hive,
Out of the devil's erse there gan to drive
A twenty thousand friars *on a rout.* *in a crowd*
And throughout hell they swarmed all about,
And came again, as fast as they may gon,
And in his erse they creeped every one:
He clapt his tail again, and lay full still.
This friar, when he looked had his fill

Upon the torments of that sorry place,
His spirit God restored of his grace
Into his body again, and he awoke;
But natheless for feare yet he quoke,
So was the devil's erse aye in his mind;
That is his heritage, *of very kind* *by his very nature*
God save you alle, save this cursed Frere;
My prologue will I end in this mannere."

THE TALE

Lordings, there is in Yorkshire, as I guess,
A marshy country called Holderness,
In which there went a limitour about
To preach, and eke to beg, it is no doubt.
And so befell that on a day this frere
Had preached at a church in his mannere,
And specially, above every thing,
Excited he the people in his preaching
To trentals, and to give, for Godde's sake,
Wherewith men mighte holy houses make,
There as divine service is honour'd,
Not there as it is wasted and devour'd,
Nor where it needeth not for to be given,
As to possessioners, that may liven,
Thanked be God, in wealth and abundance.
"Trentals," said he, "deliver from penance
Their friendes' soules, as well old as young,
Yea, when that they be hastily y-sung, —
Not for to hold a priest jolly and gay,
He singeth not but one mass in a day.
"Deliver out," quoth he, "anon the souls.
Full hard it is, with flesh-hook or with owls* *awls
To be y-clawed, or to burn or bake:
Now speed you hastily, for Christe's sake."

And when this friar had said all his intent,
With *qui cum patre* forth his way he went,
When folk in church had giv'n him what them lest;* *pleased
He went his way, no longer would he rest,
With scrip and tipped staff, *y-tucked high:* *with his robe
    tucked up high*
In every house he gan to pore* and pry, *peer
And begged meal and cheese, or elles corn.
His fellow had a staff tipped with horn,
A pair of tables* all of ivory, *writing tablets
And a pointel* y-polish'd fetisly,** *pencil **daintily
And wrote alway the names, as he stood;
Of all the folk that gave them any good,
Askaunce that he woulde for them pray.
"Give us a bushel wheat, or malt, or rey,* *rye
A Godde's kichel,* or a trip** of cheese, *little cake **scrap
Or elles what you list, we may not chese;* *choose
A Godde's halfpenny, or a mass penny;
Or give us of your brawn, if ye have any;
A dagon* of your blanket, leve dame, *remnant
Our sister dear, — lo, here I write your name,—
Bacon or beef, or such thing as ye find."
A sturdy harlot* went them aye behind, *manservant
That was their hoste's man, and bare a sack,
And what men gave them, laid it on his back
And when that he was out at door, anon
He *planed away* the names every one, *rubbed out*
That he before had written in his tables:
He served them with nifles* and with fables. — *silly tales

"Nay, there thou liest, thou Sompnour," quoth the Frere.
"Peace," quoth our Host, "for Christe's mother dear;
Tell forth thy tale, and spare it not at all."
"So thrive I," quoth this Sompnour, "so I shall." —

So long he went from house to house, till he
Came to a house, where he was wont to be
Refreshed more than in a hundred places
Sick lay the husband man, whose that the place is,
Bed-rid upon a couche low he lay:
*"*Deus hic*,"* quoth he; "O Thomas friend, good day," *God
    be here*
Said this friar, all courteously and soft.
"Thomas," quoth he, "God *yield it you,* full oft *reward you for*
Have I upon this bench fared full well,
Here have I eaten many a merry meal."
And from the bench he drove away the cat,
And laid adown his potent* and his hat, *staff
And eke his scrip, and sat himself adown:
His fellow was y-walked into town
Forth with his knave,* into that hostelry *servant
Where as he shope* him that night to lie. *shaped, purposed

"O deare master," quoth this sicke man,
"How have ye fared since that March began?
I saw you not this fortenight and more."
"God wot," quoth he, "labour'd have I full sore;
And specially for thy salvation
Have I said many a precious orison,
And for mine other friendes, God them bless.
I have this day been at your church at mess,* *mass
And said sermon after my simple wit,
Not all after the text of Holy Writ;
For it is hard to you, as I suppose,
And therefore will I teach you aye the glose.* *gloss, comment
Glosing is a full glorious thing certain,
For letter slayeth, as we clerkes* sayn. *scholars
There have I taught them to be charitable,
And spend their good where it is reasonable.
And there I saw our dame; where is she?"

"Yonder I trow that in the yard she be,"
Saide this man; "and she will come anon."
"Hey master, welcome be ye by Saint John,"
Saide this wife; "how fare ye heartily?"

This friar riseth up full courteously,
And her embraceth *in his armes narrow,* *closely
And kiss'th her sweet, and chirketh as a sparrow
With his lippes: "Dame," quoth he, "right well,
As he that is your servant every deal.* *whit
Thanked be God, that gave you soul and life,
Yet saw I not this day so fair a wife
In all the churche, God so save me,"
"Yea, God amend defaultes, Sir," quoth she;
"Algates* welcome be ye, by my fay." *always
"Grand mercy, Dame; that have I found alway.
But of your greate goodness, by your leave,
I woulde pray you that ye not you grieve,
I will with Thomas speak *a little throw:* *a little while*
These curates be so negligent and slow
To grope tenderly a conscience.
In shrift* and preaching is my diligence *confession
And study in Peter's wordes and in Paul's;
I walk and fishe Christian menne's souls,
To yield our Lord Jesus his proper rent;
To spread his word is alle mine intent."
"Now by your faith, O deare Sir," quoth she,
"Chide him right well, for sainte charity.
He is aye angry as is a pismire,* *ant
Though that he have all that he can desire,
Though I him wrie* at night, and make him warm, *cover
And ov'r him lay my leg and eke mine arm,
He groaneth as our boar that lies in sty:
Other disport of him right none have I,
I may not please him in no manner case."

"O Thomas, *je vous dis,* Thomas, Thomas, *I tell you*
This *maketh the fiend,* this must be amended. *is the devil's
    work*
Ire is a thing that high God hath defended,* *forbidden
And thereof will I speak a word or two."
"Now, master," quoth the wife, "ere that I go,
What will ye dine? I will go thereabout."
"Now, Dame," quoth he, "*je vous dis sans doute,*
Had I not of a capon but the liver,
And of your white bread not but a shiver,* *thin slice
And after that a roasted pigge's head,
(But I would that for me no beast were dead,)
Then had I with you homely suffisance.
I am a man of little sustenance.
My spirit hath its fost'ring in the Bible.
My body is aye so ready and penible* *painstaking
To wake,* that my stomach is destroy'd. *watch
I pray you, Dame, that ye be not annoy'd,
Though I so friendly you my counsel shew;
By God, I would have told it but to few."
"Now, Sir," quoth she, "but one word ere I go;
My child is dead within these weeke's two,
Soon after that ye went out of this town."

"His death saw I by revelatioun,"
Said this friar, "at home in our dortour.* *dormitory
I dare well say, that less than half an hour
After his death, I saw him borne to bliss
In mine vision, so God me wiss.* *direct
So did our sexton, and our fermerere,* *infirmary-keeper
That have been true friars fifty year, —
They may now, God be thanked of his love,
Make their jubilee, and walk above.
And up I rose, and all our convent eke,
With many a teare trilling on my cheek,

Withoute noise or clattering of bells,
Te Deum was our song, and nothing else,
Save that to Christ I bade an orison,
Thanking him of my revelation.
For, Sir and Dame, truste me right well,
Our orisons be more effectuel,
And more we see of Christe's secret things,
Than *borel folk,* although that they be kings. *laymen*
We live in povert', and in abstinence,
And borel folk in riches and dispence
Of meat and drink, and in their foul delight.
We have this worlde's lust* all in despight** *pleasure
      **contempt
Lazar and Dives lived diversely,
And diverse guerdon* hadde they thereby. *reward
Whoso will pray, he must fast and be clean,
And fat his soul, and keep his body lean
We fare as saith th' apostle; cloth* and food *clothing
Suffice us, although they be not full good.
The cleanness and the fasting of us freres
Maketh that Christ accepteth our prayeres.
Lo, Moses forty days and forty night
Fasted, ere that the high God full of might
Spake with him in the mountain of Sinai:
With empty womb* of fasting many a day *stomach
Received he the lawe, that was writ
With Godde's finger; and Eli, well ye wit,* *know
In Mount Horeb, ere he had any speech
With highe God, that is our live's leech,* *physician, healer
He fasted long, and was in contemplance.
Aaron, that had the temple in governance,
And eke the other priestes every one,
Into the temple when they shoulde gon
To praye for the people, and do service,
They woulde drinken in no manner wise

No drinke, which that might them drunken make,
But there in abstinence pray and wake,
Lest that they died: take heed what I say —
But* they be sober that for the people pray — *unless
Ware that, I say — no more: for it sufficeth.
Our Lord Jesus, as Holy Writ deviseth,* *narrates
Gave us example of fasting and prayeres:
Therefore we mendicants, we sely* freres, *simple, lowly
Be wedded to povert' and continence,
To charity, humbless, and abstinence,
To persecution for righteousness,
To weeping, misericorde,* and to cleanness. *compassion
And therefore may ye see that our prayeres
(I speak of us, we mendicants, we freres),
Be to the highe God more acceptable
Than youres, with your feastes at your table.
From Paradise first, if I shall not lie,
Was man out chased for his gluttony,
And chaste was man in Paradise certain.
But hark now, Thomas, what I shall thee sayn;
I have no text of it, as I suppose,
But I shall find it in *a manner glose;* *a kind of comment*
That specially our sweet Lord Jesus
Spake this of friars, when he saide thus,
'Blessed be they that poor in spirit be'
And so forth all the gospel may ye see,
Whether it be liker our profession,
Or theirs that swimmen in possession;
Fy on their pomp, and on their gluttony,
And on their lewedness! I them defy.
Me thinketh they be like Jovinian,
Fat as a whale, and walking as a swan;
All vinolent* as bottle in the spence;** *full of wine
    **store-room
Their prayer is of full great reverence;

When they for soules say the Psalm of David,
Lo, 'Buf' they say, *Cor meum eructavit*.
Who follow Christe's gospel and his lore* *doctrine
But we, that humble be, and chaste, and pore,* *poor
Workers of Godde's word, not auditours?* *hearers
Therefore right as a hawk *upon a sours* *rising*
Up springs into the air, right so prayeres
Of charitable and chaste busy freres
Make their sours to Godde's eares two. *rise*
Thomas, Thomas, so may I ride or go,
And by that lord that called is Saint Ive,
N'ere thou our brother, shouldest thou not thrive;
In our chapiter pray we day and night
To Christ, that he thee sende health and might,
Thy body for to *wielde hastily."* *soon be able to move freely*

"God wot," quoth he, "nothing thereof feel I;
So help me Christ, as I in fewe years
Have spended upon *divers manner freres* *friars of various
    sorts*
Full many a pound, yet fare I ne'er the bet;* *better
Certain my good have I almost beset:* *spent
Farewell my gold, for it is all ago."* *gone
The friar answer'd, "O Thomas, dost thou so?
What needest thou diverse friars to seech?* *seek
What needeth him that hath a perfect leech,* *healer
To seeken other leeches in the town?
Your inconstance is your confusioun.
Hold ye then me, or elles our convent,
To praye for you insufficient?
Thomas, that jape* it is not worth a mite; *jest
Your malady is *for we have too lite.* *because we have too
    little*
Ah, give that convent half a quarter oats;
And give that convent four and twenty groats;

And give that friar a penny, and let him go!
Nay, nay, Thomas, it may no thing be so.
What is a farthing worth parted on twelve?
Lo, each thing that is oned* in himselve   *made one, united
Is more strong than when it is y-scatter'd.
Thomas, of me thou shalt not be y-flatter'd,
Thou wouldest have our labour all for nought.
The highe God, that all this world hath wrought,
Saith, that the workman worthy is his hire
Thomas, nought of your treasure I desire
As for myself, but that all our convent
To pray for you is aye so diligent:
And for to builde Christe's owen church.
Thomas, if ye will learne for to wirch,*   *work
Of building up of churches may ye find
If it be good, in Thomas' life of Ind.
Ye lie here full of anger and of ire,
With which the devil sets your heart on fire,
And chide here this holy innocent
Your wife, that is so meek and patient.
And therefore trow* me, Thomas, if thee lest,**   *believe
                                                   **please
Ne strive not with thy wife, as for the best.
And bear this word away now, by thy faith,
Touching such thing, lo, what the wise man saith:
'Within thy house be thou no lion;
To thy subjects do none oppression;
Nor make thou thine acquaintance for to flee.'
And yet, Thomas, eftsoones* charge I thee,   *again
Beware from ire that in thy bosom sleeps,
Ware from the serpent, that so slily creeps
Under the grass, and stingeth subtilly.
Beware, my son, and hearken patiently,
That twenty thousand men have lost their lives
For striving with their lemans* and their wives.   *mistresses

Now since ye have so holy and meek a wife,
What needeth you, Thomas, to make strife?
There is, y-wis,* no serpent so cruel, *certainly
When men tread on his tail nor half so fell,* *fierce
As woman is, when she hath caught an ire;
Very* vengeance is then all her desire. *pure, only
Ire is a sin, one of the greate seven,
Abominable to the God of heaven,
And to himself it is destruction.
This every lewed* vicar and parson *ignorant
Can say, how ire engenders homicide;
Ire is in sooth th' executor* of pride. *executioner
I could of ire you say so muche sorrow,
My tale shoulde last until to-morrow.
And therefore pray I God both day and night,
An irous* man God send him little might. *passionate
It is great harm, and certes great pity
To set an irous man in high degree.

"Whilom* there was an irous potestate,** *once **judge
As saith Senec, that during his estate* *term of office
Upon a day out rode knightes two;
And, as fortune would that it were so,
The one of them came home, the other not.
Anon the knight before the judge is brought,
That saide thus; 'Thou hast thy fellow slain,
For which I doom thee to the death certain.'
And to another knight commanded he;
'Go, lead him to the death, I charge thee.'
And happened, as they went by the way
Toward the place where as he should dey,* *die
The knight came, which men weened* had been dead
    *thought
Then thoughte they it was the beste rede* *counsel
To lead them both unto the judge again.

235

They saide, 'Lord, the knight hath not y-slain
His fellow; here he standeth whole alive.'
'Ye shall be dead,' quoth he, 'so may I thrive,
That is to say, both one, and two, and three.'
And to the firste knight right thus spake he:
'I damned thee, thou must algate* be dead: *at all events
And thou also must needes lose thine head,
For thou the cause art why thy fellow dieth.'
And to the thirde knight right thus he sayeth,
'Thou hast not done that I commanded thee.'
And thus he did do slay them alle three.

Irous Cambyses was eke dronkelew,* *a drunkard
And aye delighted him to be a shrew.* *vicious,
        ill-tempered
And so befell, a lord of his meinie,* *suite
That loved virtuous morality,
Said on a day betwixt them two right thus:
'A lord is lost, if he be vicious.
An irous man is like a frantic beast,
In which there is of wisdom *none arrest*; *no control*
And drunkenness is eke a foul record
Of any man, and namely* of a lord. *especially
There is full many an eye and many an ear
Awaiting on a lord, he knows not where. *watching
For Godde's love, drink more attemperly:* *temperately
Wine maketh man to lose wretchedly
His mind, and eke his limbes every one.'
'The reverse shalt thou see,' quoth he, 'anon,
And prove it by thine own experience,
That wine doth to folk no such offence.
There is no wine bereaveth me my might
Of hand, nor foot, nor of mine eyen sight.'
And for despite he dranke muche more
A hundred part* than he had done before, *times

And right anon this cursed irous wretch
This knighte's sone let* before him fetch,   *caused
Commanding him he should before him stand:
And suddenly he took his bow in hand,
And up the string he pulled to his ear,
And with an arrow slew the child right there.
'Now whether have I a sicker* hand or non?'** *sure **not
Quoth he; 'Is all my might and mind agone?
Hath wine bereaved me mine eyen sight?'
Why should I tell the answer of the knight?
His son was slain, there is no more to say.
Beware therefore with lordes how ye play,*   *use freedom
Sing placebo; and I shall if I can,
But if it be unto a poore man: *unless
To a poor man men should his vices tell,
But not t' a lord, though he should go to hell.
Lo, irous Cyrus, thilke* Persian,   *that
How he destroy'd the river of Gisen,
For that a horse of his was drowned therein,
When that he wente Babylon to win:
He made that the river was so small,
That women mighte wade it *over all.*   *everywhere
Lo, what said he, that so well teache can,
'Be thou no fellow to an irous man,
Nor with no wood* man walke by the way,   *furious
Lest thee repent;' I will no farther say.

"Now, Thomas, leve* brother, leave thine ire,   *dear
Thou shalt me find as just as is as squire;
Hold not the devil's knife aye at thine heart;
Thine anger doth thee all too sore smart;*   *pain
But shew to me all thy confession."
"Nay," quoth the sicke man, "by Saint Simon
I have been shriven* this day of my curate;   *confessed
I have him told all wholly mine estate.

237

Needeth no more to speak of it, saith he,
But if me list of mine humility."
"Give me then of thy good to make our cloister,"
Quoth he, "for many a mussel and many an oyster,
When other men have been full well at ease,
Hath been our food, our cloister for to rese:* *raise, build
And yet, God wot, unneth* the foundement** *scarcely
      **foundation
Performed is, nor of our pavement
Is not a tile yet within our wones:* *habitation
By God, we owe forty pound for stones.
Now help, Thomas, for *him that harrow'd hell,* *Christ
For elles must we oure bookes sell,
And if ye lack our predication,
Then goes this world all to destruction.
For whoso from this world would us bereave,
So God me save, Thomas, by your leave,
He would bereave out of this world the sun
For who can teach and worken as we conne?* *know how to
      do
And that is not of little time" (quoth he),
"But since Elijah was, and Elisee,* *Elisha
Have friars been, that find I of record,
In charity, y-thanked be our Lord.
Now, Thomas, help for sainte charity."
And down anon he set him on his knee,
The sick man waxed well-nigh wood* for ire, *mad
He woulde that the friar had been a-fire
With his false dissimulation.
"Such thing as is in my possession,"
Quoth he, "that may I give you and none other:
Ye say me thus, how that I am your brother."
"Yea, certes," quoth this friar, "yea, truste well;
I took our Dame the letter of our seal"
"Now well," quoth he, "and somewhat shall I give

Unto your holy convent while I live;
And in thine hand thou shalt it have anon,
On this condition, and other none,
That thou depart* it so, my deare brother, *divide
That every friar have as much as other:
This shalt thou swear on thy profession,
Withoute fraud or cavillation."* *quibbling
"I swear it," quoth the friar, "upon my faith."
And therewithal his hand in his he lay'th;
"Lo here my faith, in me shall be no lack."
"Then put thine hand adown right by my back,"
Saide this man, "and grope well behind,
Beneath my buttock, there thou shalt find
A thing, that I have hid in privity."
"Ah," thought this friar, "that shall go with me."
And down his hand he launched to the clift,* *cleft
In hope for to finde there a gift.
And when this sicke man felte this frere
About his taile groping there and here,
Amid his hand he let the friar a fart;
There is no capel* drawing in a cart, *horse
That might have let a fart of such a soun'.
The friar up start, as doth a wood* lioun: *fierce
"Ah, false churl," quoth he, "for Godde's bones,
This hast thou in despite done for the nones:* *on purpose
Thou shalt abie* this fart, if that I may." *suffer for
His meinie,* which that heard of this affray, *servants
Came leaping in, and chased out the frere,
And forth he went with a full angry cheer* *countenance
And fetch'd his fellow, there as lay his store:
He looked as it were a wilde boar,
And grounde with his teeth, so was he wroth.
A sturdy pace down to the court he go'th,
Where as there wonn'd* a man of great honour, *dwelt
To whom that he was always confessour:

This worthy man was lord of that village.
This friar came, as he were in a rage,
Where as this lord sat eating at his board:
Unnethes* might the friar speak one word, *with difficulty
Till at the last he saide, "God you see."* *save

This lord gan look, and said, "Ben'dicite!
What? Friar John, what manner world is this?
I see well that there something is amiss;
Ye look as though the wood were full of thieves.
Sit down anon, and tell me what your grieve* is, *grievance,
    grief
And it shall be amended, if I may."
"I have," quoth he, "had a despite to-day,
God *yielde you,* adown in your village, *reward you
That in this world is none so poor a page,
That would not have abominatioun
Of that I have received in your town:
And yet ne grieveth me nothing so sore,
As that the olde churl, with lockes hoar,
Blasphemed hath our holy convent eke."
"Now, master," quoth this lord, "I you beseek" —
"No master, Sir," quoth he, "but servitour,
Though I have had in schoole that honour.
God liketh not, that men us Rabbi call
Neither in market, nor in your large hall."
"No force," quoth he; "but tell me all your grief." *no
    matter*
"Sir," quoth this friar, "an odious mischief
This day betid* is to mine order and me, *befallen
And so par consequence to each degree
Of holy churche, God amend it soon."
"Sir," quoth the lord, "ye know what is to doon:* *do
Distemp'r you not, ye be my confessour. *be not impatient*
Ye be the salt of th' earth, and the savour;

For Godde's love your patience now hold;
Tell me your grief." And he anon him told
As ye have heard before, ye know well what.
The lady of the house aye stiller sat,
Till she had hearde what the friar said,
"Hey, Godde's mother;" quoth she; "blissful maid,
Is there ought elles? tell me faithfully."
"Madame," quoth he, "how thinketh you thereby?"
"How thinketh me?" quoth she; "so God me speed,
I say, a churl hath done a churlish deed,
What should I say? God let him never the;* *thrive
His sicke head is full of vanity;
I hold him in *a manner phrenesy."* *a sort of frenzy*
"Madame," quoth he, "by God, I shall not lie,
But I in other wise may be awreke,* *revenged
I shall defame him *ov'r all there* I speak; *wherever
This false blasphemour, that charged me
To parte that will not departed be,
To every man alike, with mischance."

The lord sat still, as he were in a trance,
And in his heart he rolled up and down,
How had this churl imaginatioun
To shewe such a problem to the frere.
Never ere now heard I of such mattere;
I trow* the Devil put it in his mind. *believe
In all arsmetrik* shall there no man find, *arithmetic
Before this day, of such a question.
Who shoulde make a demonstration,
That every man should have alike his part
As of the sound and savour of a fart?
O nice* proude churl, I shrew** his face. *foolish **curse
"Lo, Sires," quoth the lord, "with harde grace,
Who ever heard of such a thing ere now?
To every man alike? tell me how.

It is impossible, it may not be.
Hey nice* churl, God let him never the.** *foolish **thrive
The rumbling of a fart, and every soun',
Is but of air reverberatioun,
And ever wasteth lite* and lite* away; *little
There is no man can deemen,* by my fay, *judge, decide
If that it were departed* equally. *divided
What? lo, my churl, lo yet how shrewedly* *impiously,
    wickedly
Unto my confessour to-day he spake;
I hold him certain a demoniac.
Now eat your meat, and let the churl go play,
Let him go hang himself a devil way!"

Now stood the lorde's squier at the board,
That carv'd his meat, and hearde word by word
Of all this thing, which that I have you said.
"My lord," quoth he, "be ye not *evil paid,* *displeased*
I coulde telle, for a gowne-cloth,* *cloth for a gown*
To you, Sir Friar, so that ye be not wrot,
How that this fart should even* dealed be *equally
Among your convent, if it liked thee."
"Tell," quoth the lord, "and thou shalt have anon
A gowne-cloth, by God and by Saint John."
"My lord," quoth he, "when that the weather is fair,
Withoute wind, or perturbing of air,
Let* bring a cart-wheel here into this hall, *cause
But looke that it have its spokes all;
Twelve spokes hath a cart-wheel commonly;
And bring me then twelve friars, know ye why?
For thirteen is a convent as I guess;
Your confessor here, for his worthiness,
Shall *perform up* the number of his convent. *complete*
Then shall they kneel adown by one assent,
And to each spoke's end, in this mannere,

Full sadly* lay his nose shall a frere;   *carefully, steadily
Your noble confessor there, God him save,
Shall hold his nose upright under the nave.
Then shall this churl, with belly stiff and tought*   *tight
As any tabour,* hither be y-brought;   *drum
And set him on the wheel right of this cart
Upon the nave, and make him let a fart,
And ye shall see, on peril of my life,
By very proof that is demonstrative,
That equally the sound of it will wend,*   *go
And eke the stink, unto the spokes' end,
Save that this worthy man, your confessour'
(Because he is a man of great honour),
Shall have the firste fruit, as reason is;
The noble usage of friars yet it is,
The worthy men of them shall first be served,
And certainly he hath it well deserved;
He hath to-day taught us so muche good
With preaching in the pulpit where he stood,
That I may vouchesafe, I say for me,
He had the firste smell of fartes three;
And so would all his brethren hardily;
He beareth him so fair and holily."

The lord, the lady, and each man, save the frere,
Saide, that Jankin spake in this mattere
As well as Euclid, or as Ptolemy.
Touching the churl, they said that subtilty
And high wit made him speaken as he spake;
He is no fool, nor no demoniac.
And Jankin hath y-won a newe gown;
My tale is done, we are almost at town.

THE CLERK'S TALE

"SIR Clerk of Oxenford," our Hoste said,
"Ye ride as still and coy, as doth a maid
That were new spoused, sitting at the board:
This day I heard not of your tongue a word.
I trow ye study about some sophime:* *sophism
But Solomon saith, every thing hath time.
For Godde's sake, be of *better cheer,* *livelier mien*
It is no time for to study here.
Tell us some merry tale, by your fay;* *faith
For what man that is entered in a play,
He needes must unto that play assent.
But preache not, as friars do in Lent,
To make us for our olde sinnes weep,
Nor that thy tale make us not to sleep.
Tell us some merry thing of aventures.
Your terms, your coloures, and your figures,
Keep them in store, till so be ye indite
High style, as when that men to kinges write.
Speake so plain at this time, I you pray,
That we may understande what ye say."

This worthy Clerk benignely answer'd;
"Hoste," quoth he, "I am under your yerd,* *rod
Ye have of us as now the governance,
And therefore would I do you obeisance,
As far as reason asketh, hardily:* *boldly, truly
I will you tell a tale, which that I
Learn'd at Padova of a worthy clerk,
As proved by his wordes and his werk.
He is now dead, and nailed in his chest,
I pray to God to give his soul good rest.
Francis Petrarc', the laureate poet,
Highte* this clerk, whose rhetoric so sweet *was called
Illumin'd all Itale of poetry,

As Linian did of philosophy,
Or law, or other art particulere:
But death, that will not suffer us dwell here
But as it were a twinkling of an eye,
Them both hath slain, and alle we shall die.

"But forth to tellen of this worthy man,
That taughte me this tale, as I began,
I say that first he with high style inditeth
(Ere he the body of his tale writeth)
A proem, in the which describeth he
Piedmont, and of Saluces the country,
And speaketh of the Pennine hilles high,
That be the bounds of all West Lombardy:
And of Mount Vesulus in special,
Where as the Po out of a welle small
Taketh his firste springing and his source,
That eastward aye increaseth in his course
T'Emilia-ward, to Ferraro, and Venice,
The which a long thing were to devise.* *narrate
And truely, as to my judgement,
Me thinketh it a thing impertinent,* *irrelevant
Save that he would conveye his mattere:
But this is the tale, which that ye shall hear."

THE TALE

Pars Prima. *First Part*
There is, right at the west side of Itale,
Down at the root of Vesulus the cold,
A lusty* plain, abundant of vitaille;** *pleasant **victuals
There many a town and tow'r thou may'st behold,
That founded were in time of fathers old,
And many another delectable sight;
And Saluces this noble country hight.

A marquis whilom lord was of that land,
As were his worthy elders* him before, *ancestors
And obedient, aye ready to his hand,
Were all his lieges, bothe less and more:
Thus in delight he liv'd, and had done yore,* *long
Belov'd and drad,* through favour of fortune, *held in
    reverence
Both of his lordes and of his commune.* *commonalty

Therewith he was, to speak of lineage,
The gentilest y-born of Lombardy,
A fair person, and strong, and young of age,
And full of honour and of courtesy:
Discreet enough his country for to gie,* *guide, rule
Saving in some things that he was to blame;
And Walter was this younge lordes name.

I blame him thus, that he consider'd not
In time coming what might him betide,
But on his present lust* was all his thought, *pleasure
And for to hawk and hunt on every side;
Well nigh all other cares let he slide,
And eke he would (that was the worst of all)
Wedde no wife for aught that might befall.

Only that point his people bare so sore,
That flockmel* on a day to him they went, *in a body
And one of them, that wisest was of lore
(Or elles that the lord would best assent
That he should tell him what the people meant,
Or elles could he well shew such mattere),
He to the marquis said as ye shall hear.

"O noble Marquis! your humanity
Assureth us and gives us hardiness,

As oft as time is of necessity,
That we to you may tell our heaviness:
Accepte, Lord, now of your gentleness,
What we with piteous heart unto you plain,* *complain of
And let your ears my voice not disdain.

"All* have I nought to do in this mattere *although
More than another man hath in this place,
Yet forasmuch as ye, my Lord so dear,
Have always shewed me favour and grace,
I dare the better ask of you a space
Of audience, to shewen our request,
And ye, my Lord, to do right *as you lest.* *as pleaseth you*

"For certes, Lord, so well us like you
And all your work, and ev'r have done, that we
Ne coulde not ourselves devise how
We mighte live in more felicity:
Save one thing, Lord, if that your will it be,
That for to be a wedded man you lest;
Then were your people *in sovereign hearte's rest.* *completely

"Bowe your neck under the blissful yoke
Of sovereignty, and not of service,
Which that men call espousal or wedlock:
And thinke, Lord, among your thoughtes wise,
How that our dayes pass in sundry wise;
For though we sleep, or wake, or roam, or ride,
Aye fleeth time, it will no man abide.

"And though your greene youthe flow'r as yet,
In creepeth age always as still as stone,
And death menaceth every age, and smit* *smiteth
In each estate, for there escapeth none:
And all so certain as we know each one

247

That we shall die, as uncertain we all
Be of that day when death shall on us fall.

"Accepte then of us the true intent,* *mind, desire
That never yet refused youre hest,* *command
And we will, Lord, if that ye will assent,
Choose you a wife, in short time at the lest,* *least
Born of the gentilest and of the best
Of all this land, so that it ought to seem
Honour to God and you, as we can deem.

"Deliver us out of all this busy dread,* *doubt
And take a wife, for highe Godde's sake:
For if it so befell, as God forbid,
That through your death your lineage should slake,* *become
    extinct
And that a strange successor shoulde take
Your heritage, oh! woe were us on live:* *alive
Wherefore we pray you hastily to wive."

Their meeke prayer and their piteous cheer
Made the marquis for to have pity.
"Ye will," quoth he, "mine owen people dear,
To that I ne'er ere* thought constraine me. *before
I me rejoiced of my liberty,
That seldom time is found in marriage;
Where I was free, I must be in servage!* *servitude

"But natheless I see your true intent,
And trust upon your wit, and have done aye:
Wherefore of my free will I will assent
To wedde me, as soon as e'er I may.
But whereas ye have proffer'd me to-day
To choose me a wife, I you release
That choice, and pray you of that proffer cease.

"For God it wot, that children often been
Unlike their worthy elders them before,
Bounte* comes all of God, not of the strene**   *goodness **stock,
     race
Of which they be engender'd and y-bore:
I trust in Godde's bounte, and therefore
My marriage, and mine estate and rest,
I *him betake;* he may do as him lest.   *commend to him

"Let me alone in choosing of my wife;
That charge upon my back I will endure:
But I you pray, and charge upon your life,
That what wife that I take, ye me assure
To worship* her, while that her life may dure,   *honour
In word and work both here and elleswhere,
As she an emperore's daughter were.

"And farthermore this shall ye swear, that ye
Against my choice shall never grudge* nor strive.   *murmur
For since I shall forego my liberty
At your request, as ever may I thrive,
Where as mine heart is set, there will I live
And but* ye will assent in such mannere,   *unless
I pray you speak no more of this mattere."

With heartly will they sworen and assent
To all this thing, there said not one wight nay:
Beseeching him of grace, ere that they went,
That he would grante them a certain day
Of his espousal, soon as e'er he may,
For yet always the people somewhat dread*   *were in fear or doubt
Lest that the marquis woulde no wife wed.

He granted them a day, such as him lest,
On which he would be wedded sickerly,*   *certainly

And said he did all this at their request;
And they with humble heart full buxomly,* *obediently
Kneeling upon their knees full reverently,
Him thanked all; and thus they have an end
Of their intent, and home again they wend.

And hereupon he to his officers
Commanded for the feaste to purvey.* *provide
And to his privy knightes and squiers
Such charge he gave, as him list on them lay:
And they to his commandement obey,
And each of them doth all his diligence
To do unto the feast all reverence.

Pars Secunda *Second Part*
Not far from thilke* palace honourable, *that
Where as this marquis shope* his marriage, *prepared;
    resolved on
There stood a thorp,* of sighte delectable, *hamlet
In which the poore folk of that village
Hadde their beastes and their harbourage,* *dwelling
And of their labour took their sustenance,
After the earthe gave them abundance.

Among this poore folk there dwelt a man
Which that was holden poorest of them all;
But highe God sometimes sende can
His grace unto a little ox's stall;
Janicola men of that thorp him call.
A daughter had he, fair enough to sight,
And Griseldis this younge maiden hight.

But for to speak of virtuous beauty,
Then was she one the fairest under sun:
Full poorely y-foster'd up was she;

No *likerous lust* was in her heart y-run; *luxurious
    pleasure*
Well ofter of the well than of the tun
She drank, and, for* she woulde virtue please *because
She knew well labour, but no idle ease.

But though this maiden tender were of age;
Yet in the breast of her virginity
There was inclos'd a *sad and ripe corage;* *steadfast and
    mature spirit*
And in great reverence and charity
Her olde poore father foster'd she.
A few sheep, spinning, on the field she kept,
She woulde not be idle till she slept.

And when she homeward came, she would bring
Wortes,* and other herbes, times oft, *plants, cabbages
The which she shred and seeth'd for her living,
And made her bed full hard, and nothing soft:
And aye she kept her father's life on loft* *up, aloft
With ev'ry obeisance and diligence,
That child may do to father's reverence.

Upon Griselda, this poor creature,
Full often sithes* this marquis set his eye, *times
As he on hunting rode, paraventure:* *by chance
And when it fell that he might her espy,
He not with wanton looking of folly
His eyen cast on her, but in sad* wise *serious
Upon her cheer* he would him oft advise;** *countenance
    **consider

Commending in his heart her womanhead,
And eke her virtue, passing any wight
Of so young age, as well in cheer as deed.

For though the people have no great insight
In virtue, he considered full right
Her bounte,* and disposed that he would   *goodness
Wed only her, if ever wed he should.

The day of wedding came, but no wight can
Telle what woman that it shoulde be;
For which marvail wonder'd many a man,
And saide, when they were in privity,
"Will not our lord yet leave his vanity?
Will he not wed? Alas, alas the while!
Why will he thus himself and us beguile?"

But natheless this marquis had *done make*   *caused to be made*
Of gemmes, set in gold and in azure,
Brooches and ringes, for Griselda's sake,
And of her clothing took he the measure
Of a maiden like unto her stature,
And eke of other ornamentes all
That unto such a wedding shoulde fall.*   *befit

The time of undern* of the same day   *evening
Approached, that this wedding shoulde be,
And all the palace put was in array,
Both hall and chamber, each in its degree,
Houses of office stuffed with plenty
There may'st thou see of dainteous vitaille,*   *victuals,
    provisions
That may be found, as far as lasts Itale.

This royal marquis, richely array'd,
Lordes and ladies in his company,
The which unto the feaste were pray'd,
And of his retinue the bach'lery,
With many a sound of sundry melody,

Unto the village, of the which I told,
In this array the right way did they hold.

Griseld' of this (God wot) full innocent,
That for her shapen* was all this array,   *prepared
To fetche water at a well is went,
And home she came as soon as e'er she may.
For well she had heard say, that on that day
The marquis shoulde wed, and, if she might,
She fain would have seen somewhat of that sight.

She thought, "I will with other maidens stand,
That be my fellows, in our door, and see
The marchioness; and therefore will I fand*   *strive
To do at home, as soon as it may be,
The labour which belongeth unto me,
And then I may at leisure her behold,
If she this way unto the castle hold."

And as she would over the threshold gon,
The marquis came and gan for her to call,
And she set down her water-pot anon
Beside the threshold, in an ox's stall,
And down upon her knees she gan to fall,
And with sad* countenance kneeled still,   *steady
Till she had heard what was the lorde's will.

The thoughtful marquis spake unto the maid
Full soberly, and said in this mannere:
"Where is your father, Griseldis?" he said.
And she with reverence, *in humble cheer,*   *with humble air*
Answered, "Lord, he is all ready here."
And in she went withoute longer let*   *delay
And to the marquis she her father fet.*   *fetched

253

He by the hand then took the poore man,
And saide thus, when he him had aside:
"Janicola, I neither may nor can
Longer the pleasance of mine hearte hide;
If that thou vouchesafe, whatso betide,
Thy daughter will I take, ere that I wend,* *go
As for my wife, unto her life's end.

"Thou lovest me, that know I well certain,
And art my faithful liegeman y-bore,* *born
And all that liketh me, I dare well sayn
It liketh thee; and specially therefore
Tell me that point, that I have said before, —
If that thou wilt unto this purpose draw,
To take me as for thy son-in-law."

This sudden case* the man astonied so, *event
That red he wax'd, abash'd,* and all quaking *amazed
He stood; unnethes* said he wordes mo', *scarcely
But only thus; "Lord," quoth he, "my willing
Is as ye will, nor against your liking
I will no thing, mine owen lord so dear;
Right as you list governe this mattere."

"Then will I," quoth the marquis softly,
"That in thy chamber I, and thou, and she,
Have a collation;* and know'st thou why? *conference
For I will ask her, if her will it be
To be my wife, and rule her after me:
And all this shall be done in thy presence,
I will not speak out of thine audience."* *hearing

And in the chamber while they were about
The treaty, which ye shall hereafter hear,
The people came into the house without,

And wonder'd them in how honest mannere
And tenderly she kept her father dear;
But utterly Griseldis wonder might,
For never erst* ne saw she such a sight. *before

No wonder is though that she be astoned,* *astonished
To see so great a guest come in that place,
She never was to no such guestes woned;* *accustomed,
    wont
For which she looked with full pale face.
But shortly forth this matter for to chase,* *push on, pursue
These are the wordes that the marquis said
To this benigne, very,* faithful maid. *true

"Griseld'," he said, "ye shall well understand,
It liketh to your father and to me
That I you wed, and eke it may so stand,
As I suppose ye will that it so be:
But these demandes ask I first," quoth he,
"Since that it shall be done in hasty wise;
Will ye assent, or elles you advise?* *consider

"I say this, be ye ready with good heart
To all my lust,* and that I freely may, *pleasure
As me best thinketh, *do you* laugh or smart, *cause you to*
And never ye to grudge,* night nor day, *murmur
And eke when I say Yea, ye say not Nay,
Neither by word, nor frowning countenance?
Swear this, and here I swear our alliance."

Wond'ring upon this word, quaking for dread,
She saide; "Lord, indigne and unworthy
Am I to this honour that ye me bede,* *offer
But as ye will yourself, right so will I:
And here I swear, that never willingly

In word or thought I will you disobey,
For to be dead; though me were loth to dey."* *die

"This is enough, Griselda mine," quoth he.
And forth he went with a full sober cheer,
Out at the door, and after then came she,
And to the people he said in this mannere:
"This is my wife," quoth he, "that standeth here.
Honoure her, and love her, I you pray,
Whoso me loves; there is no more to say."

And, for that nothing of her olde gear
She shoulde bring into his house, he bade
That women should despoile* her right there; *strip
Of which these ladies were nothing glad
To handle her clothes wherein she was clad:
But natheless this maiden bright of hue
From foot to head they clothed have all new.

Her haires have they comb'd that lay untress'd* *loose
Full rudely, and with their fingers small
A crown upon her head they have dress'd,
And set her full of nouches great and small:
Of her array why should I make a tale?
Unneth* the people her knew for her fairness, *scarcely
When she transmuted was in such richess.

The marquis hath her spoused with a ring
Brought for the same cause, and then her set
Upon a horse snow-white, and well ambling,
And to his palace, ere he longer let* *delayed
With joyful people, that her led and met,
Conveyed her; and thus the day they spend
In revel, till the sunne gan descend.

And, shortly forth this tale for to chase,
I say, that to this newe marchioness
God hath such favour sent her of his grace,
That it ne seemed not by likeliness
That she was born and fed in rudeness, —
As in a cot, or in an ox's stall, —
But nourish'd in an emperore's hall.

To every wight she waxen* is so dear   *grown
And worshipful, that folk where she was born,
That from her birthe knew her year by year,
Unnethes trowed they, but durst have sworn, *scarcely
    believed*
That to Janicol' of whom I spake before,
She was not daughter, for by conjecture
Them thought she was another creature.

For though that ever virtuous was she,
She was increased in such excellence
Of thewes* good, y-set in high bounte,   *qualities
And so discreet, and fair of eloquence,
So benign, and so digne* of reverence,   *worthy
And coulde so the people's heart embrace,
That each her lov'd that looked on her face.

Not only of Saluces in the town
Published was the bounte of her name,
But eke besides in many a regioun;
If one said well, another said the same:
So spread of here high bounte the fame,
That men and women, young as well as old,
Went to Saluces, her for to behold.

Thus Walter lowly, — nay, but royally, —
Wedded with fortn'ate honestete,* *virtue

In Godde's peace lived full easily
At home, and outward grace enough had he:
And, for he saw that under low degree
Was honest virtue hid, the people him held
A prudent man, and that is seen full seld'.* *seldom

Not only this Griseldis through her wit
Couth all the feat of wifely homeliness, *knew all the
    duties*
But eke, when that the case required it,
The common profit coulde she redress:
There n'as discord, rancour, nor heaviness
In all the land, that she could not appease,
And wisely bring them all in rest and ease

Though that her husband absent were or non,* *not
If gentlemen or other of that country,
Were wroth,* she woulde bringe them at one, *at feud
So wise and ripe wordes hadde she,
And judgement of so great equity,
That she from heaven sent was, as men wend,* *weened,
    imagined
People to save, and every wrong t'amend

Not longe time after that this Griseld'
Was wedded, she a daughter had y-bore;
All she had lever* borne a knave** child, *rather **boy
Glad was the marquis and his folk therefore;
For, though a maiden child came all before,
She may unto a knave child attain
By likelihood, since she is not barren.

Pars Tertia. *Third Part*
There fell, as falleth many times mo',
When that his child had sucked but a throw,* *little while

This marquis in his hearte longed so
To tempt his wife, her sadness* for to know, *steadfastness
That he might not out of his hearte throw
This marvellous desire his wife t'asssay;* *try
Needless,* God wot, he thought her to affray.** *without cause
    **alarm, disturb
He had assayed her anough before,
And found her ever good; what needed it
Her for to tempt, and always more and more?
Though some men praise it for a subtle wit,
But as for me, I say that *evil it sit* *it ill became him*
T'assay a wife when that it is no need,
And putte her in anguish and in dread.

For which this marquis wrought in this mannere:
He came at night alone there as she lay,
With sterne face and with full troubled cheer,
And saide thus; "Griseld'," quoth he "that day
That I you took out of your poor array,
And put you in estate of high nobless,
Ye have it not forgotten, as I guess.

"I say, Griseld', this present dignity,
In which that I have put you, as I trow* *believe
Maketh you not forgetful for to be
That I you took in poor estate full low,
For any weal you must yourselfe know.
Take heed of every word that I you say,
There is no wight that hears it but we tway.* *two

"Ye know yourself well how that ye came here
Into this house, it is not long ago;
And though to me ye be right lefe* and dear, *loved
Unto my gentles* ye be nothing so: *nobles, gentlefolk
They say, to them it is great shame and woe

259

For to be subject, and be in servage,
To thee, that born art of small lineage.

"And namely* since thy daughter was y-bore *especially
These wordes have they spoken doubteless;
But I desire, as I have done before,
To live my life with them in rest and peace:
I may not in this case be reckeless;
I must do with thy daughter for the best,
Not as I would, but as my gentles lest.* *please

"And yet, God wot, this is full loth* to me: *odious
But natheless withoute your weeting* *knowing
I will nought do; but this will I," quoth he,
"That ye to me assenten in this thing.
Shew now your patience in your working,
That ye me hight* and swore in your village *promised
The day that maked was our marriage."

When she had heard all this, she not amev'd* *changed
Neither in word, in cheer, nor countenance
(For, as it seemed, she was not aggriev'd);
She saide; "Lord, all lies in your pleasance,
My child and I, with hearty obeisance
Be youres all, and ye may save or spill* *destroy
Your owen thing: work then after your will.

"There may no thing, so God my soule save,
Like to you, that may displease me: *be pleasing*
Nor I desire nothing for to have,
Nor dreade for to lose, save only ye:
This will is in mine heart, and aye shall be,
No length of time, nor death, may this deface,
Nor change my corage* to another place." *spirit, heart

260

Glad was the marquis for her answering,
But yet he feigned as he were not so;
All dreary was his cheer and his looking
When that he should out of the chamber go.
Soon after this, a furlong way or two,
He privily hath told all his intent
Unto a man, and to his wife him sent.

A *manner sergeant* was this private* man, *kind of squire*
    *discreet
The which he faithful often founden had
In thinges great, and eke such folk well can
Do execution in thinges bad:
The lord knew well, that he him loved and drad.* *dreaded
And when this sergeant knew his lorde's will,
Into the chamber stalked he full still.

"Madam," he said, "ye must forgive it me,
Though I do thing to which I am constrain'd;
Ye be so wise, that right well knowe ye
That lordes' hestes may not be y-feign'd;
They may well be bewailed and complain'd,
But men must needs unto their lust* obey; *pleasure
And so will I, there is no more to say.

"This child I am commanded for to take."
And spake no more, but out the child he hent* *seized
Dispiteously,* and gan a cheer** to make *unpityingly **show,
    aspect
As though he would have slain it ere he went.
Griseldis must all suffer and consent:
And as a lamb she sat there meek and still,
And let this cruel sergeant do his will

Suspicious* was the diffame** of this man, *ominous **evil
    reputation
Suspect his face, suspect his word also,
Suspect the time in which he this began:
Alas! her daughter, that she loved so,
She weened* he would have it slain right tho,** *thought **then
But natheless she neither wept nor siked,* *sighed
Conforming her to what the marquis liked.

But at the last to speake she began,
And meekly she unto the sergeant pray'd,
So as he was a worthy gentle man,
That she might kiss her child, ere that it died:
And in her barme* this little child she laid, *lap, bosom
With full sad face, and gan the child to bless,* *cross
And lulled it, and after gan it kiss.

And thus she said in her benigne voice:
Farewell, my child, I shall thee never see;
But since I have thee marked with the cross,
Of that father y-blessed may'st thou be
That for us died upon a cross of tree:
Thy soul, my little child, I *him betake,* *commit unto him*
For this night shalt thou dien for my sake.

I trow* that to a norice** in this case *believe **nurse
It had been hard this ruthe* for to see: *pitiful sight
Well might a mother then have cried, "Alas!"
But natheless so sad steadfast was she,
That she endured all adversity,
And to the sergeant meekely she said,
"Have here again your little younge maid.

"Go now," quoth she, "and do my lord's behest.
And one thing would I pray you of your grace,

But if my lord forbade you at the least, *unless*
Bury this little body in some place,
That neither beasts nor birdes it arace."* *tear
But he no word would to that purpose say,
But took the child and went upon his way.

The sergeant came unto his lord again,
And of Griselda's words and of her cheer* *demeanour
He told him point for point, in short and plain,
And him presented with his daughter dear.
Somewhat this lord had ruth in his mannere,
But natheless his purpose held he still,
As lordes do, when they will have their will;

And bade this sergeant that he privily
Shoulde the child full softly wind and wrap,
With alle circumstances tenderly,
And carry it in a coffer, or in lap;
But, upon pain his head off for to swap,* *strike
That no man shoulde know of his intent,
Nor whence he came, nor whither that he went;

But at Bologna, to his sister dear,
That at that time of Panic'* was Countess, *Panico
He should it take, and shew her this mattere,
Beseeching her to do her business
This child to foster in all gentleness,
And whose child it was he bade her hide
From every wight, for aught that might betide.

The sergeant went, and hath fulfill'd this thing.
But to the marquis now returne we;
For now went he full fast imagining
If by his wife's cheer he mighte see,
Or by her wordes apperceive, that she

Were changed; but he never could her find,
But ever-in-one* alike sad** and kind. *constantly **steadfast

As glad, as humble, as busy in service,
And eke in love, as she was wont to be,
Was she to him, in every *manner wise;* *sort of way*
And of her daughter not a word spake she;
No accident for no adversity *no change of humour resulting
    from her affliction*
Was seen in her, nor e'er her daughter's name
She named, or in earnest or in game.

Pars Quarta *Fourth Part*
In this estate there passed be four year
Ere she with childe was; but, as God wo'ld,
A knave* child she bare by this Waltere, *boy
Full gracious and fair for to behold;
And when that folk it to his father told,
Not only he, but all his country, merry
Were for this child, and God they thank and hery.* *praise

When it was two year old, and from the breast
Departed* of the norice, on a day *taken, weaned
This marquis *caughte yet another lest* *was seized by yet
    another desire*
To tempt his wife yet farther, if he may.
Oh! needless was she tempted in as say;* *trial
But wedded men *not connen no measure,* *know no
    moderation*
When that they find a patient creature.

"Wife," quoth the marquis, "ye have heard ere this
My people *sickly bear* our marriage; *regard with displeasure*
And namely* since my son y-boren is, *especially
Now is it worse than ever in all our age:

The murmur slays mine heart and my corage,
For to mine ears cometh the voice so smart,* *painfully
That it well nigh destroyed hath mine heart.

"Now say they thus, 'When Walter is y-gone,
Then shall the blood of Janicol' succeed,
And be our lord, for other have we none:'
Such wordes say my people, out of drede.* *doubt
Well ought I of such murmur take heed,
For certainly I dread all such sentence,* *expression of opinion
Though they not *plainen in mine audience.* *complain in my
          hearing*

"I woulde live in peace, if that I might;
Wherefore I am disposed utterly,
As I his sister served ere* by night, *before
Right so think I to serve him privily.
This warn I you, that ye not suddenly
Out of yourself for no woe should outraie;* *become
          outrageous, rave
Be patient, and thereof I you pray."

"I have," quoth she, "said thus, and ever shall,
I will no thing, nor n'ill no thing, certain,
But as you list; not grieveth me at all
Though that my daughter and my son be slain
At your commandement; that is to sayn,
I have not had no part of children twain,
But first sickness, and after woe and pain.

"Ye be my lord, do with your owen thing
Right as you list, and ask no rede of me:
For, as I left at home all my clothing
When I came first to you, right so," quoth she,
"Left I my will and all my liberty,

265

And took your clothing: wherefore I you pray,
Do your pleasance, I will your lust* obey. *will

"And, certes, if I hadde prescience
Your will to know, ere ye your lust* me told, *will
I would it do withoute negligence:
But, now I know your lust, and what ye wo'ld,
All your pleasance firm and stable I hold;
For, wist I that my death might do you ease,
Right gladly would I dien you to please.

"Death may not make no comparisoun
Unto your love." And when this marquis say* *saw
The constance of his wife, he cast adown
His eyen two, and wonder'd how she may
In patience suffer all this array;
And forth he went with dreary countenance;
But to his heart it was full great pleasance.

This ugly sergeant, in the same wise
That he her daughter caught, right so hath he
(Or worse, if men can any worse devise,)
Y-hent* her son, that full was of beauty: *seized
And ever-in-one* so patient was she, *unvaryingly
That she no cheere made of heaviness,
But kiss'd her son, and after gan him bless.

Save this she prayed him, if that he might,
Her little son he would in earthe grave,* *bury
His tender limbes, delicate to sight,
From fowles and from beastes for to save.
But she none answer of him mighte have;
He went his way, as him nothing ne raught,* *cared
But to Bologna tenderly it brought.

The marquis wonder'd ever longer more
Upon her patience; and, if that he
Not hadde soothly knowen therebefore
That perfectly her children loved she,
He would have ween'd* that of some subtilty, *thought
And of malice, or for cruel corage,* *disposition
She hadde suffer'd this with sad* visage. *steadfast, unmoved

But well he knew, that, next himself, certain
She lov'd her children best in every wise.
But now of women would I aske fain,
If these assayes mighte not suffice?
What could a sturdy* husband more devise *stern
To prove her wifehood and her steadfastness,
And he continuing ev'r in sturdiness?

But there be folk of such condition,
That, when they have a certain purpose take,
They cannot stint* of their intention, *cease
But, right as they were bound unto a stake,
They will not of their firste purpose slake:* *slacken, abate
Right so this marquis fully hath purpos'd
To tempt his wife, as he was first dispos'd.

He waited, if by word or countenance
That she to him was changed of corage:* *spirit
But never could he finde variance,
She was aye one in heart and in visage,
And aye the farther that she was in age,
The more true (if that it were possible)
She was to him in love, and more penible.* *painstaking in
    devotion

For which it seemed thus, that of them two
There was but one will; for, as Walter lest,* *pleased

The same pleasance was her lust* also; *pleasure
And, God be thanked, all fell for the best.
She shewed well, for no worldly unrest,
A wife as of herself no thinge should
Will, in effect, but as her husbaud would.

The sland'r of Walter wondrous wide sprad,
That of a cruel heart he wickedly,
For* he a poore woman wedded had, *because
Had murder'd both his children privily:
Such murmur was among them commonly.
No wonder is: for to the people's ear
There came no word, but that they murder'd were.

For which, whereas his people therebefore
Had lov'd him well, the sland'r of his diffame* *infamy
Made them that they him hated therefore.
To be a murd'rer is a hateful name.
But natheless, for earnest or for game,
He of his cruel purpose would not stent;
To tempt his wife was set all his intent.

When that his daughter twelve year was of age,
He to the Court of Rome, in subtle wise
Informed of his will, sent his message,* *messenger
Commanding him such bulles to devise
As to his cruel purpose may suffice,
How that the Pope, for his people's rest,
Bade him to wed another, if him lest.* *wished

I say he bade they shoulde counterfeit
The Pope's bulles, making mention
That he had leave his firste wife to lete,* *leave
To stinte* rancour and dissension *put an end to

Betwixt his people and him: thus spake the bull,
The which they have published at full.

The rude people, as no wonder is,
Weened* full well that it had been right so: *thought, believed
But, when these tidings came to Griseldis.
I deeme that her heart was full of woe;
But she, alike sad* for evermo', *steadfast
Disposed was, this humble creature,
Th' adversity of fortune all t' endure;

Abiding ever his lust and his pleasance,
To whom that she was given, heart and all,
As *to her very worldly suffisance.* *to the utmost extent of
        her power*
But, shortly if this story tell I shall,
The marquis written hath in special
A letter, in which he shewed his intent,
And secretly it to Bologna sent.

To th' earl of Panico, which hadde tho* *there
Wedded his sister, pray'd he specially
To bringe home again his children two
In honourable estate all openly:
But one thing he him prayed utterly,
That he to no wight, though men would inquere,
Shoulde not tell whose children that they were,

But say, the maiden should y-wedded be
Unto the marquis of Saluce anon.
And as this earl was prayed, so did he,
For, at day set, he on his way is gone
Toward Saluce, and lorde's many a one
In rich array, this maiden for to guide, —

Her younge brother riding her beside.
Arrayed was toward* her marriage   *as if for
This freshe maiden, full of gemmes clear;
Her brother, which that seven year was of age,
Arrayed eke full fresh in his mannere:
And thus, in great nobless, and with glad cheer,
Toward Saluces shaping their journey,
From day to day they rode upon their way.

Pars Quinta.   *Fifth Part*
Among all this, after his wick' usage,   *while all this was
    going on*
The marquis, yet his wife to tempte more
To the uttermost proof of her corage,
Fully to have experience and lore*   *knowledge
If that she were as steadfast as before,
He on a day, in open audience,
Full boisterously said her this sentence:

"Certes, Griseld', I had enough pleasance
To have you to my wife, for your goodness,
And for your truth, and for your obeisance,
Not for your lineage, nor for your richess;
But now know I, in very soothfastness,
That in great lordship, if I well advise,
There is great servitude in sundry wise.

"I may not do as every ploughman may:
My people me constraineth for to take
Another wife, and cryeth day by day;
And eke the Pope, rancour for to slake,
Consenteth it, that dare I undertake:
And truely, thus much I will you say,
My newe wife is coming by the way.

"Be strong of heart, and *void anon* her place; *immediately
    vacate*
And thilke* dower that ye brought to me, *that
Take it again, I grant it of my grace.
Returne to your father's house," quoth he;
"No man may always have prosperity;
With even heart I rede* you to endure *counsel
The stroke of fortune or of aventure."

And she again answer'd in patience:
"My Lord," quoth she, "I know, and knew alway,
How that betwixte your magnificence
And my povert' no wight nor can nor may
Make comparison, it *is no nay;* *cannot be denied*
I held me never digne* in no mannere *worthy
To be your wife, nor yet your chamberere.* *chamber-maid

"And in this house, where ye me lady made,
(The highe God take I for my witness,
And all so wisly* he my soule glade),** *surely **gladdened
I never held me lady nor mistress,
But humble servant to your worthiness,
And ever shall, while that my life may dure,
Aboven every worldly creature.

"That ye so long, of your benignity,
Have holden me in honour and nobley,* *nobility
Where as I was not worthy for to be,
That thank I God and you, to whom I pray
Foryield* it you; there is no more to say: *reward
Unto my father gladly will I wend,* *go
And with him dwell, unto my lifes end,

"Where I was foster'd as a child full small,
Till I be dead my life there will I lead,

A widow clean in body, heart, and all.
For since I gave to you my maidenhead,
And am your true wife, it is no dread,* *doubt
God shielde* such a lordes wife to take *forbid
Another man to husband or to make.* *mate

"And of your newe wife, God of his grace
So grant you weal and all prosperity:
For I will gladly yield to her my place,
In which that I was blissful wont to be.
For since it liketh you, my Lord," quoth she,
"That whilom weren all mine hearte's rest,
That I shall go, I will go when you lest.

"But whereas ye me proffer such dowaire
As I first brought, it is well in my mind,
It was my wretched clothes, nothing fair,
The which to me were hard now for to find.
O goode God! how gentle and how kind
Ye seemed by your speech and your visage,
The day that maked was our marriage!

"But sooth is said, — algate* I find it true, *at all events
For in effect it proved is on me, —
Love is not old as when that it is new.
But certes, Lord, for no adversity,
To dien in this case, it shall not be
That e'er in word or work I shall repent
That I you gave mine heart in whole intent.

"My Lord, ye know that in my father's place
Ye did me strip out of my poore weed,* *raiment
And richely ye clad me of your grace;
To you brought I nought elles, out of dread,
But faith, and nakedness, and maidenhead;

And here again your clothing I restore,
And eke your wedding ring for evermore.
"The remnant of your jewels ready be
Within your chamber, I dare safely sayn:
Naked out of my father's house," quoth she,
"I came, and naked I must turn again.
All your pleasance would I follow fain:* *cheerfully
But yet I hope it be not your intent
That smockless* I out of your palace went. *naked

"Ye could not do so dishonest* a thing, *dishonourable
That thilke* womb, in which your children lay, *that
Shoulde before the people, in my walking,
Be seen all bare: and therefore I you pray,
Let me not like a worm go by the way:
Remember you, mine owen Lord so dear,
I was your wife, though I unworthy were.

"Wherefore, in guerdon* of my maidenhead, *reward
Which that I brought and not again I bear,
As vouchesafe to give me to my meed* *reward
But such a smock as I was wont to wear,
That I therewith may wrie* the womb of her *cover
That was your wife: and here I take my leave
Of you, mine owen Lord, lest I you grieve."

"The smock," quoth he, "that thou hast on thy back,
Let it be still, and bear it forth with thee."
But well unnethes* thilke word he spake, *with difficulty
But went his way for ruth and for pity.
Before the folk herselfe stripped she,
And in her smock, with foot and head all bare,
Toward her father's house forth is she fare.* *gone

The folk her follow'd weeping on her way,
And fortune aye they cursed as they gon:* *go
But she from weeping kept her eyen drey,* *dry
Nor in this time worde spake she none.
Her father, that this tiding heard anon,
Cursed the day and time, that nature
Shope* him to be a living creature. *formed, ordained

For, out of doubt, this olde poore man
Was ever in suspect of her marriage:
For ever deem'd he, since it first began,
That when the lord *fulfill'd had his corage,* *had gratified
    his whim*
He woulde think it were a disparage* *disparagement
To his estate, so low for to alight,
And voide* her as soon as e'er he might. *dismiss

Against* his daughter hastily went he *to meet
(For he by noise of folk knew her coming),
And with her olde coat, as it might be,
He cover'd her, full sorrowfully weeping:
But on her body might he it not bring,
For rude was the cloth, and more of age
By dayes fele* than at her marriage. *many

Thus with her father for a certain space
Dwelled this flow'r of wifely patience,
That neither by her words nor by her face,
Before the folk nor eke in their absence,
Ne shewed she that her was done offence,
Nor of her high estate no remembrance
Ne hadde she, *as by* her countenance. *to judge from*

No wonder is, for in her great estate
Her ghost* was ever in plein** humility; *spirit **full

No tender mouth, no hearte delicate,
No pomp, and no semblant of royalty;
But full of patient benignity,
Discreet and prideless, aye honourable,
And to her husband ever meek and stable.

Men speak of Job, and most for his humbless,
As clerkes, when them list, can well indite,
Namely* of men; but, as in soothfastness,   *particularly
Though clerkes praise women but a lite,*   *little
There can no man in humbless him acquite
As women can, nor can be half so true
As women be, *but it be fall of new.*   *unless it has lately
                                          come to pass*

Pars Sexta *Sixth Part*
From Bologn' is the earl of Panic' come,
Of which the fame up sprang to more and less;
And to the people's eares all and some
Was know'n eke, that a newe marchioness
He with him brought, in such pomp and richess
That never was there seen with manne's eye
So noble array in all West Lombardy.

The marquis, which that shope* and knew all this,   *arranged
Ere that the earl was come, sent his message*   *messenger
For thilke poore sely* Griseldis;   *innocent
And she, with humble heart and glad visage,
Nor with no swelling thought in her corage,*   *mind
Came at his hest,* and on her knees her set,   *command
And rev'rently and wisely she him gret.*   *greeted

"Griseld'," quoth he, "my will is utterly,
This maiden, that shall wedded be to me,
Received be to-morrow as royally

As it possible is in my house to be;
And eke that every wight in his degree
Have *his estate* in sitting and service, *what befits his
And in high pleasance, as I can devise. condition*

"I have no women sufficient, certain,
The chambers to array in ordinance
After my lust;* and therefore would I fain *pleasure
That thine were all such manner governance:
Thou knowest eke of old all my pleasance;
Though thine array be bad, and ill besey,* *poor to look on
Do thou thy devoir at the leaste way." * do your duty in the
     quickest manner*
"Not only, Lord, that I am glad," quoth she,
"To do your lust, but I desire also
You for to serve and please in my degree,
Withoute fainting, and shall evermo':
Nor ever for no weal, nor for no woe,
Ne shall the ghost* within mine hearte stent** *spirit **cease
To love you best with all my true intent."

And with that word she gan the house to dight,* *arrange
And tables for to set, and beds to make,
And *pained her* to do all that she might, *she took pains*
Praying the chambereres* for Godde's sake *chamber-maids
To hasten them, and faste sweep and shake,
And she the most serviceable of all
Hath ev'ry chamber arrayed, and his hall.

Aboute undern* gan the earl alight, *afternoon
That with him brought these noble children tway;
For which the people ran to see the sight
Of their array, so *richely besey;* *rich to behold*
And then *at erst* amonges them they say, *for the first time*
That Walter was no fool, though that him lest* *pleased

To change his wife; for it was for the best.
For she is fairer, as they deemen* all,   *think
Than is Griseld', and more tender of age,
And fairer fruit between them shoulde fall,
And more pleasant, for her high lineage:
Her brother eke so fair was of visage,
That them to see the people hath caught pleasance,
Commending now the marquis' governance.

"O stormy people, unsad* and ev'r untrue,   *variable
And undiscreet, and changing as a vane,
Delighting ev'r in rumour that is new,
For like the moon so waxe ye and wane:
Aye full of clapping, *dear enough a jane,*   *worth nothing *
Your doom* is false, your constance evil preveth,**   *judgment
        **proveth
A full great fool is he that you believeth."

Thus saide the sad* folk in that city,   *sedate
When that the people gazed up and down;
For they were glad, right for the novelty,
To have a newe lady of their town.
No more of this now make I mentioun,
But to Griseld' again I will me dress,
And tell her constancy and business.

Full busy was Griseld' in ev'ry thing
That to the feaste was appertinent;
Right nought was she abash'd* of her clothing,   *ashamed
Though it were rude, and somedeal eke to-rent;*   *tattered
But with glad cheer* unto the gate she went   *expression
With other folk, to greet the marchioness,
And after that did forth her business.

With so glad cheer* his guestes she receiv'd *expression
And so conningly* each in his degree, *cleverly, skilfully
That no defaulte no man apperceiv'd,
But aye they wonder'd what she mighte be
That in so poor array was for to see,
And coude* such honour and reverence; *knew, understood
And worthily they praise her prudence.

In all this meane while she not stent* *ceased
This maid, and eke her brother, to commend
With all her heart in full benign intent,
So well, that no man could her praise amend:
But at the last, when that these lordes wend* *go
To sitte down to meat, he gan to call
Griseld', as she was busy in the hall.

"Griseld'," quoth he, as it were in his play,
"How liketh thee my wife, and her beauty?"
"Right well, my Lord," quoth she, "for, in good fay,* *faith
A fairer saw I never none than she:
I pray to God give you prosperity;
And so I hope, that he will to you send
Pleasance enough unto your lives end.

"One thing beseech I you, and warn also,
That ye not pricke with no tormenting
This tender maiden, as ye have done mo:* *me
For she is foster'd in her nourishing
More tenderly, and, to my supposing,
She mighte not adversity endure
As could a poore foster'd creature."

And when this Walter saw her patience,
Her gladde cheer, and no malice at all,
And* he so often had her done offence, *although

And she aye sad* and constant as a wall, *steadfast
Continuing ev'r her innocence o'er all,
The sturdy marquis gan his hearte dress* *prepare
To rue upon her wifely steadfastness.

"This is enough, Griselda mine," quoth he,
"Be now no more *aghast, nor evil paid,* *afraid, nor
    displeased*
I have thy faith and thy benignity
As well as ever woman was, assay'd,
In great estate and poorely array'd:
Now know I, deare wife, thy steadfastness;"
And her in arms he took, and gan to kiss.

And she for wonder took of it no keep;* *notice
She hearde not what thing he to her said:
She far'd as she had start out of a sleep,
Till she out of her mazedness abraid.* *awoke
"Griseld'," quoth he, "by God that for us died,
Thou art my wife, none other I have,
Nor ever had, as God my soule save.

"This is thy daughter, which thou hast suppos'd
To be my wife; that other faithfully
Shall be mine heir, as I have aye dispos'd;
Thou bare them of thy body truely:
At Bologna kept I them privily:
Take them again, for now may'st thou not say
That thou hast lorn* none of thy children tway. *lost

"And folk, that otherwise have said of me,
I warn them well, that I have done this deed
For no malice, nor for no cruelty,
But to assay in thee thy womanhead:
And not to slay my children (God forbid),

But for to keep them privily and still,
Till I thy purpose knew, and all thy will."

When she this heard, in swoon adown she falleth
For piteous joy; and after her swooning,
She both her younge children to her calleth,
And in her armes piteously weeping
Embraced them, and tenderly kissing,
Full like a mother, with her salte tears
She bathed both their visage and their hairs.

O, what a piteous thing it was to see
Her swooning, and her humble voice to hear!
"Grand mercy, Lord, God thank it you," quoth she,
That ye have saved me my children dear;
Now reck* I never to be dead right here;   *care
Since I stand in your love, and in your grace,
No *force of* death, nor when my spirit pace.*   *no matter for*
      *pass

"O tender, O dear, O young children mine,
Your woeful mother *weened steadfastly*   *believed firmly*
That cruel houndes, or some foul vermine,
Had eaten you; but God of his mercy,
And your benigne father tenderly
Have *done you keep:*" and in that same stound*   *caused
      you to be preserved* *hour
All suddenly she swapt* down to the ground.   *fell
And in her swoon so sadly* holdeth she   *firmly
Her children two, when she gan them embrace,
That with great sleight* and great difficulty   *art
The children from her arm they can arace,*   *pull away
O! many a tear on many a piteous face
Down ran of them that stoode her beside,
Unneth'* aboute her might they abide.   *scarcely

Walter her gladdeth, and her sorrow slaketh:*   *assuages
She riseth up abashed* from her trance,   *astonished
And every wight her joy and feaste maketh,
Till she hath caught again her countenance.
Walter her doth so faithfully pleasance,
That it was dainty for to see the cheer
Betwixt them two, since they be met in fere.*   *together

The ladies, when that they their time sey,*   *saw
Have taken her, and into chamber gone,
And stripped her out of her rude array,
And in a cloth of gold that brightly shone,
And with a crown of many a riche stone
Upon her head, they into hall her brought:
And there she was honoured as her ought.

Thus had this piteous day a blissful end;
For every man and woman did his might
This day in mirth and revel to dispend,
Till on the welkin* shone the starres bright: *firmament
For more solemn in every mannes sight
This feaste was, and greater of costage,*   *expense
Than was the revel of her marriage.

Full many a year in high prosperity
Lived these two in concord and in rest;
And richely his daughter married he
Unto a lord, one of the worthiest
Of all Itale; and then in peace and rest
His wife's father in his court he kept,
Till that the soul out of his body crept.

His son succeeded in his heritage,
In rest and peace, after his father's day:
And fortunate was eke in marriage,

All* he put not his wife in great assay: *although
This world is not so strong, it *is no nay,* *not to be denied*
As it hath been in olde times yore;
And hearken what this author saith, therefore;

This story is said, not for that wives should
Follow Griselda in humility,
For it were importable* though they would; *not to be borne
But for that every wight in his degree
Shoulde be constant in adversity,
As was Griselda; therefore Petrarch writeth
This story, which with high style he inditeth.

For, since a woman was so patient
Unto a mortal man, well more we ought
Receiven all in gree* that God us sent. *good-will
For great skill is he proved that he wrought:
But he tempteth no man that he hath bought,
As saith Saint James, if ye his 'pistle read;
He proveth folk all day, it is no dread.* *doubt

And suffereth us, for our exercise,
With sharpe scourges of adversity
Full often to be beat in sundry wise;
Not for to know our will, for certes he,
Ere we were born, knew all our frailty;
And for our best is all his governance;
Let us then live in virtuous sufferance.

But one word, lordings, hearken, ere I go:
It were full hard to finde now-a-days
In all a town Griseldas three or two:
For, if that they were put to such assays,
The gold of them hath now so bad allays* *alloys

With brass, that though the coin be fair *at eye,* *to see*
It woulde rather break in two than ply.* *bend

For which here, for the Wife's love of Bath, —
Whose life and all her sex may God maintain
In high mast'ry, and elles were it scath,* — *damage, pity
I will, with lusty hearte fresh and green,
Say you a song to gladden you, I ween:
And let us stint of earnestful mattere.
Hearken my song, that saith in this mannere.

L'Envoy of Chaucer.
"Griseld' is dead, and eke her patience,
And both at once are buried in Itale:
For which I cry in open audience,
No wedded man so hardy be t'assail
His wife's patience, in trust to find
Griselda's, for in certain he shall fail.

"O noble wives, full of high prudence,
Let no humility your tongues nail:
Nor let no clerk have cause or diligence
To write of you a story of such marvail,
As of Griselda patient and kind,
Lest Chichevache you swallow in her entrail.

"Follow Echo, that holdeth no silence,
But ever answereth at the countertail;* *counter-tally
Be not bedaffed* for your innocence, *befooled
But sharply take on you the governail;* *helm
Imprinte well this lesson in your mind,
For common profit, since it may avail.

GEOFFREY CHAUCER

"Ye archiwives,* stand aye at defence, *wives of rank
Since ye be strong as is a great camail,* *camel
Nor suffer not that men do you offence.
And slender wives, feeble in battail,
Be eager as a tiger yond in Ind;
Aye clapping as a mill, I you counsail.

"Nor dread them not, nor do them reverence;
For though thine husband armed be in mail,
The arrows of thy crabbed eloquence
Shall pierce his breast, and eke his aventail;
In jealousy I rede* eke thou him bind, *advise
And thou shalt make him couch* as doth a quail. *submit, shrink

"If thou be fair, where folk be in presence
Shew thou thy visage and thine apparail:
If thou be foul, be free of thy dispence;
To get thee friendes aye do thy travail:
Be aye of cheer as light as leaf on lind,* *linden, lime-tree
And let him care, and weep, and wring, and wail."

THE MERCHANT'S TALE

"Weeping and wailing, care and other sorrow,
I have enough, on even and on morrow,"
Quoth the Merchant, "and so have other mo',
That wedded be; I trow* that it be so; *believe
For well I wot it fareth so by me.
I have a wife, the worste that may be,
For though the fiend to her y-coupled were,
She would him overmatch, I dare well swear.
Why should I you rehearse in special
Her high malice? she is *a shrew at all.* *thoroughly, in
   everything wicked*
There is a long and large difference

284

Betwixt Griselda's greate patience,
And of my wife the passing cruelty.
Were I unbounden, all so may I the,* *thrive
I woulde never eft* come in the snare. *again
We wedded men live in sorrow and care;
Assay it whoso will, and he shall find
That I say sooth, by Saint Thomas of Ind,
As for the more part; I say not all, —
God shielde* that it shoulde so befall. *forbid
Ah! good Sir Host, I have y-wedded be
These moneths two, and more not, pardie;
And yet I trow* that he that all his life *believe
Wifeless hath been, though that men would him rive*
    *wound
Into the hearte, could in no mannere
Telle so much sorrow, as I you here
Could tellen of my wife's cursedness."* *wickedness

"Now," quoth our Host, "Merchant, so God you bless,
Since ye so muche knowen of that art,
Full heartily I pray you tell us part."
"Gladly," quoth he; "but of mine owen sore,
For sorry heart, I telle may no more."

THE TALE

Whilom there was dwelling in Lombardy
A worthy knight, that born was at Pavie,
In which he liv'd in great prosperity;
And forty years a wifeless man was he,
And follow'd aye his bodily delight
On women, where as was his appetite,
As do these fooles that be seculeres.
And, when that he was passed sixty years,
Were it for holiness, or for dotage,

I cannot say, but such a great corage* *inclination
Hadde this knight to be a wedded man,
That day and night he did all that he can
To espy where that he might wedded be;
Praying our Lord to grante him, that he
Mighte once knowen of that blissful life
That is betwixt a husband and his wife,
And for to live under that holy bond
With which God firste man and woman bond.
"None other life," said he, "is worth a bean;
For wedlock is so easy, and so clean,
That in this world it is a paradise."
Thus said this olde knight, that was so wise.
And certainly, as sooth* as God is king, *true
To take a wife it is a glorious thing,
And namely* when a man is old and hoar, *especially
Then is a wife the fruit of his treasor;
Then should he take a young wife and a fair,
On which he might engender him an heir,
And lead his life in joy and in solace;* *mirth, delight
Whereas these bachelors singen "Alas!"
When that they find any adversity
In love, which is but childish vanity.
And truely it sits* well to be so, *becomes, befits
That bachelors have often pain and woe:
On brittle ground they build, and brittleness
They finde when they *weene sickerness:* *think that there
    is security*
They live but as a bird or as a beast,
In liberty, and under no arrest;* *check, control
Whereas a wedded man in his estate
Liveth a life blissful and ordinate,
Under the yoke of marriage y-bound;
Well may his heart in joy and bliss abound.
For who can be so buxom* as a wife? *obedient

Who is so true, and eke so attentive
To keep* him, sick and whole, as is his make?** *care for **mate
For weal or woe she will him not forsake:
She is not weary him to love and serve,
Though that he lie bedrid until he sterve.* *die
And yet some clerkes say it is not so;
Of which he, Theophrast, is one of tho:* *those
What force though Theophrast list for to lie? *what matter*

"Take no wife," quoth he, "for husbandry,* *thrift
As for to spare in household thy dispence;
A true servant doth more diligence
Thy good to keep, than doth thine owen wife,
For she will claim a half part all her life.
And if that thou be sick, so God me save,
Thy very friendes, or a true knave,* *servant
Will keep thee bet than she, that *waiteth aye *always waits
    to inherit your property*
After thy good,* and hath done many a day."
This sentence, and a hundred times worse,
Writeth this man, there God his bones curse.
But take no keep* of all such vanity, *notice
Defy* Theophrast, and hearken to me. *distrust

A wife is Godde's gifte verily;
All other manner giftes hardily,* *truly
As handes, rentes, pasture, or commune,* *common land
Or mebles,* all be giftes of fortune, *furniture
That passen as a shadow on the wall:
But dread* thou not, if plainly speak I shall, *doubt
A wife will last, and in thine house endure,
Well longer than thee list, paraventure.* *perhaps
Marriage is a full great sacrament;
He which that hath no wife, I hold him shent;* *ruined
He liveth helpless, and all desolate

(I speak of folk *in secular estate*): *who are not of the clergy*
And hearken why, I say not this for nought, —
That woman is for manne's help y-wrought.
The highe God, when he had Adam maked,
And saw him all alone belly naked,
God of his great goodness saide then,
Let us now make a help unto this man
Like to himself; and then he made him Eve.
Here may ye see, and hereby may ye preve,* *prove
That a wife is mans' help and his comfort,
His paradise terrestre and his disport.
So buxom* and so virtuous is she, *obedient, complying
They muste needes live in unity;
One flesh they be, and one blood, as I guess,
With but one heart in weal and in distress.
A wife? Ah! Saint Mary, ben'dicite,
How might a man have any adversity
That hath a wife? certes I cannot say
The bliss the which that is betwixt them tway,
There may no tongue it tell, or hearte think.
If he be poor, she helpeth him to swink;* *labour
She keeps his good, and wasteth never a deal;* *whit
All that her husband list, her liketh* well; *pleaseth
She saith not ones Nay, when he saith Yea;
"Do this," saith he; "All ready, Sir," saith she.
O blissful order, wedlock precious!
Thou art so merry, and eke so virtuous,
And so commended and approved eke,
That every man that holds him worth a leek
Upon his bare knees ought all his life
To thank his God, that him hath sent a wife;
Or elles pray to God him for to send
A wife, to last unto his life's end.
For then his life is set in sickerness,* *security
He may not be deceived, as I guess,

So that he work after his wife's rede;* *counsel
Then may he boldely bear up his head,
They be so true, and therewithal so wise.
For which, if thou wilt worken as the wise,
Do alway so as women will thee rede.* *counsel
Lo how that Jacob, as these clerkes read,
By good counsel of his mother Rebecc'
Bounde the kiddes skin about his neck;
For which his father's benison* he wan. *benediction
Lo Judith, as the story telle can,
By good counsel she Godde's people kept,
And slew him, Holofernes, while he slept.
Lo Abigail, by good counsel, how she
Saved her husband Nabal, when that he
Should have been slain. And lo, Esther also
By counsel good deliver'd out of woe
The people of God, and made him, Mardoche,
Of Assuere enhanced* for to be. *advanced in dignity
There is nothing *in gree superlative* *of higher esteem*
(As saith Senec) above a humble wife.
Suffer thy wife's tongue, as Cato bit;* *bid
She shall command, and thou shalt suffer it,
And yet she will obey of courtesy.
A wife is keeper of thine husbandry:
Well may the sicke man bewail and weep,
There as there is no wife the house to keep.
I warne thee, if wisely thou wilt wirch,* *work
Love well thy wife, as Christ loveth his church:
Thou lov'st thyself, if thou lovest thy wife.
No man hateth his flesh, but in his life
He fost'reth it; and therefore bid I thee
Cherish thy wife, or thou shalt never the.* *thrive
Husband and wife, what *so men jape or play,* *although men
      joke and jeer*
Of worldly folk holde the sicker* way; *certain

They be so knit there may no harm betide,
And namely* upon the wife's side. *especially

For which this January, of whom I told,
Consider'd hath within his dayes old,
The lusty life, the virtuous quiet,
That is in marriage honey-sweet.
And for his friends upon a day he sent
To tell them the effect of his intent.
With face sad,* his tale he hath them told: *grave, earnest
He saide, "Friendes, I am hoar and old,
And almost (God wot) on my pitte's* brink, *grave's
Upon my soule somewhat must I think.
I have my body foolishly dispended,
Blessed be God that it shall be amended;
For I will be certain a wedded man,
And that anon in all the haste I can,
Unto some maiden, fair and tender of age;
I pray you shape* for my marriage *arrange, contrive
All suddenly, for I will not abide:
And I will fond* to espy, on my side, *try
To whom I may be wedded hastily.
But forasmuch as ye be more than,
Ye shalle rather* such a thing espy
Than I, and where me best were to ally.
But one thing warn I you, my friendes dear,
I will none old wife have in no mannere:
She shall not passe sixteen year certain.
Old fish and younge flesh would I have fain.
Better," quoth he, "a pike than a pickerel,* *young pike
And better than old beef is tender veal.
I will no woman thirty year of age,
It is but beanestraw and great forage.
And eke these olde widows (God it wot)
They conne* so much craft on Wade's boat, *know

So muche brooke harm when that them lest, *they can do
    so much harm when they wish*
That with them should I never live in rest.
For sundry schooles make subtle clerkes;
Woman of many schooles half a clerk is.
But certainly a young thing men may guy,* *guide
Right as men may warm wax with handes ply.* *bend,
    mould
Wherefore I say you plainly in a clause,
I will none old wife have, right for this cause.
For if so were I hadde such mischance,
That I in her could have no pleasance,
Then should I lead my life in avoutrie,* *adultery
And go straight to the devil when I die.
Nor children should I none upon her getten:
Yet *were me lever* houndes had me eaten *I would rather*
Than that mine heritage shoulde fall
In strange hands: and this I tell you all.
I doubte not I know the cause why
Men shoulde wed: and farthermore know I
There speaketh many a man of marriage
That knows no more of it than doth my page,
For what causes a man should take a wife.
If he ne may not live chaste his life,
Take him a wife with great devotion,
Because of lawful procreation
Of children, to th' honour of God above,
And not only for paramour or love;
And for they shoulde lechery eschew,
And yield their debte when that it is due:
Or for that each of them should help the other
In mischief,* as a sister shall the brother, *trouble
And live in chastity full holily.
But, Sires, by your leave, that am not I,
For, God be thanked, I dare make avaunt,* *boast

291

I feel my limbes stark* and suffisant *strong
To do all that a man belongeth to:
I wot myselfe best what I may do.
Though I be hoar, I fare as doth a tree,
That blossoms ere the fruit y-waxen* be; *grown
The blossomy tree is neither dry nor dead;
I feel me now here hoar but on my head.
Mine heart and all my limbes are as green
As laurel through the year is for to seen.* *see
And, since that ye have heard all mine intent,
I pray you to my will ye would assent."

Diverse men diversely him told
Of marriage many examples old;
Some blamed it, some praised it, certain;
But at the haste, shortly for to sayn
(As all day* falleth altercation *constantly, every day
Betwixte friends in disputation),
There fell a strife betwixt his brethren two,
Of which that one was called Placebo,
Justinus soothly called was that other.

Placebo said; "O January, brother,
Full little need have ye, my lord so dear,
Counsel to ask of any that is here:
But that ye be so full of sapience,
That you not liketh, for your high prudence,
To waive* from the word of Solomon. *depart, deviate
This word said he unto us every one;
Work alle thing by counsel, — thus said he, —
And thenne shalt thou not repente thee
But though that Solomon spake such a word,
Mine owen deare brother and my lord,
So wisly* God my soule bring at rest, *surely
I hold your owen counsel is the best.

For, brother mine, take of me this motive;* *advice,
    encouragement
I have now been a court-man all my life,
And, God it wot, though I unworthy be,
I have standen in full great degree
Aboute lordes of full high estate;
Yet had I ne'er with none of them debate;
I never them contraried truely.
I know well that my lord can* more than I; *knows
What that he saith I hold it firm and stable,
I say the same, or else a thing semblable.
A full great fool is any counsellor
That serveth any lord of high honour
That dare presume, or ones thinken it;
That his counsel should pass his lorde's wit.
Nay, lordes be no fooles by my fay.
Ye have yourselfe shewed here to day
So high sentence,* so holily and well *judgment, sentiment
That I consent, and confirm *every deal* *in every point*
Your wordes all, and your opinioun
By God, there is no man in all this town
Nor in Itale, could better have y-said.
Christ holds him of this counsel well apaid.* *satisfied
And truely it is a high courage
Of any man that stopen* is in age, *advanced
To take a young wife, by my father's kin;
Your hearte hangeth on a jolly pin.
Do now in this matter right as you lest,
For finally I hold it for the best."

Justinus, that aye stille sat and heard,
Right in this wise to Placebo answer'd.
"Now, brother mine, be patient I pray,
Since ye have said, and hearken what I say.
Senec, among his other wordes wise,

Saith, that a man ought him right well advise,* *consider
To whom he gives his hand or his chattel.
And since I ought advise me right well
To whom I give my good away from me,
Well more I ought advise me, pardie,
To whom I give my body: for alway
I warn you well it is no childe's play
To take a wife without advisement.
Men must inquire (this is mine assent)
Whe'er she be wise, or sober, or dronkelew,* *given to drink
Or proud, or any other ways a shrew,
A chidester,* or a waster of thy good, *a scold
Or rich or poor; or else a man is wood.* *mad
Albeit so, that no man finde shall
None in this world, that *trotteth whole in all,* *is sound in
        every point*
No man, nor beast, such as men can devise,* *describe
But natheless it ought enough suffice
With any wife, if so were that she had
More goode thewes* than her vices bad: *qualities
And all this asketh leisure to inquere.
For, God it wot, I have wept many a tear
Full privily, since I have had a wife.
Praise whoso will a wedded manne's life,
Certes, I find in it but cost and care,
And observances of all blisses bare.
And yet, God wot, my neighebours about,
And namely* of women many a rout,** *especially **company
Say that I have the moste steadfast wife,
And eke the meekest one, that beareth life.
But I know best where wringeth* me my shoe, *pinches
Ye may for me right as you like do
Advise you, ye be a man of age,
How that ye enter into marriage;
And namely* with a young wife and a fair, * especially

By him that made water, fire, earth, air,
The youngest man that is in all this rout* *company
Is busy enough to bringen it about
To have his wife alone, truste me:
Ye shall not please her fully yeares three,
This is to say, to do her full pleasance.
A wife asketh full many an observance.
I pray you that ye be not *evil apaid."* *displeased*

"Well," quoth this January, "and hast thou said?
Straw for thy Senec, and for thy proverbs,
I counte not a pannier full of herbs
Of schoole termes; wiser men than thou,
As thou hast heard, assented here right now
To my purpose: Placebo, what say ye?"
"I say it is a cursed* man," quoth he, *ill-natured, wicked
"That letteth* matrimony, sickerly." *hindereth
And with that word they rise up suddenly,
And be assented fully, that he should
Be wedded when him list, and where he would.

High fantasy and curious business
From day to day gan in the soul impress* *imprint themselves
Of January about his marriage
Many a fair shape, and many a fair visage
There passed through his hearte night by night.
As whoso took a mirror polish'd bright,
And set it in a common market-place,
Then should he see many a figure pace
By his mirror; and in the same wise
Gan January in his thought devise
Of maidens, which that dwelte him beside:
He wiste not where that he might abide.* *stay, fix his choice
For if that one had beauty in her face,
Another stood so in the people's grace

For her sadness* and her benignity,   *sedateness
That of the people greatest voice had she:
And some were rich and had a badde name.
But natheless, betwixt earnest and game,
He at the last appointed him on one,
And let all others from his hearte gon,
And chose her of his own authority;
For love is blind all day, and may not see.
And when that he was into bed y-brought,
He pourtray'd in his heart and in his thought
Her freshe beauty, and her age tender,
Her middle small, her armes long and slender,
Her wise governance, her gentleness,
Her womanly bearing, and her sadness.*   *sedateness
And when that he *on her was condescended,* *had selected her*
He thought his choice might not be amended;
For when that he himself concluded had,
He thought each other manne's wit so bad,
That impossible it were to reply
Against his choice; this was his fantasy.
His friendes sent he to, at his instance,
And prayed them to do him that pleasance,
That hastily they would unto him come;
He would abridge their labour all and some:
Needed no more for them to go nor ride,
He was appointed where he would abide.   *he had definitively
        made his choice*

Placebo came, and eke his friendes soon,
And *alderfirst he bade them all a boon,*   *first of all he asked
        a favour of them*
That none of them no arguments would make
Against the purpose that he had y-take:
Which purpose was pleasant to God, said he,
And very ground of his prosperity.

He said, there was a maiden in the town,
Which that of beauty hadde great renown;
All* were it so she were of small degree, *although
Sufficed him her youth and her beauty;
Which maid, he said, he would have to his wife,
To lead in ease and holiness his life;
And thanked God, that he might have her all,
That no wight with his blisse parte* shall; *have a share
And prayed them to labour in this need,
And shape that he faile not to speed:
For then, he said, his spirit was at ease.
"Then is," quoth he, "nothing may me displease,
Save one thing pricketh in my conscience,
The which I will rehearse in your presence.
I have," quoth he, "heard said, full yore* ago, *long
There may no man have perfect blisses two,
This is to say, on earth and eke in heaven.
For though he keep him from the sinne's seven,
And eke from every branch of thilke tree,
Yet is there so perfect felicity,
And so great *ease and lust,* in marriage, *comfort and
    pleasure*
That ev'r I am aghast,* now in mine age *ashamed, afraid
That I shall head now so merry a life,
So delicate, withoute woe or strife,
That I shall have mine heav'n on earthe here.
For since that very heav'n is bought so dear,
With tribulation and great penance,
How should I then, living in such pleasance
As alle wedded men do with their wives,
Come to the bliss where Christ *etern on live is?* *lives
    eternally*
This is my dread;* and ye, my brethren tway, *doubt
Assoile* me this question, I you pray." *resolve, answer

297

Justinus, which that hated his folly,
Answer'd anon right in his japery;* *mockery, jesting way
And, for he would his longe tale abridge,
He woulde no authority* allege, *written texts
But saide; "Sir, so there be none obstacle
Other than this, God of his high miracle,
And of his mercy, may so for you wirch,* *work
That, ere ye have your rights of holy church,
Ye may repent of wedded manne's life,
In which ye say there is no woe nor strife:
And elles God forbid, *but if* he sent *unless
A wedded man his grace him to repent
Well often, rather than a single man.
And therefore, Sir, *the beste rede I can,* *this is the best
     counsel that I know*
Despair you not, but have in your memory,
Paraventure she may be your purgatory;
She may be Godde's means, and Godde's whip;
And then your soul shall up to heaven skip
Swifter than doth an arrow from a bow.
I hope to God hereafter ye shall know
That there is none so great felicity
In marriage, nor ever more shall be,
That you shall let* of your salvation; *hinder
So that ye use, as skill is and reason,
The lustes* of your wife attemperly,** *pleasures **moderately
And that ye please her not too amorously,
And that ye keep you eke from other sin.
My tale is done, for my wit is but thin.
Be not aghast* hereof, my brother dear, *alarmed, afraid
But let us waden out of this mattere,
The Wife of Bath, if ye have understand,
Of marriage, which ye have now in hand,
Declared hath full well in little space;
Fare ye now well, God have you in his grace."

And with this word this Justin' and his brother
Have ta'en their leave, and each of them of other.
And when they saw that it must needes be,
They wroughte so, by sleight and wise treaty,
That she, this maiden, which that *Maius hight,* *was named
    May*
As hastily as ever that she might,
Shall wedded be unto this January.
I trow it were too longe you to tarry,
If I told you of every *script and band* *written bond*
By which she was feoffed in his hand;
Or for to reckon of her rich array
But finally y-comen is the day
That to the churche bothe be they went,
For to receive the holy sacrament,
Forth came the priest, with stole about his neck,
And bade her be like Sarah and Rebecc'
In wisdom and in truth of marriage;
And said his orisons, as is usage,
And crouched* them, and prayed God should them bless,
    *crossed
And made all sicker* enough with holiness. *certain

Thus be they wedded with solemnity;
And at the feaste sat both he and she,
With other worthy folk, upon the dais.
All full of joy and bliss is the palace,
And full of instruments, and of vitaille,* *victuals, food
The moste dainteous* of all Itale. *delicate
Before them stood such instruments of soun',
That Orpheus, nor of Thebes Amphioun,
Ne made never such a melody.
At every course came in loud minstrelsy,
That never Joab trumped for to hear,
Nor he, Theodomas, yet half so clear

At Thebes, when the city was in doubt.
Bacchus the wine them skinked* all about. *poured
And Venus laughed upon every wight
(For January was become her knight,
And woulde both assaye his courage
In liberty, and eke in marriage),
And with her firebrand in her hand about
Danced before the bride and all the rout.
And certainly I dare right well say this,
Hymeneus, that god of wedding is,
Saw never his life so merry a wedded man.
Hold thou thy peace, thou poet Marcian,
That writest us that ilke* wedding merry *same
Of her Philology and him Mercury,
And of the songes that the Muses sung;
Too small is both thy pen, and eke thy tongue
For to describen of this marriage.
When tender youth hath wedded stooping age,
There is such mirth that it may not be writ;
Assay it youreself, then may ye wit* *know
If that I lie or no in this mattere.

Maius, that sat with so benign a cheer,* *countenance
Her to behold it seemed faerie;
Queen Esther never look'd with such an eye
On Assuere, so meek a look had she;
I may you not devise all her beauty;
But thus much of her beauty tell I may,
That she was hike the bright morrow of May
Full filled of all beauty and pleasance.
This January is ravish'd in a trance,
At every time he looked in her face;
But in his heart he gan her to menace,
That he that night in armes would her strain
Harder than ever Paris did Helene.

But natheless yet had he great pity
That thilke night offende her must he,
And thought, "Alas, O tender creature,
Now woulde God ye mighte well endure
All my courage, it is so sharp and keen;
I am aghast* ye shall it not sustene.   *afraid
But God forbid that I did all my might.
Now woulde God that it were waxen night,
And that the night would lasten evermo'.
I would that all this people were y-go."*   *gone away
And finally he did all his labour,
As he best mighte, saving his honour,
To haste them from the meat in subtle wise.

The time came that reason was to rise;
And after that men dance, and drinke fast,
And spices all about the house they cast,
And full of joy and bliss is every man,
All but a squire, that highte Damian,
Who carv'd before the knight full many a day;
He was so ravish'd on his lady May,
That for the very pain he was nigh wood;*   *mad
Almost he swelt* and swooned where he stood, *fainted
So sore had Venus hurt him with her brand,
As that she bare it dancing in her hand.
And to his bed he went him hastily;
No more of him as at this time speak I;
But there I let him weep enough and plain,*   *bewail
Till freshe May will rue upon his pain.
O perilous fire, that in the bedstraw breedeth!
O foe familiar,* that his service bedeth!**   *domestic **offers
O servant traitor, O false homely hewe,*   *servant
Like to the adder in bosom shy untrue,
God shield us alle from your acquaintance!
O January, drunken in pleasance

Of marriage, see how thy Damian,
Thine owen squier and thy boren* man, *born
Intendeth for to do thee villainy:* *dishonour, outrage
God grante thee thine *homely foe* t'espy. *enemy in the
    household*
For in this world is no worse pestilence
Than homely foe, all day in thy presence.

Performed hath the sun his arc diurn,* *daily
No longer may the body of him sojourn
On the horizon, in that latitude:
Night with his mantle, that is dark and rude,
Gan overspread the hemisphere about:
For which departed is this *lusty rout* *pleasant company*
From January, with thank on every side.
Home to their houses lustily they ride,
Where as they do their thinges as them lest,
And when they see their time they go to rest.
Soon after that this hasty* January *eager
Will go to bed, he will no longer tarry.
He dranke hippocras, clarre, and vernage
Of spices hot, to increase his courage;
And many a lectuary* had he full fine, *potion
Such as the cursed monk Dan Constantine
Hath written in his book *de Coitu;* *of sexual intercourse*
To eat them all he would nothing eschew:
And to his privy friendes thus said he:
"For Godde's love, as soon as it may be,
Let *voiden all* this house in courteous wise." *everyone leave*
And they have done right as he will devise.
Men drinken, and the travers* draw anon; *curtains
The bride is brought to bed as still as stone;
And when the bed was with the priest y-bless'd,
Out of the chamber every wight him dress'd,
And January hath fast in arms y-take

His freshe May, his paradise, his make.* *mate
He lulled her, he kissed her full oft;
With thicke bristles of his beard unsoft,
Like to the skin of houndfish,* sharp as brere** *dogfish **briar
(For he was shav'n all new in his mannere),
He rubbed her upon her tender face,
And saide thus; "Alas! I must trespace
To you, my spouse, and you greatly offend,
Ere time come that I will down descend.
But natheless consider this," quoth he,
"There is no workman, whatsoe'er he be,
That may both worke well and hastily:
This will be done at leisure perfectly.
It is *no force* how longe that we play; *no matter*
In true wedlock coupled be we tway;
And blessed be the yoke that we be in,
For in our actes may there be no sin.
A man may do no sinne with his wife,
Nor hurt himselfe with his owen knife;
For we have leave to play us by the law."

Thus labour'd he, till that the day gan daw,
And then he took a sop in fine clarre,
And upright in his bedde then sat he.
And after that he sang full loud and clear,
And kiss'd his wife, and made wanton cheer.
He was all coltish, full of ragerie * *wantonness
And full of jargon as a flecked pie.
The slacke skin about his necke shaked,
While that he sang, so chanted he and craked.* *quavered
But God wot what that May thought in her heart,
When she him saw up sitting in his shirt
In his night-cap, and with his necke lean:
She praised not his playing worth a bean.
Then said he thus; "My reste will I take

303

Now day is come, I may no longer wake;
And down he laid his head and slept till prime.
And afterward, when that he saw his time,
Up rose January, but freshe May
Helde her chamber till the fourthe day,
As usage is of wives for the best.
For every labour some time must have rest,
Or elles longe may he not endure;
This is to say, no life of creature,
Be it of fish, or bird, or beast, or man.

Now will I speak of woeful Damian,
That languisheth for love, as ye shall hear;
Therefore I speak to him in this manneare.
I say. "O silly Damian, alas!
Answer to this demand, as in this case,
How shalt thou to thy lady, freshe May,
Telle thy woe? She will alway say nay;
Eke if thou speak, she will thy woe bewray;* *betray
God be thine help, I can no better say.
This sicke Damian in Venus' fire
So burned that he died for desire;
For which he put his life *in aventure,* *at risk*
No longer might he in this wise endure;
But privily a penner* gan he borrow, *writing-case
And in a letter wrote he all his sorrow,
In manner of a complaint or a lay,
Unto his faire freshe lady May.
And in a purse of silk, hung on his shirt,
He hath it put, and laid it at his heart.

The moone, that at noon was thilke* day *that
That January had wedded freshe May,
In ten of Taure, was into Cancer glided;
So long had Maius in her chamber abided,

As custom is unto these nobles all.
A bride shall not eaten in the ball
Till dayes four, or three days at the least,
Y-passed be; then let her go to feast.
The fourthe day complete from noon to noon,
When that the highe masse was y-done,
In halle sat this January, and May,
As fresh as is the brighte summer's day.
And so befell, how that this goode man
Remember'd him upon this Damian.
And saide; "Saint Mary, how may this be,
That Damian attendeth not to me?
Is he aye sick? or how may this betide?"
His squiers, which that stoode there beside,
Excused him, because of his sickness,
Which letted* him to do his business: *hindered
None other cause mighte make him tarry.
"That me forthinketh,"* quoth this January   *grieves, causes
                                                         uneasiness
"He is a gentle squier, by my truth;
If that he died, it were great harm and ruth.
He is as wise, as discreet, and secre',*   *secret, trusty
As any man I know of his degree,
And thereto manly and eke serviceble,
And for to be a thrifty man right able.
But after meat, as soon as ever I may
I will myself visit him, and eke May,
To do him all the comfort that I can."
And for that word him blessed every man,
That of his bounty and his gentleness
He woulde so comforten in sickness
His squier, for it was a gentle deed.

"Dame," quoth this January, "take good heed,
At after meat, ye with your women all

(When that ye be in chamb'r out of this hall),
That all ye go to see this Damian:
Do him disport, he is a gentle man;
And telle him that I will him visite,
Have I nothing but rested me a lite: *when only I have rested
    me a little*
And speed you faste, for I will abide
Till that ye sleepe faste by my side."
And with that word he gan unto him call
A squier, that was marshal of his hall,
And told him certain thinges that he wo'ld.
This freshe May hath straight her way y-hold,
With all her women, unto Damian.
Down by his beddes side sat she than,* *then
Comforting him as goodly as she may.
This Damian, when that his time he say,* *saw
In secret wise his purse, and eke his bill,
In which that he y-written had his will,
Hath put into her hand withoute more,
Save that he sighed wondrous deep and sore,
And softely to her right thus said he:
"Mercy, and that ye not discover me:
For I am dead if that this thing be kid."* *discovered
The purse hath she in her bosom hid,
And went her way; ye get no more of me;
But unto January come is she,
That on his bedde's side sat full soft.
He took her, and he kissed her full oft,
And laid him down to sleep, and that anon.
She feigned her as that she muste gon
There as ye know that every wight must need;
And when she of this bill had taken heed,
She rent it all to cloutes* at the last, *fragments
And in the privy softely it cast.
Who studieth* now but faire freshe May? *is thoughtful

Adown by olde January she lay,
That slepte, till the cough had him awaked:
Anon he pray'd her strippe her all naked,
He would of her, he said, have some pleasance;
And said her clothes did him incumbrance.
And she obey'd him, be her *lefe or loth.* *willing or unwilling*
But, lest that precious* folk be with me wroth, *over-nice
How that he wrought I dare not to you tell,
Or whether she thought it paradise or hell;
But there I let them worken in their wise
Till evensong ring, and they must arise.

Were it by destiny, or aventure,* *chance
Were it by influence, or by nature,
Or constellation, that in such estate
The heaven stood at that time fortunate
As for to put a bill of Venus' works
(For alle thing hath time, as say these clerks),
To any woman for to get her love,
I cannot say; but greate God above,
That knoweth that none act is causeless,
He deem of all, for I will hold my peace. *let him judge*
But sooth is this, how that this freshe May
Hath taken such impression that day
Of pity on this sicke Damian,
That from her hearte she not drive can
The remembrance for *to do him ease.* *to satisfy his desire*
"Certain," thought she, "whom that this thing displease
I recke not, for here I him assure,
To love him best of any creature,
Though he no more haddee than his shirt."
Lo, pity runneth soon in gentle heart.
Here may ye see, how excellent franchise* *generosity
In women is when they them *narrow advise.* *closely consider*
Some tyrant is, — as there be many a one, —

That hath a heart as hard as any stone,
Which would have let him sterven* in the place   *die
Well rather than have granted him her grace;
And then rejoicen in her cruel pride.
And reckon not to be a homicide.
This gentle May, full filled of pity,
Right of her hand a letter maked she,
In which she granted him her very grace;
There lacked nought, but only day and place,
Where that she might unto his lust suffice:
For it shall be right as he will devise.
And when she saw her time upon a day
To visit this Damian went this May,
And subtilly this letter down she thrust
Under his pillow, read it if him lust.*   *pleased
She took him by the hand, and hard him twist
So secretly, that no wight of it wist,
And bade him be all whole; and forth she went
To January, when he for her sent.
Up rose Damian the nexte morrow,
All passed was his sickness and his sorrow.
He combed him, he proined him and picked,
He did all that unto his lady liked;
And eke to January he went as low
As ever did a dogge for the bow.
He is so pleasant unto every man
(For craft is all, whoso that do it can),
Every wight is fain to speak him good;
And fully in his lady's grace he stood.
Thus leave I Damian about his need,
And in my tale forth I will proceed.

Some clerke* holde that felicity   *writers, scholars
Stands in delight; and therefore certain he,
This noble January, with all his might

In honest wise as longeth* to a knight,   *belongeth
Shope* him to live full deliciously: *prepared, arranged
His housing, his array, as honestly*   *honourably, suitably
To his degree was maked as a king's.
Amonges other of his honest things
He had a garden walled all with stone;
So fair a garden wot I nowhere none.
For out of doubt I verily suppose
That he that wrote the *Romance of the Rose*
Could not of it the beauty well devise;*   *describe
Nor Priapus mighte not well suffice,
Though he be god of gardens, for to tell
The beauty of the garden, and the well*   *fountain
That stood under a laurel always green.
Full often time he, Pluto, and his queen
Proserpina, and all their faerie,
Disported them and made melody
About that well, and danced, as men told.
This noble knight, this January old
Such dainty* had in it to walk and play,   *pleasure
That he would suffer no wight to bear the key,
Save he himself, for of the small wicket
He bare always of silver a cliket,*   *key
With which, when that him list, he it unshet.*   *opened
And when that he would pay his wife's debt,
In summer season, thither would he go,
And May his wife, and no wight but they two;
And thinges which that were not done in bed,
He in the garden them perform'd and sped.
And in this wise many a merry day
Lived this January and fresh May,
But worldly joy may not always endure
To January, nor to no creatucere.

O sudden hap! O thou fortune unstable!
Like to the scorpion so deceivable,* *deceitful
That flatt'rest with thy head when thou wilt sting;
Thy tail is death, through thine envenoming.
O brittle joy! O sweete poison quaint!* *strange
O monster, that so subtilly canst paint
Thy giftes, under hue of steadfastness,
That thou deceivest bothe *more and less!* *great and small*
Why hast thou January thus deceiv'd,
That haddest him for thy full friend receiv'd?
And now thou hast bereft him both his eyen,
For sorrow of which desireth he to dien.
Alas! this noble January free,
Amid his lust* and his prosperity *pleasure
Is waxen blind, and that all suddenly.
He weeped and he wailed piteously;
And therewithal the fire of jealousy
(Lest that his wife should fall in some folly)
So burnt his hearte, that he woulde fain,
That some man bothe him and her had slain;
For neither after his death, nor in his life,
Ne would he that she were no love nor wife,
But ever live as widow in clothes black,
Sole as the turtle that hath lost her make.* *mate
But at the last, after a month or tway,
His sorrow gan assuage, soothe to say.
For, when he wist it might none other be,
He patiently took his adversity:
Save out of doubte he may not foregon
That he was jealous evermore-in-one:* *continually
Which jealousy was so outrageous,
That neither in hall, nor in none other house,
Nor in none other place never the mo'
He woulde suffer her to ride or go,
But if that he had hand on her alway. *unless

For which full often wepte freshe May,
That loved Damian so burningly
That she must either dien suddenly,
Or elles she must have him as her lest:* *pleased
She waited* when her hearte woulde brest.** *expected **burst
Upon that other side Damian
Becomen is the sorrowfullest man
That ever was; for neither night nor day
He mighte speak a word to freshe May,
As to his purpose, of no such mattere,
But if that January must it hear, *unless*
That had a hand upon her evermo'.
But natheless, by writing to and fro,
And privy signes, wist he what she meant,
And she knew eke the fine* of his intent. *end, aim

O January, what might it thee avail,
Though thou might see as far as shippes sail?
For as good is it blind deceiv'd to be,
As be deceived when a man may see.
Lo, Argus, which that had a hundred eyen,
For all that ever he could pore or pryen,
Yet was he blent;* and, God wot, so be mo', *deceived
That *weene wisly* that it be not so: *think confidently*
Pass over is an ease, I say no more.
This freshe May, of which I spake yore,* *previously
In warm wax hath *imprinted the cliket* *taken an impression
        of the key*
That January bare of the small wicket
By which into his garden oft he went;
And Damian, that knew all her intent,
The cliket counterfeited privily;
There is no more to say, but hastily
Some wonder by this cliket shall betide,
Which ye shall hearen, if ye will abide.

O noble Ovid, sooth say'st thou, God wot,
What sleight is it, if love be long and hot,
That he'll not find it out in some mannere?
By Pyramus and Thisbe may men lear;* *learn
Though they were kept full long and strait o'er all,
They be accorded,* rowning** through a wall, *agreed
    **whispering
Where no wight could have found out such a sleight.
But now to purpose; ere that dayes eight
Were passed of the month of July, fill* *it befell
That January caught so great a will,
Through egging* of his wife, him for to play *inciting
In his garden, and no wight but they tway,
That in a morning to this May said he:
"Rise up, my wife, my love, my lady free;
The turtle's voice is heard, mine owen sweet;
The winter is gone, with all his raines weet.* *wet
Come forth now with thine *eyen columbine* *eyes like the
    doves*
Well fairer be thy breasts than any wine.
The garden is enclosed all about;
Come forth, my white spouse; for, out of doubt,
Thou hast me wounded in mine heart, O wife:
No spot in thee was e'er in all thy life.
Come forth, and let us taken our disport;
I choose thee for my wife and my comfort."
Such olde lewed* wordes used he. *foolish, ignorant
On Damian a signe made she,
That he should go before with his cliket.
This Damian then hath opened the wicket,
And in he start, and that in such mannere
That no wight might him either see or hear;
And still he sat under a bush. Anon
This January, as blind as is a stone,
With Maius in his hand, and no wight mo',

Into this freshe garden is y-go,
And clapped to the wicket suddenly.
"Now, wife," quoth he, "here is but thou and I;
Thou art the creature that I beste love:
For, by that Lord that sits in heav'n above,
Lever* I had to dien on a knife,   *rather
Than thee offende, deare true wife.
For Godde's sake, think how I thee chees,*   *chose
Not for no covetise* doubteless,   *covetousness
But only for the love I had to thee.
And though that I be old, and may not see,
Be to me true, and I will tell you why.
Certes three thinges shall ye win thereby:
First, love of Christ, and to yourself honour,
And all mine heritage, town and tow'r.
I give it you, make charters as you lest;
This shall be done to-morrow ere sun rest,
So wisly* God my soule bring to bliss!   *surely
I pray you, on this covenant me kiss.
And though that I be jealous, wite* me not;   *blame
Ye be so deep imprinted in my thought,
That when that I consider your beauty,
And therewithal *th'unlikely eld* of me,   *dissimilar age*
I may not, certes, though I shoulde die,
Forbear to be out of your company,
For very love; this is withoute doubt:
Now kiss me, wife, and let us roam about."

This freshe May, when she these wordes heard,
Benignely to January answer'd;
But first and forward she began to weep:
"I have," quoth she, "a soule for to keep
As well as ye, and also mine honour,
And of my wifehood thilke* tender flow'r   *that same
Which that I have assured in your hond,

When that the priest to you my body bond:
Wherefore I will answer in this mannere,
With leave of you mine owen lord so dear.
I pray to God, that never dawn the day
That I *no sterve,* as foul as woman may, *do not die*
If e'er I do unto my kin that shame,
Or elles I impaire so my name,
That I bee false; and if I do that lack,
Do strippe me, and put me in a sack,
And in the nexte river do me drench:* *drown
I am a gentle woman, and no wench.
Why speak ye thus? but men be e'er untrue,
And women have reproof of you aye new.
Ye know none other dalliance, I believe,
But speak to us of untrust and repreve."* *reproof

And with that word she saw where Damian
Sat in the bush, and coughe she began;
And with her finger signe made she,
That Damian should climb upon a tree
That charged was with fruit; and up he went:
For verily he knew all her intent,
And every signe that she coulde make,
Better than January her own make.* *mate
For in a letter she had told him all
Of this matter, how that he worke shall.
And thus I leave him sitting in the perry,* *pear-tree
And January and May roaming full merry.

Bright was the day, and blue the firmament;
Phoebus of gold his streames down had sent
To gladden every flow'r with his warmness;
He was that time in Geminis, I guess,
But little from his declination
Of Cancer, Jove's exaltation.

And so befell, in that bright morning-tide,
That in the garden, on the farther side,
Pluto, that is the king of Faerie,
And many a lady in his company
Following his wife, the queen Proserpina, —
Which that he ravished out of Ethna,
While that she gather'd flowers in the mead
(In Claudian ye may the story read,
How in his grisly chariot he her fet*), — *fetched
This king of Faerie adown him set
Upon a bank of turfes fresh and green,
And right anon thus said he to his queen.
"My wife," quoth he, "there may no wight say nay, —
Experience so proves it every day, —
The treason which that woman doth to man.
Ten hundred thousand stories tell I can
Notable of your untruth and brittleness* *inconstancy
O Solomon, richest of all richess,
Full fill'd of sapience and worldly glory,
Full worthy be thy wordes of memory
To every wight that wit and reason can.* *knows
Thus praised he yet the bounte* of man: *goodness
'Among a thousand men yet found I one,
But of all women found I never none.'
Thus said this king, that knew your wickedness;
And Jesus, Filius Sirach, as I guess,
He spake of you but seldom reverence.
A wilde fire and corrupt pestilence
So fall upon your bodies yet to-night!
Ne see ye not this honourable knight?
Because, alas! that he is blind and old,
His owen man shall make him cuckold.
Lo, where he sits, the lechour, in the tree.
Now will I granten, of my majesty,
Unto this olde blinde worthy knight,

That he shall have again his eyen sight,
When that his wife will do him villainy;
Then shall be knowen all her harlotry,
Both in reproof of her and other mo'."
"Yea, Sir," quoth Proserpine," and will ye so?
Now by my mother Ceres' soul I swear
That I shall give her suffisant answer,
And alle women after, for her sake;
That though they be in any guilt y-take,
With face bold they shall themselves excuse,
And bear them down that woulde them accuse.
For lack of answer, none of them shall dien.

All* had ye seen a thing with both your eyen,   *although
Yet shall *we visage it* so hardily,   *confront it*
And weep, and swear, and chide subtilly,
That ye shall be as lewed* as be geese.   *ignorant, confounded
What recketh me of your authorities?
I wot well that this Jew, this Solomon,
Found of us women fooles many one:
But though that he founde no good woman,
Yet there hath found many another man
Women full good, and true, and virtuous;
Witness on them that dwelt in Christes house;
With martyrdom they proved their constance.
The Roman gestes make remembrance
Of many a very true wife also.
But, Sire, be not wroth, albeit so,
Though that he said he found no good woman,
I pray you take the sentence* of the man: *opinion, real meaning
He meant thus, that in *sovereign bounte*   *perfect goodness
Is none but God, no, neither *he nor she.*   *man nor woman*
Hey, for the very God that is but one,
Why make ye so much of Solomon?
What though he made a temple, Godde's house?

What though he were rich and glorious?
So made he eke a temple of false goddes;
How might he do a thing that more forbode* is? *forbidden
Pardie, as fair as ye his name emplaster,* *plaster over,
    "whitewash"
He was a lechour, and an idolaster,* *idolater
And in his eld he very* God forsook. *the true
And if that God had not (as saith the book)
Spared him for his father's sake, he should
Have lost his regne* rather** than he would. *kingdom **sooner
I *sette not of* all the villainy *value not*
That he of women wrote, a butterfly.
I am a woman, needes must I speak,
Or elles swell until mine hearte break.
For since he said that we be jangleresses,* *chatterers
As ever may I brooke* whole my tresses, *preserve
I shall not spare for no courtesy
To speak him harm, that said us villainy."
"Dame," quoth this Pluto, "be no longer wroth;
I give it up: but, since I swore mine oath
That I would grant to him his sight again,
My word shall stand, that warn I you certain:
I am a king; it sits* me not to lie." *becomes, befits
"And I," quoth she, "am queen of Faerie.
Her answer she shall have, I undertake,
Let us no more wordes of it make.
Forsooth, I will no longer you contrary."

Now let us turn again to January,
That in the garden with his faire May
Singeth well merrier than the popinjay:* *parrot
"You love I best, and shall, and other none."
So long about the alleys is he gone,
Till he was come to *that ilke perry,* *the same pear-tree*
Where as this Damian satte full merry

On high, among the freshe leaves green.
This freshe May, that is so bright and sheen,
Gan for to sigh, and said, "Alas my side!
Now, Sir," quoth she, "for aught that may betide,
I must have of the peares that I see,
Or I must die, so sore longeth me
To eaten of the smalle peares green;
Help, for her love that is of heaven queen!
I tell you well, a woman in my plight
May have to fruit so great an appetite,
That she may dien, but* she of it have." *unless
"Alas!" quoth he, "that I had here a knave* *servant
That coulde climb; alas! alas!" quoth he,
"For I am blind." "Yea, Sir, *no force,"* quoth she; *no matter*
"But would ye vouchesafe, for Godde's sake,
The perry in your armes for to take
(For well I wot that ye mistruste me),
Then would I climbe well enough," quoth she,
"So I my foot might set upon your back."
"Certes," said he, "therein shall be no lack,
Might I you helpe with mine hearte's blood."
He stooped down, and on his back she stood,
And caught her by a twist,* and up she go'th. *twig, bough
(Ladies, I pray you that ye be not wroth,
I cannot glose,* I am a rude man): *mince matters
And suddenly anon this Damian
Gan pullen up the smock, and in he throng.* *rushed
And when that Pluto saw this greate wrong,
To January he gave again his sight,
And made him see as well as ever he might.
And when he thus had caught his sight again,
Was never man of anything so fain:
But on his wife his thought was evermo'.
Up to the tree he cast his eyen two,
And saw how Damian his wife had dress'd,

In such mannere, it may not be express'd,
But if I woulde speak uncourteously.   *unless*
And up he gave a roaring and a cry,
As doth the mother when the child shall die;
"Out! help! alas! harow!" he gan to cry;
"O stronge, lady, stowre! what doest thou?"

And she answered: "Sir, what aileth you?
Have patience and reason in your mind,
I have you help'd on both your eyen blind.
On peril of my soul, I shall not lien,
As me was taught to helpe with your eyen,
Was nothing better for to make you see,
Than struggle with a man upon a tree:
God wot, I did it in full good intent."
"Struggle!" quoth he, "yea, algate* in it went.   *whatever way
God give you both one shame's death to dien!
He swived* thee; I saw it with mine eyen;   *enjoyed carnally
And elles be I hanged by the halse."*   *neck
"Then is," quoth she, "my medicine all false;
For certainly, if that ye mighte see,
Ye would not say these wordes unto me.
Ye have some glimpsing,* and no perfect sight." *glimmering
"I see," quoth he, "as well as ever I might,
(Thanked be God!) with both mine eyen two,
And by my faith me thought he did thee so."
"Ye maze,* ye maze, goode Sir," quoth she; *rave, are confused
"This thank have I for I have made you see:
Alas!" quoth she, "that e'er I was so kind."
"Now, Dame," quoth he, "let all pass out of mind;
Come down, my lefe,* and if I have missaid,   *love
God help me so, as I am *evil apaid.*   *dissatisfied*
But, by my father's soul, I ween'd have seen
How that this Damian had by thee lain,
And that thy smock had lain upon his breast."

"Yea, Sir," quoth she, "ye may *ween as ye lest:* *think as you
    please*
But, Sir, a man that wakes out of his sleep,
He may not suddenly well take keep* *notice
Upon a thing, nor see it perfectly,
Till that he be adawed* verily. *awakened
Right so a man, that long hath blind y-be,
He may not suddenly so well y-see,
First when his sight is newe come again,
As he that hath a day or two y-seen.
Till that your sight establish'd be a while,
There may full many a sighte you beguile.
Beware, I pray you, for, by heaven's king,
Full many a man weeneth to see a thing,
And it is all another than it seemeth;
He which that misconceiveth oft misdeemeth."
And with that word she leapt down from the tree.
This January, who is glad but he?
He kissed her, and clipped* her full oft, *embraced
And on her womb he stroked her full soft;
And to his palace home he hath her lad.* *led
Now, goode men, I pray you to be glad.
Thus endeth here my tale of January,
God bless us, and his mother, Sainte Mary.

THE SQUIRE'S TALE

"HEY! Godde's mercy!" said our Hoste tho,* *then
"Now such a wife I pray God keep me fro'.
Lo, suche sleightes and subtilities
In women be; for aye as busy as bees
Are they us silly men for to deceive,
And from the soothe* will they ever weive,** *truth **swerve,
    depart
As this Merchante's tale it proveth well.

But natheless, as true as any steel,
I have a wife, though that she poore be;
But of her tongue a labbing* shrew is she; *chattering
And yet* she hath a heap of vices mo'. *moreover
Thereof *no force;* let all such thinges go. *no matter*
But wit* ye what? in counsel** be it said, *know **secret,
    confidence
Me rueth sore I am unto her tied;
For, an'* I shoulde reckon every vice *if
Which that she hath, y-wis* I were too nice;** *certainly
    **foolish
And cause why, it should reported be
And told her by some of this company
(By whom, it needeth not for to declare,
Since women connen utter such chaffare),
And eke my wit sufficeth not thereto
To tellen all; wherefore my tale is do.* *done
Squier, come near, if it your wille be,
And say somewhat of love, for certes ye
Conne thereon as much as any man." *know about it*
"Nay, Sir," quoth he; "but such thing as I can,
With hearty will, — for I will not rebel
Against your lust,* — a tale will I tell. *pleasure
Have me excused if I speak amiss;
My will is good; and lo, my tale is this."

THE TALE

Pars Prima. *First part*
At Sarra, in the land of Tartary,
There dwelt a king that warrayed* Russie, *made war on
Through which there died many a doughty man;
This noble king was called Cambuscan,
Which in his time was of so great renown,
That there was nowhere in no regioun

So excellent a lord in alle thing:
Him lacked nought that longeth to a king,
As of the sect of which that he was born.
He kept his law to which he was y-sworn,
And thereto* he was hardy, wise, and rich, *moreover, besides
And piteous and just, always y-lich;* *alike, even-tempered
True of his word, benign and honourable;
Of his corage as any centre stable; *firm, immovable of spirit*
Young, fresh, and strong, in armes desirous
As any bachelor of all his house.
A fair person he was, and fortunate,
And kept alway so well his royal estate,
That there was nowhere such another man.
This noble king, this Tartar Cambuscan,
Hadde two sons by Elfeta his wife,
Of which the eldest highte Algarsife,
The other was y-called Camballo.
A daughter had this worthy king also,
That youngest was, and highte Canace:
But for to telle you all her beauty,
It lies not in my tongue, nor my conning;* *skill
I dare not undertake so high a thing:
Mine English eke is insufficient,
It muste be a rhetor* excellent, *orator
That couth his colours longing for that art,
If he should her describen any part;
I am none such, I must speak as I can.

And so befell, that when this Cambuscan
Had twenty winters borne his diadem,
As he was wont from year to year, I deem,
He let *the feast of his nativity* *his birthday party*
Do crye, throughout Sarra his city, *be proclaimed*
The last Idus of March, after the year.
Phoebus the sun full jolly was and clear,

For he was nigh his exaltation
In Marte's face, and in his mansion
In Aries, the choleric hot sign:
Full lusty* was the weather and benign; *pleasant
For which the fowls against the sunne sheen,* *bright
What for the season and the younge green,
Full loude sange their affections:
Them seemed to have got protections
Against the sword of winter keen and cold.
This Cambuscan, of which I have you told,
In royal vesture, sat upon his dais,
With diadem, full high in his palace;
And held his feast so solemn and so rich,
That in this worlde was there none it lich.* *like
Of which if I should tell all the array,
Then would it occupy a summer's day;
And eke it needeth not for to devise* *describe
At every course the order of service.
I will not tellen of their strange sewes,* *dishes
Nor of their swannes, nor their heronsews.* *young herons
Eke in that land, as telle knightes old,
There is some meat that is full dainty hold,
That in this land men *reck of* it full small: *care for*
There is no man that may reporten all.
I will not tarry you, for it is prime,
And for it is no fruit, but loss of time;
Unto my purpose* I will have recourse. *story
And so befell that, after the third course,
While that this king sat thus in his nobley,* *noble array
Hearing his ministreles their thinges play
Before him at his board deliciously,
In at the halle door all suddenly
There came a knight upon a steed of brass,
And in his hand a broad mirror of glass;
Upon his thumb he had of gold a ring,

And by his side a naked sword hanging:
And up he rode unto the highe board.
In all the hall was there not spoke a word,
For marvel of this knight; him to behold
Full busily they waited,* young and old.   *watched

This strange knight, that came thus suddenly,
All armed, save his head, full richely,
Saluted king, and queen, and lordes all,
By order as they satten in the hall,
With so high reverence and observance,
As well in speech as in his countenance,
That Gawain with his olde courtesy,
Though he were come again out of Faerie,
Him *coulde not amende with a word.*   *could not better him
    by one word*
And after this, before the highe board,
He with a manly voice said his message,
After the form used in his language,
Withoute vice* of syllable or letter.   *fault
And, for his tale shoulde seem the better,
Accordant to his worde's was his cheer,*   *demeanour
As teacheth art of speech them that it lear.*   *learn
Albeit that I cannot sound his style,
Nor cannot climb over so high a stile,
Yet say I this, as to *commune intent,*   *general sense or meaning*
Thus much amounteth all that ever he meant,   *this is the
    sum of*
If it so be that I have it in mind.
He said; "The king of Araby and Ind,
My liege lord, on this solemne day
Saluteth you as he best can and may,
And sendeth you, in honour of your feast,
By me, that am all ready at your hest,*   *command
This steed of brass, that easily and well

Can in the space of one day naturel
(This is to say, in four-and-twenty hours),
Whereso you list, in drought or else in show'rs,
Beare your body into every place
To which your hearte willeth for to pace,*   *pass, go
Withoute wem* of you, through foul or fair.   *hurt, injury
Or if you list to fly as high in air
As doth an eagle, when him list to soar,
This same steed shall bear you evermore
Withoute harm, till ye be where *you lest*   *it pleases you*
(Though that ye sleepen on his back, or rest),
And turn again, with writhing* of a pin.   *twisting
He that it wrought, he coude* many a gin;**   *knew
    **contrivance
He waited* in any a constellation,   *observed
Ere he had done this operation,
And knew full many a seal and many a bond
This mirror eke, that I have in mine hond,
Hath such a might, that men may in it see
When there shall fall any adversity
Unto your realm, or to yourself also,
And openly who is your friend or foe.
And over all this, if any lady bright
Hath set her heart on any manner wight,
If he be false, she shall his treason see,
His newe love, and all his subtlety,
So openly that there shall nothing hide.
Wherefore, against this lusty summer-tide,
This mirror, and this ring that ye may see,
He hath sent to my lady Canace,
Your excellente daughter that is here.
The virtue of this ring, if ye will hear,
Is this, that if her list it for to wear
Upon her thumb, or in her purse it bear,
There is no fowl that flyeth under heaven,

That she shall not well understand his steven,* *speech, sound
And know his meaning openly and plain,
And answer him in his language again:
And every grass that groweth upon root
She shall eke know, to whom it will do boot,* *remedy
All be his woundes ne'er so deep and wide.
This naked sword, that hangeth by my side,
Such virtue hath, that what man that it smite,
Throughout his armour it will carve and bite,
Were it as thick as is a branched oak:
And what man is y-wounded with the stroke
Shall ne'er be whole, till that you list, of grace,
To stroke him with the flat in thilke* place *the same
Where he is hurt; this is as much to sayn,
Ye muste with the flatte sword again
Stroke him upon the wound, and it will close.
This is the very sooth, withoute glose;* *deceit
It faileth not, while it is in your hold."

And when this knight had thus his tale told,
He rode out of the hall, and down he light.
His steede, which that shone as sunne bright,
Stood in the court as still as any stone.
The knight is to his chamber led anon,
And is unarmed, and to meat y-set.* *seated
These presents be full richely y-fet,* — *fetched
This is to say, the sword and the mirrour, —
And borne anon into the highe tow'r,
With certain officers ordain'd therefor;
And unto Canace the ring is bore
Solemnely, where she sat at the table;
But sickerly, withouten any fable,
The horse of brass, that may not be remued.* *removed
It stood as it were to the ground y-glued;
There may no man out of the place it drive

For no engine of windlass or polive; * *pulley
And cause why, for they *can not the craft;* *know not the
      cunning of the mechanism*
And therefore in the place they have it laft,
Till that the knight hath taught them the mannere
To voide* him, as ye shall after hear. *remove

Great was the press, that swarmed to and fro
To gauren* on this horse that stoode so: *gaze
For it so high was, and so broad and long,
So well proportioned for to be strong,
Right as it were a steed of Lombardy;
Therewith so horsely, and so quick of eye,
As it a gentle Poileis courser were:
For certes, from his tail unto his ear
Nature nor art ne could him not amend
In no degree, as all the people wend.* *weened, thought
But evermore their moste wonder was
How that it coulde go, and was of brass;
It was of Faerie, as the people seem'd.
Diverse folk diversely they deem'd;
As many heads, as many wittes been.
They murmured, as doth a swarm of been,* *bees
And made skills* after their fantasies, *reasons
Rehearsing of the olde poetries,
And said that it was like the Pegasee,* *Pegasus
The horse that hadde winges for to flee;* *fly
Or else it was the Greeke's horse Sinon,
That broughte Troye to destruction,
As men may in the olde gestes* read. *tales of adventures
"Mine heart," quoth one, "is evermore in dread;
I trow some men of armes be therein,
That shape* them this city for to win: *design, prepare
It were right good that all such thing were know."
Another rowned* to his fellow low, *whispered

And said, "He lies; for it is rather like
An apparence made by some magic,
As jugglers playen at these feastes great."
Of sundry doubts they jangle thus and treat.
As lewed* people deeme commonly *ignorant
Of thinges that be made more subtilly
Than they can in their lewdness comprehend;
They *deeme gladly to the badder end.* *are ready to think
    the worst*
And some of them wonder'd on the mirrour,
That borne was up into the master* tow'r, *chief
How men might in it suche thinges see.
Another answer'd and said, it might well be
Naturally by compositions
Of angles, and of sly reflections;
And saide that in Rome was such a one.
They speak of Alhazen and Vitellon,
And Aristotle, that wrote in their lives
Of quainte* mirrors, and of prospectives, *curious
As knowe they that have their bookes heard.
And other folk have wonder'd on the swerd,* *sword
That woulde pierce throughout every thing;
And fell in speech of Telephus the king,
And of Achilles for his quainte spear,
For he could with it bothe heal and dere,* *wound
Right in such wise as men may with the swerd
Of which right now ye have yourselves heard.
They spake of sundry hard'ning of metal,
And spake of medicines therewithal,
And how, and when, it shoulde harden'd be,
Which is unknowen algate* unto me. *however
Then spake they of Canace's ring,
And saiden all, that such a wondrous thing
Of craft of rings heard they never none,
Save that he, Moses, and King Solomon,

Hadden *a name of conning* in such art. *a reputation for
   knowledge*
Thus said the people, and drew them apart.
Put natheless some saide that it was
Wonder to maken of fern ashes glass,
And yet is glass nought like ashes of fern;
But for they have y-knowen it so ferne** *because **before
Therefore ceaseth their jangling and their wonder.
As sore wonder some on cause of thunder,
On ebb and flood, on gossamer and mist,
And on all things, till that the cause is wist.* *known
Thus jangle they, and deemen and devise,
Till that the king gan from his board arise.

Phoebus had left the angle meridional,
And yet ascending was the beast royal,
The gentle Lion, with his Aldrian,
When that this Tartar king, this Cambuscan,
Rose from the board, there as he sat full high
Before him went the loude minstrelsy,
Till he came to his chamber of parements,
There as they sounded diverse instruments,
That it was like a heaven for to hear.
Now danced lusty Venus' children dear:
For in the Fish* their lady sat full *Pisces
And looked on them with a friendly eye.
This noble king is set upon his throne;
This strange knight is fetched to him full sone.* *soon
And on the dance he goes with Canace.
Here is the revel and the jollity,
That is not able a dull man to devise:* *describe
He must have knowen love and his service,
And been a feastly* man, as fresh as May, *merry, gay
That shoulde you devise such array.
Who coulde telle you the form of dances

GEOFFREY CHAUCER

So uncouth,* and so freshe countenances**   *unfamliar
    **gestures
Such subtle lookings and dissimulances,
For dread of jealous men's apperceivings?
No man but Launcelot, and he is dead.
Therefore I pass o'er all this lustihead* *pleasantness
I say no more, but in this jolliness
I leave them, till to supper men them dress.
The steward bids the spices for to hie* *haste
And eke the wine, in all this melody;
The ushers and the squiers be y-gone,
The spices and the wine is come anon;
They eat and drink, and when this hath an end,
Unto the temple, as reason was, they wend;
The service done, they suppen all by day
What needeth you rehearse their array?
Each man wot well, that at a kinge's feast
Is plenty, to the most*, and to the least, *highest
And dainties more than be in my knowing.

At after supper went this noble king
To see the horse of brass, with all a rout
Of lordes and of ladies him about.
Such wond'ring was there on this horse of brass,
That, since the great siege of Troye was,
There as men wonder'd on a horse also,
Ne'er was there such a wond'ring as was tho.* *there
But finally the king asked the knight
The virtue of this courser, and the might,
And prayed him to tell his governance.* *mode of managing him
The horse anon began to trip and dance,
When that the knight laid hand upon his rein,
And saide, "Sir, there is no more to sayn,
But when you list to riden anywhere,
Ye muste trill* a pin, stands in his ear, *turn

330

Which I shall telle you betwixt us two;
Ye muste name him to what place also,
Or to what country that you list to ride.
And when ye come where you list abide,
Bid him descend, and trill another pin
(For therein lies th' effect of all the gin*), *contrivance
And he will down descend and do your will,
And in that place he will abide still;
Though all the world had the contrary swore,
He shall not thence be thrown nor be bore.
Or, if you list to bid him thennes gon,
Trill this pin, and he will vanish anon
Out of the sight of every manner wight,
And come again, be it by day or night,
When that you list to clepe* him again *call
In such a guise, as I shall to you sayn
Betwixte you and me, and that full soon.
Ride when you list, there is no more to do'n."
Informed when the king was of the knight,
And had conceived in his wit aright
The manner and the form of all this thing,
Full glad and blithe, this noble doughty king
Repaired to his revel as beforn.
The bridle is into the tower borne,
And kept among his jewels lefe* and dear; *cherished
The horse vanish'd, I n'ot* in what mannere, *know not
Out of their sight; ye get no more of me:
But thus I leave in lust and jollity
This Cambuscan his lordes feastying,* *entertaining
Until well nigh the day began to spring.

Pars Secunda. *Second Part*
The norice* of digestion, the sleep, *nurse
Gan on them wink, and bade them take keep,* *heed
That muche mirth and labour will have rest.

And with a gaping* mouth he all them kest,** *yawning **kissed
And said, that it was time to lie down,
For blood was in his dominatioun:
"Cherish the blood, nature's friend," quoth he.
They thanked him gaping, by two and three;
And every wight gan draw him to his rest;
As sleep them bade, they took it for the best.
Their dreames shall not now be told for me;
Full are their heades of fumosity,
That caused dreams *of which there is no charge:* *of no
     significance*
They slepte; till that, it was *prime large,* *late morning*
The moste part, but* it was Canace; *except
She was full measurable,* as women be: *moderate
For of her father had she ta'en her leave
To go to rest, soon after it was eve;
Her liste not appalled* for to be; *to look pale
Nor on the morrow *unfeastly for to see;* *to look sad,
     depressed*
And slept her firste sleep; and then awoke.
For such a joy she in her hearte took
Both of her quainte a ring and her mirrour,.
That twenty times she changed her colour;
And in her sleep, right for th' impression
Of her mirror, she had a vision.
Wherefore, ere that the sunne gan up glide,
She call'd upon her mistress'* her beside, *governesses
And saide, that her liste for to rise.

These olde women, that be gladly wise
As are her mistresses answer'd anon,
And said; "Madame, whither will ye gon
Thus early? for the folk be all in rest."
"I will," quoth she, "arise; for me lest
No longer for to sleep, and walk about."

Her mistresses call'd women a great rout,
And up they rose, well a ten or twelve;
Up rose freshe Canace herselve,
As ruddy and bright as is the yonnge sun
That in the Ram is four degrees y-run;
No higher was he, when she ready was;
And forth she walked easily a pace,
Array'd after the lusty* season swoot,** *pleasant **sweet
Lightely for to play, and walk on foot,
Nought but with five or six of her meinie;
And in a trench* forth in the park went she. *sunken path
The vapour, which up from the earthe glode,* *glided
Made the sun to seem ruddy and broad:
But, natheless, it was so fair a sight
That it made all their heartes for to light,* *be lightened, glad
What for the season and the morrowning,
And for the fowles that she hearde sing.
For right anon she wiste* what they meant *knew
Right by their song, and knew all their intent.
The knotte,* why that every tale is told, *nucleus, chief matter
If it be tarried* till the list* be cold *delayed **inclination
Of them that have it hearken'd *after yore,* *for a long time*
The savour passeth ever longer more;
For fulsomness of the prolixity:
And by that same reason thinketh me.
I shoulde unto the knotte condescend,
And maken of her walking soon an end.

Amid a tree fordry*, as white as chalk, *thoroughly dried up
There sat a falcon o'er her head full high,
That with a piteous voice so gan to cry;
That all the wood resounded of her cry,
And beat she had herself so piteously
With both her winges, till the redde blood
Ran endelong* the tree, there as she stood *from top to bottom

And ever-in-one* alway she cried and shright;** *incessantly
  **shrieked
And with her beak herselfe she so pight,* *wounded
That there is no tiger, nor cruel beast,
That dwelleth either in wood or in forest;
But would have wept, if that he weepe could,
For sorrow of her; she shriek'd alway so loud.
For there was never yet no man alive,
If that he could a falcon well descrive;* *describe
That heard of such another of fairness
As well of plumage, as of gentleness;
Of shape, of all that mighte reckon'd be.
A falcon peregrine seemed she,
Of fremde* land; and ever as she stood *foreign
She swooned now and now for lack of blood;
Till well-nigh is she fallen from the tree.

This faire kinge's daughter Canace,
That on her finger bare the quainte ring,
Through which she understood well every thing
That any fowl may in his leden* sayn, *language
And could him answer in his leden again;
Hath understoode what this falcon said,
And well-nigh for the ruth* almost she died. *pity
And to the tree she went, full hastily,
And on this falcon looked piteously;
And held her lap abroad; for well she wist
The falcon muste falle from the twist* *twig, bough
When that she swooned next, for lack of blood.
A longe while to waite her she stood;
Till at the last she apake in this mannere
Unto the hawk, as ye shall after hear:
"What is the cause, if it be for to tell,
That ye be in this furial* pain of hell?" *raging, furious
Quoth Canace unto this hawk above;

"Is this for sorrow of death; or loss of love?
For; as I trow,* these be the causes two; *believe
That cause most a gentle hearte woe:
Of other harm it needeth not to speak.
For ye yourself upon yourself awreak;* *inflict
Which proveth well, that either ire or dread* *fear
Must be occasion of your cruel deed,
Since that I see none other wight you chase:
For love of God, as *do yourselfe grace;* *have mercy on yourself*
Or what may be your help? for, west nor east,
I never saw ere now no bird nor beast
That fared with himself so piteously
Ye slay me with your sorrow verily;
I have of you so great compassioun.
For Godde's love come from the tree adown
And, as I am a kinge's daughter true,
If that I verily the causes knew
Of your disease,* if it lay in my might, *distress
I would amend it, ere that it were night,
So wisly* help me the great God of kind.** *surely **nature
And herbes shall I right enoughe find,
To heale with your hurtes hastily."
Then shriek'd this falcon yet more piteously
Than ever she did, and fell to ground anon,
And lay aswoon, as dead as lies a stone,
Till Canace had in her lap her take,
Unto that time she gan of swoon awake:
And, after that she out of swoon abraid,* *awoke
Right in her hawke's leden thus she said:

"That pity runneth soon in gentle heart
(Feeling his simil'tude in paines smart),
Is proved every day, as men may see,
As well *by work as by authority;* *by experience as by doctrine*
For gentle hearte kitheth* gentleness. *sheweth

I see well, that ye have on my distress
Compassion, my faire Canace,
Of very womanly benignity
That nature in your princples hath set.
But for no hope for to fare the bet,* *better
But for t'obey unto your hearte free,
And for to make others aware by me,
As by the whelp chastis'd* is the lion, *instructed, corrected
Right for that cause and that conclusion,
While that I have a leisure and a space,
Mine harm I will confessen ere I pace."* *depart
And ever while the one her sorrow told,
The other wept, *as she to water wo'ld,* *as if she would
    dissolve into water*
Till that the falcon bade her to be still,
And with a sigh right thus she said *her till:* *to her*
"Where I was bred (alas that ilke* day!) *same
And foster'd in a rock of marble gray
So tenderly, that nothing ailed me,
I wiste* not what was adversity, *knew
Till I could flee* full high under the sky. *fly
Then dwell'd a tercelet me faste by,
That seem'd a well of alle gentleness;
All were he full of treason and falseness, *although he was*
It was so wrapped *under humble cheer,* *under an aspect of
    humility*
And under hue of truth, in such mannere,
Under pleasance, and under busy pain,
That no wight weened that he coulde feign,
So deep in grain he dyed his colours.
Right as a serpent hides him under flow'rs,
Till he may see his time for to bite,
Right so this god of love's hypocrite
Did so his ceremonies and obeisances,
And kept in semblance all his observances,

That *sounden unto* gentleness of love. *are consonant to*
As on a tomb is all the fair above,
And under is the corpse, which that ye wet,
Such was this hypocrite, both cold and hot;
And in this wise he served his intent,
That, save the fiend, none wiste what he meant:
Till he so long had weeped and complain'd,
And many a year his service to me feign'd,
Till that mine heart, too piteous and too nice,* *foolish, simple
All innocent of his crowned malice,
Forfeared of his death, as thoughte me, *greatly afraid lest
      he should die*
Upon his oathes and his surety
Granted him love, on this conditioun,
That evermore mine honour and renown
Were saved, bothe *privy and apert;* *privately and in public*
This is to say, that, after his desert,
I gave him all my heart and all my thought
(God wot, and he, that *other wayes nought*), *in no other way*
And took his heart in change of mine for aye.
But sooth is said, gone since many a day,
A true wight and a thiefe *think not one.* *do not think alike*
And when he saw the thing so far y-gone,
That I had granted him fully my love,
In such a wise as I have said above,
And given him my true heart as free
As he swore that he gave his heart to me,
Anon this tiger, full of doubleness,
Fell on his knees with so great humbleness,
With so high reverence, as by his cheer,* *mien
So like a gentle lover in mannere,
So ravish'd, as it seemed, for the joy,
That never Jason, nor Paris of Troy, —
Jason? certes, nor ever other man,
Since Lamech was, that alderfirst* began *first of all

To love two, as write folk beforn,
Nor ever since the firste man was born,
Coulde no man, by twenty thousand
Counterfeit the sophimes* of his art; *sophistries, beguilements
Where doubleness of feigning should approach,
Nor worthy were t'unbuckle his galoche,* *shoe
Nor could so thank a wight, as he did me.
His manner was a heaven for to see
To any woman, were she ne'er so wise;
So painted he and kempt,* *at point devise,* *combed, studied
As well his wordes as his countenance. *with perfect
    precision*
And I so lov'd him for his obeisance,
And for the truth I deemed in his heart,
That, if so were that any thing him smart,* *pained
All were it ne'er so lite,* and I it wist, *little
Methought I felt death at my hearte twist.
And shortly, so farforth this thing is went,* *gone
That my will was his wille's instrument;
That is to say, my will obey'd his will
In alle thing, as far as reason fill,* *fell; allowed
Keeping the boundes of my worship ever;
And never had I thing *so lefe, or lever,* *so dear, or dearer*
As him, God wot, nor never shall no mo'.

"This lasted longer than a year or two,
That I supposed of him naught but good.
But finally, thus at the last it stood,
That fortune woulde that he muste twin* *depart, separate
Out of that place which that I was in.
Whe'er* me was woe, it is no question; *whether
I cannot make of it description.
For one thing dare I telle boldely,
I know what is the pain of death thereby;
Such harm I felt, for he might not byleve.* *stay

So on a day of me he took his leave,
So sorrowful eke, that I ween'd verily,
That he had felt as muche harm as I,
When that I heard him speak, and saw his hue.
But natheless, I thought he was so true,
And eke that he repaire should again
Within a little while, sooth to sayn,
And reason would eke that he muste go
For his honour, as often happ'neth so,
That I made virtue of necessity,
And took it well, since that it muste be.
As I best might, I hid from him my sorrow,
And took him by the hand, Saint John to borrow,* *witness, pledge
And said him thus; 'Lo, I am youres all;
Be such as I have been to you, and shall.'
What he answer'd, it needs not to rehearse;
Who can say bet* than he, who can do worse? *better
When he had all well said, then had he done.
Therefore behoveth him a full long spoon,
That shall eat with a fiend; thus heard I say.
So at the last he muste forth his way,
And forth he flew, till he came where him lest.
When it came him to purpose for to rest,
I trow that he had thilke text in mind,
That alle thing repairing to his kind
Gladdeth himself; thus say men, as I guess;
Men love of [proper] kind newfangleness,
As birdes do, that men in cages feed.
For though thou night and day take of them heed,
And strew their cage fair and soft as silk,
And give them sugar, honey, bread, and milk,
Yet, *right anon as that his door is up,* *immediately on his
    door being opened*
He with his feet will spurne down his cup,
And to the wood he will, and wormes eat;

So newefangle be they of their meat,
And love novelties, of proper kind;
No gentleness of bloode may them bind.
So far'd this tercelet, alas the day!
Though he were gentle born, and fresh, and gay,
And goodly for to see, and humble, and free,
He saw upon a time a kite flee,* *fly
And suddenly he loved this kite so,
That all his love is clean from me y-go:
And hath his trothe falsed in this wise.
Thus hath the kite my love in her service,
And I am lorn* withoute remedy." *lost, undone

And with that word this falcon gan to cry,
And swooned eft* in Canace's barme** *again **lap
Great was the sorrow, for that hawke's harm,
That Canace and all her women made;
They wist not how they might the falcon glade.* *gladden
But Canace home bare her in her lap,
And softely in plasters gan her wrap,
There as she with her beak had hurt herselve.
Now cannot Canace but herbes delve
Out of the ground, and make salves new
Of herbes precious and fine of hue,
To heale with this hawk; from day to night
She did her business, and all her might.
And by her bedde's head she made a mew,* *bird cage
And cover'd it with velouettes* blue, *velvets
In sign of truth that is in woman seen;
And all without the mew is painted green,
In which were painted all these false fowls,
As be these tidifes,* tercelets, and owls; *titmice
And pies, on them for to cry and chide,
Right for despite were painted them beside.

Thus leave I Canace her hawk keeping.
I will no more as now speak of her ring,
Till it come eft* to purpose for to sayn *again
How that this falcon got her love again
Repentant, as the story telleth us,
By mediation of Camballus,
The kinge's son of which that I you told.
But henceforth I will my process hold
To speak of aventures, and of battailes,
That yet was never heard so great marvailles.
First I will telle you of Cambuscan,
That in his time many a city wan;
And after will I speak of Algarsife,
How he won Theodora to his wife,
For whom full oft in great peril he was,
N'had he been holpen by the horse of brass. *had he not*
And after will I speak of Camballo,
That fought in listes with the brethren two
For Canace, ere that he might her win;
And where I left I will again begin.

. . . .

THE FRANKLIN'S TALE

"In faith, Squier, thou hast thee well acquit,
And gentilly; I praise well thy wit,"
Quoth the Franklin; "considering thy youthe
So feelingly thou speak'st, Sir, I aloue* thee, *allow, approve
As to my doom, there is none that is here *so far as my
     judgment goes*
Of eloquence that shall be thy peer,
If that thou live; God give thee goode chance,
And in virtue send thee continuance,
For of thy speaking I have great dainty.* *value, esteem
I have a son, and, by the Trinity;

It were me lever than twenty pound worth land, *I would
    rather*
Though it right now were fallen in my hand,
He were a man of such discretion
As that ye be: fy on possession,
But if a man be virtuous withal. *unless
I have my sone snibbed* and yet shall, *rebuked, snubbed
For he to virtue *listeth not t'intend,* *does not wish to apply
    himself*
But for to play at dice, and to dispend,
And lose all that he hath, is his usage;
And he had lever talke with a page,
Than to commune with any gentle wight,
There he might learen gentilless aright."

"Straw for your gentillesse!" quoth our Host.
"What? Frankelin, pardie, Sir, well thou wost* *knowest
That each of you must tellen at the least
A tale or two, or breake his behest."* *promise
"That know I well, Sir," quoth the Frankelin;
"I pray you have me not in disdain,
Though I to this man speak a word or two."
"Tell on thy tale, withoute wordes mo'."
"Gladly, Sir Host," quoth he, "I will obey
Unto your will; now hearken what I say;
I will you not contrary* in no wise, *disobey
As far as that my wittes may suffice.
I pray to God that it may please you,
Then wot I well that it is good enow.

"These olde gentle Bretons, in their days,
Of divers aventures made lays,
Rhymeden in their firste Breton tongue;
Which layes with their instruments they sung,
Or elles reade them for their pleasance;

And one of them have I in remembrance,
Which I shall say with good will as I can.
But, Sirs, because I am a borel* man,   *rude, unlearned
At my beginning first I you beseech
Have me excused of my rude speech.
I learned never rhetoric, certain;
Thing that I speak, it must be bare and plain.
I slept never on the mount of Parnasso,
Nor learned Marcus Tullius Cicero.
Coloures know I none, withoute dread,*   *doubt
But such colours as growen in the mead,
Or elles such as men dye with or paint;
Colours of rhetoric be to me quaint;*   *strange
My spirit feeleth not of such mattere.
But, if you list, my tale shall ye hear."

THE TALE

In Armoric', that called is Bretagne,
There was a knight, that lov'd and *did his pain*   *devoted
   himself, strove*
To serve a lady in his beste wise;
And many a labour, many a great emprise,*   *enterprise
He for his lady wrought, ere she were won:
For she was one the fairest under sun,
And eke thereto come of so high kindred,
That *well unnethes durst this knight for dread,
Tell her his woe, his pain, and his distress
But, at the last, she for his worthiness,
And namely* for his meek obeisance,   *especially
Hath such a pity caught of his penance,*   *suffering, distress
That privily she fell of his accord
To take him for her husband and her lord
(Of such lordship as men have o'er their wives);
And, for to lead the more in bliss their lives,

Of his free will he swore her as a knight,
That never in all his life he day nor night
Should take upon himself no mastery
Against her will, nor kithe* her jealousy, *show
But her obey, and follow her will in all,
As any lover to his lady shall;
Save that the name of sovereignty
That would he have, for shame of his degree.
She thanked him, and with full great humbless
She saide; "Sir, since of your gentleness
Ye proffer me to have so large a reign,
*Ne woulde God never betwixt us twain,
As in my guilt, were either war or strife:
Sir, I will be your humble true wife,
Have here my troth, till that my hearte brest."* *burst
Thus be they both in quiet and in rest.

For one thing, Sires, safely dare I say,
That friends ever each other must obey,
If they will longe hold in company.
Love will not be constrain'd by mastery.
When mast'ry comes, the god of love anon
Beateth his wings, and, farewell, he is gone.
Love is a thing as any spirit free.
Women *of kind* desire liberty, *by nature*
And not to be constrained as a thrall,* *slave
And so do men, if soothly I say shall.
Look who that is most patient in love,
He *is at his advantage all above.* *enjoys the highest advantages
  of all*
Patience is a high virtue certain,
For it vanquisheth, as these clerkes sayn,
Thinges that rigour never should attain.
For every word men may not chide or plain.
Learne to suffer, or, so may I go,* *prosper

Ye shall it learn whether ye will or no.
For in this world certain no wight there is,
That he not doth or saith sometimes amiss.
Ire, or sickness, or constellation,* *the influence of the planets*
Wine, woe, or changing of complexion,
Causeth full oft to do amiss or speaken:
On every wrong a man may not be wreaken.* *revenged
After* the time must be temperance *according to
To every wight that *can of* governance. *is capable of*
And therefore hath this worthy wise knight
(To live in ease) sufferance her behight;* *promised
And she to him full wisly* gan to swear *surely
That never should there be default in her.
Here may men see a humble wife accord;
Thus hath she ta'en her servant and her lord,
Servant in love, and lord in marriage.
Then was he both in lordship and servage?
Servage? nay, but in lordship all above,
Since he had both his lady and his love:
His lady certes, and his wife also,
The which that law of love accordeth to.
And when he was in this prosperrity,
Home with his wife he went to his country,
Not far from Penmark, where his dwelling was,
And there he liv'd in bliss and in solace.* *delight
Who coulde tell, but* he had wedded be, *unless
The joy, the ease, and the prosperity,
That is betwixt a husband and his wife?
A year and more lasted this blissful life,
Till that this knight, of whom I spake thus,
That of Cairrud was call'd Arviragus,
Shope* him to go and dwell a year or twain *prepared, arranged
In Engleland, that call'd was eke Britain,

To seek in armes worship and honour
(For all his lust* he set in such labour); *pleasure
And dwelled there two years; the book saith thus.

Now will I stint* of this Arviragus, *cease speaking
And speak I will of Dorigen his wife,
That lov'd her husband as her hearte's life.
For his absence weepeth she and siketh,* *sigheth
As do these noble wives when them liketh;
She mourneth, waketh, waileth, fasteth, plaineth;
Desire of his presence her so distraineth,
That all this wide world she set at nought.
Her friendes, which that knew her heavy thought,
Comforte her in all that ever they may;
They preache her, they tell her night and day,
That causeless she slays herself, alas!
And every comfort possible in this case
They do to her, with all their business,* *assiduity
And all to make her leave her heaviness.
By process, as ye knowen every one,
Men may so longe graven in a stone,
Till some figure therein imprinted be:
So long have they comforted her, till she
Received hath, by hope and by reason,
Th' imprinting of their consolation,
Through which her greate sorrow gan assuage;
She may not always duren in such rage.
And eke Arviragus, in all this care,
Hath sent his letters home of his welfare,
And that he will come hastily again,
Or elles had this sorrow her hearty-slain.
Her friendes saw her sorrow gin to slake,* *slacken, diminish
And prayed her on knees for Godde's sake
To come and roamen in their company,
Away to drive her darke fantasy;

And finally she granted that request,
For well she saw that it was for the best.

Now stood her castle faste by the sea,
And often with her friendes walked she,
Her to disport upon the bank on high,
There as many a ship and barge sigh,* *saw
Sailing their courses, where them list to go.
But then was that a parcel* of her woe, *part
For to herself full oft, "Alas!" said she,
Is there no ship, of so many as I see,
Will bringe home my lord? then were my heart
All warish'd* of this bitter paine's smart." *cured
Another time would she sit and think,
And cast her eyen downward from the brink;
But when she saw the grisly rockes blake,* *black
For very fear so would her hearte quake,
That on her feet she might her not sustene* *sustain
Then would she sit adown upon the green,
And piteously *into the sea behold,* *look out on the sea*
And say right thus, with *careful sikes* cold: *painful sighs*
"Eternal God! that through thy purveyance
Leadest this world by certain governance,
In idle, as men say, ye nothing make; *idly, in vain*
But, Lord, these grisly fiendly rockes blake,
That seem rather a foul confusion
Of work, than any fair creation
Of such a perfect wise God and stable,
Why have ye wrought this work unreasonable?
For by this work, north, south, or west, or east,
There is not foster'd man, nor bird, nor beast:
It doth no good, to my wit, but *annoyeth.* *works mischief*
See ye not, Lord, how mankind it destroyeth?
A hundred thousand bodies of mankind

Have rockes slain, *all be they not in mind;* *though they are
    forgotten*
Which mankind is so fair part of thy work,
Thou madest it like to thine owen mark.* *image
Then seemed it ye had a great cherte* *love, affection
Toward mankind; but how then may it be
That ye such meanes make it to destroy?
Which meanes do no good, but ever annoy.
I wot well, clerkes will say as them lest,* *please
By arguments, that all is for the best,
Although I can the causes not y-know;
But thilke* God that made the wind to blow, *that
As keep my lord, this is my conclusion:
To clerks leave I all disputation:
But would to God that all these rockes blake
Were sunken into helle for his sake
These rockes slay mine hearte for the fear."
Thus would she say, with many a piteous tear.

Her friendes saw that it was no disport
To roame by the sea, but discomfort,
And shope* them for to playe somewhere else. *arranged
They leade her by rivers and by wells,
And eke in other places delectables;
They dancen, and they play at chess and tables.* *backgammon
So on a day, right in the morning-tide,
Unto a garden that was there beside,
In which that they had made their ordinance* *provision,
    arrangement
Of victual, and of other purveyance,
They go and play them all the longe day:
And this was on the sixth morrow of May,
Which May had painted with his softe showers
This garden full of leaves and of flowers:
And craft of manne's hand so curiously

Arrayed had this garden truely,
That never was there garden of such price,* *value, praise
But if it were the very Paradise. *unless*
Th'odour of flowers, and the freshe sight,
Would have maked any hearte light
That e'er was born, *but if* too great sickness *unless*
Or too great sorrow held it in distress;
So full it was of beauty and pleasance.
And after dinner they began to dance
And sing also, save Dorigen alone
Who made alway her complaint and her moan,
For she saw not him on the dance go
That was her husband, and her love also;
But natheless she must a time abide
And with good hope let her sorrow slide.

Upon this dance, amonge other men,
Danced a squier before Dorigen
That fresher was, and jollier of array
As to my doom, than is the month of May. *in my judgment*
He sang and danced, passing any man,
That is or was since that the world began;
Therewith he was, if men should him descrive,
One of the *beste faring* men alive, *most accomplished*
Young, strong, and virtuous, and rich, and wise,
And well beloved, and holden in great price.* *esteem, value
And, shortly if the sooth I telle shall,
Unweeting of this Dorigen at all, *unknown to*
This lusty squier, servant to Venus,
Which that y-called was Aurelius,
Had lov'd her best of any creature
Two year and more, as was his aventure;* *fortune
But never durst he tell her his grievance;
Withoute cup he drank all his penance.
He was despaired, nothing durst he say,

Save in his songes somewhat would he wray* *betray
His woe, as in a general complaining;
He said, he lov'd, and was belov'd nothing.
Of suche matter made he many lays,
Songes, complaintes, roundels, virelays
How that he durste not his sorrow tell,
But languished, as doth a Fury in hell;
And die he must, he said, as did Echo
For Narcissus, that durst not tell her woe.
In other manner than ye hear me say,
He durste not to her his woe bewray,
Save that paraventure sometimes at dances,
Where younge folke keep their observances,
It may well be he looked on her face
In such a wise, as man that asketh grace,
But nothing wiste she of his intent.
Nath'less it happen'd, ere they thennes* went, *thence
    (from the garden)*
Because that he was her neighebour,
And was a man of worship and honour,
And she had knowen him *of time yore,* *for a long time*
They fell in speech, and forth aye more and more
Unto his purpose drew Aurelius;
And when he saw his time, he saide thus:
"Madam," quoth he, "by God that this world made,
So that I wist it might your hearte glade,* *gladden
I would, that day that your Arviragus
Went over sea, that I, Aurelius,
Had gone where I should never come again;
For well I wot my service is in vain.
My guerdon* is but bursting of mine heart. *reward
Madame, rue upon my paine's smart,
For with a word ye may me slay or save.
Here at your feet God would that I were grave.
I have now no leisure more to say:

Have mercy, sweet, or you will *do me dey."* *cause me
   to die*

She gan to look upon Aurelius;
"Is this your will," quoth she, "and say ye thus?
Ne'er erst,"* quoth she, "I wiste what ye meant: *before
But now, Aurelius, I know your intent.
By thilke* God that gave me soul and life, *that
Never shall I be an untrue wife
In word nor work, as far as I have wit;
I will be his to whom that I am knit;
Take this for final answer as of me."
But after that *in play* thus saide she. *playfully, in jest*
"Aurelius," quoth she, "by high God above,
Yet will I grante you to be your love
(Since I you see so piteously complain);
Looke, what day that endelong* Bretagne *from end to
   end of
Ye remove all the rockes, stone by stone,
That they not lette* ship nor boat to gon, *prevent
I say, when ye have made this coast so clean
Of rockes, that there is no stone seen,
Then will I love you best of any man;
Have here my troth, in all that ever I can;
For well I wot that it shall ne'er betide.
Let such folly out of your hearte glide.
What dainty* should a man have in his life *value, pleasure
For to go love another manne's wife,
That hath her body when that ever him liketh?"
Aurelius full often sore siketh;* *sigheth
"Is there none other grace in you?" quoth he,
"No, by that Lord," quoth she, "that maked me."
Woe was Aurelius when that he this heard,
And with a sorrowful heart he thus answer'd.
"Madame," quoth he, "this were an impossible.

Then must I die of sudden death horrible."
And with that word he turned him anon.

Then came her other friends many a one,
And in the alleys roamed up and down,
And nothing wist of this conclusion,
But suddenly began to revel new,
Till that the brighte sun had lost his hue,
For th' horizon had reft the sun his light
(This is as much to say as it was night);
And home they go in mirth and in solace;
Save only wretch'd Aurelius, alas
He to his house is gone with sorrowful heart.
He said, he may not from his death astart.* *escape
Him seemed, that he felt his hearte cold.
Up to the heav'n his handes gan he hold,
And on his knees bare he set him down.
And in his raving said his orisoun.* *prayer
For very woe out of his wit he braid;* *wandered
He wist not what he spake, but thus he said;
With piteous heart his plaint hath he begun
Unto the gods, and first unto the Sun.
He said; "Apollo God and governour
Of every plante, herbe, tree, and flower,
That giv'st, after thy declination,
To each of them his time and his season,
As thine herberow* changeth low and high; *dwelling, situation
Lord Phoebus: cast thy merciable eye
On wretched Aurelius, which that am but lorn.* *undone
Lo, lord, my lady hath my death y-sworn,
Withoute guilt, but* thy benignity *unless
Upon my deadly heart have some pity.
For well I wot, Lord Phoebus, if you lest,* *please
Ye may me helpe, save my lady, best.
Now vouchsafe, that I may you devise* *tell, explain

How that I may be holp,* and in what wise. *helped
Your blissful sister, Lucina the sheen,
That of the sea is chief goddess and queen, —
Though Neptunus have deity in the sea,
Yet emperess above him is she; —
Ye know well, lord, that, right as her desire
Is to be quick'd* and lighted of your fire, *quickened
For which she followeth you full busily,
Right so the sea desireth naturally
To follow her, as she that is goddess
Both in the sea and rivers more and less.
Wherefore, Lord Phoebus, this is my request,
Do this miracle, or *do mine hearte brest;* *cause my heart
    to burst*
That flow, next at this opposition,
Which in the sign shall be of the Lion,
As praye her so great a flood to bring,
That five fathom at least it overspring
The highest rock in Armoric Bretagne,
And let this flood endure yeares twain:
Then certes to my lady may I say,
"Holde your hest," the rockes be away.
Lord Phoebus, this miracle do for me,
Pray her she go no faster course than ye;
I say this, pray your sister that she go
No faster course than ye these yeares two:
Then shall she be even at full alway,
And spring-flood laste bothe night and day.
And *but she* vouchesafe in such mannere *if she do not*
To grante me my sov'reign lady dear,
Pray her to sink every rock adown
Into her owen darke regioun
Under the ground, where Pluto dwelleth in
Or nevermore shall I my lady win.
Thy temple in Delphos will I barefoot seek.

Lord Phoebus! see the teares on my cheek
And on my pain have some compassioun."
And with that word in sorrow he fell down,
And longe time he lay forth in a trance.
His brother, which that knew of his penance,* *distress
Up caught him, and to bed he hath him brought,
Despaired in this torment and this thought
Let I this woeful creature lie;
Choose he for me whe'er* he will live or die. *whether

Arviragus with health and great honour
(As he that was of chivalry the flow'r)
Is come home, and other worthy men.
Oh, blissful art thou now, thou Dorigen!
Thou hast thy lusty husband in thine arms,
The freshe knight, the worthy man of arms,
That loveth thee as his own hearte's life:
Nothing list him to be imaginatif *he cared not to fancy*
If any wight had spoke, while he was out,
To her of love; he had of that no doubt;* *fear, suspicion
He not intended* to no such mattere, *occupied himself with
But danced, jousted, and made merry cheer.
And thus in joy and bliss I let them dwell,
And of the sick Aurelius will I tell
In languor and in torment furious
Two year and more lay wretch'd Aurelius,
Ere any foot on earth he mighte gon;
Nor comfort in this time had he none,
Save of his brother, which that was a clerk.* *scholar
He knew of all this woe and all this work;
For to none other creature certain
Of this matter he durst no worde sayn;
Under his breast he bare it more secree
Than e'er did Pamphilus for Galatee.
His breast was whole withoute for to seen,

But in his heart aye was the arrow keen,
And well ye know that of a sursanure
In surgery is perilous the cure,
But* men might touch the arrow or come thereby. *except
His brother wept and wailed privily,
Till at the last him fell in remembrance,
That while he was at Orleans in France, —
As younge clerkes, that be likerous* — *eager
To readen artes that be curious,
Seeken in every *halk and every hern* *nook and corner*
Particular sciences for to learn,—
He him remember'd, that upon a day
At Orleans in study a book he say* *saw
Of magic natural, which his fellaw,
That was that time a bachelor of law
All* were he there to learn another craft, *though
Had privily upon his desk y-laft;
Which book spake much of operations
Touching the eight and-twenty mansions
That longe to the Moon, and such folly
As in our dayes is not worth a fly;
For holy church's faith, in our believe,* *belief, creed
Us suff'reth none illusion to grieve.
And when this book was in his remembrance
Anon for joy his heart began to dance,
And to himself he saide privily;
"My brother shall be warish'd* hastily *cured
For I am sicker* that there be sciences, *certain
By which men make divers apparences,
Such as these subtle tregetoures play. *tricksters
For oft at feaste's have I well heard say,
That tregetours, within a halle large,
Have made come in a water and a barge,
And in the halle rowen up and down.
Sometimes hath seemed come a grim lioun,

And sometimes flowers spring as in a mead;
Sometimes a vine, and grapes white and red;
Sometimes a castle all of lime and stone;
And, when them liked, voided* it anon: *vanished
Thus seemed it to every manne's sight.
Now then conclude I thus; if that I might
At Orleans some olde fellow find,
That hath these Moone's mansions in mind,
Or other magic natural above.
He should well make my brother have his love.
For with an appearance a clerk* may make, *learned man
To manne's sight, that all the rockes blake
Of Bretagne were voided* every one, *removed
And shippes by the brinke come and gon,
And in such form endure a day or two;
Then were my brother warish'd* of his woe, *cured
Then must she needes *holde her behest,* *keep her promise*
Or elles he shall shame her at the least."
Why should I make a longer tale of this?
Unto his brother's bed he comen is,
And such comfort he gave him, for to gon
To Orleans, that he upstart anon,
And on his way forth-ward then is he fare,* *gone
In hope for to be lissed* of his care. *eased of

When they were come almost to that city,
But if it were a two furlong or three, *all but*
A young clerk roaming by himself they met,
Which that in Latin *thriftily them gret.* *greeted them civilly*
And after that he said a wondrous thing;
"I know," quoth he, "the cause of your coming;"
Aud ere they farther any foote went,
He told them all that was in their intent.
The Breton clerk him asked of fellaws
The which he hadde known in olde daws,* *days

And he answer'd him that they deade were,
For which he wept full often many a tear.
Down off his horse Aurelius light anon,
And forth with this magician is be gone
Home to his house, and made him well at ease;
Them lacked no vitail* that might them please. *victuals,
    food
So well-array'd a house as there was one,
Aurelius in his life saw never none.
He shewed him, ere they went to suppere,
Forestes, parkes, full of wilde deer.
There saw he hartes with their hornes high,
The greatest that were ever seen with eye.
He saw of them an hundred slain with hounds,
And some with arrows bleed of bitter wounds.
He saw, when voided* were the wilde deer, *passed away
These falconers upon a fair rivere,
That with their hawkes have the heron slain.
Then saw he knightes jousting in a plain.
And after this he did him such pleasance,
That he him shew'd his lady on a dance,
In which himselfe danced, as him thought.
And when this master, that this magic wrought,
Saw it was time, he clapp'd his handes two,
And farewell, all the revel is y-go.* *gone, removed
And yet remov'd they never out of the house,
While they saw all the sightes marvellous;
But in his study, where his bookes be,
They satte still, and no wight but they three.
To him this master called his squier,

And said him thus, "May we go to supper?
Almost an hour it is, I undertake,
Since I you bade our supper for to make,
When that these worthy men wente with me

Into my study, where my bookes be."
"Sir," quoth this squier, "when it liketh you.
It is all ready, though ye will right now."
"Go we then sup," quoth he, "as for the best;
These amorous folk some time must have rest."
At after supper fell they in treaty
What summe should this master's guerdon* be, *reward
To remove all the rockes of Bretagne,
And eke from Gironde to the mouth of Seine.
He made it strange,* and swore, so God him save, *a matter of
    difficulty*
Less than a thousand pound he would not have,
Nor gladly for that sum he would not gon.
Aurelius with blissful heart anon
Answered thus; "Fie on a thousand pound!
This wide world, which that men say is round,
I would it give, if I were lord of it.
This bargain is full-driv'n, for we be knit;* *agreed
Ye shall be payed truly by my troth.
But looke, for no negligence or sloth,
Ye tarry us here no longer than to-morrow."
"Nay," quoth the clerk, *"have here my faith to borrow."*
    I pledge my faith on it
To bed is gone Aurelius when him lest,
And well-nigh all that night he had his rest,
What for his labour, and his hope of bliss,
His woeful heart *of penance had a liss.* *had a respite from
    suffering*
Upon the morrow, when that it was day,
Unto Bretagne they took the righte way,
Aurelius and this magician beside,
And be descended where they would abide:
And this was, as the bookes me remember,
The colde frosty season of December.
Phoebus wax'd old, and hued like latoun,* *brass

That in his hote declinatioun
Shone as the burned gold, with streames* bright; *beams
But now in Capricorn adown he light,
Where as he shone full pale, I dare well sayn.
The bitter frostes, with the sleet and rain,
Destroyed have the green in every yard. *courtyard, garden
Janus sits by the fire with double beard,
And drinketh of his bugle horn the wine:
Before him stands the brawn of tusked swine
And "nowel"* crieth every lusty man *Noel
Aurelius, in all that ev'r he can,
Did to his master cheer and reverence,
And prayed him to do his diligence
To bringe him out of his paines smart,
Or with a sword that he would slit his heart.
This subtle clerk such ruth* had on this man, *pity
That night and day he sped him, that he can,
To wait a time of his conclusion;
This is to say, to make illusion,
By such an appearance of jugglery
(I know no termes of astrology),
That she and every wight should ween and say,
That of Bretagne the rockes were away,
Or else they were sunken under ground.
So at the last he hath a time found
To make his japes* and his wretchedness *tricks
Of such a *superstitious cursedness.* *detestable villainy*
His tables Toletanes forth he brought,
Full well corrected, that there lacked nought,
Neither his collect, nor his expanse years,
Neither his rootes, nor his other gears,
As be his centres, and his arguments,
And his proportional convenients
For his equations in everything.
And by his eighte spheres in his working,

359

He knew full well how far Alnath was shove
From the head of that fix'd Aries above,
That in the ninthe sphere consider'd is.
Full subtilly he calcul'd all this.
When he had found his firste mansion,
He knew the remnant by proportion;
And knew the rising of his moone well,
And in whose face, and term, and every deal;
And knew full well the moone's mansion
Accordant to his operation;
And knew also his other observances,
For such illusions and such meschances,* *wicked devices
As heathen folk used in thilke days.
For which no longer made he delays;
But through his magic, for a day or tway,
It seemed all the rockes were away.

Aurelius, which yet despaired is
Whe'er* he shall have his love, or fare amiss, *whether
Awaited night and day on this miracle:
And when he knew that there was none obstacle,
That voided* were these rockes every one, *removed
Down at his master's feet he fell anon,
And said; "I, woeful wretch'd Aurelius,
Thank you, my Lord, and lady mine Venus,
That me have holpen from my cares cold."
And to the temple his way forth hath he hold,
Where as he knew he should his lady see.
And when he saw his time, anon right he
With dreadful* heart and with full humble cheer** *fearful **mien
Saluteth hath his sovereign lady dear.
"My rightful Lady," quoth this woeful man,
"Whom I most dread, and love as I best can,
And lothest were of all this world displease,
Were't not that I for you have such disease,* *distress, affliction

That I must die here at your foot anon,
Nought would I tell how me is woebegone.
But certes either must I die or plain;* *bewail
Ye slay me guilteless for very pain.
But of my death though that ye have no ruth,
Advise you, ere that ye break your truth:
Repente you, for thilke God above,
Ere ye me slay because that I you love.
For, Madame, well ye wot what ye have hight;* *promised
Not that I challenge anything of right
Of you, my sovereign lady, but of grace:
But in a garden yond', in such a place,
Ye wot right well what ye behighte* me, *promised
And in mine hand your trothe plighted ye,
To love me best; God wot ye saide so,
Albeit that I unworthy am thereto;
Madame, I speak it for th' honour of you,
More than to save my hearte's life right now;
I have done so as ye commanded me,
And if ye vouchesafe, ye may go see.
Do as you list, have your behest in mind,
For, quick or dead, right there ye shall me find;
In you hes all to *do me live or dey;* *cause me to live or die*
But well I wot the rockes be away."

He took his leave, and she astonish'd stood;
In all her face was not one drop of blood:
She never ween'd t'have come in such a trap.
"Alas!" quoth she, "that ever this should hap!
For ween'd I ne'er, by possibility,
That such a monster or marvail might be;
It is against the process of nature."
And home she went a sorrowful creature;
For very fear unnethes* may she go. *scarcely
She weeped, wailed, all a day or two,

And swooned, that it ruthe was to see:
But why it was, to no wight tolde she,
For out of town was gone Arviragus.
But to herself she spake, and saide thus,
With face pale, and full sorrowful cheer,
In her complaint, as ye shall after hear.
"Alas!" quoth she, "on thee, Fortune, I plain,* *complain
That unware hast me wrapped in thy chain,
From which to scape, wot I no succour,
Save only death, or elles dishonour;
One of these two behoveth me to choose.
But natheless, yet had I lever* lose *sooner, rather
My life, than of my body have shame,
Or know myselfe false, or lose my name;
And with my death *I may be quit y-wis.* *I may certainly
      purchase my exemption*
Hath there not many a noble wife, ere this,
And many a maiden, slain herself, alas!
Rather than with her body do trespass?
Yes, certes; lo, these stories bear witness.
When thirty tyrants full of cursedness* *wickedness
Had slain Phidon in Athens at the feast,
They commanded his daughters to arrest,
And bringe them before them, in despite,
All naked, to fulfil their foul delight;
And in their father's blood they made them dance
Upon the pavement, — God give them mischance.
For which these woeful maidens, full of dread,
Rather than they would lose their maidenhead,
They privily *be start* into a well, *suddenly leaped*
And drowned themselves, as the bookes tell.
They of Messene let inquire and seek
Of Lacedaemon fifty maidens eke,
On which they woulde do their lechery:
But there was none of all that company

That was not slain, and with a glad intent
Chose rather for to die, than to assent
To be oppressed* of her maidenhead.   *forcibly bereft
Why should I then to dien be in dread?
Lo, eke the tyrant Aristoclides,
That lov'd a maiden hight Stimphalides,
When that her father slain was on a night,
Unto Diana's temple went she right,
And hent* the image in her handes two,   *caught, clasped
From which image she woulde never go;
No wight her handes might off it arace,*   *pluck away by force
Till she was slain right in the selfe* place.   *same
Now since that maidens hadde such despite
To be defouled with man's foul delight,
Well ought a wife rather herself to sle,*   *slay
Than be defouled, as it thinketh me.
What shall I say of Hasdrubale's wife,
That at Carthage bereft herself of life?
For, when she saw the Romans win the town,
She took her children all, and skipt adown
Into the fire, and rather chose to die,
Than any Roman did her villainy.
Hath not Lucretia slain herself, alas!
At Rome, when that she oppressed* was   *ravished
Of Tarquin? for her thought it was a shame
To live, when she hadde lost her name.
The seven maidens of Milesie also
Have slain themselves for very dread and woe,
Rather than folk of Gaul them should oppress.
More than a thousand stories, as I guess,
Could I now tell as touching this mattere.
When Abradate was slain, his wife so dear
Herselfe slew, and let her blood to glide
In Abradate's woundes, deep and wide,
And said, 'My body at the leaste way

There shall no wight defoul, if that I may.'
Why should I more examples hereof sayn?
Since that so many have themselves slain,
Well rather than they would defouled be,
I will conclude that it is bet* for me   *better
To slay myself, than be defouled thus.
I will be true unto Arviragus,
Or elles slay myself in some mannere,
As did Demotione's daughter dear,
Because she woulde not defouled be.
O Sedasus, it is full great pity
To reade how thy daughters died, alas!
That slew themselves *for suche manner cas.* *in circumstances
          of the same kind*
As great a pity was it, or well more,
The Theban maiden, that for Nicanor
Herselfe slew, right for such manner woe.
Another Theban maiden did right so;
For one of Macedon had her oppress'd,
She with her death her maidenhead redress'd.* *vindicated
What shall I say of Niceratus' wife,
That for such case bereft herself her life?
How true was eke to Alcibiades
His love, that for to dien rather chese,* *chose
Than for to suffer his body unburied be?
"Lo, what a wife was Alceste?" quoth she.
"What saith Homer of good Penelope?
All Greece knoweth of her chastity.
Pardie, of Laedamia is written thus,
That when at Troy was slain Protesilaus,
No longer would she live after his day.
The same of noble Porcia tell I may;
Withoute Brutus coulde she not live,
To whom she did all whole her hearte give.
The perfect wifehood of Artemisie

Honoured is throughout all Barbarie.
O Teuta queen, thy wifely chastity
To alle wives may a mirror be."

Thus plained Dorigen a day or tway,
Purposing ever that she woulde dey;* *die
But natheless upon the thirde night
Home came Arviragus, the worthy knight,
And asked her why that she wept so sore.
And she gan weepen ever longer more.
"Alas," quoth she, "that ever I was born!
Thus have I said," quoth she; "thus have I sworn."
And told him all, as ye have heard before:
It needeth not rehearse it you no more.
This husband with glad cheer,* in friendly wise, *demeanour
Answer'd and said, as I shall you devise.* *relate
"Is there aught elles, Dorigen, but this?"
"Nay, nay," quoth she, "God help me so, *as wis* *assuredly*
This is too much, an* it were Godde's will." *if
"Yea, wife," quoth he, "let sleepe what is still,
It may be well par'venture yet to-day.
Ye shall your trothe holde, by my fay.
For, God so wisly* have mercy on me, *certainly
I had well lever sticked for to be, *I had rather be slain*
For very love which I to you have,
But if ye should your trothe keep and save.
Truth is the highest thing that man may keep."
But with that word he burst anon to weep,
And said; "I you forbid, on pain of death,
That never, while you lasteth life or breath,
To no wight tell ye this misaventure;
As I may best, I will my woe endure,
Nor make no countenance of heaviness,
That folk of you may deeme harm, or guess."
And forth he call'd a squier and a maid.

"Go forth anon with Dorigen," he said,
"And bringe her to such a place anon."
They take their leave, and on their way they gon:
But they not wiste why she thither went;
He would to no wight telle his intent.

This squier, which that hight Aurelius,
On Dorigen that was so amorous,
Of aventure happen'd her to meet
Amid the town, right in the quickest* street, *nearest
As she was bound* to go the way forthright *prepared, going
Toward the garden, there as she had hight.* *promised
And he was to the garden-ward also;
For well he spied when she woulde go
Out of her house, to any manner place;
But thus they met, of aventure or grace,
And he saluted her with glad intent,
And asked of her whitherward she went.
And she answered, half as she were mad,
"Unto the garden, as my husband bade,
My trothe for to hold, alas! alas!"
Aurelius gan to wonder on this case,
And in his heart had great compassion
Of her, and of her lamentation,
And of Arviragus, the worthy knight,
That bade her hold all that she hadde hight;
So loth him was his wife should break her truth* *troth,
      pledged word
And in his heart he caught of it great ruth,* *pity
Considering the best on every side,
That from his lust yet were him lever abide,
Than do so high a churlish wretchedness* *wickedness
Against franchise,* and alle gentleness; *generosity
For which in fewe words he saide thus;
"Madame, say to your lord Arviragus,

That since I see the greate gentleness
Of him, and eke I see well your distress,
That him were lever* have shame (and that were ruth)** *rather
    **pity
Than ye to me should breake thus your truth,
I had well lever aye* to suffer woe, *forever
Than to depart* the love betwixt you two. *sunder, split up
I you release, Madame, into your hond,
Quit ev'ry surement* and ev'ry bond, *surety
That ye have made to me as herebeforn,
Since thilke time that ye were born.
Have here my truth, I shall you ne'er repreve* *reproach
Of no behest; and here I take my leave, *of no (breach of)*
As of the truest and the beste wife promise*
That ever yet I knew in all my life.
But every wife beware of her behest;
On Dorigen remember at the least.
Thus can a squier do a gentle deed,
As well as can a knight, withoute drede."* *doubt

She thanked him upon her knees bare,
And home unto her husband is she fare,* *gone
And told him all, as ye have hearde said;
And, truste me, he was so *well apaid,* *satisfied*
That it were impossible me to write.
Why should I longer of this case indite?
Arviragus and Dorigen his wife
In sov'reign blisse ledde forth their life;
Ne'er after was there anger them between;
He cherish'd her as though she were a queen,
And she was to him true for evermore;
Of these two folk ye get of me no more.

Aurelius, that his cost had *all forlorn,* *utterly lost*
Cursed the time that ever he was born.

"Alas!" quoth he, "alas that I behight* *promised
Of pured* gold a thousand pound of weight *refined
To this philosopher! how shall I do?
I see no more, but that I am fordo.* *ruined, undone
Mine heritage must I needes sell,
And be a beggar; here I will not dwell,
And shamen all my kindred in this place,
But* I of him may gette better grace. *unless
But natheless I will of him assay
At certain dayes year by year to pay,
And thank him of his greate courtesy.
My trothe will I keep, I will not he."
With hearte sore he went unto his coffer,
And broughte gold unto this philosopher,
The value of five hundred pound, I guess,
And him beseeched, of his gentleness,
To grant him *dayes of* the remenant; *time to pay up*
And said; "Master, I dare well make avaunt,
I failed never of my truth as yet.
For sickerly my debte shall be quit
Towardes you how so that e'er I fare
To go a-begging in my kirtle bare:
But would ye vouchesafe, upon surety,
Two year, or three, for to respite me,
Then were I well, for elles must I sell
Mine heritage; there is no more to tell."

This philosopher soberly* answer'd, *gravely
And saide thus, when he these wordes heard;
"Have I not holden covenant to thee?"
"Yes, certes, well and truely," quoth he.
"Hast thou not had thy lady as thee liked?"
"No, no," quoth he, and sorrowfully siked.* *sighed
"What was the cause? tell me if thou can."
Aurelius his tale anon began,

And told him all as ye have heard before,
It needeth not to you rehearse it more.
He said, "Arviragus of gentleness
Had lever* die in sorrow and distress,   *rather
Than that his wife were of her trothe false."
The sorrow of Dorigen he told him als',*   *also
How loth her was to be a wicked wife,
And that she lever had lost that day her life;
And that her troth she swore through innocence;
She ne'er erst* had heard speak of apparence   *before
That made me have of her so great pity,
And right as freely as he sent her to me,
As freely sent I her to him again:
This is all and some, there is no more to sayn."

The philosopher answer'd; "Leve* brother,   *dear
Evereach of you did gently to the other;
Thou art a squier, and he is a knight,
But God forbidde, for his blissful might,
But if a clerk could do a gentle deed
As well as any of you, it is no drede*   *doubt
Sir, I release thee thy thousand pound,
As thou right now were crept out of the ground,
Nor ever ere now haddest knowen me.
For, Sir, I will not take a penny of thee
For all my craft, nor naught for my travail;*   *labour, pains
Thou hast y-payed well for my vitaille;
It is enough; and farewell, have good day."
And took his horse, and forth he went his way.
Lordings, this question would I aske now,
Which was the moste free,* as thinketh you?   *generous
Now telle me, ere that ye farther wend.
I can* no more, my tale is at an end.   *know, can tell

THE DOCTOR'S TALE

"YEA, let that passe," quoth our Host, "as now.
Sir Doctor of Physik, I praye you,
Tell us a tale of some honest mattere."
"It shall be done, if that ye will it hear,"
Said this Doctor; and his tale gan anon.
"Now, good men," quoth he, "hearken everyone."

THE TALE

There was, as telleth Titus Livius,
A knight, that called was Virginius,
Full filled of honour and worthiness,
And strong of friendes, and of great richess.
This knight one daughter hadde by his wife;
No children had he more in all his life.
Fair was this maid in excellent beauty
Aboven ev'ry wight that man may see:
For nature had with sov'reign diligence
Y-formed her in so great excellence,
As though she woulde say, "Lo, I, Nature,
Thus can I form and paint a creature,
When that me list; who can me counterfeit?
Pygmalion? not though he aye forge and beat,
Or grave or painte: for I dare well sayn,
Apelles, Zeuxis, shoulde work in vain,
Either to grave, or paint, or forge, or beat,
If they presumed me to counterfeit.
For he that is the former principal,
Hath made me his vicar-general
To form and painten earthly creatures
Right as me list, and all thing in my cure* is, *care
Under the moone, that may wane and wax.
And for my work right nothing will I ax* *ask
My lord and I be full of one accord.

I made her to the worship of my lord;
So do I all mine other creatures,
What colour that they have, or what figures."
Thus seemeth me that Nature woulde say.

This maiden was of age twelve year and tway,*   *two
In which that Nature hadde such delight.
For right as she can paint a lily white,
And red a rose, right with such painture
She painted had this noble creature,
Ere she was born, upon her limbes free,
Where as by right such colours shoulde be:
And Phoebus dyed had her tresses great,
Like to the streames* of his burned heat.   *beams, rays
And if that excellent was her beauty,
A thousand-fold more virtuous was she.
In her there lacked no condition,
That is to praise, as by discretion.
As well in ghost* as body chaste was she: *mind, spirit
For which she flower'd in virginity,
With all humility and abstinence,
With alle temperance and patience,
With measure* eke of bearing and array.   *moderation
Discreet she was in answering alway,
Though she were wise as Pallas, dare I sayn;
Her faconde* eke full womanly and plain,   *speech
No counterfeited termes hadde she
To seeme wise; but after her degree
She spake, and all her worde's more and less
Sounding in virtue and in gentleness.
Shamefast she was in maiden's shamefastness,
Constant in heart, and ever *in business*   *diligent, eager*
To drive her out of idle sluggardy:
Bacchus had of her mouth right no mast'ry.
For wine and slothe do Venus increase,

As men in fire will casten oil and grease.
And of her owen virtue, unconstrain'd,
She had herself full often sick y-feign'd,
For that she woulde flee the company,
Where likely was to treaten of folly,
As is at feasts, at revels, and at dances,
That be occasions of dalliances.
Such thinges make children for to be
Too soone ripe and bold, as men may see,
Which is full perilous, and hath been yore;* *of old
For all too soone may she learne lore
Of boldeness, when that she is a wife.

And ye mistresses,* in your olde life *governesses, duennas
That lordes' daughters have in governance,
Take not of my wordes displeasance
Thinke that ye be set in governings
Of lordes' daughters only for two things;
Either for ye have kept your honesty,
Or else for ye have fallen in frailty
And knowe well enough the olde dance,
And have forsaken fully such meschance* *wickedness
For evermore; therefore, for Christe's sake,
To teach them virtue look that ye not slake.* *be slack, fail
A thief of venison, that hath forlaft* *forsaken, left
His lik'rousness,* and all his olde craft, *gluttony
Can keep a forest best of any man;
Now keep them well, for if ye will ye can.
Look well, that ye unto no vice assent,
Lest ye be damned for your wick'* intent, *wicked, evil
For whoso doth, a traitor is certain;
And take keep* of that I shall you sayn; *heed
Of alle treason, sov'reign pestilence
Is when a wight betrayeth innocence.
Ye fathers, and ye mothers eke also,

Though ye have children, be it one or mo',
Yours is the charge of all their surveyance,* *supervision
While that they be under your governance.
Beware, that by example of your living,
Or by your negligence in chastising,
That they not perish for I dare well say,
If that they do, ye shall it dear abeye.* *pay for, suffer for
Under a shepherd soft and negligent
The wolf hath many a sheep and lamb to-rent.
Suffice this example now as here,
For I must turn again to my mattere.

This maid, of which I tell my tale express,
She kept herself, her needed no mistress;
For in her living maidens mighte read,
As in a book, ev'ry good word and deed
That longeth to a maiden virtuous;
She was so prudent and so bounteous.
For which the fame out sprang on every side
Both of her beauty and her bounte* wide: *goodness
That through the land they praised her each one
That loved virtue, save envy alone,
That sorry is of other manne's weal,
And glad is of his sorrow and unheal* — *misfortune
The Doctor maketh this descriptioun. —
This maiden on a day went in the town
Toward a temple, with her mother dear,
As is of younge maidens the mannere.
Now was there then a justice in that town,
That governor was of that regioun:
And so befell, this judge his eyen cast
Upon this maid, avising* her full fast, *observing
As she came forth by where this judge stood;
Anon his hearte changed and his mood,
So was he caught with beauty of this maid

And to himself full privily he said,
"This maiden shall be mine *for any man."* *despite what any
  man may do*
Anon the fiend into his hearte ran,
And taught him suddenly, that he by sleight
This maiden to his purpose winne might.
For certes, by no force, nor by no meed,* *bribe, reward
Him thought he was not able for to speed;
For she was strong of friendes, and eke she
Confirmed was in such sov'reign bounte,
That well he wist he might her never win,
As for to make her with her body sin.
For which, with great deliberatioun,
He sent after a clerk was in the town,
The which he knew for subtle and for bold.
This judge unto this clerk his tale told
In secret wise, and made him to assure
He shoulde tell it to no creature,
And if he did, he shoulde lose his head.
And when assented was this cursed rede,* *counsel, plot
Glad was the judge, and made him greate cheer,
And gave him giftes precious and dear.
When shapen* was all their conspiracy *arranged
From point to point, how that his lechery
Performed shoulde be full subtilly,
As ye shall hear it after openly,
Home went this clerk, that highte Claudius.
This false judge, that highte Appius, —
(So was his name, for it is no fable,
But knowen for a storial* thing notable; *historical, authentic
The sentence* of it sooth** is out of doubt); — *account **true
This false judge went now fast about
To hasten his delight all that he may.
And so befell, soon after on a day,
This false judge, as telleth us the story,

As he was wont, sat in his consistory,
And gave his doomes* upon sundry case'; *judgments
This false clerk came forth *a full great pace,* *in haste*
And saide; "Lord, if that it be your will,
As do me right upon this piteous bill,* *petition
In which I plain upon Virginius.
And if that he will say it is not thus,
I will it prove, and finde good witness,
That sooth is what my bille will express."
The judge answer'd, "Of this, in his absence,
I may not give definitive sentence.
Let do* him call, and I will gladly hear; *cause
Thou shalt have alle right, and no wrong here."
Virginius came to weet* the judge's will, *know, learn
And right anon was read this cursed bill;
The sentence of it was as ye shall hear
"To you, my lord, Sir Appius so clear,
Sheweth your poore servant Claudius,
How that a knight called Virginius,
Against the law, against all equity,
Holdeth, express against the will of me,
My servant, which that is my thrall* by right, *slave
Which from my house was stolen on a night,
While that she was full young; I will it preve* *prove
By witness, lord, so that it you *not grieve;* *be not displeasing*
She is his daughter not, what so he say.
Wherefore to you, my lord the judge, I pray,
Yield me my thrall, if that it be your will."
Lo, this was all the sentence of the bill.
Virginius gan upon the clerk behold;
But hastily, ere he his tale told,
And would have proved it, as should a knight,
And eke by witnessing of many a wight,
That all was false that said his adversary,
This cursed judge would no longer tarry,

Nor hear a word more of Virginius,
But gave his judgement, and saide thus:
"I deem* anon this clerk his servant have; *pronounce,
     determine
Thou shalt no longer in thy house her save.
Go, bring her forth, and put her in our ward
The clerk shall have his thrall: thus I award."

And when this worthy knight, Virginius,
Through sentence of this justice Appius,
Muste by force his deare daughter give
Unto the judge, in lechery to live,
He went him home, and sat him in his hall,
And let anon his deare daughter call;
And with a face dead as ashes cold
Upon her humble face he gan behold,
With father's pity sticking* through his heart, *piercing
All* would he from his purpose not convert.** *although **turn
     aside
"Daughter," quoth he, "Virginia by name,
There be two wayes, either death or shame,
That thou must suffer, — alas that I was bore!* *born
For never thou deservedest wherefore
To dien with a sword or with a knife,
O deare daughter, ender of my life,
Whom I have foster'd up with such pleasance
That thou were ne'er out of my remembrance;
O daughter, which that art my laste woe,
And in this life my laste joy also,
O gem of chastity, in patience
Take thou thy death, for this is my sentence:
For love and not for hate thou must be dead;
My piteous hand must smiten off thine head.
Alas, that ever Appius thee say!* *saw
Thus hath he falsely judged thee to-day."

And told her all the case, as ye before
Have heard; it needeth not to tell it more.

"O mercy, deare father," quoth the maid.
And with that word she both her armes laid
About his neck, as she was wont to do,
(The teares burst out of her eyen two),
And said, "O goode father, shall I die?
Is there no grace? is there no remedy?"
"No, certes, deare daughter mine," quoth he.
"Then give me leisure, father mine," quoth she,
"My death for to complain* a little space   *bewail
For, pardie, Jephthah gave his daughter grace
For to complain, ere he her slew, alas!
And, God it wot, nothing was her trespass,*   *offence
But for she ran her father first to see,
To welcome him with great solemnity."
And with that word she fell a-swoon anon;
And after, when her swooning was y-gone,
She rose up, and unto her father said:
"Blessed be God, that I shall die a maid.
Give me my death, ere that I have shame;
Do with your child your will, in Godde's name."
And with that word she prayed him full oft
That with his sword he woulde smite her soft;
And with that word, a-swoon again she fell.
Her father, with full sorrowful heart and fell,*   *stern, cruel
Her head off smote, and by the top it hent,*   *took
And to the judge he went it to present,
As he sat yet in doom* in consistory.   *judgment

And when the judge it saw, as saith the story,
He bade to take him, and to hang him fast.
But right anon a thousand people *in thrast*   *rushed in*
To save the knight, for ruth and for pity

377

For knowen was the false iniquity.
The people anon had suspect* in this thing, *suspicion
By manner of the clerke's challenging,
That it was by th'assent of Appius;
They wiste well that he was lecherous.
For which unto this Appius they gon,
And cast him in a prison right anon,
Where as he slew himself: and Claudius,
That servant was unto this Appius,
Was doomed for to hang upon a tree;
But that Virginius, of his pity,
So prayed for him, that he was exil'd;
And elles certes had he been beguil'd;
The remenant were hanged, more and less,
That were consenting to this cursedness.* *villainy
Here men may see how sin hath his merite:* *deserts
Beware, for no man knows how God will smite
In no degree, nor in which manner wise
The worm of conscience may agrise* *frighten, horrify
Of wicked life, though it so privy be,
That no man knows thereof, save God and he;
For be he lewed* man or elles lear'd,** *ignorant **learned
He knows not how soon he shall be afear'd;
Therefore I rede* you this counsel take, *advise
Forsake sin, ere sinne you forsake.

THE PARDONER'S TALE

OUR Hoste gan to swear as he were wood;
"Harow!" quoth he, "by nailes and by blood,
This was a cursed thief, a false justice.
As shameful death as hearte can devise
Come to these judges and their advoca's.* *advocates,
  counsellors
Algate* this sely** maid is slain, alas! *nevertheless **innocent

Alas! too deare bought she her beauty.
Wherefore I say, that all day man may see
That giftes of fortune and of nature
Be cause of death to many a creature.
Her beauty was her death, I dare well sayn;
Alas! so piteously as she was slain.
Of bothe giftes, that I speak of now
Men have full often more harm than prow,* *profit
But truely, mine owen master dear,
This was a piteous tale for to hear;
But natheless, pass over; 'tis *no force.* *no matter*
I pray to God to save thy gentle corse,* *body
And eke thine urinals, and thy jordans,
Thine Hippocras, and eke thy Galliens,
And every boist* full of thy lectuary, *box
God bless them, and our lady Sainte Mary.
So may I the',* thou art a proper man, *thrive
And like a prelate, by Saint Ronian;
Said I not well? Can I not speak *in term?* *in set form*
But well I wot thou dost* mine heart to erme,** *makest
    **grieve
That I have almost caught a cardiacle:* *heartache
By corpus Domini, but* I have triacle,** *unless **a remedy
Or else a draught of moist and corny ale,
Or but* I hear anon a merry tale, *unless
Mine heart is brost* for pity of this maid. *burst, broken
Thou *bel ami,* thou Pardoner," he said, *good friend*
"Tell us some mirth of japes* right anon." *jokes
"It shall be done," quoth he, "by Saint Ronion.
But first," quoth he, "here at this ale-stake* *ale-house sign
I will both drink, and biten on a cake."
But right anon the gentles gan to cry,
"Nay, let him tell us of no ribaldry.
Tell us some moral thing, that we may lear* *learn
Some wit,* and thenne will we gladly hear." *wisdom, sense

"I grant y-wis,"* quoth he; "but I must think *surely
Upon some honest thing while that I drink."

Lordings (quoth he), in churche when I preach,
I paine me* to have an hautein** speech, *take pains **loud
And ring it out, as round as doth a bell,
For I know all by rote that I tell.
My theme is always one, and ever was;
Radix malorum est cupiditas.
First I pronounce whence that I come,
And then my bulles shew I all and some;
Our liege lorde's seal on my patent,
That shew I first, *my body to warrent,* *for the protection
      of my person*
That no man be so hardy, priest nor clerk,
Me to disturb of Christe's holy werk.
And after that then tell I forth my tales.
Bulles of popes, and of cardinales,
Of patriarchs, and of bishops I shew,
And in Latin I speak a wordes few,
To savour with my predication,
And for to stir men to devotion
Then show I forth my longe crystal stones,
Y-crammed fall of cloutes* and of bones; *rags, fragments
Relics they be, as *weene they* each one. *as my listeners
      think*
Then have I in latoun* a shoulder-bone *brass
Which that was of a holy Jewe's sheep.
"Good men," say I, "take of my wordes keep;* *heed
If that this bone be wash'd in any well,
If cow, or calf, or sheep, or oxe swell,
That any worm hath eat, or worm y-stung,
Take water of that well, and wash his tongue,
And it is whole anon; and farthermore
Of pockes, and of scab, and every sore

Shall every sheep be whole, that of this well
Drinketh a draught; take keep* of that I tell. *heed

"If that the goodman, that the beastes oweth,* *owneth
Will every week, ere that the cock him croweth,
Fasting, y-drinken of this well a draught,
As thilke holy Jew our elders taught,
His beastes and his store shall multiply.
And, Sirs, also it healeth jealousy;
For though a man be fall'n in jealous rage,
Let make with this water his pottage,
And never shall he more his wife mistrist,* *mistrust
Though he the sooth of her defaute wist; *though he truly
      knew her sin*
All had she taken priestes two or three.
Here is a mittain* eke, that ye may see; *glove, mitten
He that his hand will put in this mittain,
He shall have multiplying of his grain,
When he hath sowen, be it wheat or oats,
So that he offer pence, or elles groats.
And, men and women, one thing warn I you;
If any wight be in this churche now
That hath done sin horrible, so that he
Dare not for shame of it y-shriven* be; *confessed
Or any woman, be she young or old,
That hath y-made her husband cokewold,* *cuckold
Such folk shall have no power nor no grace
To offer to my relics in this place.
And whoso findeth him out of such blame,
He will come up and offer in God's name;
And I assoil* him by the authority *absolve
Which that by bull y-granted was to me."

By this gaud* have I wonne year by year *jest, trick
A hundred marks, since I was pardonere.

I stande like a clerk in my pulpit,
And when the lewed* people down is set, *ignorant
I preache so as ye have heard before,
And telle them a hundred japes* more. *jests, deceits
Then pain I me to stretche forth my neck,
And east and west upon the people I beck,
As doth a dove, sitting on a bern;* *barn
My handes and my tongue go so yern,* *briskly
That it is joy to see my business.
Of avarice and of such cursedness* *wickedness
Is all my preaching, for to make them free
To give their pence, and namely* unto me. *especially
For mine intent is not but for to win,
And nothing for correction of sin.
I recke never, when that they be buried,
Though that their soules go a blackburied.
For certes *many a predication
Cometh oft-time of evil intention;* *preaching is often inspired
        by evil motives*
Some for pleasance of folk, and flattery,
To be advanced by hypocrisy;
And some for vainglory, and some for hate.
For, when I dare not otherwise debate,
Then will I sting him with my tongue smart* *sharply
In preaching, so that he shall not astart* *escape
To be defamed falsely, if that he
Hath trespass'd* to my brethren or to me. *offended
For, though I telle not his proper name,
Men shall well knowe that it is the same
By signes, and by other circumstances.
Thus *quite I* folk that do us displeasances: *I am revenged on*
Thus spit I out my venom, under hue
Of holiness, to seem holy and true.
But, shortly mine intent I will devise,
I preach of nothing but of covetise.

Therefore my theme is yet, and ever was, —
Radix malorum est cupiditas.
Thus can I preach against the same vice
Which that I use, and that is avarice.
But though myself be guilty in that sin,
Yet can I maken other folk to twin*   *depart
From avarice, and sore them repent.
But that is not my principal intent;
I preache nothing but for covetise.
Of this mattere it ought enough suffice.
Then tell I them examples many a one,
Of olde stories longe time gone;
For lewed* people love tales old;   *unlearned
Such thinges can they well report and hold.
What? trowe ye, that whiles I may preach
And winne gold and silver for* I teach,   *because
That I will live in povert' wilfully?
Nay, nay, I thought it never truely.
For I will preach and beg in sundry lands;
I will not do no labour with mine hands,
Nor make baskets for to live thereby,
Because I will not beggen idlely.
I will none of the apostles counterfeit;*   *imitate (in poverty)
I will have money, wool, and cheese, and wheat,
All* were it given of the poorest page,   *even if
Or of the pooreste widow in a village:
All should her children sterve* for famine.   *die
Nay, I will drink the liquor of the vine,
And have a jolly wench in every town.
But hearken, lordings, in conclusioun;
Your liking is, that I shall tell a tale
Now I have drunk a draught of corny ale,
By God, I hope I shall you tell a thing
That shall by reason be to your liking;
For though myself be a full vicious man,

A moral tale yet I you telle can,
Which I am wont to preache, for to win.
Now hold your peace, my tale I will begin.

THE TALE

In Flanders whilom was a company
Of younge folkes, that haunted folly,
As riot, hazard, stewes,* and taverns; *brothels
Where as with lutes, harpes, and giterns,* *guitars
They dance and play at dice both day and night,
And eat also, and drink over their might;
Through which they do the devil sacrifice
Within the devil's temple, in cursed wise,
By superfluity abominable.
Their oathes be so great and so damnable,
That it is grisly* for to hear them swear. *dreadful
Our blissful Lorde's body they to-tear;* *tore to pieces
Them thought the Jewes rent him not enough,
And each of them at other's sinne lough.* *laughed
And right anon in come tombesteres
Fetis* and small, and younge fruitesteres.** *dainty **fruit-girls
Singers with harpes, baudes,* waferers,** *revellers **cake-sellers
Which be the very devil's officers,
To kindle and blow the fire of lechery,
That is annexed unto gluttony.
The Holy Writ take I to my witness,
That luxury is in wine and drunkenness.
Lo, how that drunken Lot unkindely* *unnaturally
Lay by his daughters two unwittingly,
So drunk he was he knew not what he wrought.
Herodes, who so well the stories sought,
When he of wine replete was at his feast,
Right at his owen table gave his hest* *command
To slay the Baptist John full guilteless.

Seneca saith a good word, doubteless:
He saith he can no difference find
Betwixt a man that is out of his mind,
And a man whiche that is drunkelew:* *a drunkard
But that woodness,* y-fallen in a shrew,* *madness **one
    evil-tempered
Persevereth longer than drunkenness.

O gluttony, full of all cursedness;
O cause first of our confusion,
Original of our damnation,
Till Christ had bought us with his blood again!
Looke, how deare, shortly for to sayn,
Abought* was first this cursed villainy: *atoned for
Corrupt was all this world for gluttony.
Adam our father, and his wife also,
From Paradise, to labour and to woe,
Were driven for that vice, it is no dread.* *doubt
For while that Adam fasted, as I read,
He was in Paradise; and when that he
Ate of the fruit defended* of the tree, *forbidden
Anon he was cast out to woe and pain.
O gluttony! well ought us on thee plain.
Oh! wist a man how many maladies
Follow of excess and of gluttonies,
He woulde be the more measurable* *moderate
Of his diete, sitting at his table.
Alas! the shorte throat, the tender mouth,
Maketh that east and west, and north and south,
In earth, in air, in water, men do swink* *labour
To get a glutton dainty meat and drink.
Of this mattere, O Paul! well canst thou treat
Meat unto womb,* and womb eke unto meat, *belly
Shall God destroye both, as Paulus saith.
Alas! a foul thing is it, by my faith,

To say this word, and fouler is the deed,
When man so drinketh of the *white and red,* *i.e. wine*
That of his throat he maketh his privy
Through thilke cursed superfluity
The apostle saith, weeping full piteously,
There walk many, of which you told have I, —
I say it now weeping with piteous voice, —
That they be enemies of Christe's crois;* *cross
Of which the end is death; womb* is their God. *belly
O womb, O belly, stinking is thy cod,* *bag
Full fill'd of dung and of corruptioun;
At either end of thee foul is the soun.
How great labour and cost is thee to find!* *supply
These cookes how they stamp, and strain, and grind,
And turne substance into accident,
To fulfill all thy likerous talent!
Out of the harde bones knocke they
The marrow, for they caste naught away
That may go through the gullet soft and swoot* *sweet
Of spicery and leaves, of bark and root,
Shall be his sauce y-maked by delight,
To make him have a newer appetite.
But, certes, he that haunteth such delices
Is dead while that he liveth in those vices.

A lecherous thing is wine, and drunkenness
Is full of striving and of wretchedness.
O drunken man! disfgur'd is thy face,
Sour is thy breath, foul art thou to embrace:
And through thy drunken nose sowneth the soun',
As though thous saidest aye, Samsoun! Samsoun!
And yet, God wot, Samson drank never wine.
Thou fallest as it were a sticked swine;
Thy tongue is lost, and all thine honest cure;* *care
For drunkenness is very sepulture* *tomb

Of manne's wit and his discretion.
In whom that drink hath domination,
He can no counsel keep, it is no dread.* *doubt
Now keep you from the white and from the red,
And namely* from the white wine of Lepe, *especially
That is to sell in Fish Street and in Cheap.
This wine of Spaine creepeth subtilly —
In other wines growing faste by,
Of which there riseth such fumosity,
That when a man hath drunken draughtes three,
And weeneth that he be at home in Cheap,
He is in Spain, right at the town of Lepe,
Not at the Rochelle, nor at Bourdeaux town;
And thenne will he say, Samsoun! Samsoun!
But hearken, lordings, one word, I you pray,
That all the sovreign actes, dare I say,
Of victories in the Old Testament,
Through very God that is omnipotent,
Were done in abstinence and in prayere:
Look in the Bible, and there ye may it lear.* *learn
Look, Attila, the greate conqueror,
Died in his sleep, with shame and dishonour,
Bleeding aye at his nose in drunkenness:
A captain should aye live in soberness
And o'er all this, advise* you right well *consider, bethink
What was commanded unto Lemuel;
Not Samuel, but Lemuel, say I.
Reade the Bible, and find it expressly
Of wine giving to them that have justice.
No more of this, for it may well suffice.

And, now that I have spoke of gluttony,
Now will I you *defende hazardry.* *forbid gambling*
Hazard is very mother of leasings,* *lies
And of deceit, and cursed forswearings:

Blasphem' of Christ, manslaughter, and waste also
Of chattel* and of time; and furthermo' *property
It is repreve,* and contrar' of honour, *reproach
For to be held a common hazardour.
And ever the higher he is of estate,
The more he is holden desolate.* *undone, worthless
If that a prince use hazardry,
In alle governance and policy
He is, as by common opinion,
Y-hold the less in reputation.

Chilon, that was a wise ambassador,
Was sent to Corinth with full great honor
From Lacedemon, to make alliance;
And when he came, it happen'd him, by chance,
That all the greatest that were of that land,
Y-playing atte hazard he them fand.* *found
For which, as soon as that it mighte be,
He stole him home again to his country
And saide there, "I will not lose my name,
Nor will I take on me so great diffame,* *reproach
You to ally unto no hazardors.* *gamblers
Sende some other wise ambassadors,
For, by my troth, me were lever* die, *rather
Than I should you to hazardors ally.
For ye, that be so glorious in honours,
Shall not ally you to no hazardours,
As by my will, nor as by my treaty."
This wise philosopher thus said he.
Look eke how to the King Demetrius
The King of Parthes, as the book saith us,
Sent him a pair of dice of gold in scorn,
For he had used hazard therebeforn:
For which he held his glory and renown
At no value or reputatioun.

Lordes may finden other manner play
Honest enough to drive the day away.

Now will I speak of oathes false and great
A word or two, as olde bookes treat.
Great swearing is a thing abominable,
And false swearing is more reprovable.
The highe God forbade swearing at all;
Witness on Matthew: but in special
Of swearing saith the holy Jeremie,
Thou thalt swear sooth thine oathes, and not lie:
And swear in doom* and eke in righteousness; *judgement
But idle swearing is a cursedness.* *wickedness
Behold and see, there in the firste table
Of highe Godde's hestes* honourable, *commandments
How that the second best of him is this,
Take not my name in idle* or amiss. *in vain
Lo, rather* he forbiddeth such swearing, *sooner
Than homicide, or many a cursed thing;
I say that as by order thus it standeth;
This knoweth he that his hests* understandeth,
        *commandments
How that the second hest of God is that.
And farthermore, I will thee tell all plat,* *flatly, plainly
That vengeance shall not parte from his house,
That of his oathes is outrageous.
"By Godde's precious heart, and by his nails,
And by the blood of Christ, that is in Hailes,
Seven is my chance, and thine is cinque and trey:
By Godde's armes, if thou falsely play,
This dagger shall throughout thine hearte go."
This fruit comes of the *bicched bones two,* *two cursed bones
        (dice)*
Forswearing, ire, falseness, and homicide.
Now, for the love of Christ that for us died,

Leave your oathes, bothe great and smale.
But, Sirs, now will I ell you forth my tale.

These riotoures three, of which I tell,
Long *erst than* prime rang of any bell, *before
Were set them in a tavern for to drink;
And as they sat, they heard a belle clink
Before a corpse, was carried to the grave.
That one of them gan calle to his knave,* *servant
"Go bet," quoth he, "and aske readily
What corpse is this, that passeth here forth by;
And look that thou report his name well."
"Sir," quoth the boy, "it needeth never a deal;* *whit
It was me told ere ye came here two hours;
He was, pardie, an old fellow of yours,
And suddenly he was y-slain to-night;
Fordrunk* as he sat on his bench upright, *completely drunk
There came a privy thief, men clepe Death,
That in this country all the people slay'th,
And with his spear he smote his heart in two,
And went his way withoute wordes mo'.
He hath a thousand slain this pestilence;
And, master, ere you come in his presence,
Me thinketh that it were full necessary
For to beware of such an adversary;
Be ready for to meet him evermore.
Thus taughte me my dame; I say no more."
"By Sainte Mary," said the tavernere,
"The child saith sooth, for he hath slain this year,
Hence ov'r a mile, within a great village,
Both man and woman, child, and hind, and page;
I trow his habitation be there;
To be advised* great wisdom it were, *watchful, on one's guard
Ere* that he did a man a dishonour." *lest

"Yea, Godde's armes," quoth this riotour,
"Is it such peril with him for to meet?
I shall him seek, by stile and eke by street.
I make a vow, by Godde's digne* bones. *worthy
Hearken, fellows, we three be alle ones:* *at one
Let each of us hold up his hand to other,
And each of us become the other's brother,
And we will slay this false traitor Death;
He shall be slain, he that so many slay'th,
By Godde's dignity, ere it be night."
Together have these three their trothe plight
To live and die each one of them for other
As though he were his owen sworen brother.
And up they start, all drunken, in this rage,
And forth they go towardes that village
Of which the taverner had spoke beforn,
And many a grisly* oathe have they sworn, *dreadful
And Christe's blessed body they to-rent;* *tore to pieces
"Death shall be dead, if that we may him hent."* *catch
When they had gone not fully half a mile,
Right as they would have trodden o'er a stile,
An old man and a poore with them met.
This olde man full meekely them gret,* *greeted
And saide thus; "Now, lordes, God you see!"* *look on
    graciously
The proudest of these riotoures three
Answer'd again; "What? churl, with sorry grace,
Why art thou all forwrapped* save thy face? *closely wrapt up
Why livest thou so long in so great age?"
This olde man gan look on his visage,
And saide thus; "For that I cannot find
A man, though that I walked unto Ind,
Neither in city, nor in no village go,
That woulde change his youthe for mine age;
And therefore must I have mine age still

As longe time as it is Godde's will.
And Death, alas! he will not have my life.
Thus walk I like a resteless caitife,* *miserable wretch
And on the ground, which is my mother's gate,
I knocke with my staff, early and late,
And say to her, 'Leve* mother, let me in. *dear
Lo, how I wane, flesh, and blood, and skin;
Alas! when shall my bones be at rest?
Mother, with you I woulde change my chest,
That in my chamber longe time hath be,
Yea, for an hairy clout to *wrap in me.'* *wrap myself in*
But yet to me she will not do that grace,
For which full pale and welked* is my face. *withered
But, Sirs, to you it is no courtesy
To speak unto an old man villainy,
But* he trespass in word or else in deed. *except
In Holy Writ ye may yourselves read;
'Against* an old man, hoar upon his head, *to meet
Ye should arise:' therefore I you rede,* *advise
Ne do unto an old man no harm now,
No more than ye would a man did you
In age, if that ye may so long abide.
And God be with you, whether ye go or ride
I must go thither as I have to go."

"Nay, olde churl, by God thou shalt not so,"
Saide this other hazardor anon;
"Thou partest not so lightly, by Saint John.
Thou spakest right now of that traitor Death,
That in this country all our friendes slay'th;
Have here my troth, as thou art his espy;* *spy
Tell where he is, or thou shalt it abie,* *suffer for
By God and by the holy sacrament;
For soothly thou art one of his assent
To slay us younge folk, thou false thief."

"Now, Sirs," quoth he, "if it be you so lief*   *desire
To finde Death, turn up this crooked way,
For in that grove I left him, by my fay,
Under a tree, and there he will abide;
Nor for your boast he will him nothing hide.
See ye that oak? right there ye shall him find.
God save you, that bought again mankind,
And you amend!" Thus said this olde man;
And evereach of these riotoures ran,
Till they came to the tree, and there they found
Of florins fine, of gold y-coined round,
Well nigh a seven bushels, as them thought.
No longer as then after Death they sought;
But each of them so glad was of the sight,
For that the florins were so fair and bright,
That down they sat them by the precious hoard.
The youngest of them spake the firste word:
"Brethren," quoth he, "*take keep* what I shall say;   *heed*
My wit is great, though that I bourde* and play   *joke, frolic
This treasure hath Fortune unto us given
In mirth and jollity our life to liven;
And lightly as it comes, so will we spend.
Hey! Godde's precious dignity! who wend*   *weened, thought
Today that we should have so fair a grace?
But might this gold be carried from this place
Home to my house, or elles unto yours
(For well I wot that all this gold is ours),
Then were we in high felicity.
But truely by day it may not be;
Men woulde say that we were thieves strong,
And for our owen treasure do us hong.*   *have us hanged
This treasure muste carried be by night,
As wisely and as slily as it might.
Wherefore I rede,* that cut** among us all   *advise **lots
We draw, and let see where the cut will fall:

And he that hath the cut, with hearte blithe
Shall run unto the town, and that full swithe,* *quickly
And bring us bread and wine full privily:
And two of us shall keepe subtilly
This treasure well: and if he will not tarry,
When it is night, we will this treasure carry,
By one assent, where as us thinketh best."
Then one of them the cut brought in his fist,
And bade them draw, and look where it would fall;
And it fell on the youngest of them all;
And forth toward the town he went anon.
And all so soon as that he was y-gone,
The one of them spake thus unto the other;
"Thou knowest well that thou art my sworn brother,
Thy profit will I tell thee right anon. *what is for thine
     advantage*
Thou knowest well that our fellow is gone,
And here is gold, and that full great plenty,
That shall departed* he among us three. *divided
But natheless, if I could shape* it so *contrive
That it departed were among us two,
Had I not done a friende's turn to thee?"
Th' other answer'd, "I n'ot* how that may be; *know not
He knows well that the gold is with us tway.
What shall we do? what shall we to him say?"
"Shall it be counsel?"* said the firste shrew;** *secret **wretch
"And I shall tell to thee in wordes few
What we shall do, and bring it well about."
"I grante," quoth the other, "out of doubt,
That by my truth I will thee not bewray."* *betray
"Now," quoth the first, "thou know'st well we be tway,
And two of us shall stronger be than one.
Look; when that he is set,* thou right anon *sat down
Arise, as though thou wouldest with him play;
And I shall rive* him through the sides tway, *stab

While that thou strugglest with him as in game;
And with thy dagger look thou do the same.
And then shall all this gold departed* be, *divided
My deare friend, betwixte thee and me:
Then may we both our lustes* all fulfil, *pleasures
And play at dice right at our owen will."
And thus accorded* be these shrewes** tway *agreed **wretches
To slay the third, as ye have heard me say.

The youngest, which that wente to the town,
Full oft in heart he rolled up and down
The beauty of these florins new and bright.
"O Lord!" quoth he, "if so were that I might
Have all this treasure to myself alone,
There is no man that lives under the throne
Of God, that shoulde have so merry as I."
And at the last the fiend our enemy
Put in his thought, that he should poison buy,
With which he mighte slay his fellows twy.* *two
For why, the fiend found him *in such living,* *leading such a
        (bad) life*
That he had leave to sorrow him to bring.
For this was utterly his full intent
To slay them both, and never to repent.
And forth he went, no longer would he tarry,
Into the town to an apothecary,
And prayed him that he him woulde sell
Some poison, that he might *his rattes quell,* *kill his rats*
And eke there was a polecat in his haw,* *farm-yard, hedge
That, as he said, his eapons had y-slaw:* *slain
And fain he would him wreak,* if that he might, *revenge
Of vermin that destroyed him by night.
Th'apothecary answer'd, "Thou shalt have
A thing, as wisly* God my soule save, *surely
In all this world there is no creature

That eat or drank hath of this confecture,
Not but the mountance* of a corn of wheat, *amount
That he shall not his life *anon forlete;* *immediately lay down*
Yea, sterve* he shall, and that in lesse while *die
Than thou wilt go apace* nought but a mile: *quickly
This poison is so strong and violent."
This cursed man hath in his hand y-hent* *taken
This poison in a box, and swift he ran
Into the nexte street, unto a man,
And borrow'd of him large bottles three;
And in the two the poison poured he;
The third he kepte clean for his own drink,
For all the night he shope him* for to swink** *purposed **labour
In carrying off the gold out of that place.
And when this riotour, with sorry grace,
Had fill'd with wine his greate bottles three,

To his fellows again repaired he.
What needeth it thereof to sermon* more? *talk, discourse
For, right as they had cast* his death before, *plotted
Right so they have him slain, and that anon.
And when that this was done, thus spake the one;
"Now let us sit and drink, and make us merry,
And afterward we will his body bury."
And with that word it happen'd him *par cas* *by chance*
To take the bottle where the poison was,
And drank, and gave his fellow drink also,
For which anon they sterved* both the two. *died
But certes I suppose that Avicen
Wrote never in no canon, nor no *fen*,
More wondrous signes of empoisoning,
Than had these wretches two ere their ending.
Thus ended be these homicides two,
And eke the false empoisoner also.

O cursed sin, full of all cursedness!
O trait'rous homicide! O wickedness!
O glutt'ny, luxury, and hazardry!
Thou blasphemer of Christ with villany,* *outrage, impiety
And oathes great, of usage and of pride!
Alas! mankinde, how may it betide,
That to thy Creator, which that thee wrought,
And with his precious hearte-blood thee bought,
Thou art so false and so unkind,* alas! *unnatural
Now, good men, God forgive you your trespass,
And ware* you from the sin of avarice. *keep
Mine holy pardon may you all warice,* *heal
So that ye offer *nobles or sterlings,* *gold or silver coins*
Or elles silver brooches, spoons, or rings.
Bowe your head under this holy bull.
Come up, ye wives, and offer of your will;
Your names I enter in my roll anon;
Into the bliss of heaven shall ye gon;
I you assoil* by mine high powere, *absolve
You that will offer, as clean and eke as clear
As ye were born. Lo, Sires, thus I preach;
And Jesus Christ, that is our soules' leech,* *healer
So grante you his pardon to receive;
For that is best, I will not deceive.

But, Sirs, one word forgot I in my tale;
I have relics and pardon in my mail,
As fair as any man in Engleland,
Which were me given by the Pope's hand.
If any of you will of devotion
Offer, and have mine absolution,
Come forth anon, and kneele here adown
And meekely receive my pardoun.
Or elles take pardon, as ye wend,* *go
All new and fresh at every towne's end,

So that ye offer, always new and new,
Nobles or pence which that be good and true.
'Tis an honour to evereach* that is here,   *each one
That ye have a suffisant* pardonere   *suitable
T'assoile* you in country as ye ride,   *absolve
For aventures which that may betide.
Paraventure there may fall one or two
Down of his horse, and break his neck in two.
Look, what a surety is it to you all,
That I am in your fellowship y-fall,
That may assoil* you bothe *more and lass,*   *absolve *great and
    small*
When that the soul shall from the body pass.
I rede* that our Hoste shall begin,   *advise
For he is most enveloped in sin.
Come forth, Sir Host, and offer first anon,
And thou shalt kiss; the relics every one,
Yea, for a groat; unbuckle anon thy purse.

"Nay, nay," quoth he, "then have I Christe's curse!
Let be," quoth he, "it shall not be, *so the'ch.*   *so may I thrive*
Thou wouldest make me kiss thine olde breech,
And swear it were a relic of a saint,
Though it were with thy *fundament depaint'.*   *stained by
    your bottom*
But, by the cross which that Saint Helen fand,*   *found
I would I had thy coilons* in mine hand,   *testicles
Instead of relics, or of sanctuary.
Let cut them off, I will thee help them carry;
They shall be shrined in a hogge's turd."
The Pardoner answered not one word;
So wroth he was, no worde would he say.

"Now," quoth our Host, "I will no longer play
With thee, nor with none other angry man."

But right anon the worthy Knight began
(When that he saw that all the people lough*),   *laughed
"No more of this, for it is right enough.
Sir Pardoner, be merry and glad of cheer;
And ye, Sir Host, that be to me so dear,
I pray you that ye kiss the Pardoner;
And, Pardoner, I pray thee draw thee ner,*   *nearer
And as we didde, let us laugh and play."
Anon they kiss'd, and rode forth their way.

THE SHIPMAN'S TALE

Our Host upon his stirrups stood anon,
And saide; "Good men, hearken every one,
This was a thrifty* tale for the nones.   *discreet, profitable
Sir Parish Priest," quoth he, "for Godde's bones,
Tell us a tale, as was thy *forword yore:*   *promise formerly*
I see well that ye learned men in lore
Can* muche good, by Godde's dignity."   *know
The Parson him answer'd, "Ben'dicite!
What ails the man, so sinfully to swear?"
Our Host answer'd, "O Jankin, be ye there?
Now, good men," quoth our Host, "hearken to me.
I smell a Lollard in the wind," quoth he.
"Abide, for Godde's digne* passion,   *worthy
For we shall have a predication:
This Lollard here will preachen us somewhat."
"Nay, by my father's soul, that shall he not,
Saide the Shipman; "Here shall he not preach,
He shall no gospel glose* here nor teach.   *comment upon
We all believe in the great God," quoth he.
"He woulde sowe some difficulty,
Or springe cockle in our cleane corn.
And therefore, Host, I warne thee beforn,
My jolly body shall a tale tell,

And I shall clinke you so merry a bell,
That I shall waken all this company;
But it shall not be of philosophy,
Nor of physic, nor termes quaint of law;
There is but little Latin in my maw."* *belly

THE TALE

A Merchant whilom dwell'd at Saint Denise,
That riche was, for which men held him wise.
A wife he had of excellent beauty,
And *companiable and revellous* was she, *fond of society and
          merry making*
Which is a thing that causeth more dispence
Than worth is all the cheer and reverence
That men them do at feastes and at dances.
Such salutations and countenances
Passen, as doth the shadow on the wall;
Put woe is him that paye must for all.
The sely* husband algate** he must pay, *innocent **always
He must us clothe and he must us array
All for his owen worship richely:
In which array we dance jollily.
And if that he may not, paraventure,
Or elles list not such dispence endure,
But thinketh it is wasted and y-lost,
Then must another paye for our cost,
Or lend us gold, and that is perilous.

This noble merchant held a noble house;
For which he had all day so great repair,* *resort of visitors
For his largesse, and for his wife was fair,
That wonder is; but hearken to my tale.
Amonges all these guestes great and smale,
There was a monk, a fair man and a bold,

I trow a thirty winter he was old,
That ever-in-one* was drawing to that place. *constantly
This younge monk, that was so fair of face,
Acquainted was so with this goode man,
Since that their firste knowledge began,
That in his house as familiar was he
As it is possible any friend to be.
And, for as muchel as this goode man,
And eke this monk of which that I began,
Were both the two y-born in one village,
The monk *him claimed, as for cousinage,** *claimed kindred
    with him*
And he again him said not once nay,
But was as glad thereof as fowl of day;
For to his heart it was a great pleasance.
Thus be they knit with etern' alliance,
And each of them gan other to assure
Of brotherhood while that their life may dure.
Free was Dan John, and namely* of dispence,** *especially
    **spending
As in that house, and full of diligence
To do pleasance, and also *great costage;* *liberal outlay*
He not forgot to give the leaste page
In all that house; but, after their degree,
He gave the lord, and sithen* his meinie,** *afterwards **servants
When that he came, some manner honest thing;
For which they were as glad of his coming
As fowl is fain when that the sun upriseth.
No more of this as now, for it sufficeth.

But so befell, this merchant on a day
Shope* him to make ready his array *resolved, arranged
Toward the town of Bruges for to fare,
To buye there a portion of ware;* *merchandise
For which he hath to Paris sent anon

A messenger, and prayed hath Dan John
That he should come to Saint Denis, and play* *enjoy himself
With him, and with his wife, a day or tway,
Ere he to Bruges went, in alle wise.
This noble monk, of which I you devise,* *tell
Had of his abbot, as him list, licence,
(Because he was a man of high prudence,
And eke an officer out for to ride,
To see their granges and their barnes wide);
And unto Saint Denis he came anon.
Who was so welcome as my lord Dan John,
Our deare cousin, full of courtesy?
With him he brought a jub* of malvesie, *jug
And eke another full of fine vernage,
And volatile,* as aye was his usage: *wild-fowl
And thus I let them eat, and drink, and play,
This merchant and this monk, a day or tway.
The thirde day the merchant up ariseth,
And on his needeis sadly him adviseth;
And up into his countour-house* went he, *counting-house
To reckon with himself as well may be,
Of thilke* year, how that it with him stood, *that
And how that he dispended bad his good,
And if that he increased were or non.
His bookes and his bagges many a one
He laid before him on his counting-board.
Full riche was his treasure and his hoard;
For which full fast his countour door he shet;
And eke he would that no man should him let* *hinder
Of his accountes, for the meane time:
And thus he sat, till it was passed prime.

Dan John was risen in the morn also,
And in the garden walked to and fro,
And had his thinges said full courteously.

The good wife came walking full privily
Into the garden, where he walked soft,
And him saluted, as she had done oft;
A maiden child came in her company,
Which as her list she might govern and gie,* *guide
For yet under the yarde* was the maid. *rod
"O deare cousin mine, Dan John," she said,
"What aileth you so rath* for to arise?" *early
"Niece," quoth he, "it ought enough suffice
Five houres for to sleep upon a night;
But* it were for an old appalled** wight, *unless **pallid,
    wasted
As be these wedded men, that lie and dare,* *stare
As in a forme sits a weary hare,
Alle forstraught* with houndes great and smale; *distracted,
    confounded
But, deare niece, why be ye so pale?
I trowe certes that our goode man
Hath you so laboured, since this night began,
That you were need to reste hastily."
And with that word he laugh'd full merrily,
And of his owen thought he wax'd all red.
This faire wife gan for to shake her head,
And saide thus; "Yea, God wot all" quoth she.
"Nay, cousin mine, it stands not so with me;
For by that God, that gave me soul and life,
In all the realm of France is there no wife
That lesse lust hath to that sorry play;
For I may sing alas and well-away!
That I was born; but to no wight," quoth she,
"Dare I not tell how that it stands with me.
Wherefore I think out of this land to wend,
Or elles of myself to make an end,
So full am I of dread and eke of care."

This monk began upon this wife to stare,
And said, "Alas! my niece, God forbid
That ye for any sorrow, or any dread,
Fordo* yourself: but telle me your grief,   *destroy
Paraventure I may, in your mischief,*   *distress
Counsel or help; and therefore telle me
All your annoy, for it shall be secre.
For on my portos* here I make an oath,   *breviary
That never in my life, *for lief nor loth,*   *willing or unwilling*
Ne shall I of no counsel you bewray."
"The same again to you," quoth she, "I say.
By God and by this portos I you swear,
Though men me woulden all in pieces tear,
Ne shall I never, for* to go to hell,   *though I should
Bewray* one word of thing that ye me tell,   *betray
For no cousinage, nor alliance,
But verily for love and affiance."*   *confidence, promise
Thus be they sworn, and thereupon they kiss'd,
And each of them told other what them list.
"Cousin," quoth she, "if that I hadde space,
As I have none, and namely* in this place,   *specially
Then would I tell a legend of my life,
What I have suffer'd since I was a wife
With mine husband, all* be he your cousin."   *although
"Nay," quoth this monk, "by God and Saint Martin,
He is no more cousin unto me,
Than is the leaf that hangeth on the tree;
I call him so, by Saint Denis of France,
To have the more cause of acquaintance
Of you, which I have loved specially
Aboven alle women sickerly,*   *surely
This swear I you *on my professioun;*   *by my vows of religion
Tell me your grief, lest that he come adown,
And hasten you, and go away anon."

"My deare love," quoth she, "O my Dan John,
Full lief* were me this counsel for to hide, *pleasant
But out it must, I may no more abide.
My husband is to me the worste man
That ever was since that the world began;
But since I am a wife, it sits* not me *becomes
To telle no wight of our privity,
Neither in bed, nor in none other place;
God shield* I shoulde tell it for his grace; *forbid
A wife shall not say of her husband
But all honour, as I can understand;
Save unto you thus much I telle shall;
As help me God, he is nought worth at all
In no degree, the value of a fly.
But yet me grieveth most his niggardy.* *stinginess
And well ye wot, that women naturally
Desire thinges six, as well as I.
They woulde that their husbands shoulde be
Hardy,* and wise, and rich, and thereto free, *brave
And buxom* to his wife, and fresh in bed. *yielding, obedient
But, by that ilke* Lord that for us bled, *same
For his honour myself for to array,
On Sunday next I muste needes pay
A hundred francs, or elles am I lorn.* *ruined, undone
Yet *were me lever* that I were unborn, *I would rather*
Than me were done slander or villainy.
And if mine husband eke might it espy,
I were but lost; and therefore I you pray,
Lend me this sum, or elles must I dey.* *die
Dan John, I say, lend me these hundred francs;
Pardie, I will not faile you, *my thanks,* *if I can help it*
If that you list to do that I you pray;
For at a certain day I will you pay,
And do to you what pleasance and service
That I may do, right as you list devise.

And but* I do, God take on me vengeance, *unless
As foul as e'er had Ganilion of France."

This gentle monk answer'd in this mannere;
"Now truely, mine owen lady dear,
I have," quoth he, "on you so greate ruth,* *pity
That I you swear, and plighte you my truth,
That when your husband is to Flanders fare,* *gone
I will deliver you out of this care,
For I will bringe you a hundred francs."
And with that word he caught her by the flanks,
And her embraced hard, and kissed her oft.
"Go now your way," quoth he, "all still and soft,
And let us dine as soon as that ye may,
For by my cylinder* 'tis prime of day; *portable sundial
Go now, and be as true as I shall be."
"Now elles God forbidde, Sir," quoth she;
And forth she went, as jolly as a pie,
And bade the cookes that they should them hie,* *make haste
So that men mighte dine, and that anon.
Up to her husband is this wife gone,
And knocked at his contour boldely.
*"*Qui est la?*"* quoth he. "Peter! it am I," *who is there?*
Quoth she; "What, Sir, how longe all will ye fast?
How longe time will ye reckon and cast
Your summes, and your bookes, and your things?
The devil have part of all such reckonings!
Ye have enough, pardie, of Godde's sond.* *sending, gifts
Come down to-day, and let your bagges stond.* *stand
Ne be ye not ashamed, that Dan John
Shall fasting all this day elenge gon?
What? let us hear a mass, and go we dine."
"Wife," quoth this man, "little canst thou divine
The curious businesse that we have;
For of us chapmen,* all so God me save, *merchants

And by that lord that cleped is Saint Ive,
Scarcely amonges twenty, ten shall thrive
Continually, lasting unto our age.
We may well make cheer and good visage,
And drive forth the world as it may be,
And keepen our estate in privity,
Till we be dead, or elles that we play
A pilgrimage, or go out of the way.
And therefore have I great necessity
Upon this quaint* world to advise** me. *strange **consider
For evermore must we stand in dread
Of hap and fortune in our chapmanhead.* *trading
To Flanders will I go to-morrow at day,
And come again as soon as e'er I may:
For which, my deare wife, I thee beseek *beseech
As be to every wight buxom* and meek, *civil, courteous
And for to keep our good be curious,
And honestly governe well our house.
Thou hast enough, in every manner wise,
That to a thrifty household may suffice.
Thee lacketh none array, nor no vitail;
Of silver in thy purse thou shalt not fail."

And with that word his contour door he shet,* *shut
And down he went; no longer would he let;* *delay, hinder
And hastily a mass was there said,
And speedily the tables were laid,
And to the dinner faste they them sped,
And richely this monk the chapman fed.
And after dinner Dan John soberly
This chapman took apart, and privily
He said him thus: "Cousin, it standeth so,
That, well I see, to Bruges ye will go;
God and Saint Austin speede you and guide.
I pray you, cousin, wisely that ye ride:

Governe you also of your diet
Attemperly,* and namely in this heat. *moderately
Betwixt us two needeth no *strange fare;* *ado, ceremony*
Farewell, cousin, God shielde you from care.
If any thing there be, by day or night,
If it lie in my power and my might,
That ye me will command in any wise,
It shall be done, right as ye will devise.
But one thing ere ye go, if it may be;
I woulde pray you for to lend to me
A hundred frankes, for a week or twy,
For certain beastes that I muste buy,
To store with a place that is ours
(God help me so, I would that it were yours);
I shall not faile surely of my day,
Not for a thousand francs, a mile way.
But let this thing be secret, I you pray;
For yet to-night these beastes must I buy.
And fare now well, mine owen cousin dear;
Grand mercy of your cost and of your cheer." *great thanks*

This noble merchant gentilly* anon *like a gentleman
Answer'd and said, "O cousin mine, Dan John,
Now sickerly this is a small request:
My gold is youres, when that it you lest,
And not only my gold, but my chaffare;* *merchandise
Take what you list, *God shielde that ye spare.* *God forbid
    that you should take too little*
But one thing is, ye know it well enow
Of chapmen, that their money is their plough.
We may creance* while we have a name, *obtain credit
But goldless for to be it is no game.
Pay it again when it lies in your ease;
After my might full fain would I you please."

These hundred frankes set he forth anon,
And privily he took them to Dan John;
No wight in all this world wist of this loan,
Saving the merchant and Dan John alone.
They drink, and speak, and roam a while, and play,
Till that Dan John rode unto his abbay.
The morrow came, and forth this merchant rideth
To Flanders-ward, his prentice well him guideth,
Till he came unto Bruges merrily.
Now went this merchant fast and busily
About his need, and buyed and creanced;* *got credit
He neither played at the dice, nor danced;
But as a merchant, shortly for to tell,
He led his life; and there I let him dwell.

The Sunday next* the merchant was y-gone, *after
To Saint Denis y-comen is Dan John,
With crown and beard all fresh and newly shave,
In all the house was not so little a knave,* *servant-boy
Nor no wight elles that was not full fain
For that my lord Dan John was come again.
And shortly to the point right for to gon,
The faire wife accorded with Dan John,
That for these hundred francs he should all night
Have her in his armes bolt upright;
And this accord performed was in deed.
In mirth all night a busy life they lead,
Till it was day, that Dan John went his way,
And bade the meinie* "Farewell; have good day." *servants
For none of them, nor no wight in the town,
Had of Dan John right no suspicioun;
And forth he rode home to his abbay,
Or where him list; no more of him I say.

The merchant, when that ended was the fair,
To Saint Denis he gan for to repair,
And with his wife he made feast and cheer,
And tolde her that chaffare* was so dear, *merchandise
That needes must he make a chevisance;* *loan
For he was bound in a recognisance
To paye twenty thousand shields* anon. *crowns, ecus
For which this merchant is to Paris gone,
To borrow of certain friendes that he had
A certain francs, and some with him he lad.* *took
And when that he was come into the town,
For great cherte* and great affectioun *love
Unto Dan John he wente first to play;
Not for to borrow of him no money,
But for to weet* and see of his welfare, *know
And for to telle him of his chaffare,
As friendes do, when they be met in fere.* *company
Dan John him made feast and merry cheer;
And he him told again full specially,
How he had well y-bought and graciously
(Thanked be God) all whole his merchandise;
Save that he must, in alle manner wise,
Maken a chevisance, as for his best;
And then he shoulde be in joy and rest.
Dan John answered, "Certes, I am fain* *glad
That ye in health be come borne again:
And if that I were rich, as have I bliss,
Of twenty thousand shields should ye not miss,
For ye so kindely the other day
Lente me gold, and as I can and may
I thanke you, by God and by Saint Jame.
But natheless I took unto our Dame,
Your wife at home, the same gold again,
Upon your bench; she wot it well, certain,
By certain tokens that I can her tell

Now, by your leave, I may no longer dwell;
Our abbot will out of this town anon,
And in his company I muste gon.
Greet well our Dame, mine owen niece sweet,
And farewell, deare cousin, till we meet.

This merchant, which that was full ware and wise,
Creanced hath, and paid eke in Paris *had obtained credit*
To certain Lombards ready in their hond
The sum of gold, and got of them his bond,
And home he went, merry as a popinjay.* *parrot
For well he knew he stood in such array
That needes must he win in that voyage
A thousand francs, above all his costage.* *expenses
His wife full ready met him at the gate,
As she was wont of old usage algate* *always
And all that night in mirthe they beset;* *spent
For he was rich, and clearly out of debt.
When it was day, the merchant gan embrace
His wife all new, and kiss'd her in her face,
And up he went, and maked it full tough.

"No more," quoth she, "by God ye have enough;"
And wantonly again with him she play'd,
Till at the last this merchant to her said.
"By God," quoth he, "I am a little wroth
With you, my wife, although it be me loth;
And wot ye why? by God, as that I guess,
That ye have made a *manner strangeness* *a kind of
            estrangement*
Betwixte me and my cousin, Dan John.
Ye should have warned me, ere I had gone,
That he you had a hundred frankes paid
By ready token; he *had him evil apaid* *was displeased*
For that I to him spake of chevisance,* *borrowing

411

(He seemed so as by his countenance);
But natheless, by God of heaven king,
I thoughte not to ask of him no thing.
I pray thee, wife, do thou no more so.
Tell me alway, ere that I from thee go,
If any debtor hath in mine absence
Y-payed thee, lest through thy negligence
I might him ask a thing that he hath paid."

This wife was not afeared nor afraid,
But boldely she said, and that anon;
"Mary! I defy that false monk Dan John,
I keep* not of his tokens never a deal:** *care **whit
He took me certain gold, I wot it well. —
What? evil thedom* on his monke's snout! — *thriving
For, God it wot, I ween'd withoute doubt
That he had given it me, because of you,
To do therewith mine honour and my prow,* *profit
For cousinage, and eke for belle cheer
That he hath had full often here.
But since I see I stand in such disjoint,* *awkward
      position
I will answer you shortly to the point.
Ye have more slacke debtors than am I;
For I will pay you well and readily,
From day to day, and if so be I fail,
I am your wife, score it upon my tail,
And I shall pay as soon as ever I may.
For, by my troth, I have on mine array,
And not in waste, bestow'd it every deal.
And, for I have bestowed it so well,
For your honour, for Godde's sake I say,
As be not wroth, but let us laugh and play.
Ye shall my jolly body have *to wed;* *in pledge*
By God, I will not pay you but in bed;

Forgive it me, mine owen spouse dear;
Turn hitherward, and make better cheer."

The merchant saw none other remedy;
And for to chide, it were but a folly,
Since that the thing might not amended be.
"Now, wife," he said, "and I forgive it thee;
But by thy life be no more so large;* *liberal, lavish
Keep better my good, this give I thee in charge."
Thus endeth now my tale; and God us send
Taling enough, until our lives' end!

THE PRIORESS'S TALE

"Well said, by *corpus Domini*,"* quoth our Host; *the Lord's
      body*
"Now longe may'st thou saile by the coast,
Thou gentle Master, gentle Marinere.
God give the monk *a thousand last quad year!* *ever so much
      evil*
Aha! fellows, beware of such a jape.* *trick
The monk *put in the manne's hood an ape,* *fooled him*
And in his wife's eke, by Saint Austin.
Drawe no monkes more into your inn.
But now pass over, and let us seek about,
Who shall now telle first of all this rout
Another tale;" and with that word he said,
As courteously as it had been a maid;
"My Lady Prioresse, by your leave,
So that I wist I shoulde you not grieve,* *offend
I woulde deeme* that ye telle should *judge, decide
A tale next, if so were that ye would.
Now will ye vouchesafe, my lady dear?"
"Gladly," quoth she; and said as ye shall hear.

413

THE TALE

O Lord our Lord! thy name how marvellous
Is in this large world y-spread! (quoth she)
For not only thy laude* precious   *praise
Performed is by men of high degree,
But by the mouth of children thy bounte*   *goodness
Performed is, for on the breast sucking
Sometimes showe they thy herying.*   *glory

Wherefore in laud, as I best can or may
Of thee, and of the white lily flow'r
Which that thee bare, and is a maid alway,
To tell a story I will do my labour;
Not that I may increase her honour,
For she herselven is honour and root
Of bounte, next her son, and soules' boot.*   *help

O mother maid, O maid and mother free!*   *bounteous
O bush unburnt, burning in Moses' sight,
That ravished'st down from the deity,
Through thy humbless, the ghost that in thee light;
Of whose virtue, when he thine hearte light,*   *lightened,
      gladdened
Conceived was the Father's sapience;
Help me to tell it to thy reverence.

Lady! thy bounty, thy magnificence,
Thy virtue, and thy great humility,
There may no tongue express in no science:
For sometimes, Lady! ere men pray to thee,
Thou go'st before, of thy benignity,
And gettest us the light, through thy prayere,
To guiden us unto thy son so dear.

My conning* is so weak, O blissful queen, *skill, ability
For to declare thy great worthiness,
That I not may the weight of it sustene;
But as a child of twelvemonth old, or less,
That can unnethes* any word express, *scarcely
Right so fare I; and therefore, I you pray,
Guide my song that I shall of you say.

There was in Asia, in a great city,
Amonges Christian folk, a Jewery,
Sustained by a lord of that country,
For foul usure, and lucre of villainy,
Hateful to Christ, and to his company;
And through the street men mighte ride and wend,* *go, walk
For it was free, and open at each end.

A little school of Christian folk there stood
Down at the farther end, in which there were
Children an heap y-come of Christian blood,
That learned in that schoole year by year
Such manner doctrine as men used there;
This is to say, to singen and to read,
As smalle children do in their childhead.

Among these children was a widow's son,
A little clergion,* seven year of age, *young clerk or scholar
That day by day to scholay* was his won,** *study **wont
And eke also, whereso he saw th' image
Of Christe's mother, had he in usage,
As him was taught, to kneel adown, and say
Ave Maria as he went by the way.

Thus had this widow her little son y-taught
Our blissful Lady, Christe's mother dear,

To worship aye, and he forgot it not;
For sely* child will always soone lear.**   *innocent **learn
But aye when I remember on this mattere,
Saint Nicholas stands ever in my presence;
For he so young to Christ did reverence.

This little child his little book learning,
As he sat in the school at his primere,
He *Alma redemptoris* hearde sing,
As children learned their antiphonere;
And as he durst, he drew him nere and nere,*   *nearer
And hearken'd aye the wordes and the note,
Till he the firste verse knew all by rote.

Nought wist he what this Latin was to say,*   *meant
For he so young and tender was of age;
But on a day his fellow gan he pray
To expound him this song in his language,
Or tell him why this song was in usage:
This pray'd he him to construe and declare,
Full oftentime upon his knees bare.

His fellow, which that elder was than he,
Answer'd him thus: "This song, I have heard say,
Was maked of our blissful Lady free,
Her to salute, and eke her to pray
To be our help and succour when we dey.*   *die
I can no more expound in this mattere:
I learne song, I know but small grammere."

"And is this song y-made in reverence
Of Christe's mother?" said this innocent;
Now certes I will do my diligence
To conne* it all, ere Christemas be went;   *learn
Though that I for my primer shall be shent,*   *disgraced

416

And shall be beaten thries in an hour,
I will it conne, our Lady to honour."

His fellow taught him homeward* privily   *on the way home
From day to day, till he coud* it by rote,   *knew
And then he sang it well and boldely
From word to word according with the note;
Twice in a day it passed through his throat;
To schoole-ward, and homeward when he went;
On Christ's mother was set all his intent.

As I have said, throughout the Jewery,
This little child, as he came to and fro,
Full merrily then would he sing and cry,
O Alma redemptoris, evermo';
The sweetness hath his hearte pierced so
Of Christe's mother, that to her to pray
He cannot stint* of singing by the way.   *cease

Our firste foe, the serpent Satanas,
That hath in Jewes' heart his waspe's nest,
Upswell'd and said, "O Hebrew people, alas!
Is this to you a thing that is honest,*   *creditable, becoming
That such a boy shall walken as him lest
In your despite, and sing of such sentence,
Which is against your lawe's reverence?"

From thenceforth the Jewes have conspired
This innocent out of the world to chase;
A homicide thereto have they hired,
That in an alley had a privy place,
And, as the child gan forth by for to pace,
This cursed Jew him hent,* and held him fast   *seized
And cut his throat, and in a pit him cast.

417

I say that in a wardrobe* he him threw, *privy
Where as the Jewes purged their entrail.
O cursed folk! O Herodes all new!
What may your evil intente you avail?
Murder will out, certain it will not fail,
And namely* where th' honour of God shall spread;
    *especially
The blood out crieth on your cursed deed.

O martyr souded* to virginity, *confirmed
Now may'st thou sing, and follow ever-in-one* *continually
The white Lamb celestial (quoth she),
Of which the great Evangelist Saint John
In Patmos wrote, which saith that they that gon
Before this Lamb, and sing a song all new,
That never fleshly woman they ne knew.

This poore widow waited all that night
After her little child, but he came not;
For which, as soon as it was daye's light,
With face pale, in dread and busy thought,
She hath at school and elleswhere him sought,
Till finally she gan so far espy,
That he was last seen in the Jewery.

With mother's pity in her breast enclosed,
She went, as she were half out of her mind,
To every place, where she hath supposed
By likelihood her little child to find:
And ever on Christ's mother meek and kind
She cried, and at the laste thus she wrought,
Among the cursed Jewes she him sought.

She freined,* and she prayed piteously *asked*
To every Jew that dwelled in that place,

To tell her, if her childe went thereby;
They saide, "Nay;" but Jesus of his grace
Gave in her thought, within a little space,
That in that place after her son she cried,
Where he was cast into a pit beside.

O greate God, that preformest thy laud
By mouth of innocents, lo here thy might!
This gem of chastity, this emeraud,* *emerald
And eke of martyrdom the ruby bright,
Where he with throat y-carven* lay upright, *cut
He *Alma redemptoris* gan to sing
So loud, that all the place began to ring.

The Christian folk, that through the streete went,
In came, for to wonder on this thing:
And hastily they for the provost sent.
He came anon withoute tarrying,
And heried* Christ, that is of heaven king, *praised
And eke his mother, honour of mankind;
And after that the Jewes let* he bind. *caused

With torment, and with shameful death each one
The provost did* these Jewes for to sterve** *caused **die
That of this murder wist, and that anon;
He woulde no such cursedness observe* *overlook
Evil shall have that evil will deserve;
Therefore with horses wild he did them draw,
And after that he hung them by the law.

The child, with piteous lamentation,
Was taken up, singing his song alway:
And with honour and great procession,
They carry him unto the next abbay.
His mother swooning by the biere lay;

Unnethes* might the people that were there   *scarcely
This newe Rachel bringe from his bier.

Upon his biere lay this innocent
Before the altar while the masses last';*   *lasted
And, after that, th' abbot with his convent
Have sped them for to bury him full fast;
And when they holy water on him cast,
Yet spake this child, when sprinkled was the water,
And sang, *O Alma redemptoris mater!*

This abbot, which that was a holy man,
As monkes be, or elles ought to be,
This younger child to conjure he began,
And said; "O deare child! I halse* thee,   *implore
In virtue of the holy Trinity;
Tell me what is thy cause for to sing,
Since that thy throat is cut, to my seeming."

"My throat is cut unto my necke-bone,"
Saide this child, "and, as *by way of kind,*   *in course of nature*
I should have died, yea long time agone;
But Jesus Christ, as ye in bookes find,
Will that his glory last and be in mind;
And, for the worship* of his mother dear,   *glory
Yet may I sing *O Alma* loud and clear.

"This well* of mercy, Christe's mother sweet,   *fountain
I loved alway, after my conning:*   *knowledge
And when that I my life should forlete,*   *leave
To me she came, and bade me for to sing
This anthem verily in my dying,
As ye have heard; and, when that I had sung,
Me thought she laid a grain upon my tongue.

"Wherefore I sing, and sing I must certain,
In honour of that blissful maiden free,
Till from my tongue off taken is the grain.
And after that thus saide she to me;
'My little child, then will I fetche thee,
When that the grain is from thy tongue take:
Be not aghast,* I will thee not forsake.'" *afraid

This holy monk, this abbot him mean I,
His tongue out caught, and took away the grain;
And he gave up the ghost full softely.
And when this abbot had this wonder seen,
His salte teares trickled down as rain:
And groff* he fell all flat upon the ground, *prostrate, grovelling
And still he lay, as he had been y-bound.

The convent* lay eke on the pavement *all the monks
Weeping, and herying* Christ's mother dear. *praising
And after that they rose, and forth they went,
And took away this martyr from his bier,
And in a tomb of marble stones clear
Enclosed they his little body sweet;
Where he is now, God lene* us for to meet. *grant

O younge Hugh of Lincoln! slain also
With cursed Jewes, — as it is notable,
For it is but a little while ago, —
Pray eke for us, we sinful folk unstable,
That, of his mercy, God so merciable* *merciful
On us his greate mercy multiply,
For reverence of his mother Mary.

CHAUCER'S TALE OF SIR THOPAS
WHEN said was this miracle, every man
As sober* was, that wonder was to see, *serious

Till that our Host to japen* he began,   *talk lightly
And then *at erst* he looked upon me,   *for the first time*
And saide thus; "What man art thou?" quoth he;
"Thou lookest as thou wouldest find an hare,
For ever on the ground I see thee stare.

"Approache near, and look up merrily.
Now ware you, Sirs, and let this man have place.
He in the waist is shapen as well as I;
This were a puppet in an arm t'embrace
For any woman small and fair of face.
He seemeth elvish* by his countenance,   *surly, morose
For unto no wight doth he dalliance.

"Say now somewhat, since other folk have said;
Tell us a tale of mirth, and that anon."
"Hoste," quoth I, "be not evil apaid,*   *dissatisfied
For other tale certes can* I none,   *know
But of a rhyme I learned yore* agone."   *long
"Yea, that is good," quoth he; "now shall we hear
Some dainty thing, me thinketh by thy cheer."*   *expression, mien

THE TALE

The First Fit*   *part
Listen, lordings, in good intent,
And I will tell you verrament*   *truly
Of mirth and of solas,*   *delight, solace
All of a knight was fair and gent,*   *gentle
In battle and in tournament,
His name was Sir Thopas.

Y-born he was in far country,
In Flanders, all beyond the sea,
At Popering in the place;

His father was a man full free,
And lord he was of that country,
As it was Godde's grace.

Sir Thopas was a doughty swain,
White was his face as paindemain,
His lippes red as rose.
His rode* is like scarlet in grain, *complexion
And I you tell in good certain
He had a seemly nose.

His hair, his beard, was like saffroun,
That to his girdle reach'd adown,
His shoes of cordewane:
Of Bruges were his hosen brown;
His robe was of ciclatoun,
That coste many a jane.

He coulde hunt at the wild deer,
And ride on hawking *for rivere* *by the river*
With gray goshawk on hand:
Thereto he was a good archere,
Of wrestling was there none his peer,
Where any ram should stand.

Full many a maiden bright in bow'r
They mourned for him par amour,
When them were better sleep;
But he was chaste, and no lechour,
And sweet as is the bramble flow'r
That beareth the red heep.* *hip

And so it fell upon a day,
For sooth as I you telle may,
Sir Thopas would out ride;

He worth* upon his steede gray,   *mounted
And in his hand a launcegay,*   *spear
A long sword by his side.

He pricked through a fair forest,
Wherein is many a wilde beast,
Yea, bothe buck and hare;
And as he pricked north and east,
I tell it you, him had almest*   *almost
Betid* a sorry care.   *befallen

There sprange herbes great and small,
The liquorice and the setewall,*   *valerian
And many a clove-gilofre,
And nutemeg to put in ale,
Whether it be moist* or stale,   *new
Or for to lay in coffer.

The birdes sang, it is no nay,
The sperhawk* and the popinjay,**   *sparrowhawk **parrot
That joy it was to hear;
The throstle-cock made eke his lay,
The woode-dove upon the spray
She sang full loud and clear.

Sir Thopas fell in love-longing
All when he heard the throstle sing,
And *prick'd as he were wood;*   *rode as if he were mad*
His faire steed in his pricking
So sweated, that men might him wring,
His sides were all blood.

Sir Thopas eke so weary was
For pricking on the softe grass,
So fierce was his corage,*   *inclination, spirit

That down he laid him in that place,
To make his steed some solace,
And gave him good forage.

"Ah, Saint Mary, ben'dicite,
What aileth thilke* love at me *this
To binde me so sore?
Me dreamed all this night, pardie,
An elf-queen shall my leman* be, *mistress
And sleep under my gore.* *shirt

"An elf-queen will I love, y-wis,* *assuredly
For in this world no woman is
Worthy to be my make* *mate
In town;
All other women I forsake,
And to an elf-queen I me take
By dale and eke by down."

Into his saddle he clomb anon,
And pricked over stile and stone
An elf-queen for to spy,
Till he so long had ridden and gone,
That he found in a privy wonne* *haunt
The country of Faery,
So wild;
For in that country was there none
That to him durste ride or gon,
Neither wife nor child.

Till that there came a great giaunt,
His name was Sir Oliphaunt,
A perilous man of deed;
He saide, "Child,* by Termagaunt, *young man
But if thou prick out of mine haunt, *unless

Anon I slay thy steed
With mace.
Here is the Queen of Faery,
With harp, and pipe, and symphony,
Dwelling in this place."

The Child said, "All so may I the,* *thrive
To-morrow will I meete thee,
When I have mine armor;
And yet I hope, *par ma fay,* *by my faith*
That thou shalt with this launcegay
Abyen* it full sore; *suffer for
Thy maw* *belly
Shall I pierce, if I may,
Ere it be fully prime of day,
For here thou shalt be slaw."* *slain

Sir Thopas drew aback full fast;
This giant at him stones cast
Out of a fell staff sling:
But fair escaped Child Thopas,
And all it was through Godde's grace,
And through his fair bearing.

Yet listen, lordings, to my tale,
Merrier than the nightingale,
For now I will you rown,* *whisper
How Sir Thopas, with sides smale,* *small
Pricking over hill and dale,
Is come again to town.

His merry men commanded he
To make him both game and glee;
For needes must he fight
With a giant with heades three,

For paramour and jollity
Of one that shone full bright.

"*Do come,*" he saide, "my minstrales *summon*
And gestours* for to telle tales. *story-tellers
Anon in mine arming,
Of romances that be royales,
Of popes and of cardinales,
And eke of love-longing."

They fetch'd him first the sweete wine,
And mead eke in a maseline,* *drinking-bowl
And royal spicery; of maple wood
Of ginger-bread that was full fine,
And liquorice and eke cumin,
With sugar that is trie.* *refined

He didde,* next his white lere,** *put on **skin
Of cloth of lake* fine and clear, *fine linen
A breech and eke a shirt;
And next his shirt an haketon,* *cassock
And over that an habergeon,* *coat of mail
For piercing of his heart;

And over that a fine hauberk,* *plate-armour
Was all y-wrought of Jewes'* werk, *magicians'
Full strong it was of plate;
And over that his coat-armour,* *knight's surcoat
As white as is the lily flow'r,
In which he would debate.* *fight

His shield was all of gold so red
And therein was a boare's head,
A charboucle* beside; *carbuncle
And there he swore on ale and bread,

How that the giant should be dead,
Betide whatso betide.

His jambeaux* were of cuirbouly, *boots
His sworde's sheath of ivory,
His helm of latoun* bright, *brass
His saddle was of rewel bone,
His bridle as the sunne shone,
Or as the moonelight.

His speare was of fine cypress,
That bodeth war, and nothing peace;
The head full sharp y-ground.
His steede was all dapple gray,
It went an amble in the way
Full softely and round
In land.

Lo, Lordes mine, here is a fytt;
If ye will any more of it,
To tell it will I fand.* *try

The Second Fit
Now hold your mouth for charity,
Bothe knight and lady free,
And hearken to my spell;* *tale
Of battle and of chivalry,
Of ladies' love and druerie,* *gallantry
Anon I will you tell.

Men speak of romances of price* * worth, esteem
Of Horn Child, and of Ipotis,
Of Bevis, and Sir Guy,
Of Sir Libeux, and Pleindamour,

But Sir Thopas, he bears the flow'r
Of royal chivalry.

His goode steed he all bestrode,
And forth upon his way he glode,*   *shone
As sparkle out of brand;*   *torch
Upon his crest he bare a tow'r,
And therein stick'd a lily flow'r;
God shield his corse* from shand!**   *body **harm

And, for he was a knight auntrous,*   *adventurous
He woulde sleepen in none house,
But liggen* in his hood,   *lie
His brighte helm was his wanger,*   *pillow
And by him baited* his destrer**   *fed **horse
Of herbes fine and good.

Himself drank water of the well,
As did the knight Sir Percivel,
So worthy under weed;
Till on a day — . . .

CHAUCER'S TALE OF MELIBOEUS

"No more of this, for Godde's dignity!"
Quoth oure Hoste; "for thou makest me
So weary of thy very lewedness,*   *stupidity, ignorance
That, all so wisly* God my soule bless,   *surely
Mine eares ache for thy drafty* speech.   *worthless
Now such a rhyme the devil I beteche:*   *commend to
This may well be rhyme doggerel," quoth he.
"Why so?" quoth I; "why wilt thou lette* me   *prevent
More of my tale than any other man,
Since that it is the best rhyme that I can?"*   *know

"By God!" quoth he, "for, plainly at one word,
Thy drafty rhyming is not worth a tord:
Thou dost naught elles but dispendest* time. *wastest
Sir, at one word, thou shalt no longer rhyme.
Let see whether thou canst tellen aught *in gest,* *by way of
Or tell in prose somewhat, at the least, narrative*
In which there be some mirth or some doctrine."
"Gladly," quoth I, "by Godde's sweete pine,* *suffering
I will you tell a little thing in prose,
That oughte like* you, as I suppose, *please
Or else certes ye be too dangerous.* *fastidious
It is a moral tale virtuous,
All be it told sometimes in sundry wise *although it be*
By sundry folk, as I shall you devise.
As thus, ye wot that ev'ry Evangelist,
That telleth us the pain* of Jesus Christ, *passion
He saith not all thing as his fellow doth;
But natheless their sentence is all soth,* *true
And all accorden as in their sentence,* *meaning
All be there in their telling difference;
For some of them say more, and some say less,
When they his piteous passion express;
I mean of Mark and Matthew, Luke and John;
But doubteless their sentence is all one.
Therefore, lordinges all, I you beseech,
If that ye think I vary in my speech,
As thus, though that I telle somedeal more
Of proverbes, than ye have heard before
Comprehended in this little treatise here,
T'enforce with the effect of my mattere, *with which to
      enforce*
And though I not the same wordes say
As ye have heard, yet to you all I pray
Blame me not; for as in my sentence
Shall ye nowhere finde no difference

From the sentence of thilke* treatise lite,** *this **little
After the which this merry tale I write.
And therefore hearken to what I shall say,
And let me tellen all my tale, I pray."

THE TALE

A young man called Meliboeus, mighty and rich, begat upon
his wife, that called was Prudence, a daughter which that
called was Sophia. Upon a day befell, that he for his disport
went into the fields him to play. His wife and eke his daughter
hath he left within his house, of which the doors were fast
shut. Three of his old foes have it espied, and set ladders to
the walls of his house, and by the windows be entered, and
beaten his wife, and wounded his daughter with five mortal
wounds, in five sundry places; that is to say, in her feet, in
her hands, in her ears, in her nose, and in her mouth; and
left her for dead, and went away. When Meliboeus returned
was into his house, and saw all this mischief, he, like a man
mad, rending his clothes, gan weep and cry. Prudence his
wife, as farforth as she durst, besought him of his weeping
for to stint: but not forthy [notwithstanding] he gan to weep
and cry ever longer the more.

This noble wife Prudence remembered her upon the
sentence of Ovid, in his book that called is the *Remedy of
Love*, where he saith: "He is a fool that disturbeth the mother
to weep in the death of her child, till she have wept her fill,
as for a certain time; and then shall a man do his diligence
with amiable words her to recomfort and pray her of her
weeping for to stint" [cease]. For which reason this noble wife
Prudence suffered her husband for to weep and cry, as for a
certain space; and when she saw her time, she said to him in
this wise: "Alas! my lord," quoth she, "why make ye yourself
for to be like a fool? For sooth it appertaineth not to a wise
man to make such a sorrow. Your daughter, with the grace of

God, shall warish [be cured] and escape. And all [although] were it so that she right now were dead, ye ought not for her death yourself to destroy. Seneca saith, 'The wise man shall not take too great discomfort for the death of his children, but certes he should suffer it in patience, as well as he abideth the death of his own proper person'."

Meliboeus answered anon and said: "What man," quoth he, "should of his weeping stint, that hath so great a cause to weep? Jesus Christ, our Lord, himself wept for the death of Lazarus his friend." Prudence answered, "Certes, well I wot, attempered [moderate] weeping is nothing defended [forbidden] to him that sorrowful is, among folk in sorrow but it is rather granted him to weep. The Apostle Paul unto the Romans writeth, 'Man shall rejoice with them that make joy, and weep with such folk as weep.' But though temperate weeping be granted, outrageous weeping certes is defended. Measure of weeping should be conserved, after the lore [doctrine] that teacheth us Seneca. 'When that thy friend is dead', quoth he, 'let not thine eyes too moist be of tears, nor too much dry: although the tears come to thine eyes, let them not fall. And when thou hast forgone [lost] thy friend, do diligence to get again another friend: and this is more wisdom than to weep for thy friend which that thou hast lorn [lost] for therein is no boot [advantage]. And therefore if ye govern you by sapience, put away sorrow out of your heart.' Remember you that Jesus Sirach saith, 'A man that is joyous and glad in heart, it him conserveth flourishing in his age: but soothly a sorrowful heart maketh his bones dry.' He said eke thus, 'that sorrow in heart slayth full many a man.' Solomon saith 'that right as moths in the sheep's fleece annoy [do injury] to the clothes, and the small worms to the tree, right so annoyeth sorrow to the heart of man.' Wherefore us ought as well in the death of our children, as in the loss of our goods temporal, have patience. Remember you upon the patient Job, when he had lost his children and his temporal substance, and in his body endured and received full many a grievous tribulation, yet said he thus: 'Our Lord hath given it to me, our Lord hath bereft it me; right as our Lord would, right so be it done; blessed be the name of our Lord'."

To these foresaid things answered Meliboeus unto his wife Prudence: "All thy words," quoth he, "be true, and thereto [also] profitable, but truly mine heart is troubled with this sorrow so grievously, that I know not what to do." "Let call," quoth Prudence, "thy true friends all, and thy lineage, which be wise, and tell to them your case, and hearken what they say in counselling, and govern you after their sentence [opinion]. Solomon saith, 'Work all things by counsel, and thou shall never repent.'" Then, by counsel of his wife Prudence, this Meliboeus let call [sent for] a great congregation of folk, as surgeons, physicians, old folk and young, and some of his old enemies reconciled (as by their semblance) to his love and to his grace; and therewithal there come some of his neighbours, that did him reverence more for dread than for love, as happeneth oft. There come also full many subtle flatterers, and wise advocates learned in the law. And when these folk together assembled were, this Meliboeus in sorrowful wise showed them his case, and by the manner of his speech it seemed that in heart he bare a cruel ire, ready to do vengeance upon his foes, and suddenly desired that the war should begin, but nevertheless yet asked he their counsel in this matter. A surgeon, by licence and assent of such as were wise, up rose, and to Meliboeus said as ye may hear. "Sir," quoth he, "as to us surgeons appertaineth, that we do to every wight the best that we can, where as we be withholden, [employed] and to our patient that we do no damage; wherefore it happeneth many a time and oft, that when two men have wounded each other, one same surgeon healeth them both; wherefore unto our art it is not pertinent to nurse war, nor parties to support [take sides]. But certes, as to the warishing [healing] of your daughter, albeit so that perilously she be wounded, we shall do so attentive business from day to night, that, with the grace of God, she shall be whole and sound, as soon as is possible." Almost right in the same wise the physicians answered, save that they said a few words more: that right as maladies be cured by their contraries, right so shall man warish war (by peace). His neighbours full of envy, his feigned friends that seemed reconciled, and his flatterers, made semblance of weeping, and impaired and agregged [aggravated] much of this matter, in praising greatly Meliboeus of might, of power, of riches, and of friends, despising the power of his adversaries: and said utterly, that he anon should wreak him on his foes, and begin war.

Up rose then an advocate that was wise, by leave and by counsel of other that were wise, and said, "Lordings, the need [business] for which we be assembled in this place, is a full heavy thing, and an high matter, because of the wrong and of the wickedness that hath been done, and eke by reason of the great damages that in time coming be possible to fall for the same cause, and eke by reason of the great riches and power of the parties both; for which reasons, it were a full great peril to err in this matter. Wherefore, Meliboeus, this is our sentence [opinion]; we counsel you, above all things, that right anon thou do thy diligence in keeping of thy body, in such a wise that thou want no espy nor watch thy body to save. And after that, we counsel that in thine house thou set sufficient garrison, so that they may as well thy body as thy house defend. But, certes, to move war or suddenly to do vengeance, we may not deem [judge] in so little time that it were profitable. Wherefore we ask leisure and space to have deliberation in this case to deem; for the common proverb saith thus; 'He that soon deemeth soon shall repent.' And eke men say, that that judge is wise, that soon understandeth a matter, and judgeth by leisure. For albeit so that all tarrying be annoying, algates [nevertheless] it is no reproof [subject for reproach] in giving of judgement, nor in vengeance taking, when it is sufficient and reasonable. And that shewed our Lord Jesus Christ by example; for when that the woman that was taken in adultery was brought in his presence to know what should be done with her person, albeit that he wist well himself what he would answer, yet would he not answer suddenly, but he would have deliberation, and in the ground he wrote twice. And by these causes we ask deliberation and we shall then by the grace of God counsel the thing that shall be profitable."

Up started then the young folk anon at once, and the most part of that company have scorned these old wise men and begun to make noise and said, "Right as while that iron is hot men should smite, right so men should wreak their wrongs while that they be fresh and new": and with loud voice they cried. "War! War!" Up rose then one of these old wise, and with his hand made countenance [a sign, gesture] that men should hold them still, and give him audience. "Lordings," quoth he, "there is full many a man that crieth, 'War! war!' that wot full little what war amounteth. War at his beginning hath so great an entering and so large, that every wight may enter when him liketh, and lightly [easily] find war: but certes what end shall fall thereof it is not light to know. For soothly when war is once begun, there is full many a child unborn of his mother, that shall sterve [die] young by cause of that war, or else live in sorrow and die in wretchedness; and therefore, ere that any war be begun, men must have great counsel and great deliberation." And when this old man weened [thought, intended] to enforce his tale by reasons, well-nigh all at once began they to rise for to break his tale, and bid him full oft his words abridge. For soothly he that preacheth to them that list not hear his words, his sermon them annoyeth. For Jesus Sirach saith, that music in weeping is a noyous [troublesome] thing. This is to say, as much availeth to speak before folk to whom his speech annoyeth, as to sing before him that weepeth. And when this wise man saw that him wanted audience, all shamefast he sat him down again. For Solomon saith, "Where as thou mayest have no audience, enforce thee not to speak." "I see well," quoth this wise man, "that the common proverb is sooth, that good counsel wanteth, when it is most need." Yet [besides, further] had this Meliboeus in his council many folk, that privily in his ear counselled him certain thing, and counselled him the contrary in general audience. When Meliboeus had heard that the greatest part of his council were accorded [in agreement] that he should make war, anon he consented to their counselling, and fully affirmed their sentence [opinion, judgement].

(Dame Prudence, seeing her husband's resolution thus taken, in full humble wise, when she saw her time, begins to counsel him against war, by a warning against haste in requital of either good or evil. Meliboeus tells her that he will not work by her counsel, because he should be held a fool if he rejected for her advice the opinion of so many wise men; because all women are bad; because it would seem that he had given her the mastery over him; and because she could not keep his secret, if he resolved to follow her advice. To these reasons Prudence answers that it is no folly to change counsel when things, or men's judgements of them, change — especially to alter a resolution taken on the impulse of a great multitude of folk, where every man crieth and clattereth what him liketh; that if all women had been wicked, Jesus Christ would never have descended to be born of a woman, nor have showed himself first to a woman after his resurrection and that when Solomon said he had found no good woman, he meant that God alone was supremely good; that her husband would not seem to give her the mastery by following her counsel, for he had his own free choice in following or rejecting it; and that he knew well and had often tested her great silence, patience, and secrecy. And whereas he had quoted a saying, that in wicked counsel women vanquish men, she reminds him that she would counsel him against doing a wickedness on which he had set his mind, and cites instances to show that many women have been and yet are full good, and their counsel wholesome and profitable. Lastly, she quotes the words of God himself, when he was about to make woman as an help meet for man; and promises that, if her husband will trust her counsel, she will restore to him his daughter whole and sound, and make him have honour in this case. Meliboeus answers that because of his wife's sweet words, and also because he has proved and assayed her great wisdom and her great truth, he will govern him by her counsel in all things. Thus encouraged, Prudence enters on a long discourse, full of learned citations, regarding the manner in which counsellors should be chosen and consulted, and the times and reasons for changing a counsel. First, God must be besought for guidance. Then a man must well examine his own thoughts, of such things as he holds to be best for his own profit; driving out of his heart anger, covetousness, and hastiness, which perturb and pervert the judgement. Then he must keep his counsel secret, unless confiding it to another shall be more profitable; but, in so confiding it, he shall say nothing to bias the mind of the counsellor toward flattery or subserviency. After that he should consider his friends and his enemies, choosing of the former such as be most faithful and wise, and eldest and most approved in counselling; and even of these only a few. Then he must eschew the counselling of fools, of flatterers, of his old enemies that be reconciled, of servants who bear him great reverence and fear, of folk that be drunken and can hide no counsel, of such as counsel one thing privily and the contrary openly; and of young folk, for their counselling is not ripe. Then, in examining his counsel, he must truly tell his tale; he must consider whether the thing he proposes to do be reasonable, within his power, and acceptable to the more part and the better part of his counsellors; he must look at the things that may follow from that counselling, choosing the best and waiving all besides; he must consider the root whence the matter of his counsel is engendered, what fruits it may bear, and from what causes they be sprung. And having thus examined his counsel and approved it by many wise folk and old, he shall consider if he may perform it and make of it a good end; if he be in doubt, he shall choose rather to suffer than to begin; but otherwise he shall prosecute his resolution steadfastly till the enterprise be at an end. As to changing his counsel, a man may do so without reproach, if the cause cease, or when a new case betides, or if he find that by error or otherwise harm or damage may result, or if his counsel be dishonest or come of dishonest cause, or if it be impossible or may not properly be kept; and he must take it for a general rule, that every counsel which is affirmed so strongly, that it may not be changed for any condition that may betide, that counsel is wicked. Meliboeus, admitting that his wife had spoken well and suitably as to counsellors and counsel in general, prays her to tell him in especial what she thinks of the counsellors whom they have chosen in their present need. Prudence replies that his counsel in this case could not properly be called a counselling, but a movement of folly; and points out that he has erred in sundry wise against the rules which he had just laid down. Granting that he has erred, Meliboeus says that he is all ready to change his counsel right as she will devise; for, as the proverb runs, to do sin is human, but to persevere long in sin is work of the Devil. Prudence then minutely recites, analyses, and criticises the counsel given to her husband in the assembly of his friends. She commends the advice of the physicians and surgeons, and urges that they should be well rewarded for their noble speech and their services in healing Sophia; and she asks Meliboeus how he understands their proposition that one contrary must be cured by another contrary. Meliboeus answers, that he should do vengeance on his enemies, who had done him wrong. Prudence, however, insists that vengeance is not the contrary of vengeance, nor wrong of wrong, but the like; and that wickedness should be healed by goodness, discord by accord, war by peace. She proceeds to deal with the counsel of the lawyers and wise folk that advised Meliboeus to take prudent measures for the security of his body and of his house. First, she would have her husband pray for the protection and aid of Christ; then commit the keeping of his person to his true friends; then suspect and avoid all strange folk, and liars, and such people as she had already warned him against; then beware of presuming on his strength, or the weakness of his adversary, and neglecting to guard his person — for every wise man dreadeth his enemy; then he should evermore be on the watch against ambush and all espial, even in what seems a place of safety; though he should not be so cowardly, as to fear where is no cause for dread; yet he should dread to be poisoned, and therefore shun scorners, and fly their words as venom. As to the fortification of his house, she points out that towers and great edifices are costly and laborious, yet useless unless defended by true friends that be old and wise; and the greatest and strongest garrison that a rich man may have, as well to keep his person as his goods, is, that he be beloved by his subjects and by his neighbours. Warmly approving the counsel that in all this business Meliboeus should proceed with great diligence and deliberation, Prudence goes on to examine the advice given by his neighbours that do him reverence without love, his old enemies reconciled, his flatterers that counselled him certain things privily and openly counselled him the contrary, and the young folk that counselled him to avenge himself and make war at once. She reminds him that he stands alone against three powerful enemies, whose kindred are numerous and close, while his are fewer and remote in relationship; that only the judge who has jurisdiction in a case may take sudden vengeance on any man; that her husband's power does not accord with his desire; and that, if he did take vengeance, it would only breed fresh wrongs and contests. As to the causes of the wrong done to him, she holds that God, the causer of all things, has permitted him to suffer because he has drunk so much honey of sweet temporal riches, and delights, and honours of this world, that he is drunken, and has forgotten Jesus Christ his Saviour; the three enemies of mankind, the flesh, the fiend, and the world, have entered his heart by the windows of his body, and wounded his soul in five places — that is to say, the deadly sins that have entered into his heart by the five senses; and in the same manner Christ has suffered his three enemies to enter his house by the windows, and wound his daughter in the five places before specified. Meliboeus demurs, that if his wife's objections prevailed, vengeance would never be taken, and thence great mischiefs would arise; but Prudence replies that the taking of vengeance lies with the judges, to whom the private individual must have recourse. Meliboeus declares that such vengeance does not please him, and that, as Fortune has nourished and helped him from his childhood, he will now assay her, trusting, with God's help, that she will aid him to avenge his shame. Prudence warns him against trusting to Fortune, all the less because she has hitherto favoured him, for just on that account she is the more likely to fail him; and she calls on him to leave his vengeance with the Sovereign Judge, that avengeth all villainies and wrongs. Meliboeus argues that if he refrains from taking vengeance he will invite his enemies to do him further wrong, and he will be put and held over low; but Prudence contends that such a result can be brought about only by the neglect of the judges, not by the patience of the individual. Supposing that he had leave to avenge himself, she repeats that he is not strong enough, and quotes the common saw, that it is madness for a man to strive with a stronger than himself, peril to strive with one of equal strength, and folly to strive with a weaker. But, considering his own defaults and demerits — remembering the patience of Christ and the undeserved tribulations of the saints, the brevity of this life with all its trouble and sorrow, the discredit thrown on the wisdom and training of a man who cannot bear wrong with patience — he should refrain wholly from taking vengeance. Meliboeus submits that he is not at all a perfect man, and his heart will never be at peace until he is avenged; and that as his enemies disregarded the peril when they attacked him, so he might, without reproach, incur some peril in attacking them in return, even though he did a great excess in avenging one wrong by another. Prudence strongly deprecates all outrage or excess; but Meliboeus insists that he cannot see that it might greatly harm him though he took a vengeance, for he is richer and mightier than his enemies, and all things obey money. Prudence thereupon launches into a long dissertation on the advantages of riches, the evils of poverty, the means by which wealth should be gathered, and the manner in which it should be used; and concludes by counselling her husband not to move war and battle through trust in his riches, for they suffice not to maintain war, the battle is not always to the strong or the numerous, and the perils of conflict are many. Meliboeus then curtly asks her for her counsel how he shall do in this need; and she answers that certainly she counsels him to agree with his adversaries and have peace with them. Meliboeus on this cries out that plainly she loves not his honour or his worship, in counselling him to go and humble himself before his enemies, crying mercy to them that, having done him so grievous wrong, ask him not to be reconciled. Then Prudence, making semblance of wrath, retorts that she loves his honour and profit as she loves her own, and ever has done; she cites the Scriptures in support of her counsel to seek peace; and says she will leave him to his own courses, for she knows well he is so stubborn, that he will do nothing for her.

Meliboeus then relents; admits that he is angry and cannot judge aright; and puts himself wholly in her hands, promising to do just as she desires, and admitting that he is the more held to love and praise her, if she reproves him of his folly).

Then Dame Prudence discovered all her counsel and her will unto him, and said: "I counsel you," quoth she, "above all things, that ye make peace between God and you, and be reconciled unto Him and to his grace; for, as I have said to you herebefore, God hath suffered you to have this tribulation and disease [distress, trouble] for your sins; and if ye do as I say you, God will send your adversaries unto you, and make them fall at your feet, ready to do your will and your commandment. For Solomon saith, 'When the condition of man is pleasant and liking to God, he changeth the hearts of the man's adversaries, and constraineth them to beseech him of peace of grace.' And I pray you let me speak with your adversaries in privy place, for they shall not know it is by your will or your assent; and then, when I know their will and their intent, I may counsel you the more surely." "Dame," quoth Meliboeus, "do your will and your liking, for I put me wholly in your disposition and ordinance."

Then Dame Prudence, when she saw the goodwill of her husband, deliberated and took advice in herself, thinking how she might bring this need [affair, emergency] unto a good end. And when she saw her time, she sent for these adversaries to come into her into a privy place, and showed wisely into them the great goods that come of peace, and the great harms and perils that be in war; and said to them, in goodly manner, how that they ought have great repentance of the injuries and wrongs that they had done to Meliboeus her Lord, and unto her and her daughter. And when they heard the goodly words of Dame Prudence, then they were surprised and ravished, and had so great joy of her, that wonder was to tell. "Ah lady!" quoth they, "ye have showed unto us the blessing of sweetness, after the saying of David the prophet; for the reconciling which we be not worthy to have in no manner, but we ought require it with great contrition and humility, ye of your great goodness have presented unto us. Now see we well, that the science and conning [knowledge] of Solomon is full true; for he saith, that sweet words multiply and increase friends, and make shrews [the ill-natured or angry] to be debonair [gentle, courteous] and meek. Certes we put our deed, and all our matter and cause, all wholly in your goodwill, and be ready to obey unto the speech and commandment of my lord Meliboeus. And therefore, dear and benign lady, we pray you and beseech you as meekly as we can and may, that it like unto your great goodness to fulfil in deed your goodly words. For we consider and acknowledge that we have offended and grieved my lord Meliboeus out of measure, so far forth that we be not of power to make him amends; and therefore we oblige and bind us and our friends to do all his will and his commandment. But peradventure he hath such heaviness and such wrath to usward, [towards us] because of our offence, that he will enjoin us such a pain [penalty] as we may not bear nor sustain; and therefore, noble lady, we beseech to your womanly pity to take such advisement [consideration] in this need, that we, nor our friends, be not disinherited and destroyed through our folly."

"Certes," quoth Prudence, "it is an hard thing, and right perilous, that a man put him all utterly in the arbitration and judgement and in the might and power of his enemy. For Solomon saith, 'Believe me, and give credence to that that I shall say: to thy son, to thy wife, to thy friend, nor to thy brother, give thou never might nor mastery over thy body, while thou livest.' Now, since he defendeth [forbiddeth] that a man should not give to his brother, nor to his friend, the might of his body, by a stronger reason he defendeth and forbiddeth a man to give himself to his enemy. And neverthe-less, I counsel you that ye mistrust not my lord: for I wot well and know verily, that he is debonair and meek, large, courteous and nothing desirous nor envious of good nor riches: for there is nothing in this world that he desireth save only worship and honour. Furthermore I know well, and am right sure, that he shall nothing do in this need without counsel of me; and I shall so work in this case, that by the grace of our Lord God ye shall be reconciled unto us."

Then said they with one voice, "Worshipful lady, we put us and our goods all fully in your will and disposition, and be ready to come, what day that it like unto your nobleness to limit us or assign us, for to make our obligation and bond, as strong as it liketh unto your goodness, that we may fulfil the will of you and of my lord Meliboeus."

When Dame Prudence had heard the answer of these men, she bade them go again privily, and she returned to her lord Meliboeus, and told him how she found his adversaries full repentant, acknowledging full lowly their sins and trespasses, and how they were ready to suffer all pain, requiring and praying him of mercy and pity. Then said Meliboeus, "He is well worthy to have pardon and forgiveness of his sin, that excuseth not his sin, but acknowledgeth, and repenteth him, asking indulgence. For Seneca saith, 'There is the remission and forgiveness, where the confession is; for confession is neighbour to innocence.' And therefore I assent and confirm me to have peace, but it is good that we do naught without the assent and will of our friends." Then was Prudence right glad and joyful, and said, "Certes, Sir, ye be well and goodly advised; for right as by the counsel, assent, and help of your friends ye have been stirred to avenge you and make war, right so without their counsel shall ye not accord you, nor have peace with your adversaries. For the law saith, 'There is nothing so good by way of kind, [nature] as a thing to be unbound by him that it was bound.'"

And then Dame Prudence, without delay or tarrying, sent anon her messengers for their kin and for their old friends, which were true and wise; and told them by order, in the presence of Meliboeus, all this matter, as it is above expressed and declared; and prayed them that they would give their advice and counsel what were best to do in this need. And when Meliboeus' friends had taken their advice and deliberation of the foresaid matter, and had examined it by great business and great diligence, they gave full counsel for to have peace and rest, and that Meliboeus should with good heart receive his adversaries to forgiveness and mercy. And when Dame Prudence had heard the assent of her lord Meliboeus, and the counsel of his friends, accord with her will and her intention, she was wondrous glad in her heart, and said: "There is an old proverb that saith, 'The goodness that thou mayest do this day, do it, and abide not nor delay it not till to-morrow': and therefore I counsel you that ye send your messengers, such as be discreet and wise, unto your adversaries, telling them on your behalf, that if they will treat of peace and of accord, that they shape [prepare] them, without delay or tarrying, to come unto us." Which thing performed was indeed. And when these trespassers and repenting folk of their follies, that is to say, the adversaries of Meliboeus, had heard what these messengers said unto them, they were right glad and joyful, and answered full meekly and benignly, yielding graces and thanks to their lord Meliboeus, and to all his company; and shaped them without delay to go with the messengers, and obey to the commandment of their lord Meliboeus. And right anon they took their way to the court of Meliboeus, and took with them some of their true friends, to make faith for them, and for to be their borrows [sureties].

And when they were come to the presence of Meliboeus, he said to them these words; "It stands thus," quoth Meliboeus, "and sooth it is, that ye causeless, and without skill and reason, have done great injuries and wrongs to me, and to my wife Prudence, and to my daughter also; for ye have entered into my house by violence, and have done such outrage, that all men know well that ye have deserved the death: and therefore will I know and weet of you, whether ye will put the punishing and chastising, and the vengeance of this outrage, in the will of me and of my wife, or ye will not?" Then the wisest of them three answered for them all, and said; "Sir," quoth he, "we know well, that we be unworthy to come to the court of so great a lord and so worthy as ye be, for we have so greatly mistaken us, and have offended and aguilt [incurred guilt] in such wise against your high lordship, that truly we have deserved the death. But yet for the great goodness and debonairte [courtesy, gentleness] that all the world witnesseth of your person, we submit us to the excellence and benignity of your gracious lordship, and be ready to obey to all your commandments, beseeching you, that of your merciable [merciful] pity ye will consider our great repentance and low submission, and grant us forgiveness of our outrageous trespass and offence; for well we know, that your liberal grace and mercy stretch them farther into goodness, than do our outrageous guilt and trespass into wickedness; albeit that cursedly [wickedly] and damnably we have aguilt [incurred guilt] against your high lordship." Then Meliboeus took them up from the ground full benignly, and received their obligations and their bonds, by their oaths upon their pledges and borrows, [sureties] and assigned them a certain day to return unto his court for to receive and accept sentence and judgement, that Meliboeus would command to be done on them, by the causes aforesaid; which things ordained, every man returned home to his house.

And when that Dame Prudence saw her time she freined [inquired] and asked her lord Meliboeus, what vengeance he thought to take of his adversaries. To which Meliboeus answered, and said; "Certes," quoth he, "I think and purpose me fully to disinherit them of all that ever they have, and for to put them in exile for evermore." "Certes," quoth Dame Prudence, "this were a cruel sentence, and much against reason. For ye be rich enough, and have no need of other men's goods;

and ye might lightly [easily] in this wise get you a covetous name, which is a vicious thing, and ought to be eschewed of every good man: for, after the saying of the Apostle, covetousness is root of all harms. And therefore it were better for you to lose much good of your own, than for to take of their good in this manner. For better it is to lose good with worship [honour], than to win good with villainy and shame. And every man ought to do his diligence and his business to get him a good name. And yet [further] shall he not only busy him in keeping his good name, but he shall also enforce him alway to do some thing by which he may renew his good name; for it is written, that the old good los [reputation] of a man is soon gone and passed, when it is not renewed. And as touching that ye say, that ye will exile your adversaries, that thinketh ye much against reason, and out of measure, [moderation] considered the power that they have given you upon themselves. And it is written, that he is worthy to lose his privilege, that misuseth the might and the power that is given him. And I set case [if I assume] ye might enjoin them that pain by right and by law (which I trow ye may not do), I say, ye might not put it to execution peradventure, and then it were like to return to the war, as it was before. And therefore if ye will that men do you obeisance, ye must deem [decide] more courteously, that is to say, ye must give more easy sentences and judgements. For it is written, 'He that most courteously commandeth, to him men most obey.' And therefore I pray you, that in this necessity and in this need ye cast you [endeavour, devise a way] to overcome your heart. For Seneca saith, that he that overcometh his heart, overcometh twice. And Tullius saith, 'There is nothing so commendable in a great lord, as when he is debonair and meek, and appeaseth him lightly' [easily]. And I pray you, that ye will now forbear to do vengeance, in such a manner, that your good name may be kept and conserved, and that men may have cause and matter to praise you of pity and of mercy; and that ye have no cause to repent you of thing that ye do. For Seneca saith, 'He overcometh in an evil manner, that repenteth him of his victory.' Wherefore I pray you let mercy be in your heart, to the effect and intent that God Almighty have mercy upon you in his last judgement; for Saint James saith in his Epistle, 'Judgement without mercy shall be done to him, that hath no mercy of another wight.'"

When Meliboeus had heard the great skills [arguments, reasons] and reasons of Dame Prudence, and her wise inform-ation and teaching, his heart gan incline to the will of his wife, considering her true intent, he conformed him anon and assented fully to work after her counsel, and thanked God, of whom proceedeth all goodness and all virtue, that him sent a wife of so great discretion. And when the day came that his adversaries should appear in his presence, he spake to them full goodly, and said in this wise; "Albeit so, that of your pride and high presumption and folly, an of your negligence and unconning, [ignorance] ye have misborne [misbehaved] you, and trespassed [done injury] unto me, yet forasmuch as I see and behold your great humility, and that ye be sorry and repentant of your guilts, it constraineth me to do you grace and mercy. Wherefore I receive you into my grace, and forgive you utterly all the offences, injuries, and wrongs, that ye have done against me and mine, to this effect and to this end, that God of his endless mercy will at the time of our dying forgive us our guilts, that we have trespassed to him in this wretched world; for doubtless, if we be sorry and repentant of the sins and guilts which we have trespassed in the sight of our Lord God, he is so free and so merciable [merciful], that he will forgive us our guilts, and bring us to the bliss that never hath end." Amen.

THE MONK'S TALE
When ended was my tale of Melibee,
And of Prudence and her benignity,
Our Hoste said, "As I am faithful man,

And by the precious corpus Madrian,
I had lever* than a barrel of ale,   *rather
That goode lefe* my wife had heard this tale;   *dear
For she is no thing of such patience
As was this Meliboeus' wife Prudence.
By Godde's bones! when I beat my knaves
She bringeth me the great clubbed staves,
And crieth, 'Slay the dogges every one,
And break of them both back and ev'ry bone.'
And if that any neighebour of mine
Will not in church unto my wife incline,
Or be so hardy to her to trespace,*   *offend
When she comes home she rampeth* in my face,   *springs
And crieth, 'False coward, wreak* thy wife   *avenge
By corpus Domini, I will have thy knife,
And thou shalt have my distaff, and go spin.'
From day till night right thus she will begin.
'Alas!' she saith, 'that ever I was shape*   *destined
To wed a milksop, or a coward ape,
That will be overlad* with every wight!   *imposed on
Thou darest not stand by thy wife's right.'

"This is my life, *but if* that I will fight;   *unless
And out at door anon I must me dight,*   *betake myself
Or elles I am lost, but if that I
Be, like a wilde lion, fool-hardy.
I wot well she will do* me slay some day   *make
Some neighebour and thenne *go my way;*   *take to flight*
For I am perilous with knife in hand,
Albeit that I dare not her withstand;
For she is big in armes, by my faith!
That shall he find, that her misdoth or saith.
But let us pass away from this mattere.
My lord the Monk," quoth he, "be merry of cheer,
For ye shall tell a tale truely.

Lo, Rochester stands here faste by.
Ride forth, mine owen lord, break not our game.
But by my troth I cannot tell your name;
Whether shall I call you my lord Dan John,
Or Dan Thomas, or elles Dan Albon?
Of what house be ye, by your father's kin?
I vow to God, thou hast a full fair skin;
It is a gentle pasture where thou go'st;
Thou art not like a penant* or a ghost.   *penitent
Upon my faith thou art some officer,
Some worthy sexton, or some cellarer.
For by my father's soul, *as to my dome,*   *in my judgement*
Thou art a master when thou art at home;
No poore cloisterer, nor no novice,
But a governor, both wily and wise,
And therewithal, of brawnes* and of bones,   *sinews
A right well-faring person for the nonce.
I pray to God give him confusion
That first thee brought into religion.
Thou would'st have been a treade-fowl* aright;   *cock
Hadst thou as greate leave, as thou hast might,
To perform all thy lust in engendrure,*   *generation, begettting
Thou hadst begotten many a creature.
Alas! why wearest thou so wide a cope?
God give me sorrow, but, an* I were pope,   *if
Not only thou, but every mighty man,
Though he were shorn full high upon his pan,*   *crown
Should have a wife; for all this world is lorn;*   *undone,
        ruined
Religion hath ta'en up all the corn
Of treading, and we borel* men be shrimps: *lay
Of feeble trees there come wretched imps.*   *shoots
This maketh that our heires be so slender
And feeble, that they may not well engender.
This maketh that our wives will assay

Religious folk, for they may better pay
Of Venus' payementes than may we:
God wot, no lusheburghes paye ye.
But be not wroth, my lord, though that I play;
Full oft in game a sooth have I heard say."

This worthy Monk took all in patience,
And said, "I will do all my diligence,
As far as *souneth unto honesty,* *agrees with good
    manners*
To telle you a tale, or two or three.
And if you list to hearken hitherward,
I will you say the life of Saint Edward;
Or elles first tragedies I will tell,
Of which I have an hundred in my cell.
Tragedy *is to say* a certain story, *means*
As olde bookes maken us memory,
Of him that stood in great prosperity,
And is y-fallen out of high degree
In misery, and endeth wretchedly.
And they be versified commonly
Of six feet, which men call hexametron;
In prose eke* be indited many a one, *also
And eke in metre, in many a sundry wise.
Lo, this declaring ought enough suffice.
Now hearken, if ye like for to hear.
But first I you beseech in this mattere,
Though I by order telle not these things,
Be it of popes, emperors, or kings,
After their ages, as men written find, *in chronological
    order*
But tell them some before and some behind,
As it now cometh to my remembrance,
Have me excused of mine ignorance."

THE TALE

I will bewail, in manner of tragedy,
The harm of them that stood in high degree,
And felle so, that there was no remedy
To bring them out of their adversity.
For, certain, when that Fortune list to flee,
There may no man the course of her wheel hold:
Let no man trust in blind prosperity;
Beware by these examples true and old.

At Lucifer, though he an angel were,
And not a man, at him I will begin.
For though Fortune may no angel dere,*   *hurt
From high degree yet fell he for his sin
Down into hell, where as he yet is in.
O Lucifer! brightest of angels all,
Now art thou Satanas, that may'st not twin*   *depart
Out of the misery in which thou art fall.

Lo Adam, in the field of Damascene
With Godde's owen finger wrought was he,
And not begotten of man's sperm unclean;
And welt* all Paradise saving one tree: *commanded
Had never worldly man so high degree
As Adam, till he for misgovernance*   *misbehaviour
Was driven out of his prosperity
To labour, and to hell, and to mischance.

Lo Sampson, which that was annunciate
By the angel, long ere his nativity;
And was to God Almighty consecrate,
And stood in nobless while that he might see;
Was never such another as was he,
To speak of strength, and thereto hardiness;*   *courage

But to his wives told he his secre,
Through which he slew himself for wretchedness.

Sampson, this noble and mighty champion,
Withoute weapon, save his handes tway,
He slew and all to-rente* the lion,   *tore to pieces
Toward his wedding walking by the way.
His false wife could him so please, and pray,
Till she his counsel knew; and she, untrue,
Unto his foes his counsel gan bewray,
And him forsook, and took another new.

Three hundred foxes Sampson took for ire,
And all their tailes he together band,
And set the foxes' tailes all on fire,
For he in every tail had knit a brand,
And they burnt all the combs of that lend,
And all their oliveres* and vines eke.   *olive trees
A thousand men he slew eke with his hand,
And had no weapon but an ass's cheek.

When they were slain, so thirsted him, that he
Was *well-nigh lorn,* for which he gan to pray   *near to perishing*
That God would on his pain have some pity,
And send him drink, or elles must he die;
And of this ass's check, that was so dry,
Out of a wang-tooth* sprang anon a well,   *cheek-tooth
Of which, he drank enough, shortly to say.
Thus help'd him God, as Judicum can tell.

By very force, at Gaza, on a night,
Maugre* the Philistines of that city,   *in spite of
The gates of the town he hath up plight,*   *plucked, wrenched
And on his back y-carried them hath he

High on an hill, where as men might them see.
O noble mighty Sampson, lefe* and dear, *loved
Hadst thou not told to women thy secre,
In all this world there had not been thy peer.

This Sampson never cider drank nor wine,
Nor on his head came razor none nor shear,
By precept of the messenger divine;
For all his strengthes in his haires were;
And fully twenty winters, year by year,
He had of Israel the governance;
But soone shall he weepe many a tear,
For women shall him bringe to mischance.

Unto his leman* Dalila he told, *mistress
That in his haires all his strengthe lay;
And falsely to his foemen she him sold,
And sleeping in her barme* upon a day *lap
She made to clip or shear his hair away,
And made his foemen all his craft espien.
And when they founde him in this array,
They bound him fast, and put out both his eyen.

But, ere his hair was clipped or y-shave,
There was no bond with which men might him bind;
But now is he in prison in a cave,
Where as they made him at the querne* grind. *mill
O noble Sampson, strongest of mankind!
O whilom judge in glory and richess!
Now may'st thou weepe with thine eyen blind,
Since thou from weal art fall'n to wretchedness.

Th'end of this caitiff* was as I shall say; *wretched man
His foemen made a feast upon a day,
And made him as their fool before them play;

And this was in a temple of great array.
But at the last he made a foul affray,
For he two pillars shook, and made them fall,
And down fell temple and all, and there it lay,
And slew himself and eke his foemen all;

This is to say, the princes every one;
And eke three thousand bodies were there slain
With falling of the great temple of stone.
Of Sampson now will I no more sayn;
Beware by this example old and plain,
That no man tell his counsel to his wife
Of such thing as he would *have secret fain,* *wish to be secret*
If that it touch his limbes or his life.

Of Hercules the sov'reign conquerour
Singe his workes' land and high renown;
For in his time of strength he bare the flow'r.
He slew and reft the skin of the lion
He of the Centaurs laid the boast adown;
He Harpies slew, the cruel birdes fell;
He golden apples reft from the dragon
He drew out Cerberus the hound of hell.

He slew the cruel tyrant Busirus.
And made his horse to fret* him flesh and bone; *devour
He slew the fiery serpent venomous;
Of Achelous' two hornes brake he one.
And he slew Cacus in a cave of stone;
He slew the giant Antaeus the strong;
He slew the grisly boar, and that anon;
And bare the heav'n upon his necke long.

Was never wight, since that the world began,
That slew so many monsters as did he;

Throughout the wide world his name ran,
What for his strength, and for his high bounte;
And every realme went he for to see;
He was so strong that no man might him let;* *withstand
At both the worlde's ends, as saith Trophee,
Instead of boundes he a pillar set.

A leman had this noble champion,
That highte Dejanira, fresh as May;
And, as these clerkes make mention,
She hath him sent a shirte fresh and gay;
Alas! this shirt, alas and well-away!
Envenomed was subtilly withal,
That ere that he had worn it half a day,
It made his flesh all from his bones fall.

But natheless some clerkes her excuse
By one, that highte Nessus, that it maked;
Be as he may, I will not her accuse;
But on his back this shirt he wore all naked,
Till that his flesh was for the venom blaked.* *blackened
And when he saw none other remedy,
In hote coals he hath himselfe raked,
For with no venom deigned he to die.

Thus sterf* this worthy mighty Hercules. *died
Lo, who may trust on Fortune *any throw?* *for a
        moment*
For him that followeth all this world of pres,* *near
Ere he be ware, is often laid full low;
Full wise is he that can himselfe know.
Beware, for when that Fortune list to glose
Then waiteth she her man to overthrow,
By such a way as he would least suppose.

The mighty throne, the precious treasor,
The glorious sceptre, and royal majesty,
That had the king Nabuchodonosor
With tongue unnethes* may described be. *scarcely
He twice won Jerusalem the city,
The vessels of the temple he with him lad;*
    *took away
At Babylone was his sov'reign see,* *seat
In which his glory and delight he had.

The fairest children of the blood royal
Of Israel he *did do geld* anon, *caused to be castrated*
And maked each of them to be his thrall.* *slave
Amonges others Daniel was one,
That was the wisest child of every one;
For he the dreames of the king expounded,
Where in Chaldaea clerkes was there none
That wiste to what fine* his dreames sounded. *end

This proude king let make a statue of gold
Sixty cubites long, and seven in bread',
To which image hathe young and old
Commanded he to lout,* and have in dread, *bow
    down to
Or in a furnace, full of flames red,
He should be burnt that woulde not obey:
But never would assente to that deed
Daniel, nor his younge fellows tway.

This king of kinges proud was and elate;* *lofty
He ween'd* that God, that sits in majesty, *thought
Mighte him not bereave of his estate;
But suddenly he lost his dignity,
And like a beast he seemed for to be,
And ate hay as an ox, and lay thereout

In rain, with wilde beastes walked he,
Till certain time was y-come about.

And like an eagle's feathers wax'd his hairs,
His nailes like a birde's clawes were,
Till God released him at certain years,
And gave him wit; and then with many a tear
He thanked God, and ever his life in fear
Was he to do amiss, or more trespace:
And till that time he laid was on his bier,
He knew that God was full of might and grace.

His sone, which that highte Balthasar,
That *held the regne* after his father's day, *possessed the
    kingdom*
He by his father coulde not beware,
For proud he was of heart and of array;
And eke an idolaster was he aye.
His high estate assured* him in pride; *confirmed
But Fortune cast him down, and there he lay,
And suddenly his regne gan divide.

A feast he made unto his lordes all
Upon a time, and made them blithe be,
And then his officeres gan he call;
"Go, bringe forth the vessels," saide he,
"Which that my father in his prosperity
Out of the temple of Jerusalem reft,
And to our highe goddes thanks we
Of honour, that our elders* with us left." *forefathers

His wife, his lordes, and his concubines
Aye dranke, while their appetites did last,
Out of these noble vessels sundry wines.
And on a wall this king his eyen cast,

And saw an hand, armless, that wrote full fast;
For fear of which he quaked, and sighed sore.
This hand, that Balthasar so sore aghast,* *dismayed
Wrote Mane, tekel, phares, and no more.

In all that land magician was there none
That could expounde what this letter meant.
But Daniel expounded it anon,
And said, "O King, God to thy father lent
Glory and honour, regne, treasure, rent;* *revenue
And he was proud, and nothing God he drad;* *dreaded
And therefore God great wreche* upon him sent,
        *vengeance
And him bereft the regne that he had.

"He was cast out of manne's company;
With asses was his habitation
And ate hay, as a beast, in wet and dry,
Till that he knew by grace and by reason
That God of heaven hath domination
O'er every regne, and every creature;
And then had God of him compassion,
And him restor'd his regne and his figure.

"Eke thou, that art his son, art proud also,
And knowest all these thinges verily;
And art rebel to God, and art his foe.
Thou drankest of his vessels boldely;
Thy wife eke, and thy wenches, sinfully
Drank of the same vessels sundry wines,
And heried* false goddes cursedly; *praised
Therefore *to thee y-shapen full great pine is.* *great
        punishment is prepared for thee*

"This hand was sent from God, that on the wall
Wrote Mane, tekel, phares, truste me;
Thy reign is done; thou weighest naught at all;
Divided is thy regne, and it shall be
To Medes and to Persians giv'n," quoth he.
And thilke same night this king was slaw* *slain
And Darius occupied his degree,
Though he thereto had neither right nor law.

Lordings, example hereby may ye take,
How that in lordship is no sickerness;* *security
For when that Fortune will a man forsake,
She bears away his regne and his richess,
And eke his friendes bothe more and less,
For what man that hath friendes through fortune,
Mishap will make them enemies, I guess;
This proverb is full sooth, and full commune.

Zenobia, of Palmyrie the queen,
As write Persians of her nobless,
So worthy was in armes, and so keen,
That no wight passed her in hardiness,
Nor in lineage, nor other gentleness.* *noble qualities
Of the king's blood of Perse* is she descended; *Persia
I say not that she hadde most fairness,
But of her shape she might not he amended.

From her childhood I finde that she fled
Office of woman, and to woods she went,
And many a wilde harte's blood she shed
With arrows broad that she against them sent;
She was so swift, that she anon them hent.* *caught
And when that she was older, she would kill
Lions, leopards, and beares all to-rent,* *torn to pieces
And in her armes wield them at her will.

She durst the wilde beastes' dennes seek,
And runnen in the mountains all the night,
And sleep under a bush; and she could eke
Wrestle by very force and very might
With any young man, were he ne'er so wight;* *active,
    nimble
There mighte nothing in her armes stond.
She kept her maidenhood from every wight,
To no man deigned she for to be bond.

But at the last her friendes have her married
To Odenate, a prince of that country;
All were it so, that she them longe tarried.
And ye shall understande how that he
Hadde such fantasies as hadde she;
But natheless, when they were knit in fere,* *together
They liv'd in joy, and in felicity,
For each of them had other lefe* and dear. *loved

Save one thing, that she never would assent,
By no way, that he shoulde by her lie
But ones, for it was her plain intent
To have a child, the world to multiply;
And all so soon as that she might espy
That she was not with childe by that deed,
Then would she suffer him do his fantasy
Eftsoon,* and not but ones, *out of dread.* *again *without
    doubt*

And if she were with child at thilke* cast, *that
No more should he playe thilke game
Till fully forty dayes were past;
Then would she once suffer him do the same.
All* were this Odenatus wild or tame, *whether
He got no more of her; for thus she said,

461

It was to wives lechery and shame
In other case* if that men with them play'd. *on other terms

Two sones, by this Odenate had she,
The which she kept in virtue and lettrure.* *learning
But now unto our tale turne we;
I say, so worshipful a creature,
And wise therewith, and large* with measure,** *bountiful
    **moderation
So penible* in the war, and courteous eke, *laborious
Nor more labour might in war endure,
Was none, though all this worlde men should seek.

Her rich array it mighte not be told,
As well in vessel as in her clothing:
She was all clad in pierrie* and in gold, *jewellery
And eke she *lefte not,* for no hunting, *did not neglect*
To have of sundry tongues full knowing,
When that she leisure had, and for t'intend* *apply
To learne bookes was all her liking,
How she in virtue might her life dispend.

And, shortly of this story for to treat,
So doughty was her husband and eke she,
That they conquered many regnes great
In th'Orient, with many a fair city
Appertinent unto the majesty
Of Rome, and with strong hande held them fast,
Nor ever might their foemen do* them flee, *make
Aye while that Odenatus' dayes last'.

Her battles, whoso list them for to read,
Against Sapor the king, and other mo',
And how that all this process fell in deed,
Why she conquer'd, and what title thereto,

And after of her mischief* and her woe, *misfortune
How that she was besieged and y-take,
Let him unto my master Petrarch go,
That writes enough of this, I undertake.

When Odenate was dead, she mightily
The regne held, and with her proper hand
Against her foes she fought so cruelly,
That there n'as* king nor prince in all that land, *was not
That was not glad, if be that grace fand
That she would not upon his land warray;* *make war
With her they maden alliance by bond,
To be in peace, and let her ride and play.

The emperor of Rome, Claudius,
Nor, him before, the Roman Gallien,
Durste never be so courageous,
Nor no Armenian, nor Egyptien,
Nor Syrian, nor no Arabien,
Within the fielde durste with her fight,
Lest that she would them with her handes slen,* *slay
Or with her meinie* putte them to flight. *troops

In kinges' habit went her sones two,
As heires of their father's regnes all;
And Heremanno and Timolao
Their names were, as Persians them call
But aye Fortune hath in her honey gall;
This mighty queene may no while endure;
Fortune out of her regne made her fall
To wretchedness and to misadventure.

Aurelian, when that the governance
Of Rome came into his handes tway,
He shope* upon this queen to do vengeance; *prepared

463

And with his legions he took his way
Toward Zenobie, and, shortly for to say,
He made her flee, and at the last her hent,* *took
And fetter'd her, and eke her children tway,
And won the land, and home to Rome he went.

Amonges other thinges that he wan,
Her car, that was with gold wrought and pierrie,* *jewels
This greate Roman, this Aurelian
Hath with him led, for that men should it see.
Before in his triumphe walked she
With gilte chains upon her neck hanging;
Crowned she was, as after* her degree, *according to
And full of pierrie her clothing.

Alas, Fortune! she that whilom was
Dreadful to kinges and to emperours,
Now galeth* all the people on her, alas! *yelleth
And she that *helmed was in starke stowres,* *wore a helmet in
    obstinate battles*
And won by force townes strong and tow'rs,
Shall on her head now wear a vitremite;
And she that bare the sceptre full of flow'rs
Shall bear a distaff, *her cost for to quite.* * to make her
    living*

Although that Nero were so vicious
As any fiend that lies full low adown,
Yet he, as telleth us Suetonius,
This wide world had in subjectioun,
Both East and West, South and Septentrioun.
Of rubies, sapphires, and of pearles white
Were all his clothes embroider'd up and down,
For he in gemmes greatly gan delight.

More delicate, more pompous of array,
More proud, was never emperor than he;
That *ilke cloth* that he had worn one day, *same robe*
After that time he would it never see;
Nettes of gold thread had he great plenty,
To fish in Tiber, when him list to play;
His lustes* were as law, in his degree, *pleasures
For Fortune as his friend would him obey.

He Rome burnt for his delicacy;* *pleasure
The senators he slew upon a day,
To heare how that men would weep and cry;
And slew his brother, and by his sister lay.
His mother made he in piteous array;
For he her wombe slitte, to behold
Where he conceived was; so well-away!
That he so little of his mother told.* *valued

No tear out of his eyen for that sight
Came; but he said, a fair woman was she.
Great wonder is, how that he could or might
Be doomesman* of her deade beauty: *judge
The wine to bringe him commanded he,
And drank anon; none other woe he made,
When might is joined unto cruelty,
Alas! too deepe will the venom wade.

In youth a master had this emperour,
To teache him lettrure* and courtesy; *literature, learning
For of morality he was the flow'r,
As in his time, *but if* bookes lie. *unless
And while this master had of him mast'ry,
He made him so conning and so souple,* *subtle
That longe time it was ere tyranny,
Or any vice, durst in him uncouple.* *be let loose

465

This Seneca, of which that I devise,* *tell
Because Nero had of him suche dread,
For he from vices would him aye chastise
Discreetly, as by word, and not by deed;
"Sir," he would say, "an emperor must need
Be virtuous, and hate tyranny."
For which he made him in a bath to bleed
On both his armes, till he muste die.

This Nero had eke of a custumance* *habit
In youth against his master for to rise;* *stand in his
  presence
Which afterward he thought a great grievance;
Therefore he made him dien in this wise.
But natheless this Seneca the wise
Chose in a bath to die in this mannere,
Rather than have another tormentise;* *torture
And thus hath Nero slain his master dear.

Now fell it so, that Fortune list no longer
The highe pride of Nero to cherice;* *cherish
For though he were strong, yet was she stronger.
She thoughte thus; "By God, I am too nice* *foolish
To set a man, that is full fill'd of vice,
In high degree, and emperor him call!
By God, out of his seat I will him trice!* *thrust
When he least weeneth,* soonest shall he fall." *expecteth

The people rose upon him on a night,
For his default; and when he it espied,
Out of his doors anon he hath him dight* *betaken himself
Alone, and where he ween'd t'have been allied,* *regarded
  with friendship
He knocked fast, and aye the more he cried
The faster shutte they their doores all;

Then wist he well he had himself misgied,* *misled
And went his way, no longer durst he call.

The people cried and rumbled up and down,
That with his eares heard he how they said;
"Where is this false tyrant, this Neroun?"
For fear almost out of his wit he braid,* *went
And to his goddes piteously he pray'd
For succour, but it mighte not betide
For dread of this he thoughte that died,
And ran into a garden him to hide.

And in this garden found he churles tway,
That satte by a fire great and red;
And to these churles two he gan to pray
To slay him, and to girdon* off his head, *strike
That to his body, when that he were dead,
Were no despite done for his defame.* *infamy
Himself he slew, *he coud no better rede;* *he knew no
    better counsel*
Of which Fortune laugh'd and hadde game.

Was never capitain under a king,
That regnes more put in subjectioun,
Nor stronger was in field of alle thing
As in his time, nor greater of renown,
Nor more pompous in high presumptioun,
Than Holofernes, whom Fortune aye kiss'd
So lik'rously, and led him up and down,
Till that his head was off *ere that he wist.* *before he knew it*

Not only that this world had of him awe,
For losing of richess and liberty;
But he made every man *reny his law.* *renounce his religion
Nabuchodonosor was God, said he;

467

None other Godde should honoured be.
Against his hest* there dare no wight trespace, *command
Save in Bethulia, a strong city,
Where Eliachim priest was of that place.

But take keep* of the death of Holofern; *notice
Amid his host he drunken lay at night
Within his tente, large as is a bern;* *barn
And yet, for all his pomp and all his might,
Judith, a woman, as he lay upright
Sleeping, his head off smote, and from his tent
Full privily she stole from every wight,
And with his head unto her town she went.

What needeth it of king Antiochus
To tell his high and royal majesty,
His great pride, and his workes venomous?
For such another was there none as he;
Reade what that he was in Maccabee.
And read the proude wordes that he said,
And why he fell from his prosperity,
And in an hill how wretchedly he died.

Fortune him had enhanced so in pride,
That verily he ween'd he might attain
Unto the starres upon every side,
And in a balance weighen each mountain,
And all the floodes of the sea restrain.
And Godde's people had he most in hate
Them would he slay in torment and in pain,
Weening that God might not his pride abate.

And for that Nicanor and Timothee
With Jewes were vanquish'd mightily,
Unto the Jewes such an hate had he,

That he bade *graith his car* full hastily, *prepare his chariot*
And swore and saide full dispiteously,
Unto Jerusalem he would eftsoon,* *immediately
To wreak his ire on it full cruelly
But of his purpose was he let* full soon. *prevented

God for his menace him so sore smote,
With invisible wound incurable,
That in his guttes carf* it so and bote,** *cut **gnawed
Till that his paines were importable;* *unendurable
And certainly the wreche* was reasonable, *vengeance
For many a manne's guttes did he pain;
But from his purpose, curs'd* and damnable, *impious
For all his smart he would him not restrain;
But bade anon apparaile* his host. *prepare

And suddenly, ere he was of it ware,
God daunted all his pride, and all his boast
For he so sore fell out of his chare,* *chariot
That it his limbes and his skin to-tare,
So that he neither mighte go nor ride
But in a chaire men about him bare,
Alle forbruised bothe back and side.

The wreche* of God him smote so cruelly, *vengeance
That through his body wicked wormes crept,
And therewithal he stank so horribly
That none of all his meinie* that him kept, *servants
Whether so that he woke or elles slept,
Ne mighte not of him the stink endure.
In this mischief he wailed and eke wept,
And knew God Lord of every creature.

To all his host, and to himself also,
Full wlatsem* was the stink of his carrain;** *loathsome **body

No manne might him beare to and fro.
And in this stink, and this horrible pain,
He starf* full wretchedly in a mountain. *dies
Thus hath this robber, and this homicide,
That many a manne made to weep and plain,
Such guerdon* as belongeth unto pride. *reward

The story of Alexander is so commune,
That ev'ry wight that hath discretion
Hath heard somewhat or all of his fortune.
This wide world, as in conclusion,
He won by strength; or, for his high renown,
They were glad for peace to him to send.
The pride and boast of man he laid adown,
Whereso he came, unto the worlde's end.

Comparison yet never might be maked
Between him and another conqueror;
For all this world for dread of him had quaked
He was of knighthood and of freedom flow'r:
Fortune him made the heir of her honour.
Save wine and women, nothing might assuage
His high intent in arms and labour,
So was he full of leonine courage.

What praise were it to him, though I you told
Of Darius, and a hundred thousand mo',
Of kinges, princes, dukes, and earles bold,
Which he conquer'd, and brought them into woe?
I say, as far as man may ride or go,
The world was his, why should I more devise?* *tell
For, though I wrote or told you evermo',
Of his knighthood it mighte not suffice.

Twelve years he reigned, as saith Maccabee
Philippe's son of Macedon he was,
That first was king in Greece the country.
O worthy gentle* Alexander, alas   *noble
That ever should thee falle such a case!
Empoison'd of thine owen folk thou were;
Thy six Fortune hath turn'd into an ace,
And yet for thee she wepte never a tear.

Who shall me give teares to complain
The death of gentiless, and of franchise,*   *generosity
That all this worlde had in his demaine,*   *dominion
And yet he thought it mighte not suffice,
So full was his corage* of high emprise?   *spirit
Alas! who shall me helpe to indite
False Fortune, and poison to despise?
The whiche two of all this woe I wite.*   *blame

By wisdom, manhood, and by great labour,
From humbleness to royal majesty
Up rose he, Julius the Conquerour,
That won all th' Occident,* by land and sea,   *West
By strength of hand or elles by treaty,
And unto Rome made them tributary;
And since* of Rome the emperor was he,   *afterwards
Till that Fortune wax'd his adversary.

O mighty Caesar, that in Thessaly
Against Pompeius, father thine in law,
That of th' Orient had all the chivalry,
As far as that the day begins to daw,
That through thy knighthood hast them take and slaw,*   *slain*
Save fewe folk that with Pompeius fled;
Through which thou put all th' Orient in awe;
Thanke Fortune that so well thee sped.

But now a little while I will bewail
This Pompeius, this noble governor
Of Rome, which that fled at this battaile
I say, one of his men, a false traitor,
His head off smote, to winne him favor
Of Julius, and him the head he brought;
Alas! Pompey, of th' Orient conqueror,
That Fortune unto such a fine* thee brought! *end

To Rome again repaired Julius,
With his triumphe laureate full high;
But on a time Brutus and Cassius,
That ever had of his estate envy,
Full privily have made conspiracy
Against this Julius in subtle wise
And cast* the place in which he shoulde die, *arranged
With bodekins,* as I shall you devise.** *daggers **tell

This Julius to the Capitole went
Upon a day, as he was wont to gon;
And in the Capitol anon him hent* *seized
This false Brutus, and his other fone,* *foes
And sticked him with bodekins anon
With many a wound, and thus they let him lie.
But never groan'd he at no stroke but one,
Or else at two, *but if* the story lie. *unless

So manly was this Julius of heart,
And so well loved *estately honesty *dignified propriety*
That, though his deadly woundes sore smart,* *pained him
His mantle o'er his hippes caste he,
That ne man shoulde see his privity
And as he lay a-dying in a trance,
And wiste verily that dead was he,
Of honesty yet had he remembrance.

Lucan, to thee this story I recommend,
And to Sueton', and Valerie also,
That of this story write *word and end* *the whole*
How that to these great conquerores two
Fortune was first a friend, and since* a foe. *afterwards
No manne trust upon her favour long,
But *have her in await for evermo';* *ever be watchful against
  her*
Witness on all these conquerores strong.

The riche Croesus, whilom king of Lyde, —
Of which Croesus Cyrus him sore drad,* — *dreaded
Yet was he caught amiddes all his pride,
And to be burnt men to the fire him lad;
But such a rain down *from the welkin shad,* *poured from
  the sky*
That slew the fire, and made him to escape:
But to beware no grace yet he had,
Till fortune on the gallows made him gape.

When he escaped was, he could not stint* *refrain
For to begin a newe war again;
He weened well, for that Fortune him sent
Such hap, that he escaped through the rain,
That of his foes he mighte not be slain.
And eke a sweven* on a night he mette,** *dream **dreamed
Of which he was so proud, and eke so fain,* *glad
That he in vengeance all his hearte set.

Upon a tree he was set, as he thought,
Where Jupiter him wash'd, both back and side,
And Phoebus eke a fair towel him brought
To dry him with; and therefore wax'd his pride.
And to his daughter that stood him beside,
Which he knew in high science to abound,

473

He bade her tell him what it signified;
And she his dream began right thus expound.

"The tree," quoth she, "the gallows is to mean,
And Jupiter betokens snow and rain,
And Phoebus, with his towel clear and clean,
These be the sunne's streames* sooth to sayn; *rays
Thou shalt y-hangeth be, father, certain;
Rain shall thee wash, and sunne shall thee dry."
Thus warned him full plat and eke full plain
His daughter, which that called was Phanie.

And hanged was Croesus the proude king;
His royal throne might him not avail.
Tragedy is none other manner thing,
Nor can in singing crien nor bewail,
But for that Fortune all day will assail
With unware stroke the regnes* that be proud: *kingdoms
For when men truste her, then will she fail,
And cover her bright face with a cloud.

O noble, O worthy Pedro, glory of Spain,
Whem Fortune held so high in majesty,
Well oughte men thy piteous death complain.
Out of thy land thy brother made thee flee,
And after, at a siege, by subtlety,
Thou wert betray'd, and led unto his tent,
Where as he with his owen hand slew thee,
Succeeding in thy regne* and in thy rent.** *kingdom **revenues

The field of snow, with th' eagle of black therein,
Caught with the lion, red-colour'd as the glede,* *burning coal
He brew'd this cursedness,* and all this sin; *wickedness, villainy
The wicked nest was worker of this deed;
Not Charles' Oliver, that took aye heed

Of truth and honour, but of Armorike
Ganilien Oliver, corrupt for meed,* *reward, bribe
Broughte this worthy king in such a brike.* *breach, ruin

O worthy Petro, King of Cypre also,
That Alexandre won by high mast'ry,
Full many a heathnen wroughtest thou full woe,
Of which thine owen lieges had envy;
And, for no thing but for thy chivalry,
They in thy bed have slain thee by the morrow;
Thus can Fortune her wheel govern and gie,* *guide
And out of joy bringe men into sorrow.

Of Milan greate Barnabo Viscount,
God of delight, and scourge of Lombardy,
Why should I not thine clomben* wert so high? *climbed
Thy brother's son, that was thy double ally,
For he thy nephew was and son-in-law,
Within his prison made thee to die,
But why, nor how, *n'ot I* that thou were slaw.* *I know not*
    slain

Of th' Earl Hugolin of Pise the languour* *agony
There may no tongue telle for pity.
But little out of Pisa stands a tow'r,
In whiche tow'r in prison put was he,
Aud with him be his little children three;
The eldest scarcely five years was of age;
Alas! Fortune, it was great cruelty
Such birdes for to put in such a cage.

Damned was he to die in that prison;
For Roger, which that bishop was of Pise,
Had on him made a false suggestion,
Through which the people gan upon him rise,

And put him in prison, in such a wise
As ye have heard; and meat and drink he had
So small, that well unneth* it might suffice, *scarcely
And therewithal it was full poor and bad.

And on a day befell, that in that hour
When that his meate wont was to be brought,
The jailor shut the doores of the tow'r;
He heard it right well, but he spake nought.
And in his heart anon there fell a thought,
That they for hunger woulde *do him dien;* *cause him
    to die*
"Alas!" quoth he, "alas that I was wrought!"* *made, born
Therewith the teares fell from his eyen.

His youngest son, that three years was of age,
Unto him said, "Father, why do ye weep?
When will the jailor bringen our pottage?
Is there no morsel bread that ye do keep?
I am so hungry, that I may not sleep.
Now woulde God that I might sleepen ever!
Then should not hunger in my wombe* creep; *stomach
There is no thing, save bread, that one were lever."* *dearer

Thus day by day this child begun to cry,
Till in his father's barme* adown he lay, *lap
And saide, "Farewell, father, I must die;"
And kiss'd his father, and died the same day.
And when the woeful father did it sey,* *see
For woe his armes two he gan to bite,
And said, "Alas! Fortune, and well-away!
To thy false wheel my woe all may I wite."* *blame

His children ween'd that it for hunger was
That he his armes gnaw'd, and not for woe,

And saide, "Father, do not so, alas!
But rather eat the flesh upon us two.
Our flesh thou gave us, our flesh take us fro',
And eat enough"; right thus they to him said.
And after that, within a day or two,
They laid them in his lap adown, and died.

Himself, despaired, eke for hunger starf.* *died
Thus ended is this Earl of Pise;
From high estate Fortune away him carf.* *cut off
Of this tragedy it ought enough suffice
Whoso will hear it *in a longer wise,* *at greater length*
Reade the greate poet of Itale,
That Dante hight, for he can it devise
From point to point, not one word will he fail.

THE NUN'S PRIEST'S TALE

"Ho!" quoth the Knight, "good sir, no more of this;
That ye have said is right enough, y-wis,* *of a surety
And muche more; for little heaviness
Is right enough to muche folk, I guess.
I say for me, it is a great disease,* *source of distress,
        annoyance
Where as men have been in great wealth and ease,
To hearen of their sudden fall, alas!
And the contrary is joy and great solas,* *delight, comfort
As when a man hath been in poor estate,
And climbeth up, and waxeth fortunate,
And there abideth in prosperity;
Such thing is gladsome, as it thinketh me,
And of such thing were goodly for to tell."

"Yea," quoth our Hoste, "by Saint Paule's bell.
Ye say right sooth; this monk hath clapped* loud; *talked

477

He spake how Fortune cover'd with a cloud
I wot not what, and als' of a tragedy
Right now ye heard: and pardie no remedy
It is for to bewaile, nor complain
That that is done, and also it is pain,
As ye have said, to hear of heaviness.
Sir Monk, no more of this, so God you bless;
Your tale annoyeth all this company;
Such talking is not worth a butterfly,
For therein is there no sport nor game;
Therefore, Sir Monke, Dan Piers by your name,
I pray you heart'ly, tell us somewhat else,
For sickerly, n'ere* clinking of your bells, *were it not for
    the
That on your bridle hang on every side,
By heaven's king, that for us alle died,
I should ere this have fallen down for sleep,
Although the slough had been never so deep;
Then had your tale been all told in vain.
For certainly, as these clerkes sayn,
Where as a man may have no audience,
Nought helpeth it to telle his sentence.
And well I wot the substance is in me,
If anything shall well reported be.
Sir, say somewhat of hunting, I you pray."

"Nay," quoth the Monk, "I have *no lust to play;* *no fondness
    for jesting*
Now let another tell, as I have told."
Then spake our Host with rude speech and bold,
And said unto the Nunne's Priest anon,
"Come near, thou Priest, come hither, thou Sir John,
Tell us such thing as may our heartes glade.* *gladden
Be blithe, although thou ride upon a jade.
What though thine horse be bothe foul and lean?

If he will serve thee, reck thou not a bean;
Look that thine heart be merry evermo'."

"Yes, Host," quoth he, "so may I ride or go,
But* I be merry, y-wis I will be blamed." *unless
And right anon his tale he hath attamed* *commenced
And thus he said unto us every one,
This sweete priest, this goodly man, Sir John.

THE TALE

A poor widow, *somedeal y-stept* in age, *somewhat advanced*
Was whilom dwelling in a poor cottage,
Beside a grove, standing in a dale.
This widow, of which I telle you my tale,
Since thilke day that she was last a wife,
In patience led a full simple life,
For little was *her chattel and her rent.* *her goods and her
    income*
By husbandry* of such as God her sent, *thrifty
    management
She found* herself, and eke her daughters two. *maintained
Three large sowes had she, and no mo';
Three kine, and eke a sheep that highte Mall.
Full sooty was her bow'r,* and eke her hall, *chamber
In which she ate full many a slender meal.
Of poignant sauce knew she never a deal.* *whit
No dainty morsel passed through her throat;
Her diet was *accordant to her cote.* *in keeping with her
    cottage*
Repletion her made never sick;
Attemper* diet was all her physic, *moderate
And exercise, and *hearte's suffisance.* *contentment of heart*
The goute *let her nothing for to dance,* *did not prevent her
    from dancing*

Nor apoplexy shente* not her head. *hurt
No wine drank she, neither white nor red:
Her board was served most with white and black,
Milk and brown bread, in which she found no lack,
Seind* bacon, and sometimes an egg or tway; *singed
For she was as it were *a manner dey.* *kind of day labourer*
A yard she had, enclosed all about
With stickes, and a drye ditch without,
In which she had a cock, hight Chanticleer;
In all the land of crowing *n'as his peer.* *was not his equal*
His voice was merrier than the merry orgon,* *organ
On masse days that in the churches gon.
Well sickerer* was his crowing in his lodge, *more punctual*
Than is a clock, or an abbay horloge.* *clock
By nature he knew each ascension
Of th' equinoctial in thilke town;
For when degrees fiftene were ascended,
Then crew he, that it might not be amended.
His comb was redder than the fine coral,
Embattell'd as it were a castle wall.
His bill was black, and as the jet it shone;
Like azure were his legges and his tone;* *toes
His nailes whiter than the lily flow'r,
And like the burnish'd gold was his colour,
This gentle cock had in his governance
Sev'n hennes, for to do all his pleasance,
Which were his sisters and his paramours,
And wondrous like to him as of colours.
Of which the fairest-hued in the throat
Was called Damoselle Partelote,
Courteous she was, discreet, and debonair,
And companiable,* and bare herself so fair, *sociable
Since the day that she sev'n night was old,
That truely she had the heart in hold
Of Chanticleer, locked in every lith;* *limb

He lov'd her so, that well was him therewith,
But such a joy it was to hear them sing,
When that the brighte sunne gan to spring,
In sweet accord, *My Lefe is Fare in Land.* *My Love is Gone
    Abroad*
For, at that time, as I have understand,
Beastes and birdes coulde speak and sing.

And so befell, that in a dawening,
As Chanticleer among his wives all
Sat on his perche, that was in the hall,
And next him sat this faire Partelote,
This Chanticleer gan groanen in his throat,
As man that in his dream is dretched* sore,   *oppressed
And when that Partelote thus heard him roar,
She was aghast,* and saide, "Hearte dear,   *afraid
What aileth you to groan in this mannere?
Ye be a very sleeper, fy for shame!"
And he answer'd and saide thus; "Madame,
I pray you that ye take it not agrief;*   *amiss, in umbrage
By God, *me mette* I was in such mischief,** *I dreamed* **trouble
Right now, that yet mine heart is sore affright'.
Now God," quoth he, "my sweven* read aright   *dream, vision
And keep my body out of foul prisoun.
Me mette, how that I roamed up and down   *I dreamed*
Within our yard, where as I saw a beast
Was like an hound, and would have *made arrest*   *seized*
Upon my body, and would have had me dead.
His colour was betwixt yellow and red;
And tipped was his tail, and both his ears,
With black, unlike the remnant of his hairs.
His snout was small, with glowing eyen tway;
Yet of his look almost for fear I dey;*   *died
This caused me my groaning, doubtless."

"Away," quoth she, "fy on you, heartless!* *coward
Alas!" quoth she, "for, by that God above!
Now have ye lost my heart and all my love;
I cannot love a coward, by my faith.
For certes, what so any woman saith,
We all desiren, if it mighte be,
To have husbandes hardy, wise, and free,
And secret,* and no niggard nor no fool, *discreet
Nor him that is aghast* of every tool,** *afraid **rag, trifle
Nor no avantour,* by that God above! *braggart
How durste ye for shame say to your love
That anything might make you afear'd?
Have ye no manne's heart, and have a beard?
Alas! and can ye be aghast of swevenes?* *dreams
Nothing but vanity, God wot, in sweven is,
Swevens *engender of repletions,* *are caused by over-eating*
And oft of fume,* and of complexions, *drunkenness
When humours be too abundant in a wight.
Certes this dream, which ye have mette tonight,
Cometh of the great supefluity
Of youre rede cholera,* pardie, *bile
Which causeth folk to dreaden in their dreams
Of arrows, and of fire with redde beams,
Of redde beastes, that they will them bite,
Of conteke,* and of whelpes great and lite;** *contention **little
Right as the humour of melancholy
Causeth full many a man in sleep to cry,
For fear of bulles, or of beares blake,
Or elles that black devils will them take,
Of other humours could I tell also,
That worke many a man in sleep much woe;
That I will pass as lightly as I can.
Lo, Cato, which that was so wise a man,
Said he not thus, *'Ne do no force of* dreams,' *attach no
        weight to*

Now, Sir," quoth she, "when we fly from these beams,
For Godde's love, as take some laxatife;
On peril of my soul, and of my life,
I counsel you the best, I will not lie,
That both of choler, and melancholy,
Ye purge you; and, for ye shall not tarry,
Though in this town is no apothecary,
I shall myself two herbes teache you,
That shall be for your health, and for your prow;* *profit
And in our yard the herbes shall I find,
The which have of their property by kind* *nature
To purge you beneath, and eke above.
Sire, forget not this for Godde's love;
Ye be full choleric of complexion;
Ware that the sun, in his ascension,
You finde not replete of humours hot;
And if it do, I dare well lay a groat,
That ye shall have a fever tertiane,
Or else an ague, that may be your bane,
A day or two ye shall have digestives
Of wormes, ere ye take your laxatives,
Of laurel, centaury, and fumeterere,
Or else of elder-berry, that groweth there,
Of catapuce, or of the gaitre-berries,
Or herb ivy growing in our yard, that merry is:
Pick them right as they grow, and eat them in,
Be merry, husband, for your father's kin;
Dreade no dream; I can say you no more."

"Madame," quoth he, "grand mercy of your lore,
But natheless, as touching *Dan Catoun,* *Cato
That hath of wisdom such a great renown,
Though that he bade no dreames for to dread,
By God, men may in olde bookes read
Of many a man more of authority

Than ever Cato was, so may I the,* *thrive
That all the reverse say of his sentence,* *opinion
And have well founden by experience
That dreames be significations
As well of joy, as tribulations
That folk enduren in this life present.
There needeth make of this no argument;
The very preve* sheweth it indeed. *trial, experience
One of the greatest authors that men read
Saith thus, that whilom two fellowes went
On pilgrimage in a full good intent;
And happen'd so, they came into a town
Where there was such a congregatioun
Of people, and eke so *strait of herbergage,* *without
    lodging*
That they found not as much as one cottage
In which they bothe might y-lodged be:
Wherefore they musten of necessity,
As for that night, departe company;
And each of them went to his hostelry,* *inn
And took his lodging as it woulde fall.
The one of them was lodged in a stall,
Far in a yard, with oxen of the plough;
That other man was lodged well enow,
As was his aventure, or his fortune,
That us governeth all, as in commune.
And so befell, that, long ere it were day,
This man mette* in his bed, there: as he lay, *dreamed
How that his fellow gan upon him call,
And said, 'Alas! for in an ox's stall
This night shall I be murder'd, where I lie
Now help me, deare brother, or I die;
In alle haste come to me,' he said.
This man out of his sleep for fear abraid;* *started
But when that he was wak'd out of his sleep,

He turned him, and *took of this no keep;* *paid this no
    attention*
He thought his dream was but a vanity.
Thus twies* in his sleeping dreamed he, *twice
And at the thirde time yet his fellaw again
Came, as he thought, and said, 'I am now slaw;* *slain
Behold my bloody woundes, deep and wide.
Arise up early, in the morning, tide,
And at the west gate of the town,' quoth he,
'A carte full of dung there shalt thou see,
In which my body is hid privily.
Do thilke cart arroste* boldely. *stop
My gold caused my murder, sooth to sayn.'
And told him every point how he was slain,
With a full piteous face, and pale of hue.

"And, truste well, his dream he found full true;
For on the morrow, as soon as it was day,
To his fellowes inn he took his way;
And when that he came to this ox's stall,
After his fellow he began to call.
The hostelere answered him anon,
And saide, 'Sir, your fellow is y-gone,
As soon as day he went out of the town.'
This man gan fallen in suspicioun,
Rememb'ring on his dreames that he mette,* *dreamed
And forth he went, no longer would he let,* *delay
Unto the west gate of the town, and fand* *found
A dung cart, as it went for to dung land,
That was arrayed in the same wise
As ye have heard the deade man devise;* *describe
And with an hardy heart he gan to cry,
'Vengeance and justice of this felony:
My fellow murder'd in this same night
And in this cart he lies, gaping upright.

I cry out on the ministers,' quoth he.
'That shoulde keep and rule this city;
Harow! alas! here lies my fellow slain.'
What should I more unto this tale sayn?
The people out start, and cast the cart to ground
And in the middle of the dung they found
The deade man, that murder'd was all new.
O blissful God! that art so good and true,
Lo, how that thou bewray'st murder alway.
Murder will out, that see we day by day.
Murder is so wlatsom* and abominable   *loathsome
To God, that is so just and reasonable,
That he will not suffer it heled* be;   *concealed
Though it abide a year, or two, or three,
Murder will out, this is my conclusioun,
And right anon, the ministers of the town
Have hent* the carter, and so sore him pined,**   *seized
        **tortured
And eke the hostelere so sore engined,*   *racked
That they beknew* their wickedness anon,   *confessed
And were hanged by the necke bone.

"Here may ye see that dreames be to dread.
And certes in the same book I read,
Right in the nexte chapter after this
(I gabbe* not, so have I joy and bliss),   *talk idly
Two men that would, have passed over sea,
For certain cause, into a far country,
If that the wind not hadde been contrary,
That made them in a city for to tarry,
That stood full merry upon an haven side;
But on a day, against the even-tide,
The wind gan change, and blew right *as them lest.*   *as they
        wished*
Jolly and glad they wente to their rest,

And caste* them full early for to sail. *resolved
But to the one man fell a great marvail
That one of them, in sleeping as he lay,
He mette* a wondrous dream, against the day: *dreamed
He thought a man stood by his bedde's side,
And him commanded that he should abide;
And said him thus; 'If thou to-morrow wend,
Thou shalt be drown'd; my tale is at an end.'
He woke, and told his follow what he mette,
And prayed him his voyage for to let;* *delay
As for that day, he pray'd him to abide.
His fellow, that lay by his bedde's side,
Gan for to laugh, and scorned him full fast.
'No dream,' quoth he, 'may so my heart aghast,* *frighten
That I will lette* for to do my things.* *delay
I sette not a straw by thy dreamings,
For swevens* be but vanities and japes.** *dreams **jokes, deceits
Men dream all day of owles and of apes,
And eke of many a maze* therewithal; *wild imagining
Men dream of thing that never was, nor shall.
But since I see, that thou wilt here abide,
And thus forslothe* wilfully thy tide,** **idle away **time
God wot, *it rueth me;* and have good day.' *I am sorry for it*
And thus he took his leave, and went his way.
But, ere that he had half his course sail'd,
I know not why, nor what mischance it ail'd,
But casually* the ship's bottom rent, *by accident
And ship and man under the water went,
In sight of other shippes there beside
That with him sailed at the same tide.

"And therefore, faire Partelote so dear,
By such examples olde may'st thou lear,* *learn
That no man shoulde be too reckless
Of dreames, for I say thee doubteless,

That many a dream full sore is for to dread.
Lo, in the life of Saint Kenelm I read,
That was Kenulphus' son, the noble king
Of Mercenrike, how Kenelm mette a thing.
A little ere he was murder'd on a day,
His murder in his vision he say.* *saw
His norice* him expounded every deal** *nurse **part
His sweven, and bade him to keep* him well *guard
For treason; but he was but seven years old,
And therefore *little tale hath he told* *he attached little
    significance to*
Of any dream, so holy was his heart.
By God, I hadde lever than my shirt
That ye had read his legend, as have I.
Dame Partelote, I say you truely,
Macrobius, that wrote the *Vision*
In Afric' of the worthy Scipion,
Affirmeth dreames, and saith that they be
'Warnings of thinges that men after see.'
And furthermore, I pray you looke well
In the Old Testament, of Daniel,
If he held dreames any vanity.
Read eke of Joseph, and there shall ye see
Whether dreams be sometimes (I say not all)
Warnings of thinges that shall after fall.
Look of Egypt the king, Dan Pharaoh,
His baker and his buteler also,
Whether they felte none effect* in dreams. *significance
Whoso will seek the acts of sundry remes* *realms
May read of dreames many a wondrous thing.
Lo Croesus, which that was of Lydia king,
Mette he not that he sat upon a tree,
Which signified he shoulde hanged be?
Lo here, Andromache, Hectore's wife,
That day that Hector shoulde lose his life,

She dreamed on the same night beforn,
How that the life of Hector should be lorn,* *lost
If thilke day he went into battaile;
She warned him, but it might not avail;
He wente forth to fighte natheless,
And was y-slain anon of Achilles.
But thilke tale is all too long to tell;
And eke it is nigh day, I may not dwell.
Shortly I say, as for conclusion,
That I shall have of this avision
Adversity; and I say furthermore,
That I ne *tell of laxatives no store,* *hold laxatives of no value*
For they be venomous, I wot it well;
I them defy,* I love them never a del.** *distrust **whit

"But let us speak of mirth, and stint* all this; *cease
Madame Partelote, so have I bliss,
Of one thing God hath sent me large* grace; liberal
For when I see the beauty of your face,
Ye be so scarlet-hued about your eyen,
I maketh all my dreade for to dien,
For, all so sicker* as *In principio*, *certain
Mulier est hominis confusio.
Madam, the sentence* of this Latin is, *meaning
Woman is manne's joy and manne's bliss.
For when I feel at night your softe side, —
Albeit that I may not on you ride,
For that our perch is made so narrow, Alas! –
I am so full of joy and of solas,* *delight
That I defy both sweven and eke dream."
And with that word he flew down from the beam,
For it was day, and eke his hennes all;
And with a chuck he gan them for to call,
For he had found a corn, lay in the yard.
Royal he was, he was no more afear'd;

He feather'd Partelote twenty time,
And as oft trode her, ere that it was prime.
He looked as it were a grim lion,
And on his toes he roamed up and down;
He deigned not to set his feet to ground;
He chucked, when he had a corn y-found,
And to him ranne then his wives all.
Thus royal, as a prince is in his hall,
Leave I this Chanticleer in his pasture;
And after will I tell his aventure.

When that the month in which the world began,
That highte March, when God first maked man,
Was complete, and y-passed were also,
Since March ended, thirty days and two,
Befell that Chanticleer in all his pride,
His seven wives walking him beside,
Cast up his eyen to the brighte sun,
That in the sign of Taurus had y-run
Twenty degrees and one, and somewhat more;
He knew by kind,* and by none other lore,** *nature **learning
That it was prime, and crew with blissful steven.* *voice
"The sun," he said, "is clomben up in heaven
Twenty degrees and one, and more y-wis.* *assuredly
Madame Partelote, my worlde's bliss,
Hearken these blissful birdes how they sing,
And see the freshe flowers how they spring;
Full is mine heart of revel and solace."
But suddenly him fell a sorrowful case;* *casualty
For ever the latter end of joy is woe:
God wot that worldly joy is soon y-go:
And, if a rhetor* coulde fair indite, *orator
He in a chronicle might it safely write,
As for *a sov'reign notability* *a thing supremely notable*
Now every wise man, let him hearken me;

This story is all as true, I undertake,
As is the book of *Launcelot du Lake*,
That women hold in full great reverence.
Now will I turn again to my sentence.

A col-fox, full of sly iniquity,
That in the grove had wonned* yeares three,   *dwelt
By high imagination forecast,
The same night through the hedges brast*   *burst
Into the yard, where Chanticleer the fair
Was wont, and eke his wives, to repair;
And in a bed of wortes* still he lay,   *cabbages
Till it was passed undern of the day,
Waiting his time on Chanticleer to fall:
As gladly do these homicides all,
That in awaite lie to murder men.
O false murd'rer! Rouking* in thy den!   *crouching, lurking
O new Iscariot, new Ganilion!
O false dissimuler, O Greek Sinon,
That broughtest Troy all utterly to sorrow!
O Chanticleer! accursed be the morrow
That thou into thy yard flew from the beams;*   *rafters
Thou wert full well y-warned by thy dreams
That thilke day was perilous to thee.
But what that God forewot* must needes be,   *foreknows
After th' opinion of certain clerkes.
Witness on him that any perfect clerk is,
That in school is great altercation
In this matter, and great disputation,
And hath been of an hundred thousand men.
But I ne cannot *boult it to the bren,*   *examine it thoroughly*
As can the holy doctor Augustine,
Or Boece, or the bishop Bradwardine,
Whether that Godde's worthy foreweeting*   *foreknowledge
Straineth me needly for to do a thing   *forces me*

(Needly call I simple necessity),
Or elles if free choice be granted me
To do that same thing, or do it not,
Though God forewot* it ere that it was wrought; *knew in advance
Or if *his weeting straineth never a deal,* *his knowing
    constrains not at all*
But by necessity conditionel.
I will not have to do of such mattere;
My tale is of a cock, as ye may hear,
That took his counsel of his wife, with sorrow,
To walken in the yard upon the morrow
That he had mette the dream, as I you told.
Womane's counsels be full often cold;* *mischievous, unwise
Womane's counsel brought us first to woe,
And made Adam from Paradise to go,
There as he was full merry and well at case.
But, for I n'ot* to whom I might displease *know not
If I counsel of women woulde blame,
Pass over, for I said it in my game.* *jest
Read authors, where they treat of such mattere
And what they say of women ye may hear.
These be the cocke's wordes, and not mine;
I can no harm of no woman divine.* *conjecture, imagine
Fair in the sand, to bathe* her merrily, *bask
Lies Partelote, and all her sisters by,
Against the sun, and Chanticleer so free
Sang merrier than the mermaid in the sea;
For Physiologus saith sickerly,* *certainly
How that they singe well and merrily.
And so befell that, as he cast his eye
Among the wortes,* on a butterfly, *cabbages
He was ware of this fox that lay full low.
Nothing *ne list him thenne* for to crow, *he had no
    inclination*
But cried anon "Cock! cock!" and up he start,

As man that was affrayed in his heart.
For naturally a beast desireth flee
From his contrary,* if he may it see, *enemy
Though he *ne'er erst* had soon it with his eye *never before*
This Chanticleer, when he gan him espy,
He would have fled, but that the fox anon
Said, "Gentle Sir, alas! why will ye gon?
Be ye afraid of me that am your friend?
Now, certes, I were worse than any fiend,
If I to you would harm or villainy.
I am not come your counsel to espy.
But truely the cause of my coming
Was only for to hearken how ye sing;
For truely ye have as merry a steven,* *voice
As any angel hath that is in heaven;
Therewith ye have of music more feeling,
Than had Boece, or any that can sing.
My lord your father (God his soule bless)
And eke your mother of her gentleness,
Have in mine house been, to my great ease:* *satisfaction
And certes, Sir, full fain would I you please.
But, for men speak of singing, I will say,
So may I brooke* well mine eyen tway, *enjoy, possess, or use
Save you, I hearde never man so sing
As did your father in the morrowning.
Certes it was of heart all that he sung.
And, for to make his voice the more strong,
He would *so pain him,* that with both his eyen *make
    such an exertion*
He muste wink, so loud he woulde cryen,
And standen on his tiptoes therewithal,
And stretche forth his necke long and small.
And eke he was of such discretion,
That there was no man, in no region,
That him in song or wisdom mighte pass.

I have well read in *Dan Burnel the Ass*,
Among his verse, how that there was a cock
That, for* a prieste's son gave him a knock   *because
Upon his leg, while he was young and nice,*   *foolish
He made him for to lose his benefice.
But certain there is no comparison
Betwixt the wisdom and discretion
Of youre father, and his subtilty.
Now singe, Sir, for sainte charity,
Let see, can ye your father counterfeit?"

This Chanticleer his wings began to beat,
As man that could not his treason espy,
So was he ravish'd with his flattery.
Alas! ye lordes, many a false flattour*   *flatterer
Is in your court, and many a losengeour,*   *deceiver
That please you well more, by my faith,
Than he that soothfastness* unto you saith.   *truth
Read in Ecclesiast' of flattery;
Beware, ye lordes, of their treachery.
This Chanticleer stood high upon his toes,
Stretching his neck, and held his eyen close,
And gan to crowe loude for the nonce
And Dan Russel the fox start up at once,
And *by the gorge hente* Chanticleer,   *seized by the throat*
And on his back toward the wood him bare.
For yet was there no man that him pursu'd.
O destiny, that may'st not be eschew'd!*   *escaped
Alas, that Chanticleer flew from the beams!
Alas, his wife raughte* nought of dreams!   *regarded
And on a Friday fell all this mischance.
O Venus, that art goddess of pleasance,
Since that thy servant was this Chanticleer
And in thy service did all his powere,
More for delight, than the world to multiply,

Why wilt thou suffer him on thy day to die?
O Gaufrid, deare master sovereign,
That, when thy worthy king Richard was slain
With shot, complainedest his death so sore,
Why n'had I now thy sentence and thy lore,
The Friday for to chiden, as did ye?
(For on a Friday, soothly, slain was he),
Then would I shew you how that I could plain*   *lament
For Chanticleer's dread, and for his pain.

Certes such cry nor lamentation
Was ne'er of ladies made, when Ilion
Was won, and Pyrrhus with his straighte sword,
When he had hent* king Priam by the beard,   *seized
And slain him (as saith us *Eneidos*),   *the *Aeneid*
As maden all the hennes in the close,*   *yard
When they had seen of Chanticleer the sight.
But sov'reignly* Dame Partelote shright,**   *above all others
     **shrieked
Full louder than did Hasdrubale's wife,
When that her husband hadde lost his life,
And that the Romans had y-burnt Carthage;
She was so full of torment and of rage,
That wilfully into the fire she start,
And burnt herselfe with a steadfast heart.
O woeful hennes! right so cried ye,
As, when that Nero burned the city
Of Rome, cried the senatores' wives,
For that their husbands losten all their lives;
Withoute guilt this Nero hath them slain.
Now will I turn unto my tale again;

The sely* widow, and her daughters two,   *simple, honest
Hearde these hennes cry and make woe,
And at the doors out started they anon,

And saw the fox toward the wood is gone,
And bare upon his back the cock away:
They cried, "Out! harow! and well-away!
Aha! the fox!" and after him they ran,
And eke with staves many another man
Ran Coll our dog, and Talbot, and Garland;
And Malkin, with her distaff in her hand
Ran cow and calf, and eke the very hogges
So fear'd they were for barking of the dogges,
And shouting of the men and women eke.
They ranne so, them thought their hearts would break.
They yelled as the fiendes do in hell;
The duckes cried as men would them quell;* *kill, destroy
The geese for feare flewen o'er the trees,
Out of the hive came the swarm of bees,
So hideous was the noise, ben'dicite!
Certes he, Jacke Straw, and his meinie,* *followers
Ne made never shoutes half so shrill
When that they woulden any Fleming kill,
As thilke day was made upon the fox.
Of brass they broughte beames* and of box, *trumpets
Of horn and bone, in which they blew and pooped,* *tooted
And therewithal they shrieked and they hooped;
It seemed as the heaven shoulde fall

Now, goode men, I pray you hearken all;
Lo, how Fortune turneth suddenly
The hope and pride eke of her enemy.
This cock, that lay upon the fox's back,
In all his dread unto the fox he spake,
And saide, "Sir, if that I were as ye,
Yet would I say (as wisly* God help me), *surely
'Turn ye again, ye proude churles all;
A very pestilence upon you fall.
Now am I come unto the woode's side,

Maugre your head, the cock shall here abide;
I will him eat, in faith, and that anon.'"
The fox answer'd, "In faith it shall be done:"
And, as he spake the word, all suddenly
The cock brake from his mouth deliverly,* *nimbly
And high upon a tree he flew anon.
And when the fox saw that the cock was gone,
"Alas!" quoth he, "O Chanticleer, alas!
I have," quoth he, "y-done to you trespass,* *offence
Inasmuch as I maked you afear'd,
When I you hent,* and brought out of your yard; *took
But, Sir, I did it in no wick' intent;
Come down, and I shall tell you what I meant.
I shall say sooth to you, God help me so."
"Nay then," quoth he, "I shrew* us both the two, *curse
And first I shrew myself, both blood and bones,
If thou beguile me oftener than once.
Thou shalt no more through thy flattery
Do* me to sing and winke with mine eye; *cause
For he that winketh when he shoulde see,
All wilfully, God let him never the."* *thrive
"Nay," quoth the fox; "but God give him mischance
That is so indiscreet of governance,
That jangleth* when that he should hold his peace." *chatters

Lo, what it is for to be reckeless
And negligent, and trust on flattery.
But ye that holde this tale a folly,
As of a fox, or of a cock or hen,
Take the morality thereof, good men.
For Saint Paul saith, that all that written is,
To our doctrine it written is y-wis. *is surely written for our
    instruction*
Take the fruit, and let the chaff be still.

Now goode God, if that it be thy will,
As saith my Lord, so make us all good men;
And bring us all to thy high bliss. Amen.

THE EPILOGUE

"Sir Nunne's Priest," our hoste said anon,
"Y-blessed be thy breech, and every stone;
This was a merry tale of Chanticleer.
But by my truth, if thou wert seculere,* *a layman
Thou wouldest be a treadefowl* aright; *cock
For if thou have courage as thou hast might,
Thee were need of hennes, as I ween,
Yea more than seven times seventeen.
See, whate brawnes* hath this gentle priest, *muscles, sinews
So great a neck, and such a large breast
He looketh as a sperhawk with his eyen
Him needeth not his colour for to dyen
With Brazil, nor with grain of Portugale.
But, Sir, faire fall you for your tale."
And, after that, he with full merry cheer
Said to another, as ye shall hear.

THE SECOND NUN'S TALE

The minister and norice* unto vices, *nurse
Which that men call in English idleness,
The porter at the gate is of delices;* *delights
T'eschew, and by her contrar' her oppress, —
That is to say, by lawful business,* — *occupation, activity
Well oughte we to *do our all intent* *apply ourselves*
Lest that the fiend through idleness us hent.* *seize

For he, that with his thousand cordes sly
Continually us waiteth to beclap,* *entangle, bind

When he may man in idleness espy,
He can so lightly catch him in his trap,
Till that a man be hent* right by the lappe,** *seized
    **hem
He is not ware the fiend hath him in hand;
Well ought we work, and idleness withstand.

And though men dreaded never for to die,
Yet see men well by reason, doubteless,
That idleness is root of sluggardy,
Of which there cometh never good increase;
And see that sloth them holdeth in a leas,* *leash
Only to sleep, and for to eat and drink,
And to devouren all that others swink.* *labour

And, for to put us from such idleness,
That cause is of so great confusion,
I have here done my faithful business,
After the Legend, in translation
Right of thy glorious life and passion, —
Thou with thy garland wrought of rose and lily,
Thee mean I, maid and martyr, Saint Cecilie.

And thou, thou art the flow'r of virgins all,
Of whom that Bernard list so well to write,
To thee at my beginning first I call;
Thou comfort of us wretches, do me indite
Thy maiden's death, that won through her merite
Th' eternal life, and o'er the fiend victory,
As man may after readen in her story.

Thou maid and mother, daughter of thy Son,
Thou well of mercy, sinful soules' cure,
In whom that God of bounte chose to won;* *dwell
Thou humble and high o'er every creature,

Thou nobilest, *so far forth our nature,* *as far as our nature
    admits*
That no disdain the Maker had of kind,* *nature
His Son in blood and flesh to clothe and wind.* *wrap

Within the cloister of thy blissful sides
Took manne's shape th' eternal love and peace,
That of *the trine compass* Lord and guide is *the trinity*
Whom earth, and sea, and heav'n, *out of release,*
    *unceasingly
Aye hery; and thou, Virgin wemmeless,* *forever praise*
    *immaculate
Bare of thy body, and dweltest maiden pure,
The Creator of every creature.

Assembled is in thee magnificence
With mercy, goodness, and with such pity,
That thou, that art the sun of excellence,
Not only helpest them that pray to thee,
But oftentime, of thy benignity,
Full freely, ere that men thine help beseech,
Thou go'st before, and art their lives' leech.* *healer, saviour.

Now help, thou meek and blissful faire maid,
Me, flemed* wretch, in this desert of gall; *banished, outcast
Think on the woman Cananee that said
That whelpes eat some of the crumbes all
That from their Lorde's table be y-fall;
And though that I, unworthy son of Eve,
Be sinful, yet accepte my believe.* *faith

And, for that faith is dead withoute werkes,
For to worke give me wit and space,
That I be *quit from thennes that most derk is;* *freed from
    the most dark place (Hell)*

O thou, that art so fair and full of grace,
Be thou mine advocate in that high place,
Where as withouten end is sung Osanne,
Thou Christe's mother, daughter dear of
    Anne.

And of thy light my soul in prison light,
That troubled is by the contagion
Of my body, and also by the weight
Of earthly lust and false affection;
O hav'n of refuge, O salvation
Of them that be in sorrow and distress,
Now help, for to my work I will me dress.

Yet pray I you, that reade what I write,
Forgive me that I do no diligence
This ilke* story subtilly t' indite. *same
For both have I the wordes and sentence
Of him that at the sainte's reverence
The story wrote, and follow her legend;
And pray you that you will my work amend.

First will I you the name of Saint Cecilie
Expound, as men may in her story see.
It is to say in English, Heaven's lily,
For pure chasteness of virginity;
Or, for she whiteness had of honesty,* *purity
And green of conscience, and of good fame
The sweete savour, Lilie was her name.

Or Cecilie is to say, the way of blind;
For she example was by good teaching;
Or else Cecilie, as I written find,
Is joined by a manner conjoining
Of heaven and Lia, and herein figuring

The heaven is set for thought of holiness,
And Lia for her lasting business.

Cecilie may eke be said in this mannere,
Wanting of blindness, for her greate light
Of sapience, and for her thewes* clear. *qualities
Or elles, lo, this maiden's name bright
Of heaven and Leos comes, for which by right
Men might her well the heaven of people call,
Example of good and wise workes all;

For Leos people in English is to say;
And right as men may in the heaven see
The sun and moon, and starres every way,
Right so men ghostly,* in this maiden free, *spiritually
Sawen of faith the magnanimity,
And eke the clearness whole of sapience,
And sundry workes bright of excellence.

And right so as these philosophers write,
That heav'n is swift and round, and eke burning,
Right so was faire Cecilie the white
Full swift and busy in every good working,
And round and whole in good persevering,
And burning ever in charity full bright;
Now have I you declared *what she hight.* *why she had her name*

This maiden bright Cecilie, as her life saith,
Was come of Romans, and of noble kind,
And from her cradle foster'd in the faith
Of Christ, and bare his Gospel in her mind:
She never ceased, as I written find,
Of her prayere, and God to love and dread,
Beseeching him to keep her maidenhead.

And when this maiden should unto a man
Y-wedded be, that was full young of age,
Which that y-called was Valerian,
And come was the day of marriage,
She, full devout and humble in her corage,* *heart
Under her robe of gold, that sat full fair,
Had next her flesh y-clad her in an hair.* *garment of
    hair-cloth

And while the organs made melody,
To God alone thus in her heart sang she;
"O Lord, my soul and eke my body gie* *guide
Unwemmed,* lest that I confounded be." *unblemished
And, for his love that died upon the tree,
Every second or third day she fast',
Aye bidding* in her orisons full fast. *praying

The night came, and to bedde must she gon
With her husband, as it is the mannere;
And privily she said to him anon;
"O sweet and well-beloved spouse dear,
There is a counsel,* an'** ye will it hear, *secret **if
Which that right fain I would unto you say,
So that ye swear ye will it not bewray."* *betray

Valerian gan fast unto her swear
That for no case nor thing that mighte be,
He never should to none bewrayen her;
And then at erst* thus to him saide she; *for the first time
"I have an angel which that loveth me,
That with great love, whether I wake or sleep,
Is ready aye my body for to keep;

"And if that he may feelen, *out of dread,* *without doubt*
That ye me touch or love in villainy,

503

He right anon will slay you with the deed,
And in your youthe thus ye shoulde die.
And if that ye in cleane love me gie,* *guide
He will you love as me, for your cleanness,
And shew to you his joy and his brightness."

Valerian, corrected as God wo'ld,
Answer'd again, "If I shall truste thee,
Let me that angel see, and him behold;
And if that it a very angel be,
Then will I do as thou hast prayed me;
And if thou love another man, forsooth
Right with this sword then will I slay you both."

Cecilie answer'd anon right in this wise;
"If that you list, the angel shall ye see,
So that ye trow* of Christ, and you baptise; *know
Go forth to Via Appia," quoth she,
"That from this towne stands but miles three,
And to the poore folkes that there dwell
Say them right thus, as that I shall you tell,

"Tell them, that I, Cecilie, you to them sent
To shewe you the good Urban the old,
For secret needes,* and for good intent; *business
And when that ye Saint Urban have behold,
Tell him the wordes which I to you told
And when that he hath purged you from sin,
Then shall ye see that angel ere ye twin* *depart

Valerian is to the place gone;
And, right as he was taught by her learning
He found this holy old Urban anon
Among the saintes' burials louting;* *lying concealed
And he anon, withoute tarrying,

Did his message, and when that he it told,
Urban for joy his handes gan uphold.

The teares from his eyen let he fall;
"Almighty Lord, O Jesus Christ,"
Quoth he, "Sower of chaste counsel, herd* of us all; *shepherd
The fruit of thilke* seed of chastity *that
That thou hast sown in Cecilie, take to thee
Lo, like a busy bee, withoute guile,
Thee serveth aye thine owen thrall* Cecilie, *servant

"For thilke spouse, that she took *but now,* *lately*
Full like a fierce lion, she sendeth here,
As meek as e'er was any lamb to owe."
And with that word anon there gan appear
An old man, clad in white clothes clear,
That had a book with letters of gold in hand,
And gan before Valerian to stand.

Valerian, as dead, fell down for dread,
When he him saw; and he up hent* him tho,** *took **there
And on his book right thus he gan to read;
"One Lord, one faith, one God withoute mo',
One Christendom, one Father of all also,
Aboven all, and over all everywhere."
These wordes all with gold y-written were.

When this was read, then said this olde man,
"Believ'st thou this or no? say yea or nay."
"I believe all this," quoth Valerian,
"For soother* thing than this, I dare well say, *truer
Under the Heaven no wight thinke may."
Then vanish'd the old man, he wist not where
And Pope Urban him christened right there.

Valerian went home, and found Cecilie
Within his chamber with an angel stand;
This angel had of roses and of lily
Corones* two, the which he bare in hand,   *crowns
And first to Cecilie, as I understand,
He gave the one, and after gan he take
The other to Valerian her make.*   *mate, husband

"With body clean, and with unwemmed* thought,   *unspotted,
    blameless
Keep aye well these corones two," quoth he;
"From Paradise to you I have them brought,
Nor ever more shall they rotten be,
Nor lose their sweet savour, truste me,
Nor ever wight shall see them with his eye,
But he be chaste, and hate villainy.

"And thou, Valerian, for thou so soon
Assented hast to good counsel, also
Say what thee list,* and thou shalt have thy boon."**   *wish **desire
"I have a brother," quoth Valerian tho,*   *then
"That in this world I love no man so;
I pray you that my brother may have grace
To know the truth, as I do in this place."

The angel said, "God liketh thy request,
And bothe, with the palm of martyrdom,
Ye shalle come unto this blissful rest."
And, with that word, Tiburce his brother came.
And when that he the savour undernome*   *perceived
Which that the roses and the lilies cast,
Within his heart he gan to wonder fast;

And said; "I wonder, this time of the year,
Whence that sweete savour cometh so

Of rose and lilies, that I smelle here;
For though I had them in mine handes two,
The savour might in me no deeper go;
The sweete smell, that in my heart I find,
Hath changed me all in another kind."

Valerian said, "Two crownes here have we,
Snow-white and rose-red, that shine clear,
Which that thine eyen have no might to see;
And, as thou smellest them through my prayere,
So shalt thou see them, leve* brother dear,   *beloved
If it so be thou wilt withoute sloth
Believe aright, and know the very troth."

Tiburce answered, "Say'st thou this to me
In soothness, or in dreame hear I this?"
"In dreames," quoth Valorian, "have we be
Unto this time, brother mine, y-wis
But now *at erst* in truth our dwelling is."   *for the first time*
How know'st thou this," quoth Tiburce; "in what wise?"
Quoth Valerian, "That shall I thee devise*   *describe

"The angel of God hath me the truth y-taught,
Which thou shalt see, if that thou wilt reny*   *renounce
The idols, and be clean, and elles nought."
[And of the miracle of these crownes tway
Saint Ambrose in his preface list to say;
Solemnely this noble doctor dear
Commendeth it, and saith in this mannere

"The palm of martyrdom for to receive,
Saint Cecilie, full filled of God's gift,
The world and eke her chamber gan to weive;*   *forsake
Witness Tiburce's and Cecilie's shrift,*   *confession
To which God of his bounty woulde shift

507

Corones two, of flowers well smelling,
And made his angel them the crownes bring.

"The maid hath brought these men to bliss above;
The world hath wist what it is worth, certain,
Devotion of chastity to love."
Then showed him Cecilie all open and plain,
That idols all are but a thing in vain,
For they be dumb, and thereto* they be deave;** *therefore **deaf
And charged him his idols for to leave.

"Whoso that troweth* not this, a beast he is," *believeth
Quoth this Tiburce, "if that I shall not lie."
And she gan kiss his breast when she heard this,
And was full glad he could the truth espy:
"This day I take thee for mine ally."* *chosen friend
Saide this blissful faire maiden dear;
And after that she said as ye may hear.

"Lo, right so as the love of Christ," quoth she,
"Made me thy brother's wife, right in that wise
Anon for mine ally here take I thee,
Since that thou wilt thine idoles despise.
Go with thy brother now and thee baptise,
And make thee clean, so that thou may'st behold
The angel's face, of which thy brother told."

Tiburce answer'd, and saide, "Brother dear,
First tell me whither I shall, and to what man?"
"To whom?" quoth he, "come forth with goode cheer,
I will thee lead unto the Pope Urban."
"To Urban? brother mine Valerian,"
Quoth then Tiburce; "wilt thou me thither lead?
Me thinketh that it were a wondrous deed.

"Meanest thou not that Urban," quoth he tho,* *then
"That is so often damned to be dead,
And wons* in halkes** always to and fro, *dwells **corners
And dare not ones putte forth his head?
Men should him brennen* in a fire so red, *burn
If he were found, or if men might him spy:
And us also, to bear him company.

"And while we seeke that Divinity
That is y-hid in heaven privily,
Algate* burnt in this world should we be." *nevertheless
To whom Cecilie answer'd boldely;
"Men mighte dreade well and skilfully* *reasonably
This life to lose, mine owen deare brother,
If this were living only, and none other.

"But there is better life in other place,
That never shall be loste, dread thee nought;
Which Godde's Son us tolde through his grace
That Father's Son which alle thinges wrought;
And all that wrought is with a skilful* thought, *reasonable
The Ghost,* that from the Father gan proceed, *Holy Spirit
Hath souled* them, withouten any drede.** *endowed them
    with a soul **doubt

By word and by miracle, high God's Son,
When he was in this world, declared here.
That there is other life where men may won."* *dwell
To whom answer'd Tiburce, "O sister dear,
Saidest thou not right now in this mannere,
There was but one God, Lord in soothfastness,* *truth
And now of three how may'st thou bear witness?"

"That shall I tell," quoth she, "ere that I go.
Right as a man hath sapiences* three, *mental faculties

509

Memory, engine,* and intellect also, *wit
So in one being of divinity
Three persones there maye right well be."
Then gan she him full busily to preach
Of Christe's coming, and his paines teach,

And many pointes of his passion;
How Godde's Son in this world was withhold* *employed
To do mankinde plein* remission, *full
That was y-bound in sin and cares cold.* *wretched
All this thing she unto Tiburce told,
And after that Tiburce, in good intent,
With Valerian to Pope Urban he went.

That thanked God, and with glad heart and light
He christen'd him, and made him in that place
Perfect in his learning, and Godde's knight.
And after this Tiburce got such grace,
That every day he saw in time and space
Th' angel of God, and every manner boon* *request, favour
That he God asked, it was sped* full anon. *granted,
     successful

It were full hard by order for to sayn
How many wonders Jesus for them wrought,
But at the last, to telle short and plain,
The sergeants of the town of Rome them sought,
And them before Almach the Prefect brought,
Which them apposed,* and knew all their intent, *questioned
And to th'image of Jupiter them sent.

And said, "Whoso will not do sacrifice,
Swap* off his head, this is my sentence here." *strike
Anon these martyrs, *that I you devise,* *of whom I tell you*
One Maximus, that was an officere

Of the prefect's, and his corniculere
Them hent,* and when he forth the saintes lad,** *seized
    **led
Himself he wept for pity that he had.

When Maximus had heard the saintes lore,* *doctrine,
    teaching
He got him of the tormentores* leave, *torturers
And led them to his house withoute more;
And with their preaching, ere that it were eve,
They gonnen* from the tormentors to reave,** *began **wrest,
    root out
And from Maxim', and from his folk each one,
The false faith, to trow* in God alone. *believe

Cecilie came, when it was waxen night,
With priestes, that them christen'd *all in fere;* *in a
    company*
And afterward, when day was waxen light,
Cecilie them said with a full steadfast cheer,* *mien
"Now, Christe's owen knightes lefe* and dear, *beloved
Cast all away the workes of darkness,
And arme you in armour of brightness.

Ye have forsooth y-done a great battaile,
Your course is done, your faith have ye conserved;
O to the crown of life that may not fail;
The rightful Judge, which that ye have served
Shall give it you, as ye have it deserved."
And when this thing was said, as I devise,* relate
Men led them forth to do the sacrifice.

But when they were unto the place brought
To telle shortly the conclusion,
They would incense nor sacrifice right nought

But on their knees they sette them adown,
With humble heart and sad* devotion,   *steadfast
And loste both their heades in the place;
Their soules wente to the King of grace.

This Maximus, that saw this thing betide,
With piteous teares told it anon right,
That he their soules saw to heaven glide
With angels, full of clearness and of light
And with his word converted many a wight.
For which Almachius did him to-beat
With whip of lead, till he his life gan lete.*   *quit

Cecilie him took, and buried him anon
By Tiburce and Valerian softely,
Within their burying-place, under the stone.
And after this Almachius hastily
Bade his ministers fetchen openly
Cecilie, so that she might in his presence
Do sacrifice, and Jupiter incense.*   *burn incense to

But they, converted at her wise lore,*   *teaching
Wepte full sore, and gave full credence
Unto her word, and cried more and more;
"Christ, Godde's Son, withoute difference,
Is very God, this is all our sentence,*   *opinion
That hath so good a servant him to serve
Thus with one voice we trowe,* though we sterve."**   *believe
      **die

Almachius, that heard of this doing,
Bade fetch Cecilie, that he might her see;
And alderfirst,* lo, this was his asking;   *first of all
"What manner woman arte thou?" quoth he,
"I am a gentle woman born," quoth she.

"I aske thee," quoth he, "though it thee grieve,
Of thy religion and of thy believe."

"Ye have begun your question foolishly,"
Quoth she, "that wouldest two answers conclude
In one demand? ye aske lewedly."* *ignorantly
Almachius answer'd to that similitude,
"Of whence comes thine answering so rude?"
"Of whence?" quoth she, when that she was freined,* *asked
"Of conscience, and of good faith unfeigned."

Almachius saide; "Takest thou no heed
Of my power?" and she him answer'd this;
"Your might," quoth she, "full little is to dread;
For every mortal manne's power is
But like a bladder full of wind, y-wis;* *certainly
For with a needle's point, when it is blow',
May all the boast of it be laid full low."

"Full wrongfully begunnest thou," quoth he,
"And yet in wrong is thy perseverance.
Know'st thou not how our mighty princes free
Have thus commanded and made ordinance,
That every Christian wight shall have penance,* *punishment
But if that he his Christendom withsay,* *deny
And go all quit, if he will it renay?"* *renounce

"Your princes erren, as your nobley* doth," *nobility
Quoth then Cecilie, "and with a *wood sentence* *mad judgment*
Ye make us guilty, and it is not sooth:* *true
For ye that knowe well our innocence,
Forasmuch as we do aye reverence
To Christ, and for we bear a Christian name,
Ye put on us a crime and eke a blame.

513

"But we that knowe thilke name so
For virtuous, we may it not withsay."
Almachius answered, "Choose one of these two,
Do sacrifice, or Christendom renay,
That thou may'st now escape by that way."
At which the holy blissful faire maid
Gan for to laugh, and to the judge said;

"O judge, *confused in thy nicety,* *confounded in thy folly*
Wouldest thou that I reny innocence?
To make me a wicked wight," quoth she,
"Lo, he dissimuleth* here in audience; *dissembles
He stareth and woodeth* in his advertence."** *grows furious
    **thought
To whom Almachius said, "Unsely* wretch, *unhappy
Knowest thou not how far my might may stretch?

"Have not our mighty princes to me given
Yea bothe power and eke authority
To make folk to dien or to liven?
Why speakest thou so proudly then to me?"
"I speake not but steadfastly," quoth she,
Not proudly, for I say, as for my side,
We hate deadly* thilke vice of pride. *mortally

"And, if thou dreade not a sooth* to hear, *truth
Then will I shew all openly by right,
That thou hast made a full great leasing* here. *falsehood
Thou say'st thy princes have thee given might
Both for to slay and for to quick* a wight, — *give life to
Thou that may'st not but only life bereave;
Thou hast none other power nor no leave.

"But thou may'st say, thy princes have thee maked
Minister of death; for if thou speak of mo',

Thou liest; for thy power is full naked."
"Do away thy boldness," said Almachius tho,* *then
"And sacrifice to our gods, ere thou go.
I recke not what wrong that thou me proffer,
For I can suffer it as a philosopher.

"But those wronges may I not endure,
That thou speak'st of our goddes here," quoth he.
Cecilie answer'd, "O nice* creature, *foolish
Thou saidest no word, since thou spake to me,
That I knew not therewith thy nicety,* *folly
And that thou wert in *every manner wise* *every sort of way*
A lewed* officer, a vain justice. *ignorant

"There lacketh nothing to thine outward eyen
That thou art blind; for thing that we see all
That it is stone, that men may well espyen,
That ilke* stone a god thou wilt it call. *very, selfsame
I rede* thee let thine hand upon it fall, *advise
And taste* it well, and stone thou shalt it find; *examine, test
Since that thou see'st not with thine eyen blind.

"It is a shame that the people shall
So scorne thee, and laugh at thy folly;
For commonly men *wot it well over all,* *know it
    everywhere*
That mighty God is in his heaven high;
And these images, well may'st thou espy,
To thee nor to themselves may not profite,
For in effect they be not worth a mite."

These wordes and such others saide she,
And he wax'd wroth, and bade men should her lead
Home to her house; "And in her house," quoth he,
"Burn her right in a bath, with flames red."

And as he bade, right so was done the deed;
For in a bath they gan her faste shetten,*   *shut, confine
And night and day great fire they under betten.*   *kindled,
    applied

The longe night, and eke a day also,
For all the fire, and eke the bathe's heat,
She sat all cold, and felt of it no woe,
It made her not one droppe for to sweat;
But in that bath her life she must lete.*   *leave
For he, Almachius, with full wick' intent,
To slay her in the bath his sonde* sent.   *message, order

Three strokes in the neck he smote her tho,*   *there
The tormentor,* but for no manner chance   *executioner
He might not smite her faire neck in two:
And, for there was that time an ordinance
That no man should do man such penance,*   *severity, torture
The fourthe stroke to smite, soft or sore,
This tormentor he durste do no more;

But half dead, with her necke carven* there   *gashed
He let her lie, and on his way is went.
The Christian folk, which that about her were,
With sheetes have the blood full fair y-hent;   *taken up
Three dayes lived she in this torment,
And never ceased them the faith to teach,
That she had foster'd them, she gan to preach.

And them she gave her mebles* and her thing,   *goods
And to the Pope Urban betook* them tho;**   *commended
    **then
And said, "I ask this of heaven's king,
To have respite three dayes and no mo',
To recommend to you, ere that I go,

These soules, lo; and that *I might do wirch* *cause to be
    made*
Here of mine house perpetually a church."

Saint Urban, with his deacons, privily
The body fetch'd, and buried it by night
Among his other saintes honestly;
Her house the church of Saint Cecilie hight;* *is called
Saint Urban hallow'd it, as he well might;
In which unto this day, in noble wise,
Men do to Christ and to his saint service.

THE CANON'S YEOMAN'S TALE

When ended was the life of Saint Cecilie,
Ere we had ridden fully five mile,
At Boughton-under-Blee us gan o'ertake
A man, that clothed was in clothes black,
And underneath he wore a white surplice.
His hackenay,* which was all pomely-gris,** *nag
    **dapple-gray
So sweated, that it wonder was to see;
It seem'd as he had pricked* miles three. *spurred
The horse eke that his yeoman rode upon
So sweated, that unnethes* might he gon.** *hardly **go
About the peytrel stood the foam full high;
He was of foam, as *flecked as a pie.* *spotted like a magpie*
A maile twyfold on his crupper lay;
It seemed that he carried little array;
All light for summer rode this worthy man.
And in my heart to wonder I began
What that he was, till that I understood
How that his cloak was sewed to his hood;
For which, when I had long advised* me, *considered
I deemed him some Canon for to be.

His hat hung at his back down by a lace,* *cord
For he had ridden more than trot or pace;
He hadde pricked like as he were wood.* *mad
A clote-leaf* he had laid under his hood, *burdock-leaf
For sweat, and for to keep his head from heat.
But it was joye for to see him sweat;
His forehead dropped as a stillatory* *still
Were full of plantain or of paritory.* *wallflower
And when that he was come, he gan to cry,
"God save," quoth he, "this jolly company.
Fast have I pricked," quoth he, "for your sake,
Because that I would you overtake,
To riden in this merry company."
His Yeoman was eke full of courtesy,
And saide, "Sirs, now in the morning tide
Out of your hostelry I saw you ride,
And warned here my lord and sovereign,
Which that to ride with you is full fain,
For his disport; he loveth dalliance."
"Friend, for thy warning God give thee good chance,"*
    *fortune
Said oure Host; "certain it woulde seem
Thy lord were wise, and so I may well deem;
He is full jocund also, dare I lay;
Can he aught tell a merry tale or tway,
With which he gladden may this company?"
"Who, Sir? my lord? Yea, Sir, withoute lie,
He can* of mirth and eke of jollity *knows
Not but enough; also, Sir, truste me, *not less than*
An* ye him knew all so well as do I, *if
Ye would wonder how well and craftily
He coulde work, and that in sundry wise.
He hath take on him many a great emprise,* *task,
        undertaking
Which were full hard for any that is here

To bring about, but* they of him it lear.** *unless **learn
As homely as he rides amonges you,
If ye him knew, it would be for your prow:* *advantage
Ye woulde not forego his acquaintance
For muche good, I dare lay in balance
All that I have in my possession.
He is a man of high discretion.
I warn you well, he is a passing* man." *surpassing,
    extraordinary
"Well," quoth our Host, "I pray thee tell me than,
Is he a clerk,* or no? Tell what he is." *scholar, priest
"Nay, he is greater than a clerk, y-wis,"* *certainly
Saide this Yeoman; "and, in wordes few,
Host, of his craft somewhat I will you shew,
I say, my lord can* such a subtlety *knows
(But all his craft ye may not weet* of me, *learn
And somewhat help I yet to his working),
That all the ground on which we be riding
Till that we come to Canterbury town,
He could all cleane turnen up so down,
And pave it all of silver and of gold."
And when this Yeoman had this tale told
Unto our Host, he said; "Ben'dicite!
This thing is wonder marvellous to me,
Since that thy lord is of so high prudence,
Because of which men should him reverence,
That of his worship* recketh he so lite;** *honour **little
His *overest slop* it is not worth a mite *upper garment*
As in effect to him, so may I go;
It is all baudy* and to-tore also. *slovenly
Why is thy lord so sluttish, I thee pray,
And is of power better clothes to bey,* *buy
If that his deed accordeth with thy speech?
Telle me that, and that I thee beseech."

"Why?" quoth this Yeoman, "whereto ask ye me?
God help me so, for he shall never the* *thrive
(But I will not avowe* that I say, *admit
And therefore keep it secret, I you pray);
He is too wise, in faith, as I believe.
Thing that is overdone, it will not preve* *stand the test
Aright, as clerkes say; it is a vice;
Wherefore in that I hold him *lewd and nice.* *ignorant and
    foolish*
For when a man hath over great a wit,
Full oft him happens to misusen it;
So doth my lord, and that me grieveth sore.
God it amend; I can say now no more."

"Thereof *no force,* good Yeoman," quoth our Host; *no
    matter*
"Since of the conning* of thy lord, thou know'st, *knowledge
Tell how he doth, I pray thee heartily,
Since that be is so crafty and so sly.* *wise
Where dwelle ye, if it to telle be?"
"In the suburbes of a town," quoth he,
"Lurking in hernes* and in lanes blind, *corners
Where as these robbers and these thieves by kind* *nature
Holde their privy fearful residence,
As they that dare not show their presence,
So fare we, if I shall say the soothe."* *truth
"Yet," quoth our Hoste, "let me talke to thee;
Why art thou so discolour'd of thy face?"
"Peter!" quoth he, "God give it harde grace,
I am so us'd the hote fire to blow,
That it hath changed my colour, I trow;
I am not wont in no mirror to pry,
But swinke* sore, and learn to multiply. *labour
We blunder* ever, and poren** in the fire, *toil **peer
And, for all that, we fail of our desire

For ever we lack our conclusion
To muche folk we do illusion,
And borrow gold, be it a pound or two,
Or ten or twelve, or many summes mo',
And make them weenen,* at the leaste way, *fancy
That of a pounde we can make tway.
Yet is it false; and aye we have good hope
It for to do, and after it we grope:* *search, strive
But that science is so far us beforn,
That we may not, although we had it sworn,
It overtake, it slides away so fast;
It will us make beggars at the last."
While this Yeoman was thus in his talking,
This Canon drew him near, and heard all thing
Which this Yeoman spake, for suspicion
Of menne's speech ever had this Canon:
For Cato saith, that he that guilty is,
Deemeth all things be spoken of him y-wis;* *surely
Because of that he gan so nigh to draw
To his Yeoman, that he heard all his saw;
And thus he said unto his Yeoman tho* *then
"Hold thou thy peace, and speak no wordes mo':
For if thou do, thou shalt *it dear abie.* *pay dearly for it*
Thou slanderest me here in this company
And eke discoverest that thou shouldest hide."
"Yea," quoth our Host, "tell on, whatso betide;
Of all his threatening reck not a mite."
"In faith," quoth he, "no more do I but lite."* *little
And when this Canon saw it would not be
But his Yeoman would tell his privity,* *secrets
He fled away for very sorrow and shame.

"Ah!" quoth the Yeoman, "here shall rise a game;* *some
    diversion
All that I can anon I will you tell,

Since he is gone; the foule fiend him quell!* *destroy
For ne'er hereafter will I with him meet,
For penny nor for pound, I you behete.* *promise
He that me broughte first unto that game,
Ere that he die, sorrow have he and shame.
For it is earnest* to me, by my faith; *a serious matter
That feel I well, what so any man saith;
And yet for all my smart, and all my grief,
For all my sorrow, labour, and mischief,* *trouble
I coulde never leave it in no wise.
Now would to God my witte might suffice
To tellen all that longeth to that art!
But natheless yet will I telle part;
Since that my lord is gone, I will not spare;
Such thing as that I know, I will declare."

THE TALE

With this Canon I dwelt have seven year,
And of his science am I ne'er the near* *nearer
All that I had I have lost thereby,
And, God wot, so have many more than I.
Where I was wont to be right fresh and gay
Of clothing, and of other good array
Now may I wear an hose upon mine head;
And where my colour was both fresh and red,
Now is it wan, and of a leaden hue
(Whoso it useth, sore shall he it rue);
And of my swink* yet bleared is mine eye; *labour
Lo what advantage is to multiply!
That sliding* science hath me made so bare, *slippery,
    deceptive
That I have no good,* where that ever I fare; *property
And yet I am indebted so thereby
Of gold, that I have borrow'd truely,

That, while I live, I shall it quite* never; *repay
Let every man beware by me for ever.
What manner man that casteth* him thereto, *betaketh
If he continue, I hold *his thrift y-do;* *prosperity at an end*
So help me God, thereby shall he not win,
But empty his purse, and make his wittes thin.
And when he, through his madness and folly,
Hath lost his owen good through jupartie,* *hazard
Then he exciteth other men thereto,
To lose their good as he himself hath do'.
For unto shrewes* joy it is and ease *wicked folk
To have their fellows in pain and disease.* *trouble
Thus was I ones learned of a clerk;
Of that no charge;* I will speak of our work. *matter

When we be there as we shall exercise
Our elvish* craft, we seeme wonder wise, *fantastic, wicked
Our termes be so *clergial and quaint.* *learned and strange
I blow the fire till that mine hearte faint.
Why should I tellen each proportion
Of thinges, whiche that we work upon,
As on five or six ounces, may well be,
Of silver, or some other quantity?
And busy me to telle you the names,
As orpiment, burnt bones, iron squames,* *scales
That into powder grounden be full small?
And in an earthen pot how put is all,
And, salt y-put in, and also peppere,
Before these powders that I speak of here,
And well y-cover'd with a lamp of glass?
And of much other thing which that there was?
And of the pots and glasses engluting,* *sealing up
That of the air might passen out no thing?
And of the easy* fire, and smart** also, *slow **quick
Which that was made? and of the care and woe

That we had in our matters subliming,
And in amalgaming, and calcining
Of quicksilver, called mercury crude?
For all our sleightes we can not conclude.
Our orpiment, and sublim'd mercury,
Our ground litharge* eke on the porphyry,   *white lead
Of each of these of ounces a certain,*   *certain proportion
Not helpeth us, our labour is in vain.
Nor neither our spirits' ascensioun,
Nor our matters that lie all fix'd adown,
May in our working nothing us avail;
For lost is all our labour and travail,
And all the cost, a twenty devil way,
Is lost also, which we upon it lay.

There is also full many another thing
That is unto our craft appertaining,
Though I by order them not rehearse can,
Because that I am a lewed* man;   *unlearned
Yet will I tell them as they come to mind,
Although I cannot set them in their kind,
As sal-armoniac, verdigris, borace;
And sundry vessels made of earth and glass;
Our urinales, and our descensories,
Phials, and croslets, and sublimatories,
Cucurbites, and alembikes eke,
And other suche, *dear enough a leek,*   *worth less than a
       leek*
It needeth not for to rehearse them all.
Waters rubifying, and bulles' gall,
Arsenic, sal-armoniac, and brimstone,
And herbes could I tell eke many a one,
As egremoine,* valerian, and lunary,**   *agrimony **moon-wort
And other such, if that me list to tarry;
Our lampes burning bothe night and day,

To bring about our craft if that we may;
Our furnace eke of calcination,
And of waters albification,
Unslaked lime, chalk, and *glair of an ey,* *egg-white
Powders diverse, ashes, dung, piss, and clay,
Seared pokettes, saltpetre, and vitriol;
And divers fires made of wood and coal;
Sal-tartar, alkali, salt preparate,
And combust matters, and coagulate;
Clay made with horse and manne's hair, and oil
Of tartar, alum, glass, barm, wort, argoil,* *potter's clay
Rosalgar,* and other matters imbibing; *flowers of antimony
And eke of our matters encorporing,* *incorporating
And of our silver citrination,
Our cementing, and fermentation,
Our ingots,* tests, and many thinges mo'. *moulds
I will you tell, as was me taught also,
The foure spirits, and the bodies seven,
By order, as oft I heard my lord them neven.* *name
The first spirit Quicksilver called is;
The second Orpiment; the third, y-wis,
Sal-Armoniac, and the fourth Brimstone.
The bodies sev'n eke, lo them here anon.
Sol gold is, and Luna silver we threpe* *name
Mars iron, Mercury quicksilver we clepe;* *call
Saturnus lead, and Jupiter is tin,
And Venus copper, by my father's kin.

This cursed craft whoso will exercise,
He shall no good have that him may suffice;
For all the good he spendeth thereabout,
He lose shall, thereof have I no doubt.
Whoso that list to utter* his folly, *display
Let him come forth and learn to multiply:
And every man that hath aught in his coffer,

Let him appear, and wax a philosopher;
Ascaunce* that craft is so light to lear.** *as if **learn
Nay, nay, God wot, all be he monk or frere,
Priest or canon, or any other wight;
Though he sit at his book both day and night;
In learning of this *elvish nice* lore, * fantastic, foolish
All is in vain; and pardie muche more,
Is to learn a lew'd* man this subtlety; *ignorant
Fie! speak not thereof, for it will not be.
And *conne he letterure,* or conne he none, *if he knows
    learning*
As in effect, he shall it find all one;
For bothe two, by my salvation,
Concluden in multiplication* *transmutation by alchemy
Alike well, when they have all y-do;
This is to say, they faile bothe two.
Yet forgot I to make rehearsale
Of waters corrosive, and of limaile,* *metal filings
And of bodies' mollification,
And also of their induration,
Oiles, ablutions, metal fusible,
To tellen all, would passen any Bible
That owhere* is; wherefore, as for the best, *anywhere
Of all these names now will I me rest;
For, as I trow, I have you told enough
To raise a fiend, all look he ne'er so rough.

Ah! nay, let be; the philosopher's stone,
Elixir call'd, we seeke fast each one;
For had we him, then were we sicker* enow; *secure
But unto God of heaven I make avow,* *confession
For all our craft, when we have all y-do,
And all our sleight, he will not come us to.
He hath y-made us spende muche good,
For sorrow of which almost we waxed wood,* *mad

But that good hope creeped in our heart,
Supposing ever, though we sore smart,
To be relieved by him afterward.
Such supposing and hope is sharp and hard.
I warn you well it is to seeken ever.
That future temps* hath made men dissever,** *time **part from
In trust thereof, from all that ever they had,
Yet of that art they cannot waxe sad,* *repentant
For unto them it is a bitter sweet;
So seemeth it; for had they but a sheet
Which that they mighte wrap them in at night,
And a bratt* to walk in by dayelight, *cloak
They would them sell, and spend it on this craft;
They cannot stint,* until no thing be laft. *cease
And evermore, wherever that they gon,
Men may them knowe by smell of brimstone;
For all the world they stinken as a goat;
Their savour is so rammish and so hot,
That though a man a mile from them be,
The savour will infect him, truste me.
Lo, thus by smelling and threadbare array,
If that men list, this folk they knowe may.
And if a man will ask them privily,
Why they be clothed so unthriftily,* *shabbily
They right anon will rownen* in his ear, *whisper
And sayen, if that they espied were,
Men would them slay, because of their science:
Lo, thus these folk betrayen innocence!

Pass over this; I go my tale unto.
Ere that the pot be on the fire y-do* *placed
Of metals, with a certain quantity
My lord them tempers,* and no man but he *adjusts the
        proportions
(Now he is gone, I dare say boldely);

For as men say, he can do craftily,
Algate* I wot well he hath such a name, *although
And yet full oft he runneth into blame;
And know ye how? full oft it happ'neth so,
The pot to-breaks, and farewell! all is go'.* *gone
These metals be of so great violence,
Our walles may not make them resistence,
But if they were wrought of lime and stone; *unless*
They pierce so, that through the wall they gon;
And some of them sink down into the ground
(Thus have we lost by times many a pound),
And some are scatter'd all the floor about;
Some leap into the roof withoute doubt.
Though that the fiend not in our sight him show,
I trowe that he be with us, that shrew;* *impious wretch
In helle, where that he is lord and sire,
Is there no more woe, rancour, nor ire.
When that our pot is broke, as I have said,
Every man chides, and holds him *evil apaid.* *dissatisfied*
Some said it was *long on* the fire-making; *because of *
Some saide nay, it was on the blowing
(Then was I fear'd, for that was mine office);
"Straw!" quoth the third, "ye be *lewed and **nice,
        *ignorant **foolish
It was not temper'd* as it ought to be." *mixed in due
        proportions
"Nay," quoth the fourthe, "stint* and hearken me; *stop
Because our fire was not y-made of beech,
That is the cause, and other none, *so the'ch.* *so may I thrive*
I cannot tell whereon it was along,
But well I wot great strife is us among."
"What?" quoth my lord, "there is no more to do'n,
Of these perils I will beware eftsoon.* *another time
I am right sicker* that the pot was crazed.** *sure **cracked
Be as be may, be ye no thing amazed.* *confounded

As usage is, let sweep the floor as swithe;* *quickly
Pluck up your heartes and be glad and blithe."

The mullok* on a heap y-sweeped was, *rubbish
And on the floor y-cast a canevas,
And all this mullok in a sieve y-throw,
And sifted, and y-picked many a throw.* *time
"Pardie," quoth one, "somewhat of our metal
Yet is there here, though that we have not all.
And though this thing *mishapped hath as now,* *has gone
    amiss at present*
Another time it may be well enow.
We muste *put our good in adventure; * *risk our property*
A merchant, pardie, may not aye endure,
Truste me well, in his prosperity:
Sometimes his good is drenched* in the sea, *drowned, sunk
And sometimes comes it safe unto the land."
"Peace," quoth my lord; "the next time I will fand* *endeavour
To bring our craft *all in another plight,* *to a different
    conclusion*
And but I do, Sirs, let me have the wite;* *blame
There was default in somewhat, well I wot."
Another said, the fire was over hot.
But be it hot or cold, I dare say this,
That we concluden evermore amiss;
We fail alway of that which we would have;
And in our madness evermore we rave.
And when we be together every one,
Every man seemeth a Solomon.
But all thing, which that shineth as the gold,
It is not gold, as I have heard it told;
Nor every apple that is fair at eye,
It is not good, what so men clap* or cry. *assert
Right so, lo, fareth it amonges us.
He that the wisest seemeth, by Jesus,

Is most fool, when it cometh to the prefe;* *proof, test
And he that seemeth truest, is a thief.
That shall ye know, ere that I from you wend;
By that I of my tale have made an end.

There was a canon of religioun
Amonges us, would infect* all a town, *deceive
Though it as great were as was Nineveh,
Rome, Alisandre,* Troy, or other three. *Alexandria
His sleightes* and his infinite falseness *cunning tricks
There coulde no man writen, as I guess,
Though that he mighte live a thousand year;
In all this world of falseness n'is* his peer. *there is not
For in his termes he will him so wind,
And speak his wordes in so sly a kind,
When he commune shall with any wight,
That he will make him doat* anon aright, *become foolishly
    fond of him*
But it a fiende be, as himself is.
Full many a man hath he beguil'd ere this,
And will, if that he may live any while;
And yet men go and ride many a mile
Him for to seek, and have his acquaintance,
Not knowing of his false governance.* *deceitful conduct
And if you list to give me audience,
I will it telle here in your presence.
But, worshipful canons religious,
Ne deeme not that I slander your house,
Although that my tale of a canon be.
Of every order some shrew is, pardie;
And God forbid that all a company
Should rue a singular* manne's folly. *individual
To slander you is no thing mine intent;
But to correct that is amiss I meant.
This tale was not only told for you,

But eke for other more; ye wot well how
That amonges Christe's apostles twelve
There was no traitor but Judas himselve;
Then why should all the remenant have blame,
That guiltless were? By you I say the same.
Save only this, if ye will hearken me,
If any Judas in your convent be,
Remove him betimes, I you rede,*   *counsel
If shame or loss may causen any dread.
And be no thing displeased, I you pray;
But in this case hearken what I say.

In London was a priest, an annualere,
That therein dwelled hadde many a year,
Which was so pleasant and so serviceable
Unto the wife, where as he was at table,
That she would suffer him no thing to pay
For board nor clothing, went he ne'er so gay;
And spending silver had he right enow;
Thereof no force;* will proceed as now,   *no matter
And telle forth my tale of the canon,
That brought this prieste to confusion.
This false canon came upon a day
Unto the prieste's chamber, where he lay,
Beseeching him to lend him a certain
Of gold, and he would quit it him again.
"Lend me a mark," quoth he, "but dayes three,
And at my day I will it quite thee.
And if it so be that thou find me false,
Another day hang me up by the halse."*   *neck
This priest him took a mark, and that as swithe,*   *quickly
And this canon him thanked often sithe,*   *times
And took his leave, and wente forth his way;
And at the thirde day brought his money;
And to the priest he took his gold again,

Whereof this priest was wondrous glad and fain.* *pleased
"Certes," quoth he, *"nothing annoyeth me* *I am not unwilling*
To lend a man a noble, or two, or three,
Or what thing were in my possession,
When he so true is of condition,
That in no wise he breake will his day;
To such a man I never can say nay."
"What," quoth this canon, "should I be untrue?
Nay, that were *thing y-fallen all of new!* *a new thing to happen*
Truth is a thing that I will ever keep,
Unto the day in which that I shall creep
Into my grave; and elles God forbid;
Believe this as sicker* as your creed. *sure
God thank I, and in good time be it said,
That there was never man yet *evil apaid* *displeased,
      dissatisfied*
For gold nor silver that he to me lent,
Nor ever falsehood in mine heart I meant.
And Sir," quoth he, "now of my privity,
Since ye so goodly have been unto me,
And kithed* to me so great gentleness, *shown
Somewhat, to quite with your kindeness,
I will you shew, and if you list to lear,* *learn
I will you teache plainly the mannere
How I can worken in philosophy.
Take good heed, ye shall well see *at eye* *with your own eyes*
That I will do a mas'try ere I go."
"Yea," quoth the priest; "yea, Sir, and will ye so?
Mary! thereof I pray you heartily."
"At your commandement, Sir, truely,"
Quoth the canon, "and elles God forbid."
Lo, how this thiefe could his service bede!* *offer

Full sooth it is that such proffer'd service
Stinketh, as witnesse *these olde wise;* *those wise folk of old*

And that full soon I will it verify
In this canon, root of all treachery,
That evermore delight had and gladness
(Such fiendly thoughtes *in his heart impress*) *press into
    his heart*
How Christe's people he may to mischief bring.
God keep us from his false dissimuling!
What wiste this priest with whom that he dealt?
Nor of his harm coming he nothing felt.
O sely* priest, O sely innocent! *simple
With covetise anon thou shalt be blent;* *blinded;
    beguiled
O graceless, full blind is thy conceit!
For nothing art thou ware of the deceit
Which that this fox y-shapen* hath to thee; *contrived
His wily wrenches* thou not mayest flee. *snares
Wherefore, to go to the conclusioun
That referreth to thy confusion,
Unhappy man, anon I will me hie* *hasten
To telle thine unwit* and thy folly, *stupidity
And eke the falseness of that other wretch,
As farforth as that my conning* will stretch.
    *knowledge
This canon was my lord, ye woulde ween;* *imagine
Sir Host, in faith, and by the heaven's queen,
It was another canon, and not he,
That can* an hundred fold more subtlety. *knows
He hath betrayed folkes many a time;
Of his falseness it doleth* me to rhyme. *paineth
And ever, when I speak of his falsehead,
For shame of him my cheekes waxe red;
Algates* they beginne for to glow, *at least
For redness have I none, right well I know,
In my visage; for fumes diverse
Of metals, which ye have me heard rehearse,

Consumed have and wasted my redness.
Now take heed of this canon's cursedness.* *villainy

"Sir," quoth he to the priest, "let your man gon
For quicksilver, that we it had anon;
And let him bringen ounces two or three;
And when he comes, as faste shall ye see
A wondrous thing, which ye saw ne'er ere this."
"Sir," quoth the priest, "it shall be done, y-wis."* *certainly
He bade his servant fetche him this thing,
And he all ready was at his bidding,
And went him forth, and came anon again
With this quicksilver, shortly for to sayn;
And took these ounces three to the canoun;
And he them laide well and fair adown,
And bade the servant coales for to bring,
That he anon might go to his working.
The coales right anon weren y-fet,* *fetched
And this canon y-took a crosselet* *crucible
Out of his bosom, and shew'd to the priest.
"This instrument," quoth he, "which that thou seest,
Take in thine hand, and put thyself therein
Of this quicksilver an ounce, and here begin,
In the name of Christ, to wax a philosopher.
There be full few, which that I woulde proffer
To shewe them thus much of my science;
For here shall ye see by experience
That this quicksilver I will mortify,
Right in your sight anon withoute lie,
And make it as good silver, and as fine,
As there is any in your purse, or mine,
Or elleswhere; and make it malleable,
And elles holde me false and unable
Amonge folk for ever to appear.
I have a powder here that cost me dear,

Shall make all good, for it is cause of all
My conning,* which that I you shewe shall. *knowledge
Voide* your man, and let him be thereout; *send away
And shut the doore, while we be about
Our privity, that no man us espy,
While that we work in this philosophy."
All, as he bade, fulfilled was in deed.
This ilke servant right anon out yede,* *went
And his master y-shut the door anon,
And to their labour speedily they gon.

This priest, at this cursed canon's bidding,
Upon the fire anon he set this thing,
And blew the fire, and busied him full fast.
And this canon into the croslet cast
A powder, I know not whereof it was
Y-made, either of chalk, either of glass,
Or somewhat elles, was not worth a fly,
To blinden* with this priest; and bade him hie** *deceive
     **make haste
The coales for to couchen* all above *lay in order
The croslet; "for, in token I thee love,"
Quoth this canon, "thine owen handes two
Shall work all thing that here shall be do'."
"Grand mercy," quoth the priest, and was full glad, *great
     thanks*
And couch'd the coales as the canon bade.
And while he busy was, this fiendly wretch,
This false canon (the foule fiend him fetch),
Out of his bosom took a beechen coal,
In which full subtifly was made a hole,
And therein put was of silver limaile* *filings
An ounce, and stopped was withoute fail
The hole with wax, to keep the limaile in.
And understande, that this false gin* *contrivance

Was not made there, but it was made before;
And other thinges I shall tell you more,
Hereafterward, which that he with him brought;
Ere he came there, him to beguile he thought,
And so he did, ere that they *went atwin;* *separated*
Till he had turned him, could he not blin.* *cease
It doleth* me, when that I of him speak; *paineth
On his falsehood fain would I me awreak,* *revenge myself
If I wist how, but he is here and there;
He is so variant,* he abides nowhere. *changeable

But take heed, Sirs, now for Godde's love.
He took his coal, of which I spake above,
And in his hand he bare it privily,
And while the prieste couched busily
The coales, as I tolde you ere this,
This canon saide, "Friend, ye do amiss;
This is not couched as it ought to be,
But soon I shall amenden it," quoth he.
"Now let me meddle therewith but a while,
For of you have I pity, by Saint Gile.
Ye be right hot, I see well how ye sweat;
Have here a cloth, and wipe away the wet."
And while that the prieste wip'd his face,
This canon took his coal, — *with sorry grace,* — *evil fortune
        attend him!*
And layed it above on the midward
Of the croslet, and blew well afterward,
Till that the coals beganne fast to brenn.* *burn
"Now give us drinke," quoth this canon then,
"And swithe* all shall be well, I undertake. *quickly
Sitte we down, and let us merry make."
And whenne that this canon's beechen coal
Was burnt, all the limaile out of the hole
Into the crosselet anon fell down;

And so it muste needes, by reasoun,
Since it above so *even couched* was; *exactly laid*
But thereof wist the priest no thing, alas!
He deemed all the coals alike good,
For of the sleight he nothing understood.

And when this alchemister saw his time,
"Rise up, Sir Priest," quoth he, "and stand by me;
And, for I wot well ingot* have ye none; *mould
Go, walke forth, and bring me a chalk stone;
For I will make it of the same shape
That is an ingot, if I may have hap.
Bring eke with you a bowl, or else a pan,
Full of water, and ye shall well see than* *then
How that our business shall *hap and preve* *succeed*
And yet, for ye shall have no misbelieve* *mistrust
Nor wrong conceit of me, in your absence,
I wille not be out of your presence,
But go with you, and come with you again."
The chamber-doore, shortly for to sayn,
They opened and shut, and went their way,
And forth with them they carried the key;
And came again without any delay.
Why should I tarry all the longe day?
He took the chalk, and shap'd it in the wise
Of an ingot, as I shall you devise;* *describe
I say, he took out of his owen sleeve
A teine* of silver (evil may he cheve!**) *little piece **prosper
Which that ne was but a just ounce of weight.
And take heed now of his cursed sleight;
He shap'd his ingot, in length and in brede* *breadth
Of this teine, withouten any drede,* *doubt
So slily, that the priest it not espied;
And in his sleeve again he gan it hide;
And from the fire he took up his mattere,

And in th' ingot put it with merry cheer;
And in the water-vessel he it cast,
When that him list, and bade the priest as fast
Look what there is; "Put in thine hand and grope;
There shalt thou finde silver, as I hope."
What, devil of helle! should it elles be?
Shaving of silver, silver is, pardie.
He put his hand in, and took up a teine
Of silver fine; and glad in every vein
Was this priest, when he saw that it was so.
"Godde's blessing, and his mother's also,
And alle hallows,* have ye, Sir Canon!" *saints
Saide this priest, "and I their malison* *curse
But, an'* ye vouchesafe to teache me *if
This noble craft and this subtility,
I will be yours in all that ever I may."
Quoth the canon, "Yet will I make assay
The second time, that ye may take heed,
And be expert of this, and, in your need,
Another day assay in mine absence
This discipline, and this crafty science.
Let take another ounce," quoth he tho,* *then
"Of quicksilver, withoute wordes mo',
And do therewith as ye have done ere this
With that other, which that now silver is."

The priest him busied, all that e'er he can,
To do as this canon, this cursed man,
Commanded him, and fast he blew the fire
For to come to th' effect of his desire.
And this canon right in the meanewhile
All ready was this priest eft* to beguile, *again
and, for a countenance,* in his hande bare *stratagem
An hollow sticke (take keep* and beware); *heed
Of silver limaile put was, as before

Was in his coal, and stopped with wax well
For to keep in his limaile every deal.* *particle
And while this priest was in his business,
This canon with his sticke gan him dress* *apply
To him anon, and his powder cast in,
As he did erst (the devil out of his skin
Him turn, I pray to God, for his falsehead,
For he was ever false in thought and deed),
And with his stick, above the crosselet,
That was ordained* with that false get,** *provided **contrivance
He stirr'd the coales, till relente gan
The wax against the fire, as every man,
But he a fool be, knows well it must need.
And all that in the sticke was out yede,* *went
And in the croslet hastily* it fell. *quickly
Now, goode Sirs, what will ye bet* than well? *better
When that this priest was thus beguil'd again,
Supposing naught but truthe, sooth to sayn,
He was so glad, that I can not express
In no mannere his mirth and his gladness;
And to the canon he proffer'd eftsoon* *forthwith; again
Body and good. "Yea," quoth the canon soon,
"Though poor I be, crafty* thou shalt me find; *skilful
I warn thee well, yet is there more behind.
Is any copper here within?" said he.
"Yea, Sir," the prieste said, "I trow there be."
"Elles go buy us some, and that as swithe.* *swiftly
Now, goode Sir, go forth thy way and hie* thee." *hasten
He went his way, and with the copper came,
And this canon it in his handes name,* *took
And of that copper weighed out an ounce.
Too simple is my tongue to pronounce,
As minister of my wit, the doubleness
Of this canon, root of all cursedness.
He friendly seem'd to them that knew him not;

But he was fiendly, both in work and thought.
It wearieth me to tell of his falseness;
And natheless yet will I it express,
To that intent men may beware thereby,
And for none other cause truely.
He put this copper in the crosselet,
And on the fire as swithe* he hath it set,   *swiftly
And cast in powder, and made the priest to blow,
And in his working for to stoope low,
As he did erst,* and all was but a jape;**   *before **trick
Right as him list the priest *he made his ape.*   *befooled him*
And afterward in the ingot he it cast,
And in the pan he put it at the last
Of water, and in he put his own hand;
And in his sleeve, as ye beforehand
Hearde me tell, he had a silver teine;*   *small piece
He silly took it out, this cursèd heine*   *wretch
(Unweeting* this priest of his false craft),   *unsuspecting
And in the panne's bottom he it laft*   *left
And in the water rumbleth to and fro,
And wondrous privily took up also
The copper teine (not knowing thilke priest),
And hid it, and him hente* by the breast,   *took
And to him spake, and thus said in his game;
"Stoop now adown; by God, ye be to blame;
Helpe me now, as I did you whilere;*   *before
Put in your hand, and looke what is there."

This priest took up this silver teine anon;
And thenne said the canon, "Let us gon,
With these three teines which that we have wrought,
To some goldsmith, and *weet if they be aught:*   *find out if
     they are worth anything*
For, by my faith, I would not for my hood
But if they were silver fine and good,   *unless

And that as swithe* well proved shall it be." *quickly
Unto the goldsmith with these teines three
They went anon, and put them in assay* *proof
To fire and hammer; might no man say nay,
But that they weren as they ought to be.
This sotted* priest, who gladder was than he? *stupid, besotted
Was never bird gladder against the day;
Nor nightingale in the season of May
Was never none, that better list to sing;
Nor lady lustier in carolling,
Or for to speak of love and womanhead;
Nor knight in arms to do a hardy deed,
To standen in grace of his lady dear,
Than had this priest this crafte for to lear;
And to the canon thus he spake and said;
"For love of God, that for us alle died,
And as I may deserve it unto you,
What shall this receipt coste? tell me now."
"By our Lady," quoth this canon, "it is dear.
I warn you well, that, save I and a frere,
In Engleland there can no man it make."
"No force," quoth he; "now, Sir, for Godde's sake, *no matter*
What shall I pay? telle me, I you pray."
"Y-wis,"* quoth he, "it is full dear, I say. *certainly
Sir, at one word, if that you list it have,
Ye shall pay forty pound, so God me save;
And n'ere* the friendship that ye did ere this *were it not for
To me, ye shoulde paye more, y-wis."
This priest the sum of forty pound anon
Of nobles fet,* and took them every one *fetched
To this canon, for this ilke receipt.
All his working was but fraud and deceit.
"Sir Priest," he said, "I keep* to have no los** *care **praise
Of my craft, for I would it were kept close;
And as ye love me, keep it secre:

For if men knewen all my subtlety,
By God, they woulde have so great envy
To me, because of my philosophy,
I should be dead, there were no other way."
"God it forbid," quoth the priest, "what ye say.
Yet had I lever* spenden all the good   *rather
Which that I have (and elles were I wood*),   *mad
Than that ye shoulde fall in such mischief."
"For your good will, Sir, have ye right good prefe,"*   *results
      of your experiments*
Quoth the canon; "and farewell, grand mercy."
He went his way, and never the priest him sey *   *saw
After that day; and when that this priest should
Maken assay, at such time as he would,
Of this receipt, farewell! it would not be.
Lo, thus bejaped* and beguil'd was he;   *tricked
Thus made he his introduction
To bringe folk to their destruction.

Consider, Sirs, how that in each estate
Betwixte men and gold there is debate,
So farforth that *unnethes is there none.*   *scarcely is there any*
This multiplying blint* so many a one,   *blinds, deceives
That in good faith I trowe that it be
The cause greatest of such scarcity.
These philosophers speak so mistily
In this craft, that men cannot come thereby,
For any wit that men have how-a-days.
They may well chatter, as do these jays,
And in their termes set their *lust and pain,*   *pleasure and
      exertion*
But to their purpose shall they ne'er attain.
A man may lightly* learn, if he have aught,   *easily
To multiply, and bring his good to naught.
Lo, such a lucre* is in this lusty** game;   *profit **pleasant

A manne's mirth it will turn all to grame,* *sorrow
And empty also great and heavy purses,
And make folke for to purchase curses
Of them that have thereto their good y-lent.
Oh, fy for shame! they that have been brent,* *burnt
Alas! can they not flee the fire's heat?
Ye that it use, I rede* that ye it lete,** *advise **leave
Lest ye lose all; for better than never is late;
Never to thrive, were too long a date.
Though ye prowl aye, ye shall it never find;
Ye be as bold as is Bayard the blind,
That blunders forth, and *peril casteth none;* *perceives no
   danger*
He is as bold to run against a stone,
As for to go beside it in the way:
So fare ye that multiply, I say.
If that your eyen cannot see aright,
Look that your minde lacke not his sight.
For though you look never so broad, and stare,
Ye shall not win a mite on that chaffare,* *traffic, commerce
But wasten all that ye may *rape and renn.* *get by hook or
   crook*
Withdraw the fire, lest it too faste brenn;* *burn
Meddle no more with that art, I mean;
For if ye do, your thrift* is gone full clean. *prosperity
And right as swithe* I will you telle here *quickly
What philosophers say in this mattere.

Lo, thus saith Arnold of the newe town,
As his Rosary maketh mentioun,
He saith right thus, withouten any lie;
"There may no man mercury mortify,
But* it be with his brother's knowledging." *except
Lo, how that he, which firste said this thing,
Of philosophers father was, Hermes;

He saith, how that the dragon doubteless
He dieth not, but if that he be slain
With his brother. And this is for to sayn,
By the dragon, Mercury, and none other,
He understood, and Brimstone by his brother,
That out of Sol and Luna were y-draw.* *drawn, derived
"And therefore," said he, "take heed to my saw.* *saying
Let no man busy him this art to seech,* *study, explore
But if that he th'intention and speech *unless
Of philosophers understande can;
And if he do, he is a lewed* man. *ignorant, foolish
For this science and this conning,"* quoth he, *knowledge
"Is of the secret of secrets pardie."
Also there was a disciple of Plato,
That on a time said his master to,
As his book, Senior, will bear witness,
And this was his demand in soothfastness:
"Tell me the name of thilke* privy** stone." *that **secret
And Plato answer'd unto him anon;
"Take the stone that Titanos men name."
"Which is that?" quoth he. "Magnesia is the same,"
Saide Plato. "Yea, Sir, and is it thus?
This is *ignotum per ignotius.*
What is Magnesia, good Sir, I pray?"
"It is a water that is made, I say,
Of th' elementes foure," quoth Plato.
"Tell me the roote, good Sir," quoth he tho,* *then
"Of that water, if that it be your will."
"Nay, nay," quoth Plato, "certain that I n'ill.* *will not
The philosophers sworn were every one,
That they should not discover it to none,
Nor in no book it write in no mannere;
For unto God it is so lefe* and dear, *precious
That he will not that it discover'd be,
But where it liketh to his deity

Man for to inspire, and eke for to defend* *protect
Whom that he liketh; lo, this is the end."

Then thus conclude I, since that God of heaven
Will not that these philosophers neven* *name
How that a man shall come unto this stone,
I rede* as for the best to let it gon. *counsel
For whoso maketh God his adversary,
As for to work any thing in contrary
Of his will, certes never shall he thrive,
Though that he multiply term of his live.
And there a point;* for ended is my tale. *end
God send ev'ry good man *boot of his bale.* *remedy for his
    sorrow*

THE MANCIPLE'S TALE

Weet* ye not where there stands a little town, *know
Which that y-called is Bob-up-and-down,
Under the Blee, in Canterbury way?
There gan our Hoste for to jape and play,
And saide, "Sirs, what? Dun is in the mire.
Is there no man, for prayer nor for hire,
That will awaken our fellow behind?
A thief him might full* rob and bind *easily
See how he nappeth, see, for cocke's bones,
As he would falle from his horse at ones.
Is that a Cook of London, with mischance?
Do* him come forth, he knoweth his penance; *make
For he shall tell a tale, by my fay,* *faith
Although it be not worth a bottle hay.

Awake, thou Cook," quoth he; "God give thee sorrow
What aileth thee to sleepe *by the morrow?* *in the day time*
Hast thou had fleas all night, or art drunk?

Or had thou with some quean* all night y-swunk,**   *whore
    **laboured
So that thou mayest not hold up thine head?"
The Cook, that was full pale and nothing red,
Said to Host, "So God my soule bless,
As there is fall'n on me such heaviness,
I know not why, that me were lever* sleep,   *rather
Than the best gallon wine that is in Cheap."
"Well," quoth the Manciple, "if it may do ease
To thee, Sir Cook, and to no wight displease
Which that here rideth in this company,
And that our Host will of his courtesy,
I will as now excuse thee of thy tale;
For in good faith thy visage is full pale:
Thine eyen daze,* soothly as me thinketh,   *are dim
And well I wot, thy breath full soure stinketh,
That sheweth well thou art not well disposed;
Of me certain thou shalt not be y-glosed.*   *flattered
See how he yawneth, lo, this drunken wight,
As though he would us swallow anon right.
Hold close thy mouth, man, by thy father's kin;
The devil of helle set his foot therein!
Thy cursed breath infecte will us all:
Fy! stinking swine, fy! foul may thee befall.
Ah! take heed, Sirs, of this lusty man.
Now, sweete Sir, will ye joust at the fan?
Thereto, me thinketh, ye be well y-shape.
I trow that ye have drunken wine of ape,
And that is when men playe with a straw."

And with this speech the Cook waxed all wraw,*   *wrathful
And on the Manciple he gan nod fast
For lack of speech; and down his horse him cast,
Where as he lay, till that men him up took.
This was a fair chevachie* of a cook: *cavalry expedition

Alas! that he had held him by his ladle!
And ere that he again were in the saddle
There was great shoving bothe to and fro
To lift him up, and muche care and woe,
So unwieldy was this silly paled ghost.
And to the Manciple then spake our Host:
"Because that drink hath domination
Upon this man, by my salvation
I trow he lewedly* will tell his tale. *stupidly
For were it wine, or old or moisty* ale, *new
That he hath drunk, he speaketh in his nose,
And sneezeth fast, and eke he hath the pose
He also hath to do more than enough
To keep him on his capel* out of the slough; *horse
And if he fall from off his capel eftsoon,* *again
Then shall we alle have enough to do'n
In lifting up his heavy drunken corse.
Tell on thy tale, of him *make I no force.* *I take no account*
But yet, Manciple, in faith thou art too nice* *foolish
Thus openly to reprove him of his vice;
Another day he will paraventure
Reclaime thee, and bring thee to the lure;
I mean, he speake will of smalle things,
As for to *pinchen at* thy reckonings, *pick flaws in*
That were not honest, if it came to prefe."* *test, proof
Quoth the Manciple, "That were a great mischief;
So might he lightly bring me in the snare.
Yet had I lever* paye for the mare *rather
Which he rides on, than he should with me strive.
(I will not wrathe him, so may I thrive)
That that I spake, I said it in my bourde.* *jest
And weet ye what? I have here in my gourd
A draught of wine, yea, of a ripe grape,
And right anon ye shall see a good jape.* *trick
This Cook shall drink thereof, if that I may;

On pain of my life he will not say nay."
And certainly, to tellen as it was,
Of this vessel the cook drank fast (alas!
What needed it? he drank enough beforn),
And when he hadde *pouped in his horn,* *belched*
To the Manciple he took the gourd again.
And of that drink the Cook was wondrous fain,
And thanked him in such wise as he could.

Then gan our Host to laughe wondrous loud,
And said, "I see well it is necessary
Where that we go good drink with us to carry;
For that will turne rancour and disease* *trouble, annoyance
T'accord and love, and many a wrong appease.
O Bacchus, Bacchus, blessed be thy name,
That so canst turnen earnest into game!
Worship and thank be to thy deity.
Of that mattere ye get no more of me.
Tell on thy tale, Manciple, I thee pray."
"Well, Sir," quoth he, "now hearken what I say."

THE TALE

When Phoebus dwelled here in earth adown,
As olde bookes make mentioun,
He was the moste lusty* bacheler *pleasant
Of all this world, and eke* the best archer. *also
He slew Python the serpent, as he lay
Sleeping against the sun upon a day;
And many another noble worthy deed
He with his bow wrought, as men maye read.
Playen he could on every minstrelsy,
And singe, that it was a melody
To hearen of his cleare voice the soun'.
Certes the king of Thebes, Amphioun,

That with his singing walled the city,
Could never singe half so well as he.
Thereto he was the seemlieste man
That is, or was since that the world began;
What needeth it his features to descrive?
For in this world is none so fair alive.
He was therewith full fill'd of gentleness,
Of honour, and of perfect worthiness.

This Phoebus, that was flower of bach'lery,
As well in freedom* as in chivalry,   *generosity
For his disport, in sign eke of victory
Of Python, so as telleth us the story,
Was wont to bearen in his hand a bow.
Now had this Phoebus in his house a crow,
Which in a cage he foster'd many a day,
And taught it speaken, as men teach a jay.
White was this crow, as is a snow-white swan,
And counterfeit the speech of every man
He coulde, when he shoulde tell a tale.
Therewith in all this world no nightingale
Ne coulde by an hundred thousand deal* *part
Singe so wondrous merrily and well.
Now had this Phoebus in his house a wife;
Which that he loved more than his life.
And night and day did ever his diligence
Her for to please, and do her reverence:
Save only, if that I the sooth shall sayn,
Jealous he was, and would have kept her fain.
For him were loth y-japed* for to be; *tricked, deceived
And so is every wight in such degree;
But all for nought, for it availeth nought.
A good wife, that is clean of work and thought,
Should not be kept in none await* certain: *observation
And truely the labour is in vain

To keep a shrewe,* for it will not be. *ill-disposed woman
This hold I for a very nicety,* *sheer folly
To spille* labour for to keepe wives; *lose
Thus writen olde clerkes in their lives.

But now to purpose, as I first began.
This worthy Phoebus did all that he can
To please her, weening, through such pleasance,
And for his manhood and his governance,
That no man should have put him from her grace;
But, God it wot, there may no man embrace
As to distrain* a thing, which that nature *succeed in
    constraining
Hath naturally set in a creature.
Take any bird, and put it in a cage,
And do all thine intent, and thy corage,* *what thy heart
    prompts
To foster it tenderly with meat and drink
Of alle dainties that thou canst bethink,
And keep it all so cleanly as thou may;
Although the cage of gold be never so gay,
Yet had this bird, by twenty thousand fold,
Lever* in a forest, both wild and cold, *rather
Go eate wormes, and such wretchedness.
For ever this bird will do his business
T'escape out of his cage when that he may:
His liberty the bird desireth aye.
Let take a cat, and foster her with milk
And tender flesh, and make her couch of silk,
And let her see a mouse go by the wall,
Anon she weiveth* milk, and flesh, and all, *forsaketh
And every dainty that is in that house,
Such appetite hath she to eat the mouse.
Lo, here hath kind* her domination, *nature
And appetite flemeth* discretion. *drives out

A she-wolf hath also a villain's kind
The lewedeste wolf that she may find,
Or least of reputation, will she take
In time when *her lust* to have a make.* *she desires* *mate
All these examples speak I by* these men *with reference to
That be untrue, and nothing by women.
For men have ever a lik'rous appetite
On lower things to perform their delight
Than on their wives, be they never so fair,
Never so true, nor so debonair.* *gentle, mild
Flesh is so newefangled, *with mischance,* *ill luck to it*
That we can in no thinge have pleasance
That *souneth unto* virtue any while. *accords with*

This Phoebus, which that thought upon no guile,
Deceived was for all his jollity;
For under him another hadde she,
A man of little reputation,
Nought worth to Phoebus in comparison.
The more harm is; it happens often so,
Of which there cometh muche harm and woe.
And so befell, when Phoebus was absent,
His wife anon hath for her leman* sent. *unlawful lover
Her leman! certes that is a knavish speech.
Forgive it me, and that I you beseech.
The wise Plato saith, as ye may read,
The word must needs accorde with the deed;
If men shall telle properly a thing,
The word must cousin be to the working.
I am a boistous* man, right thus I say. *rough-spoken,
    downright
There is no difference truely
Betwixt a wife that is of high degree
(If of her body dishonest she be),
And any poore wench, other than this

551

(If it so be they worke both amiss),
But, for* the gentle is in estate above,   *because
She shall be call'd his lady and his love;
And, for that other is a poor woman,
She shall be call'd his wench and his leman:
And God it wot, mine owen deare brother,
Men lay the one as low as lies the other.
Right so betwixt a *titleless tyrant* *usurper
And an outlaw, or else a thief errant,* *wandering
The same I say, there is no difference
(To Alexander told was this sentence),
But, for the tyrant is of greater might
By force of meinie* for to slay downright, *followers
And burn both house and home, and make all plain,* *level
Lo, therefore is he call'd a capitain;
And, for the outlaw hath but small meinie,
And may not do so great an harm as he,
Nor bring a country to so great mischief,
Men calle him an outlaw or a thief.
But, for I am a man not textuel,* *learned in texts
I will not tell of texts never a deal;* *whit
I will go to my tale, as I began.

When Phoebus' wife had sent for her leman,
Anon they wroughten all their *lust volage.* *light or rash
     pleasure*
This white crow, that hung aye in the cage,
Beheld their work, and said never a word;
And when that home was come Phoebus the lord,
This crowe sung, "Cuckoo, cuckoo, cuckoo!"
"What? bird," quoth Phoebus, "what song sing'st thou now?
Wert thou not wont so merrily to sing,
That to my heart it was a rejoicing
To hear thy voice? alas! what song is this?"
"By God," quoth he, "I singe not amiss.

Phoebus," quoth he, "for all thy worthiness,
For all thy beauty, and all thy gentleness,
For all thy song, and all thy minstrelsy,
For all thy waiting, bleared is thine eye *despite all thy
      watching, thou art befooled*
With one of little reputation,
Not worth to thee, as in comparison,
The mountance* of a gnat, so may I thrive; *value
For on thy bed thy wife I saw him swive."
What will ye more? the crow anon him told,
By sade* tokens, and by wordes bold, *grave, trustworthy
How that his wife had done her lechery,
To his great shame and his great villainy;
And told him oft, he saw it with his eyen.
This Phoebus gan awayward for to wrien;* *turn aside
Him thought his woeful hearte burst in two.
His bow he bent, and set therein a flo,* *arrow
And in his ire he hath his wife slain;
This is th' effect, there is no more to sayn.
For sorrow of which he brake his minstrelsy,
Both harp and lute, gitern* and psaltery; *guitar
And eke he brake his arrows and his bow;
And after that thus spake he to the crow.

"Traitor," quoth he, "with tongue of scorpion,
Thou hast me brought to my confusion;
Alas that I was wrought!* why n'ere** I dead? *made **was not
O deare wife, O gem of lustihead,* *pleasantness
That wert to me so sad,* and eke so true, *steadfast
Now liest thou dead, with face pale of hue,
Full guiltless, that durst I swear y-wis!* *certainly
O rakel* hand, to do so foul amiss *rash, hasty
O troubled wit, O ire reckeless,
That unadvised smit'st the guiltless!
O wantrust,* full of false suspicion! *distrust

Where was thy wit and thy discretion?
O! every man beware of rakelness,* *rashness
Nor trow* no thing withoute strong witness. *believe
Smite not too soon, ere that ye weete* why, *know
And *be advised* well and sickerly** *consider* *surely
Ere ye *do any execution* *take any action*
Upon your ire* for suspicion. anger*
Alas! a thousand folk hath rakel ire
Foully fordone, and brought them in the mire.
Alas! for sorrow I will myself slee* *slay
And to the crow, "O false thief," said he,
"I will thee quite anon thy false tale.
Thou sung whilom* like any nightingale, *once on a time
Now shalt thou, false thief, thy song foregon,* *lose
And eke thy white feathers every one,
Nor ever in all thy life shalt thou speak;
Thus shall men on a traitor be awreak. *revenged
Thou and thine offspring ever shall be blake,* *black
Nor ever sweete noise shall ye make,
But ever cry against* tempest and rain, *before, in warning of
In token that through thee my wife is slain."
And to the crow he start,* and that anon, *sprang
And pull'd his white feathers every one,
And made him black, and reft him all his song,
And eke his speech, and out at door him flung
Unto the devil, *which I him betake;* *to whom I commend him*
And for this cause be all crowes blake.
Lordings, by this ensample, I you pray,
Beware, and take keep* what that ye say; *heed
Nor telle never man in all your life
How that another man hath dight his wife;
He will you hate mortally certain.
Dan Solomon, as wise clerkes sayn,
Teacheth a man to keep his tongue well;
But, as I said, I am not textuel.

But natheless thus taughte me my dame;
"My son, think on the crow, in Godde's name.
My son, keep well thy tongue, and keep thy friend;
A wicked tongue is worse than is a fiend:
My son, from a fiend men may them bless.* *defend by
    crossing
My son, God of his endless goodness themselves
Walled a tongue with teeth, and lippes eke,
For* man should him advise,** what he speak. *because
    **consider
My son, full often for too muche speech
Hath many a man been spilt,* as clerkes teach; *destroyed
But for a little speech advisedly
Is no man shent,* to speak generally. *ruined
My son, thy tongue shouldest thou restrain
At alle time, *but when thou dost thy pain* *except when you
    do your best effort*
To speak of God in honour and prayere.
The firste virtue, son, if thou wilt lear,* *learn
Is to restrain and keepe well thy tongue;
Thus learne children, when that they be young.
My son, of muche speaking evil advis'd,
Where lesse speaking had enough suffic'd,
Cometh much harm; thus was me told and taught;
In muche speeche sinne wanteth not.
Wost* thou whereof a rakel** tongue serveth? *knowest **hasty
Right as a sword forcutteth and forcarveth
An arm in two, my deare son, right so
A tongue cutteth friendship all in two.
A jangler* is to God abominable. *prating man
Read Solomon, so wise and honourable;
Read David in his Psalms, and read Senec'.
My son, speak not, but with thine head thou beck,* *beckon,
    nod
Dissimule as thou wert deaf, if that thou hear

A jangler speak of perilous mattere.
The Fleming saith, and learn *if that thee lest,* *if it please
    thee*
That little jangling causeth muche rest.
My son, if thou no wicked word hast said,
Thee thar not dreade for to be bewray'd; *thou hast no
    need to fear to be betrayed*
But he that hath missaid, I dare well sayn,
He may by no way call his word again.
Thing that is said is said, and forth it go'th,
Though him repent, or be he ne'er so loth;
He is his thrall,* to whom that he hath said *slave
A tale, *of which he is now evil apaid.* *which he now regrets*
My son, beware, and be no author new
Of tidings, whether they be false or true;
Whereso thou come, amonges high or low,
Keep well thy tongue, and think upon the crow."

THE PARSON'S TALE

By that the Manciple his tale had ended,
The sunne from the south line was descended
So lowe, that it was not to my sight
Degrees nine-and-twenty as in height.
Four of the clock it was then, as I guess,
For eleven foot, a little more or less,
My shadow was at thilke time, as there,
Of such feet as my lengthe parted were
In six feet equal of proportion.
Therewith the moone's exaltation,* *rising
In meane Libra, gan alway ascend, *in the middle of*
As we were ent'ring at a thorpe's* end. *village's
For which our Host, as he was wont to gie,* *govern
As in this case, our jolly company,
Said in this wise; "Lordings every one,

Now lacketh us no more tales than one.
Fulfill'd is my sentence and my decree;
I trow that we have heard of each degree.* *from each class
    or rank in the company
Almost fulfilled is mine ordinance;
I pray to God so give him right good chance
That telleth us this tale lustily.
Sir Priest," quoth he, "art thou a vicary?* *vicar
Or art thou a Parson? say sooth by thy fay.* *faith
Be what thou be, breake thou not our play;
For every man, save thou, hath told his tale.
Unbuckle, and shew us what is in thy mail.* *wallet
For truely me thinketh by thy cheer
Thou shouldest knit up well a great mattere.
Tell us a fable anon, for cocke's bones."

This Parson him answered all at ones;
"Thou gettest fable none y-told for me,
For Paul, that writeth unto Timothy,
Reproveth them that *weive soothfastness,* *forsake truth*
And telle fables, and such wretchedness.
Why should I sowe draff* out of my fist, *chaff, refuse
When I may sowe wheat, if that me list?
For which I say, if that you list to hear
Morality and virtuous mattere,
And then that ye will give me audience,
I would full fain at Christe's reverence
Do you pleasance lawful, as I can.
But, truste well, I am a southern man,
I cannot gest,* rom, ram, ruf, by my letter; *relate stories
And, God wot, rhyme hold I but little better.
And therefore if you list, I will not glose,* *mince matters
I will you tell a little tale in prose,
To knit up all this feast, and make an end.
And Jesus for his grace wit me send

To shewe you the way, in this voyage,
Of thilke perfect glorious pilgrimage,
That hight Jerusalem celestial.
And if ye vouchesafe, anon I shall
Begin upon my tale, for which I pray
Tell your advice,* I can no better say. *opinion
But natheless this meditation
I put it aye under correction
Of clerkes,* for I am not textuel; *scholars
I take but the sentence,* trust me well. *meaning, sense
Therefore I make a protestation,
That I will stande to correction."
Upon this word we have assented soon;
For, as us seemed, it was *for to do'n,* *a thing worth doing*
To enden in some virtuous sentence,* *discourse
And for to give him space and audience;
And bade our Host he shoulde to him say
That alle we to tell his tale him pray.
Our Hoste had the wordes for us all:
"Sir Priest," quoth he, "now faire you befall;
Say what you list, and we shall gladly hear."
And with that word he said in this mannere;
"Telle," quoth he, "your meditatioun,
But hasten you, the sunne will adown.
Be fructuous,* and that in little space; *fruitful; profitable
And to do well God sende you his grace."

THE TALE

[The Parson begins his "little treatise" (which, if given at length, would extend to about thirty of these pages, and which cannot by any stretch of courtesy or fancy be said to merit the title of a "Tale") in these words: —]

Our sweet Lord God of Heaven, that no man will perish, but will that we come all to the knowledge of him, and to the blissful life that is perdurable [everlasting], admonishes us by the prophet Jeremiah, that saith in this wise: "Stand upon the ways, and see and ask of old paths, that is to say, of old sentences, which is the good way, and walk in that way, and ye shall find refreshing for your souls," &c. Many be the spiritual ways that lead folk to our Lord Jesus Christ, and to the reign of glory; of which ways there is a full noble way, and full convenable, which may not fail to man nor to woman, that through sin hath misgone from the right way of Jerusalem celestial; and this way is called penitence. Of which men should gladly hearken and inquire with all their hearts, to wit what is penitence, and whence it is called penitence, and in what manner, and in how many manners, be the actions or workings of penitence, and how many species there be of penitences, and what things appertain and behove to penitence, and what things disturb penitence.

[Penitence is described, on the authority of Saints Ambrose, Isidore, and Gregory, as the bewailing of sin that has been wrought, with the purpose never again to do that thing, or any other thing which a man should bewail; for weeping and not ceasing to do the sin will not avail — though it is to be hoped that after every time that a man falls, be it ever so often, he may find grace to arise through penitence. And repentant folk that leave their sin ere sin leave them, are accounted by Holy Church sure of their salvation, even though the repentance be at the last hour. There are three actions of penitence; that a man be baptized after he has sinned; that he do no deadly sin after receiving baptism; and that he fall into no venial sins from day to day. "Thereof saith St Augustine, that penitence of good and humble folk is the penitence of every day." The species of penitence are three: solemn, when a man is openly expelled from Holy Church in Lent, or is compelled by Holy Church to do open penance for an open sin openly talked of in the country; common penance, enjoined by priests in certain cases, as to go on pilgrimage naked or barefoot; and privy penance, which men do daily for private sins, of which they confess privately and receive private penance. To very perfect penitence are behoveful and necessary three things: contrition of heart, confession of mouth, and satisfaction; which are fruitful penitence against delight in thinking, reckless speech, and wicked sinful works.

Penitence may be likened to a tree, having its root in contrition, biding itself in the heart as a tree-root does in the earth; out of this root springs a stalk, that bears branches and leaves of confession, and fruit of satisfaction. Of this root also springs a seed of grace, which is mother of all security, and this seed is eager and hot; and the grace of this seed springs of God, through remembrance on the day of judgment and on the pains of hell. The heat of this seed is the love of God, and the desire of everlasting joy; and this heat draws the heart of man to God, and makes him hate his sin. Penance is the tree of life to them that receive it. In penance or contrition man shall understand four things: what is contrition; what are the causes that move a man to contrition; how he should be contrite; and what contrition availeth to the soul. Contrition is the heavy and grievous sorrow that a man receiveth in his heart for his sins, with earnest purpose to confess and do penance, and never more to sin. Six causes ought to move a man to contrition: 1. He should remember him of his sins; 2. He should reflect that sin putteth a man in great thraldom, and all the greater the higher is the estate from which he falls; 3. He should dread the day of doom and the horrible pains of hell; 4. The sorrowful remembrance of the good deeds that man hath omitted to do here on earth, and also the good that he hath lost, ought to make him have contrition; 5. So also ought the remembrance of the passion that our Lord Jesus Christ suffered for our sins; 6. And so ought the hope of three things, that is to say, forgiveness of sin, the gift of grace to do well, and the glory of heaven with which God shall reward man for his good deeds. — All these points the

Parson illustrates and enforces at length; waxing especially eloquent under the third head, and plainly setting forth the sternly realistic notions regarding future punishments that were entertained in the time of Chaucer: –]

Certes, all the sorrow that a man might make from the beginning of the world, is but a little thing, at retard of [in comparison with] the sorrow of hell. The cause why that Job calleth hell the land of darkness; understand, that he calleth it land or earth, for it is stable and never shall fail, and dark, for he that is in hell hath default [is devoid] of light natural; for certes the dark light, that shall come out of the fire that ever shall burn, shall turn them all to pain that be in hell, for it sheweth them the horrible devils that them torment. Covered with the darkness of death; that is to say, that he that is in hell shall have default of the sight of God; for certes the sight of God is the life perdurable [everlasting]. The darkness of death, be the sins that the wretched man hath done, which that disturb [prevent] him to see the face of God, right as a dark cloud doth between us and the sun. Land of misease, because there be three manner of defaults against three things that folk of this world have in this present life; that is to say, honours, delights, and riches. Against honour have they in hell shame and confusion: for well ye wot, that men call honour the reverence that man doth to man; but in hell is no honour nor reverence; for certes no more reverence shall be done there to a king than to a knave [servant]. For which God saith by the prophet Jeremiah; "The folk that me despise shall be in despite." Honour is also called great lordship. There shall no wight serve other, but of harm and torment. Honour is also called great dignity and highness; but in hell shall they be all fortrodden [trampled under foot] of devils. As God saith, "The horrible devils shall go and come upon the heads of damned folk;" and this is, forasmuch as the higher that they were in this present life, the more shall they be abated [abased] and defouled in hell. Against the riches of this world shall they have misease [trouble, torment] of poverty, and this poverty shall be in four things: in default [want] of treasure; of which David saith, "The rich folk that embraced and oned [united] all their heart to treasure of this world, shall sleep in the sleeping of death, and nothing shall they find in their hands of all their treasure." And moreover, the misease of hell shall be in default of meat and drink. For God saith thus by Moses, "They shall be wasted with hunger, and the birds of hell shall devour them with bitter death, and the gall of the dragon shall be their drink, and the venom of the dragon their morsels." And furthermore, their misease shall be in default of clothing, for they shall be naked in body, as of clothing, save the fire in which they burn, and other filths; and naked shall they be in soul, of all manner virtues, which that is the clothing of the soul. Where be then the gay robes, and the soft sheets, and the fine shirts? Lo, what saith of them the prophet Isaiah, that under them shall be strewed moths, and their covertures shall be of worms of hell. And furthermore, their misease shall be in default of friends, for he is not poor that hath good friends: but there is no friend; for neither God nor any good creature shall be friend to them, and evereach of them shall hate other with deadly hate. The Sons and the daughters shall rebel against father and mother, and kindred against kindred, and chide and despise each other, both day and night, as God saith by the prophet Micah. And the loving children, that whom loved so fleshly each other, would each of them eat the other if they might. For how should they love together in the pains of hell, when they hated each other in the prosperity of this life? For trust well, their fleshly love was deadly hate; as saith the prophet David; "Whoso loveth wickedness, he hateth his own soul:" and whoso hateth his own soul, certes he may love none other wight in no manner: and therefore in hell is no solace nor no friendship, but ever

the more kindreds that be in hell, the more cursing, the more chiding, and the more deadly hate there is among them. And furtherover, they shall have default of all manner delights; for certes delights be after the appetites of the five wits [senses]; as sight, hearing, smelling, savouring [tasting], and touching. But in hell their sight shall be full of darkness and of smoke, and their eyes full of tears; and their hearing full of waimenting [lamenting] and grinting [gnashing] of teeth, as saith Jesus Christ; their nostrils shall be full of stinking; and, as saith Isaiah the prophet, their savouring [tasting] shall be full of bitter gall; and touching of all their body shall be covered with fire that never shall quench, and with worms that never shall die, as God saith by the mouth of Isaiah. And forasmuch as they shall not ween that they may die for pain, and by death flee from pain, that may they understand in the word of Job, that saith, "There is the shadow of death." Certes a shadow hath the likeness of the thing of which it is shadowed, but the shadow is not the same thing of which it is shadowed: right so fareth the pain of hell; it is like death, for the horrible anguish; and why? for it paineth them ever as though they should die anon; but certes they shall not die. For, as saith Saint Gregory, "To wretched caitiffs shall be given death without death, and end without end, and default without failing; for their death shall always live, and their end shall evermore begin, and their default shall never fail." And therefore saith Saint John the Evangelist, "They shall follow death, and they shall not find him, and they shall desire to die, and death shall flee from them." And eke Job saith, that in hell is no order of rule. And albeit that God hath created all things in right order, and nothing without order, but all things be ordered and numbered, yet nevertheless they that be damned be not in order, nor hold no order. For the earth shall bear them no fruit (for, as the prophet David saith, "God shall destroy the fruit of the earth, as for them"); nor water shall give them no moisture, nor the air no refreshing, nor the fire no light. For as saith Saint Basil, "The burning of the fire of this world shall God give in hell to them that be damned, but the light and the clearness shall be given in heaven to his children; right as the good man giveth flesh to his children, and bones to his hounds." And for they shall have no hope to escape, saith Job at last, that there shall horror and grisly dread dwell without end. Horror is always dread of harm that is to come, and this dread shall ever dwell in the hearts of them that be damned. And therefore have they lost all their hope for seven causes. First, for God that is their judge shall be without mercy to them; nor they may not please him; nor none of his hallows [saints]; nor they may give nothing for their ransom; nor they have no voice to speak to him; nor they may not flee from pain; nor they have no goodness in them that they may shew to deliver them from pain.

[Under the fourth head, of good works, the Parson says: —]

The courteous Lord Jesus Christ will that no good work be lost, for in somewhat it shall avail. But forasmuch as the good works that men do while they be in good life be all amortised [killed, deadened] by sin following, and also since all the good works that men do while they be in deadly sin be utterly dead, as for to have the life perdurable [everlasting], well may that man that no good works doth, sing that new French song, *J'ai tout perdu — mon temps et mon labour.* For certes, sin bereaveth a man both the goodness of nature, and eke the goodness of grace. For soothly the grace of the Holy Ghost fareth like fire, that may not be idle; for fire faileth anon as it forleteth [leaveth] its working, and right so grace faileth anon as it forleteth its working. Then loseth the sinful man the goodness of glory, that only is to good men that labour and work. Well may he be sorry then, that oweth all his life to God, as long as he hath lived, and also as long as he shall live, that no goodness hath to pay with his debt to God, to whom he oweth all his life: for trust well he shall give account, as saith Saint Bernard, of all the goods that have been given him in his present life, and how he hath them dispended, insomuch that there shall not perish an hair of his head, nor a moment of an hour shall not perish of his time, that he shall not give thereof a reckoning.

[Having treated of the causes, the Parson comes to the manner, of contrition — which should be universal and total, not merely of outward deeds of sin, but also of wicked delights and thoughts and words; "for certes Almighty God is all good, and therefore either he forgiveth all, or else right naught." Further, contrition should be "wonder sorrowful and anguishous", and also continual, with steadfast purpose of confession and amendment. Lastly, of what contrition availeth, the Parson says, that sometimes it delivereth man from sin; that without it neither confession nor satisfaction is of any worth; that it "destroyeth the prison of hell, and maketh weak and feeble all the strengths of the devils, and restoreth the gifts of the Holy Ghost and of all good virtues, and cleanseth the soul of sin, and delivereth it from the pain of hell, and from the company of the devil, and from the servage [slavery] of sin, and restoreth it to all goods spiritual, and to the company and communion of Holy Church." He who should set his intent to these things, would no longer be inclined to sin, but would give his heart and body to the service of Jesus Christ, and thereof do him homage. "For, certes, our Lord Jesus Christ hath spared us so benignly in our follies, that if he had not pity on man's soul, a sorry song might we all sing."

The Second Part of the Parson's Tale or Treatise opens with an explanation of what is confession — which is termed "the second part of penitence, that is, sign of contrition"; whether it ought needs be done or not; and what things be convenable to true confession. Confession is true shewing of sins to the priest, without excusing, hiding, or forwrapping [disguising] of anything, and without vaunting of good works. "Also, it is necessary to understand whence that sins spring, and how they increase, and which they be." From Adam we took original sin; "from him fleshly descended be we all, and engendered of vile and corrupt matter"; and the penalty of Adam's transgression dwelleth with us as to temptation, which penalty is called concupiscence. "This concupiscence, when it is wrongfully disposed or ordained in a man, it maketh him covet, by covetise of flesh, fleshly sin by sight of his eyes, as to earthly things, and also covetise of highness by pride of heart." The Parson proceeds to shew how man is tempted in his flesh to sin; how, after his natural concupiscence, comes suggestion of the devil, that is to say the devil's bellows, with which he bloweth in man the fire of concupiscence; and how man then bethinketh him whether he will do or no the thing to which he is tempted. If he flame up into pleasure at the thought, and give way, then is he all dead in soul; "and thus is sin accomplished, by temptation, by delight, and by consenting; and then is the sin actual." Sin is either venial, or deadly; deadly, when a man loves any creature more than Jesus Christ our Creator, venial, if he love Jesus Christ less than he ought. Venial sins diminish man's love to God more and more, and may in this wise skip into deadly sin; for many small make a great. "And hearken this example: A great wave of the sea cometh sometimes with so great a violence, that it drencheth [causes to sink] the ship: and the same harm do sometimes the small drops, of water that enter through a little crevice in the thurrok [hold, bilge], and in the bottom of the ship, if men be so negligent that they discharge them not betimes. And therefore, although there be difference betwixt these two causes of drenching, algates [in any case] the ship is dreint [sunk]. Right so fareth it sometimes of deadly sin", and of venial sins when they multiply in a man so greatly as to make him love worldly things more than God. The Parson then enumerates specially a number of sins which many a man peradventure deems no sins, and confesses them not, and yet nevertheless they are truly sins:–]

This is to say, at every time that a man eateth and drinketh more than sufficeth to the sustenance of his body, in certain he doth sin; eke when he speaketh more than it needeth, he doth sin; eke when he heareth not benignly the complaint of the poor; eke when he is in health of body, and will not fast when other folk fast, without cause reasonable; eke when he sleepeth more than needeth, or when he cometh by that occasion too late to church, or to other works of charity; eke when he useth his wife without sovereign desire of engendrure, to the honour of God, or for the intent to yield his wife his debt of his body; eke when he will not visit the sick, or the prisoner, if he may; eke if he love wife, or child, or other worldly thing, more than reason requireth; eke if he flatter or blandish more than he ought for any necessity; eke if he minish or withdraw the alms of the poor; eke if he apparail [prepare] his meat more deliciously than need is, or eat it too hastily by likerousness [gluttony]; eke if he talk vanities in the church, or at God's service, or that he be a talker of idle words of folly or villainy, for he shall yield account of them at the day of doom; eke when he behighteth [promiseth] or assureth to do things that he may not perform; eke when that by lightness of folly he missayeth or scorneth his neighbour; eke when he hath any wicked suspicion of thing, that he wot of it no soothfastness: these things, and more without number, be sins, as saith Saint Augustine.

[No earthly man may eschew all venial sins; yet may he refrain him, by the burning love that he hath to our Lord Jesus Christ, and by prayer and confession, and other good works, so that it shall but little grieve. "Furthermore, men may also refrain and put away venial sin, by receiving worthily the precious body of Jesus Christ; by receiving eke of holy water; by alms-deed; by general confession of

Confiteor at mass, and at prime, and at compline [evening service]; and by blessing of bishops and priests, and by other good works." The Parson then proceeds to weightier matters: —]

Now it is behovely [profitable, necessary] to tell which be deadly sins, that is to say, chieftains of sins; forasmuch as all they run in one leash, but in diverse manners. Now be they called chieftains, forasmuch as they be chief, and of them spring all other sins. The root of these sins, then, is pride, the general root of all harms. For of this root spring certain branches: as ire, envy, accidie or sloth, avarice or covetousness (to common understanding), gluttony, and lechery: and each of these sins hath his branches and his twigs, as shall be declared in their chapters following. And though so be, that no man can tell utterly the number of the twigs, and of the harms that come of pride, yet will I shew a part of them, as ye shall understand. There is inobedience, vaunting, hypocrisy, despite, arrogance, impudence, swelling of hearte, insolence, elation, impatience, strife, contumacy, presumption, irreverence, pertinacity, vainglory and many another twig that I cannot tell nor declare . . .]

And yet [moreover] there is a privy species of pride that waiteth first to be saluted ere he will salute, all [although] be he less worthy than that other is; and eke he waiteth [expecteth] or desireth to sit or to go above him in the way, or kiss the pax, or be incensed, or go to offering before his neighbour, and such semblable [like] things, against his duty peradventure, but that he hath his heart and his intent in such a proud desire to be magnified and honoured before the people. Now be there two manner of prides; the one of them is within the heart of a man, and the other is without. Of which soothly these foresaid things, and more than I have said, appertain to pride that is within the heart of a man and there be other species of pride that be without: but nevertheless, the one of these species of pride is sign of the other, right as the gay levesell [bush] at the tavern is sign of the wine that is in the cellar. And this is in many things: as in speech and countenance, and outrageous array of clothing; for certes, if there had been no sin in clothing, Christ would not so soon have noted and spoken of the clothing of that rich man in the gospel. And Saint Gregory saith, that precious clothing is culpable for the dearth [dearness] of it, and for its softness, and for its strangeness and disguising, and for the superfluity or for the inordinate scantness of it; alas! may not a man see in our days the sinful costly array of clothing, and namely [specially] in too much superfluity, or else in too disordinate scantness? As to the first sin, in superfluity of clothing, which that maketh it so dear, to the harm of the people, not only the cost of the embroidering, the disguising, indenting or barring, ounding, paling, winding, or banding, and semblable [similar] waste of cloth in vanity; but there is also the costly furring [lining or edging with fur] in their gowns, so much punching of chisels to make holes, so much dagging [cutting] of shears, with the superfluity in length of the foresaid gowns, trailing in the dung and in the mire, on horse and eke on foot, as well of man as of woman, that all that trailing is verily (as in effect) wasted, consumed, threadbare, and rotten with dung, rather than it is given to the poor, to great damage of the foresaid poor folk, and that in sundry wise: this is to say, the more that cloth is wasted, the more must it cost to the poor people for the scarceness; and furthermore, if so be that they would give such punched and dagged clothing to the poor people, it is not convenient to wear for their estate, nor sufficient to boot [help, remedy] their necessity, to keep them from the distemperance [inclemency] of the firmament. Upon the other side, to speak of the horrible disordinate scantness of clothing, as be these cutted slops or hanselines [breeches], that through their shortness cover not the shameful member of man, to wicked intent alas! some of them shew the boss and the shape of the horrible swollen members, that seem like to the malady of hernia, in the wrapping of their hosen, and eke the buttocks of them, that fare as it were the hinder part of a she-ape in the full of the moon. And more over the wretched swollen members that they shew through disguising, in departing [dividing] of their hosen in white and red, seemeth that half their shameful privy members were flain [flayed]. And if so be that they depart their hosen in other colours, as is white and blue, or white and black, or black and red, and so forth; then seemeth it, by variance of colour, that the half part of their privy members be corrupt by the fire of Saint Anthony, or by canker, or other such mischance. And of the hinder part of their buttocks it is full horrible to see, for certes, in that part of their body where they purge their stinking ordure, that foul part shew they to the people proudly in despite of honesty [decency], which honesty Jesus Christ and his friends observed to shew in his life. Now as of the outrageous array of women, God wot, that though the visages of some of them seem full chaste and debonair [gentle], yet notify they, in their array of attire, likerousness and pride. I say not that honesty [reasonable and appropriate style] in clothing of man or woman unconvenable but, certes, the superfluity or disordinate scarcity of clothing is reprovable. Also the sin of their ornament, or of apparel, as in things that appertain to riding, as in too many delicate horses, that be holden for delight, that be so fair, fat, and costly; and also in many a vicious knave, [servant] that is sustained because of them; in curious harness, as in saddles, cruppers, peytrels, [breast-plates] and bridles, covered with precious cloth and rich bars and plates of gold and silver. For which God saith by Zechariah the prophet, "I will confound the riders of such horses." These folk take little regard of the riding of God's Son of heaven, and of his harness, when he rode upon an ass, and had no other harness but the poor clothes of his disciples; nor we read not that ever he rode on any other beast. I speak this for the sin of superfluity, and not for reasonable honesty [seemliness], when reason it requireth. And moreover, certes, pride is greatly notified in holding of great meinie [retinue of servants], when they be of little profit or of right no profit, and namely [especially] when that meinie is felonous [violent] and damageous [harmful] to the people by hardiness [arrogance] of high lordship, or by way of office; for certes, such lords sell then their lordship to the devil of hell, when they sustain the wickedness of their meinie. Or else, when these folk of low degree, as they that hold hostelries, sustain theft of their hostellers, and that is in many manner of deceits: that manner of folk be the flies that follow the honey, or else the hounds that follow the carrion. Such foresaid folk strangle spiritually their lordships; for which thus saith David the prophet, "Wicked death may come unto these lordships, and God give that they may descend into hell adown; for in their houses is iniquity and shrewedness, [impiety] and not God of heaven." And certes, but if [unless] they do amendment, right as God gave his benison [blessing] to Laban by the service of Jacob, and to Pharaoh by the service of Joseph; right so God will give his malison [condemnation] to such lordships as sustain the wickedness of their servants, but [unless] they come to amendment. Pride of the table apaireth [worketh harm] eke full oft; for, certes, rich men be called to feasts, and poor folk be put away and rebuked; also in excess of divers meats and drinks, and namely [specially] such manner bake-meats and dish-meats burning of wild fire, and painted and castled with paper, and semblable [similar] waste, so that it is abuse to think. And eke in too great preciousness of vessel, [plate] and curiosity of minstrelsy, by which a man is stirred more to the delights of luxury, if so be that he set his heart the less upon our Lord Jesus Christ, certain it is a sin; and certainly the delights might be so great in this case, that a man might lightly [easily] fall by them into deadly sin.

[The sins that arise of pride advisedly and habitually are deadly; those that arise by frailty unadvised suddenly, and suddenly withdraw again, though grievous, are not deadly. Pride itself springs sometimes of the goods of nature, sometimes of the goods of fortune, sometimes of the goods of grace; but the Parson, enumerating and examining all these in turn, points out how little security they possess and how little ground for pride they furnish, and goes on to enforce the remedy against pride — which is humility or meekness, a virtue through which a man hath true knowledge of himself, and holdeth no high esteem of himself in regard of his deserts, considering ever his frailty.]

Now be there three manners [kinds] of humility; as humility in heart, and another in the mouth, and the third in works. The humility in the heart is in four manners: the one is, when a man holdeth himself as nought worth before God of heaven; the second is, when he despiseth no other man; the third is, when he recketh not though men hold him nought worth; the fourth is, when he is not sorry of his humiliation. Also the humility of mouth is in four things: in temperate speech; in humility of speech; and when he confesseth with his own mouth that he is such as he thinketh that he is in his heart; another is, when he praiseth the bounte [goodness] of another man and nothing thereof diminisheth. Humility eke in works is in four manners: the first is, when he putteth other men before him; the second is, to choose the lowest place of all; the third is, gladly to assent to good counsel; the fourth is, to stand gladly by the award [judgment] of his sovereign, or of him that is higher in degree: certain this is a great work of humility.

[The Parson proceeds to treat of the other cardinal sins, and their remedies: (2.) Envy, with its remedy, the love of God principally and of our neighbours as ourselves: (3.) Anger, with all its fruits in revenge, rancour, hate, discord, manslaughter, blasphemy, swearing, falsehood, flattery, chiding and reproving, scorning, treachery, sowing of strife, doubleness of tongue, betraying of counsel to a man's disgrace,

menacing, idle words, jangling, japery or buffoonery, &c. —
and its remedy in the virtues called mansuetude, debonairte,
or gentleness, and patience or sufferance: (4.) Sloth, or
"Accidie", which comes after the sin of Anger, because Envy
blinds the eyes of a man, and Anger troubleth a man, and
Sloth maketh him heavy, thoughtful, and peevish. It is opposed
to every estate of man — as unfallen, and held to work in
praising and adoring God; as sinful, and held to labour in
praying for deliverance from sin; and as in the state of grace,
and held to works of penitence. It resembles the heavy and
sluggish condition of those in hell; it will suffer no hardness
and no penance; it prevents any beginning of good works; it
causes despair of God's mercy, which is the sin against the
Holy Ghost; it induces somnolency and neglect of communion
in prayer with God; and it breeds negligence or recklessness,
that cares for nothing, and is the nurse of all mischiefs, if
ignorance is their mother. Against Sloth, and these and other
branches and fruits of it, the remedy lies in the virtue of
fortitude or strength, in its various species of magnanimity or
great courage; faith and hope in God and his saints; surety or
sickerness, when a man fears nothing that can oppose the
good works he has undertaken; magnificence, when he carries
out great works of goodness begun; constancy or stableness
of heart; and other incentives to energy and laborious service:
(5.) Avarice, or Covetousness, which is the root of all harms,
since its votaries are idolaters, oppressors and enslavers of
men, deceivers of their equals in business, simoniacs, gamblers,
liars, thieves, false swearers, blasphemers, murderers, and
sacrilegious. Its remedy lies in compassion and pity largely
exercised, and in reasonable liberality — for those who spend
on "fool-largesse", or ostentation of worldly estate and luxury,
shall receive the malison [condemnation] that Christ shall give
at the day of doom to them that shall be damned: (6.) Gluttony;
— of which the Parson treats so briefly that the chapter may
be given in full:—]

After Avarice cometh Gluttony, which is express against the commandment of God. Gluttony is unmeasurable appetite to eat or to drink; or else to do in aught to the unmeasurable appetite and disordered covetousness [craving] to eat or drink. This sin corrupted all this world, as is well shewed in the sin of Adam and of Eve. Look also what saith Saint Paul of gluttony: "Many", saith he, "go, of which I have oft said to you, and now I say it weeping, that they be enemies of the cross of Christ, of which the end is death, and of which their womb [stomach] is their God and their glory"; in confusion of them that so savour [take delight in] earthly things. He that is usant [accustomed, addicted] to this sin of gluttony, he may no sin withstand, he must be in servage [bondage] of all vices, for it is the devil's hoard, [lair, lurking-place] where he hideth him in and resteth. This sin hath many species. The first is drunkenness, that is the horrible sepulture of man's reason: and therefore when a man is drunken, he hath lost his reason; and this is deadly sin. But soothly, when that a man is not wont to strong drink, and peradventure knoweth not the strength of the drink, or hath feebleness in his head, or hath travailed [laboured], through which he drinketh the more, all [although] be he suddenly caught with drink, it is no deadly sin, but venial. The second species of gluttony is, that the spirit of a man waxeth all troubled for drunkenness, and bereaveth a man the discretion of his wit. The third species of gluttony is, when a man devoureth his meat, and hath no rightful manner of eating. The fourth is, when, through the great abundance of his meat, the humours of his body be distempered. The fifth is, forgetfulness by too much drinking, for which a man sometimes forgetteth by the morrow what be did at eve. In other manner be distinct the species of gluttony, after Saint Gregory. The first is, for to eat or drink before time. The second is, when a man getteth him too delicate meat or drink. The third is, when men take too much over measure [immoderately]. The fourth is curiosity [nicety] with great intent [application, pains] to make and apparel [prepare] his meat. The fifth is, for to eat too greedily. These be the five fingers of the devil's hand, by which he draweth folk to the sin.

Against gluttony the remedy is abstinence, as saith Galen; but that I hold not meritorious, if he do it only for the health of his body. Saint Augustine will that abstinence be done for virtue, and with patience. Abstinence, saith he, is little worth, but if [unless] a man have good will thereto, and but it be enforced by patience and by charity, and that men do it for God's sake, and in hope to have the bliss in heaven. The fellows of abstinence be temperance, that holdeth the mean in all things; also shame, that escheweth all dishonesty [indecency, impropriety], sufficiency, that seeketh no rich meats nor drinks, nor doth no force of [sets no value on] no outrageous apparelling of meat; measure [moderation] also, that restraineth by reason the unmeasurable appetite of eating; soberness also, that restraineth the outrage of drink; sparing also, that restraineth the delicate ease to sit long at meat, wherefore some folk stand of their own will to eat, because they will eat at less leisure.

[At great length the Parson then points out the many varieties of the sin of (7.) Lechery, and its remedy in chastity and continence, alike in marriage and in widowhood; also in the abstaining from all such indulgences of eating, drinking, and sleeping as inflame the passions, and from the company of all who may tempt to the sin. Minute guidance is given as to the duty of confessing fully and faithfully the circumstances that attend and may aggravate this sin; and the Treatise then passes to the consideration of the conditions that are essential to a true and profitable confession of sin in general. First, it must be in sorrowful bitterness of spirit; a condition that has five signs — shamefastness, humility in heart and outward sign, weeping with the bodily eyes or in the heart, disregard of the shame that might curtail or garble confession, and obedience to the penance enjoined. Secondly, true confession must be promptly made, for dread of death, of increase of sinfulness, of forgetfulness of what should be confessed, of Christ's refusal to hear if it be put off to the last day of life; and this condition has four terms; that confession be well pondered beforehand, that the man confessing have comprehended in his mind the number and greatness of his sins and how long he has lain in sin, that he be contrite for and eschew his sins, and that he fear and flee the occasions for that sin to which he is inclined. — What follows under this head is of some interest for the light which it throws on the rigorous government wielded by the Romish Church in those days —]

Also thou shalt shrive thee of all thy sins to one man, and not a parcel [portion] to one man, and a parcel to another; that is to understand, in intent to depart [divide] thy confession for shame or dread; for it is but strangling of thy soul. For certes Jesus Christ is entirely all good, in him is none imperfection, and therefore either he forgiveth all perfectly, or else never a deal [not at all]. I say not that if thou be assigned to thy penitencer for a certain sin, that thou art bound to shew him all the remnant of thy sins, of which thou hast been shriven of thy curate, but if it like thee [unless thou be pleased] of thy humility; this is no departing [division] of shrift. And I say not, where I speak of division of confession, that if thou have license to shrive thee to a discreet and an honest priest, and where thee liketh, and by the license of thy curate, that thou mayest not well shrive thee to him of all thy sins: but let no blot be behind, let no sin be untold as far as thou hast remembrance. And when thou shalt be shriven of thy curate, tell him eke all the sins that thou hast done since thou wert last shriven. This is no wicked intent of division of shrift. Also, very shrift [true confession] asketh certain conditions. First, that thou shrive thee by thy free will, not constrained, nor for shame of folk, nor for malady [sickness], or such things: for it is reason, that he that trespasseth by his free will, that by his free will he confess his trespass; and that no other man tell his sin but himself; nor he shall not nay nor deny his sin, nor wrath him against the priest for admonishing him to leave his sin. The second condition is, that thy shrift be lawful, that is to say, that thou that shrivest thee, and eke the priest that heareth thy confession, be verily in the faith of Holy Church, and that a man be not despaired of the mercy of Jesus Christ, as Cain and Judas were. And eke a man must accuse himself of his own trespass, and not another: but he shall blame and wite [accuse] himself of his own malice and of his sin, and none other: but nevertheless, if that another man be occasion or else enticer of his sin, or the estate of the person be such by which his sin is aggravated, or else that be may not plainly shrive him but [unless] he tell the person with which he hath sinned, then may he tell, so that his intent be not to backbite the person, but only to declare his confession. Thou shalt not eke make no leasings [falsehoods] in thy confession for humility, peradventure, to say that thou hast committed and done such sins of which that thou wert never guilty. For Saint Augustine saith, "If that thou, because of humility, makest a leasing on thyself, though thou were not in sin before, yet art thou then in sin through thy leasing." Thou must also shew thy sin by thine own proper mouth, but [unless] thou be dumb, and not by letter; for thou that hast done the sin, thou shalt have the shame of the confession. Thou shalt not paint thy confession with fair and subtle words, to cover the more thy sin; for then beguilest thou thyself, and not the priest; thou must tell it plainly, be it never so foul nor so horrible. Thou shalt eke shrive thee to a priest that is discreet to counsel thee; and eke thou shalt not shrive thee for vainglory, nor for hypocrisy, nor for no cause but only for the doubt [fear] of Jesus Christ and the health of thy soul. Thou shalt not run to the priest all suddenly, to tell him lightly thy sin, as who telleth a jape [jest] or a tale, but advisedly and with good devotion; and generally shrive thee oft; if thou oft fall, oft arise by confession. And though thou shrive thee oftener than once of sin of which thou hast been shriven, it is more merit; and, as saith Saint Augustine, thou shalt have the more lightly [easily] release and grace of God, both of sin and of pain. And certes, once a year at the least way, it is lawful to be houseled, for soothly once a year all things in the earth renovelen [renew themselves].

[Here ends the Second Part of the Treatise; the Third Part, which contains the practical application of the whole, follows entire, along with the remarkable "Prayer of Chaucer", as it stands in the Harleian Manuscript:—]

De Tertia Parte Poenitentiae. [Of the third part of penitence].

Now have I told you of very [true] confession, that is the second part of penitence: The third part of penitence is satisfaction, and that standeth generally in almsdeed and bodily pain. Now be there three manner of almsdeed: contrition of heart, where a man offereth himself to God; the second is, to have pity of the default of his neighbour; the third is, in giving of good counsel and comfort, ghostly and bodily, where men have need, and namely [specially] sustenance of man's food. And take keep [heed] that a man hath need of these things generally; he hath need of food, of clothing, and of herberow [lodging], he hath need of charitable counsel and visiting in prison and malady, and sepulture of his dead body. And if thou mayest not visit the needful with thy person, visit them by thy message and by thy gifts. These be generally alms or works of charity of them that have temporal riches or discretion in counselling. Of these works shalt thou hear at the day of doom. This alms shouldest thou do of thine own proper things, and hastily [promptly], and privily [secretly] if thou mayest; but nevertheless, if thou mayest not do it privily, thou shalt not forbear to do alms, though men see it, so that it be not done for thank of the world, but only for thank of Jesus Christ. For, as witnesseth

Saint Matthew, chap. v., "A city may not be hid that is set on a mountain, nor men light not a lantern and put it under a bushel, but men set it on a candlestick, to light the men in the house; right so shall your light lighten before men, that they may see your good works, and glorify your Father that is in heaven."

Now as to speak of bodily pain, it is in prayer, in wakings, [watchings] in fastings, and in virtuous teachings. Of orisons ye shall understand, that orisons or prayers is to say a piteous will of heart, that redresseth it in God, and expresseth it by word outward, to remove harms, and to have things spiritual and durable, and sometimes temporal things. Of which orisons, certes in the orison of the Pater noster hath our Lord Jesus Christ enclosed most things. Certes, it is privileged of three things in its dignity, for which it is more digne [worthy] than any other prayer: for Jesus Christ himself made it: and it is short, for [in order] it should be coude the more lightly, [be more easily conned or learned] and to withhold [retain] it the more easy in heart, and help himself the oftener with this orison; and for a man should be the less weary to say it; and for a man may not excuse him to learn it, it is so short and so easy: and for it comprehendeth in itself all good prayers. The exposition of this holy prayer, that is so excellent and so digne, I betake [commit] to these masters of theology; save thus much will I say, when thou prayest that God should forgive thee thy guilts, as thou forgivest them that they guilt to thee, be full well ware that thou be not out of charity. This holy orison aminisheth [lesseneth] eke venial sin, and therefore it appertaineth specially to penitence. This prayer must be truly said, and in very faith, and that men pray to God ordinately, discreetly, and devoutly; and always a man shall put his will to be subject to the will of God. This orison must eke be said with great humbleness and full pure, and honestly, and not to the annoyance of any man or woman. It must eke be continued with the works of charity. It availeth against the vices of the soul; for, assaith Saint Jerome, by fasting be saved the vices of the flesh, and by prayer the vices of the soul.

After this thou shalt understand, that bodily pain stands in waking [watching]. For Jesus Christ saith "Wake and pray, that ye enter not into temptation." Ye shall understand also, that fasting stands in three things: in forbearing of bodily meat and drink, and in forbearing of worldly jollity, and in forbearing of deadly sin; this is to say, that a man shall keep him from deadly sin in all that he may. And thou shalt understand eke, that God ordained fasting; and to fasting appertain four things: largeness [generosity] to poor folk; gladness of heart spiritual; not to be angry nor annoyed nor grudge [murmur] for he fasteth; and also reasonable hour for to eat by measure; that is to say, a man should not eat in untime [out of time], nor sit the longer at his meal for [because] he fasteth. Then shalt thou understand, that bodily pain standeth in discipline, or teaching, by word, or by writing, or by ensample. Also in wearing of hairs [haircloth] or of stamin [coarse hempen cloth], or of habergeons [mail-shirts] on their naked flesh for Christ's sake; but ware thee well that such manner penance of thy flesh make not thine heart bitter or angry, nor annoyed of thyself; for better is to cast away thine hair than to cast away the sweetness of our Lord Jesus Christ. And therefore saith Saint Paul, "Clothe you, as they that be chosen of God in heart, of misericorde [with compassion], debonairte [gentleness], sufferance [patience], and such manner of clothing", of which Jesus Christ is more apaid [better pleased] than of hairs or of hauberks. Then is discipline eke in knocking of thy breast, in scourging with yards [rods], in kneelings, in tribulations, in suffering patiently wrongs that be done to him, and eke in patient sufferance of maladies, or losing of worldly catel [chattels], or of wife, or of child, or of other friends.

Then shalt thou understand which things disturb penance, and this is in four things; that is dread, shame, hope, and wanhope, that is, desperation. And for to speak first of dread, for which he weeneth that he may suffer no penance, there-against is remedy for to think that bodily penance is but short and little at the regard of [in comparison with] the pain of hell, that is so cruel and so long, that it lasteth without end. Now against the shame that a man hath to shrive him, and namely [specially] these hypocrites, that would be holden so perfect, that they have no need to shrive them; against that shame should a man think, that by way of reason he that hath not been ashamed to do foul things, certes he ought not to be ashamed to do fair things, and that is confession. A man should eke think, that God seeth and knoweth all thy thoughts, and all thy works; to him may nothing be hid nor covered. Men should eke remember them of the shame that is to come at the day of doom, to them that be not penitent and shriven in this present life; for all the creatures in heaven, and in earth, and in hell, shall see apertly [openly] all that he hideth in this world.

Now for to speak of them that be so negligent and slow to shrive them; that stands in two manners. The one is, that he hopeth to live long, and to purchase [acquire] much riches for his delight, and then he will shrive him: and, as he sayeth, he may, as him seemeth, timely enough come to shrift: another is, the surquedrie [presumption] that he hath in Christ's mercy. Against the first vice, he shall think that our life is in no sickerness, [security] and eke that all the riches in this world be in adventure, and pass as a shadow on the wall; and, as saith St Gregory, that it appertaineth to the great righteous-ness of God, that never shall the pain stint [cease] of them, that never would withdraw them from sin, their thanks [with their goodwill], but aye continue in sin; for that perpetual will to do sin shall they have perpetual pain. Wanhope [despair] is in two manners [of two kinds]. The first wanhope is, in the mercy of God: the other is, that they think they might not long persevere in goodness. The first wanhope cometh of that he deemeth that he sinned so highly and so oft, and so long hath lain in sin, that he shall not be saved. Certes against that cursed wanhope should he think, that the passion of Jesus Christ is more strong for to unbind, than sin is strong for to bind. Against the second wanhope he shall think, that as oft as he falleth, he may arise again by penitence; and though he never so long hath lain in sin, the mercy of Christ is always ready to receive him to mercy. Against the wanhope that he thinketh he should not long persevere in goodness, he shall think that the feebleness of the devil may nothing do, but [unless] men will suffer him; and eke he shall have strength of the help of God, and of all Holy Church, and of the protection of angels, if him list.

Then shall men understand, what is the fruit of penance; and after the word of Jesus Christ, it is the endless bliss of heaven, where joy hath no contrariety of woe nor of penance nor grievance; there all harms be passed of this present life; there as is the sickerness [security] from the pain of hell; there as is the blissful company, that rejoice them evermore each of the other's joy; there as the body of man, that whilom was foul and dark, is more clear than the sun; there as the body of man that whilom was sick and frail, feeble and mortal, is immortal, and so strong and so whole, that there may nothing apair [impair, injure] it; there is neither hunger, nor thirst, nor cold, but every soul replenished with the sight of the perfect knowing of God. This blissful regne [kingdom] may men purchase by poverty spiritual, and the glory by lowliness, the plenty of joy by hunger and thirst, the rest by travail, and the life by death and mortification of sin; to which life He us bring, that bought us with his precious blood! Amen.

PRECES DE CHAUCERES *Prayer of Chaucer*
Now pray I to you all that hear this little treatise or read it, that if there be anything in it that likes them, that thereof they

thank our Lord Jesus Christ, of whom proceedeth all wit and all goodness; and if there be anything that displeaseth them, I pray them also that they arette [impute] it to the default of mine unconning [unskilfulness], and not to my will, that would fain have said better if I had had conning; for the book saith, all that is written for our doctrine is written. Wherefore I beseech you meekly for the mercy of God that ye pray for me, that God have mercy on me and forgive me my guilts, and namely [specially] my translations and of inditing in worldly vanities, which I revoke in my Retractions, as is the Book of Troilus, the Book also of Fame, the Book of Twenty-five Ladies, the Book of the Duchess, the Book of Saint Valentine's Day and of the Parliament of Birds, the *Tales of Canterbury*, all those that sounen unto sin, [are sinful, tend towards sin] the Book of the Lion, and many other books, if they were in my mind or remembrance, and many a song and many a lecherous lay, of the which Christ for his great mercy forgive me the sins. But of the translation of Boece de Consolatione, and other books of consolation and of legend of lives of saints, and homilies, and moralities, and devotion, that thank I our Lord Jesus Christ, and his mother, and all the saints in heaven, beseeching them that they from henceforth unto my life's end send me grace to bewail my guilts, and to study to the salvation of my soul, and grant me grace and space of very repentance, penitence, confession, and satisfaction, to do in this present life, through the benign grace of Him that is King of kings and Priest of all priests, that bought us with his precious blood of his heart, so that I may be one of them at the day of doom that shall be saved: *Qui cum Patre et Spiritu Sancto vivis et regnas Deus per omnia secula.* Amen.

Classic Literature: Words and Phrases
adapted from the Collins English Dictionary

Accoucheur NOUN a male midwife or doctor ❑ *I think my sister must have had some general idea that I was a young offender whom an Accoucheur Policemen had taken up (on my birthday) and delivered over to her* (*Great Expectations* by Charles Dickens)

addled ADJ confused and unable to think properly ❑ *But she counted and counted till she got that addled* (*The Adventures of Huckleberry Finn* by Mark Twain)

admiration NOUN amazement or wonder ❑ *lifting up his hands and eyes by way of admiration* (*Gulliver's Travels* by Jonathan Swift)

afeard ADJ afeard means afraid ❑ *shake it – and don't be afeard* (*The Adventures of Huckleberry Finn* by Mark Twain)

affected VERB affected means followed ❑ *Hadst thou affected sweet divinity* (*Doctor Faustus 5.2* by Christopher Marlowe)

aground ADV when a boat runs aground, it touches the ground in a shallow part of the water and gets stuck ❑ *what kep' you?–boat get aground?* (*The Adventures of Huckleberry Finn* by Mark Twain)

ague NOUN a fever in which the patient has alternate hot and cold shivering fits ❑ *his exposure to the wet and cold had brought on fever and ague* (*Oliver Twist* by Charles Dickens)

alchemy ADJ false or worthless ❑ *all wealth alchemy* (*The Sun Rising* by John Donne)

all alike PHRASE the same all the time ❑ *Love, all alike* (*The Sun Rising* by John Donne)

alow and aloft PHRASE alow means in the lower part or bottom, and aloft means on the top, so alow and aloft means on the top and in the bottom or throughout ❑ *Someone's turned the chest out alow and aloft* (*Treasure Island* by Robert Louis Stevenson)

ambuscade NOUN ambuscade is not a proper word. Tom means an ambush, which is when a group of people attack their enemies, after hiding and waiting for them ❑ *and so we would lie in ambuscade, as he called it* (*The Adventures of Huckleberry Finn* by Mark Twain)

amiable ADJ likeable or pleasant ❑ *Such amiable qualities must speak for themselves* (*Pride and Prejudice* by Jane Austen)

amulet NOUN an amulet is a charm thought to drive away evil spirits. ❑ *uttered phrases at once occult and familiar, like the amulet worn on the heart* (*Silas Marner* by George Eliot)

amusement NOUN here amusement means a strange and disturbing puzzle ❑ *this was an amusement the other way* (*Robinson Crusoe* by Daniel Defoe)

ancient NOUN an ancient was the flag displayed on a ship to show which country it belongs to. It is also called the ensign ❑ *her ancient and pendants out* (*Robinson Crusoe* by Daniel Defoe)

antic ADJ here antic means horrible or grotesque ❑ *armed and dressed after a very antic manner* (*Gulliver's Travels* by Jonathan Swift)

antics NOUN antics is an old word meaning clowns, or people who do silly things to make other people laugh ❑ *And point like antics at his triple crown* (*Doctor Faustus 3.2* by Christopher Marlowe)

appanage NOUN an appanage is a living allowance ❑ *As if loveliness were not the special prerogative of woman–her legitimate appanage* *and heritage!* (*Jane Eyre* by Charlotte Brontë)

appended VERB appended means attached or added to ❑ *and these words appended* (*Treasure Island* by Robert Louis Stevenson)

approver NOUN an approver is someone who gives evidence against someone he used to work with ❑ *Mr. Noah Claypole: receiving a free pardon from the Crown in consequence of being admitted approver against Fagin* (*Oliver Twist* by Charles Dickens)

areas NOUN the areas is the space, below street level, in front of the basement of a house ❑ *The Dodger had a vicious propensity, too, of pulling the caps from the heads of small boys and tossing them down areas* (*Oliver Twist* by Charles Dickens)

argument NOUN theme or important idea or subject which runs through a piece of writing ❑ *Thrice needful to the argument which now* (*The Prelude* by William Wordsworth).

artificially ADJ artfully or cleverly ❑ *and he with a sharp flint sharpened very artificially* (*Gulliver's Travels* by Jonathan Swift)

artist NOUN here artist means a skilled workman ❑ *This man was a most ingenious artist* (*Gulliver's Travels* by Jonathan Swift)

assizes NOUN assizes were regular court sessions which a visiting judge was in charge of ❑ *you shall hang at the next assizes* (*Treasure Island* by Robert Louis Stevenson)

attraction NOUN gravitation, or Newton's theory of gravitation ❑ *he predicted the same fate to attraction* (*Gulliver's Travels* by Jonathan Swift)

aver VERB to aver is to claim something strongly ❑ *for Jem Rodney, the mole catcher, averred that one evening as he was returning homeward* (*Silas Marner* by George Eliot)

baby NOUN here baby means doll, which is a child's toy that looks like a small

person ❑ *and skilful dressing her baby* (*Gulliver's Travels* by Jonathan Swift)

bagatelle NOUN bagatelle is a game rather like billiards and pool ❑ *Breakfast had been ordered at a pleasant little tavern, a mile or so away upon the rising ground beyond the green; and there was a bagatelle board in the room, in case we should desire to unbend our minds after the solemnity.* (*Great Expectations* by Charles Dickens)

bah EXCLAM Bah is an exclamation of frustration or anger ❑ *"Bah," said Scrooge.* (*A Christmas Carol* by Charles Dickens)

bairn NOUN a northern word for child ❑ *Who has taught you those fine words, my bairn?* (*Wuthering Heights* by Emily Brontë)

bait VERB to bait means to stop on a journey to take refreshment ❑ *So, when they stopped to bait the horse, and ate and drank and enjoyed themselves, I could touch nothing that they touched, but kept my fast unbroken.* (*David Copperfield* by Charles Dickens)

balustrade NOUN a balustrade is a row of vertical columns that form railings ❑ *but I mean to say you might have got a hearse up that staircase, and taken it broadwise, with the splinter-bar towards the wall, and the door towards the balustrades: and done it easy* (*A Christmas Carol* by Charles Dickens)

bandbox NOUN a large lightweight box for carrying bonnets or hats ❑ *I am glad I bought my bonnet, if it is only for the fun of having another bandbox* (*Pride and Prejudice* by Jane Austen)

barren NOUN a barren here is a stretch or expanse of barren land ❑ *a line of upright stones, continued the length of the barren* (*Wuthering Heights* by Emily Brontë)

basin NOUN a basin was a cup without a handle ❑ *who is drinking his tea out of a basin* (*Wuthering Heights* by Emily Brontë)

battalia NOUN the order of battle ❑ *till I saw part of his army in battalia* (*Gulliver's Travels* by Jonathan Swift)

battery NOUN a Battery is a fort or a place where guns are positioned ❑ *You bring the lot to me, at that old Battery over yonder* (*Great Expectations* by Charles Dickens)

battledore and shuttlecock NOUN The game battledore and shuttlecock was an early version of the game now known as badminton. The aim of the early game was simply to keep the shuttlecock from hitting the ground. ❑ *Battledore and shuttlecock's a wery good game vhen you an't the shuttlecock and two lawyers the battledores, in which case it gets too excitin' to be pleasant* (*Pickwick Papers* by Charles Dickens)

beadle NOUN a beadle was a local official who had power over the poor ❑ *But these impertinences were speedily checked by the evidence of the surgeon, and the testimony of the beadle* (*Oliver Twist* by Charles Dickens)

bearings NOUN the bearings of a place are the measurements or directions that are used to find or locate it ❑ *the bearings of the island* (*Treasure Island* by Robert Louis Stevenson)

beaufet NOUN a beaufet was a sideboard ❑ *and sweet-cake from the beaufet* (*Emma* by Jane Austen)

beck NOUN a beck is a small stream ❑ *a beck which follows the bend of the glen* (*Wuthering Heights* by Emily Brontë)

bedight VERB decorated ❑ *and bedight with Christmas holly stuck into the top.* (*A Christmas Carol* by Charles Dickens)

Bedlam NOUN Bedlam was a lunatic asylum in London which had statues carved by Caius Gabriel Cibber at its entrance ❑ *Bedlam, and those carved maniacs at the gates* (*The Prelude* by William Wordsworth)

beeves NOUN oxen or castrated bulls which are animals used for pulling vehicles or carrying things ❑ *to deliver in every morning six beeves* (*Gulliver's Travels* by Jonathan Swift)

begot VERB created or caused ❑ *Begot in thee* (*On His Mistress* by John Donne)

behoof NOUN behoof means benefit ❑ *"Yes, young man," said he, releasing the handle of the article in question, retiring a step or two from my table, and speaking for the behoof of the landlord and waiter at the door* (*Great Expectations* by Charles Dickens)

berth NOUN a berth is a bed on a boat ❑ *this is the berth for me* (*Treasure Island* by Robert Louis Stevenson)

bevers NOUN a bever was a snack, or small portion of food, eaten between main meals ❑ *that buys me thirty meals a day and ten bevers* (*Doctor Faustus 2.1* by Christopher Marlowe)

bilge water NOUN the bilge is the widest part of a ship's bottom, and the bilge water is the dirty water that collects there ❑ *no gush of bilge-water had turned it to fetid puddle* (*Jane Eyre* by Charlotte Brontë)

bills NOUN bills is an old term meaning prescription. A prescription is the piece of paper on which your doctor writes an order for medicine and which you give to a chemist to get the medicine ❑ *Are not thy bills hung up as monuments* (*Doctor Faustus 1.1* by Christopher Marlowe)

black cap NOUN a judge wore a black cap when he was about to sentence a prisoner to death ❑ *The judge assumed the black cap, and the prisoner still stood with the same air and gesture.* (*Oliver Twist* by Charles Dickens)

boot-jack NOUN a wooden device to help take boots off ❑ *The speaker appeared to throw a boot-jack, or some such article, at the person he* addressed (*Oliver Twist* by Charles Dickens)

booty NOUN booty means treasure or prizes ❑ *would be inclined to give up their booty in payment of the dead man's debts* (*Treasure Island* by Robert Louis Stevenson)

Bow Street runner PHRASE Bow Street runners were the first British police force, set up by the author Henry Fielding in the eighteenth century ❑ *as would have convinced a judge or a Bow Street runner* (*Treasure Island* by Robert Louis Stevenson)

brawn NOUN brawn is a dish of meat which is set in jelly ❑ *Heaped up upon the floor, to form a kind of throne, were turkeys, geese, game, poultry, brawn, great joints of meat, sucking-pigs* (*A Christmas Carol* by Charles Dickens)

bray VERB when a donkey brays, it makes a loud, harsh sound ❑ *and she doesn't bray like a jackass* (*The Adventures of Huckleberry Finn* by Mark Twain)

break VERB in order to train a horse you first have to break it ❑ *"If a high-mettled creature like this," said he, "can't be broken by fair means, she will never be good for anything"* (*Black Beauty* by Anna Sewell)

bullyragging VERB bullyragging is an old word which means bullying. To bullyrag someone is to threaten or force someone to do something they don't want to do ❑ *and a lot of loafers bullyragging him for sport* (*The Adventures of Huckleberry Finn* by Mark Twain)

but PREP except for (this) ❑ *but this, all pleasures fancies be* (*The Good-Morrow* by John Donne)

by hand PHRASE by hand was a common expression of the time meaning that baby had been fed either using a spoon or a bottle rather than by breast-feeding ❑ *My sister, Mrs. Joe Gargery, was more than twenty years older than I, and had established a great reputation with herself . . . because she had bought*

me up 'by hand' (*Great Expectations* by Charles Dickens)

bye-spots NOUN bye-spots are lonely places ❑ *and bye-spots of tales rich with indigenous produce* (*The Prelude* by William Wordsworth)

calico NOUN calico is plain white fabric made from cotton ❑ *There was two old dirty calico dresses* (*The Adventures of Huckleberry Finn* by Mark Twain)

camp-fever NOUN camp-fever was another word for the disease typhus ❑ *during a severe camp-fever* (*Emma* by Jane Austen)

cant NOUN cant is insincere or empty talk ❑ *"Man," said the Ghost, "if man you be in heart, not adamant, forbear that wicked cant until you have discovered What the surplus is, and Where it is."* (*A Christmas Carol* by Charles Dickens)

canty ADJ canty means lively, full of life ❑ *My mother lived til eighty, a canty dame to the last* (*Wuthering Heights* by Emily Brontë)

canvas VERB to canvas is to discuss ❑ *We think so very differently on this point Mr Knightley, that there can be no use in canvassing it* (*Emma* by Jane Austen)

capital ADJ capital means excellent or extremely good ❑ *for it's capital, so shady, light, and big* (*Little Women* by Louisa May Alcott)

capstan NOUN a capstan is a device used on a ship to lift sails and anchors ❑ *capstans going, ships going out to sea, and unintelligible sea creatures roaring curses over the bulwarks at respondent lightermen* (*Great Expectations* by Charles Dickens)

case-bottle NOUN a square bottle designed to fit with others into a case ❑ *The spirit being set before him in a huge case-bottle, which had originally come out of some ship's locker* (*The Old Curiosity Shop* by Charles Dickens)

casement NOUN casement is a word meaning window. The teacher in Nicholas Nickleby misspells window showing what a bad teacher he is ❏ *W-i-n, win, d-e-r, der, winder, a casement.'* (*Nicholas Nickleby* by Charles Dickens)

cataleptic ADJ a cataleptic fit is one in which the victim goes into a trance-like state and remains still for a long time ❏ *It was at this point in their history that Silas's cataleptic fit occurred during the prayer-meeting* (*Silas Marner* by George Eliot)

cauldron NOUN a cauldron is a large cooking pot made of metal ❏ *stirring a large cauldron which seemed to be full of soup* (*Alice's Adventures in Wonderland* by Lewis Carroll)

cephalic ADJ cephalic means to do with the head ❏ *with ink composed of a cephalic tincture* (*Gulliver's Travels* by Jonathan Swift)

chaise and four NOUN a closed four-wheel carriage pulled by four horses ❏ *he came down on Monday in a chaise and four to see the place* (*Pride and Prejudice* by Jane Austen)

chamberlain NOUN the main servant in a household ❏ *In those times a bed was always to be got there at any hour of the night, and the chamberlain, letting me in at his ready wicket, lighted the candle next in order on his shelf* (*Great Expectations* by Charles Dickens)

characters NOUN distinguishing marks ❏ *Impressed upon all forms the characters* (*The Prelude* by William Wordsworth)

chary ADJ cautious ❏ *I should have been chary of discussing my guardian too freely even with her* (*Great Expectations* by Charles Dickens)

cherishes VERB here cherishes means cheers or brightens ❏ *some philosophic song of Truth that cherishes our daily life* (*The Prelude* by William Wordsworth)

chickens' meat PHRASE chickens' meat is an old term which means chickens' feed or food ❏ *I had shook a bag of chickens' meat out in that place* (*Robinson Crusoe* by Daniel Defoe)

chimeras NOUN a chimera is an unrealistic idea or a wish which is unlikely to be fulfilled ❏ *with many other wild impossible chimeras* (*Gulliver's Travels* by Jonathan Swift)

chines NOUN chine is a cut of meat that includes part or all of the backbone of the animal ❏ *and they found hams and chines uncut* (*Silas Marner* by George Eliot)

chits NOUN chits is a slang word which means girls ❏ *I hate affected, niminy-piminy chits!* (*Little Women* by Louisa May Alcott)

chopped VERB chopped means come suddenly or accidentally ❏ *if I had chopped upon them* (*Robinson Crusoe* by Daniel Defoe)

chute NOUN a narrow channel ❏ *One morning about day-break, I found a canoe and crossed over a chute to the main shore* (*The Adventures of Huckleberry Finn* by Mark Twain)

circumspection NOUN careful observation of events and circumstances; caution ❏ *I honour your circumspection* (*Pride and Prejudice* by Jane Austen)

clambered VERB clambered means to climb somewhere with difficulty, usually using your hands and your feet ❏ *he clambered up and down stairs* (*Treasure Island* by Robert Louis Stevenson)

clime NOUN climate ❏ *no season knows nor clime* (*The Sun Rising* by John Donne)

clinched VERB clenched ❏ *the tops whereof I could but just reach with my fist clinched* (*Gulliver's Travels* by Jonathan Swift)

close chair NOUN a close chair is a sedan chair, which is an covered chair which has room for one person. The sedan chair is carried on two poles by two men, one in front and one behind ❏ *persuaded even the Empress herself to let me hold her in her close chair* (*Gulliver's Travels* by Jonathan Swift)

clown NOUN clown here means peasant or person who lives off the land ❏ *In* ancient days by emperor and clown (*Ode on a Nightingale* by John Keats)

coalheaver NOUN a coalheaver loaded coal onto ships using a spade ❏ *Good, strong, wholesome medicine, as was given with great success to two Irish labourers and a coalheaver* (*Oliver Twist* by Charles Dickens)

coal-whippers NOUN men who worked at docks using machines to load coal onto ships ❏ *here, were colliers by the score and score, with the coal-whippers plunging off stages on deck* (*Great Expectations* by Charles Dickens)

cobweb NOUN a cobweb is the net which a spider makes for catching insects ❏ *the walls and ceilings were all hung round with cobwebs* (*Gulliver's Travels* by Jonathan Swift)

coddling VERB coddling means to treat someone too kindly or protect them too much ❏ *and I've been coddling the fellow as if I'd been his grandmother* (*Little Women* by Louisa May Alcott)

coil NOUN coil means noise or fuss or disturbance ❏ *What a coil is there?* (*Doctor Faustus 4.7* by Christopher Marlowe)

collared VERB to collar something is a slang term which means to capture. In this sentence, it means he stole it [the money] ❏ *he collared it* (*The Adventures of Huckleberry Finn* by Mark Twain)

colling VERB colling is an old word which means to embrace and kiss ❏ *and no clasping and colling at all* (*Tess of the D'Urbervilles* by Thomas Hardy)

colloquies NOUN colloquy is a formal conversation or dialogue ❏ *Such colloquies have occupied many a pair of pale-faced weavers* (*Silas Marner* by George Eliot)

comfit NOUN sugar-covered pieces of fruit or nut eaten as sweets ❏ *and pulled out a box of comfits* (*Alice's Adventures in Wonderland* by Lewis Carroll)

coming out VERB when a girl came out in society it meant she was of marriageable age. In order to 'come out' girls were expecting to attend balls and other parties during a season ❏ *The younger girls formed hopes of coming out a year or two sooner than they might otherwise have done* (*Pride and Prejudice* by Jane Austen)

commit VERB commit means arrest or stop ❏ *Commit the rascals* (*Doctor Faustus 4.7* by Christopher Marlowe)

commodious ADJ commodious means convenient ❏ *the most commodious and effectual ways* (*Gulliver's Travels* by Jonathan Swift)

commons NOUN commons is an old term meaning food shared with others ❏ *his pauper assistants ranged themselves behind him; the gruel was served out; and a long grace was said over the short commons.* (*Oliver Twist* by Charles Dickens)

complacency NOUN here complacency means a desire to please others. To-day complacency means feeling pleased with oneself without good reason. ❏ *Twas thy power that raised the first complacency in me* (*The Prelude* by William Wordsworth)

complaisance NOUN complaisance was eagerness to please ❏ *we cannot wonder at his complaisance* (*Pride and Prejudice* by Jane Austen)

complaisant ADJ complaisant means polite ❏ *extremely cheerful and complaisant to their guest* (*Gulliver's Travels* by Jonathan Swift)

conning VERB conning means learning by heart ❏ *Or conning more* (*The Prelude* by William Wordsworth)

consequent NOUN consequence ❏ *as avarice is the necessary consequent of old age* (*Gulliver's Travels* by Jonathan Swift)

consorts NOUN concerts ❏ *The King, who delighted in music, had frequent consorts at Court* (*Gulliver's Travels* by Jonathan Swift)

conversible ADJ conversible meant easy to talk to, companionable ❏ *He can be* *a conversible companion (Pride and Prejudice* by Jane Austen)

copper NOUN a copper is a large pot that can be heated directly over a fire ❑ *He gazed in stupefied astonishment on the small rebel for some seconds, and then clung for support to the copper (Oliver Twist* by Charles Dickens)

copper-stick NOUN a copper-stick is the long piece of wood used to stir washing in the copper (or boiler) which was usually the biggest cooking pot in the house ❑ *It was Christmas Eve, and I had to stir the pudding for next day, with a copper-stick, from seven to eight by the Dutch clock (Great Expectations* by Charles Dickens)

counting-house NOUN a counting house is a place where accountants work ❑ *Once upon a time–of all the good days in the year, on Christmas Eve–old Scrooge sat busy in his counting-house (A Christmas Carol* by Charles Dickens)

courtier NOUN a courtier is someone who attends the king or queen–a member of the court ❑ *next the ten courtiers; (Alice's Adventures in Wonderland* by Lewis Carroll)

covies NOUN covies were flocks of partridges ❑ *and will save all of the best covies for you (Pride and Prejudice* by Jane Austen)

cowed VERB cowed means frightened or intimidated ❑ *it cowed me more than the pain (Treasure Island* by Robert Louis Stevenson)

cozened VERB cozened means tricked or deceived ❑ *Do you remember, sir, how you cozened me (Doctor Faustus 4.7* by Christopher Marlowe)

cravats NOUN a cravat is a folded cloth that a man wears wrapped around his neck as a decorative item of clothing ❑ *we'd a' slept in our cravats to-night (The Adventures of Huckleberry Finn* by Mark Twain)

crock and dirt PHRASE crock and dirt is an old expression meaning soot and dirt ❑ *and the mare catching cold at the door, and the boy grimed with crock and dirt (Great Expectations* by Charles Dickens)

crockery NOUN here crockery means pottery ❑ *By one of the parrots was a cat made of crockery (The Adventures of Huckleberry Finn* by Mark Twain)

crooked sixpence PHRASE it was considered unlucky to have a bent sixpence ❑ *You've got the beauty, you see, and I've got the luck, so you must keep me by you for your crooked sixpence (Silas Marner* by George Eliot)

croquet NOUN croquet is a traditional English summer game in which players try to hit wooden balls through hoops ❑ *and once she remembered trying to box her own ears for having cheated herself in a game of croquet (Alice's Adventures in Wonderland* by Lewis Carroll)

cross PREP across ❑ *The two great streets, which run cross and divide it into four quarters (Gulliver's Travels* by Jonathan Swift)

culpable ADJ if you are culpable for something it means you are to blame ❑ *deep are the sorrows that spring from false ideas for which no man is culpable. (Silas Marner* by George Eliot)

cultured ADJ cultivated ❑ *Nor less when spring had warmed the cultured Vale (The Prelude* by William Wordsworth)

cupidity NOUN cupidity is greed ❑ *These people hated me with the hatred of cupidity and disappointment. (Great Expectations* by Charles Dickens)

curricle NOUN an open two-wheeled carriage with one seat for the driver and space for a single passenger ❑ *and they saw a lady and a gentleman in a curricle (Pride and Prejudice* by Jane Austen)

cynosure NOUN a cynosure is something that strongly attracts attention or admiration ❑ *Then I thought of Eliza and Georgiana; I beheld one the cynosure of a ballroom, the other the inmate of a convent cell (Jane Eyre* by Charlotte Brontë)

dalliance NOUN someone's dalliance with something is a brief involvement with it ❑ *nor sporting in the dalliance of love* (*Doctor Faustus Chorus* by Christopher Marlowe)

darkling ADV darkling is an archaic way of saying in the dark ❑ *Darkling I listen* (*Ode on a Nightingale* by John Keats)

delf-case NOUN a sideboard for holding dishes and crockery ❑ *at the pewter dishes and delf-case* (*Wuthering Heights* by Emily Brontë)

determined ■ VERB here determined means ended ❑ *and be out of vogue when that was determined* (*Gulliver's Travels* by Jonathan Swift) ■ VERB determined can mean to have been learned or found especially by investigation or experience ❑ *All the sensitive feelings it wounded so cruelly, all the shame and misery it kept alive within my breast, became more poignant as I thought of this; and I determined that the life was unendurable* (*David Copperfield* by Charles Dickens)

Deuce NOUN a slang term for the Devil ❑ *Ah, I dare say I did. Deuce take me, he added suddenly, I know I did. I find I am not quite unscrewed yet.* (*Great Expectations* by Charles Dickens)

diabolical ADJ diabolical means devilish or evil ❑ *and with a thousand diabolical expressions* (*Treasure Island* by Robert Louis Stevenson)

direction NOUN here direction means address ❑ *Elizabeth was not surprised at it, as Jane had written the direction remarkably ill* (*Pride and Prejudice* by Jane Austen)

discover VERB to make known or announce ❑ *the Emperor would discover the secret while I was out of his power* (*Gulliver's Travels* by Jonathan Swift)

dissemble VERB hide or conceal ❑ *Dissemble nothing* (*On His Mistress* by John Donne)

dissolve VERB dissolve here means to release from life, to die ❑ *Fade far away,*

dissolve, and quite forget (*Ode on a Nightingale* by John Keats)

distrain VERB to distrain is to seize the property of someone who is in debt in compensation for the money owed ❑ *for he's threatening to distrain for it* (*Silas Marner* by George Eliot)

Divan NOUN a Divan was originally a Turkish council of state—the name was transferred to the couches they sat on and is used to mean this in English ❑ *Mr Brass applauded this picture very much, and the bed being soft and comfortable, Mr Quilp determined to use it, both as a sleeping place by night and as a kind of Divan by day.* (*The Old Curiosity Shop* by Charles Dickens)

divorcement NOUN separation ❑ *By all pains which want and divorcement hath* (*On His Mistress* by John Donne)

dog in the manger, PHRASE this phrase describes someone who prevents you from enjoying something that they themselves have no need for ❑ *You are a dog in the manger, Cathy, and desire no one to be loved but yourself* (*Wuthering Heights* by Emily Brontë)

dolorifuge NOUN dolorifuge is a word which Thomas Hardy invented. It means pain-killer or comfort ❑ *as a species of dolorifuge* (*Tess of the D'Urbervilles* by Thomas Hardy)

dome NOUN building ❑ *that river and that mouldering dome* (*The Prelude* by William Wordsworth)

domestic PHRASE here domestic means a person's management of the house ❑ *to give some account of my domestic* (*Gulliver's Travels* by Jonathan Swift)

dunce NOUN a dunce is another word for idiot ❑ *Do you take me for a dunce? Go on?* (*Alice's Adventures in Wonderland* by Lewis Carroll)

Ecod EXCLAM a slang exclamation meaning 'oh God!' ❑ *"Ecod," replied Wemmick, shaking his head, "that's not my trade."* (*Great Expectations* by Charles Dickens)

egg-hot NOUN an egg-hot (see also 'flip' and 'negus') was a hot drink made from beer and eggs, sweetened with nutmeg ❑ *She fainted when she saw me return, and made a little jug of egg-hot afterwards to console us while we talked it over.* (*David Copperfield* by Charles Dickens)

encores NOUN an encore is a short extra performance at the end of a longer one, which the entertainer gives because the audience has enthusiastically asked for it ❑ *we want a little something to answer encores with, anyway* (*The Adventures of Huckleberry Finn* by Mark Twain)

equipage NOUN an elegant and impressive carriage ❑ *and besides, the equipage did not answer to any of their neighbours* (*Pride and Prejudice* by Jane Austen)

exordium NOUN an exordium is the opening part of a speech ❑ *"Now, Handel," as if it were the grave beginning of a portentous business exordium, he had suddenly given up that tone* (*Great Expectations* by Charles Dickens)

expect VERB here expect means to wait for ❑ *to expect his farther commands* (*Gulliver's Travels* by Jonathan Swift)

familiars NOUN familiars means spirits or devils who come to someone when they are called ❑ *I'll turn all the lice about thee into familiars* (*Doctor Faustus 1.4* by Christopher Marlowe)

fantods NOUN a fantod is a person who fidgets or can't stop moving nervously ❑ *It most give me the fantods* (*The Adventures of Huckleberry Finn* by Mark Twain)

farthing NOUN a farthing is an old unit of British currency which was worth a quarter of a penny ❑ *Not a farthing less. A great many back-payments are included in it, I assure you.* (*A Christmas Carol* by Charles Dickens)

farthingale NOUN a hoop worn under a skirt to extend it ❑ *A bell with an old voice–which I dare say in its time had often said to the house, Here is the green farthingale* (*Great Expectations* by Charles Dickens)

favours NOUN here favours is an old word which means ribbons ❑ *A group of humble mourners entered the gate: wearing white favours* (*Oliver Twist* by Charles Dickens)

feigned VERB pretend or pretending ❑ *not my feigned page* (*On His Mistress* by John Donne)

fence ◼ NOUN a fence is someone who receives and sells stolen goods ❑ *What are you up to? Ill-treating the boys, you covetous, avaricious, in-sa-ti-a-ble old fence?* (*Oliver Twist* by Charles Dickens) ◼ NOUN defence or protection ❑ *but honesty hath no fence against superior cunning* (*Gulliver's Travels* by Jonathan Swift)

fess ADJ fess is an old word which means pleased or proud ❑ *You'll be fess enough, my poppet* (*Tess of the D'Urbervilles* by Thomas Hardy)

fettered ADJ fettered means bound in chains or chained ❑ *"You are fettered," said Scrooge, trembling. "Tell me why?"* (*A Christmas Carol* by Charles Dickens)

fidges VERB fidges means fidgets, which is to keep moving your hands slightly because you are nervous or excited ❑ *Look, Jim, how my fingers fidges* (*Treasure Island* by Robert Louis Stevenson)

finger-post NOUN a finger-post is a sign-post showing the direction to different places ❑ *"The gallows," continued Fagin, "the gallows, my dear, is an ugly finger-post, which points out a very short and sharp turning that has stopped many a bold fellow's career on the broad highway."* (*Oliver Twist* by Charles Dickens)

fire-irons NOUN fire-irons are tools kept by the side of the fire to either cook with or look after the fire ❑ *the fire-irons came first* (*Alice's Adventures in Wonderland* by Lewis Carroll)

fire-plug NOUN a fire-plug is another word for a fire hydrant ❑ *The pony* looked with great attention into a fire-plug, which was near him, and appeared to be quite absorbed in contemplating it (*The Old Curiosity Shop* by Charles Dickens)

flank NOUN flank is the side of an animal ❑ *And all her silken flanks with garlands dressed* (*Ode on a Grecian Urn* by John Keats)

flip NOUN a flip is a drink made from warmed ale, sugar, spice and beaten egg ❑ *The events of the day, in combination with the twins, if not with the flip, had made Mrs. Micawber hysterical, and she shed tears as she replied* (*David Copperfield* by Charles Dickens)

flit VERB flit means to move quickly ❑ *and if he had meant to flit to Thrushcross Grange* (*Wuthering Heights* by Emily Brontë)

floorcloth NOUN a floorcloth was a hard-wearing piece of canvas used instead of carpet ❑ *This avenging phantom was ordered to be on duty at eight on Tuesday morning in the hall (it was two feet square, as charged for floorcloth)* (*Great Expectations* by Charles Dickens)

fly-driver NOUN a fly-driver is a carriage drawn by a single horse ❑ *The fly-drivers, among whom I inquired next, were equally jocose and equally disrespectful* (*David Copperfield* by Charles Dickens)

fob NOUN a small pocket in which a watch is kept ❑ *"Certain," replied the man, drawing a gold watch from his fob* (*Oliver Twist* by Charles Dickens)

folly NOUN folly means foolishness or stupidity ❑ *the folly of beginning a work* (*Robinson Crusoe* by Daniel Defoe)

fond ADJ fond means foolish ❑ *Fond worldling* (*Doctor Faustus 5.2* by Christopher Marlowe)

fondness NOUN silly or foolish affection ❑ *They have no fondness for their colts or foals* (*Gulliver's Travels* by Jonathan Swift)

for his fancy PHRASE for his fancy means for

his liking or as he wanted ❑ *and as I did not obey quick enough for his fancy* (*Treasure Island* by Robert Louis Stevenson)

forlorn ADJ lost or very upset ❑ *you are from that day forlorn* (*Gulliver's Travels* by Jonathan Swift)

foster-sister NOUN a foster-sister was someone brought up by the same nurse or in the same household ❑ *I had been his foster-sister* (*Wuthering Heights* by Emily Brontë)

fox-fire NOUN fox-fire is a weak glow that is given off by decaying, rotten wood ❑ *what we must have was a lot of them rotten chunks that's called fox-fire* (*The Adventures of Huckleberry Finn* by Mark Twain)

frozen sea PHRASE the Arctic Ocean ❑ *into the frozen sea* (*Gulliver's Travels* by Jonathan Swift)

gainsay VERB to gainsay something is to say it isn't true or to deny it ❑ *"So she had," cried Scrooge. "You're right. I'll not gainsay it, Spirit. God forbid!"* (*A Christmas Carol* by Charles Dickens)

gaiters NOUN gaiters were leggings made of a cloth or piece of leather which covered the leg from the knee to the ankle ❑ *Mr Knightley was hard at work upon the lower buttons of his thick leather gaiters* (*Emma* by Jane Austen)

galluses NOUN galluses is an old spelling of gallows, and here means suspenders. Suspenders are straps worn over someone's shoulders and fastened to their trousers to prevent the trousers falling down ❑ *and home-knit galluses* (*The Adventures of Huckleberry Finn* by Mark Twain)

galoot NOUN a sailor but also a clumsy person ❑ *and maybe a galoot on it chopping* (*The Adventures of Huckleberry Finn* by Mark Twain)

gayest ADJ gayest means the most lively and bright or merry ❑ *Beth played her gayest march* (*Little Women* by Louisa May Alcott)

gem NOUN here gem means jewellery ❑ *the*

mountain shook off turf and flower, had only heath for raiment and crag for gem (*Jane Eyre* by Charlotte Brontë)

giddy ADJ giddy means dizzy ❑ and I wish you wouldn't keep appearing and vanishing so suddenly; you make one quite giddy. (*Alice's Adventures in Wonderland* by Lewis Carroll)

gig NOUN a light two-wheeled carriage ❑ *when a gig drove up to the garden gate: out of which there jumped a fat gentleman* (*Oliver Twist* by Charles Dickens)

gladsome ADJ gladsome is an old word meaning glad or happy ❑ *Nobody ever stopped him in the street to say, with gladsome looks* (*A Christmas Carol* by Charles Dickens)

glen NOUN a glen is a small valley; the word is used commonly in Scotland ❑ *a beck which follows the bend of the glen* (*Wuthering Heights* by Emily Brontë)

gravelled VERB gravelled is an old term which means to baffle or defeat someone ❑ *Gravelled the pastors of the German Church* (*Doctor Faustus 1.1* by Christopher Marlowe)

grinder NOUN a grinder was a private tutor ❑ *but that when he had had the happiness of marrying Mrs Pocket very early in his life, he had impaired his prospects and taken up the calling of a Grinder* (*Great Expectations* by Charles Dickens)

gruel NOUN gruel is a thin, watery cornmeal or oatmeal soup ❑ *and the little saucepan of gruel (Scrooge had a cold in his head) upon the hob.* (*A Christmas Carol* by Charles Dickens)

guinea, half a NOUN a half guinea was ten shillings and sixpence ❑ *but lay out half a guinea at Ford's* (*Emma* by Jane Austen)

gull VERB gull is an old term which means to fool or deceive someone ❑ *Hush, I'll gull him supernaturally* (*Doctor Faustus 3.4* by Christopher Marlowe)

gunnel NOUN the gunnel, or gunwhale, is the upper edge of a boat's side ❑ *But he put his foot on the gunnel and rocked her* (*The Adventures of Huckleberry Finn* by Mark Twain)

gunwale NOUN the side of a ship ❑ *He dipped his hand in the water over the boat's gunwale* (*Great Expectations* by Charles Dickens)

Gytrash NOUN a Gytrash is an omen of misfortune to the superstitious, usually taking the form of a hound ❑ *I remembered certain of Bessie's tales, wherein figured a North-of-England spirit, called a 'Gytrash'* (*Jane Eyre* by Charlotte Brontë)

hackney-cabriolet NOUN a two-wheeled carriage with four seats for hire and pulled by a horse ❑ *A hackney-cabriolet was in waiting; with the same vehemence which she had exhibited in addressing Oliver, the girl pulled him in with her, and drew the curtains close.* (*Oliver Twist* by Charles Dickens)

hackney-coach NOUN a four-wheeled horse-drawn vehicle for hire ❑ *The twilight was beginning to close in, when Mr. Brownlow alighted from a hackney-coach at his own door, and knocked softly.* (*Oliver Twist* by Charles Dickens)

haggler NOUN a haggler is someone who travels from place to place selling small goods and items ❑ *when I be plain Jack Durbeyfield, the haggler* (*Tess of the 'Urbervilles* by Thomas Hardy)

halter NOUN a halter is a rope or strap used to lead an animal or to tie it up ❑ *I had of course long been used to a halter and a headstall* (*Black Beauty* by Anna Sewell)

hamlet NOUN a hamlet is a small village or a group of houses in the countryside ❑ *down from the hamlet* (*Treasure Island* by Robert Louis Stevenson)

hand-barrow NOUN a hand-barrow is a device for carrying heavy objects. It is like a wheelbarrow except that it has handles, rather than wheels, for moving the barrow ❑ *his sea chest* *following behind him in a hand-barrow* (*Treasure Island* by Robert Louis Stevenson)

handspike NOUN a handspike was a stick which was used as a lever ❑ *a bit of stick like a handspike* (*Treasure Island* by Robert Louis Stevenson)

haply ADV haply means by chance or perhaps ❑ *And haply the Queen-Moon is on her throne* (*Ode on a Nightingale* by John Keats)

harem NOUN the harem was the part of the house where the women lived ❑ *mostly they hang round the harem* (*The Adventures of Huckleberry Finn* by Mark Twain)

hautboys NOUN hautboys are oboes ❑ *sausages and puddings resembling flutes and hautboys* (*Gulliver's Travels* by Jonathan Swift)

hawker NOUN a hawker is someone who sells goods to people as he travels rather than from a fixed place like a shop ❑ *to buy some stockings from a hawker* (*Treasure Island* by Robert Louis Stevenson)

hawser NOUN a hawser is a rope used to tie up or tow a ship or boat ❑ *Again among the tiers of shipping, in and out, avoiding rusty chain-cables, frayed hempen hawsers* (*Great Expectations* by Charles Dickens)

headstall NOUN the headstall is the part of the bridle or halter that goes around a horse's head ❑ *I had of course long been used to a halter and a headstall* (*Black Beauty* by Anna Sewell)

hearken VERB hearken means to listen ❑ *though we sometimes stopped to lay hold of each other and hearken* (*Treasure Island* by Robert Louis Stevenson)

heartless ADJ here heartless means without heart or dejected ❑ *I am not heartless* (*The Prelude* by William Wordsworth)

hebdomadal ADJ hebdomadal means weekly ❑ *It was the hebdomadal treat to which we all looked forward from Sabbath to Sabbath* (*Jane Eyre* by Charlotte Brontë)

highwaymen NOUN highwaymen were people who stopped travellers and robbed them ❑ *We are highwaymen* (*The Adventures of Huckleberry Finn* by Mark Twain)

hinds NOUN hinds means farm hands, or people who work on a farm ❑ *He called his hinds about him* (*Gulliver's Travels* by Jonathan Swift)

histrionic ADJ if you refer to someone's behaviour as histrionic, you are being critical of it because it is dramatic and exaggerated ❑ *But the histrionic muse is the darling* (*The Adventures of Huckleberry Finn* by Mark Twain)

hogs NOUN hogs is another word for pigs ❑ *Tom called the hogs 'ingots'* (*The Adventures of Huckleberry Finn* by Mark Twain)

horrors NOUN the horrors are a fit, called delirium tremens, which is caused by drinking too much alcohol ❑ *I'll have the horrors* (*Treasure Island* by Robert Louis Stevenson)

huffy ADJ huffy means to be obviously annoyed or offended about something ❑ *They will feel that more than angry speeches or huffy actions* (*Little Women* by Louisa May Alcott)

hulks NOUN hulks were prison-ships ❑ *The miserable companion of thieves and ruffians, the fallen outcast of low haunts, the associate of the scourings of the jails and hulks* (*Oliver Twist* by Charles Dickens)

humbug NOUN humbug means nonsense or rubbish ❑ *"Bah," said Scrooge. "Humbug!"* (*A Christmas Carol* by Charles Dickens)

humours NOUN it was believed that there were four fluids in the body called humours which decided the temperament of a person depending on how much of each fluid was present ❑ *other peccant humours* (*Gulliver's Travels* by Jonathan Swift)

husbandry NOUN husbandry is farming animals ❑ *bad husbandry were plentifully anointing their wheels* (*Silas Marner* by George Eliot)

huswife NOUN a huswife was a small sewing kit ❑ *but I had put my huswife on it* (*Emma* by Jane Austen)

ideal ADJ ideal in this context means imaginary ❑ *I discovered the yell was not ideal* (*Wuthering Heights* by Emily Brontë)

If our two PHRASE if both our ❑ *If our two loves be one* (*The Good-Morrow* by John Donne)

ignis-fatuus NOUN ignis-fatuus is the light given out by burning marsh gases, which lead careless travellers into danger ❑ *it is madness in all women to let a secret love kindle within them, which, if unreturned and unknown, must devour the life that feeds it; and, if discovered and responded to, must lead ignis-fatuus-like, into miry wilds whence there is no extrication.* (*Jane Eyre* by Charlotte Brontë)

imaginations NOUN here imaginations means schemes or plans ❑ *soon drove out those imaginations* (*Gulliver's Travels* by Jonathan Swift)

impressible ADJ impressible means open or impressionable ❑ *for Marner had one of those impressible, self-doubting natures* (*Silas Marner* by George Eliot)

in good intelligence PHRASE friendly with each other ❑ *that these two persons were in good intelligence with each other* (*Gulliver's Travels* by Jonathan Swift)

inanity NOUN inanity is silliness or dull stupidity ❑ *Do we not wile away moments of inanity* (*Silas Marner* by George Eliot)

incivility NOUN incivility means rudeness or impoliteness ❑ *if it's only for a piece of incivility like to-night's* (*Treasure Island* by Robert Louis Stevenson)

indigenae NOUN indigenae means natives or people from that area ❑ *an exotic that the surly indigenae will not recognise for kin* (*Wuthering Heights* by Emily Brontë)

indocible ADJ unteachable ❑ *so they were the most restive and indocible*

(*Gulliver's Travels* by Jonathan Swift)

ingenuity NOUN inventiveness ❑ *entreated me to give him something as an encouragement to ingenuity* (*Gulliver's Travels* by Jonathan Swift)

ingots NOUN an ingot is a lump of a valuable metal like gold, usually shaped like a brick ❑ *Tom called the hogs 'ingots'* (*The Adventures of Huckleberry Finn* by Mark Twain)

inkstand NOUN an inkstand is a pot which was put on a desk to contain either ink or pencils and pens ❑ *throwing an inkstand at the Lizard as she spoke* (*Alice's Adventures in Wonderland* by Lewis Carroll)

inordinate ADJ without order. To-day inordinate means 'excessive'. ❑ *Though yet untutored and inordinate* (*The Prelude* by William Wordsworth)

intellectuals NOUN here intellectuals means the minds (of the workmen) ❑ *those instructions they give being too refined for the intellectuals of their workmen* (*Gulliver's Travels* by Jonathan Swift)

interview NOUN meeting ❑ *By our first strange and fatal interview* (*On His Mistress* by John Donne)

jacks NOUN jacks are rods for turning a spit over a fire ❑ *It was a small bit of pork suspended from the kettle hanger by a string passed through a large door key, in a way known to primitive housekeepers unpossessed of jacks* (*Silas Marner* by George Eliot)

jews-harp NOUN a jews-harp is a small, metal, musical instrument that is played by the mouth ❑ *A jews-harp's plenty good enough for a rat* (*The Adventures of Huckleberry Finn* by Mark Twain)

jorum NOUN a large bowl ❑ *while Miss Skiffins brewed such a jorum of tea, that the pig in the back premises became strongly excited* (*Great Expectations* by Charles Dickens)

jostled VERB jostled means bumped or

pushed by someone or some people ❏ *being jostled himself into the kennel* (*Gulliver's Travels* by Jonathan Swift)

keepsake NOUN a keepsake is a gift which reminds someone of an event or of the person who gave it to them. ❏ *books and ornaments they had in their boudoirs at home: keepsakes that different relations had presented to them* (*Jane Eyre* by Charlotte Brontë)

kenned VERB kenned means knew ❏ *though little kenned the lamplighter that he had any company but Christmas!* (*A Christmas Carol* by Charles Dickens)

kennel NOUN kennel means gutter, which is the edge of a road next to the pavement, where rain water collects and flows away ❏ *being jostled himself into the kennel* (*Gulliver's Travels* by Jonathan Swift)

knock-knee ADJ knock-knee means slanted, at an angle. ❏ *LOT 1 was marked in whitewashed knock-knee letters on the brewhouse* (*Great Expectations* by Charles Dickens)

ladylike ADJ to be ladylike is to behave in a polite, dignified and graceful way ❏ *No, winking isn't ladylike* (*Little Women* by Louisa May Alcott)

lapse NOUN flow ❏ *Stealing with silent lapse to join the brook* (*The Prelude* by William Wordsworth)

larry NOUN larry is an old word which means commotion or noisy celebration ❏ *That was all a part of the larry!* (*Tess of the D'Urbervilles* by Thomas Hardy)

laths NOUN laths are strips of wood ❏ *The panels shrunk, the windows cracked; fragments of plaster fell out of the ceiling, and the naked laths were shown instead* (*A Christmas Carol* by Charles Dickens)

leer NOUN a leer is an unpleasant smile ❏ *with a kind of leer* (*Treasure Island* by Robert Louis Stevenson)

lenitives NOUN these are different kinds of drugs or medicines: lenitives and palliatives were pain

relievers; aperitives were laxatives; abstersives caused vomiting; corrosives destroyed human tissue; restringents caused constipation; cephalalgics stopped headaches; icterics were used as medicine for jaundice; apophlegmatics were cough medicine, and acoustics were cures for the loss of hearing ❏ *lenitives, aperitives, abstersives, corrosives, restringents, palliatives, laxatives, cephalalgics, icterics, apophlegmatics, acoustics* (*Gulliver's Travels* by Jonathan Swift)

lest CONJ in case. If you do something lest something (usually) unpleasant happens you do it to try to prevent it happening ❏ *She went in without knocking, and hurried upstairs, in great fear lest she should meet the real Mary Ann* (*Alice's Adventures in Wonderland* by Lewis Carroll)

levee NOUN a levee is an old term for a meeting held in the morning, shortly after the person holding the meeting has got out of bed ❏ *I used to attend the King's levee once or twice a week* (*Gulliver's Travels* by Jonathan Swift)

life-preserver NOUN a club which had lead inside it to make it heavier and therefore more dangerous ❏ *and with no more suspicious articles displayed to view than two or three heavy bludgeons which stood in a corner, and a 'life-preserver' that hung over the chimney-piece.* (*Oliver Twist* by Charles Dickens)

lighterman NOUN a lighterman is another word for sailor ❏ *in and out, hammers going in ship-builders' yards, saws going at timber, clashing engines going at things unknown, pumps going in leaky ships, capstans going, ships going out to sea, and unintelligible sea creatures roaring curses over the bulwarks at respondent lightermen* (*Great Expectations* by Charles Dickens)

livery NOUN servants often wore a uniform known as a livery ❏ *suddenly a footman in livery came running out of the wood* (*Alice's Adventures in Wonderland* by Lewis Carroll)

livid ADJ livid means pale or ash coloured. Livid also means very angry ❏ *a dirty, livid white* (*Treasure Island* by Robert Louis Stevenson)

lottery-tickets NOUN a popular card game ❏ *and Mrs. Philips protested that they would have a nice comfortable noisy game of lottery tickets* (*Pride and Prejudice* by Jane Austen)

lower and upper world PHRASE the earth and the heavens are the lower and upper worlds ❏ *the changes in the lower and upper world* (*Gulliver's Travels* by Jonathan Swift)

lustres NOUN lustres are chandeliers. A chandelier is a large, decorative frame which holds light bulbs or candles and hangs from the ceiling ❏ *the lustres, lights, the carving and the guilding* (*The Prelude* by William Wordsworth)

lynched VERB killed without a criminal trial by a crowd of people ❏ *He'll never know how nigh he come to getting lynched* (*The Adventures of Huckleberry Finn* by Mark Twain)

malingering VERB if someone is malingering they are pretending to be ill to avoid working ❏ *And you stand there malingering* (*Treasure Island* by Robert Louis Stevenson)

managing PHRASE treating with consideration ❏ *to think the honour of my own kind not worth managing* (*Gulliver's Travels* by Jonathan Swift)

manhood PHRASE manhood means human nature ❏ *concerning the nature of manhood* (*Gulliver's Travels* by Jonathan Swift)

man-trap NOUN a man-trap is a set of steel jaws that snap shut when trodden on and trap a person's leg ❏ *"Don't go to him," I called out of the window, "he's an assassin! A man-trap!"* (*Oliver Twist* by Charles Dickens)

maps NOUN charts of the night sky ❏ *Let maps to others, worlds on worlds have shown* (*The Good-Morrow* by John Donne)

mark VERB look at or notice ❏ *Mark but this flea, and mark in this* (*The Flea* by John Donne)

maroons NOUN A maroon is someone who has been left in a place which is difficult for them to escape from, like a small island ❏ *if schooners, islands, and maroons* (*Treasure Island* by Robert Louis Stevenson)

mast NOUN here mast means the fruit of forest trees ❏ *a quantity of acorns, dates, chestnuts, and other mast* (*Gulliver's Travels* by Jonathan Swift)

mate VERB defeat ❏ *Where Mars did mate the warlike Carthigens* (*Doctor Faustus Chorus* by Christopher Marlowe)

mealy ADJ Mealy when used to describe a face meant pallid, pale or colourless ❏ *I only know two sorts of boys. Mealy boys, and beef-faced boys* (*Oliver Twist* by Charles Dickens)

middling ADJ fairly or moderately ❏ *she worked me middling hard for about an hour* (*The Adventures of Huckleberry Finn* by Mark Twain)

mill NOUN a mill, or treadmill, was a device for hard labour or punishment in prison ❏ *Was you never on the mill?* (*Oliver Twist* by Charles Dickens)

milliner's shop NOUN a milliner's sold fabrics, clothing, lace and accessories; as time went on they specialized more and more in hats ❏ *to pay their duty to their aunt and to a milliner's shop just over the way* (*Pride and Prejudice* by Jane Austen)

minching un' munching PHRASE how people in the north of England used to describe the way people from the south speak ❏ *Minching un' munching!* (*Wuthering Heights* by Emily Brontë)

mine NOUN gold ❏ *Whether both th'Indias of spice and mine* (*The Sun Rising* by John Donne)

mire NOUN mud ❏ *Tis my fate to be always ground into the mire under the iron heel of oppression* (*The Adventures of Huckleberry Finn* by Mark Twain)

miscellany NOUN a miscellany is a collection of many different kinds of things ❑ *under that, the miscellany began* (*Treasure Island* by Robert Louis Stevenson)

mistarshers NOUN mistarshers means moustache, which is the hair that grows on a man's upper lip ❑ *when he put his hand up to his mistarshers* (*Tess of the D'Urbervilles* by Thomas Hardy)

morrow NOUN here good-morrow means tomorrow and a new and better life ❑ *And now good-morrow to our waking souls* (*The Good-Morrow* by John Donne) ·

mortification NOUN mortification is an old word for gangrene which is when part of the body decays or 'dies' because of disease ❑ *Yes, it was a mortification—that was it* (*The Adventures of Huckleberry Finn* by Mark Twain)

mought PARTICIPLE mought is an old spelling of might ❑ *what you mought call me? You mought call me captain* (*Treasure Island* by Robert Louis Stevenson)

move VERB move me not means do not make me angry ❑ *Move me not, Faustus* (*Doctor Faustus 2.1* by Christopher Marlowe)

muffin-cap NOUN a muffin cap is a flat cap made from wool ❑ *the old one, remained stationary in the muffin-cap and leathers* (*Oliver Twist* by Charles Dickens)

mulatter NOUN a mulatter was another word for mulatto, which is a person with parents who are from different races ❑ *a mulatter, most as white as a white man* (*The Adventures of Huckleberry Finn* by Mark Twain)

mummery NOUN mummery is an old word that meant meaningless (or pretentious) ceremony ❑ *When they were all gone, and when Trabb and his men—but not his boy: I looked for him—had crammed their mummery into bags, and were gone too, the house felt wholesomer.* (*Great Expectations* by Charles Dickens)

nap NOUN the nap is the woolly surface on a new item of clothing. Here the surface has been worn away so it looks bare ❑ *like an old hat with the nap rubbed off* (*The Adventures of Huckleberry Finn* by Mark Twain)

natural ■ NOUN a natural is a person born with learning difficulties ❑ *though he had been left to his particular care by their deceased father, who thought him almost a natural.* (*David Copperfield* by Charles Dickens) ■ ADJ natural meant illegitimate ❑ *Harriet Smith was the natural daughter of somebody* (*Emma* by Jane Austen)

navigator NOUN a navigator was originally someone employed to dig canals. It is the origin of the word 'navvy' meaning a labourer ❑ *She ascertained from me in a few words what it was all about, comforted Dora, and gradually convinced her that I was not a labourer—from my manner of stating the case I believe Dora concluded that I was a navigator, and went balancing myself up and down a plank all day with a wheelbarrow—and so brought us together in peace.* (*David Copperfield* by Charles Dickens)

necromancy NOUN necromancy means a kind of magic where the magician speaks to spirits or ghosts to find out what will happen in the future ❑ *He surfeits upon cursed necromancy* (*Doctor Faustus chorus* by Christopher Marlowe)

negus NOUN a negus is a hot drink made from sweetened wine and water ❑ *He sat placidly perusing the newspaper, with his little head on one side, and a glass of warm sherry negus at his elbow.* (*David Copperfield* by Charles Dickens)

nice ADJ discriminating. Able to make good judgements or choices ❑ *consequently a claim to be nice* (*Emma* by Jane Austen)

nigh ADV nigh means near ❑ *He'll never know how nigh he come to getting lynched* (*The Adventures of Huckleberry Finn* by Mark Twain)

nimbleness NOUN nimbleness means being able to move very quickly or skillfully ❑ *and with incredible accuracy and nimbleness* (*Treasure Island* by Robert Louis Stevenson)

noggin NOUN a noggin is a small mug or a wooden cup ❑ *you'll bring me one noggin of rum* (*Treasure Island* by Robert Louis Stevenson)

none ADJ neither ❑ *none can die* (*The Good-Morrow* by John Donne)

notices NOUN observations ❑ *Arch are his notices* (*The Prelude* by William Wordsworth)

occiput NOUN occiput means the back of the head ❑ *saw off the occiput of each couple* (*Gulliver's Travels* by Jonathan Swift)

officiously ADJ kindly ❑ *the governess who attended Glumdalclitch very officiously lifted me up* (*Gulliver's Travels* by Jonathan Swift)

old salt PHRASE old salt is a slang term for an experienced sailor ❑ *a 'true sea-dog', and a 'real old salt'* (*Treasure Island* by Robert Louis Stevenson)

or ere PHRASE before ❑ *or ere the Hall was built* (*The Prelude* by William Wordsworth)

ostler NOUN one who looks after horses at an inn ❑ *The bill paid, and the waiter remembered, and the ostler not forgotten, and the chambermaid taken into consideration* (*Great Expectations* by Charles Dickens)

ostry NOUN an ostry is an old word for a pub or hotel ❑ *lest I send you into the ostry with a vengeance* (*Doctor Faustus 2.2* by Christopher Marlowe)

outrunning the constable PHRASE outrunning the constable meant spending more than you earn ❑ *but I shall by this means be able to check your bills and to pull you up if I find you outrunning the constable.* (*Great Expectations* by Charles Dickens)

over ADJ across ❑ *It is in length six yards, and in the thickest part at least three yards over* (*Gulliver's Travels* by Jonathan Swift)

over the broomstick PHRASE this is a phrase meaning 'getting married without a formal ceremony' ❑ *They both led tramping lives, and this woman in Gerrard-street here, had been married very young, over the broomstick (as we say), to a tramping man, and was a perfect fury in point of jealousy.* (*Great Expectations* by Charles Dickens)

own VERB own means to admit or to acknowledge ❑ *It's my old girl that advises. She has the head. But I never own to it before her. Discipline must be maintained* (*Bleak House* by Charles Dickens)

page NOUN here page means a boy employed to run errands ❑ *not my feigned page* (*On His Mistress* by John Donne)

paid pretty dear PHRASE paid pretty dear means paid a high price or suffered quite a lot ❑ *I paid pretty dear for my monthly fourpenny piece* (*Treasure Island* by Robert Louis Stevenson)

pannikins NOUN pannikins were small tin cups ❑ *of lifting light glasses and cups to his lips, as if they were clumsy pannikins* (*Great Expectations* by Charles Dickens)

pards NOUN pards are leopards ❑ *Not charioted by Bacchus and his pards* (*Ode on a Nightingale* by John Keats)

parlour boarder NOUN a pupil who lived with the family ❑ *and somebody had lately raised her from the condition of scholar to parlour boarder* (*Emma* by Jane Austen)

particular, a London PHRASE London in Victorian times and up to the 1950s was famous for having very dense fog–which was a combination of real fog and the smog of pollution from factories ❑ *This is a London particular . . . A fog, miss'* (*Bleak House* by Charles Dickens)

patten NOUN pattens were wooden soles which were fixed to shoes by straps to protect the shoes in wet weather ❑ *carrying a basket like the Great Seal of England in plaited straw, a pair of pattens, a spare shawl, and* *an umbrella, though it was a fine bright day* (*Great Expectations* by Charles Dickens)

paviour NOUN a paviour was a labourer who worked on the street pavement ❏ *the paviour his pickaxe* (*Oliver Twist* by Charles Dickens)

peccant ADJ peccant means unhealthy ❏ *other peccant humours* (*Gulliver's Travels* by Jonathan Swift)

penetralium NOUN penetralium is a word used to describe the inner rooms of the house ❏ *and I had no desire to aggravate his impatience previous to inspecting the penetralium* (*Wuthering Heights* by Emily Brontë)

pensive ADV pensive means deep in thought or thinking seriously about something ❏ *and she was leaning pensive on a tomb-stone on her right elbow* (*The Adventures of Huckleberry Finn* by Mark Twain)

penury NOUN penury is the state of being extremely poor ❏ *Distress, if not penury, loomed in the distance* (*Tess of the D'Urbervilles* by Thomas Hardy)

perspective NOUN telescope ❏ *a pocket perspective* (*Gulliver's Travels* by Jonathan Swift)

phaeton NOUN a phaeton was an open carriage for four people ❏ *often condescends to drive by my humble abode in her little phaeton and ponies* (*Pride and Prejudice* by Jane Austen)

phantasm NOUN a phantasm is an illusion, something that is not real. It is sometimes used to mean ghost ❏ *Experience had bred no fancies in him that could raise the phantasm of appetite* (*Silas Marner* by George Eliot)

physic NOUN here physic means medicine ❏ *there I studied physic two years and seven months* (*Gulliver's Travels* by Jonathan Swift)

pinioned VERB to pinion is to hold both arms so that a person cannot move them ❏ *But the relentless Ghost pinioned him in both his arms, and forced him to observe what happened next.* (*A Christmas Carol* by Charles Dickens)

piquet NOUN piquet was a popular card game in the C18th ❏ *Mr Hurst and Mr Bingley were at piquet* (*Pride and Prejudice* by Jane Austen)

plaister NOUN a plaister is a piece of cloth on which an apothecary (or pharmacist) would spread ointment. The cloth is then applied to wounds or bruises to treat them ❏ *Then, she gave the knife a final smart wipe on the edge of the plaister, and then sawed a very thick round off the loaf: which she finally, before separating from the loaf, hewed into two halves, of which Joe got one, and I the other.* (*Great Expectations* by Charles Dickens)

plantations NOUN here plantations means colonies, which are countries controlled by a more powerful country ❏ *besides our plantations in America* (*Gulliver's Travels* by Jonathan Swift)

plastic ADV here plastic is an old term meaning shaping or a power that was forming ❏ *A plastic power abode with me* (*The Prelude* by William Wordsworth)

players NOUN actors ❏ *of players which upon the world's stage be* (*On His Mistress* by John Donne)

plump ADV all at once, suddenly ❏ *But it took a bit of time to get it well round, the change come so uncommon plump, didn't it?* (*Great Expectations* by Charles Dickens)

plundered VERB to plunder is to rob or steal from ❏ *These crosses stand for the names of ships or towns that they sank or plundered* (*Treasure Island* by Robert Louis Stevenson)

pommel ■ VERB to pommel someone is to hit them repeatedly with your fists ❏ *hug him round the neck, pommel his back, and kick his legs in irrepressible affection!* (*A Christmas Carol* by Charles Dickens) ■ NOUN a pommel is the part of a saddle that rises up at the front ❏ *He had his gun across his pommel* (*The*

Adventures of Huckleberry Finn by Mark Twain)

poor's rates NOUN poor's rates were property taxes which were used to support the poor ❑ *"Oh!" replied the undertaker; "why, you know, Mr. Bumble, I pay a good deal towards the poor's rates." (Oliver Twist* by Charles Dickens)

popular ADJ popular means ruled by the people, or Republican, rather than ruled by a monarch ❑ *With those of Greece compared and popular Rome (The Prelude* by William Wordsworth)

porringer NOUN a porringer is a small bowl ❑ *Of this festive composition each boy had one porringer, and no more (Oliver Twist* by Charles Dickens)

postboy NOUN a postboy was the driver of a horse-drawn carriage ❑ *He spoke to a postboy who was dozing under the gateway (Oliver Twist* by Charles Dickens)

post-chaise NOUN a fast carriage for two or four passengers ❑ *Looking round, he saw that it was a post-chaise, driven at great speed (Oliver Twist* by Charles Dickens)

postern NOUN a small gate usually at the back of a building ❑ *The little servant happening to be entering the fortress with two hot rolls, I passed through the postern and crossed the drawbridge, in her company (Great Expectations* by Charles Dickens)

pottle NOUN a pottle was a small basket ❑ *He had a paper-bag under each arm and a pottle of strawberries in one hand . . . (Great Expectations* by Charles Dickens)

pounce NOUN pounce is a fine powder used to prevent ink spreading on untreated paper ❑ *in that grim atmosphere of pounce and parchment, red-tape, dusty wafers, ink-jars, brief and draft paper, law reports, writs, declarations, and bills of costs (David Copperfield* by Charles Dickens)

pox NOUN pox means sexually transmitted diseases like syphilis ❑ *how the pox in all its consequences and*

denominations (Gulliver's Travels by Jonathan Swift)

prelibation NOUN prelibation means a foretaste of or an example of something to come ❑ *A prelibation to the mower's scythe (The Prelude* by William Wordsworth)

prentice NOUN an apprentice ❑ *and Joe, sitting on an old gun, had told me that when I was 'prentice to him regularly bound, we would have such Larks there! (Great Expectations* by Charles Dickens)

presently ADV immediately ❑ *I presently knew what they meant (Gulliver's Travels* by Jonathan Swift)

pumpion NOUN pumpkin ❑ *for it was almost as large as a small pumpion (Gulliver's Travels* by Jonathan Swift)

punctual ADJ kept in one place ❑ *was not a punctual presence, but a spirit (The Prelude* by William Wordsworth)

quadrille ■ NOUN a quadrille is a dance invented in France which is usually performed by four couples ❑ *However, Mr Swiveller had Miss Sophy's hand for the first quadrille (country-dances being low, were utterly proscribed) (The Old Curiosity Shop* by Charles Dickens) ■ NOUN quadrille was a card game for four people ❑ *to make up her pool of quadrille in the evening (Pride and Prejudice* by Jane Austen)

quality NOUN gentry or upper-class people ❑ *if you are with the quality (The Adventures of Huckleberry Finn* by Mark Twain)

quick parts PHRASE quick-witted ❑ *Mr Bennet was so odd a mixture of quick parts (Pride and Prejudice* by Jane Austen)

quid NOUN a quid is something chewed or kept in the mouth, like a piece of tobacco ❑ *rolling his quid (Treasure Island* by Robert Louis Stevenson)

quit VERB quit means to avenge or to make even ❑ *But Faustus's death shall quit my infamy (Doctor Faustus 4.3* by Christopher Marlowe)

rags NOUN divisions ❑ *Nor hours, days,*

months, which are the rags of time
(*The Sun Rising* by John Donne)

raiment NOUN raiment means clothing ❏
*the mountain shook off turf and
flower, had only heath for raiment
and crag for gem* (*Jane Eyre* by
Charlotte Brontë)

rain cats and dogs PHRASE an expression
meaning rain heavily. The origin of
the expression is unclear ❏ *But it'll
perhaps rain cats and dogs
to-morrow* (*Silas Marner* by George
Eliot)

raised Cain PHRASE raised Cain means caused
a lot of trouble. Cain is a character
in the Bible who killed his brother
Abel ❏ *and every time he got drunk
he raised Cain around town* (*The
Adventures of Huckleberry Finn* by
Mark Twain)

rambling ADJ rambling means confused
and not very clear ❏ *my head
began to be filled very early with
rambling thoughts* (*Robinson Crusoe*
by Daniel Defoe)

raree-show NOUN a raree-show is an old
term for a peep-show or a fair-
ground entertainment ❏ *A raree-
show is here, with children gathered
round* (*The Prelude* by William
Wordsworth)

recusants NOUN people who resisted
authority ❏ *hardy recusants* (*The
Prelude* by William Wordsworth)

redounding VERB eddying. An eddy is a
movement in water or air which
goes round and round instead of
flowing in one direction ❏ *mists
and steam-like fogs redounding
everywhere* (*The Prelude* by William
Wordsworth)

redundant ADJ here redundant means
overflowing but Wordsworth also
uses it to mean excessively large or
too big ❏ *A tempest, a redundant
energy* (*The Prelude* by William
Wordsworth)

reflex NOUN reflex is a shortened version of
reflexion, which is an alternative
spelling of reflection ❏ *To cut
across the reflex of a star* (*The
Prelude* by William Wordsworth)

Reformatory NOUN a prison for young
offenders/criminals ❏ *Even when I
was taken to have a new suit of
clothes, the tailor had orders to make
them like a kind of Reformatory,
and on no account to let me have the
free use of my limbs.* (*Great
Expectations* by Charles Dickens)

remorse NOUN pity or compassion ❏ *by that
remorse* (*On His Mistress* by John
Donne)

render VERB in this context render means
give. ❏ *and Sarah could render no
reason that would be sanctioned by
the feeling of the community.* (*Silas
Marner* by George Eliot)

repeater NOUN a repeater was a watch that
chimed the last hour when a
button was pressed–as a result it
was useful in the dark ❏ *And his
watch is a gold repeater, and worth
a hundred pound if it's worth a
penny.* (*Great Expectations* by
Charles Dickens)

repugnance NOUN repugnance means a
strong dislike of something or
someone ❏ *overcoming a strong
repugnance* (*Treasure Island* by
Robert Louis Stevenson)

reverence NOUN reverence means bow.
When you bow to someone, you
briefly bend your body towards
them as a formal way of showing
them respect ❏ *made my reverence*
(*Gulliver's Travels* by Jonathan
Swift)

reverie NOUN a reverie is a day dream ❏ *I
can guess the subject of your reverie*
(*Pride and Prejudice* by Jane
Austen)

revival NOUN a religious meeting held in
public ❏ *well I'd ben a-running' a
little temperance revival thar' bout
a week* (*The Adventures of
Huckleberry Finn* by Mark Twain)

revolt VERB revolt means turn back or stop
your present course of action and
go back to what you were doing
before ❏ *Revolt, or I'll in piecemeal
tear thy flesh* (*Doctor Faustus 5.1*
by Christopher Marlowe)

rheumatics/rheumatism NOUN rheumatics
[rheumatism] is an illness that

makes your joints or muscles stiff and painful ❏ *a new cure for the rheumatics* (*Treasure Island* by Robert Louis Stevenson)

riddance NOUN riddance is usually used in the form good riddance which you say when you are pleased that something has gone or been left behind ❏ *I'd better go into the house, and die and be a riddance* (*David Copperfield* by Charles Dickens)

rimy ADJ rimy is an ADJECTIVE which means covered in ice or frost ❏ *It was a rimy morning, and very damp* (*Great Expectations* by Charles Dickens)

riper ADJ riper means more mature or older ❏ *At riper years to Wittenberg he went* (*Doctor Faustus chorus* by Christopher Marlowe)

rubber NOUN a set of games in whist or backgammon ❏ *her father was sure of his rubber* (*Emma* by Jane Austen)

ruffian NOUN a ruffian is a person who behaves violently ❏ *and when the ruffian had told him* (*Treasure Island* by Robert Louis Stevenson)

sadness NOUN sadness is an old term meaning seriousness ❏ *But I prithee tell me, in good sadness* (*Doctor Faustus 2.2* by Christopher Marlowe)

sailed before the mast PHRASE this phrase meant someone who did not look like a sailor ❏ *he had none of the appearance of a man that sailed before the mast* (*Treasure Island* by Robert Louis Stevenson)

scabbard NOUN a scabbard is the covering for a sword or dagger ❏ *Girded round its middle was an antique scabbard; but no sword was in it, and the ancient sheath was eaten up with rust* (*A Christmas Carol* by Charles Dickens)

schooners NOUN A schooner is a fast, medium-sized sailing ship ❏ *if schooners, islands, and maroons* (*Treasure Island* by Robert Louis Stevenson)

science NOUN learning or knowledge ❏ *Even Science, too, at hand* (*The Prelude* by William Wordsworth)

scrouge VERB to scrouge means to squeeze or to crowd ❏ *to scrouge in and get a sight* (*The Adventures of Huckleberry Finn* by Mark Twain)

scrutore NOUN a scrutore, or escritoire, was a writing table ❏ *set me gently on my feet upon the scrutore* (*Gulliver's Travels* by Jonathan Swift)

scutcheon/escutcheon NOUN an escutcheon is a shield with a coat of arms, or the symbols of a family name, engraved on it ❏ *On the scutcheon we'll have a bend* (*The Adventures of Huckleberry Finn* by Mark Twain)

sea-dog PHRASE sea-dog is a slang term for an experienced sailor or pirate ❏ *a 'true sea-dog', and a 'real old salt,'* (*Treasure Island* by Robert Louis Stevenson)

see the lions PHRASE to see the lions was to go and see the sights of London. Originally the phrase referred to the menagerie in the Tower of London and later in Regent's Park ❏ *We will go and see the lions for an hour or two–it's something to have a fresh fellow like you to show them to, Copperfield* (*David Copperfield* by Charles Dickens)

self-conceit NOUN self-conceit is an old term which means having too high an opinion of oneself, or deceiving yourself ❏ *Till swollen with cunning, of a self-conceit* (*Doctor Faustus chorus* by Christopher Marlowe)

seneschal NOUN a steward ❏ *where a grey-headed seneschal sings a funny chorus with a funnier body of vassals* (*Oliver Twist* by Charles Dickens)

sensible ADJ if you were sensible of something you are aware or conscious of something ❏ *If my children are silly I must hope to be always sensible of it* (*Pride and Prejudice* by Jane Austen)

sessions NOUN court cases were heard at specific times of the year called

sessions ❏ *He lay in prison very ill, during the whole interval between his committal for trial, and the coming round of the Sessions.* (*Great Expectations* by Charles Dickens)

shabby ADJ shabby places look old and in bad condition ❏ *a little bit of a shabby village named Pikesville* (*The Adventures of Huckleberry Finn* by Mark Twain)

shay-cart NOUN a shay-cart was a small cart drawn by one horse ❏ *"I were at the Bargemen t'other night, Pip;" whenever he subsided into affection, he called me Pip, and whenever he relapsed into politeness he called me Sir; "when there come up in his shay-cart Pumblechook."* (*Great Expectations* by Charles Dickens)

shilling NOUN a shilling is an old unit of currency. There were twenty shillings in every British pound ❏ *"Ten shillings too much," said the gentleman in the white waistcoat.* (*Oliver Twist* by Charles Dickens)

shines NOUN tricks or games ❏ *well, it would make a cow laugh to see the shines that old idiot cut* (*The Adventures of Huckleberry Finn* by Mark Twain)

shirking VERB shirking means not doing what you are meant to be doing, or evading your duties ❏ *some of you shirking lubbers* (*Treasure Island* by Robert Louis Stevenson)

shiver my timbers PHRASE shiver my timbers is an expression which was used by sailors and pirates to express surprise ❏ *why, shiver my timbers, if I hadn't forgotten my score!* (*Treasure Island* by Robert Louis Stevenson)

shoe-roses NOUN shoe-roses were roses made from ribbons which were stuck on to shoes as decoration ❏ *the very shoe-roses for Netherfield were got by proxy* (*Pride and Prejudice* by Jane Austen)

singular ADJ singular means very great and remarkable or strange ❏ *"Singular dream," he says* (*The Adventures of Huckleberry Finn* by Mark Twain)

sire NOUN sire is an old word which means lord or master or elder ❏ *She also defied her sire* (*Little Women* by Louisa May Alcott)

sixpence NOUN a sixpence was half of a shilling ❏ *if she had only a shilling in the world, she would be very lilkely to give away sixpence of it* (*Emma* by Jane Austen)

slavey NOUN the word slavey was used when there was only one servant in a house or boarding-house–so she had to perform all the duties of a larger staff ❏ *Two distinct knocks, sir, will produce the slavey at any time* (*The Old Curiosity Shop* by Charles Dickens)

slender ADJ weak ❏ *In slender accents of sweet verse* (*The Prelude* by William Wordsworth)

slop-shops NOUN slop-shops were shops where cheap ready-made clothes were sold. They mainly sold clothes to sailors ❏ *Accordingly, I took the jacket off, that I might learn to do without it; and carrying it under my arm, began a tour of inspection of the various slop-shops.* (*David Copperfield* by Charles Dickens)

sluggard NOUN a lazy person ❏ *"Stand up and repeat 'Tis the voice of the sluggard,'" said the Gryphon.* (*Alice's Adventures in Wonderland* by Lewis Carroll)

smallpox NOUN smallpox is a serious infectious disease ❏ *by telling the men we had smallpox aboard* (*The Adventures of Huckleberry Finn* by Mark Twain)

smalls NOUN smalls are short trousers ❏ *It is difficult for a large-headed, small-eyed youth, of lumbering make and heavy countenance, to look dignified under any circumstances; but it is more especially so, when superadded to these personal attractions are a red nose and yellow smalls* (*Oliver Twist* by Charles Dickens)

sneeze-box NOUN a box for snuff was called a sneeze-box because sniffing snuff makes the user sneeze ❏ *To think of Jack Dawkins — lummy Jack — the Dodger — the Artful Dodger*

— *going abroad for a common twopenny-halfpenny sneeze-box!* (*Oliver Twist* by Charles Dickens)

snorted VERB slept ❏ *Or snorted we in the Seven Sleepers' den?* (*The Good-Morrow* by John Donne)

snuff NOUN snuff is tobacco in powder form which is taken by sniffing ❏ *as he thrust his thumb and forefinger into the proffered snuff-box of the under-taker: which was an ingenious little model of a patent coffin.* (*Oliver Twist* by Charles Dickens)

soliloquized VERB to soliloquize is when an actor in a play speaks to himself or herself rather than to another actor ❏ *"A new servitude! There is some-thing in that," I soliloquized (mentally, be it understood; I did not talk aloud)* (*Jane Eyre* by Charlotte Brontë)

sough NOUN a sough is a drain or a ditch ❏ *as you may have noticed the sough that runs from the marshes* (*Wuthering Heights* by Emily Brontë)

spirits NOUN a spirit is the nonphysical part of a person which is believed to remain alive after their death ❏ *that I might raise up spirits when I please* (*Doctor Faustus* 1.5 by Christopher Marlowe)

spleen ■ NOUN here spleen means a type of sadness or depression which was thought to only affect the wealthy ❏ *yet here I could plainly discover the true seeds of spleen* (*Gulliver's Travels* by Jonathan Swift) ■ NOUN irritability and low spirits ❏ *Adieu to disappoint-ment and spleen* (*Pride and Prejudice* by Jane Austen)

spondulicks NOUN spondulicks is a slang word which means money ❏ *not for all his spondulicks and as much more on top of it* (*The Adventures of Huckleberry Finn* by Mark Twain)

stalled of VERB to be stalled of something is to be bored with it ❏ *I'm stalled of doing naught* (*Wuthering Heights* by Emily Brontë)

stanchion NOUN a stanchion is a pole or bar that stands upright and is used as a buidling support ❏ *and slid down a*

stanchion (*The Adventures of Huckleberry Finn* by Mark Twain)

stang NOUN stang is another word for pole which was an old measurement ❏ *These fields were intermingled with woods of half a stang* (*Gulliver's Travels* by Jonathan Swift)

starlings NOUN a starling is a wall built around the pillars that support a bridge to protect the pillars ❏ *There were states of the tide when, having been down the river, I could not get back through the eddy-chafed arches and starlings of old London Bridge* (*Great Expectations* by Charles Dickens)

startings NOUN twitching or night-time movements of the body ❏ *with midnight's startings* (*On His Mistress* by John Donne)

stomacher NOUN a panel at the front of a dress ❏ *but send her aunt the pattern of a stomacher* (*Emma* by Jane Austen)

stoop VERB swoop ❏ *Once a kite hovering over the garden made a stoop at me* (*Gulliver's Travels* by Jonathan Swift)

succedaneum NOUN a succedaneum is a substitute ❏ *But as a succedaneum* (*The Prelude* by William Wordsworth)

suet NOUN a hard animal fat used in cooking ❏ *and your jaws are too weak For anything tougher than suet* (*Alice's Adventures in Wonderland* by Lewis Carroll)

sultry ADJ sultry weather is hot and damp. Here sultry means unpleasant or risky ❏ *for it was getting pretty sultry for us* (*The Adventures of Huckleberry Finn* by Mark Twain)

summerset NOUN summerset is an old spelling of somersault. If someone does a somersault, they turn over completely in the air ❏ *I have seen him do the summerset* (*Gulliver's Travels* by Jonathan Swift)

supper NOUN supper was a light meal taken late in the evening. The main meal was dinner which was eaten at four or five in the afternoon ❏ *and the* *supper table was all set out* (*Emma* by Jane Austen)

surfeits VERB to surfeit in something is to have far too much of it, or to overindulge in it to an unhealthy degree ❑ *He surfeits upon cursed necromancy* (*Doctor Faustus chorus* by Christopher Marlowe)

surtout NOUN a surtout is a long close-fitting overcoat ❑ *He wore a long black surtout reaching nearly to his ankles* (*The Old Curiosity Shop* by Charles Dickens)

swath NOUN swath is the width of corn cut by a scythe ❑ *while thy hook Spares the next swath* (*Ode to Autumn* by John Keats)

sylvan ADJ sylvan means belonging to the woods ❑ *Sylvan historian* (*Ode on a Grecian Urn* by John Keats)

taction NOUN taction means touch. This means that the people had to be touched on the mouth or the ears to get their attention ❑ *without being roused by some external taction upon the organs of speech and hearing* (*Gulliver's Travels* by Jonathan Swift)

Tag and Rag and Bobtail PHRASE the riff-raff, or lower classes. Used in an insulting way ❑ *"No," said he; "not till it got about that there was no protection on the premises, and it come to be considered dangerous, with convicts and Tag and Rag and Bobtail going up and down."* (*Great Expectations* by Charles Dickens)

tallow NOUN tallow is hard animal fat that is used to make candles and soap ❑ *and a lot of tallow candles* (*The Adventures of Huckleberry Finn* by Mark Twain)

tan VERB to tan means to beat or whip ❑ *and if I catch you about that school I'll tan you good* (*The Adventures of Huckleberry Finn* by Mark Twain)

tanyard NOUN the tanyard is part of a tannery, which is a place where leather is made from animal skins ❑ *hid in the old tanyard* (*The Adventures of Huckleberry Finn* by Mark Twain)

tarry ADJ tarry means the colour of tar or black ❑ *his tarry pig-tail* (*Treasure Island* by Robert Louis Stevenson)

thereof PHRASE from there❑ *By all desires which thereof did ensue* (*On His Mistress* by John Donne)

thick with, be PHRASE if you are 'thick with someone' you are very close, sharing secrets–it is often used to describe people who are planning something secret ❑ *Hasn't he been thick with Mr Heathcliff lately?* (*Wuthering Heights* by Emily Brontë)

thimble NOUN a thimble is a small cover used to protect the finger while sewing ❑ *The paper had been sealed in several places by a thimble* (*Treasure Island* by Robert Louis Stevenson)

thirtover ADJ thirtover is an old word which means obstinate or that someone is very determined to do want they want and can not be persuaded to do something in another way ❑ *I have been living on in a thirtover, lackadaisical way* (*Tess of the D'Urbervilles* by Thomas Hardy)

timbrel NOUN timbrel is a tambourine ❑ *What pipes and timbrels?* (*Ode on a Grecian Urn* by John Keats)

tin NOUN tin is slang for money/cash ❑ *Then the plain question is, an't it a pity that this state of things should continue, and how much better would it be for the old gentleman to hand over a reasonable amount of tin, and make it all right and comfortable* (*The Old Curiosity Shop* by Charles Dickens)

tincture NOUN a tincture is a medicine made with alcohol and a small amount of a drug ❑ *with ink composed of a cephalic tincture* (*Gulliver's Travels* by Jonathan Swift)

tithe NOUN a tithe is a tax paid to the church ❑ *and held farms which, speaking from a spiritual point of view, paid highly-desirable* *tithes* (*Silas Marner* by George Eliot)

towardly ADJ a towardly child is dutiful or obedient ❏ *and a towardly child* (*Gulliver's Travels* by Jonathan Swift)

toys NOUN trifles are things which are considered to have little importance, value, or significance ❏ *purchase my life from them bysome bracelets, glass rings, and other toys* (*Gulliver's Travels* by Jonathan Swift)

tract NOUN a tract is a religious pamphlet or leaflet ❏ *and Joe Harper got a hymn-book and a tract* (*The Adventures of Huckleberry Finn* by Mark Twain)

train-oil NOUN train-oil is oil from whale blubber ❏ *The train-oil and gunpowder were shoved out of sight in a minute* (*Wuthering Heights* by Emily Brontë)

tribulation NOUN tribulation means the suffering or difficulty you experience in a particular situation ❏ *Amy was learning this distinction through much tribulation* (*Little Women* by Louisa May Alcott)

trivet NOUN a trivet is a three-legged stand for resting a pot or kettle ❏ *a pocket-knife in his right; and a pewter pot on the trivet* (*Oliver Twist* by Charles Dickens)

trot line NOUN a trot line is a fishing line to which a row of smaller fishing lines are attached ❏ *when he got along I was hard at it taking up a trot line* (*The Adventures of Huckleberry Finn* by Mark Twain)

troth NOUN oath or pledge ❏ *I wonder, by my troth* (*The Good-Morrow* by John Donne)

truckle NOUN a truckle bedstead is a bed that is on wheels and can be slid under another bed to save space ❏ *It rose under my hand, and the door yielded. Looking in, I saw a lighted candle on a table, a bench, and a mattress on a truckle bedstead.* (*Great Expectations* by Charles Dickens)

trump NOUN a trump is a good, reliable person wo can be trusted ❏ *This lad Hawkins is a trump, I perceive* (*Treasure Island* by Robert Louis Stevenson)

tucker NOUN a tucker is a frilly lace collar which is worn around the neck ❏ *Whereat Scrooge's niece's sister – the plump one with the lace tucker: not the one with the roses – blushed.* (*A Christmas Carol* by Charles Dickens)

tureen NOUN a large bowl with a lid from which soup or vegetables are served ❏ *Waiting in a hot tureen!* (*Alice's Adventures in Wonderland* by Lewis Carroll)

turnkey NOUN a prison officer; jailer ❏ *As we came out of the prison through the lodge, I found that the great importance of my guardian was appreciated by the turnkeys, no less than by those whom they held in charge.* (*Great Expectations* by Charles Dickens)

turnpike NOUN the upkeep of many roads of the time was paid for by tolls (fees) collected at posts along the road. There was a gate to prevent people travelling further along the road until the toll had been paid. ❏ *Traddles, whom I have taken up by appointment at the turnpike, presents a dazzling combination of cream colour and light blue; and both he and Mr. Dick have a general effect about them of being all gloves.* (*David Copperfield* by Charles Dickens)

twas PHRASE it was ❏ *twas but a dream of thee* (*The Good-Morrow* by John Donne)

tyrannized VERB tyrannized means bullied or forced to do things against their will ❏ *for people would soon cease coming there to be tyrannized over and put down* (*Treasure Island* by Robert Louis Stevenson)

'un NOUN 'un is a slang term for one – usually used to refer to a person ❏ *She's been thinking the old 'un* (*David Copperfield* by Charles Dickens)

undistinguished ADJ undiscriminating or incapable of making a distinction between good and bad things ❏

their undistinguished appetite to devour everything (*Gulliver's Travels* by Jonathan Swift)

use NOUN habit ❑ *Though use make you apt to kill me* (*The Flea* by John Donne)

vacant ADJ vacant usually means empty, but here Wordsworth uses it to mean carefree ❑ *To vacant musing, unreproved neglect* (*The Prelude* by William Wordsworth)

valetudinarian NOUN one too concerned with his or her own health. ❑ *for having been a valetudinarian all his life* (*Emma* by Jane Austen)

vamp VERB vamp means to walk or tramp to somewhere ❑ *Well, vamp on to Marlott, will 'ee* (*Tess of the D'Urbervilles* by Thomas Hardy)

vapours NOUN the vapours is an old term which means unpleasant and strange thoughts, which make the person feel nervous and unhappy ❑ *and my head was full of vapours* (*Robinson Crusoe* by Daniel Defoe)

vegetables NOUN here vegetables means plants ❑ *the other vegetables are in the same proportion* (*Gulliver's Travels* by Jonathan Swift)

venturesome ADJ if you are venturesome you are willing to take risks ❑ *he must be either hopelessly stupid or a venturesome fool* (*Wuthering Heights* by Emily Brontë)

verily ADJ verily means really or truly ❑ *though I believe verily* (*Robinson Crusoe* by Daniel Defoe)

vicinage NOUN vicinage is an area or the residents of an area ❑ *and to his thought the whole vicinage was haunted by her.* (*Silas Marner* by George Eliot)

victuals NOUN victuals means food ❑ *grumble a little over the victuals* (*The Adventures of Huckleberry Finn* by Mark Twain)

vintage NOUN vintage in this context means wine ❑ *Oh, for a draught of vintage!* (*Ode on a Nightingale* by John Keats)

virtual ADJ here virtual means powerful

or strong ❑ *had virtual faith* (*The Prelude* by William Wordsworth)

vittles NOUN vittles is a slang word which means food ❑ *There never was such a woman for givin' away vittles and drink* (*Little Women* by Louisa May Alcott)

voided straight PHRASE voided straight is an old expression which means emptied immediately ❑ *see the rooms be voided straight* (*Doctor Faustus 4.1* by Christopher Marlowe)

wainscot NOUN wainscot is wood panel lining in a room so wainscoted means a room lined with wooden panels ❑ *in the dark wainscoted parlor* (*Silas Marner* by George Eliot)

walking the plank PHRASE walking the plank was a punishment in which a prisoner would be made to walk along a plank on the side of the ship and fall into the sea, where they would be abandoned ❑ *about hanging, and walking the plank* (*Treasure Island* by Robert Louis Stevenson)

want VERB want means to be lacking or short of ❑ *The next thing wanted was to get the picture framed* (*Emma* by Jane Austen)

wanting ADJ wanting means lacking or missing ❑ *wanting two fingers of the left hand* (*Treasure Island* by Robert Louis Stevenson)

wanting, I was not PHRASE I was not wanting means I did not fail ❑ *I was not wanting to lay a foundation of religious knowledge in his mind* (*Robinson Crusoe* by Daniel Defoe)

ward NOUN a ward is, usually, a child who has been put under the protection of the court or a guardian for his or her protection ❑ *I call the Wards in Jarndyce. The are caged up with all the others.* (*Bleak House* by Charles Dickens)

waylay VERB to waylay someone is to lie in wait for them or to intercept them ❑ *I must go up the road and waylay him* (*The Adventures of Huckleberry Finn* by Mark Twain)

weazen NOUN weazen is a slang word for throat. It actually means shrivelled ❏ *You with a uncle too! Why, I knowed you at Gargery's when you was so small a wolf that I could have took your weazen betwixt this finger and thumb and chucked you away dead* (*Great Expectations* by Charles Dickens)

wery ■ ADV very ❏ *Be wery careful o' vidders all your life* (*Pickwick Papers* by Charles Dickens) ■ *See* wibrated

wherry NOUN a wherry is a small swift rowing boat for one person ❏ *It was flood tide when Daniel Quilp sat himself down in the wherry to cross to the opposite shore.* (*The Old Curiosity Shop* by Charles Dickens)

whether PREP whether means which of the two in this example ❏ *we came in full view of a great island or continent (for we knew not whether)* (*Gulliver's Travels* by Jonathan Swift)

whetstone NOUN a whetstone is a stone used to sharpen knives and other tools ❏ *I dropped pap's whetstone there too* (*The Adventures of Huckleberry Finn* by Mark Twain)

wibrated VERB in Dickens's use of the English language 'w' often replaces 'v' when he is reporting speech. So here 'wibrated' means 'vibrated'. In Pickwick Papers a judge asks Sam Weller (who constantly confuses the two letters) 'Do you spell it with a 'v' or a 'w'?' to which Weller replies 'That depends upon the taste and fancy of the speller, my Lord' ❏ *There are strings . . . in the human heart that had better not be wibrated'* (*Barnaby Rudge* by Charles Dickens)

wicket NOUN a wicket is a little door in a larger entrance ❏ *Having rested here, for a minute or so, to collect a good burst of sobs and an imposing show of tears and terror, he knocked loudly at the wicket;* (*Oliver Twist* by Charles Dickens)

without CONJ without means unless ❏ *You don't know about me, without you have read a book by the name of* The Adventures of Tom Sawyer (*The Adventures of Huckleberry Finn* by Mark Twain)

wittles ■ NOUN wittles is a slang word which means food ❏ *I live on broken wittles–and I sleep on the coals* (*David Copperfield* by Charles Dickens) ■ *See* wibrated

woo VERB courts or forms a proper relationship with ❏ *before it woo* (*The Flea* by John Donne)

words, to have PHRASE if you have words with someone you have a disagreement or an argument ❏ *I do not want to have words with a young thing like you.* (*Black Beauty* by Anna Sewell)

workhouse NOUN workhouses were places where the homeless were given food and a place to live in return for doing very hard work ❏ *And the Union workhouses? demanded Scrooge. Are they still in operation?* (*A Christmas Carol* by Charles Dickens)

yawl NOUN a yawl is a small boat kept on a bigger boat for short trips. Yawl is also the name for a small fishing boat ❏ *She sent out her yawl, and we went aboard* (*The Adventures of Huckleberry Finn* by Mark Twain)

yeomanry NOUN the yeomanry was a collective term for the middle classes involved in agriculture ❏ *The yeomanry are precisely the order of people with whom I feel I can have nothing to do* (*Emma* by Jane Austen)

yonder ADV yonder means over there ❏ *all in the same second we seem to hear low voices in yonder!* (*The Adventures of Huckleberry Finn* by Mark Twain)